Geoffrey gripped Rosalind's arm and pulled her close. "I want to know why you'd go to such extremes to keep me from your bed, madam. I want to know why our marriage hasn't been consummated."

"You want a great deal, it seems. How much did my father pay you to sway me with your pretty lovemaking? How much was it worth to you to trick me to the altar? I hope it was plenty for you'll not see another cent."

"I was not paid to wed you, Rosalind," he protested.

"If not for the money, then why? Love?" Her laugh was mocking. "If you had loved me, you would have told me so. Convince me or leave me now. I want nothing more to do with you."

Geoffrey's kiss stunned her into silence. As she struggled to regain her composure, he gently stroked the fine line of her jaw.

"Believe what you will, Roz. You're not going to drive me off with your bold bluff of indifference. I'm not going to let you end our marriage because I want it and I want you."

Her quivering lips parted as his head lowered, but his mouth passed them by to tease the tender flesh of her throat. Shivery darts of pleasure radiated beneath his attentive touch, warm and seductive in their promise of what would follow . . .

Bartered Bride

LAUREN GIDDINGS

ZEBRA BOOKS
KENSINGTON PUBLISHING CORP.

ZEBRA BOOKS

are published by

Kensington Publishing Corp.
475 Park Avenue South
New York, NY 10016

First printing: March, 1989
Printed in the United States of America

For Mom and Dad

Thanks for giving me the dreams
and the opportunities

Chapter One

The tinkling of glass and boom of the casement woke Rosalind Dunstan but it was the rush of damp, chilling air that prompted her from the warm cocoon of blankets. She drew a hissing breath as bare feet touched cold planking. The past two weeks had been unceasingly disagreeable so why had she expected her first blissful night's rest to go undisturbed?

Weary and stiff from the long carriage ride and head aching from the endless prattle of its occupants, she sought her room the way one would a refuge, a thankfully quiet refuge. The storm that forced them from the roads had filled the remote country inn to near double its capacity. Sharing rooms brought yet another subject for moaning and complaints. She was hailed as an admirable sport for taking the lowly servant's room. Martyrdom had little to do with it. She would have chosen the stables over another night in the same room with the gabby, snoring Everard girls. Though small and sparsely furnished, she found her quarters inoffensive and retired early. As she sank into the unexpectedly yielding bed, she hoped the heavy rains would delay an early departure so she could savor some more of the luxurious silence. To be pulled from that snug comfort to brave the icy onslaught of wind did little for a temperament already stretched taut.

The intruding gust of wet midnight made Rosalind shiver in her thin nightdress as she hurried across the darkened room to secure the window. She drew up with a soft cry as slivers of glass pricked the delicate pads of her feet. The discomfort and chill were quickly forgotten. That there was broken glass on the floor when the window opened outward seemed an ominous warning of something she had yet to grasp. Angered to think someone would throw a stone through her window on such a night, she frowned and turned, intending to light the lamp at her bedside so she could clean up the unwelcomed mess. She took a step, then stopped, or rather was stopped.

Rosalind's surprise was such that she didn't use the precious second to cry out. The figure she collided with was as solid as a restraining wall and very wet. Before she could draw another breath to let loose a scream, a large hand spanned her mouth from either side of her jaw, effectively muzzling the sound. A steely arm curved behind her back and jerked her up to the cold, hard chest. His very volume was sufficient to subdue her frightened struggles.

"Shh," came a low, intense whisper. "I'm not going to harm you."

Rosalind's mind spun frantically. She carried a small case of common jewelry with her and just a little money. Would he be satisfied with such a meager amount or would he demand . . . more? She refused to give way to the fit of trembling that shivered through her insides. She never considered believing his words. Men who meant no harm didn't break into rooms in the dead of night. She stood quite still in the overwhelming embrace.

"Are you alone?"

Her head began to nod before her thoughts quickened enough to give a denying shake. If he didn't know, why hand him the knowledge of her vulnerability? The contrary movement didn't convince her assailant.

"Yes or no?" he urged with a deep, severe rumbling.

Meekly, her imprisoned chin moved up and down. She felt some of the rigid purpose ease from him.

"I'm going to release you now. Don't scream."

Gingerly, the powerful fingers loosened, then came away. Rosalind gathered a slow, measured breath to fill her lungs. Her intended shriek was little more than a squeak as his hand returned to silence her and to exact an impatient shake.

"Stop that, you silly creature," he warned and crushed her close to contain her renewed struggles. His tone was sharp with annoyance rather than menace. "I told you I mean no harm. I'm not bent on robbery or anything of that sordid nature. The vines beneath your window were the only ones that promised to support my weight. Now, are you going to behave or am I going to have to gag you to control your hysterics?"

The feminine figure stiffened in his grasp and her breath seethed indignantly over the back of his hand. That rebellious stance weakened as her position shifted. He didn't understand her muffled whimper of hurt until his boots crunched on the scattering of glass. In an easy motion, his arm tightened about her waist so her feet cleared the floor and he walked with her across the room. Hand still affixed, he settled her on the edge of the bed, not heeding her alarm at that destination as he went down on one knee before her. They faced each other directly in the dimness.

"Promise you won't cry out and I'll take away my hand. Your word on it, madam."

His words were well spoken. The palm that sealed her lips wasn't coarse and the grasp of his fingers, though firm, wasn't hurtful. Warily, she chose to believe his assurances, and in her eagerness to draw a proper breath, nodded. He turned up the light and, more cautiously, removed his hand. Rosalind had lost interest in crying for help, at least for the moment, as she observed him candidly in the mellow glow of lamplight. He was bareheaded and dripping wet, and, also, very handsome. That fact may have held sway over her decision. His sweeping glance assessed her just as boldly, prompting her to color in the awkwardness of her position. Her words were tart.

"I am not going to fall into hysterics, sir, and I demand to know what you want of me."

His features broke into a wide, deeply dimpled smile. It was an engaging gesture, one that made her breath falter slightly. "Normally, when alone with a beautiful woman in a wet nightdress, my answer would be more flattering, but for now, all I ask is your indulgence for a brief moment."

Rosalind's arms crossed protectively over the damp bodice of her gown but her maidenly reaction was wasted, for his attention was drawn away. Carefully, he lifted her bare feet to brush the splinters of glass from the tiny cuts that scored the tender flesh. The unexpected contact of his cold hands made her gasp.

"Am I hurting you?" His touch gentled to match his tone.

"No," she murmured hoarsely. Despite the chill of his fingers, her skin seemed to burn beneath his handling. The idea of a man seeing, let alone caressing, her bare limbs was shocking, yet thoughts of impropriety were held at temporary bay in lieu of that strange warming. Finally, as if prodded by conscience, she pulled her feet away to tuck them beneath the hem of her gown.

"No great harm done," he pronounced, standing. "Though I regret my arrival has caused you any hurt."

Her eyes followed his ascension in wordless awe. He soared above her in the flowing Garrick, its many capes cloaking him like the surrounding foliage of a giant oak. His size and presence intimidated her more than the circumstance. She began to shiver in an odd excitement.

Seeing her tremble, he crossed to the window. With a careful glance below, he reached out for the buffeted frame and, after a moment's struggle with the tearing winds, secured it soundly. Air still leaked through the small, broken square but it was minimal.

Rosalind measured the distance between him and the door and wondered if she could reach it in time to escape him. Even from where she sat, a hearty scream would wake most of the inn's patrons. However, she no longer considered herself in need of aid, her curiosity outweighing any threat. She quizzed her uninvited guest more thoroughly as he shed the sodden great coat. His garments were finely made, speaking of no little coin, at least not that a common thief could afford. His manner was that of a gentleman if, indeed, a roguish one.

"Who are you hiding from?" she asked as he turned back toward her.

He smiled at her forthrightness even as he recognized the hesitancy behind it. "Not the authorities, so rest easy."

"A jealous husband then?" Her own frankness startled her. She was not one for artless speculation, least of all of an intimate nature with someone so obviously male. Her courage was born of the strange situation and, therefore, to her thinking, allowable.

He grinned, not at all offended. "Not this time. The weather forced me to lay over in a rather disreputable establishment. I got into a game and let's just say the outcome didn't please all parties. I was encouraged to make a hasty exit."

Rosalind recalled seeing such a place a goodly distance away. He did seem winded, his wetness and the heavy splattering of mud on boots and trousers suggesting a lengthy trek in the inclement weather. "You walked here?"

"No, in all prudence, I ran."

"What of your horse?"

"I prefer my own two legs to a saddle atop four unreliable ones," he vowed. He returned to the window but his furtive gaze yielded only blackness.

She asked in a hushed tone, "You're being pursued?"

"Why else would I risk my neck on a slippery trellis and a questionable welcome? Surely there are simpler ways to get in out of the rain."

The dry retort brought a deep flush and her eyes swept downward. The puddles of mud and water that circled his filthy boots contained another, darker pattern. She looked up in concern to search out the source of his injury. The knuckles and the back of his hand were deeply scored from breaking the glass. The cold had numbed his awareness of the pain. He took a startled step back when she caught his hand, then stared in amazement at the welling gashes.

"I've cut myself," he remarked inanely. He tried to draw the hand away but she held on with surprising tenacity.

"These are hardly of no consequence," she scolded in response to his frown. "Sit and let me bind them." When he wavered indecisively, she gave him a stern look to win compliance. While he looked on a bit apprehensively, she dipped a cloth into her washbasin and laid it across the cuts. The muscles in his arm gave a spasm of protest as the contact woke all manner of discomforts but he made no sound. She carefully completed the cleansing with a gentleness not unlike that he had used with her earlier, then snugly wrapped the damaged hand with several of her handkerchiefs.

The Samaritan deed done, Rosalind was abruptly aware of him, of the long legs she knelt between and the curious eyes that observed her. She moved away in confusion as he tested the bandage by wiggling his fingers in cautious experimentation. He nodded that it would do.

A loud knock at the door brought him off the bed, his relaxed pose overturned by one of desperation. He seized her roughly, assuming the threatening attitude once again. A small hand touched to his chest, bidding him to be calm.

"If I don't answer, they'll know something's amiss," she told him with a quiet logic.

Slowly, his grip loosened but his eyes were dark and distrustful. "I beg of you not to give me away," he said softly, then stepped into the shadows behind the bed.

Rosalind pulled her dressing gown about her, securing it as she did her countenance. With a steadying breath, she opened the door to the red-faced innkeeper. He was flanked by a pair of burly men who looked past her into the scant section of the room the slight part of the door would allow.

"Begging your pardon, mum, but these here — gentlemen

be wanting to search your room."

"My room? What ever for?"

"They were following a thief, a very dangerous man. His footprints end below your window. They would like to look within." The ruddy features grew even darker.

Rosalind clutched her robe together and gave him a cool, leveling stare. "If there was a man in my room, I would know of it. It is late and I am very weary," she concluded in freezing accents. "If there is nothing else, good night, sir."

The innkeeper was eager to withdraw but the two men held him there, arguing in a mixture of French and thickly accented English while making threatening gestures that made interpretation of their awkward phrases very clear. He turned back apologetically.

"I'm sorry, mum, but I must insist." He sounded unconvincing.

"Insist?" She drew herself up with an indignant hauteur. "I, sir, insist that my privacy be respected. Would you impugn my word and my honor at the uncertain accusations of such men? I will not have my personal belongings handled or my honesty questioned. Good evening, sir."

"Yes, mum," the innkeeper murmured, bobbing in abject embarrassment as the door closed in his face. He pushed the grumbling men along, refusing to heed any further nonsense from them if it meant intruding upon his guests.

Rosalind leaned against the door with a gusty sigh of relief. The sound was echoed by the figure who sat heavily on the edge of her bed. She looked at the slumped shadow for an anxious moment, beginning to doubt the wisdom of what she had done.

"They said you were a thief and—and dangerous."

His low chuckle soothed her taut nerves. "I assure you, I am neither. What I am is very much in your debt and quite done in. It should be safe for me to go soon, if I might ask your kindness to extend that far."

Rosalind made a soft sound of protest as he lay back on the bed, but the weary groan he uttered held her silent. As she considered her position, a soft tap sounded. He came up in wide-eyed alarm to have her reassure him with the motion of her hand. She opened the door slightly to the concerned features of her maid, Jessup.

"Are you all right, miss? What was that commotion?"

Rosalind smiled at the severe woman who had been with

her mother before her. She couldn't remember a time when her hair wasn't shot with gray or the pinched face relieved in a smile.

"Just some mix-up, but most disturbing." She thought of her guest and added, "I fear my rest has been shaken and there is a dreadful draft in this room. Could you fetch me a bottle of something—comforting from below?"

Nearly cross-eyed with surprise at the request, Jessup scuffled to do as bid and returned with a bottle of sherry and a single glass. When they were taken with a crisp thank you, the door closed firmly. She shook her head wonderingly and went back to her crowded quarters.

Latching the door, Rosalind began, "I thought you could use some warming after being out in the weather." Upon turning, the words died away and she gave a helpless sigh. Her companion had curled atop her covers and was soundly asleep. Mud darkened the linens about the boots he hadn't bothered to shed.

Nonplussed, she sat on the single, hard chair and stared at him, not knowing what to do. She couldn't send him out into the treacherous night where danger might still await him, and calling Nathaniel was out of the question. He would never understand her irrational action in harboring an unknown fugitive. She wasn't sure she did, either. Such impulsiveness was not in her character. She poured a healthy glass of wine and sipped it while she mulled over the incredible events of the evening.

Thief, they had called him. He didn't look like a thief in his fine clothes. In truth, his accusers looked more suspect. She didn't think him dangerous. If he had meant to harm her, he had had ample opportunity to do so. What he was, was a very attractive man, the kind she never thought to have in her bed even under these unlikely circumstances. Exciting intrigues didn't happen to plain, somber-minded Rosalind Dunstan. But, excited she was, by the adventure and undeniably by the man. It warmed and tingled through her on the seditious lull of the wine and unused to either the sensation or the spirits, she was soon giddy with them.

Her eyes lingered over the long, well-made contours of the sleeping man. She had never indulged hereself in such scrutiny before and found it absorbing. She studied the back that was to her as she refilled her glass reflexively. How broad his shoulders were, tapering to lean waist and hips and long,

13

shapely legs. She hadn't appreciated the male form quite so thoroughly and this was a prime example, she was sure. The transgression of her thoughts brought her to a deep blush. Certain the wine was to blame for such improper considerations, she set the glass down next to the bottle. Her brows rose in surprise. There was less than a half glass left. Surely she couldn't have finished the rest.

The chill from the broken pane settled about her, making her twist and shiver uncomfortably in the straight chair. Its narrow seat wasn't meant to cradle a weary soul or support a precariously tipsy one. Through drooping eyes, Rosalind coveted the empty sheets on the nearer half of the bed. Their warmth and comfort were beckoning. The slumbering form hadn't so much as twitched since she'd been watching him. Surely there'd be no harm in just lying on the edge of the bed for a few minutes, just until the room stopped wavering quite so much. Then, she'd wake him and send him on his way. And besides, she argued, he was fully clothed and atop the covers. It all seemed safe enough to her muffled thinking. Without further ado, she tottered to the bed and slipped beneath the wonderfully accommodating blankets to fall instantly asleep.

It was a delightful dream, one that teased her to the edge of consciousness with the promise of tantalizing unknowns. She drifted with it, reveling in each hazy touch, each lingering kiss. And it was so warm. Never had she felt so secure and content as in this rapturous free-float of bliss. Her hand came up unsteadily to fall upon slightly damp hair, plying and threading through it for several timeless seconds until the reality of that slick texture brought her eyes fully open with a snap of surprise.

He was no longer atop the covers or fully dressed. Both those observations stumbled through her foggy mind. He wasn't even on his side of the bed. It was the heat of his bare skin against her that created the delicious warmth, the feel of his large hand beneath the tangle of her nightdress that provoked the tremors rippling through her, the cushion of his wide mouth upon her own that woke the lazy passion weaving so pleasantly betwixt her half-realized dreams.

Drugged with heavy sleep and sherry, her responses were slow to show resistance. It took an absurd effort for her hands to find his shoulders and push. Somehow, they clung instead. Even her protest was faint and unconvincing.

His voice was a deep, rumbling vibration that shivered through her consciousness as purposefully seductive as his touch. "I wanted to thank you properly. Let me repay you, precious one.

Rosalind's lips parted to voice a stronger objection but his silenced her as effectively as his hand had earlier. Without meaning to, she tested the full, yielding luxury of his wide mouth and her claim to reality trembled as fraily as her body. Instead of fighting to form a defense, her mind fastened in feverish recall on his earlier words. He had called her beautiful. No one had ever done that before and only under the numbing effects of the liquor and her own blossoming desire could she believe it now. She was beautiful. What he was doing to her was beautiful. The budding feelings within her were beautiful.

Having never experienced a man's kiss before, she relished the feel and taste of it. It was nearly as intoxicating as the wine and much more enjoyable. Noting that he closed his eyes, she did the same and easily sank into a deeper velvety darkness where sensation faded to a whisper and awareness slipped into oblivion.

She wandered through that vague blackness for an eternity. Or mere minutes. Comfortable and completely relaxed, she had no inclination to stir. Her hand caressed the empty space beside her until her mind sharpened into disturbing focus. With a gasp, she bolted upright then moaned aloud at the see-sawing dizziness the movement brought to her head and stomach. She was alone. It had been a crazy dream brought on by weariness and too much wine at dinner. But the wine had come later, her dulled memory argued. She'd had it in this room while she watched him sleep. Him . . .

Her eyes flashed to the window. The morning light gleamed on the fragments of glass, glistening on the wood floor like diamonds. The bottoms of her feet pained her. That was no dream. The bottle of wine and glass were there, though emptied and placed on the night table. That had been as real as her persistent headache. But what of the rest? Tremors of shock, disbelief, and wonder shook through her, threatening to spill forth in uncontrolled tears as she looked upon the caking of dried mud at the foot of the bed and, more damning still, at the speckling of blood on the rough linens. His or hers? She bit her lip fiercely and hurried her thoughts through the hazy line of her recall to their abrupt end. Crimson with shame, she struggled to breach that gap of memory lapse but there was nothing that would give the slightest clue. She closed her eyes to the race of frantic thoughts of consequence and strove for a balancing calm. It was too late to weep over what had happened on the narrow, borrowed bed but the questionable facts couldn't be ignored. Whether the passionate moments she remembered had continued beyond the end of her awareness, she couldn't guess. Only he would know that. She had been wrong about him. He was a thief, a clever, seductive thief who'd proved far more dangerous than she could have imagined. Yet she had let him stay and to her deepening disgrace had shared a not-so-innocent bed with him. She had allowed, no welcomed, the lovemaking of not just any man, but a stranger, one whose name she didn't even know.

That thought pierced through her misery of self-reproach with a more alarming fact. She didn't even know his name. She hadn't thought to ask but now the importance of it was overwhelming. How would she find him, this dream-lover who stole into her room, stole her heart and perhaps much more? How would she ever find him again?

Her dazed eyes fixed on something bright upon the pillows. Curiously, she lifted the small circle of rubies and diamonds set in a mesh of gold. It was a woman's ring. She stared at it without comprehension. Let me repay you, he had said. Another long minute passed, then a limited understanding dawned.

He had left it for her, a token, a payment, the way one would reward a service rendered. She considered her quarters and frowned. He had thought her some lowly serving girl and paid her for the comforts of the night, comforts she couldn't remember bestowing. Yet why else would he leave the brilliant stones worth the innocent blood of a dozen virgins?

16

Chapter Two

The quiet tap on her door shook Rosalind from her wanderings. It was followed by a call from her maid.

"Lady Rosalind, will you be wanting breakfast before we travel on to London?"

Flustered at being called to the present, she stammered, "No, Jessup, I think not. Just have some hot water sent up so I can refresh myself."

There was a slight pause. Did she sound that odd?

"Yes my lady."

Gathering her fractured wits with a new determination, Rosalind left the bed. She had to rid the room of all traces that would hint she hadn't spent the night alone. Limping on tender feet, she went to the window and swept the splinters of glass into the hem of her nightdress, then shook them outside into the cool morning air. With the soiled towel she'd used to tend his hand, she washed away the tracks of mud on the floor. It followed the glass out the window to the bushes below. The sheets presented a more serious problem. She could brush the dirt away but what of the accusing stains? Her cheeks fused a guilty color as thoughts chased one another through the muddle of her brain until she seized on an answer that would preserve her honor.

Her party of travelers was breakfasting in a private saloon purchased with an ample weight of coin. As she stood unnoticed in the open doors, she was able to observe them dispassionately for several minutes.

The Everards were a fine old family with a lineage as solid as English soil. Percy Everard, the Viscount Chappingham, hadn't managed to tarnish that sterling name with his fondness for gaming and the disciples of the Wilson sisters. Unfortunately, their finances hadn't fared as well. The Dowager Viscountess was a nearsighted, bellowing, birdlike creature whose menacing squint was the only gruff quality she possessed. Her doting indulgence of her son and the silence of his meek wife had led the viscount to his many vices.

17

Thankfully, none of them passed to his heir, Nathaniel. He was a sober individual, prepossessed with the creative arts rather than the frivolous ones. The table was rounded out by the four Everard girls, all of whom were of high-strung nature and little physical beauty. Without a sizable turnabout in their fortune, their futures looked unpromising. And that was where Rosalind intervened.

James Dunstan had more than a sizable fortune; he was a varitable Midas. As his only child, Rosalind appeared the salvation of the debt-plagued Everards. It wasn't as coldly calculating as it seemed. Rosalind had known Nathaniel since childhood and their relationship flourished into a comfortable friendship. He had asked her to the Everard estates in hopes of molding that friendship in a more permanent cast. She was surprised to learn he had already spoken to her father of it and, doubtlessly, he was already anticipating the hefty dowry he planned to bargain for. Her failure to give an answer to his awkward proposal was only one of the reasons she had been anxious to escape their expectant faces.

Nathaniel's long face brightened when he spied her in the doorway and he rose quickly to seat her.

"Good morning, Rosalind. How fair you look today."

She murmured a polite response while her mind chided, only fair, not beautiful. Nathaniel may have had the soul of a poet but his honesty was unimaginative.

"What a storm last night," the youngest Everard girl chimed. "It had me so rattled, I nearly hid under my bed the whole night."

"What's that?" the dowager bawled out. "You say someone was under your bed?"

"No, madam," her son explained in a loud voice, repeating what the girl had said.

The wrinkled harridan sniffed and murmured, "Shameful business. Not safe in one's own room."

As Rosalind reached for a cup of tea, Nathaniel was quick to note the kerchief that wrapped her hand. "What's this?" he exclaimed. "Have you hurt yourself?"

Rosalind wasn't brave enough to lift her eyes, muttering into her cup, "The wind knocked a branch through my window and I cut myself picking up the pieces of glass." She didn't know if there were any branches near her window that could have done the deed, but then, neither would he.

"Are you sure you're all right? I could see about a surgeon."

18

"No, really, Nate," she cried in genuine alarm. "I'm fine. Just a small wound. It doesn't pain me." The consternation in his eyes forced her to look away uncomfortably. It was her conscience that caused her pain. "When are we leaving?"

"As soon as the coach is brought around."

"Receiving?" the dowager crowed. "What a time to be receiving. Who's here?"

"No one, Mama," Chappingham soothed patiently. "We're leaving."

"Leaving just when we're expecting guests? I say, Percy, that don't seem quite the civil thing."

He gave an exasperated sigh.

Their conveyances were under way within the hour, the travel slow and far from comfortable with the washout from the rain. Nathaniel finally gave up his attempts to engage his future fiancée in pleasant talk. She was in an odd mood. He was used to her silences but not to the vague, dreamy wistfulness that occupied her so completely. Dare he hope she was thinking of their exchange of the prior eve? He repressed an encouraging smile and wished he dared take up her hand. Knowing how such affectionate displays embarrassed her, he merely watched her with devoted eyes and congratulated himself on disturbing her reserved demeanor.

Rosalind had never been so relieved to see the line of stately plane trees that shaded Berkeley Square. Her father's large private home was on Charles Street just off the prestigious square and her eyes strained ahead for the sight of it. Even though her place as its questionable mistress had been succeeded by her father's new wife, it was still her home, her haven, and she couldn't wait to get within its welcoming walls.

She dismissed Nathaniel and his noisy entourage with unbecoming curtness, eager to be free of the twisting guilt she felt under his fond stare. Her mind was too full of turmoil to endure any further complications. She wanted only to retreat to her cool, serene suite of rooms to recoup her flagging spirits. But before she could mount the wide sweeping stairs, a commanding voice called her to task.

"Well, Daughter? What news have you for me?"

Rosalind would have dreaded the interview under the best of circumstances. Considering what lay on her conscience, it had her in a quake. She turned slowly to greet her father with a respectful smile. She went to the door of his library to

19

present a pale cheek.

James Dunstan was an intimidating figure. He was tall, unbent, and unsilvered despite his near fifty years of hard living. His dark eyes had a piercing directness that brooked no nonsense or excuse. The efficient staff of his huge household tiptoed about when he was in one of his attitudes, as did his daughter. An angry Lord Dunstan was a fearsome sight. He leveled that expectant gaze on the timid miss before him and scowled, unused to repeating himself.

"Well?"

"I had a tolerable time. The viscount provided some delightful entertainments and there were several outings—"

"Never mind that." His booming voice made her jump. "You know what I want to hear. What of young Everard?"

Rosalind wrung her hands and murmured obligingly, "He asked me to be his wife."

Dunstan expelled his breath in a long-suffering roar. "About time. And?"

"I told him I would think on it."

The thunderclouds gathered on the stern brow. "What? This is not the time to play the shy coquette. You cannot claim this took you by surprise. You knew the way of it when you went with him and his family."

"Well, yes," she stammered.

"Then why the hesitation?"

Meekly, she whispered, "I'm not sure he's the man I want to wed."

"Not certain?" he charged in accents that cleared the ground floor of its servants. Rosalind wished for a like retreat. "Not certain? I grow old waiting for an heir and you are not certain."

Rosalind drew a fortifying breath for the trimming she knew would follow. Her spiritless resignation only served to increase his rage.

"I have waited for five years for you to be certain. I have seen an endless parade of fine London bloods wait on a word from you. I have given balls, tiresome routs, arranged countless introductions only to have you pull in your head like a frightened turtle at the sight of anything in trousers. I thought you liked Everard or, at least, that you weren't scared whiskerless when in the same room with him. He wouldn't have been my choice but I would have given my blessing. At this point, I would settle for the lantern lighter on Grosvenor

Square if he would beget me grandsons." He stared narrowly at the downcast face, so submissive in all but this one thing. He sighed heavily and tried yet another time.

"What is it you want, Rosalind? Name it and if it be in my power, you shall have it."

"I want a man who cares more for me than for my fortune," she replied unhappily

Dunstan gave an unkind laugh, not seeing how it made his daughter shrink into herself. "Rosalind, you were not blessed with the countenance to charm the man of your dreams. You were blessed with a wealth that could gain you whoever you fancy. I fail to see your complaint."

"The best your money can buy," she murmured. If he hadn't known her better, he would have believed them the words of a hardened cynic.

"And what is wrong with that?" he challenged. "You've always had the best I could give you — the best clothing, the best instruction, the best companions. You pick a poor time to make a stand opposed to all you have enjoyed well enough to this point."

He paused, but she remained silent, still avoiding his eyes. Her silences were more aggravating than a direct argument and it angered him that he never knew if he was winning the discussion or if she was even listening to him. He had reached the end of his endurance and minimal patience. When he spoke, his words were clipped and exacting.

"It's my fault, I know, for indulging you to this point. I allowed you to hide in the country after your mother's death. I let you neglect your social upbringing. If I hadn't been so preoccupied, I would have called you to task earlier but that is no excuse for your stubbornness now. Enough of this, Daughter. If my wealth is such a stumbling block, I will give you the option of doing without it." At least that gained her attention. She peered up at him through the sweep of her lashes. "If you've not given me a son in one year's time, I will make other provisions in my will."

She was looking at him squarely then, eyes round with disbelief.

"You'd best say a pretty yes to your beau or find another in his stead within the month. If you cannot decide, I will pick for you. You forced me to this, Rosalind, but, by God, I will have an heir and in my lifetime!"

"Really, my lord, must you sound like such an ogre?"

Only Camilla, his lovely bride, dared speak to him so. She hurried up in a rustle of silk to slip a supporting arm about her stepdaughter's sagging shoulders. Though the woman was less than three years her senior, Rosalind took comfort in her gentle yet spirited presence.

"Camilla, I will thank you not to interfere," he grumbled with no true threat in his tone.

"I must. It would serve you right if she brought home some groomsman to satisfy your vanity."

A smile quirked his severe lips but he wouldn't relent. "Then I leave it to you to see she brings in someone worthy." His look hardened when he turned to his dismayed daughter. "You'd best be at the altar in two months time and hope your chosen is virile."

Upstairs, Rosalind collapsed on her bed with a moan of "Oh, Cammy, what am I to do?"

The older woman sat beside her and gave her arm a pat. "Don't despair of it, Lindy. I'm sure he won't be so cruel as to cut you out."

"I wish I could have your confidence. He is quite vexed with me and rightly so. Why am I so particular when I've no reason to give myself such airs? I should have married years ago and given him the children he deserves instead of bringing all to such a disagreeable turn."

"Are you so certain that Everard would not suit?"

Rosalind rolled onto her back and knuckled her damp eyes. "Oh, I don't know. He's kind and considerate and we're ever such good friends."

"But you don't have any feelings of love for him," she summed up sympathetically.

"I don't think so."

"Is there any other who would do?"

Rosalind came close to blurting out the whole truth. There was another but she chose to keep his existence secret from even Camilla who had become such a friend and mentor to her. Instead, she said, "No, none."

"Then we shall go and have a look about. Surely there is some lucky fellow you've overlooked. We'll make it into a game. I think I'll quite enjoy helping you shop for a husband. It's much more challenging than finding a string of matched pearls to wear with my Chantilly court dress."

That brought a doubtful giggle. "Really, Cammy. You are the outside of too much."

"There's a rout tomorrow evening at Oatlands. The duchess always manages a delightful crush in spite of those beasts she keeps."

"Not a rout," she cried miserably. "I fare so poorly at conversation. I'm always tongue-tied and bird-witted."

"You'd do fine if you'd let yourself have fun."

"It's easy for you. You always know just what to say. You even have Papa in your pockets."

She gazed admiringly at her stepmother without a trace of envy in her heart. Camilla Dunstan was stunningly beautiful. She possessed a willowy figure, perfect skin, masses of shiny black curls, and beguiling blue eyes that were both innocent and mischievous. Men loved just to look at her, yet she was doubly favored with a lively tongue. If only she had a trace of that spontaneous poise, Rosalind thought wistfully.

With their closeness in age, resentment would have been a natural thing, yet it had never taken root between the two women in the Dunstan household. Rosalind was only too glad to surrender the duties of hostess and have a buffer in her strained relationship with her father. He hadn't been quite correct in his summation of her years in the country. It hadn't been hiding as much as a hibernation. She loved the solitary freedom there. When forced to London to face its regimented rules of etiquette and propriety, she suffered from having no one to show her the outs and her ignorance manifested in a desperate shyness. Camilla was a savior, an example of feminine grace and wiles that had no equal. She hadn't shunned Dunstan's awkward daughter but had accepted her openly as a friend instead of a threat. And for that, Rosalind would always be grateful.

"Come, Lindy. What do you say? I'll find you something to wear that won't show the dog hair."

It was hard to deny Camilla anything and, pleased to have won her case, she left with a satisfied smile and a vow to make things easier between her and her father by the time they met over supper.

For a time, Rosalind stared reflectively at the canopy overhead, then drew out the ring she carried in the bodice of her gown. It was a splendid creation, the fire of rubies and cool elegance of diamonds meshed in a fine work of gold. Impulsively, she slipped it on her right hand. The fit was snug and familiar. She turned it this way and that so it flashed and sparkled. It was a token of perhaps the only night

23

of love she would ever know. Looking back from the secure comforts of her room, it was like a dream: the charming stranger, the thrill of danger, the passionate interlude, and even the incredible words he had spoken to her. All the fanciful dream of a lonely heart, for what else could it be?

She rose and looked pessimistically into her mirror. What she saw encouraged no confidence. She saw plain Rosalind Dunstan, twenty-three-might-as-well-be-forty, of the nondescript brown hair and eyes. Brown, she thought disgustedly. Why couldn't her eyes have been a dazzling blue or enchanting green? Why couldn't she have been blessed with curls of cornsilk or midnight instead of her father's fortune? How unfair that among all the graceful reeds she should look as solid as a post. Even those faults might have been overlooked if she had a vivacious nature, a pleasing laugh, or a confident manner. When in the company of more than one, her voice suffered an odd paralysis. Her laugh was a nervous giggle. Her response to conversation was a frozen stare that tottered between blankness and terror. If it hadn't been for her wealth, few would have approached her out of sympathy for her genuine distress at being singled out.

Her position as heiress had brought forth several stalwart souls. Even their greed couldn't prompt them to endure hours of her monosyllabic replies and frightfully pained aloofness. Nathaniel seemed her only recourse. With him, she could talk with relative ease, sharing bits of a poem or discussions. He didn't mind her habitual shyness, or perhaps his case was more desperate than most. She knew he offered for her only out of necessity, though she didn't blame him for it. He was doing his duty to his family and was to be admired for that. And now, it was time for her to do her duty to her own. She had two months to choose, court, and marry. That didn't give her the luxury of finding true love, only of striking the least objectionable bargain.

She twisted the ring on her finger and gave a tiny sigh. If only there was more time, perhaps . . . No, there was no hope there. She had to find her lifelong mate in the crowded Mayfair parlors, not in a cold servant's room in a distant inn. That happened only in dreams.

Chapter Three

The rooms of the Duchess of York's apartments were overly full. It seemed that every inch of space was occupied even with the furniture pushed back against the walls to allow freer movement. Rosalind stood very still against one of the walls, hoping to blend in with the draperies or to be mistaken for a piece of statuary. The duchess's reputation for hospitality always drew the cream of ton and she felt quite helpless in that social glitter. Brummell was sure to attend any function given by his good friend and that automatically included his circle of dandified reflections flocking as birds of like feather in their blue tailcoats with brass buttons, white waistcoats, and blue stockinette pantaloons strapped over black slippers. To the aspiring, this blanket imitation was all the crack. Rosalind thought it tedious and unimaginative.

Except for a brief, amusing respite in which one of the duchess's titled guests chased one of her large, dirty, and embarrassing dogs with a cane after it chose to relieve itself on his trouser leg, Rosalind spent her time trying to look inconspicuous while searching the mob for Camilla. She hoped to sway her with the plea of a headache, for the tension, the heat, and the noise were creating an unpleasant din between her temples. Instead, she was spotted by Amelia Grantham and her cousins, all of whom were as ill-behaved and unkempt as the duchess's favored pets. They surrounded Rosalind because she was the only one without the quickness or simple rudeness to avoid them.

"Hallo, Lindy," Amelia called cheerily. When she pressed close, the scent she applied so liberally was nearly choking. "Marvelous squeeze, ain't it?"

Rosalind smiled politely and cast a desperate glance for Camilla.

Amelia leaned in to whisper with forced intimation, "I hear you're casting out lures for a husband. Lucky you've got such a credit line to sustain you."

Rosalind crimsoned to the roots of her hair at the bold disclosure. Amelia never got any news firsthand. Was it common knowledge that she was desperate for a husband? She couldn't bear the humiliation of it. Oh, where was Camilla? She had to escape. She could well envision the smug tittering behind gloved hands and innocently raised fans and the line of fortune hunters readying for the attack. What a miserable month it was going to be. Vaguely, she heard the grating voice continue, taking full advantage of a willing ear.

"There is one man you must meet," Amelia gushed and squeezed her arm with raptured promise. "Lord Chilton." The sighing way his name was said was enough to dim Rosalind's enthusiasm. Amelia's taste in men was highly suspect. "Oh, Lindy, he is famously handsome and fabulously rich."

"Why is it that I've never heard of him then?" she murmured ingraciously.

"He's just arrived from Paris."

"But we've no treaty with France to date."

Pleased to have won some interest, Amelia breathed excitedly, "He been living there for over twenty years. Surely you recall the scandal. It was the most whispered on-dit for months."

Before she could claim no passion for idle talk, the confiding girl leaned closer. Her perfume clogged Rosalind's nose and set up a painful tempo in her head.

"His mother was sent to the Continent supposedly for her health, but it was rumored she had an affair and ran away. One couldn't blame her. The old viscount was an odious creature when in his cups. Drank himself to death, finally. There was a younger brother, I recall. You've heard of Nigel Chilton. Touched in the upper works, they say. He never married and hasn't been seen in polite circles for years. The viscount is the last in line for all that money and the title of Earl Harlech. His uncle succeeded to it through the fifth earl when the direct line died out. I'm certain such a warrant will be granted. Just think, an earldom and such a pleasing face. I vow he won't last long on the market. Oh, look. There he is next to Alvany and that fop, Rutherford. The tall one. Ain't he of the first stare?"

Stare, she did. For long moments, Rosalind was rooted with astonishment as she took in the figure of Lord Chilton.

He was every bit as handsome as Amelia boasted, but that was no surprise to her. She was well acquainted with the smooth, even planes of his face that yielded deep, boyish dimples at the rendering of his broad smile. She knew his eyes were as dark and changeable as a stormy sky when uneasy and a dusky blue when warmed with their sultry slant of humor. She was uncomfortably familiar as well with the large, sturdy form, now elegantly draped in dry clothing. The rich beige cloth of his coat contrasted intriguingly with the sea of blue and brass and was cut to perfection to delineate wide shoulders in a way that was constrained yet subtly, undeniably powerful. Snug pantaloons skimmed long, well muscled legs but Rosalind feared to let her eyes traverse there least her heated cheeks betray her. The only aspect of Lord Chilton she wasn't aware of was the color of his hair without the darkening dampness. It was a rich, burnished gold, the color of deep, brilliant autumn, and the remembered scent of rain upon it assailed her like a freshening breath in the stifling room.

For the first time, the surrounding company no longer mattered. Her preoccupation with keeping notice away from herself fell away and, unconsciously, her stance grew bolder. For once, she desperately wanted to be seen. Obligingly, the dusky eyes rose to touch on hers. A quick word was spoken to his companion and the two of them started through the crush.

"He's coming this way," squeaked one of the homely cousins. "I shall positively expire if he speaks to me."

"What shall I say?" Amelia babbled. "Which of you knows Rutherford so we can beg an introduction?"

It was Rosalind who kept her countenance and murmured a tart aside. "Amelia, do be silent. You are driving me to distraction with your pittle-pattling."

The unexpected cut had her color rising at a variance with her unfortunate choice of cheek rouge but Amelia, for once, held her tongue.

Dabney Rutherford made an admirable leg to the ladies and exchanged greetings with Rosalind, with whom he had a passing acquaintance. Then he made a generous motion to the tall man at his side.

"Lady Rosalind, might I present to you Lord Geoffrey Chilton."

With remarkable calm, Rosalind extended her hand and

managed not to tremble when it was lightly taken in large, warm fingers.

"How delightful, to be formally introduced at last, my lady."

"The pleasure is mine as well, sir," she said prettily. She saw his gaze pause at the sight of his ring upon her finger; then he lifted her hand in an easy gesture. Instead of touching his lips to its back, he turned it so his kiss fell upon her salty palm and lingered there for an indecent time. She was torn between proper dismay that demanded she snatch it back and the impulse to touch his face encouragingly. In the end, he saved her by relinquishing his grasp.

Introductions were made to the other girls and acknowledged civilly but the deep blue eyes never wavered from Rosalind's.

"Are you enjoying your evening, my lady?" She had forgotten how low and silky his voice was and it made her shiver deliciously.

"In all truth, no." Rosalind heard Amelia's scandalized gasp. "It's too much of a squeeze for me."

"Forces together some rather odd bedfellows, eh?"

Rosalind didn't blush. Her gaze was locked into his. "Indeed it does, my lord."

"Perhaps we shall meet again under more rewarding circumstances." His brow lifted in question.

"In all likelihood, my lord. I usually take in the park at four."

"Perhaps we will come upon one another," he said in lower, hopeful tones.

"I would not take exception to that."

He gave his slow, spreading smile and retrieved her hand for a proper kiss. "Lady Rosalind. Ladies."

The cousins mooned after his retreating figure but Rosalind alone failed to return to earth. She made vague responses to the girlish tittering and finally, discouraged, Amelia withdrew.

"Good heavens, Lindy," Camilla exclaimed, coming upon her in the mash. "Are you a bit bosky?" the girl's high color prompted her to ask.

"I'm fine, Cammy. Truly," she said in a dreamy fashion that made her stepmother cast a surprised glance about to see the reason for her uncharacteristic glow. Finding no probable cause, she sighed and took up the girl's arm.

"I've had enough of this elbow-knocking. More feet have trod upon mine than the carpet. Are you for home?"

"Whatever you like."

Camilla gave her another shrewd stare. Rosalind was usually begging to leave moments after their arrival. This evening, she seemed in no hurry.

No, she was in no hurry. She had a name now. Geoffrey Chilton. Things no longer appeared so bleak.

For Geoffrey, the evening had begun as a questionable success. As a guest of the dandyish Rutherford, he had gained entry into the exclusive rout only to face offended stares at his choice of unconventional dress. Annoyed by the obvious censure, he adopted an attitude of commanding hauteur and gave the blue-coated group a thorough quizzing through his long-stemmed glass.

He horrified Rutherford by declaring coolly, "I find it inconceivable that the grandson of a valet should dictate fashion to me. How impertinent when all of Europe views the British as ridiculously stuffy."

"And where do you receive your dictates, sir?" asked Brummell, not to be outmatched by the newcomer's arrogance.

"Paris, of course, where anything of consequence originates."

The two men observed each other with regal disdain that softened into a grudging admiration. Rutherford was wishing he'd never brought this plague down upon his head.

"You must be Chilton," the Beau remarked with an affected brush of his sleeve. "I heard you had just arrived."

"And who on either continent has not heard of you, sir." He produced a Sèvres snuff box with an understated flourish and flicked it open with his thumbnail. At the invitation, Brummell took a pinch of the brown, flaky stuff with his left hand.

"King's Martinique," he pronounced knowledgeably.

"Blended with Brazil and a touch of this and that."

"Interesting."

"I am rather impressed with the creases of your cravat. My man is forever putting the scorch to mine."

Growing more comfortable with the exchange of compliments, Brummell was moved to remark, "Fine cloth you're wearing."

"Umm. I applaud the cut of yours as well, though the color

is not to my taste. Perhaps you could recommend me a good tailor. I shall need some new duds."

"I let no one but Weston cover my back. He has a shop in Old Bond Street."

"Thank you for the suggestion."

"Once you're fitted for some proper English clothes, come by White's so I might admire them."

Geoffrey took the languidly proffered card with a slight bow. Rutherford exhaled with obvious relief once the encounter was over. His new acquaintance had played bold with the Lord of Style's vanity, but it had earned him the desired result. With Brummell's patronage, his in at the exclusive gaming club was assured.

"You've won a weighty friend, Chilton. Most scheme for months to secure an introduction alone."

The viscount gave an indifferent shrug. "I have little patience for waiting. I've always gone after what I want down the quickest, most direct path. Adopt a lazy air, my friend, but never a lazy mind."

Rutherford gauged the tall man appreciatively, at the same time wondering how he would look in a beige tailcoat.

"Bearing in mind my fondness for the direct, if I was to look for the best match among the Mayfair misses, where would I cast my eye?"

Dabney thought for a moment, then replied, "Lady Rosalind Dunstan is a considerable heiress. I'll wager she's the primest of the plump-pocketed."

"You mean that exquisite creature you pointed out earlier?" he asked hopefully.

"No, no. That's the mama."

"Good gracious This lady must be little more than a babe!"

"Lady Camilla is Dunstan's second wife. Rosalind is his daughter and heir apparent. You'll have rocky going there if you think to court her. Many have tried to breech that thorny bower but none have succeeded."

Geoffrey cocked a curious brow. "Is the lady full of herself, then?"

Rutherford chuckled at his ignorance. "Quite the opposite. She's timid as a ghost. Nearly swoons if you look her way. Ain't a man here whose been able to coax two words out of her, let alone kindle her to even the remotest thoughts of passion. I suggest you set your sights on a lesser purse."

"Where is this blushing paragon of chastity? I'm quite

intrigued to meet someone immune to my charm." His glib inquiring gaze followed Rutherford's direction. The amusement fled his features. "That's Rosalind Dunstan?"

"Plain as porridge but with the bank of a Gold Bowl."

For a moment, he wasn't certain it was the same woman. As Dabney cited, she was no first-stepper. In fact, she was only a shade above passable and that wasn't how Geoffrey remembered the bold chit who had saved his skin then had come sweetly into his arms. They couldn't be one in the same, for this retiring miss was a titled lady, not a serving girl. No highborn lady would have given herself to his caresses. He thought back to that night, to the lovely creature who had feigned a meager protest only to fire his passion to the limit with her tender acquiescence. He had been moved to leave more than impersonal coin as a sign of his gratitude. The surrender of his mother's ring had wrought only the tiniest regret. Even unto this hour, he had considered a return to that inn, but as he studied the woman across the room, he knew he wouldn't find her there. She was here and she was far from what he had believed her to be.

Geoffrey assessed Lady Rosalind with a puzzled frown. Little of what he saw was appealing. Hunched among several other unattractive females, her demureness bordered on the fainthearted as she tried to fade into obscurity. The too-tight shift of apple green was appalling. The color sallowed her skin and the flirty material was at a variance with her demeanor. Its snug fit drew attention to a figure not designed for the day's fashion. Her hair was drawn back in a severe style unbecoming to her sharp bone structure. It highlighted her apprehensive eyes and the thin press of her lips.

Thoroughly confused, Geoffrey was about to concede to a mistake when those haunted eyes rose. They sparkled when they met his and the quick flush of animation assured he wasn't wrong. Smiling, he turned to his companion.

"If you're a betting man, Rutherford, I'll wager you twenty guineas that I get not only more than two words but an invitation to share more.

"You're on, Chilton. Lud, but you like to play deep."

He wasn't certain of what the lady's reaction would be to seeing him again. He didn't know her well enough to anticipate a fit of temper or a wailing of remorse over the ending of their evening together. Discovering her identity shed new light on his interpretation of that eve. She had objected, though not forcefully. Could it be he had cowed her into reluctant submission? Would there be a price to pay with some outraged father? He swallowed hard, thinking of how far he'd come only to be tumbled by an indiscreet desire.

His worries proved groundless. The Lady Rosalind greeted him with enviable aplomb, never batting an eye as they exchanged pleasantries. If he looked no farther than her dark, depthless eyes, he could see again the woman who had braced him without fear, had knelt at his feet to tend his injured hand, and had lied to protect him. He wanted very much to know that woman inside the timid shell.

When he had said his good nights, he collected his guineas with a confident hope that there was much more to be won. He was in considerable spirits as he walked the streets to the Chilton family townhouse on Grosvenor Square. His tone-less whistling announced him to the only other occupant in the ornate dwelling.

"Mon frère, was it a success?"

"I was the consummate snob, Henri. You would have been so proud." He grinned at the older man who joined him. He was dressed in the sober cloth of servitude. "A pity you couldn't have seen me."

"Impossible. A gentleman does not bring his valet to such affairs. He leaves him at home to waste away in laborious tedium and starvation."

Geoffrey laughed and tossed him a carefully wrapped parcel from out of the folds of his coat as they moved into the front room. All the furnishings were still shrouded in their dusty coverings. The lanky Frenchman gave an appreciative cry at the sight of pilfered slices of rare beef and hard rolls.

"Now, if we only had a decent French wine," he murmured.

A bottle was produced with a showy flourish. Geoffrey squinted in the dim light. "A fair port. Will it suffice?"

"He asks me if I will settle for dog spittle. Ah well, if it was the best you could do *mon ami,* I will not complain."

"Thank you for your graciousness." Geoffrey dropped into one of the covered chairs and regarded the man who called him brother. Henri Girard was his stepbrother, but more than that, his trusted friend. That link was as strong as any forged of blood. He had a fine aristocratic bearing and features chiseled to an arrogant perfection. "Coming here was your idea if you'll recall, so don't moan of your discomfort to me. I shall not be sympathetic. I'm the one who has to

32

endure the dreadful gatherings of London's boring elite. I suppose I'll need more of this stuff." He drew out the snuff box with a distasteful grimace. "Disgusting," he pronounced adamantly before he turned to his own preference and lit a slim, dark cheroot. He expelled a stream of smoke and watched it filter up toward the high, muraled ceiling.

"Geoff, you have the cultivated tastes of an ostler."

Grinning, he swung one long, well-made leg over the arm of the chair with a lethargic grace and finished his smoke while the other made quick work of his makeshift supper.

While they split the bottle of wine, he said casually, "You've done wonders with the house."

Henri frowned at the sarcasm and declared, "I have no intention of becoming your housemaid. If you wish it cleaned, I am more than willing to watch. It seems as though it's been empty for a hundred years rather than a mere twenty."

"At least it's costing us nothing, which is about all we can afford at the moment. If you prefer Grillion's Hotel, be my guest."

"I am content here. You've made your point. As you said, it is a roof over our heads."

Neither wanted to think of the sundry places they had found to sleep over the last few years. The dusty, cavernous rooms were by far better than most. As it was temporary, anything could be endured.

"Be thankful my uncle kept up his rents. I'm surprised it's in this good condition. I'm sure he's not going to mind us borrowing it for the short time we're in London." He took another drink and said casually, "I'm opening an account with Weston to have some coats made." He felt the keen, dark eyes pierce him with displeasure. There was a long silence and finally, he ventured a glance at the figure seated on the floor.

"Coats? Geoff, you know we haven't enough left to afford a good wine let alone to clothe you like a king."

"Not a king, Henri, a viscount. If I'm to sell the package it must be properly wrapped. None of these fine merchants will press us right away."

"And when they do, how are you going to pay them?"

"I'll simply order more. They can hardly dun me when I've given them more business. That's how things are done in civilized circles. I'll need some cards, as well, and five shil-

33

lings for the General Post so I can get the early London delivery. Stop shooting daggers at me, Hank."

Henri shook his head wonderingly. "You have the greatest talent for spending what you do not have. You will have markers all over the city."

"See how far this goes then." He tossed fifteen guineas into his brother's lap in hopes of dispelling his pout.

"Where did you find this fortune?" His inquiring glance fell on the smallest finger of his hand. In an anguished tone, he said, "Not your ring. You didn't sell it, did you? Geoff, things are not that desperate." He knew how cherished the heirloom was. "You haven't thought to use it the same way as the necklace, have you?"

"No, I put it to much better use. Don't worry over our funds. Soon, all will be right with us. You'll see. Soon we'll be able to spend without a care."

"I fear you do that already. Have you some scheme in the works?" The gloomy shadow was gone from the handsome face.

"Decidedly so. If we can hold on to this masquerade, our futures are secured. No more borrowing port or sleeping under borrowed roofs. We shall be men of consequence, you and I."

Henri lifted the bottle in an agreeable toast to whatever plot brought the speculative glint to the slanting blue eyes. "To our future."

Chapter Four

Rosalind tipped her small parasol so it shielded her, more from curious onlookers than from the afternoon sun. For a lady to take a tour of Hyde Park between the fashionable hours of four and five was all the fashion, but for Lady Rosalind it was a novelty. Her fondness for the outdoors and horses had never coaxed her into that high society rendezvous. She found nothing relaxing about being posed in a carriage for the bucks to ogle from horseback in the ridiculous crush of vehicles. For her to request an outing and insist on going alone raised more than one brow.

Rosalind had chosen the earlier hour in hopes of avoiding the majority of the social circus. While crowded, the park's broad avenues were yet uncongested and the stylish barouche spun along smoothly behind the pair of perfectly matched greys. She struggled to maintain a casual semblance while her eyes chased along the shady byways in search of a single figure among the many. Her sights were set high to scan the numerous riders so she nearly missed the lone figure strolling at an easy pace. In her haste to stop the carriage, she was almost unseated. She managed to rearrange her skirts and compose herself before calling out nonchalantly.

"Good afternoon, Lord Chilton."

Her heart took a sudden stagger when his eyes turned to her and the broad smile flashed in greeting. He made his way to the side of her carriage and leaned upon his walking cane.

"Lady Rosalind, how good it is to see you. A fine day to take in the air."

"Yes, it is. I had forgotten your preference for two legs over four. Does that forbid you from the comfort of a conveyance?"

Her hesitant boldness made him chuckle. "Not at all."

Rosalind took a deep breath. She was being very forward but she wanted private words with him. "Would you care to join me in a turn about the park?"

"I'd be delighted."

When he stepped up, he was surprised when she swept her skirts to one side, offering him a place next to her. He settled into it not knowing she reasoned his nearness would be easier to bear than his scrutiny from the opposite seat.

His closeness was more difficult than she could have predicted. It brought back reminders of a more intimate warmth and, unbidden, her pulse began an erratic race. She had spent long hours thinking of what she would say to him but now her tongue felt thick and awkward and her mind went embarrassingly blank. Thankfully, he didn't stare at her in impatience, waiting for her to speak. He was resting leisurely back into the seat, apparently content to take in the passing spectacle. She hazarded a glance at him and her eyes lingered overlong, enthralled in his cleanly cut profile. He caught her gaze and tendered a brief, unpressuring smile.

"I understand you've been living in Paris," she began a bit weakly. "Is this your first visit to London?"

"That I can truly remember, yes. My mother told me much about it so I don't feel a stranger."

"A stranger to your own country? How odd."

"I feel more French than English. I left here when I was quite young. I never planned to return."

The tang of bitterness in his tone prompted a puzzled look. "Yet, here you are."

"Yes." That calm monosyllable invited no further questions.

They were silent for a time, Rosalind trying to use the quiet to summon her courage and Geoffrey covertly gauging the expensive equipage with its liveried footmen and be-wigged coachman. He priced every detail from the magnificent Thoroughbreds to the three-cornered hats and French gloves of the servants and filed it all away.

"How is your hand?" she asked tentatively, nudging toward the topic she longed to discuss with this elegant stranger who was also contrarily well known to her.

He flexed gloved fingers. "Healing nicely. Thank you. Thank you for many things," he added in a husky undervoice.

Rosalind said nothing. Color flamed in her face. She felt hot. She didn't dare use her fan for fear the trembling of her hands would draw notice. She couldn't look at him as he continued in a low timbre.

36

"I never would have presumed so much had I known your station. I am not some self-serving rake who feels he must make a conquest in every bed he passes."

"Why then?" she asked of him. The words quavered. Her parasol twirled in nervous fingers.

"You were in a servant's room," he began.

"And you suffer no qualms in bedding them?" There was a slight bite to her tone that took him aback.

"No . . . I mean, yes. What I mean has nothing to do with that. You took me in, a stranger. You cared for me. You lied for me. You came into bed with me. I thought—"

"You were mistaken," she cried as if in pain, then lowered her voice to explain in tremulous urgency. "The inn was full. That was the only room available. You fell asleep and I didn't have the heart to wake you. It was cold. I drank too much wine. I only thought to rest for a moment. I never imagined that you—that you would—"

She took the handkerchief he offered and pressed it to quivering lips. Geoffrey sat helplessly while dampness welled in the injured dark eyes. Their words may have been private but their actions were on display for all those passing and he didn't want to compromise her further by making an attempt to comfort her. Wretchedly, he said, "Lady Rosalind, my behavior was inexcusable. I took advantage of your kindness and your vulnerability and I beg you to forgive me. I am willing to do the honorable thing if that be your wish."

He heard her draw a long, shaky breath. The handkerchief lowered to her lap where it was tortured by restless hands. Eyes downcast and voice faint, she said, "I would not demand that kind of sacrifice."

"Perhaps it would not be one. Are you suggesting we forget anything happened?" he challenged gently.

"There's not much chance of that, sir." The snap of anger was more apparent now, as if her pride rather than her honor suffered. "It is not as though I am forgiving a thoughtless word or rude slight."

How, indeed, could she forget the way he had made her feel, the way she felt even now just being with him? She felt light-headed, she felt ill with anxiety, she felt confused and at the same time, marvelously clear-sighted. She wanted to hide in shame and, contrarily, to turn to him and kiss that wide, sensuous mouth in desperate longing.

"Rosalind, I would like very much to call on you."

The low, encouraging tone gave her a chill of warning and of delight. More than anything, she wanted to see him again. And again. And again. Instead, she told him very quietly, "I don't think so, Lord Chilton."

She motioned for the carriage to halt and with cool dignity extended her hand. He took it respectfully. Her hand had been kissed many times but never had it felt scorched. He lavished it with the same attention he would her lips and it left her with the same breathless feeling. He stared long into her eyes, waiting, until she realized she still clung to his hand. Flushing, she let him go.

"I shall be near should you change your mind." His voice rumbled with seductive promise.

"Good afternoon, my lord."

Rosalind discovered on her return that Nathaniel Everard had called no less than three times and was anxious to remind her of her promise to attend at Almack's that evening. Though wishing she might cry off, her father made it plain that she was to make herself available and that he himself would be on hand to see that she did. That knowledge alone sealed her night with the stamp of misery. She went through the necessary preparations with a resigned moping, yielding to Camilla's choice of a straw-colored gown, though privately she frowned over the fussy rows of swags and frills. The stylish Camilla insisted it would make her all the thing. She thought it made her look like a well-stuffed pastry.

Nathaniel was ever prompt and remarked on her fine elbow-length gloves, making her certain the dress was ghastly. His banal conversation did much to relax her mounting dread and she managed to give him an encouraging smile. Faithful Nate looked so grateful, she was almost ashamed for her casual treatment of his suit. She resolved to be an agreeable escort. He deserved that much and it would placate her father for the time being.

Rosalind had been in the fashionable assembly hall for less than the time it took for whispers to run from one side to the next before she was aware of the substance of the talk. Lady Rosalind was desperate for a husband. She, who was usually ignored, became the uncomfortable focus of attention. Nathaniel became a thankful foil, staying close by her side to protect his position as well as to save her from the insincere crush of admirers. Still, she was deluged with flowery greetings, hopeful suggestions of later meetings and invitations to dance. Rosalind was polite, carefully vague and quite adamant. Only her dancing surpassed her conversation in gracelessness. She would have been content to cling to Nathaniel's arm all evening, but her father was of a different mind. He interceded neatly, sending young Everard off on his wife's arm to guarantee a private word with his daughter.

"You are putting up a discouraging front, Rosalind. Have you chosen Everard, then, or a martyred future?"

"Papa, please," she murmured, horrified lest someone overhear and add scandalous fuel to their rumor machine.

"He'll do, I suppose. He's a bit thin-blooded. I'd hoped you'd choose from a more vital stock, one with good, strong lines and promise. Everard looks a bit weak-hocked and short of wind."

"Good heavens, Papa, we're not discussing horseflesh. Next, you'll be wanting to see the bottom of their feet and their teeth." She couldn't repress an annoyed sigh. It was all too absurd.

"Good breeding is good breeding. I didn't develop the best string of Thoroughbreds in the country by guess work. You want a strong line, you get a lusty stallion full of heart and stamina. If I were to choose betwixt the blooded stock at this gathering, I'd pick Chilton's heir. Now that's a virile-looking buck. I'll wager he'd get a fine string of sons on you."

Rosalind went rigid with shock and outrage. In low, freezing accents, she exclaimed, "If all you are interested in is breeding a line of heirs, I suggest you forget marriage. Just tether me in the barn, pay him the serving fee, and be done with it."

She turned to stalk away and collided squarely with a familiar, immovable form. She made as if to recoil in alarm but her hand and waist were firmly caught to whirl her out amongst the waltzing couples.

Rosalind felt faint with dismay and embarrassment. There was no way Geoffrey could have missed the exchange between her and her father. To have her desperate predicament aired before him of all people was a humiliation too great to swallow. While she gulped noisy breaths in an attempt to restore her composure, he moved her glidingly about the floor. She was too distraught to be awkward in his arms and, for once, the steps came naturally.

Feeling the eddies of distress ripple through her, Geoffrey

held Rosalind close as he dared, hoping that his nearness might fortify instead of provoke her further. In a teasing humor, he said, "I came to rescue you from the crush of your admirers. Should I have waited for your father to have examined my teeth?"

A laugh trembled from her. Remarkably, the worst of the moment seemed to pass and she was able to see the ridiculousness of it. As upset subsided, a warm tingle of awareness rose. The large hand that opened wide upon the small of her back pressed her toward the welcoming expanse of his chest and it was a struggle to resist the pull. Shyly, her gaze settled on the elaborate folds of his showy cravat as if entranced by its intricate twists. Slowly, it rose to the corded neck and sturdy chin, then lifted another degree. As she detailed the ripe, sensual contours of his mouth, it began to stretch and curve until dimples creased the lean cheeks.

"I'm sure he would approve of my teeth, Miss Dunstan."

Rosalind flushed and gathered the courage to force her stare higher. His smoky eyes crinkled with amusement but not at her expense. It was an intimate look, one that implied a shared secret that they could enjoy together. It coaxed an answering smile from her, and that relaxed gesture softened her pinched features, giving him a glimpse of the woman within.

"I'm sure your teeth are fine, Lord Chilton," she countered lightly.

"Then would you consider me?"

"As what, sir?" The husky question made her wary.

"As one of your prospective suitors. I did say I planned to rescue you."

Her laugh was nervous and uncertain. He was smiling but his slanted eyes were intense in their probing of her own.

"I'm not in need of rescue, my lord."

"Indeed? If you need no champion, I shall be forced to join the ranks."

She swallowed in agitation and licked dry lips. His stare had grown too warm, too persistent. "We are barely acquainted, sir."

"What more would you like to know?"

Rosalind colored at that silky chiding. It was too difficult to think when he was touching her. It made her thoughts transgress in disturbing directions. "I know enough."

"Mad, bad, and dangerous to know, is that it? Is that

description befitting me as well as your infamous Byron? Can you say what you already know isn't enough to make you want more?"

She stepped away from him in confusion and left the dance floor. Providently, her departure was well timed with the end of the waltz so no one knew she was fleeing in a panic. Except herself and Lord Chilton.

Watching his daughter with Geoffrey Chilton, James Dunstan's eyes narrowed thoughtfully. Oddly enough, they made an attractive pairing, solid and earthy in tones of brown and gold. It was more than his size that detracted from her inelegance. She seemed to lose that graceless hesitancy when turning on his arm. Her features took on a delicate glow of color when tilted up toward his, and damn if she wasn't lovely to behold. That surprised him. He'd never seen his reserved, bookish daughter in that light before. He'd always thought it a shame that she had inherited none of her mother's beauty, yet here it was, sparkling up like a fresh, bubbly well to reflect the lowered eyes of her handsome partner. The scholarly Everard had never struck that spark, nor had any of a dozen others.

He was thinking of her angry suggestion when she rejoined him moments later looking flushed and breathless. Without a word, he looped his arm through hers, gratified when she hugged it close. He was smiling faintly as his eyes followed the tall, able figure of Geoffrey Chilton back to William, second baron of Alvanly who had procured his invitation to the night's festivities.

He was smiling that same smile when Chilton responded to his invitation to lunch at Garroway's in Exchange Alley. Though the coffeehouse was crowded with its usual array of prominent auctioneers and merchandise brokers, the viscount had no trouble finding him at his secluded table.

After they exchanged pleasantries, Dunstan gave the younger man a chance to order a drink and a meal. Then the dark, dusk-colored eyes regarded him directly, waiting to hear the reason for their meeting.

"Do you know who I am, Chilton?"

"Yes, sir. I make it a practice to know everyone of wealth and influence and you have a considerable amount of both." And who didn't know James Dunstan, fifth earl, also Viscount Alnwick and Baron of Stalbridge. As if the revenue brought by titles alone wasn't sufficient, Dunstan had accumulated his own personal fortune, one that was unentailed and destined to his only daughter.

Dunstan nodded, pleased by the observation and the blunt way in which it was given. "I have considerably more than anyone else." He tapped the copy of *Lloyd's List*. He'd been reading the maritime news while waiting. "I have extensive interests here as well as abroad. I have dealings in the Colonies, on the Continent and anywhere else there is a profit to be had. My horses are the finest fencers you' ll ever see. Even the poorest would fetch over a thousand guineas. I've spent my life building a fortune to pass on with pride and now, I fear it all ends with me."

"A shame to see such a legacy die."

"I mean to see it doesn't. I need to know the line will continue, strong and vital, and that my interests, all of them, will be well tended."

"You are an admirable steward, my lord."

Dunstan gauged his companion closely. Chilton was lounging comfortably in his chair, long legs carelessly crossed, but the leisurely posture ended at his eyes. They were alert and attentive, grasping every nuance of what was being said. Casually, the young lord drew out a snuff box and made a polite offering. His manner was smooth but affected.

"No, thank you. I'm not a nose man," he said curtly.

Chilton flashed a brilliant smile. "You didn' t have the look of one." The box disappeared, replaced by thin cheroots. The two men smoked in silence while assessing each other.

Geoffrey saw in James Dunstan everything he admired — wealth, position, power, and an unshakable control over all in his grasp. He was too shrewd to be fooled by silky words and flattery. He was a simple man who saw things in black and white, loss or gain. He saw his greatest accomplishment as one passed down through his loins, a continuation of himself, his piece of eternity, and Geoffrey waited patiently, knowing if he did, all would come to him in one neat package.

"How well do you know my daughter Rosalind?"

The bold question was greeted unblinkingly. "We met informally on the road to London and several times thereafter."

"And how did she strike you?"

He didn't have to explain where his conversation was leading and Chilton followed easily.

"She is no great beauty but she has a well-regulated mind.

42

We get on quite well and I don't believe she takes any exception to me. And she is also your daughter, my lord."

"Are you planning to court her?"

"Do you advise it?"

Dunstan gave a slow smile. "Can you afford not to? Rosalind is my daughter. But what good is a fortune if there is no heir? The knowledge of a proper heir would be worth a great deal to me."

"That makes my suit very attractive."

"With my endorsement, Rosalind could find it irresistible."

"If that were true, you would already have your heirs."

Dunstan flushed darkly at the impertinent observation, then chuckled. He liked Chilton. He was clever and ambitious and bright enough to see beyond the obvious. "Just so."

"You know nothing about me, sir."

"I don't care about your politics or your personal habits. I am a selfish man. Will you give me what I want?"

"It seems that we want the same things, my lord." He raised his glass and Dunstan responded to the salute with a satisfied nod.

"You will make a fine son-in-law."

"And if your daughter doesn't agree?"

"That, my dear Chilton, is how you are going to earn your way."

Chapter Five

Whereas Nathaniel had been patient before, even tolerant of her indecisiveness, he was pressured to grow bolder by the attractive lure of Rosalind's fortune. He wasn't blind to the interest stirred by rumors of her urgent need to be wedded. He was a quiet, methodical man but these were desperate times. His need to commit the lady to an answer overwhelmed his normal reflective passivity. Determinedly, he vowed to woo her by sheer perseverance.

Nathaniel was encouraged when she agreed to accompany him for a carriage ride. She sat opposite him, eyes wandering wistfully while he read verse to her in the pleasant spring sunshine. This was one time he'd hoped to touch on her emotions rather than her intellect and he had chosen the text appropriately. It appeared a success, for her cheeks held a becoming pink and her look was distracted as she listened. When they spun through Berkeley Square on the return, she met his suggestion that they stop for a cooling ice with a nod of approval.

Sitting comfortably in the shaded barouche, Rosalind let her fancies drift over the amorous verses Nathaniel had spoken. He would have been crushed to learn that her thoughts hadn't once touched on him. Her musings had another source and so involved was she in the depth of those daydreams that she blinked in alarm to find their focus so close at hand.

Geoffrey Ghilton lounged by the rail and smiled to affirm he had been watching her for some moments. He looked away only long enough to pay the waiter who dashed across the street from the famed confectioner's shop with its pineapple address instead of a number. He took two tinkling glasses from the tray and approached her carriage to give an elegant bow.

"Lady Rosalind, how nice to see you."

Rosalind had begun to frown in irrational pique at the

44

sight of the two frosty glasses. She wondered which of the waiting lovelies he was catering to until he extended one of the sorbets to her. It was the heat of his fingers rather than the chill of the glass that made her shiver. He received her murmur of thanks with a bold smile.

"You looked a bit overwarm. From Byron, I see." He lifted the open book from the opposite seat and quoted with a mocking breathlessness, " 'Thru sin's long labyrinth had run, with pleasure drugged, he almost longed for woe.' " He arched a brow as she snatched the volume of *Childe Harold's Pilgrimage* from him. "Miss Dunstan, you didn' t strike me as the type of giddy female who would swoon in lovesick delight over Byron's glowing rhetoric."

She glowered at him, wishing he would go away yet helplessly admiring him as he leaned his elbows on the gilded door beside her. His chin rested atop folded hands and the tall glass dangled precariously beneath that indolent arch. His look was provokingly personal. The sun gleamed off his deep gold hair in an exciting invitation to feel the warmth of those bared locks. She was overly warm and growing increasingly so under his sultry stare and insinuating smirk.

"It must be the verse, for I can see nothing in your gangling companion to inspire such a passion. I could read you more to keep you simmering while you await his return."

"You are impertinent, sir," she clipped out in a show of annoyance, which was quickly calmed when he began to recite from memory. His voice was low, velvet seduction, giving the words of forbidden romance an unbearable, throbbing pulse. The dusky eyes held hers entranced, enticing her with their smoldering lure. His nearness created a magnetism that made her blood pump too rapidly in response to its exciting pull. The words were a disturbing reminder of what already lay between them.

When the recitation was complete, Rosalind shook herself from his charmed spell. She gave a sound of dismay to find the moisture from her tightly gripped glass had puddled damply on her skirt.

"Let me."

Without invitation, Geoffrey dabbed at the wetness with his handkerchief. The feel of his purposefully indelicate fumbling upon the tops of her thighs gave her an abrupt jolt of indecent want. In her agitation, more of the crystalline drink sloshed out and he set industriously to mopping it up.

"Stop," she cried hoarsely. She seized his hand and for a moment, their gazes locked.

"I beg your pardon" came a stiff remark. "Am I intruding here?"

Rosalind thrust the offending hand away and faced Nathaniel with a look of wide-eyed panic. "Don't be a goose, Nate. Of course you're not." She returned the half-spilled glass back to the smug lord and smiled sweetly up at her escort as she took the icy treat he brought her.

"Nathaniel, I don't believe you've met the viscount. Chilton, this is the Honorable Nathaniel Everard."

The two men exchanged crisply civil howdy-dos.

Nathaniel settled territorially into the barouche and eyed the other pointedly until he straightened from his casual lolling upon the door. "I wasn't aware you were acquainted," he said brittely.

"Most intimately," Geoffrey said with a meaningful smile. He looked to Rosalind for confirmation, but she sat silent, eyes downcast and features suddenly pale. "I can see I am intruding now. A good day to you. Miss Dunstan, always a pleasure."

He sauntered away and Rosalind's gust of expelled breath was more damning than his brash words had been. Nathaniel observed her closely and his apprehension grew. He may not have been a terribly clever man but he wasn't dim enough not to realize something disquieting had passed between the two, something he'd never been able to incite with all his torrid verses and proper lovemaking. This was something deep and very different and he didn't like it or Lord Chilton at all.

Before he had a chance to discuss any of his suspicions, Rosalind seemed herself again and gave him a hopeful glance.

"You remembered the invitation to dine with us tonight, didn't you, Nate? I'd be most distressed if you've made other plans."

Her inexpert cajolery lifted him from his mood to exclaim, "Forget? Never! I always anticipate the time I spend with you, would that it be more."

She looked away from the expectant expression and gave a wan smile.

Dinner with the Dunstans would have been a solemn affair

if not for the determined animation of Camilla. She could keep up a gay chatter to fill in the lack of response from both husband and daughter and make it appear natural. If Rosalind had ever a reason to be thankful to her for being the perfect hostess, it was that night.

Rosalind appeared late, having broken the clasp on the necklace she intended to wear. Having nothing else to wear with the pink tulle Camilla had suggested, she was forced to dig through her closets to find a replacement. Her groping fingers were stayed by the touch of silk. Puzzled, she drew out a gown of deep ruby silk and blond lace. She had purchased it long ago, having taken an instant fancy to the sumptuous fabric, but Camilla's insistence that it was too old for her doomed it to hang untried. Seeing it again made her smile with remembered pleasure and, impulsively, she slipped it on, adding a short rope of pearls before hurrying downstairs.

Everyone was already assembled in the main saloon. Camilla's look made her hesitate, her fingers clutching in the flowing skirt. The older woman seemed almost angry. Before she could withdraw, Nathaniel saw her and gaped for a moment before rushing to take up her hand. His fervent kiss upon it surprised her.

"Rosalind, how—how very fine you look," he murmured. His cheeks were flushed, making her wonder if he was a trifle foxed.

Then she saw the reason for his strange behavior. Her father had been speaking with another man when she entered the room. Now, they both turned toward her politely. Her dark eyes stood out in wide relief against the sudden pallor of her skin.

"There you are, Daughter," Dunstan scolded. He was emphatic about punctuality. "I was about to order dinner served without you. I hope you don't mind a last-minute addition to our table."

Her smile was frozen. "Of course not, Father. Good evening, Lord Chilton."

He had been leaning against the mantel and straightened. That simple movement contained a ripple and flex of power not concealed by his well-tailored evening clothes. There was something disturbingly sensual in the way he moved as if all the languid grace was a pretense to cover what he really was. Whatever that might be, Rosalind knew it was a danger to her. His smoky eyes traveled over her in a quick, thorough summation that left her blushing. His smile was frankly carnal, reminding her that he had seen her in a much different light. That blatant look in the private setting of her home instilled a panic within her breast as if suddenly she was no longer safe from the threat of him and her own weakness to it.

Rosalind managed to force down her portion of the braised ham and larded sweetbreads, retaining a meager appetite as long as her eyes didn't lift to those that were steadily watching her from across the table. At her side, the normally quiet Nathaniel was laboring over his end of the conversation in obvious competition with one who excelled far beyond his scope of stilted charm. Geoffrey Chilton was unfailingly at ease. When he couldn't draw Rosalind out, he kept up an animated discourse with Camilla who insisted he tell her all about Paris. With the years of tiresome war, the tiny island seemed horribly isolated from the glamorous vitality of the Continent. While Nathaniel could only moan of his inability to take the Grand Tour to polish his manners and languages, Chilton was a fount of information. Camilla sighed as he spoke of eating *cotelle à la Soubise* at Beauvilliers in the rue de Richelieu. She exclaimed at his telling of duels between French and English officers in the Bois de Boulogne and at their aftermath, when the survivor would treat his friends to champagne at Tortani's. She gasped in horror at his description of Frenchwomen's enormous bonnets. From that, she shifted skillfully into a deep discussion of maritime treaties in the Americas with her husband. In those political waters, Nathaniel floundered and sank in silence.

Rosalind couldn't help but admire the way Geoffrey held to his part with her father. Dunstan was opinionated to the extreme, yet the young viscount managed to disagree with such smooth and well-tempered aggression that voices never raised. The earl let only those who he truly respected harbor contentions. Nathaniel was not of that mold.

As they picked from a basket of pastries, Dunstan announced casually, "Chilton, if you have the time, come down to Lloyd's tomorrow. I'd be interested to hear how your ideas fare among the knowledgeable."

"I'd be honored, sir."

Everard was crushed. He had never received an invitation to meet with Rosalind's father at any but social functions. As

48

the meal ended, he hoped for a chance to recoup when the earl suggested he might enjoy viewing some of J.M.W. Turner's landscapes he had purchased for Camilla, who was very fond of the reclusive artist's water colors. But even that bright glimmer dimmed with his next words.

"Rosalind, take Chilton down to the stables and show him that new fencer you're so proud of. You've never seen horseflesh until you've looked into our barns. Don't fidget about, girl. It will be dark soon."

Thusly dismissed into his company, Rosalind led Geoffrey through the rear gardens to the elaborate mews from which the wicker of horses and the pungent scent of straw drifted into the cool night. He was respectfully silent as they walked, not urging her to entertain him and apparently content with her awkward stillness. Once inside the warm, cavernous stable, she began a quiet tour from stall to stall. Geoffrey half-listened, counting the satiny Thoroughbreds and adding guineas by the thousands in his head.

It wasn't until she stopped at the last stall that Rosalind captured his full attention. When she spoke in a low, husky voice, a coal black muzzle stretched over the stall door to nudge her shoulder.

"This is Pericles. I stole him from Tattersall's at a mere two thousand guineas. Look at that chest and those legs. He's every inch a champion."

"I'm sure he has good teeth, too."

Rosalind ignored the wry remark and whispered softly into the sharply pricked ears. "His offspring are going to be everything that's the best in horseflesh. He's been matched with my best mare and if the result is what I expect, he'll be paired with the finest mares at our manor."

"Sounds like an enviable life, cropping clover and lazing about while the fillies are brought to you."

She glanced at him then, trying to maintain her frown. He was lounging against the stall, one foot crossed over the other, a blade of straw twirling between his teeth. His eyes glimmered roguishly. "But only for the deserving," she told him coolly, then turned back to the stallion. "The best are always deserving, aren't they, baby," she crooned into the shell-like ears.

Geoffrey watched her with the horse as she rubbed the sleek hide and soft nose. The movements were gentle, even loving. The forbidding attitude dropped away and he

49

glimpsed the tenderness it sought to protect. In the mellow glow of lanternlight, her face radiated a warmth of caring, of deep passion and feeling. His gaze followed the hypnotic stroke of her hand along the muscled withers and his flesh began to prickle in unqualified longing. When her lips pursed to touch between the dark, liquid eyes, his own tingled in response. The sound of his quickened breathing startled him, bringing awareness to his sudden, unbidden arousal. His wish that she would lavish such affection upon him was a revelation he hadn't prepared for. Nor was coming to a smelly barn with a remote spinster to find, instead, a lovely Circe. Would that she transform him into a beast so he could suffer from her attention.

"You are so beautiful."

Rosalind jumped in alarm at the husky words spoken against her ear, then frowned at their meaning. Geoffrey had abandoned his leisurely pose and was standing close, very close. Her back was to the stall as she looked up at him in an anxious panic.

"Sir, I am not such a fool as to believe that," she said quietly.

His fingertip traced down the angular line of her jaw. "Do you call me liar because I see what I see? I see a woman who should never hide inside those spun-cotton frills made for coy schoolmisses. I see a woman whose beauty is like a precious gem with many facets of unequaled brilliance. You should dress yourself in the colors of those sparkling stones, all bold and flash but warm and secret within."

She shrunk back as his hands rose, but they went up to her hair. His fingers meshed deep to loosen the rigid coiffure until its fullness softened her features becomingly.

"Rosalind, you're going to marry me."

She stared at him. He said it so calmly, with such confidence she almost believed it a fact. His eyes gave a drooping flicker and his lips parted as he bent down. With a small cry, she ducked under his arm and began to walk rapidly toward the house. He caught up to her easily but made no move to restrain her.

"Why?" she demanded tightly. "You don't need the money."

"Is that the only reason to wed?"

"Why else in my case?" She stopped to face him, her eyes shimmering in the darkness. "Why else would anyone be interested in pressing suit? For the money. It's always been for the money. I've lived with that knowledge and accept it. Don't insult my intelligence, my lord."

"Then don't insult my good taste."

Before she could speak, he seized her up in a crushing embrace. His mouth twisted upon hers, wringing a groan akin to pain from her.

"No," she cried unevenly and tried to push away. "No?" he questioned gently, but his grasp didn't slacken. She squirmed against the solid plane of his chest, fighting her desire to yield more fervently than his aggression. "That's not the answer in your heart. Why pretend it to be otherwise?"

Rosalind couldn't think clearly. The powerful, potent signals he was sending wrecked havoc on her senses. The fists that braced against his chest trembled in their want to hold him. Her white, thin lips quivered with the need to soften beneath his. Only the edge of her will hung on to reality with a bitter tenacity.

"The answer is still no," she told him with faint yet firm defiance. "You took advantage of my weakness before but the same is not the case this time. I don't lift my skirts for any rutting buck who considers himself an unequaled catch. I may not be beautiful but you'll find I am prideful."

The mounting strength of her words made him smile strangely. His hold loosened and she jerked away to assume a straight, combative pose. How little resemblance there was to the timid wallflower from the crowded parlor at Oatlands.

"There is already a bond between us that you cannot deny. Why else would you still wear my ring?"

She glanced down at the bright flash of rubies and diamonds in surprise. Why, indeed? She hadn't questioned it before and now it angered her that he should draw such a smug conclusion. With a contrary flare of temper, she drew off the gold band.

"Take it back. As you can see, I do not need payment for your favors."

Not wanting to risk the dangerous contact with him, she gave the ring an indifferent toss. The ring struck his arm and rebounded in a twinkling arc before settling into one of the decorative ponds with an ominous plunk.

Geoffrey was instantly on his knees. His hand plunged beneath the black, glassy surface without a pause to push up his sleeve. After a moment of unfruitful groping, his search grew more desperate.

51

Rosalind frowned as she watched him, annoyed by his greedy attachment to the gems. "I am sorry," she said with a stiff graciousness. "If it was valuable, I'll see it is replaced."

"I don't care about the value," he growled. "You can't replace it. It's all I have left of my mother."

Something in the rough emotion of his voice lodged in her heart and she found herself down beside him, fishing through the cold water. Stretched out as far as she dared, her fingertips brushed tauntingly upon a small circle.

"I have it. Almost," she cried happily and reached a bit further. Her bracing palm slid on the mossy edge. Overextended as she was, she went headlong into the pool. Her gasp of shock as the icy water rushed down the front of her gaping bodice was choked off in a sputter. One of her flailing hands was caught and used to haul her from her unexpected dunking. She coughed and floundered for a trace of composure, then all fled when she found herself cradled in Geoffrey's lap. The laughter in his eyes quieted. His large hand rose to push aside the clinging strands of her ruined coif, then steadied her rebellious head.

"Rosalind, marry me."

She drew a tortured breath and began with an objecting shake, "I will —"

He interrupted that final word of denial by kissing her. He certainly knew how to conclude a disagreement, Rosalind thought in a panic of bliss. Her lips parted in submission, innocently opening the way for a taste of passion's potential that set her mind whirling. His kisses grew deep and desire drugged. The intrusion of his tongue caused her to recoil briefly from naive shock rather than displeasure then she relaxed to savor the tantalizing quest. Of their own accord, her arms had slipped over his shoulders, remaining there as he turned them both and laid her back upon the cool grass.

With him above her and the stars and the mighty infinity of the heavens as his backdrop, the dreamlike sense returned to Rosalind. Her eyes closed tight in a wash of forbidden delight as his fingers brushed over the peaks of her breasts that had risen hard and chilled against the damp cling of silk.

"My lord," she managed in a breathy moan. "Oh, Geoffrey — please."

Uncertain if she meant for him to go on or to stop, Geoffrey hesitated. He looked down upon the flushed face and tenderly parted lips and into the eyes that opened in shy confusion and he realized that she didn't know, either. The dark, vulnerable eyes were liquid and pleading but to what end? Still, he hesitated. Her look was so unguarded, so tearfully resigned to her own weakness.

Rosalind received his kiss upon trembling lips. How different it was, slow and sweetly gentle, seeking only to share instead of dominate. Her resistance gave with a quiet sigh, yet he made no move to revel in her surrender. He sat back slowly and lifted his ring from her palm. Wordlessly, he slipped it on her left hand. A shiver of expectation shook through her at that simple, symbolic gesture.

"Come. You're wet and cold. Let's get you inside," he said softly.

She stood with his assistance, mindless of her sodden appearance, of the gown that molded to the full thrust of her breasts and clung to the long line of her legs. Geoffrey's eyes never left hers to ogle that luscious sight. Instead, he shrugged out of his coat and used it to cloak her dripping figure, then steered her to the house. She was too dazed to appreciate the discreet way he smuggled her into the hall and urged her up the stairs before awkward explanations had to be made. Nor did she see the way his smoky eyes followed her ascent.

Geoffrey was carefully close to the cuff with his own emotions until he broke into a tuneless whistle on his walk home. His own elation was hard to explain. He hadn't actually won anything, yet his enthusiasm was boundless. His plan to dazzle a prim, timid miss couldn't have been more ill-advised. Rosalind Dunstan was a complex creature, full of surprising turns and flares of cynical insight. She wouldn't be dazzled by him but could he say the same?

In the stuffy parlor, Geoffrey reached down to clear the sofa of its scattering of papers. There were stacks of maritime periodicals, books on commercial enterprise, articles on Thoroughbred bloodlines, all bits and pieces he was studying furiously in his effort to impress Dunstan. Several sheets listed the assets he'd been able to discover and an approximate tally, ever-growing, of the earl's worth. It rose to dizzying heights after seeing the inside of his posh home. Not to mention the stables. He had no interest in cataloguing them now.

He stretched out on the yielding cushions, long legs crossed and dangling over the far arm. While he drifted into unfocused wanderings, his fingertips traced the wide line of his mouth in unconscious circles. When he realized he was becoming increasingly uncomfortable, he licked his lips as if to deny he was mooning over the feel of Miss Dunstan's kisses. She had him in a strange agitation, body and mind at a variance, yet longing for the same thing. If he wasn't careful, he feared he would be a victim of his own scheming.

Chapter Six

Geoffrey was awakened by the slap of a stack of papers upon his chest. He stretched awkwardly on the sofa and eyed Henri in bleary question.

"Time for a talk, *mon ami*," the Frenchman said tersely.

"What is all this?" Geoffrey murmured. As he sat up, the pile shifted, sending a dozen or so slips to the floor. He picked up several and understood the other's glowering disposition. "Can't this wait until after I've breakfasted?" he pleaded hopefully.

"Now, *s'il vous plaît*, before that clever mind of yours begins to work at full pitch. I had a visit yesterday from a gentleman asking when you'd like your curricle delivered."

Was that all, Geoffrey thought in relief. He feared it would be about the barouche. "Hank, I can't get everywhere on foot. A man in my position doesn't take hired rigs."

"A man in your position," Henri mocked. "You've never held a set of ribbons in your life and you're nervous as a cat around horses."

"I'm going to learn to drive," he said determinedly. With less conviction, he added, "And to ride."

"Perhaps, but that won't supply the £17 tax on your fancy rig or the £5 for each horse. I assume you'll be buying horses with this imagined wealth of yours. Then you'll be wanting a groom and all the rest. You're digging us in too deep, my friend."

Geoffrey sighed and put on a penitent face. Henri snorted in disbelief.

"Don't turn those calf eyes on me. It won't work. You've no sense of conscience or remorse. If you did you won't leave me with all these bills." He snatched up the stack and sorted through them indiscriminately. "Weston's, Lock's, Hatchard's. Five pairs of boots. Five! Dog-skin gloves. A watch fob. Really, Geoff. I must protest. What do you need with another fob?"

"It was a gift for you," he said mildly.

Henri sputtered, momentarily thrown off. Then he continued in fond exasperation. "Have you any idea of the total here? It's staggering. How can you be so bright yet have such an empty head?"

"You will make someone a fine nagging wife someday," his brother drawled. "There's a good deal of cost involved in this charade. You agreed to it, Hank."

"All right. All right. The fault is mine. Only, pray, where do we find the money for these necessities?"

"I've the blunt right here." He fished into the pocket of his discarded coat to withdraw a substantial wad of notes. He passed them over with a faint smile.

Henri stared at the money for a long, silent moment, then asked, "Where did you get this?" Then louder, "Geoff, where did you get this? Tell me you won it gaming. Tell me you stole it."

"I got it from a fellow they call 'Jew' King in Clarges Street. Brummell put me on to him."

Henri cuffed the side of his head hard enough to make him wince. "Fool! Idiot! You promised me. You promised you would never go to the money lenders again. How could you be so stupid? We were nearly killed last time. You cannot play games with these people and think you'll not be caught."

"This man is different. He has a reputation—"

"They all have reputations, my friend."

"I'll be able to pay it back. There won't be any trouble. It won't be like last time. I won't borrow any more from him, Hank. My word on it. Don't go all prim and prosy on me now, at least until you've heard my plan."

Henri spread his hands wide. He rarely won an argument. Eight years older, he sometimes felt more like father than brother to his irrepressible sibling. Geoffrey was impossibly quick-witted, his thoughts ever spinning some new scheme to earn them that all-important fortune. Henri could see that sharp, covetous envy and want whenever he looked on something of value. Or when he talked of his schemes. And they were brilliant as he talked of his latest ideas over their informal breakfast. Henri's look was far less critical when he had finished. He tapped his cheek with a speculative finger.

"How much do you think the father would pay to have you in the family? Would he be fool enough to give it to you before the wedding? You might be right with this one, *mon ami.* We may have our fortunes set if you can convince them you mean to take the girl all the way to the altar."

Geoffrey said nothing. His eyes were distant and thoughtful. He was remembering the feel of her kiss.

Rosalind was thinking the same thing as she held his black tailcoat in a cautious embrace. The smell of him lingered in the rich folds to tantalize her senses. She set it aside to soberly consider the ring on her finger. Did its presence signify a proposal accepted? She wasn't sure.

She lay back on her bolster of lacy pillows and clutched the dark coat to her. Would it be so bad being the wife of Geoffrey Chilton? Despite the fact that they were nearly strangers, she knew him more intimately than her childhood friend Nathaniel. She knew he inspired her to an irrational desire with his presumptuous kisses. She knew his enslaving touch made her a willing prisoner. She knew his outrageous manners could coax a smile from her most severe temper. She knew, as well, that just looking at him caused a shortness of breath and a confusion to her logic. She was afraid to think she was falling in love with him.

He didn't need her money. That was the one thing that swayed her the most. Fearing an avarice motive had made her shy from the attentions of men. It had hardened her outlook on the prospect of marriage. Her wealth could bring a man to the altar when she, as a woman, could not. She hated her fortune with all the jealousy of a beautiful rival for, in fact, it seduced away all those she might consider.

Yet, Geoffrey was different. He had the Chilton legacy to sustain him. So why was he still interested? And why was she? Chilton was rude, overly confident, bold to the point of shocking, and smug in his own worth. She tried to make those faults of a monumental proportion but failed. She also knew another side of him, one that was unfailingly attractive. It was the odd moments so out of step with his brash character that made her take notice. There were the considerate silences when others would have ruined all with words. There was the anguished timbre in his voice at the thought of losing his mother's ring. And there was the agonizing sweetness of their last kiss. He frightened her, and fascinated her. And she didn't want to hope for more.

After Jessup completed her toilet, Rosalind looked long into her mirror, trying to imagine what Geoffrey had seen. Unconsciously, she reached up to soften the stern sleekness of her hair. The effect pleased her and her smile was pensive.

"Come, Jessup. We're going shopping."

"Lady Dunstan is off on a call this morning. She should be back shortly after eleven."

Rosalind's head gave an independent tip. "I don't need her to help me pick up a few things for myself. Go on, Jessup. See to the carriage."

As she pulled on her gloves and straightened her hat in the hall mirror, Rosalind caught sight of her father's uncompromising features over her shoulder. She put on a brave face and turned to him.

"Off so early?"

"I'm doing some shopping."

"I thought Camilla had already left on errands."

Everyone's assumption that she was incapable of making her own choices made her frown and her reply testy. "I do not need a chaperone, my lord."

Dunstan raised a brow and gave her an accessing stare. Always stingy with his praise, he wasn't lavish with it now. "You looked right comely last night. Which of the young men were you trying to sway?"

"As you well know, I wasn't aware Lord Chilton would be present."

"For young Everard, then. I cannot see the comparison between them, a soft-mouthed hobby horse to a lusty stallion, but it is your choice as long as you make it soon."

Rosalind flushed and asked, "Must we talk of this now?"

He bowed rather formally, his expression set in lines of displeasure. "Very well, miss. But tell me, have you found any favor with Chilton?"

"I find him impossibly bold and quite impertinent."

Noting her high color, Dunstan merely nodded, saving his small smile until after she had gone.

With Jessup in attendance, Rosalind spent an enjoyable morning between Clark & Debenham of Cavendish House in Wigmore Street and W. H. Botibol of Oxford Street. Once she'd made it clear that her ideas were not those of her stepmother and that cost was no object, the merchants were eager to accommodate her. When the fabrics she had chosen were strewn across the counter they glitered like a jeweler's case. There were satins in garnet and golden topaz, taffetas in ruby and amethyst, silks that shimmered like diamonds, and velvets gleaming with the richness of sapphires and emeralds. What more befitting an heiress than to wear a wealth upon her back, Rosalind thought wryly. After selecting accompanying hats and fripperies, she felt an unusual confidence and was anxious to show off her new arrayal to one in particular.

But he stayed away. Days passed and no card was left. Her father was full of praise about the quick, energetic Geoffrey Chilton who impressed even his soberest friends at Lloyd's with his inventive opinions and truculent charm. Camilla said he had the best drawing rooms under his thumb. Apparently, there wasn't a maid in all London who wasn't casting out lures for the eligible viscount. Rosalind listened to all, glumly, wondering if her chance with him had already passed.

The Church Parade was a highly fashionable event each Sunday morning during the Season. Between the end of church and luncheon, an elegant crowd gathered in Hyde Park on a strip of grass and gravel between Stanhope Gate and the Achilles Statue to promenade with their prayer books. In spite of the stately manners and quiet murmur of friends greeting one another, to Rosalind it was yet another occasion for the glamorous figures to preen and gossip.

Preferring a walk alone to the company of the imperious Lady Holland, Rosalind left her parents to attend the regal figure. She strolled quickly, her head down to discourage conversation. The sudden brush of warm fingertips along the inside of her arm gave her an abrupt start. She would have shied away like a frightened foal had those strong fingers not curled possessively in the crook of her elbow. Her eyes flew up and she could only hope that her delight wasn't too evident in that brief instant of happy recognition.

"Lord Chilton, you startled me," she said breathlessly.

"I thought I might be saving some poor soul's life the way you were bowling along like a bull with horns lowered." His grin softened the likening of his words and he fell in step beside her. His considerate silence gave her a chance to gather her flustered composure and also the opportunity to take in his magnificent appearance in frock coat and silk hat. She hadn't realized how hungry her eyes were for the sight of him.

With unaccustomed good manners, Geoffrey made no allusions to their last charged meeting. It was enough for him to note she still wore the ring. He escorted her with an easy complacence until her defenses were in a comfortable lull.

"I'm going to Tattersall's tomorrow to purchase a pair for my new curricle. Since I know of no one with your intuition when it comes to those four-legged beasts, I was hoping I could entreat you to be my guide. I can't tell a cart pony from a Thoroughbred. Have pity on me and protect my pocket from ill-advised schemers."

Pleased by the flattery and at the thought of seeing him again, she replied she was at his service only to find he was surrendering her to her family. How quickly the moments passed when she wished to hold to them a bit longer. After exchanging greetings with her parents, he vowed to come round for her in the afternoon. With a tip of his hat, he walked on to where Henri waited in a hired rig.

"So that's her," Henri voiced skeptically. "I would have gone for more countenance and less purse, myself."

Geoffrey seemed annoyed and his tone was crisp. "Remember, it's the purse I'm interested in."

Henri shrugged and motioned to the driver.

Boxes arrived from Cavendish House early the next day and Rosalind tore through them with unbridled excitement. The gowns were unquestionably elegant and a delight to handle, each with its own sumptuous feel from slippery to warmly sensuous and filled with swishes and crunches of its own melody. Hanging them in her cupboard beside the pastel tulles and muslins created a glaring contrast as if each was for a different person. But then they were. She realized the petallike confections had never become her. She had been uncomfortable with them and in them yet had yielded to Camilla's fashion sense. Had it not been for Geoffrey's coaching, she might never have rebelled, fearing her own taste too inexperienced. Determinedly, she took an armload of the pretty but inappropriate gowns and gave them to Jessup, telling her to find some good use for them, perhaps among the less fortunate.

She was admiring the fit of the sapphire velvet day dress with its ruff collar, waist sash, and pleated frills at the hem when she felt the presence of another. Her quick turn caught Camilla with an unexpectedly harsh look on her face. It was immediately masked with a smile. Of course, Rosalind thought guiltily, she was hurt by the rejection of the wardrobe she had planned so carefully.

"You look very nice, Lindy," she offered politely. "The darker shades seem to suit you."

"Do you think so?" She looked back to the mirror for confirmation. "You know how much I value your opinion, Cammy. If you say they're all right, I'll believe you."

Camilla touched a hand to her shoulder. Her voice was gentle. "They are first notch, Lindy. Why the sudden change? It's for Chilton, isn't it?" She didn't need to see the deep blush to know she'd guessed correctly. "I told Dunstan that was where your affections lay. I can see why. He's a very handsome, charming man."

"But?" Rosalind prompted uneasily.

"I've had such men court me. They flatter, they beguile, but they don't take you to the altar. Even if they did, it would be a matter of convenience only and they'd soon stray. I don't wish you unhappy, Lindy, but I can see no good of a relationship with Chilton. Everard may not be as exciting, however, you can depend on him, the way I do your father. A good match need not begin as a love match. That grows in time."

Rosalind's smile was frozen. "You needn't worry. I have no intention of marrying Lord Chilton. He is too wild by half."

"You are wise, Lindy. Let him amuse you but do not let him confuse you."

That sober warning took much of the joy from her anticipation of the day. Geoffrey found her mostly silent and restrained. He didn't try to cajole her from her mood, waiting for the smell of straw and manure to charm her back to good humor.

The change in her around horseflesh was remarkable. She was confident, knowledgeable and expounded verses on the long and short of every animal brought to auction. Her opinions were critical until a pair of high-stepping bays made her clutch his arm excitedly.

"Those are the ones you must have. Give a bid of fifteen hundred guineas." At his startled look, she added, "They're well worth it. Hurry before someone else snatches them up. If the money is a problem—"

"Oh no, nothing of a sort," he assured quickly. "If you are sure."

"You did say you trusted my judgment."

His fingertips brushed the velvet sleeve. "I do, as I see you have mine."

Her smile was faint but warmed him through, easing his

61

conscience as he made the bid with funds he didn't have. In possession of two horses that would be brought round the next morning for payment, Geoffrey took Rosalind's arm and escorted her back to the rented hack.

"Regrets, my lord?" she asked as he settled beside her.

"About what, Lady Rosalind?"

"The horses, of course."

"Of course," he responded with engaging dimples. "Only that in addition to having a shrewd eye, you're not a whip as well."

"And if I was?"

His brow soared. "You drive? But then, you would." He didn't make that sound condemning and seemed genuinely impressed. "Would you— No, never mind. It's too ridiculous."

Well baited, she insisted, "Tell me."

"Would you show me how to handle the leads?"

Her laugh was spontaneous and low music upon his ears. "Chilton, you are the outside of too much. You spend a fortune on horses you can't even drive."

Coloring a bit, he shared her amusement, adding his deep chuckle to her own. "I mean well. Sometimes I just mistake the order."

The dark eyes fell away. Rosalind turned a stony profile to him. "Yes, you do," she agreed quietly.

He paused, then hurried on boldly. "Will you teach me then? I learn quickly. I will be a good and grateful student. I cannot expect two legs to get me everywhere I want to go."

The hack pulled up on Charles Street. Without looking at him, Rosalind said, "The early morning would be best. The park is less crowded then." She took the driver's hand and stepped down, then hurried up the walk before she had time to reconsider.

Geoffrey's smile was only for the moment. He called an address to the driver and settled back somberly.

"I'm sorry, Hank," he said softly.

Chapter Seven

Henri opened the front door on Grosvenor Square and paused in a moment of sheer stupefaction. Finding creditors or even the authorities wouldn't have surprised him. Finding the Prince Regent himself couldn't have been more of a shock than discovering an unescorted Rosalind Dunstan on the doorstep. London's ways were foreign to him, but this looked to be an improper breach of etiquette on either side of the Channel.

"Good morning. Is Lord Chilton at home? Could you tell him Lady Rosalind is here for our appointment."

Henri blinked to dispel the blankness from his features, then assumed a rigidly formal posture. "Please come in, my lady. I'll advise his lordship of your presence."

When he spoke a few words in his native tongue, she gave him a curious look and said apologetically, "I'm sorry. My French is far from passable."

"If you'll step into the drawing room, mademoiselle."

There was a clatter on the stairs and a call of, "Hank, I thought I heard the door." Geoffrey stepped into view and pulled up short, his eyes growing round and nonplussed.

"I have a feeling I was unexpected," Rosalind murmured. His flustered look gave her a moment of delightful superiority. Her gaze swept over him uncontrollably. Taking in his careless appearance, her eyes lingered over his half-open shirtfront and the vee of exquisite chest it exposed, then trailed down the long legs encased in form-fitting stockinette. The sight was stimulating and decidedly one of male virility.

"You have me at a loss, Miss Dunstan," he said hastily. "Should I have been?"

"The park, this morning. Your lesson," she reminded. A trace of a smile played about her lips.

"Oh, of course. You meant *this* morning. I beg your pardon. I feel very foolish. If you'll have a little patience, Henri will make you some tea while I make myself presentable."

His valet began a rapid inundation of foreign speech to which Geoffrey replied in flawless accents. His servant looked disgruntled but bowed crisply.

"I shan't be long," Geoffrey assured and with a quick, unsettled smile, took his leave as well.

Rosalind took advantage of the time to look about the spacious room. For as long as she could remember, the address had stood empty. What she saw made her brow furrow in bemusement. Had it not been for the knocker on the door, the opened shutters, and the two obvious exceptions, she would have thought it still uninhabited. Everything was covered with drop cloths and a thin layer of dust. The scent of timeless disuse was stale upon the air. The entire setting looked untouched and unlived in.

Geoffrey's manservant returned bearing a heavy silver service which he laid upon one of the filmy tables. He flipped the covering off one of the chairs with no flicker of expression to betray this state of affairs was unusual. As Rosalind took the seat, she was aware of the man's narrow scrutiny and puzzled over such boldness. He lingered wordlessly while she poured a cup of tea under his watchful eye.

Geoffrey strode in, very much the picture of style in a well-fitted blue coat, fawn-colored waistcoat, buff nankeens, and highly glossed Hessians. He dropped his untried brown riding gloves on the tray and lifted a cup.

"Henri, go have the curricle readied. Miss Dunstan and I will be leaving in a few minutes."

The elegant valet gave a murmur of something in French and Geoffrey's retort was curt enough to exact a disdainful pout. As Henri went to do as bid, Geoffrey gave Rosalind an apologetic look.

"Henri's been with me forever. Sometimes I think he feels more an older brother than a steward. I hope you'll forgive me for making you wait."

Her dark brows rose. "It appears you weren't expecting anyone."

Geoffrey gave her his most charming smile. "Oh, the house. Quite a shambles, isn't it? I came over with only Henri and a portmanteau. My other servants and belongings were delayed by some political falderol. Until they arrive, I decided to live as the Spartans. Since I wasn't planning to entertain, I thought I'd forgo the hurly-burly of engaging a staff to set things right when I plan to redo all when my own people get here. It's a bit inconvenient but I'm not terribly spoiled to luxury." That understatement made his grin widen.

Rosalind accepted his reasoning, if a bit eccentric, with a nod.

"The horses are ready, my lord" came a stiff announcement from the door. "Will there be anything else, sir?"

Geoffrey assisted Rosalind to her feet and picked up his gloves. "No, thank you, Henri. We have all we need." The dusky eyes sought hers for lengthy exchange that warmed her cheeks to a rosy glow. "Shall we get on with it? Thy chariot awaits."

Rosalind was more than a fair hand with the ribbons. Only her sex prevented her from joining Lords Worcester, Sefton, and Barrymore, Sir John Lade and Colonel Berkeley when their Four-in-Hand Club gathered in George Street to drive to dinner at Salt Hill. She had, in fact, often joined the crush of onlookers who turned out to quiz the elegant drags and teams of matched horses. She would have loved to handle such spirited steppers to the admiration of all. As it was, she had to settle for prudent snatches of freedom at the reins while isolated in the country. The light two-wheeled carriage spun out to the leafy glades of Hyde Park under her deft hand while Geoffrey leaned back in apparent indolence. She wasn't aware of how alert he was and how atuned to her every movement.

"How did you learn to handle the reins so neatly?"

Rosalind flicked the leads to encourage a showy trot. "Before Papa remarried, we spent most of our time on our estate. There was little to do for amusement and Papa was usually busy so I pestered our head groom Pettigrew daily. You might say I grew up around more four-legged creatures than two."

"And prefer them, it would seem."

She smiled ruefully and said nothing.

"Do you hate London so very much?"

"Oh, no. It can be quite diverting. I enjoy the theater and the bookstores. Camilla quite thrives on the city life. She is bored to distraction when there is no company."

"Your stepmother is a vivacious woman," he said carefully.

"She's very beautiful," Rosalind claimed proudly. "Papa dotes on her and she's been a good friend to me. You see, I

65

never knew my mother. She died when I was very young. Cammy is the only female I've been exposed to other than the servants. She has infinite patience with me and never accuses me of being a dull dog, though I know it's true."

Geoffrey observed her anew, seeing a shy little girl growing up with a severely critical father and no feminine influence. Thrust into a sometimes savage social sea to flounder inadequately with only her wealth to keep her afloat, no wonder she had developed her timid reticence in an awkward defense for her lack of schooling. She blossomed becomingly when tended with warmth so he saw no evidence of a flaw within her sheltered soul. He placed the fault with a father who'd taken no time to nurture such a fragile bloom, a father who had cast her on arid ground and expected, no, demanded that she take root in that shallow soil. He suspected she would flower brilliantly in the rich loomy earth of her beloved estates but how so in the stuffy London drawing rooms if cared for attentively? It would be a challenge, though not an impossible one for someone of determination.

Rosalind pulled in the horses and turned to Geoffrey. He was smiling softly and she responded with a faint one of her own. "Time for you to take the reins, my lord. There doesn't seem to be anyone about that you could bowl over."

She arranged the ribbons in his large hands, trying to block out the sudden knowledge of his nearness and the warm brush of his breath upon her cheek. Rather crisply, she explained the rudiments of controlling the lively pair — then sat back.

Looking uncomfortable and even anxious, Geoffrey asked, "What do I do first?"

"Get us moving, my lord. There's little you can do until then."

He took a deep, fortifying breath. She hadn't thought anything could shake the confident Lord Chilton from his show of swaggering daring, yet he seemed quite humbled by the task of managing the two animals. He gave an experimental slap of the reins and they started off at an easy lope. Though he soon mastered the technique, his tension made his charges nervous and hard to handle.

Rosalind's hands slid over his to guide the ribbons and the pair settled instantly into a brisk trot. "Relax your grip, Geoffrey. The horses can sense you're ill at ease and will take advantage of you. They want a firm master who'll be gentle but in control." She spoke his given name without thinking until his quiet words brought it to her attention.

"And is that what you want as well, Rosalind?"

Startled by her proximity to the broad temptation of his chest and the sultry lure of his question, she shrank back on the seat, leaving him to awkwardly calm the alarmed horses and draw them to a halt. Rosalind wouldn't look at him, her head ducked as if in a fierce study of her twisting hands.

"Is it, Roz?" he asked again.

"We were not speaking of me, sir," she argued in a failing voice. Her breath quickened in a closing panic as he shifted on the seat to face her. It caught in a fearful gasp when his gloved hand cupped her chin and turned her head toward him. Her eyes lifted slowly, wide, cautious, and softly pleading.

"Isn't it time we did?"

His gaze drooped in sensual invitation. In response, hers flew about madly in search of hopeful rescue. Their shady lane was deserted. When her attention returned to him, he had drawn much closer and his large hand slipped behind the slender column of her neck to impel her forward.

She met his kiss with a rigid posture of protest, leaning away until his following weight was heavy against her hip and shoulder. His other arm circled her for balance, securing her retreat. Lips that sought to remain firm and resisting yielded with trembling reluctance to the enticing probe of his tongue. She was limp beneath that insistently intimate intrusion, feeling her will ebb in successive waves. Her hand rose to touch his cheek and the vital warmth of him was shock enough to waken her dormant senses. When her palms pried for leverage, he bowed to the ineffective strength of her denial and released her.

After tasting the submission of her sweet kiss, it was difficult not to press, but the fright and confusion in the large, dark eyes held him at bay. Her panting breaths and the unwitting pout of her moistened lips betrayed her desire for more and he was hot to give it even on the uncomfortable seat in the questionable privacy of the early hour, yet the anguished entreaty of her gaze took a checking rein. His lust melted into a pool of gentler emotion when she flinched away from the brush of his fingertips upon her pale cheek. His look was as tender as his caress longed to be.

"Roz, I don't mean to be so bold but I fear I must press my

67

case so you'll take me serious. I realize you don't feel you know me, that you don't trust or believe me sincere. I don't blame you for thinking me a self-seeking roué concerned with his own pleasures at the cost of your integrity. Believe me when I tell you how much I respect you. Perhaps I'm not the sort of man you should consider seriously. I am not sober-minded. I'm not docile or even tamed. I know I frighten you with my abruptness and my desires but I won't apologize. If you can hold the reins and demand the respect of these fiery beasts, then why not do the same with me? Marry me, Rosalind, and tame me to your lead."

She stared at him soundlessly for a long moment, then looked away. He read that response not as a denial of him but of herself and her own wants. Quietly, he concluded, "I won't ask again nor will I pressure you for an answer. If you decide the answer is yes, come to me and tell me."

With that, he picked up the reins and sent them at a good clip down the avenue. He was too preoccupied by the silent figure at his side to mind his driving and the horses responded to the instinctive guidance with a flashy gait, drawing many admiring looks as they wisked into a more populated area. He took her directly to her door and lifted her down with the utmost courtesy.

"Thank you for the lesson, Miss Dunstan," he murmured, then added meaningfully, "We may or may not be seeing each other again, but I did enjoy our morning together." With that, he nodded and hopped back up into the curricle. She caught her breath as he sent it into the path of a lumbering dray and earned himself a colorful curse. From there, he wove an uncertain path out onto Berkeley Square nearly trampling two surprised shop girls and just escaping a collision with an old-fashioned laudaulet.

Rosalind tried to slip unnoticed into the house but a booming voice from the library caught her before she reached the stairs.

"Rosalind, I want a word with you."

Cold with apprehension, she advanced into her father's dark bastion. He was standing at the window, hands clasped behind his back. When he turned, his expression was formidable. She knew her time of grace had come to an end.

"How was your outing with Chilton?"

"Very nice," she mumbled quietly.

"And?"

"What is it you wish to hear, Papa?" Her tone was tart and defensive. "You have not secured him in your breeding paddock if that's what you are wondering."

Dunstan was a monument of displeasure. He glared down at the pasty-cheeked girl who for once met his stare unblinkingly. His words were unemotional. "Everard was here in your absence. He made another appeal for your hand and we have come to tentative terms. Present me with another alternative in time to post the banns on Sunday or it will be his name and yours to be read."

She received his ultimatum unflinchingly. No sign of shock or surprise flickered in her glassy eyes. With uncommon dignity, she murmured, "As you wish, my lord."

That stately composure remained with her as she climbed to her room and sat stiffly on her yielding chaise. Her thoughts were moving precisely as if viewing the dilemma of another. She couldn't afford to relax that objective pose. It was time to settle her lot and she had three options: forgo her inheritence or choose one of two men. She knew she couldn't surrender her fortune and still secure a future without solitude and disgrace. That left the remaining two choices.

In Nathaniel Everard she would find safety. It would be a comfortable arrangement, if no love match. They knew well each other's tastes and had unfailing respect for each other. He would not make demands on her or insist she change her reclusive existence. She could map out their entire future from her place on the chaise and know there would be little deviation. They would live at the decrepit family estate where his father would quickly game away her dowry and his sisters would be parceled off with the aid of her fortune.

When her thoughts turned to an intimate nature, she realized with some surprise that Nathaniel had never kissed her. He had made gentlemanly overtures, lavished attention over her hand, gazed into her eyes and boldly brushed her cheek, but had never seized her up for a demonstration of passion. She concluded there would be little likelihood of it even after marriage. Nathaniel would be caring, considerate, and dutiful but never impulsively romantic.

When she thought of Geoffrey in the same circumstance, her cheeks stained a hot crimson. She was certain his bed would never be a spot for conversation or rest. She imagined long nights in his urgent embrace, succumbing to his kisses, his touch, his desires, freely, the way she had wanted to.

69

Restlessly, Rosalind began to pace. Camilla's warning returned to her. What if on wedding the vital Lord Chilton, his affections turned elsewhere? Was his proposal merely one of convenience? Would she have to suffer the suspicion or painful knowledge of countless distractions in the petticoat line, or worse, mistresses? Would she be able to channel his passionate nature and hold his interest or would he soon grow tired of her plain face and retiring ways and seek more exciting game? With Nathaniel, she would have no cause for worry. He would be steadfast in his devotion. But there would be no love, either. That was what she was really afraid of. She feared loving Geoffrey Chilton. Their marriage would be no casual matter, at least not to her. He would have her heart and she feared he would misuse it. That was what she was choosing between, safe and secure versus love and danger.

More than ever, Rosalind felt the pang of being alone. She longed to have someone to share her doubts with, to guide her in these mammoth decisions. There was Camilla but she was too like a friend. She didn't need someone to exchange girlish secrets with. She needed a confidant, a confessor, a mother.

Sighing, she resigned herself to making this decision, like all others without wiser counsel. She had only her own limited experience and untried heart to rely upon and that would have to do. She could only hope she would choose well and for the best of all concerned.

Though a member at White's for countless years, James Dunstan's presence was enough of an oddity to cause an immediate whisper. He was not a gambler or a force in political circles so his use of the club was purely one of status. His purpose this day was not to be seen but to find one in particular. His gaze rested on the secluded bow window from which Brummell held court. There, he found the usual inner circle of Lords Alvanly, Sefton, Worcester, and Forley, the Duke of Argyll and the spectacle of Sir Lumley Skeffington. "Skiffy," as expected, was grossly painted and reeking of cologne. In his silken suit, he was more ridiculous than ever next to the sedately garbed newcomer, Lord Chilton. When the dusky eyes rose, still in their study of amused contempt, Chilton saw the somber earl as a reprieve from affectation.

70

He was quick to excuse himself and join the older man.

"You run with a lofty crowd, Chilton."

Geoffrey grinned at the obvious censure, taking no offense. "It has its purpose, my lord."

"To know everyone of wealth and influence."

The grin widened at the accurate recollection. "Just so, sir. You were looking for me?"

They found a small table and sat with the ease of old friends reunited. Dunstan regarded the dapper viscount through gauging eyes.

"The banns for my daughter's marriage will be posted on Sunday," he remarked casually. Chilton didn't move, yet there was a sudden keen attentiveness to his gaze.

"Congratulations, Dunstan. And who is this new member to your family?"

The earl smiled silkily. "That's up to you or did I mistake your earlier interest?"

Chilton's alarm relaxed into a languorous pose. "I am interested but I feel I've missed something here. Would you mind elaborating."

"Rosalind will have a betrothed by week's end. Everard has put in his claim but I've heard no others."

"Are you selling her at auction, then?" Though coolly spoken, his words were edged with disdain.

"I'm not looking for a buyer. I'm not interested in a fortune. I have that already. What I need is an heir."

"And are Rosalind's wants of no concern?" The derision was closer to the surface now.

"She has until Sunday to pick, then I will make the decision for her."

"A very loving, paternal gesture, indeed."

Dunstan frowned at the criticism, no matter how smoothly delivered. "Will you have her or not?"

"What comes with her?" The deep blue eyes took on a hard shine. Dunstan understood business and made his proposal as if bartering for properties.

"Provide me with an heir, a male heir in a year's time and your child inherits all, the earldom and my unentailed monies."

"What if you should conceive a son of your own with your new bride?"

"Within one year and all will be yours, irregardless. Camilla and any of her children will be well provided for."

71

"And if it isn't a son?"

"Camilla will hold all in trust until the first male child of Rosalind's comes of age. Rosalind will get a sizable allowance, of course."

"All in writing?"

"As legal as the marriage papers."

Geoffrey pursed his lips thoughtfully and appeared to consider. Cautiously, he advanced another piece in the game they were playing with Rosalind's future. "My estates are rather tied up from my father's dealings and my uncle is somewhere abroad. My own finances are not terribly fluid at the moment."

"Strike whatever terms you like when you have my daughter's answer. If I make the choice, I make the terms."

"And what terms did you make with Everard?"

"That is between us and none of your concern. Your only worry is that Rosalind say yes to you."

Chapter Eight

Rosalind spent the week in a nervous agitation, refusing Nathaniel's notes and wondering why there had been none from Geoffrey. She was aware her father had met with both men though was spared the humiliating details of his bargainings. Chilton must have known of the deadline yet made no effort to rush his suit. Was he still waiting for her to come to him, she puzzled in a panic, or was he not interested enough to pursue her?

She took her meals in her room, returning them mostly untouched while she fretted through her waking hours and tossed during restless nights. Her decision consumed her until she lost sight of what was in her tormented heart. By the time Friday evening came and the hour neared for Nathaniel to escort her to supper at Vauxhall, she was hollow-eyed with fatigue and no closer to naming a betrothed than the week before. She longed for the day when the anxiety would end, believing she would welcome handing the choice to her father. Rosalind always enjoyed dinners at Vauxhall Gardens. She loved the outdoors and the sense of freedom that came when the air was clear and open. There was none of the close, stifling pressure of the drawing rooms where walls became a symbol of imprisonment. She liked taking the Grand Walk along the tree-lined promenade and pretending she could lose herself in the twelve acres of formal paths. It was almost like a return to the country when the gleam of lanternlight could be mistaken for stars. Even the arbored supper boxes held an Arcadian charm far removed from the unbearable formal affairs she hated.

Rosalind's tension eased somewhat in the crisp evening breeze as she was seated by her escort. Nathaniel was considerate enough to confine their conversation to safe subjects while they dined and Rosalind found herself quite starved. She ate leisurely, sensing from Everard's nervousness that he was waiting for her to finish before delving into a more

73

serious topic. She studied the familiar face over dinner, finding nothing in its pleasant planes to take exception to. His talk was interesting and his manner inoffensive. So why was she so uncomfortable?

Then her gaze caught on a lively foursome across the way and held with a shock of recognition. Rutherford and Geoffrey Chilton, she knew. The two young ladies, she did not. Afraid to be found staring, she dropped her glistening eyes but couldn't keep them from returning in a daze of dull agony. Was this why he hadn't called? her numbed heart seemed to cry with every anguished beat. Pretending to be indifferent, she continued the stolen glances through a hot, bitter haze. In her upset, she never heard Nathaniel clear his throat and begin a ponderous, practiced speech. She was only aware of the deep blue eyes that locked with hers across the distance, restarting her failing pulses with an excited lurch. With that single exchange, she knew how much she loved the handsome Lord Chilton and how she could never bear to lose him.

With a brief word to his companion, Geoffrey stood and walked not toward her but away. Frantically, her gaze followed his tall, elegant figure through the growing number of milling patrons.

"Oh, Nate, please excuse me," she murmured distractedly and darted from her seat to pursue the golden head bobbing above the crowd. She walked as quickly as she could without breaking into a run but still, she lost him. With a moan of despair, she searched the bustling walkways to no avail.

Then a warm hand cupped her elbow, encouraging her to fall in step. She didn't dare look up at him for fear the tangle of newly discovered emotion would give her away. She didn't want to overwhelm him with her passion when no longer certain of his.

She didn't think to object when he turned her down a deeply shadowed tunnel of greenery. None of the starlike lamps lit the secluded passage they would for not have been welcomed on the notorious Dark Walk where couples escaped for a clandestine rendezvous. When there was no danger of them being disturbed, Geoffrey turned her into a trellised niche. The darkness was deep but not complete, casting his features into intriguing obscurity when she grew brave enough to raise her head.

74

Geoffrey was silent, reading the conflict of want and caution in her uplifted eyes. He took her hand gently and pressed its palm to his cheek, holding it there when she would shy away from the contact. Slowly, he moved it beneath the guide of his own in a gliding caress, familiarizing her with the lean contours of his face and softness of his lips with a thoroughness she wouldn't have dared. When his lifted, hers continued the exploration alone. Her fingers slipped into the silken mat of his hair, finding it so glorious, her others were persuaded to join.

Rosalind was lost in the dusky enchantment of his eyes. Her breath quickened to match the urgent tempo of her heart and shivered in pants of uncharted desire. Her love had led her to this unexpected tryst but was too new and fragile to be spoken. He waited patiently, expectantly, encouragingly for her to speak of what brought her to him but her voice was held captive by the flood of potent emotion that choked within her breast. Desperate to communicate what she had discovered, her fingers laced to draw him down. Her lips fastened upon the willing part of his. As her arms tightened to bring their bodies flush, his came up to form an unyielding circle to bind her to his chest until she felt deliciously mashed.

She let her kiss convey all the things she was feeling — the love, the want, the yielding, the fear — and his told her in kind that there had been no change in his desire for her. The fiery union deepened and flamed to the edge of control, threatening reason and restraint. Finally, Geoffrey caught the sides of her tousled head and pulled her away so air and distance could revive them.

The sight of Rosalind was as stunning as an unexpected blow. Her hair had fallen from its proper coif to tumble in glossy abandon about her shoulders. Her eyes were bright, gleaming beacons to draw him down to the full, pouting lips. The swell of her heaving bosom crushed to his shirtfront, begging for release from the confines of molten satin. All was so luscious, so seductive. Yet it was her single, softly spoken word that worked his heart and soul into a spectacular crescendo.

"Yes," she whispered.

Geoffrey hesitated then asked huskily, "Yes, to what, precious one?"

"Yes to all you ask."

"You'll be my wife?"

The dark head nodded between his palms and, impulsively, he jerked her up for an exalted kiss. His mouth slanted across hers, bruising, demanding, and wildly possessing then, just as abruptly, gentled. It was like a plunging fall from a great height to be caught up on a teasing breeze just short of the bottom. Rosalind was left gasping as his lips brushed over hers in a light caress, titillating her senses with a blissful anticipation. When he leaned away, her aching lips protested the absence.

"You will marry me?" he asked again.

"Yes."

"There's so much to do and so little time. We'll have to tell your father and—"

Her hand covered his mouth. "Geoffrey, just kiss me."

She felt his smile beneath her fingertips as he gathered her into a snug embrace. Their exchange was lengthy and rich with giving one to the other. Rosalind's candid response surprised her but the benefits of the passionate union were too wonderful to resist. His wide, sensuous mouth was yielding, persuasive, provocative, knowing. The light tracing of his tongue was yet another tantalizing taste of what was to come. That expectancy had become an urgent tingling and tightness in her breasts. Desire wriggled, hot and insistent through the lush length of her body. Her flesh glowed where it pressed to the lean strength of him and cried out for attention in places where he was not. She wanted to feel the warmth of his hands adoring her the way his eyes did.

"Oh, Geoffrey," she moaned into his kiss. "Make me yours."

Determinedly, he set her apart from him, resisting the anxious plea in her gaze and the ripe invitation of her body as it swayed hopefully toward him. He took several deep gulps of the cool night air in a desperate effort to clear the lust-enflamed urges from his heart and mind. His instincts told him to bring the tumbling play of passion to a halt.

"Roz, I have to get you home," he said with difficulty. "I have to talk with your father. There's much that needs be said between us as well."

"You don't want me?"

The tiny voice almost called him to yield. He scooped her up in a careless embrace so she could feel the disastrous effect she had on him. His heart thundered madly against the soft cushion of her breast and the bold contour of his desire was unmistakable.

"What an unfair question," he rumbled thickly into the swirling mass of hair. "I've wanted you since that night at the inn but never so much as now."

Sensing his refusal in those gentle words, she argued, "You took me then as a stranger. Why not now as your betrothed?"

"Took you? Rosalind, I don't understand." He looked down into her dark eyes. Seeing the tumult of embarrassed longing in them, he took a step back. "You think—but you couldn't. Roz, do you believe that I—that we— Nothing was completed that night." Reading her doubt and confusion, he added, "I was willing but, providentially, you fell asleep. Not very flattering considering how well warmed I was. Did you think I'd take advantage of you as you lay snoring? Very loudly, too."

"And you just left?" She sounded astonished.

"You gave me little choice when I couldn't wake you. Did you find my attention that tedious? Remind me not to let you imbibe on our wedding night."

Her arms slipped over his shoulders as she languished on his chest. Her expression was weak with relief and a new respectfulness. "Hardly tedious." She stretched up to kiss him but he eluded her, features sharp and wary. "What is it, Geoffrey?" she asked in considerable alarm.

"You thought we'd been lovers. Is that the reason you agreed to marry me? Tell me the truth, Rosalind. Is that why you said yes?"

"I said yes because I love you," she told him simply.

The harshness left his face and he drew her up for a tender kiss. Cradling her to his shoulder, he murmured, "If I had made love to you that night, I fear I wouldn't have been able to leave you."

Rosalind blushed with pleasure but her modesty made her chuckle with self-deprecating doubt. "Or you never would have made me an offer. I fear you might have been disappointed."

"I haven't been yet."

"What if you find I don't please you? If you discover I'm too—plump?"

His large hands roved the ample satin curves from rounded hip to full bosom and lingered there to fondle in appreciation. "I like a woman who is soft and feminine. I don't care to bruise myself on a rack of ribs and bone. I find nothing wrong with the way you are made and I promise you, I won't be displeased."

Tears sparkled in her eyes before she let them close in joyous reconciliation. Her palms kneaded the firm muscle of his chest and arms. Her voice was deep and almost unrecognizable. "I look forward to being your wife."

"And you have my promise you won't be displeased, either." His lips pressed to the soft crown of her head. "Now I'd better see you home. Shouldn't you say something to your escort first?"

She came away from him with a guilty flush. "Oh, Nate. I quite forgot him. I left him in the lurch and he must be beside himself. How can I face him? I must be a sight."

Chilton's warm gaze followed the nervous hands that smoothed her rumpled gown and tumbled hair, seeking to do the impossible. "You are a sight," he said softly, "but one only I should see. He touched the swollen lips with a finger and gave a silken smile. "Looking as you do, he'd most certainly think the worst. Neither of us would have a shred of honor left."

"Then we might as well enjoy the fruit of their gossip."

She leaned against him in a sensual assault that nearly cost him his resolve. Smiling narrowly, he stepped back to elude her persistent charms. "Roz, you tempt me too far. Behave or face the consequences."

His threat wrought a winsome pout. "That sounds most intriguing, my lord."

"Incorrigible creature," he groaned. He gave her a sharp tap under the chin. "Let's not keep Everard chafing. I'll send someone with word that you suddenly took ill and rushed home."

"And what of your companion?"

His brow arched at her crisp tone. Then he grinned disarmingly. "Those chits are cousins of Rutherford's. Gabby, giggly little things. I hoped to provoke you and it worked quite neatly. I only came here tonight to see you."

She frowned, not liking to be tricked, but was quickly mollified by the brief touch of his mouth. "Really, Chilton, you are too bold by half."

"Yes, but you are here, aren't you?" He looked pleased

with himself and she finally relented with a chuckle.

Snuggling close to his side in the closed carriage, Rosalind knew a moment of complete happiness. No worries or doubts penetrated the secure circle of his arms. In the rapture of her first love, all was perfect. Geoffrey Chilton was more than she could ever dream of possessing, yet he would soon be hers. Like a princess born in a magical coach, she had no hint of warning that the spell might end. It was too complete, too deceivingly wonderful. That her handsome prince might not be a hero never occurred to her as she delighted in the warmth of his embrace. That he might not be a prince was inconceivable.

When the carriage stopped in Charles Street, Geoffrey's kiss was thorough enough to bind her heart in his absence. She let herself in, floating in a euphoric daze that even her father's summons couldn't threaten.

Dunstan stared at his daughter as if seeing a stranger. She stood regally in the door, hood not quite concealing the mussed cascade of her hair. The dim light only heightened her color and the brilliance of her eyes. She sparkled and glowed like the fiery stones about her throat.

"Post the banns, my lord. I am to be wed," she said in an oddly husky voice.

"Everard?" he questioned, but seeing her all flushed and giddy, he couldn't believe it.

"Lord Chilton will call on you in the morning. I hope I've finally managed to please you."

He started forward to embrace her in an uncommon gesture of fatherly affection but she retreated with a frosty smile to deny him the impulse.

"Good night, sir."

He watched the dignified withdrawal, feeling vaguely cheated from a moment of closeness that should have been reserved for such a time. After a moment, he went to pour himself a glass and made a silent toast.

The sound of a champagne cork exploding in celebration woke Henri from his slumber on the sofa. He squinted up to see Geoffrey pouring two ample glasses of the frothy stuff.

"Come, Hank. Drink with me to my wedding."

Henri blinked owlishly. In his surprise, he forgot to speak English. "I must be dreaming, *mon frère*. I thought I heard you say you were getting married. Please wake me up."

"You're not dreaming, yet I confess it feels a bit like one. Here take your glass. I'm getting all wet."

Henri sat up, firmly convinced the younger man was intoxicated until he saw the glitter in his eyes. Then, he began to frown.

"Lady Rosalind agreed to be my wife, Hank. We've finally made our fortune, my friend. Drink up so I can pour us another."

Henri gulped down the bubbly wine, desperate for composure. "Geoff, are you mad? Are you serious? You cannot mean to marry that woman. This is some joke, *non?*"

"No. I go to speak to her father tomorrow and set the foundation for our future. No more living off the necklace and pretty lies. No more pretending and running from creditors. Henri, I show you a glimpse of heaven and you sit there frowning at me."

"You said nothing of marrying her," he cried in dismay. "I thought you were going to bargain for a price then break off."

"Why settle for a taste when we can feast?" The cold brilliance of his stare was unnerving. "You should see how they live. We can, too. We should. I'm tired of running from one scheme to the next. This is my chance to have it all; our chance, and I'm not going to let it slip away. I'm going to live like a real lord."

"Geoff, you cannot stay here forever. The truth will catch up to you. Then what? Do you think your fine lady would still have you?"

"You worry too much, *mon ami*. Nigel Chilton hasn't been in this country for years. No one here knows anything, and France is an ocean and a war away," he argued reasonably as he refilled their glasses.

"The risk is too great. Take what you can and get out. That's the only way. I, too, wish it could be different. Take the father for a fortune, get the necklace back, and we'll go back to the Continent, somewhere we have no past or ties. Geoff, be sensible. *Réfléchez.*"

He was thinking. He leaned back in his chair and considered his future with the Dunstans. He saw himself stepping into the earl's well-cut, expensive shoes, controlling his monies, living in his fine home. And then there was Rosalind. No meager hint of exposure from an unknown and unlikely source was going to convince him to be cautious. He meant to plunge in, sink or swim.

Rosalind, too, was thinking. Her thoughts and emotions churned too rapidly for sleep so she lay back on her bed and let them carry her aloft. She replayed each word, each kiss, each glance until it was a torture to lie alone knowing it would be a three-week wait before she could be with the man she loved. She imagined what that moment would be like, carrying it as far as her patchy recall of the night at the inn, then dreaming the rest in ignorant ecstasy.

She didn't look beyond to what married life would be on a day-to-day basis with Lord Chilton. In truth, she knew little of him other than the passions of his nature and the way he stirred the same in her. She didn't consider how they would live or where. She didn't concern herself with questions of their compatibility. Would there be any similarities to strengthen their relationship? Would he expect her to play hostess for the social whirl? She didn't know or care. She was thinking of Geoffrey Chilton as a lover, not of Lord Chilton as a husband. She never entertained the idea that he might be disappointing as the latter. She was too mesmerized by the promise of the former.

A tap at her door distracted her from wistful anticipation and her call brought in a solemn-faced Camilla. She looked young and lovely in her pale peach silk wrapper. Rosalind was struck anew by the oddity of having her as a mother.

"May I speak to you, Lindy? Dunstan told me your news."

Rosalind sat up, features filled with an anguish of dismay. "Please say you're happy for me, Cammy. I know you don't approve of Chilton but he is the one I would be wed to."

Her smile was sweet yet poignant. "I'm for anything that makes you happy, dearest. I only hope you find it to be him."

"I am happy and I'm certain I will remain so. You see, I love him very much." The confidence was shared with an awkward shyness and engaging blush.

"And he's said the same to you?"

The pointed question brought a deeper color to her cheeks. She stammered, "N-no, not exactly."

Camilla hurried to make amends. "I'm sure he must care for you or he wouldn't have offered. Some men are not good at voicing such sentiments."

Rosalind, who would never classify the outspoken viscount in that light, murmured an uncertain affirmative.

81

Seeing her unvoiced distress, Camilla concluded with a bit too much gaiety, "I really just wanted to offer my congratulations. I'm sure you made the best choice for yourself. If there's anything I can do, please ask."

Rosalind gave a hesitant smile. "I'd like very much for you to be my chief bridesmaid. Would that be improper, you being my stepmother, too?"

Camilla was silent for a moment, then came to embrace her. The delicate scent of roses floated from the folds of her gown. "Oh, Lindy, I would be delighted. We have much to do. Get a good night's rest, for I mean to keep you very busy for the next few weeks."

But rest was long in coming. Rosalind lay back in the darkened room, puzzled and vaguely disturbed. Why hadn't Geoffrey said he loved her?

Chapter Nine

Rosalind hovered about the library's closed doors trying not to look apprehensive. It did no good to remind herself that her father liked Chilton. Dunstan didn't need a reason to be disagreeable. He had done his best to meddle in her happiness and she feared he would cast some slur upon it now. When the two men emerged smiling, both looking pleased, her relief was monumental. She started toward them, then pulled up in some confusion.

Taking passionate liberties with Geoffrey Chilton in the enchanting darkness was quite different from confronting him in her home beneath her father's eye. Here, he looked incredibly elegant, big, magnificently handsome, and somehow unapproachable. It wasn't her nervousness that made her hesitate. It was the way he looked at her, dusky eyes coolly assessing, gauging her with the same emotionless appraisal one would a work of art or valuable jewel.

"Good morning, my lord," she began uneasily. Did his sudden aloofness mean he had come to cry off?

Geoffrey took up her hand in a formal gesture. "Your father has graciously consented to you becoming my wife."

Her lips twitched in a ghostly caricature of a smile.

"Shall we take a turn in the garden? We have much to say to one another."

Rosalind greeted the suggestion with a stiff nod and walked docilely beside him into the warmth of the morning sun. They strolled in silence until a row of hedges came between them and the house. Geoffrey turned to her, his expression perplexed.

"Roz?" His fingertips touched her cheek.

With a soft cry, she was in his arms. Their kiss was eager and reaffirming but necessarily brief. He looked down into her eyes, seeing the answering warmth in them.

"Thank heavens," he exclaimed. "You looked so odd inside, I feared you'd changed your mind. Is everything all right with you?"

83

"Now it is," she sighed happily. She retained his hand as they sat side by side in one of the leafy arbors.

"Is the seventeenth all right?"

"For what?"

"Our wedding, what else, you goose," he chided gently.

"That's fine."

"We'll be living here for a time. My estate's in dreadful repair and the townhouse . . . Well, you've seen it."

"I don't care where we live," she said agreeably.

"I understand Brighton's all the vogue for after the wedding."

Rosalind's eyes dropped carefully. "That would be fine."

"Unless you'd rather go right to your estate in the country."

Her grateful cry made him grin. "Oh, could we? You wouldn't mind terribly?"

"I don't care where we go." The dark, smoky eyes slanted suggestively and she blushed with an excited warmth. His next statement dimmed some of her enthusiasm. "Your father wants us to say our vows at St. George's."

Rosalind moaned to think of the circus that would entail.

Feeling for her dismay, Geoffrey gave her a supportive hug. "We could elope if you like."

"No, Papa would never forgive me. It would break his heart if I gave him such a slight."

Geoffrey made no comment about the state or existence of James Dunstan's heart. "It will be over quickly then you never have to worry over pleasing anyone save yourself. And me, of course, but that won't be difficult."

She smiled with a shy pleasure then grew serious. Her dark eyes held a pensive look that caused him to raise a brow in question.

"Why did you ask me to marry you, Geoffrey?"

The candid query took him aback, then he was all smooth, engaging smiles. "What a question. Why do you think? A better one would be why you would say yes to someone like me, an impertinent rogue who creeps into bedroom windows in the dead of night and proposes in a fish pond."

She responded with a quiet laugh and held tight to his large hands. He felt so good, so solid, so sure. She had no doubts when she was with him. She was about to speak when she saw his attention distracted over her shoulder. She turned to an apologetic Camilla.

"Oh, do forgive me, Lindy. I thought you were alone." She

fixed a charming smile on the now-standing viscount. "Congratulations, my lord, and welcome to our ranks."

Camilla rose to press a light kiss to his cheek. His smile became fixed and he stepped back quickly. She looked to her stepdaughter with a fond exasperation.

"Lindy, have you forgotten our appointment this morning? We must leave right away. I'll await you in the house."

"I won't keep you."

Geoffrey followed the slender retreating figure with a wary frown. He hadn't imagined the caress of her fingers upon his chest during the chaste kiss.

It was some time later before Rosalind realized that he had never exactly answered her question.

Preparing for a ton wedding would have been a nightmare had it not been for Camilla's organization and efficient command. Rosalind was able to sit quietly aside while she tended the overwhelming number of details. Though the preparation time seemed to fly, the actual minutes ticked by in agonizing drudgery. Rosalind managed only brief minutes with Geoffrey and those were never alone. He treated her with a proper respectfulness that left her chafing for a taste of his passion. Each time she saw him, that urgency increased. In the final week, it had become a taut, vibrating coil deep in the seat of her frustrated emotions.

There had been a constant flux of visitors to Charles Street eager to discuss the trousseau and offer pieces of shyly taken advice. They were mostly friends of her mother or Camilla's who had little in common with the reserved bride-to-be. One visitor came just to see her and she received Nathaniel Everard on the night they opened their house up to friends and members of the wedding party with a touch of fond remorse.

After kissing her hands, Nathaniel sat close beside her on the sofa and for a moment there was an uncomfortable silence. Rosalind was finally moved to break it, touched by the anguish in his dark, soulful eyes.

"Dear Nate, thank you for coming. I feared you would be too put out with me."

"With you, Rosalind? Never. You've always been very dear to me. I do confess I wish things had taken a different turn but I care too much for you to begrudge your happiness."

"You are happy, aren't you?"

"Oh, yes, Nate, very happy. You've always been my best friend, but I love Geoffrey. I hope you don't see that as a slight to you. I don't want you to think I was leading you on. It just happened. I know my change of heart has cost you dearly and I pray you'll find some other means to escape your difficulties."

He smiled nobly to dispel the tears he saw gathering in her tender gaze and patted her hands. "Never fear, Lindy. My family will survive. My only wish now is that we can remain friends. That loss would be irreplaceable."

"Of course, we shall, Nate. Don't worry over it again. You will always be my cherished companion."

He took a deep breath and said staunchly, "And if you ever need me, if Chilton doesn't treat you as he should, if you need a friend who'll ask no questions, I'll be there."

She gave him an impulsive hug and murmured, "Thank you, Nate."

"I would have considered it an honor to have had you as my wife," he told her with more emotion than she had ever heard from him. Overcome, Rosalind pressed a heartfelt kiss to his cheek.

Geoffrey walked in upon that innocent embrace and was momentarily stunned by its implications. He checked his first hasty thoughts and waited for Rosalind to catch sight of him. Her eyes brightened with warmth and delight and no trace of guilt. That was answer enough for him.

"Good evening, my lord," she said prettily. "I wasn't aware you had arrived."

"Apparently" was his dry retort.

Everard flushed and rose to meet him, prepared to be Rosalind's protector if need be. His rival's actions surprised him. He took the extended hand cautiously.

"I won her fairly, Everard, but I respect your taste in women."

The easily offered words put Nathaniel at a loss. He mumbled a bit stiffly, "Thank you, Lord Chilton. Good of you to be so gracious." He excused himself from their company not only to be polite but to escape the sight of Rosalind's response to the handsome viscount. It brought her claim home too painfully.

Geoffrey turned to her and gave a slow smile that started a nervous flutter in her stomach. "You look lovely this evening, Roz. You do me proud.

Rosalind colored, accepting the praise with an awkward

pleasure. She did feel attractive in her high-waisted gown of ivory silk. With its glittery aerophanes, she looked like an expensive jewel, shimmering as the light reflected her every movement. His presence was all that was needed to bring an inner beauty to her features, firing her eyes and fusing her countenance with a becoming flush.

"I've something that will hopefully do you justice."

He stepped close and presented her with a long, flat box. When she hesitated, he opened it. At her hoarse gasp, he asked, "Do you like it?"

"It's fabulous," she exclaimed faintly as she stared at the array of fiery diamonds. They made a close fitting collar with a horseshoe-shaped pendant.

"I had it made for you. I could think of nothing closer to your heart. It will be a symbol of luck as well. May I?"

She turned so he could lay the weighty necklace about her throat. After fastening the clasp, his fingers lightly traced the bare column of her neck and shoulders. That brief, sensual touch quickened Rosalind's pulses to a frantic pace. She drew a tortured breath and her eyes shut in a rapturous expectation. Her supple flesh responded to his nearness, seeming to burn beneath the collar of gems and draw to a tingling excitement over her breasts. Before she could act on the delicious sensations, the door to the room opened and Geoffrey stepped to a proper distance.

"Our guests are arriving, Rosalind," Camilla said, discreetly pretending not to notice her high color.

"I'll be right there, Cammy."

The mood between them had been broken. Rosalind touched the necklace and murmured softly, "Thank you, my lord. I shall treasure this gift and its special meaning."

"We'd better join the mob." He said this reluctantly, as if he, too, was aggravated by the duties that called them apart. He tucked her hand in the crook of his elbow. "Shall we?"

The evening was a surprising success. Rosalind was the most astonished of all by her unusual poise. When she felt the feelings of panic and tongue-tied dismay rise when called upon for a response, she clung to the diamond horseshoe as if it was some strength-giving amulet. It was a symbol of Geoffrey's pride in her and she couldn't bear to fail him. Seeing his golden head nodding among the throng of guests further bolstered her determination when it was wont to lag. Her replies, while not witty or dazzling, were well spoken and did much to dispel the stigma of awkwardness attached to her. She clung to Geoffrey's encouraging gaze like a lifeline in the troublesome sea of social chatter. And she didn't sink.

With the wedding the main topic of the night, Geoffrey's gifts to the bridesmaids fanned a flurry of awed whispers. He gave each maid a diamond bracelet as an elaborate keepsake and to Camilla, in her honored position, a choker of the brilliant stones. The extravagance won much approval and would doubtlessly become a high standard for future comparisons. Much ado was made over Rosalind's necklace and she showed it off with blushing pride. The gifts made Lord Chilton appear generous to a fault. He shrugged aside the cost as if it was of no consequence.

Throughout the evening, Rosalind's eyes followed her betrothed about the room. He was a constant source of amazement and attraction to her. She admired his controlled grace with its hints of closely reined energy and his agreeable manner. While clever and somewhat biting, his humor was never caustic. His air of infinite ease made those around him comfortable. His appearance was stylish without the threat of affected posturing. That casual flair gave his elegance more appeal, a deeper, more sensual message that not only Rosalind responded to. He was a beguiling man and to say he was merely handsome would have been a grave disservice. It was shamefully simple to fall under the spell of his charm and watching him weave it about those he spoke to made Rosalind wonder anew at her luck in securing him and fear her ability to hold him.

Marriage in the exclusive circles of ton was hardly the sanctified institution it was designed to be. Rosalind wasn't privy to all the choice scandals, but she'd heard enough to know the way of them. The fine, prestigious lords kept their mistresses in grand style and shopped openly for the lovely demi-reps in Hyde Park and at the Opera House. Their haughty wives carried on just as shamefully, often bearing children out of their illicit affairs. Arrangements of convenience often threw two people together who despised each other openly. One had only to look to the Prince Regent and his estranged wife Caroline for proof. Rosalind may have been naive or just stricken with romantic idealism, but she knew she didn't want to be bound in some casually structured relationship where trust and fidelity were as antiquated as love.

Bothered by these new perceptions, Rosalind slipped from the noisy assembly into the cool gardens. Things were moving too swiftly. Had she enough time to consider what she was doing? The time she had known Geoffrey suddenly seemed very insignificant.

Then warm hands glided up her arms. She turned and cast herself upon him with a small cry.

"Roz, what is it?"

"Just hold me, Geoffrey."

He complied without hesitation, drawing her to his crisp shirtfront. He could feel shivers tremble through her and the desperation in the fingers that plied his evening coat. Whatever was troubling her, he feared it was of no minor consequence.

"Geoffrey, tell me that you love me."

The quavering plea made him frown in concern. "What is it, Roz? What has you in such a state? You weren't so havey-cavey when we spoke earlier. Has someone said something to upset you?" He pried her away so he could look into her dark, liquid eyes and demand the truth.

Rosalind stiffened her pride with a hard swallow and asked in blunt misery, "Are you planning to take mistresses?"

Geoffrey nearly choked on his surprise. He started to laugh at the absurdity of it, then sobered when a jewellike wetness penciled down her cheeks. He brushed the dampness away as he spoke with a tender chiding.

"We aren't even wed yet and you're accusing me of being unfaithful. How can you ask if I plan to tire of you when the thought of our wedding night has me in knots? Rosalind, you are the silliest creature even with that level head of yours. Who put these thoughts into your head? Have I done something to make you believe I'm not sincere?"

She blushed and cast her eyes down in foolish embarrassment. Her explanation was faint with self-reproach. "No. It's just that you are so wondrously fair."

"I could try to be less so if that would please you. I could stop bathing. I could paint my face. I could pick my teeth or bite my nails. Whatever you suggest."

She was smiling now, amused by her own insecurities when approached in his teasing light.

"Truly, Roz, what do you want of me? What can I do to assure you?"

The misgivings returned with her seriousness. She looked

at his flawless face through wistful eyes. "We don't suit, Geoffrey. A man like you shouldn't be tied to someone like me. You should be paired with someone like Camilla."

He seemed to recoil slightly, then took up her hands in earnest. "If I had been looking for a pretty face to show off upon my arm, true, I could have done better, but I wasn't. A shallow, pleasing countenance isn't the main attraction for a wife. When I thought of the woman I wanted to spend my life with, I didn't pick one for mere beauty that time would fade. I looked for one I could respect, one who offered intrigue and depth of character that would be a joy to me day after day, one who would gift me with love and passion. That woman's you, would could gift me with love and passion. That woman's you, Roz. I have no doubts. I don't want you to, either."

His hand cupped her chin and guided her up to meet the persuasive part of his mouth. It was impossible to question such delicious assurances and she found herself convinced the moment his tongue stroked with velvet insistence over hers. She held to the powerful line of his shoulders, willing his words to be true, wanting him to make her believe.

Geoffrey broke away, breath labored and eyes as dark as the night sky. His hands massaged the satiny skin between neck and shoulders, palms dipping lower to brush the swell of her ripe bosom. "You make it hard to wait three more days," he told her gruffly.

"Then let's not."

The low rumble of desire in her voice made it more difficult for him to step back and resist the sumptuous feel of her.

"No, Roz."

"What does it matter?" she pressed in growing urgency. "We'll be properly wed by week's end."

"You'd have me take you right here in your father's primroses? With a houseful of guests bound to miss us at any time?"

"Yes," she answered recklessly, but the smile that played about his tempting mouth had lessened the desperation in her tone. With a sigh, she turned away from the lure he held for her. "Three days seems an eternity. So much can happen. So much can change."

He banished her gloomy apprehension by slipping his arms about her middle and drawing her back to his chest. His kisses nibbled along her neck to punctuate his vow of, "Nothing will, precious one. In three days time, we will be man and wife and

90

nothing will come between us. Nothing. Now let's go back inside before the rumor is spread that we've eloped."

He revolved her easily within the circle of his embrace. Starlight glimmered and repeated in her gossamer gown, in the stones about her neck, and in the deep pools of her eyes. No one would have called her less than beautiful.

"It won't make the days go faster but it will make them easier to bear. I love you, Geoffrey."

His smile was small. Very respectfully, he kissed the hand that wore his ring, then tucking it in his elbow, he led her into the bright interior.

Chapter Ten

With the details all behind them, the eve of the wedding passed quietly for Rosalind and Camilla. Camilla insisted on spending the long hours with her as part of her duty as chief bridesmaid and Rosalind was grateful for her line of shallow conversation that helped calm her nervousness. Together, they went over the arrangements once again. The bride's nuptial cards had been sent to all the necessary parties. The white satin gown had been checked for creases or conspicuous wrinkles. Gloves wrapped in white paper and tied with white ribbon had been sent to each of the bridesmaids. Strips of cake had been threaded through Rosalind's wedding ring, then wrapped in ornamental papers. They would be given to the young unmarried guests at the wedding breakfast as a token of luck and love. Preparations for the *déjeuner* were concluded, its menu consisting of cold fowls, tongues, hams, botargoes, dried fruits, wines, cordials, and the cake, ordered through Gunter's. The drawing room was a showcase for the gifts already received, including a silver tea equipage, a service of choice porcelain, and purses containing money from her distant relatives. It was hard to believe that the fevered pitch would come to a conclusion in twelve hours time.

Looking fragile and sinfully young in a lacy dressing gown, Camilla shepherded Rosalind beneath the covers.

"You should get some sleep, Lindy. Tomorrow will begin all too soon. This notion of having to be wed before noon is an inconvenience to any gentleborn lady. You should have had Chilton apply for a special license. Why, no one of any breeding rises before eight or breakfasts before half past nine. On the day you have to look your best, you have to rise at an indecent hour to complete your toilet, have breakfast, see a half-a-score of well-wishers, drive to church, and still manage to look unwilted and all before twelve. Luckily, you and Chilton will be off on your honeymoon while your father and I contend with a restless houseful of guests from the end of breakfast to the evening dance. The downstairs rooms will be full of smoking men at cards and billiards, and the upstairs, of snoring bridesmaids."

"Will it be as awful as all that?" Rosalind cried in dismay.

Camilla laughed gaily. "Oh, no. Not for me. I plan to be snoring the loudest. Don't be concerned about me. You'll have other things on your mind."

She said that so ominously that Rosalind sat up, her innocent stare full of questions. "What is it like, Cammy?" she asked with a furious blush. "The wedding night, I mean."

The delicate brows arched high. "No one's told you what to expect?"

"Who would? Papa?" The irony of her situation made her tone wry. "I know about mating, of course. I've seen our mares bred since I was a child. I assume it works the same way. I just wondered if it was—pleasurable." That last was murmured with an awkward embarrassment.

Camilla looked down at her hands with a careful tact and said casually, "I believe men find it so. Of course, as a wife it's your duty to submit without complaint."

Rosalind's forehead puckered in confusion. It was indelicate to pry, but what she was hearing seemed contrary to her own feelings when she was with Geoffrey. She'd expected the event to be joyous, not one of simple duty.

Seeing her doubt, Camilla squeezed her hand and confided, "Don't worry, Lindy. It's not of long duration. If you do nothing to provoke it, I'm sure Chilton won't demand his rights more frequently than you can bear. It must be endured for the sake of begetting an heir, elsewise I would gladly avoid that part of married life. All in all, it's not a terrible sacrifice to make for the other pleasures of marriage."

Demand, endure, sacrifice? Rosalind was in a doubtful quake. Surely such terms couldn't apply. She voiced her thoughts timidly. "But I've enjoyed Geoffrey's touch thus far. I cannot believe he would hurt me."

"Nor should you let him know he is. If you convince him you're not repulsed by his crude demonstrations, he won't be so quick to turn to those who are paid to respond in kind. Men just don't understand how their baser nature offends a lady. No decent woman could welcome such a violation of her privacy yet it is our lot to bear it with dignity. Romance has little to do with what goes on in the marriage bed so go to it with your eyes open lest you be cruelly shocked."

Rosalind said nothing. Her mind was reeling with this new

information. Camilla must know the truth of it, yet how could it be so? She couldn't imagine not finding happiness in Geoffrey's arms. She was as anxious to conclude their love as he, or was that only because she didn't know what was to come?

Frowning slightly, she sank down into her covers. Her anxiety over the upcoming day was now overshadowed by the fear of the night to follow.

"Sleep well," Camilla cooed with a small smile and turned down the lights.

Across the river, a different evening was being spent by the groom at the White Hart Inn and Tavern on High Street. The Southwark Saloon had been chosen for its isolation from high ton, where the two brothers could meet as equals. Several toasts had been raised and a groggy Geoffrey Chilton leaned a heavy head into the support of his palm as he smiled across the table at the hazy figure of Henri Girard.

"I want you to stand up with me tomorrow, Hank," he mumbled. "Rutherford's a fair swell, but he's not my best friend. You are."

"A fine lord having his valet serving second." Henri laughed fondly. "What a sight that would be before all your quality guests."

Geoffrey pouted, his expression much aggrieved. "Hang them. I don't care. It's my wedding and you should be there with me. I insist on it."

"You've had too much to drink, *mon ami*. In the morning you'll see how impossible it is, but for now, I thank you."

"I'm not foxed. I'm seeing things very clearly, all two of you." His smile was silly and endearing. Then he was petulant once more. "Say you'll be there with me, Hank. It means ever so much to me. A man doesn't get married every day, does he?"

Henri smiled indulgently. "You won't be long in this one. I'll stand up with you next time."

Geoffrey frowned, his mind too confused to follow his logic. But he didn't want to differ with his brother on this special night. He wanted to celebrate his last hours in a cheerful camaraderie. That focused him on another matter and he approached it clumsily.

"There is something I would ask you, Hank?"

Henri paused in filling their glasses, bemused by the hesitant tone and deepening blush. "What is it, Geoff?"

"Tomorrow is my wedding night and I'm not sure, that is, I'm not certain I know— What I mean is—"

"Stop falling all over it and just ask, *mon ami.*"

Geoffrey cleared his throat and stared into his drink. His face was fiery. "How does one handle an inexperienced woman?" When Henri was silent, his glance slipped upward.

Henri gave a loud and hearty laugh and the embarrassed eyes dropped in misery. "You've never taken a virgin to bed?" his brother asked in amusement. The mute response was his answer. "Afraid of offending your pristine bride?"

Geoffrey looked up almost angrily and snapped, "Forget I said anything. I should never have expected you'd take me serious."

Still chuckling, Henri reached across to lay a hand on his brother's frowning face. "I'm sorry, *mon frère,* but it is very amusing to find you ignorant of such a thing. I am quite experienced in the area and if you are reluctant to do the task, I will see to her for you."

The dark blue eyes widened, then narrowed with surprising fierceness. "I fail to see the humor in your offer."

"Neither do I. I fear I wouldn't enjoy the deed in the least. I've always said *chacun à son goût* everyone to his own taste, but this time, I find yours to be a mystery."

"I am not wedding her to satisfy your limited tastes."

"Pardonnez-moi," he apologized with an elaborate gesture. He observed the sulky features for a long moment, perplexed by the vehement display. Geoffrey's good humor rarely lapsed and his occasional sullenness was never directed his way. Could it be because of the woman, the colorless heiress? He preferred not to think so. He preferred to think it was just a case of fidgets and sought to calm them. "Talk a lot," he advised and when Geoffrey's gaze lifted, he smiled and continued. "Women like that. They like to think you are sensitive. They want every man to be a poet, at least, at first. Spend a lot of time telling her she's the most beautiful, exciting woman you've ever known, that you've never felt the same about anyone before, that no one could ever compare to her. They believe that because they want to. When you've done enough talking, let the rest come slow and easy. Concentrate on her wants. You can be selfish and inconsiderate once she's used to you. Virgins aren't too much different from any other woman, unless, of course, they start screaming and fall into

hysterics."

Faintly, Geoffrey asked, "What do you do then?"

"Find a mistress."

Geoffrey snorted and drank down his drink. He gave the Frenchman a long-suffering look and pronounced, "You are an incredible cynic, Hank. How could a woman ever think you sincere?"

"Because I'm a consummate actor and an incredible lover."

Geoffrey smiled at that conceited claim and asked, "Haven't you ever cared for any of the ladies you were with?"

"Why complicate something that's meant to be simple?"

The younger man had no answer for his brother or for himself. He sighed and emptied his glass. "Perhaps you'll change your mind when you meet someone like Rosalind."

Henri reserved his judgment and gave his companion a gauging look. "You're playing it too close with this woman, *mon frère*. Remember it is all a game. Isn't it?"

"Of course. What else would it be. Just for the money. I'll be a lord until the first babe is born, then all is ours. We'll go off somewhere and live like kings."

Henri was satisfied with that selfish sentiment. It sounded more like Geoffrey than the mooning claims of a moment before. It would be the two of them, like always.

While Geoffrey dozed on the tabletop, Henri paid for the drinks and arranged for a coach to take them back to Grosvenor Square. As his brother slept against his shoulder on the ride there, he considered the scheme before them. It would prove more lucrative than plying the ruby necklace through countless hands. All they had to do was hold to the game until the money was released into Geoffrey's hands. Disclosure of his past would win a discreet divorce. Until then, they would live high and well off the Dunstans, a cozy arrangement to take them through the winter. Then they would move on, he and Geoff and whatever they could carry.

A note had been delivered for the viscount in their absence. Geoffrey stumbled into the drawing room and struggled with the lamp, cursing as he did the stiff-neck snobs of Grosvenor Square who refused to let the aesthetic impurity of gaslight intrude into their elite community. Finally, he managed to kindle a flame and squinted over the bold script. His posture straightened as he read the message. An icy chill of sobriety stiffened his spine.

"What is it, Geoff?" Henri called from the doorway, then

yawned into his hand.

"Nothing. Nothing. Just some prenuptial congratulations. Go on to bed. Remember you have to rouse me at a decent hour in the morning and that's only a few away." He flashed a broad convincing smile.

The dark head nodded. *"Bon soir, mon ami."*

"Good night, Hank."

Geoffrey sat heavily on the settee and reviewed the note. The text was brief. His debt of £18,000 was payable in Clarges Street before he left the city with his new bride. No threat was implied, but the crisp call for rendering offered no alternatives. Now wide awake and painfully clear of mind, he folded the paper and searched for options.

Rosalind held the bouquet of white rosebuds up to inhale the delicate fragrance. They had just arrived from Geoffrey. All that was left to do was dress and ride to the church. Her case of nervous qualms that prevented sleep had eased to a surprising calm when all about her was a chaos of bridesmaids and their abigails. She touched the pristine flowers and smiled. Before the morning was out, she would be Lady Chilton.

She looked up from her fanciful daydreaming to her stepmother. Camilla had donned her dress and looked very much the bride herself.

"Lindy, your father wants a word with you. He's in the book room. Do hurry. We still have to get you ready."

The ground floor was a bustle of preparations for the wedding breakfast. Rosalind had to weave her way between members of the staff to get to her father's library. The door there was slightly ajar. The sound of male voices drew her up before announcing herself with a knock. Recognition of her intended's voice held her fast in confusion. What would Geoffrey be doing at their home an hour before the ceremony?

"As you requested," her father was saying. "Don't count it here. There isn't time. You've a wedding to get to, remember? I needn't tell you that Rosalind should never hear of this. She's a strange one in matters of this kind."

"Not a word from me. I'm no fool and I am very familiar with her pride."

"Treat her wisely and in nine months time you'll have no need to bargain for paltry sums like this. Welcome to the family, Chilton. I trust you won't disappoint me."

Rosalind staggered back, mind reeling with what she'd heard. Only the quick action of a passing kitchen girl saved her from stumbling over her hem in her hasty retreat. She clung to the supporting arm for several seconds, so severely shocked she couldn't force her thoughts to focus.

"Are you all right, miss?" the worried girl asked, alarmed by the ghastly expression and pale cheeks.

Rosalind gulped for air, aware of the curious stares of no less than a dozen servants. Before one of them gathered the presence of mind to call to her father, she straightened and supplied a wan smile.

"I tripped. I'm sorry if I gave you a startle. I wasn't looking where I was going." She cast a glance at the partially opened door. "Excuse me. I have to get ready."

The girl grinned and released her arm and the others went about their business, leaving Rosalind to make her way upstairs with an iron rein on her composure. There was no relief in the crowded upper hall or in her own room where Jessup and Camilla awaited her.

"Did you chastise his lordship for calling you away at such a time?" Camilla asked in mild annoyance.

"He didn't want to see me at all," she managed in a stiff tone. Jessup hurried her to the dressing table and began work on her hair.

"Oh?" Camilla frowned in puzzlement. "He was asking over your whereabouts. I assumed the rest. Just as well. Let's get you together. This is the happiest day of your life."

Rosalind gave a pinched smile to her colorless reflection. She sat silently while her hair was bound with Roman fillets and a wreath of roses. She concentrated on her own breathing, clinging to that steady rhythm to suppress the panic of emotion that sought a dramatic escape. She could allow no tears or wailings. That wouldn't do. Not at all. Such a display before a houseful of company would be in incredibly bad form. She didn't care about her own or her father's embarrassment but she couldn't cast such a shame upon Camilla, who alone was blameless. There was no time to vent hysterics. She had to follow through the bitter charade. It was too late to do otherwise. She wouldn't think of it now. She would think of nothing but maintaining face for her family. No cracks could flaw this perfect day . . . the happiest of her life.

"Lindy, dear, is something wrong? You look so pale."

98

Rosalind smiled reassuringly at her pretty stepmother. "Just nerves, Cammy. I'll be fine."

The narrow streets near St. George's in Hanover Square were crammed with carriages. Elegantly garbed members of London's ton crowded the pews of Mayfair's parish church shoulder-to-shoulder and spilled over into the galleries. All eyes strained toward the forward rail for a glimpse of the fashionable wedding party. Descriptions of the bride in her clinging, high-waisted gown of white satin and lace would be all the talk for weeks to come. The less exclusive would beg to know exactly how her trailing scarf of Brussels lace wound from its pinning on the back of her head in a loose, flowing drape about her bare arms. They would clamor to hear about the celestial bridesmaids all in white with their glimmering keepsakes creating brilliant flashes of fire amid the yards of veils and flowers. Maids would sigh over the handsome groom in his black finery flanked by his nervous groomsman as wedding hymns were sung in the fully choral service.

After leaving the flower-banked church, the wedding group widened considerably with relatives and friends as the Dunstan home was filled to capacity for breakfast and toasts to the newly wed couple. Dunstan beamed when congratulated on the extravagant and tasteful affair. Lord Chilton accepted well wishes with a broad grin and hearty handshake. Only the bride was reserved as she stoically greeted the guests and offered her cheek for constant bussings. When her new husband tried to kiss her, she shied away with admirable modesty and a flush of becoming warmth. They didn't notice how she stiffened and balked when he caught her arm and drew her to the spectacular display of gifts. He gestured to a large straw box, his features animated with a wide, boyish grin.

"My gift to you, Lady Chilton. It's called a corbeille and is a tradition in France. Open it," he urged. At her reluctance, he gave her a slight nudge as anxious guests leaned close.

Rosalind drew off the lid of the satin-lined box and for all her forced indifference, couldn't repress a gasp at the treasures within. That sound of appreciation echoed back through the onlookers as she handled lengths of rich velvet and silks, luxurious fur pieces, yards of old Honiton lace, delicate fans, and a string of perfect pearls.

Since her neck was bare, Geoffrey lay the pearls in a

creamy circle about her throat. She seemed to freeze beneath that attentive brush of his fingertips and her tone was stilted. "Thank you, my lord. Your generosity overwhelms me."

The faint tang of sarcasm was lost to all but his ear and he gave a puzzled frown as she slipped away from him in the crowd. He followed as soon as he was able, managing to catch her hand by the flower-decked mantel. This time, her struggle to free herself was more obvious.

"Roz, what is it?" he demanded in an urgent undervoice.

"Nothing. I have a beastly headache. How soon can we leave here?"

Still perplexed, he muttered, "Whenever you like."

"I'm going to change then." She ducked quickly away from him and, with Camilla in attendance, hurried up the stairs.

"You're leaving already?" Camilla asked as she assisted her out of the exquisite gown. Jessup was rushing to lay out her traveling clothes.

"You know how I hate these affairs. I just want to be on my way to the manor. I—I—" Her voice caught in a sudden sob and she covered her mouth with an unsteady hand.

"Lindy, whatever is the matter?" Camilla's arms circled the trembling shoulders in a sheltering embrace.

Rosalind swallowed the rush of her grief and put on a brave face to satisfy her companion's concern. "I'm just so exhausted by all the fuss. I'll be better at the manor. Cammy, please come out soon. I shall miss you so dreadfully."

"If that's what you want. I would have thought you and Chilton would enjoy the privacy."

"I would like you there. Please." Her hands clasped the other's in a damp, desperate entreaty.

"Of course, Lindy. As soon as it is proper."

"Thank you. You don't know how much I depend upon you."

"I'm glad," replied the smiling woman as she supplied a fortifying hug.

James Dunstan met them at the foot of the stairs. Rosalind accepted his kiss but eluded the embrace he tried to draw her into. She kept a wary distance, eyeing him with thinly veiled contempt.

"My girl all duly wed," he mused with atypical fondness. The ceremony had him misty-eyed and sentimental. Rosalind's reaction was coldly cutting.

"I'm sure you must be very pleased that things worked out

to fit your clever schemes. Congratulations, my lord. You got your way this time, but perhaps not again."

She brushed by him to let Geoffrey take her arm in escort to the coach that would take them to the country. Amid many shouts of farewell and congratulations, she stepped up into the well-sprung carriage. She spread her skirts wide, offering no adjoining space for Geoffrey. He took the opposite seat with a curious cant of his brow but had no time to question her as the coach jolted to a start in a shower of satin slippers. Leaving the revelers behind, they hurried on alone toward their new life together.

As they spun through the gates, leaving London behind, Geoffrey turned an amorous eye on his new bride. She sat stiffly, looking determinedly out the window. His stare appraised the tilt of her narrow nose, the fixed purpose of her clear eyes, the full wanting pout of her lips, then dipped lower to ogle the press of her bosom against the soft velvet. The sight began to warm him with the knowledge that all he saw was his and he was eager to finally lay claim.

"Is it a long ride to your properties?"

The low caress of his voice made Rosalind wary. "We will be there by nightfall, my lord. If you don't mind, I should like to rest."

"Let me offer my shoulder." He started up with the intention of joining her, but her hand braced against his chest.

"I am fine, my lord. Don't trouble yourself."

He would have protested but she gave him a pointed shove back onto his own seat where he remained, slightly stunned by her cool rejection. He watched in some degree of pique while she pillowed her head on the side of the coach and closed him out by the shutting of her eyes.

Surprisingly, Rosalind did sleep. The tension of the long night and the agony of the pretense throughout the morning had worn her to a miserable low. She slept unaware of the scrutiny she was under and of the miles and hours that passed in uneventful silence. It wasn't until she heard a soft call that she stirred from her uncomfortable position.

"Rosalind, we're here."

She straightened slowly. The crink in her neck made her reevaluate pride over the cushion of her companion. She cast a cautious glance at him but his stare was held by Dunstan Manor.

The structure appeared to be one of Wyatt's huge Gothic

101

mansions. It bristled with spires, pinnacles, and crockets, resembling their towering wedding cake. Pointed, arched windows, imitation arrow slits, sharp archways, and fan-vaulting in wood and plaster helped further the illusion of medievalism. The effect was overpowering and Rosalind summed it up simply.

"Grotesque, isn't it?"

"Impressive but quite awful, I do agree. Somehow, I cannot picture your father in such a place."

"It was Camilla's dream palace. She had the additions designed, but I fear her fantasy is more a nightmare."

As if realizing they were sharing a conversation, Rosalind was instantly silent. She stepped from the coach on the arm of one of the footmen and hurried up to the house where she was formally greeted by the assembled staff. She was thankful to see Jessup had arrived before them.

"I'm going to my room, Jessup. Have a meal sent to me there," she commanded precisely. As if an afterthought, she added, "Have his lordship's things taken to the eastern suite."

"Ma'am?"

Rosalind dismissed the odd look with a cool stare and Jessup swallowed the objection. It was like challenging the old lord himself, and risky business that was.

Without waiting to see how her spouse fared, Lady Chilton went directly to her familiar suite of rooms. The first thing she noticed was that the mauve color didn't suit her and the second was her own reflection. She looked ashen and strained by the events of the day. It was hardly the look of a bride. Her lower lip quivered and she bit it fiercely, but the chill had already swept out of her control. Weeping soundlessly, she sat on the edge of her bed and let her unhappiness overtake her.

What a fool she felt. She had believed it all — the passionate kisses, the ardent gazes, the pretty words. Yet he hadn't committed the most damning sin. He hadn't lied by saying he loved her. She fingered the pearls about her throat. Knowledge that he had purchased them with her father's money brought a violent reaction. She tore them from her neck with a quick jerk. The individual orbs fell from the broken string and scattered like so many promises.

Her father had bought her a husband; bought and paid for him right under her nose. Not just any man but the one she had wanted so much to love and have love her in return. The irony of it was unbearable. Had it been Everard, she could have borne it. Nathaniel had never been anything but honest with her. Geoffrey had played a skillful game, tending to her fragile emotions and her father's vanity. How easy it had been for him to make her think all had been her choice. They had planned it between them right down to the payment on the day of her wedding. With the next due at the birth of her child.

Anger began to supplant hurt when she thought of the cruel joke played upon her passions. With his handsome face and jovial manner, Geoffrey Chilton had slipped beneath her guard. Taken unawares, he had succeeded where none of the others had, she had let herself care for him. He had courted her smoothly with just the right hint of intensity and she had crumpled at his whispered promises. She was the means to his greater fortune, her body, and her child. Then, she imagined he would have no reason to pretend interest or affection in the plain, gullible Rosalind Chilton.

That he would use her and cast her off woke a deeper rebellion in her heart, one sharper than the pain of betrayal and more bitter than the knowledge of deception. He would not find it so easy to claim that second payment. He may have been bought by her father but she didn't have to accept him. She wouldn't accept him. If Dunstan had thought her stubborn before, he had a true battle of wills ahead of him. No one was going to buy her child at any price.

When Geoffrey tapped on the door to Rosalind's suite, it was answered by her maid. He was told crisply that Lady Chilton had retired for the evening and didn't wish to be disturbed. By anyone. Then the door closed and was securely latched. He stood there, jaw unhinged and eyes round with disbelief for long minutes. She had shut him out. It was their wedding night and she had greeted him with a curt message and a locked door. He hadn't received so much as a teasing glimpse of her. He was no scholar on married life but he was certain this wasn't how it was meant to begin.

For a month, he had harbored dreams of being with her. He was tortured by his memories from the inn, all too brief and unsatisfying. She had come into his arms countless times to respond to his kisses. He had refused her pleas to hurry the conclusion of their desires and had waited in anticipation for this night. He'd imagined coming to her on her bed of innocence for a long lingering night's journey to knowledge, one they would share and fully enjoy. He had banked his needs and urged them to wait and she met him with a locked door. He was dumbfounded.

He could knock again but it would be too embarrassing to be turned away a second time. He could have forced his way in but that defeated his purpose as well as hers. He stared at the closed door and all it hid from him and heaved a sigh of disappointment. Reluctantly, he returned to the rooms assigned him. Their location didn't please him — across the hall and several doors down from his wife's rooms. It was where one put a guest, not a husband. It was not at all promising.

Geoffrey prowled his rooms, restlessly aware of his celibate state. His fingertips roved over the glossy satinwood furnishings and well-chosen art objects. He hefted a cut-glass decanter and distractedly admired its intricate faceting. His aimless stare wandered over the tasteful and expensive oils on the walls and the Aubusson carpet on the floor. Unconsciously, he began to calculate each item, assigning a worth and adding up an impressive total. The wealth of his surroundings helped soothe his abused feelings and when he settled down to sleep, he dreamed he was appraising the contents of the Gothic manse and all was his. His lips curved in his sleep.

Chapter Eleven

Awaking to the luxurious surroundings did much to restore Geoffrey's confident outlook. While he indulged in a breakfast in bed, he considered his position with Rosalind. With his passions cooled, he could make excuses for her cold behavior. Of course, she was exhausted after the excitement and stress of the wedding. He knew how much she dreaded such regimented affairs. Then there had been the long ride. And she did have a headache. How could he have expected her to respond to his selfish desires when in such a fragile state? A good night's rest, undisturbed rest, was doubtlessly what she'd needed. Now, he was sure things would warm agreeably between them and he would have what he needed.

Thinking along those lines shifted the focus of his appetite. Picking up the single white rose he'd asked be brought up with his tray, he padded down the hall in his Turkish-style slippers. He adopted a careless pose and knocked. When it swung open, he presented the delicate bud with a sultry, "For you, precious one."

Jessup regarded him in his dressing gown with a cool reproof. "My lord?"

Feeling foolish, Geoffrey straightened from his languid posture. "Is Lady Chilton about yet?" he asked with forced courtesy.

"Hours ago, sir."

"May I see her?"

"She's not within, my lord. She's gone out."

"Out?"

"Gone riding, sir. I'm sure Pettigrew can find a mount for you if you wish to join her ladyship."

"No, that's quite all right," he said quickly. Mounting a horse was not what he'd had in mind.

"Very good, sir."

When the door closed, he regarded the rose in sullen defeat. So much for early morning romancing. On returning to his room, he found Henri sprawled upon his unmade bed putting the finish to his breakfast.

"*Bonjour, mon frère*. How did your night of *amour* with your

105

chaste bride fare?"

"Oh, do be quiet, Hank," he growled peevishly and gave the blameless flower a brusque toss.

"Marital difficulties so soon? I don't believe I heard any screaming."

He scowled at the levity and grumbled, "I didn't get the opportunity to do anything." Henri's grin only increased his humiliation.

"You might as well be in London for all the good this room does you. Could you not find quarters more to your advantage?"

Geoffrey's eyes took on a thoughtful slant and he checked the hall, counting doorways. When a petite young upstairs maid passed by, he called to her and smiled at her blushing discomposure over his state of dress.

"Excuse me — ?"

"Faye, my lord," she supplied with a giggle.

"Yes, Faye. Could you tell me whose room that is next to her ladyship's?"

"That be a sitting room, sir, shared by both suites."

"And the other suite, is it occupied?"

"No, sir."

His grin deepened into charming dimples. The simple girl was flustered. "Faye, I'd like my things moved into that room. Could you see to it for me?"

She drew up in importance to be asked to do something so above her station by the new lord. She stammered, "But this room be much grander, sir."

"Perhaps but the sun comes in so early and wakes me. Could you see to the other room. Please?"

His fingertips touched under the pointed chin and the girl nearly swooned. Her voice was barely a whisper. "Of course, Lord Chilton. I'll see to it personal."

"Thank you, Faye."

Faye bobbed a quick curtsy and hurried off on her entrusted mission.

Geoffrey turned back into the room with a satisfied smile, thinking himself a step closer.

Rosalind returned from her ride feeling a high flush of exhilarated freedom. The restraining shackles of London had been kicked off as she sent her mount galloping across the open fields in the fresh, open sunshine. It was a feeling no other could replace and one that always spoke of a return home. She strode into her dressing room and began to shed her dusty garments. She didn't notice the adjoining door was open until, on turning, she saw Geoffrey leaning against the doorframe. Clutching the open shirt together, she eyed him in defensive alarm.

"My lord, I was not expecting to see you," she said breathlessly.

"We live under the same roof, dear wife. You had to know we would run into one another eventually." He stared at her odd attire as he spoke. In the baggy trousers and loose shirt, she could have passed for a fair stableboy except for the luscious curves the gaping front revealed. The sight brought a strange dryness to his mouth. "I took this room for my own. I found it much more agreeable than the other."

Rosalind's lips pressed thin with annoyance, for she could think of no reason to protest the move. Tone taut, she said, "Please excuse me, Chilton. I should like to refresh myself after my ride."

Contrarily, he didn't leave but continued his thorough assessment. "I never considered a pair of trousers could look so fetching," he mused.

Rosalind heard the dangerous rumble in his low voice and edged back toward her own room. Seeing him all grinning and agreeable threatened her angry resolve. It would be too easy to forget what she had heard between him and her father. Easy but still impossible.

Suddenly, he stood away from the door and advanced toward her. Holding her ground when her heart screamed for her to flee was no simple matter. She stood rigidly when his palm fit warmly against her cheek. His eyes were smoky and dark with desire.

"I missed you last night, Roz." His tone was all silken seduction. She was entranced by it as his head dipped down. When she felt his breath brush her lips, she jerked her head aside to avoid the peril of his kiss. Her resolution was too newly made to withstand such a trial.

"I apologize for that, my lord. My absence must have inconvenienced you."

That brittle speech made him frown. "Inconvenienced?" That was an odd term and he didn't like its connotations. "Rosalind, I wouldn't put my wants ahead of yours if you're not feeling quite the thing."

She met his anxious gaze triumphantly. "That's it. I am not myself and I beg your tolerance while I am indisposed."

"Are you ill?" He took up her hand in an urgent press.

"Nothing so awful. Just the female ailment."

Geoffrey flushed a deep crimson and dropped her hand with an embarrassed "Oh." He retreated a gallant step.

Let him talk his way around that, she thought smugly. "Please excuse me. I wish to change." She stepped into her room and closed the door between them.

For the next week, Geoffrey settled into the Dunstan household in the name-only position as Rosalind's husband. The servants treated him with a reserved respect and Rosalind treated him with a reserve so icy he was nearly frostbitten during their brief encounters. He rarely managed to see her. The huge house and endless grounds conspired to keep her whereabouts secret during the day. She was always up long before him and in the absence of any company, preferred to dine alone in her room. At night, his own modest naïveté was a greater barrier than her closed door. Though bewildered by her abrupt behavior he excused it as a symptom of her condition and tried to be extra accommodating.

While he waited for her affliction to end, Geoffrey spent his hours taking a room-to-room inventory of the manor. He began in the great entrance hall and worked his way through dining and drawing rooms on either side, back into the formal parlor, morning room, study, and billiard room. He even toured the rear kitchen with its washhouse, bakehouse, and scullery. The upstairs rooms were spacious connecting suites, and with the exception of Rosalind's and his own, unoccupied. The collection of paintings amazed him. They put a well-stocked museum to shame. His tally soared to dizzying heights when he discovered a collection of rare texts and one of exquisite porcelains. Each day was a treasure hunt. The servants admired his industry without knowing his motive. They couldn't guess that he'd become clammy with excitement when handling the jewel-encrusted sabers adorning the study walls. The continuous finds set him trembling with a covetous delight. His sincere admiration and probing questions on the origins of each piece made the household staff puff with pride. They became quite taken by the ever-smiling, energetic Lord Chilton.

As hard as it was to evade him, Rosalind was ever reminded

of Geoffrey's presence through the glowing comments of the servants, especially the girls whom he flattered and sent into transports with his easy flirtations. While she hid from him, she wracked her brain for a means to rid herself of the charming intruder. Concentrating on that kept her from thinking of how much she longed to welcome him as her husband. She had to keep reminding herself that he was not the man she fell in love with. He was the man her father had bribed to court her. Her anger grew apace with her frustrated desire until the thought or mention of Geoffrey Chilton sent her into a seething rage. The tender consideration he greeted her with smacked of mocking insincerity. How he must loathe her to play such vile tricks with her emotions. She had to be rid of him and soon.

The nights were the worst. She could hear him prowling about the sitting room. Anxiously, she watched the door, wondering how long it would remain closed between them, wondering if she could resist him if he chose to open it. He wouldn't be put off forever. He was anxious to earn the rest of his fee, her inheritance. All he had to do was fill her with his male child and his comfort would be certain. It was a tidy reward for a few minutes of unpleasant duty. She ground her teeth in impotent fury and tossed on her virginal bed. Another night passed with little sleep.

While man and wife danced about each other, Henri took quite naturally to life in the grand house. As one of the high ranking in the household regiments, he had endless privilege and took advantage of them to the fullest. The younger maids were captivated by his foreign flair and the rest resented his air of superiority. He was content with his lordly position among the below stairs population though he continued to bemoan his servile stature to bedevil Geoffrey. In truth, he preferred it to the stuffy social set where he was a nonentity. Here, he could reign supreme.

The brothers' pretense ended in Geoffrey's quarters. There, Henri would cease his catering and the two of them would lounge about, drinking good liquor and laughing over their circumstance. The Frenchman was full of delightful talk from the staff and Geoffrey, of the valuables he'd uncovered. Rosalind was their only point of contention. Henri saw her through disparaging eyes. His ceaseless remarks about her lack of beauty, grace, and charm had Geoffrey in an awkward defensiveness. He was forced to champion her without seeming to. To Henri, she was part of another scheme to be carefully played but she was more to him. His inability to define how much more was a constant frustration. As was his continued celibacy.

Henri chose a poor evening to take unfair jabs at Rosalind. Geoffrey had seen her briefly clad in a scandalously low-cut satin gown that displayed the generous curve of her bosom to his hungering stare. Just the sound of her walking, the fabric sighing in insinuating whispers as it shifted about her hips and thighs was enough to encourage his frenzied imaginings. Now was not the time to discuss her rationally.

"I rather enjoy this country life," Henri was saying as he sipped his wine. "Too bad it won't last long."

Geoffrey snapped at his baiting with an irritable, "What do you mean by that?"

"No heir in a year, no money, no reason to stay on. I don't mean to pry but it would seem easier to accomplish the necessary conception if you did more than moon over your frosty bride. Geoff, surely you realize you do have to play a part in producing this heir and that it requires more than heated glances. Is she so unappealing that you cannot bring yourself to the task?"

"That isn't it at all. It's—she's—" His furious blush made Henri raise an indolent brow. "Indisposed," he concluded awkwardly.

Henri pursed his lips, amused by his brother's delicate discomfort. Very dryly, he said, "That is not what I hear." He waited until Geoffrey shot him a surly look to go on. I hear she is in perfect health, female or otherwise. There is quite a good deal of talk as to why you haven't approached her. Shall I tell them that she tricked you into believing she was—how did you say, indisposed?"

Geoffrey was silent for a long moment. When he spoke, his flat tone impressed even the imperturbable Henri.

"See that I'm awakened in time to speak with Lady Chilton before she takes her morning ride. It seems we have much to discuss. Leave me, Henri. I've no wish for company."

Respectfully, and for once without an offered opinion, Henri withdrew.

Geoffrey stood for long minutes staring at the closed door on the other side of the sitting room. His features hid the tumult of emotion that worked behind them. Finally, he conceded defeat for yet another night but determined it would be

110

the last one. ✓

Rosalind's leisurely walk to the stables was one she looked forward to each morning. The crispness of the day cleared her head and revitalized her spirit. She drew a contented strength from the invigorating scent of dew and dawn, just as she had as a child. She found herself wishing anew that she could manage the same composure in the crowded London setting. Yet this was her haven, her idyll and London had nothing to offer her in comparison. She had everything she wanted on the sprawling grounds—freedom, companionship, the joy of having a good mount beneath her and— She broke off her thoughts, annoyed at having them disturbed and even more so at the intrusion of a low voice.

"Good morning, my lady."

"Good morning, my lord," she returned as he fell in step beside her. "Unusually early for you, isn't it?"

Her clipped words brought an increased tightness to the set of his expression. "How would you know, dear wife? You have scarcely noticed me since our arrival. You cannot be familiar with my habits."

Rosalind walked faster. Something was amiss. She had never seen Geoffrey drop his congenial pose before. The decided coolness alarmed her. Defenses up and readied, she asked, "To what do I owe this unexpected attention?"

He gripped her arm, jerking her up short. "What game are you playing with me, madam?"

"Game, my lord?" She met his stare levelly. "I don't understand."

"Yes, you do. I want to know why you'd go to such extremes to keep me from your bed. I can accept a certain degree of apprehension, but this is something else altogether. I want to know why you've been avoiding me. I want to know why our marriage hasn't been consummated."

"Do you indeed." She pulled free of his grasp and strode on. Her strides were quick with agitation.

"I want to know now."

They had reached the stables and further discussion was detained by the presence of the groom who held Rosalind's spirited stallion. Geoffrey dismissed him with a curt word, giving Rosalind time to mount. His wariness of the horse kept him at bay. His tone was low and angry.

"Rosalind, talk to me now."

She drew up the reins sharply. The stallion tossed its head and pranced nervously. Geoffrey retreated several prudent steps.

"I have no interest in talking to you. I have no interest in you at all, Lord Chilton. You cannot expect me to hold to my father's arrangement. You may have schemed your way into this family, but you have won no place in my affections. My father may be able to buy me a husband but he cannot force his will upon me, nor will you, sir. My father will be sorely disappointed and you, my lord, have outsmarted yourself. The money he paid you is all you're going to get. Stay if you like, but in a year's time, my father will be only too happy to have this convenient little folly annulled when it proves as barren as your promises. He may have bought me your name, but don't confuse yourself by trying to act as my husband."

Geoffrey's startlement was slow in ending. Finally, in a desperate move to get her to listen, he bravely gripped the reins in one hand and her knee with the other. "Roz, there's been some mistake. Please, talk to me."

"Oh, there's been a mistake all right. Yours. Take your hand from me."

Her crop slashed down on the back of his hand. The blow wasn't cutting, yet was smart enough to earn her release. She hauled her mount around with a fierceness that made Geoffrey stumble back to avoid being knocked down by the powerful haunches. She applied her heels and was off in a reckless gallop.

Rosalind expended much of her potent fury in the wild, headlong ride that wore hard on her and her mount. The thundering hoofbeats echoed the pounding of her heart and provoked passions. The sting of the wind could have been blamed for the wetness on her cheeks.

After pushing the lathered stallion to near its limit, Rosalind slowed the beast to an easy lope. Gradually, the frantic pounding within her quieted to match. A great weight of relief was lifted from her heart but the sadness remained. He would go now. There was no reason for him to stay now that she'd exposed his unwise plotting. She would no longer be troubled by his presence, but how so his absence? Discovery of his smoothly spoken deceit hadn't managed to tear him from her deep-seated emotions. Memory of the persuasive suitor in the gardens, in the curricle, and in the deep shadows of the Dark

112

Walk played cruel opposite to the conversation she'd over-heard. The irony of her finally lowering her guard to trust and take a chance on someone who proved yet another fortune hunter was too merciless. Why hadn't she seen through the charming smile and simmering attentions? Because she hadn't wanted to, she scolded. She should have heeded the warning from Camilla. If only she had listened. She heard it all too clear now and she wanted to scream for the taunts to stop. Fool. Dreamer.

Geoffrey Chilton was no longer of any consequence. In time, she would forget him, if not the bitter lesson. Her father was another matter. How could he have been so callous of her feelings, of her, his only child? She had never been more to him than an asset to be used for the greatest gain. She vowed not to be manipulated for his purpose. His fortune may have been his ruling God but not hers. She could exist easily on an allowance if it meant challenging his dictates. When she married again and had children, it would be for love, not for the sake of propagating his vanity. And if she never found that love and a reason to immortalize it, she would remain chaste without regret.

With those bold vows to sustain her, Rosalind returned to the stable, relinquishing her winded stead to the groomsman. She pulled off her gloves and started through the pungent stall area feeling confident in her new stance. At least until it met its first challenge.

"You didn't think our talk was finished, did you?"

Rosalind took a hasty step back as Geoffrey straightened from his casual pose against one of the stall posts. She scrambled internally to recover the poise his unexpected presence shook from her.

"I've said all I'm going to, sir. Now, if you'll excuse me."

Her attempt to sail by him was quickly thwarted. His large hand caught her forearm and pinwheeled her bodily into an empty stall. He trapped her between the straddling of his arms, backing her to the wall. She glared up at him, breath seething between clenched teeth and breast heaving in the passion of her anger. The sight of her fiery defiance curled exciting threads of longing throughout his taut body.

"You're not running from me until you explain this non-sense. Why are you so angry with me and what is all this bathering about your father?" When she tried to dodge past him, he bounced her back with a hard bump of his hip.

113

"Rosalind, you are going nowhere until I have some answers from you."

"What you ask, you already know," she spat at him. "How much did he pay you to sway me with your pretty lovemaking? How much was it worth to you to trick me to the altar? I hope it was plenty, for you'll not see another cent."

"Roz, I needed no bribe to make you my wife," he argued with formidable ire. "Why would you believe it so?"

"Because I heard the two of you. I heard you take his money. I heard you laugh over my ignorance. How dare you treat me as such a joke." Tears of humiliation and hurt escaped her angry eyes to trail forlornly down her cheeks and lance his heart with barbs of stabbing guilt.

"What you heard was me borrowing from your father. Nothing more. It had nothing to do with you. Roz, believe me. Please."

She searched the earnest blue eyes, hating herself for wanting to see truthfulness in them. Even now, the attraction he held was a powerful weapon against her will.

"I don't believe you," she said coldly. "A man in your position doesn't borrow on the day of his wedding. What a featherhead you must think me. I won't be taken in by you a second time. Your pretty manners are not worth the price paid you and will not earn you a place in this household. You are not going to charm your way into my trust, Lord Chilton, or into my bed. Once my father realizes that, he'll release you from your bargain. He should have given his money to Everard. At least his cause was admirable. Your greed I find deplorable."

"I was not paid to wed you, Rosalind," he protested, growing more frustrated by her anguish and chilling conclusion.

"If not for the money, then why? Love?" Her laugh was mocking. "If you had loved me, you would have told me so. Convince me or leave me now. I want nothing more to do with you."

The barrier of Geoffrey's arms collapsed, bringing him down to her with stunning abruptness. His weight carried them down to the bed of straw. Her cry of alarm was smothered by the avid press of his lips. For a moment, they were at an impasse, she neither accepting nor rejecting his urgent kiss, then her hands rose to alternately push and clutch at him. The confusion of intentions encouraged him all the more. When he leaned back, she lay motionless on the fresh hay, eyes squeezed shut while she panted for possession of her senses. His hand stroked gently along the finely cut line of her jaw, waking the huge, desperate pools of deepest brown.

"Believe what you will, Roz. You're not going to drive me off with your bold bluff of indifference. I know you love me. I'm not going to let you end our marriage because I want it and I want you. I'm your husband and I'm going to be your lover and the father of your children. Denying me is denying yourself. Don't cheat us of the pleasure of being together."

Her quivering lips parted as his head lowered, but his mouth passed them by to gently feast on the tender flesh of her throat. Her moan was one of helpless wonder as his hand slipped within the loose folds of her shirt to tease a wanting peak upon one heavy breast. The fabric parted to lay bare a downward path for his hot kisses. The whisper of his breath brought hers to a torturous halt only to begin again in sharp gasps as his tongue made a tantalizing circle. Her hands rose to the golden head, closing convulsively in the silken web of his hair. Shivery darts of pleasure radiated beneath his attentive mouth, warm and seductive in their promise of what would follow.

The sound of heavy footsteps brought her dazed eyes open with a startled snap. The reality of her position was a freezing dash to quell her kindling passions. She was nearly prostrate on the floor of the stall, holding his head to her breast like a suckling babe. The fear of discovery didn't shake her as badly as her wanton permissiveness with a man she would deprive of such favors.

"Get off me, you odious cur," she hissed, shoving him hard. He hadn't heard the approaching footfalls and was reluctant to comply. "Stop it, Geoffrey. Let me up this instant. For God's sake, let me up. Someone is coming."

Lowell Pettigrew thought of his stables the way most considered their homes. He saw they were spotlessly clean, efficiently organized, and revered by those who worked in them as though they were a shrine to the perfection of horseflesh. The last thing he would allow was one of his employees frolicking with a housemaid in his domain. Planning to give the rutting cub a good setdown, he strode forward, but his features didn't darken until he heard the frenzied voice and recognized it.

Geoffrey felt the piercing jab of a pitchfork between his shoulder blades and quickly obeyed the voice that sounded much deadlier.

"Get up from there before I run you through. Miss Lindy, are you all right?"

Rosalind pulled her clothing together and scrambled up the moment she was free of the pinning weight. She ducked behind her rescuer and clung to his beefy arm. When Geoffrey turned, the tines of the fork pricked his throat uncomfortably and didn't lower even after he was identified. The brawny man who sheltered his wife was dressed in rough-hewn work clothes; however, his manner was more fatherly than servile toward the woman he protected.

Behind the safety of Pettigrew's stocky figure, Rosalind pulled together her scattered wits and glared at Geoffrey. Her look was so coldly venomous, he wondered if she meant to see him punished as if he'd no right to the liberties he had hoped to take. Then she turned to the severe-eyed man and laid a fond hand on his arm.

"Put that down, Pettigrew. I'm in no danger. I but tripped and Chilton was helping me up." The calm of her voice forbid any contradiction.

"If you say so, ma'am." The fork lowered reluctantly, but the head groom's posture didn't relax. He hadn't imagined his lady's distress or its cause and he made sure the new lord knew it as well. His words were correct but there was no humility in his tone. "I do beg your pardon, my lord. I mistook the situation."

"No harm done," Geoffrey said graciously. His stare recognized the warning. Then the smoky eyes turned to Rosalind, intimating that he'd made no mistake with her, either. She met his slow, wide smile with a combative glower. The lines had been drawn and he had already crossed them once most successfully. His confident grin said it was only a matter of time before he took the step again. Her fierce glare replied he wouldn't find the journey so easy if he dared a second attempt.

For all her bravado, Rosalind was sick at heart. If Pettigrew hadn't interrupted, she feared her battle would have been lost on a stable floor. Was she a match for the beguiling Lord Chilton or was she deceiving herself this time?

116

Chapter Twelve

The tension in the manor house was thrown off late that afternoon by an impressive parade of London coaches. The first arrivals bore numerous lesser servants, the steward from Charles Street and footmen, followed closely by a fourgon with a mountain of luggage and essential belongings, a bevy of housemaids and kitchen porters. The ensuing hubbub prepared the way for an elegant private chaise bearing Lord and Lady Dunstan.

Rosalind greeted her stepmother with a fond hug, marveling that she could make such a trip without looking rumpled or fatigued. Her father, she met with considerably less warmth, freezing inwardly when he pressed a kiss upon her cheek and cast a speculative glance at her belly. Geoffrey offset her chilliness by welcoming the older man with a familiar camaraderie that served only to deepen her distrust of them both. The ready ease with which Geoffrey assumed the position of host angered and annoyed her. It was all she could do not to shake off the possessive hand he let fall upon her shoulder.

"Chilton, I hope you haven't found the country life too flat," Camilla sympathized. "Lindy dotes on the silence and space. Personally, I would go mad without some distraction." She rose to press a soft, scented cheek to his. Her gloved fingertips grazed the firm contour of his jaw in a would-be innocent caress that was most distracting, indeed. Geoffrey's smile was carefully bland when the bright blue eyes assessed him in a quick glance that could have meant many things.

To defuse the danger of the situation, Geoffrey's eyes slanted heavily to adore his new bride as he said, "Quite honestly, I haven't had the chance to become bored." He felt Rosalind stiffen at the hearty laugh that bold claim won from her father. Knowing she was helpless to vent her wrath, he let a tease of amusement play about his mouth. Her smile was docile. Her gaze severed his head from his shoulders.

The presence of others in the house drastically changed the

117

stalemate between the newlyweds. Rosalind was forced to endure Geoffrey's company with agonizing frequency. He had charmed his way with the staff and was privy to her daily plans, always managing to arrive and ruin any enjoyment she might have found. Riding was her only sanctuary, that and her bedroom and she kept to both as much as possible. Since his untimely intrusion, Pettigrew made it a practice to be on hand whenever she was in the stables and his stoic bulk kept Geoffrey at an arm's length. He never seemed put off by her cold snubs. He strolled along beside her as if a wanted companion, carrying on a one-sided conversation with unfailing high spirits. He joked and cajoled in attempts to provoke a smile, yet her stony resistance didn't discourage him. She tolerated him only because he never tried to persuade her with more than words when they were alone. He saved that special torture for the presence of others.

Dinner was a goading trial to her resolve. Seated at Geoffrey's left, Rosalind couldn't avoid the casual touches and warm gazes that punctuated his speech. She knew each glance, each small caress was based on a lie and wanted to shrink beneath them. Too proud to display her shame, she kept her misery to herself and wished she was free to slap the confident, smiling face.

Geoffrey was excellent at table talk. Between him and Camilla, meals were a lively discourse on varying subjects from fashion to politics. It was difficult not to admire him for his diverse opinions and the competent way he offered them. He used intelligence, logic, and a potent dose of charm to gain sway in his favor rather than loud, rude, or bullying tactics. Where Dunstan herded lambs to the slaughter, Geoffrey lured them with sweet entreaties. Rosalind felt very much the victim of both ploys.

At dinner's end, the men retired for drinks and cigars while they talked of business. Geoffrey was a compelling confidant and Dunstan found a good foil for his plans and hopes. The fresh, energetic younger man instilled new vitality in his empire just as he hoped he would in his daughter.

After an evening of particularly good dialog and port, Geoffrey found himself lingering in the sitting room. Senses pleasantly dulled by the strong, dark wine, he eyed the closed door and speculated on the joys within. Rosalind had looked fetching over dinner. The ruby taffeta gown was a favorite of his for its dramatic display of tempting cleavage. As he considered the door, his desires stirred an insistent need to plunge more than his heated gaze into that shadowed valley. The longer he thought on the subject, the harder it was to remain level-headed. Alcohol usually made him sleepy or silly, but on this night it fueled him with a foolish confidence in his own irresistible charm. Certain Rosalind would crumple beneath it, he took the bold step into her room.

Rosalind was under her covers, banked by lace-edged pillows. She lowered the novel she was reading to stare at him. Her dismay tempered to a wry annoyance when he crossed the room in a swaggering reel to clutch the bedpost for support. Lost in the bedcurtains for a brief moment, he managed to battle the devilish things and assume a carefree pose.

"Good evening, madam wife."

"My lord."

"I wanted to compliment you on your attire at dinner. Your breasts—er, your dress was most becoming." His smile was more leering than alluring as his gaze traveled over her. The contours that shaped her bedcovers tantalized his already well-encouraged imagination.

"Thank you, my lord," she said coolly. "Was there something else?"

"I thought you might like some company."

"You thought wrong, sir."

Emboldened by the wine and enticed by the hills and planes of the comforter, Geoffrey embarked on a perilous journey toward her. Odd, how he kept losing his way when he thought he was so close. "Curled up with Byron for the night?" His voice lowered to a suggestive caress. "Wouldn't you rather curl up with me?"

Before she could find a suitable retort, he dove for the bed, taking a hard bounce facefirst into her pillows. Rosalind rolled toward freedom only to have it hampered by the hem of her nightdress which was pinned beneath him. She tugged at it insistently. Discovering what trapped her, Geoffrey grinned triumphantly and used the traitorous fabric to draw her slowly toward him, exposing a great deal of nicely shaped leg in the process.

Indignantly, Rosalind tried to pull loose. "Let me go," she warned fiercely. "Get out of my room this instant." She slapped at the hand that reached for her bared knee.

"Or what, dear wife? I rather fancy cozying up to you tonight. Are you going to toss me out bodily?" His devilish

119

eyes dared her to try.

"I'll scream."

Her threat made him chuckle. "Scream away. You'll only embarrass yourself. After all, I am your dutiful husband and most eager to become so."

Rosalind's piercing shriek won her release. Geoffrey scrambled back, staring at her through wide, astonished eyes while she calmly smoothed her nightclothes.

The scream brought attention from all quarters, filling the door to her room with servants as well as her parents. She greeted their questioning looks with a sheepish smile.

"Oh, do forgive me for disturbing you. There was this mouse, you see, and it quite surprised me. His lordship frightened it away."

Dunstan looked at the odd spectacle of his son-in-law crouched atop the bedcovers and then back at his composed daughter. He could never recall her being timid around mice before. He arched a suspect brow and harrumphed. None of his affair, anyway.

"Most likely you scared it to death," he grumbled.

"Please go back to bed, all of you," Rosalind urged, then to Geoffrey, said sweetly, "Thank you, my lord. You needn't concern yourself further. I'm sure I shan't be troubled by any more unwelcomed creatures tonight."

While the crowd in the hall dispersed, she faced Geoffrey with a smug, satisfied smile. He conceded to her clearer thinking with a begrudging bow and retreated to his solitary quarters. As he shut the door, she heard his low, appreciative chuckle.

Smiling, she slipped beneath her covers and picked up her book.

Geoffrey was conspicuously absent from her heels the following day and subdued at the supper table. The change brought Rosalind's eyes to him in curious speculation. Was he feeling embarrassed by his behavior or merely pouting because it had gained him nothing? She was surprised to find she wasn't angry at him. The incident had been more amusing than threatening. Yet there was the matter of the privacy of her room being breached. In doing so once, would he feel freer in his next trespass?

She was considering that as she reposed on the sitting-room chaise paying indifferent attention to a book of poetry. She felt secure in the neutral territory between their bedrooms knowing her father would monopolize Geoffrey for at least several hours. It was with unfeigned surprise that she caught sight of him in the adjoining door. He offered an inoffensive smile. When she quickly straightened and snapped her book closed, making ready to leave, he put out a staying hand.

"Don't go, Roz. I am harmless this evening. Could we declare a truce and talk for a bit?" His hopeful gaze began a reluctant softening of her frosty attitude.

"I don't believe I have anything to say to you, Chilton." Her cool words lacked their usual bite. Could it be she was too lonely to reject the company?

"Would you listen then? I want to apologize for last night. I was a bit in my cups and fear I acted with poor judgment. I ask you to forgive me . . . for that, at least."

His pretty speech won a gracious nod. Rosalind was lulled by the lack of his usual brashness and aggressive charm. She didn't realize this quiet approach was deceivingly smooth and as potent as heady spirits even when sipped slowly.

"May I sit with you for a time? These long country days make me a bit restless."

"You may return to London any time you wish, my lord. Don't feel you must remain to attend me. I would not miss you."

"No?" He pursed his lips doubtfully. "Perhaps not, but I should miss you. I don't dislike it here. It just takes some adjustment. It's been a long time since I've been out of the city. Just dining in the light of day is hard to contend with."

"You sound like Camilla. She hates the shift to country hours. You and she are quite the kindred spirits."

Geoffrey found no pleasure in the comparison but didn't allow it to manifest in his expression. He came to sit on the edge of the chaise, keeping a careful distance from the wary figure of his wife.

"Shall I read some verse to you? I recall you enjoyed that well enough."

"Yes, Everard was a pleasing orator." Her purposeful jibe seemed to miss its mark, for he lifted the book unflinchingly.

"I shall try to do justice to your memory of him."

Geoffrey leafed through the pages for several moments before settling on a passage, then began to read. He had the perfect voice for recitation: low, fluid and filled with passionate nuances. Without meaning to, she dropped her chilly guard as the rhythmic flow of the words twined warm and melliferous about her unprotected senses. Each phrase was rendered like a physical caress and, without moving, Geoffrey soon had her shifting uncomfortably from the subtle longing he stirred with each lingering inflection.

Closing her eyes, Rosalind transformed the vocal seduction into heated recollections of his touch. The crooning intonation was like his teasing, provocative kiss, his elocution of each line like the purposeful stroke of his hands. By the time he finished the reading, she was flushed by the possessing spell woven by words and dreams.

"I'd better go."

The soft claim brought her eyes open with quick protest and her hand was on his arm before she thought to still it. His searching glance was full of hesitant expectation.

"Geoffrey," she began tightly, emotions trembling too fiercely to give her ease.

Before she could go on, a rapid tapping on the door broke the trance between them. Rosalind rose instinctively to answer, all too aware of the bemused gaze that followed.

Faye related the message she was given while her stare touched shyly on the handsome Lord Chilton. "Mr. Pettigrew says Bridgett's about to drop and that you should come direct."

Without question, Rosalind darted into her room to fetch a wrap, shouting over her shoulder for Geoffrey to find her a lamp. With one in hand, he greeted her with a question.

"Who's this Bridgett?"

"One of our best mares. She's foaling. It's Pericles's first. We almost lost her the first time," she explained briefly as he helped her into her pelisse. "I cannot let that happen with this one."

"The expectant father is missing all the excitement." He had fallen in step beside her and was pleased when she didn't think to object.

The stable was well lit by a ring of lanterns about a large box stall. Pettigrew handed her an oversized shirt in lieu of a greeting. After donning it over her clothing, Rosalind stepped into the stall with a knowledgeable air. She felt the drooping belly, then held aside its tail to reach within to check the position of the foal. Geoffrey lagged back, frankly shocked and uncertain of his decision to come along.

"Feel's right, Lowell. Let's get her down." Once the horse was lying on the bed of straw, Rosalind said without looking around, "Chilton, sit at her head and keep her down and quiet." When he made no move, she glanced back to where he hesitated in an apprehensive sweat.

"Just how do I do that?" he asked uneasily.

"Talk to her."

"To a horse?"

"Pretend she's some fair little miss. You're no stranger to sweet-talking the ladies." With that, she dismissed him from mind and turned to Pettigrew to exchange words.

Geoffrey crossed the stall reluctantly and bent down before the prone animal. A toss of the glossy head rocked him back on his heels. He cast a rather desperate look toward Rosalind, but she seemed to have forgotten him. With a heavy sigh of resignation, he put a hand out to touch the broad forehead. The mare gave a low sound that resembled a groan.

"Don't complain to me, madam. You should have known what to expect when you pranced about the fields swishing your tail in front of some clovered up stallion."

Hearing his statement, Rosalind glanced his way with an amused twitch of her lips but had no time to comment.

The foal was long in coming and required the efforts of them all to finally gain entrance into the world. As the laboring mare grew more restless, Geoffrey crouched close speaking in low, soothing tones while stroking the tossing head. He had stripped off his coat, using it to rub along the damp, lathered neck as he murmured the assurances. He turned in time to see the introduction of a slimy, impossibly spindly little creature that Pettigrew proudly announced was a fine colt. He laid the knobby foal on the straw beside Geoffrey and instructed him curtly to clean it off.

First using his coat, then the towel he was given, Geoffrey wiped the leggy baby down then watched in amazement as it struggled up on wobbly legs within the cautious circle of his arms. They had the mare up by that time and Rosalind guided the foal to its first eager meal. She turned to her elegant lordship and looked long and well as he knelt in the straw clutching the filthy coat, his face lit with a radiant grin. His shiny gaze lifted and their eyes held for a moment. Shyly, Rosalind let hers drop away as she touched the gangly colt.

"A beauty, isn't he? A life we helped bring into the world."

"What an incredible joy that must be," Geoffrey reflected in a quiet mood. Then his hand fell next to hers on the bony flank. "He'll do his papa proud, this one will." He stood and brushed the straw from his trousers then went to pat the mare's sleek neck. "Well done, madam," he said softly into the pricked ears.

"We're all done here, Miss Lindy. You best turn in. It's mighty late," Pettigrew advised, taking her smock.

Smiling, Rosalind gave him a rewarding hug. "Good night, Lowell."

They walked back to the house together, Geoffrey holding the lamp high to mark the way. He was shivering. His thin shirt was no match for the cool evening.

"You've forgotten your coat."

Geoffrey's laugh was low and delightfully warm. "Henri would never send it to be laundered. He'd insist it be buried. I'm saving his feelings."

"You were very good with Bridgett."

"Just another female to woo," he said fliply.

"It's more than that," Rosalind ventured. "You have a gentle touch, Geoffrey. She felt safe with you."

"I wish *you* did, Roz." He said it simply, without pausing or looking at her. Her hand on his arm stilled him. In the darkness, his eyes were bottomless and black, beckoning like deep, still waters, yet still dangerous. They were eyes one could drown in.

"Thank you for coming with me tonight," she said.

"And you for wanting to share it with me."

Quite impulsively, Rosalind reached up to firmly cushion her lips upon his. Geoffrey stood very still. His eyes remained closed for a long heartbeat and when they opened, Rosalind ran ahead, leaving him alone and shaken in his solitary pool of light.

Camilla paused before her mirror to check her appearance, then answered the timid knock. Looking flawless, even freshly waked, she opened her door to emit her not so well-groomed stepdaughter. Rosalind was mussed, fatigued, and visibly upset.

"What is it, Lindy?"

"I'm sorry for the hour, but I must talk with someone. If I don't, I fear I'll go quite mad."

"Gracious! Do come in." She took the other's hand and led her to the frilly bed where they both sat on its edge.

Rosalind wrung her hands in awkward misery, unable to frame the words around the picture of her anguish.

"It's Chilton, isn't it?"

The gentle question brought a shimmering wetness to the

124

forlorn eyes. "I don't know what I shall do. Oh, Cammy, it's so awful."

"Tell me."

Briefly, painfully, Rosalind told her all then concluded with a sob, "I loved him. I still want to love him and I cannot help but want him. What am I to do?"

"Are you certain he hasn't told you the truth?"

She nodded. "I heard them. He doesn't love me, Cammy. He married me for the money, that cursed money. I wish I didn't have it. Then I should know what he cared for most."

"If you mean that, there is a way," Camilla began, but then shook her head. The inky curls bobbed girlishly from beneath her sleep cap. "But no, it would be quite difficult."

Now it was Rosalind's turn to urge, "Tell me."

"If the money is all he wants, he'd not stay if you no longer had it. If he cares for you, it won't matter to him and he'd stay."

"But how will I know?"

"If no child is born in the first year, the inheritance won't be entrusted to him. All you have to do is remain chaste for another few months and you will have your answer. If you haven't conceived by then, he'll realize there's no future if it's your fortune he's after. Then you'll know for sure."

"Yes, I would," she echoed thoughtfully.

"But, dear Lindy, are you sure you don't want the money?"

Rosalind's tone was shaking with conviction. "I want a husband who loves me. That's all that matters. I've never cared to be an heiress. I would be quite comfortable on what Papa allows me, but will Geoffrey? In finding the truth, I could lose him."

"Do you want to keep him and never know?"

That question would torment her for a long while on the quiet night as she tried to calm her prowling thoughts. She did love Geoffrey. That was the hardest truth to admit. She enjoyed his company, her status as his wife, the knowledge that he was near, and the pleasure of seeing him daily. However, those simple joys didn't overshadow the doubts. His deception had hurt. It had been a near fatal pain at the time and now, a persistent ache. The fact that he'd married her for her money wasn't the worst of it. She respected honesty. Had he simply been forthright, in all likelihood she still would have agreed to his proposal. She didn't demand a vow of poverty from the man she married. Yet, he had lied and in finding the truth, her pride had taken a crippling blow.

She had had time to prevent the marriage yet had chosen not to. It had nothing to do with honor or saving face, it had to do with love. Even knowing, she couldn't bear to let him go. Geoffrey Chilton was the man she wanted to wed. His reason for taking her to the altar hadn't been as important as being there with him. Now, she suffered for that weakness. Now, what would she do? She had tried hating him, tried despising him for his shallow greed, yet there were times, like that one in the barn when he looked up at her from his knees that her love burned so strong she feared she would perish in the blaze. It had been a struggle to keep from surrendering all to him in that moment. In the end, she had fled from those desires, unable to face them boldly or submit to them freely.

If only she could believe he cared. If only he loved her.

Chapter Thirteen

Rosalind was surprised to find Geoffrey lingering outside the box stall, leaning upon forearms while he watched the tiny colt with its mother. The broad, dazzling smile he met her with threw her into a moment of palpitations, however, her calm returned a bit unsteadily after his smoky stare left her.

"What are you going to call him?"

Rosalind joined him at the gate and smiled at the sight of the knobby black foal. "I don't know. I haven't given it much thought."

"The poor fellow must have a name. Tamburlaine." At Rosalind's quizzical look, he explained. "From Marlowe's play. He's my favorite."

Her smile was wry. Of course, he would liken himself to that tragic hero whose passion for the power of rule, money, and knowledge wrought his own end. He, too, knew that striving ambition to push upward regardless of consequence.

"Yes, that will suit."

"You'll have to be more decisive when our children arrive. Never underestimate the importance of a name. It can shape an entire future."

Geoffrey's pensive mood was lost on Rosalind. She seized on the smug connotations of his words with a savage pounce. It made all her own frustrations come to a sudden head and she lashed out at him as if to make her point once and for all.

"You say 'our,' my lord, and I say you are mistaken. There will be no 'our' children because there is no 'us' to make them."

She strode down the corridor in quick, angry strides but was easily overtaken. Geoffrey caught her upper arms, holding her captive to listen to his impassioned argument.

"But there is, Roz. I want to be a husband to you. Can't we start over? Can't we forget all the doubts and mistrust?"

In freezing accents, she said, "How easy that would be for you. And how profitable. But you forget one thing. You were not purchased to be my husband. You were bought for one purpose only. Your services are no longer required, my lord. Take your unearned fee and return to London. My days as a brood mare are over. You will not be cropping clover in my

127

pastures. Go away. There is no reason for you to be here."

She jerked free and ran blindly to the house. She didn't want him to see her tears and be encouraged by that weakness. And she was weak, weak and helpless to stop the fierce conflict within her. She'd been unprepared for his attack on her emotions and her defense had been instinctive. Perhaps she did want him to go. She knew she couldn't think clearly in his presence. He always managed to juxtapose heart and mind and the balance was growing precarious. She couldn't yield to her confusion, fearing she would be lost with the slightest concession. She feared there would be no conditions in a surrender to Geoffrey Chilton.

Once she reached her room, Rosalind considered herself safe. She gave a startled gasp as the door was thrown open behind her then quickly closed. They regarded each other unblinkingly for a long moment.

"Get out."

Geoffrey countered the commanding phrase with a shake of his head. "No. I've had enough, Rosalind. If I cannot court you in a civil fashion, I will use whatever means you force me to. I am your husband, like it or not. No matter how it came about, it is still a fact." She began to back away apprehensively. He followed her retreat, matching her step for step.

"You said the words in St. George's. Neither your father nor I made you say them. You are my wife and I demand the privilege of knowing you as such." He relentlessly pushed aside the table she thought to place between them.

"You demand?" Rosalind challenged. "What effrontery! You'll make no demands upon me. I gave you no such right."

"Then I shall take it. And you."

With a quickness that gave her no chance to evade him, he snatched her up and deposited her roughly on the bed. Stunned, she didn't struggle when he came down upon her.

"No more patience. No more games. No more fencing. The moment is at hand, madam, so accept it as fact and stop pretending it is not what you want as well."

Panic flushed her with sudden vigor. Her palms rose to fend him off and her head rolled wildly from side to side to escape his kisses.

"No, my lord," she cried out in desperation. "You cannot. You must not. 'Tis morning. 'Tis daylight. Give me until nightfall to ready myself. Please, my lord. Geoffrey."

Her body gave an odd shudder beneath him and he realized

128

she was weeping. He would have taken her fighting and cursing regardless of her reasoning but the beseeching sobs curtailed his lusts with abrupt efficiency. He stood away. She remained prone on the bed, her breath coming in hurried gasps, her eyes huge and black. The sight of her defenseless fright made him weak with shame, yet there was no sign of change of heart in his gruff proclamation.

"Until tonight then, madam. After that, I shall show you no further mercy. If you barricade your door, I shall break it down. If I have to search for you, I'll lay you down where I find you. Tonight, Rosalind. Depend on it. No excuses and no delays."

He turned an indifferent back to her pale, tear-stained face and stormed downstairs. By the time he entered the study, the insanity of the moment was gone, leaving him feeling small and uncertain. He hadn't meant to let temper and desire goad him to such extremes yet there was no going back. He'd made his ultimatum, wise or not, and now he had to brazen it out. Bullying tactics sat unwell with him, he who preferred silky persuasion to shows of force. He'd never imagined Rosalind would resist him, but resist she had and their battle had become most frustrating. Her crackling wit and quick cunning had kept him at an arm's length. Arm's length was where he no longer was content to be.

"You look like you could use a drink, Chilton."

Geoffrey was startled to discover Camilla had entered the room. Being alone with his attractive mother-in-law was something he'd been careful to avoid. His instincts warned him to be wary and not without cause.

Camilla poured a generous glass of port and handed it to him. In the exchange, their hands met. To Geoffrey, the contact seemed overlong and he searched for a way to escape what he feared was developing. The last thing he wished for was an entanglement with Dunstan's wife. Then, when she began to speak, he wished it was something so simple and sordid she had in mind.

"Rosalind has confided that you have no marriage between you. Is there something you'd like to talk about?" She waved a dainty hand toward an intimate settee.

"Not with you, madam. Thank you."

His elegant rebuff earned a soft chuckle. "We are alike, Chilton, you and I. We know what we want and we go after it. Perhaps together, we can both be satisfied." Her eyes lowered invitingly and hinted at promising rewards.

"We aren't at all alike, Lady Dunstan, and I am quite satisfied where I am." He set down the untouched glass. Annoyance played about his mouth.

"Really?" she purred. "Dunstan will see she gets the annulment she seeks when he finds he'll have no heir." She smiled at his sudden attentiveness. "Then what will you have to show for your troubles? You see, I know the money is what you're after. I've known it since first seeing you. You're drawn to wealth, just as I am."

"I think this conversation is over."

"Chilton, one of us doesn't have to lose."

He halted and looked at her. Her blue eyes were hard and shiny, eyes like his own.

"I will pay you £50,000 if you leave here today. I have the money. All you have to do is take it and say nothing." She waited with a smug smile for him to snap at her offer. His nonchalance was provoking.

"And I thought your husband was the businessman. I like living here, Lady Dunstan. I've no plans to leave."

Camilla closed the distance between them and placed a hand on his chest. Her fingers began a tempting massage. "Then stay, but stay for the right reasons. Rosalind may be fool enough not to want you, but I, sir, am no fool. Give your child to me instead of her and we'll share the good fortune. You can't possibly prefer that silly goose to me. It is too absurd. Ours can be a most fruitful relationship."

The beautiful countess stretched up to place an experienced kiss on his lips. The tip of her tongue slithered across his unresponsive mouth. When she stepped back, she found his eyes still open and unmoved. Undaunted, she touched a fingertip to his damp mouth.

"Think on it, Chilton. You're a clever man. We shall make a fine pairing."

Henri listened with interest to the retelling of Camilla's offer by his less than enthused brother. He mused, not unkindly, "Who would have thought such a pretty shape could house such an unattractive heart." He smiled to himself, admiring the lady for her willingness to see to her own fate. But theirs was the fate he had to consider. "And are you thinking on it?"

"Of bedding my mother-in-law? Certainly not."

"Moral outrage? Really, Geoff. The fact that she's married could hardly hinder you after all the lusty ladies you've played for the necklace."

"I never did."

Henri's brow arched. "Never what?"

Geoffrey looked uncomfortable and muttered, "Slept with any of them." He turned away from Henri's incredulous stare.

"*Mon Dieu,* Geoff. I cannot believe what I am hearing. Not one? I cannot believe this. Why not? You speak of some of the most desirable women in all France!"

Geoffrey crossed to the window. His posture was squared with tension and his voice harsh. "Because they were married, Hank. I want no part of that. Laugh if you like, but you should know why I feel that way." The light pressure of Henri's hand on his shoulder loosened its rigid line.

"I am not laughing, *mon ami,* and I do understand. Only if you did not make love to them, how did you get the rubies back?"

Geoffrey gave a small smile. "I talked them out of it."

He did laugh then and supplied a fond embrace. "Only you could do such a thing." The speculative gleam returned to his eyes. "So what of the other offer? Do we take the money? It is a generous amount. Most generous. The ties would be severed quickly and neatly."

Geoffrey sighed and pressed his fingertips to the window. The cool of the glass formed a mist about the warm pads. It was like the haze he felt cloud his thoughts. To take the money would make him everything she believed him to be and worse. And he would never see her again. Ever.

"There may be hope for our original plan," he said quietly.

"You still want it all, don't you?"

"Yes. All."

The even softer reply made the Frenchman frown suspiciously. "Remember, it is only a game, Geoff. A game. When it is done, we are gone from here. Agreed?"

"Yes," he murmured distractedly. "Of course."

Rosalind's absence from the dinner table was a shattering blow to Geoffrey's confidence. Had he frightened her that badly or was she even now preparing to do battle? Either way, the heart had gone from his crusade upon her chastity. He wished he could call back his bold speech and return things to the slow, unhurried path they'd been taking. But there was no time. Now he was trapped into going where he no longer wanted to push his way. He had only to glance across the table to the avid blue eyes to read his other options. They were unappealing. His stalemate with Rosalind had to end. Either she accepted him or she didn't. If she didn't, his days at Dunstan Manor were over. Henri would have been alarmed if he knew the money had no part in his turmoiled thoughts.

After the meal, he lingered over cigars with Dunstan, wondering if the man knew he was planning the rape of his daughter. Sourly, he guessed he would have approved of it. As the sky grew dark, his mood followed apace until he finally forced himself to mount the stairs. He felt as solemn as an executioner climbing the gallows. Was Rosalind to be his sacrificial virgin?

At the last minute, his courage failed and he ducked into his own room. For long minutes, he considered cowardly crawling into his own bed and forgetting the whole arrangement. Perhaps she would be better disposed toward him in the morning. Realizing he couldn't leave her to fret the night away in anticipation of his *droit du seigneur*, he stepped into the sitting room.

Geoffrey was surprised to find her there. A large blaze had been kindled to cast out the evening chill and Rosalind stood near it for the comfort of its heat. Hearing him, she turned, reluctance in every inch of the slow revolution. He had misjudged her mood. She was neither fearful nor combative. The large eyes that lifted to his were oddly quiet.

"Good evening, my lady," he began tentatively. "I missed you at dinner."

"I had little appetite, my lord." Her voice was cool and even.

Probably she'd lost it dreading his brutish appearance, he thought miserably. While he considered how to phrase his apology, his gaze wandered over the length of her. She wore a pale, diaphanous nightdress. Its thin cords crisscrossed and tied beneath her breasts, defining each full, perfect globe. The clinging drape hinted maddeningly at the long line of her legs and rounded hips. Light from the fire created interesting shadows through the fine gossamer and he forgot his intention to make a noble retreat.

Rosalind watched his approach through lowered lashes. Her every muscle was bunched and ready to take flight. He seemed remarkably quiet for all his earlier blustering and as cautious as she herself was. That air of uncertainty allowed her to relax just a fraction. She had forged every bit of her nerve into a tight knot of resolve, vowing to see the inevitability of the night through. Haunting whispers of Camilla's words on intimacy made all unravel the moment he touched her. Tears swam helplessly in her eyes. She hated that sign of her frailty yet couldn't control it. Any more than she could control the ache of longing for the man she was forced to submit to.

Seeing her fitful shivering, Geoffrey frowned, angry with himself for giving her reason to quake. "I've made you afraid of me," he stated softly.

"Pay no heed to my fears, my lord. I am here as you bid me. I am determined to see this through so do as you will."

Her small, tart words quirked a faint smile upon his lips, but it faded away when she winced beneath the brush of his fingers upon her cool cheek.

"Not like this."

His husky words brought up the dark, glistening eyes. She looked so lovely, so vulnerable. Her bewildered gaze searched his rapidly.

"Rosalind, forgive me for demanding what is only yours to give."

His hand dropped heavily to his side. With a regretful sigh, he turned from the promise of her martyred offer and was about to retire when her anxious cry caught him.

"Don't you want me, Geoffrey?"

The question shot through him with a hard jolt of desire but not so much as the kiss she met him with when he turned back. Her lips were chilled but willing in their urgent press, heating as his response did. His arms came up slowly to encircle her yielding form, the movement hesitant, as if disbelieving. His hands spread wide over the smooth fan of her shoulders then brought her up close to the startled thunder of his heart. When the kiss had run its course, he released her and waited to know her intention.

Rosalind was breathless with the power his nearness commanded and with the demands of her own desire. She spoke clearly and from the heart. "Tonight, my lord. I am ready and no longer pretending. Take what I have to give."

His large hands flew up to cup her face, cradling it while his lips knew the sweetness of possessing hers. The unexpected gift of her compliance overwhelmed him and he vowed to accept it with a tender humility as it was meant to be received.

Their hands intertwined and each started away toward their own room, expecting the other to follow. Both exchanged looks of impatience over this first dissension, then Geoffrey chuckled to break the impasse.

"We've come too far to be at sixes and sevens over such a silly thing. Why not here on neutral ground?"

His suggestion was met with a brief nod. Now that the certainty of her choice was inescapable, Rosalind felt all aquiver with nervous flutters of doubt and dread. She didn't regret the decision, just the unknowns of it. She bit her lip and lowered her cowardly stare.

"Roz?" He lifted her chin in his palm. The dark liquid eyes woke an anxious pang of protectiveness.

"Are you going to hurt me, Geoffrey?"

Eager to still the fear that whispered in that quiet question, he was quick to reassure her. "No, Roz. I won't hurt you." The warming trust in her gaze brought a deeper timbre to his voice as he admitted, "I don't know. I'll do what I can to make it easy for you. Trust me to take care of you."

"I do, my lord." She said it and meant it, surrendering herself into his care without further fears. Where before there had been anxiety, an urgent anticipation began to rise. She refused to think further than this night. Tonight, she and Geoffrey would be man and wife and she would give herself without reservation because she loved him. Tonight, all her dreams would be fulfilled and tomorrow she would be free of them and all their forbidden temptation.

"You're cold," he noted, chafing her hands. "Let's sit by the fire." He led her easily to the Aubusson carpet before the hearth and encouraged her down upon its luxurious design. The fire was warm and welcoming, as was his kiss and the languorous combination overcame the last of her hesitation. She went down to the floor with him, sighing beneath the determined seduction of his mouth as it traveled from the pliant reception of her own to the arched curve of her throat. Her timid hands rose to his chest and were frustrated by the bulk of clothing that kept her from seeking the more personal heat of his body.

As if he understood her complaint, Geoffrey sat up to bare himself to the waist. His torso gleamed in the firelight, golden and intriguingly defined. When he rested beside her on one elbow, Rosalind emboldened her hand to touch him. Her fingers slid in wondering awe along the firm contour of rib and muscle then came to rest.

"How fast your heart is beating," she marveled. The quick, powerful pulse excited her own.

"That is your doing. Perhaps it would be unwise of me to ask more of it."

Contrarily, he began to untie her gown. The leisurely movements instilled that curious drawing and fullness in her breasts that intensified with his kneading caress. His other hand loosened and spread her hair in a glossy fan. The dark waves gleamed in burnished ripples like lengths of fine silk. He lowered his face into those fragrant tresses.

With a sudden wantonness, Rosalind gave his head a downward push. Obligingly, he let his kisses become lost in the generous bounty, constrained by its web of wispy fabric. Freed from its attention there, his hand slid lower, gliding down the path of taunting nightdress to its very end.

The contact of his hot palm on the cool satin of her leg made her shiver in exhilaration. A complex yearning for something she had yet to experience began to flow with heavy, honied luxury beneath his slow exploration. Her startled gasp of discovery was stilled by the return of his sensual mouth to her own trembling lips. The enticing stroke of his tongue mimicked his inquisitive touch until her ripening passions brought forth a low moaning cry. Without direction, her hands moved in restless circles along his shoulders, blindly seeking a way to stabilize the sudden delirious careening of her world. Sensations sizzled and swirled with a frightening intensity, like a fevered madness or dizzying dream and it was cling to him or be lost in those consuming spirals of uncharted delight.

He brought her back slowly, safely, his kiss gentling and his hand escaping the dampening heat of her nightgown to rest lightly on the curve of her waist. He could feel her breath shiver frantically beneath it, matching the rhythm of his own labored efforts. She met his smile shyly, then looked away, a sudden consternation showing in her eyes.

"Roz, what is it?" he asked, fearing she had changed her mind. That worry brought a frown to his features. Her reply was far from what he expected when her gaze returned, steeped in anguish and uncertainty.

"Oh, Geoffrey, is there something wrong with me? Am I terribly wicked?"

His brow furrowed. "What makes you ask such a thing?"

Her blush provoked an odd tremor in him. She said awkwardly, "I was told I shouldn't enjoy what we are doing and that decent women don't welcome it."

"And what have you discovered?" he prompted gently. His dusky eyes were warmed by a tender humor as he guessed what she would say.

"I am enjoying it very much." Her color deepened, however, she met his questioning gaze with a simple candor.

"Good. I would hate to think it otherwise." His fingertips grazed the line of her jaw and brushed across her passion-pouted lips. "And who filled your head with this nonsense?"

"Camilla," she admitted in a small voice.

Geoffrey's humor hardened with a wry twist. "How very helpful of her. And not surprising."

"Was she wrong about it all then?" Her innocent hopefulness touched him.

"Why don't you forget whatever she told you and discover for yourself. If you've enjoyed the journey so far, the rest shouldn't disappoint you."

Her tone was husky. "Show me the rest of the way, Geoffrey," she insisted, then sighed into his beckoning kiss.

The nightdress had proved a nuisance for long enough. Geoffrey skimmed it off her and gave it a toss. The vaporous fabric drifted to the floor like a settling mist. At first, Rosalind tried to hide her nakedness from him, embarrassed and reluctant for him to see her unfettered form. His soothing caress discouraged the concealment and, leisurely, his gaze appraised the creamy figure basked only in the rosy glow of firelight.

"You've nothing to be ashamed of, precious one. I can find no fault. You are beautiful."

"Truly, my lord?" she challenged faintly.

"You must trust my judgment, for I am not going to allow for another opinion."

His starchy words won a smile and a blossoming of confidence. "I will believe you then."

He busied himself with the rest of his clothing, pausing when he heard her maidenly cry of, "Oh, my!" Her widened eyes rose to fix on the center of his chest, seeing it vibrate with a low chuckle.

"That is the most flattering thing anyone has ever said to me," he claimed with a teasing conceit then lifted her head.

"You were going to trust me, remember?"

She swallowed hard and gave an ill-convinced nod.

Those misgivings were forgotten when his mouth sought hers once more. The consuming heat of his bare skin was beyond the scope of pleasures she'd experienced. It gave a new dimension to their intimacy, one that was bonding and personal. Rosalind doubted if she could ever think of warmth and comfort again without remembering the sensuous feel of flesh on flesh. The exposure went beyond mere physical to the stripping away of privacy from her inner being. It was as if they were no longer separate and it seemed unnatural for the union not to be complete.

She greeted the shift of his weight with eager arms and a deepening acceptance of his kiss. Struggling to keep his promise, Geoffrey breached the barrier of her virginity by slow, intimate degrees until his possession became one of sharing rather than invasion. Her stiff posture of expected hurt eased and her hands tentatively explored the broad slope of his back and firm cording of his neck and arms. Her breathing quickened to match the uneven rush of his and with that timid encouragement, his restraint gave way in a torrent of long-unresolved passion.

Rosalind turned her head toward the fire, feeling his breath scorch just as hot upon the side of her neck. Her unfocused stare was lost in the brilliant blaze that reflected the color of his deep gold hair and the snapping, leaping darts of her own burgeoning pleasure. All was like those flames, fiery, flickering, devouring. When she closed her eyes, she could still see them dance upon her lids and feel them race with molten fervor to consume her body. Embers exploded in a sudden shower, making her cry out in wonder and surprise. Then the sparks extinguished one by one leaving only the baking warmth of contentment within and Geoffrey's heavy covering without. She let that sated peace drift and deepen, smiling softly as it settled into a sleep. She never felt Geoffrey's tender kiss or the careful embrace that bore her to the comfort of his bed where he cuddled her close in possessing satisfaction through the remaining hours of the night.

Chapter Fourteen

The languid relaxation of his body told Geoffrey it had been no dream. He indulged in a limbering stretch, then the pleasant lethargy deserted him. Rosalind was gone and the sheets beside him lay cool. Memories of the evening anything but, he rolled from the bed and slipped on his robe. The sitting room gave no hint that they'd shared such ecstasy before the fire that now lay in cold ashes in its grate.

Feeling uneasy in her absence, Geoffrey crossed to the door of her room. Perhaps she was just being shy or had wanted to dress rather than linger in bed with him. He could accept that but he feared those were not the reasons. He tapped lightly and called her name.

"Rosalind?"

The door opened a crack and Jessup peered out at him. Her tone was crisp and discouraging. "Her ladyship is indisposed this morning, my lord. She begs not to be disturbed."

"Indisposed?" he echoed pointedly. Ironic, the choice of words, yet quite intentional he was sure. Mouth taking a bitter twist, he said, "I see. I wouldn't want to do that."

"Very good, sir." The door closed conclusively.

So that was the way of it, he thought dejectedly. His shoulders slumped with the release of a weighty sigh. The evening had won him nothing save a sharper focus for his disappointment.

Henri was engrossed in his role of valet and looked up from the selection of clothing he was laying out. He observed Geoffrey's expression and his own grew more amused.

"Good morning, *mon frère*. Sleep well?"

Geoffrey had no answer. He dropped wearily on the edge of the bed and pretended to study his bare toes.

Henri's smirk deepened. "I was by earlier. Imagine my surprise and the lady's to discover you weren't alone."

The dark blue eyes flew up. "Did you speak to her?" Henri's attitude of indecent mirth made him want to shake him soundly.

"I wouldn't have been so rude as to compromise the lady's obvious distress by starting a conversation."

"Stop dancing about, Hank. I'm in no mood for it," he growled in warning.

Henri adopted an injured moue and dismissed the uncivil threat with a sniff. "Your wife looked positively strickened by your rather telling proximity. Really, Geoff, what did you do to the poor creature to inspire such faintheartedness?"

"I don't know, Hank. I truly don't. Things were so promising last night and this morning she won't even acknowledge me."

Henri regarded his unhappy features for a long moment. He could have been mourning the elusiveness of the fortune but he suspected not. "Geoff, do your affections run deep for this woman?" The silence was damning. Henri drew a sharp breath, finding danger in this unforeseen complication. He never would have thought it of Geoffrey. His charm was shallow and superficial by nature rather than design. His greed seemed the only thing to touch him deeply. It wasn't as if he had no true feelings. He just had no time to affix an attachment to anything or anyone and seemed to prefer it that way. His life was nomadic and necessarily uninvolved. Henri recalled several hurried passions but his brother's restless energy refused to let interest take root. As long as no feelings matured, he felt no loss when they moved on. That was how he survived his peripheral circling of commitment or ties. Henri indulged his good-natured irresponsibility and kept him safe from its consequences. His protective instincts had been too slow in this case.

"It's time to get out, *mon ami*. You've forgotten the rules of the game. Take what you can. We leave tonight. It's finished here. I didn't like the play anyway. Too dangerous."

Geoffrey's eyes were wide with panic and objection. "We can't abandon our plans now. We've too much invested."

"You've too much invested. That's why we have to go. You tell me honestly that you could fill that woman with your child then walk away from them both. That part is no game. You have to think about that."

"I don't want to think about it now," he complained pettishly. That was typical Geoffrey.

"You have to face it sometime. You've found you have a tender heart whether you like it or not and I cannot believe you could turn it to stone. It's a bond you won't be able to break. Or want to."

"You're wrong, Hank. I've never let anyone interfere in what I've wanted. This is no different."

"But it is. You've never been in one place with one person for a year. It is simple to walk away from strangers but these people are going to be like family to you."

"You're my only family, Henri," he argued fiercely, then paused to heave a frustrated sigh. "Perhaps you're right. I'll have to trust your judgment because mine is none too steady. We'll go then. But I don't want to take the £50,000."

Henri stared at him. He'd never seen his brother so adamant. Knowing he wouldn' t be swayed, he silently vowed to see to the money himself. Geoffrey would be glad of it later. He gave a placating nod. "We'll pick up the necklace and move on. Perhaps to Vienna. It's a bit somber there, but it's safe. You should take on another name."

Geoffrey wasn't listening and murmured, "Whatever you want, Hank." He stared through the sitting room to the closed door and tried to tell himself he wasn't losing anything.

Rosalind was admittedly guilty of cowardice when she blockaded herself in her room. She needed to think and there was no possibility of that with the virile viscount curled beside her. One flash of his engaging smile and reason fell away, a victim of love's folly. Everything about her ralationship with Geoffrey was ill-advised rashness. Rational thought seemed not to apply to him and she needed to be very rational and very thorough in her thinking.

The facts were not pleasant but look at them she would over all the nonsensical protests of her attraction to the man. True, he was handsome and charming, quick in wit and intelligence and he could make her feel confident in herself. Those were all good things, but there was so much more she wanted and feared she would never have from him, things like trust, fidelity, honesty, and, mostly, love. There was no fault in being beguiled by a whirlwind romance. She would never regret falling under the giddy spell of his magnetism. But men like Geoffrey Chilton were meant to be fleeting lovers, passionate, consuming and brief, not thoughtful, caring husbands. A moment of unrestrained passion, as last night had been, was exhilarating, yet when it was over and the desires cooled, the moment was gone. A moment could never be a lifetime. Trying to stretch it into one would only mean disappointment and eventually disillusionment.

She knew the chance of conceiving his child would greaten each time they were together, so she could afford no further weakenings. Camilla had been right. She didn't want to keep him and never know the truth.

Acting quickly before the enticement began its subtle lure once more, Rosalind closed the study doors behind her. Determinedly, she met her father's questioning gaze.

"What has you so severe this early in the day, Rosalind?" Dunstan leaned back in his comfortable chair but didn't lay aside the sheaf of papers he'd been looking through. She noticed that with a wry smile. He would never allow her his full attention.

"I want out of my marriage to Chilton. Arrange it for me." She was gratified to know that caught his interest, at least.

"You what?"

"It was a mistake. I was foolish to believe I could make a success of it, for we don't at all suit. Fix it for me. Then, I will marry Everard and provide you with heirs through him."

Dunstan frowned. She made it sound so cold and logical. "Daughter, a marriage is not something you dissolve on a whim. What does Chilton think of this?"

"Do not credit him with a voice in this. We both know what his place in this marriage was to have been. I've already given you a replacement, so you cannot object."

"But you agreed on Chilton. You spoke vows with him."

Rosalind was very pale but very sure. Her tone was crisp and matter-of-fact. "Is it the money you gave him? Don't let it trouble you. You've contracted the services of a stallion before only to find it wouldn't take. Consider this such a loss. I will not give you heirs through Chilton. See my marriage is ended and I will do my duty through Everard. You once said you wouldn't care if I chose to mate with a groom as long as it produced the desired result. At least Everard is a respectable choice."

Dunstan was stunned. He couldn't believe such calculated reasonings of his only child, she of the meek heart and timid soul. This was more like—like he himself. "Stop this foolishness at once. You wedded Chilton and that choice stands. I don't want to know what transpired between the two of you to put you in such a disagreeable temper but it will pass."

"No, it won't. Give me what I ask or suffer for it."

His heavy brows rose.

"I will remain here at the manor, secluded in my room. You will have no heirs. Your dynasty will die with you." She smiled brittlely when that won a sharp recoil. "You know me, Papa. I am very stubborn. I mean what I say."

Dunstan stood very slowly, his features congealing with aggravation. "Don't threaten me, miss. I will not bow before this tantrum. I will speak to Chilton and see what can be done."

"Are you going to give him more money? Will you pay him to be more agreeable? It won't suffice. I will not have him."

141

"And what would you have, Daughter? What do you demand that has not been given you generously all your life?"

Rosalind laughed scornfully. "Generously? Oh, you've been so generous. With your things, your connections, your money. What of your love, Father? When have you been generous with your love?"

Dunstan was taken aback. "You know I love you, Daughter."

"Daughter," she sneered. "That's it, of course. I was a daughter, a weak, useless female, not the steel-loined son you always desired. You never forgave me for that, did you? Geoffrey would have made you a fine son. He's smart and greedy and ambitious and knows nothing of love, just like you. I spent my whole life trying to be deserving of your love and your time. I pleaded for it, I wept for it. I won't go through that with Geoffrey. I won't beg for his affection. I'm done with you high-minded selfish men. At least Everard cares for me. That is some consolation. He doesn't insult me by pretending to feel what he doesn't."

"Rosalind." Dunstan's voice was strange and strained, but she was too caught up in her own impassioned speech to hear it.

"You and Geoffrey deserve one another. I will play your pawn no longer. I will breed your heirs then I want no more to do with you. Do you hear?"

Rosalind spun away to march in icy dignity to the door. As she pulled it open, an odd sound drew her attention back into the room. Her father had taken a single step to pursue her then faltered. His face was frozen in a mask of surprise. The papers he held filtered to the floor in a haphazard snowfall of neglect. His lips moved soundlessly.

"Papa?"

Rosalind started toward him, hesitant in her alarm, then rushed to catch him as he slumped forward. She struggled with his weight, managing to get him back into the chair. His head lolled unresponsively and prompted her unthinking cry.

"Geoffrey!"

The day had been a long one and at its end, James Dunstan was resting much easier than his daughter. The weary figure sat rigidly on the edge of the sitting-room chaise. Blind, glassy eyes stared into the small, warming blaze. None of that warmth reached Rosalind. She was cold. Cold as the night. Cold as the grave.

"Here. Drink this. You have to have something."

She looked unblinkingly at the cup of honied tea which

stayed before her until she was obliged to take it. The delicate cup rattled noisily on its saucer. Finally, Geoffrey took it back and set it aside.

Not quite sure what to do with the stiff, silent woman who rejected every comfort, Geoffrey sat beside her and remained quiet.

After long minutes passed, Rosalind spoke to the fire in a leaded voice. "I don't know what I should have done had he died."

"But he didn't, Roz. The doctor said with rest, he should recover completely. He was lucky to have you there when it happened."

"Lucky?" she repeated shrilly. Her dark eyes finally acknowledged him. They were lifeless and shiny. "If I hadn't been there, nothing would have happened. Don't you see? It was my doing. I could have killed him."

When slow crystal droplets began to well and shimmer, Geoffrey shifted slightly and drew her carefully to his chest, holding her there with a hand against her glossy hair and an arm curved loosely about her slumped shoulders. She was too drained to object and the tears began to fall in a guilty stream.

"You couldn't have known," he soothed reasonably. "He seemed so strong of heart to all of us."

"Until I broke it with my cruel, unthinking words."

"What did you argue over?"

She was silent for a moment then said, "It doesn't signify now. All that's important is that he get well. I'll do anything I can to see that happens."

The heavy resignation in her tone prompted a brief frown on the handsome face before he brushed his lips against the silken crown. That tender gesture had another witness. Henri paused in the open door to observe the way his brother consoled the grieving woman. The gentle stroke of his hand upon the soft tresses was not the action of a man about to say his good-byes. Scowling, the Frenchman retreated to the bedroom and began to unpack the portmanteau with an angry disregard.

"I'm here for you, Roz, if ever you should need me," Geoffrey told her quietly.

She leaned away and wiped her face on the back of her hand. The ache of fatigue and worry dulled her, making every move an effort. "I'm very tired. I think I shall go to bed." Geoffrey stood with her. "I've sent Jessup away for the night but will need help with the fastenings on my gown," she murmured distractedly.

"I'll help you," he offered with a kind gallantry and steered her into her bedroom. He maided her efficiently, then turned down the covers while she shed the gown. Clad in her thin chemise, she slipped into bed and let him tuck her in. His hand lingered for a moment atop the coverlet, then he wished her a low good night.

Impulsively, Rosalind caught his hand. "Don't go, Geoffrey. Please stay and hold me for a time." She slid over to give him room to lay above the covers. She had forgotten the dangers of that situation and was content to have him cradle her to his shoulder. He made a wonderful pillow and within minutes, the steady hush of his breathing and thud of his pulse rocked her to a sleep that lasted deep and healing, long into the night.

The room was in complete darkness when Rosalind awoke shortly before dawn. She was momentarily startled by the relaxed arm that curled beneath her head. Then she remembered Geoffrey. He was sleeping soundly, still fully clothed in the same spot she'd left him. The sonorous rhythm of his slumber was in no way threatening.

She lay listening to him breathe while her mind considered what she must do in careful deliberation. Restlessly, she edged away from him to turn up the light. The sight of Geoffrey Chilton in sleep would stir maternal instincts in any female breast. With his vital energy at an ebb, the glossy good looks inherited a boyish innocence that was endearingly harmless and dangerous to those who would believe it so. There was nothing helpless or dependent about the dynamic viscount. It was an illusion and it made her wonder how much else about him was fiction.

Like it or not, her father wanted her to stay with Geoffrey. To ease his mind and the strain on his fragile heart, she would bow to that wish. It was too late to call back her earlier defiance but she could concede with good grace to keep him from further agitation. She would remain Lady Chilton.

Part of her secretly rejoiced, that part that avidly studied the long, powerful line of his body. Another part was terrified. Every moment she spent with him ingrained him deeper into her heart. Every time he turned to her with that dimpling smile, it was harder to maintain a cautious resistance. Even thinking of his touch made her control slip and tremble mightily. How could she keep a safe distance when what she craved was closeness? She wanted to accept him readily as husband and lover but the falseness of both soured that desire. If she relented, Geoffrey would use and hurt her. She knew it as certainly as she knew he wasn't the sweet angel he appeared to be in sleep. Every inch of ground she lost to him made her footing that much more precarious. If she wasn't extremely careful, he would pull it out from under her altogether. It would be no easy task to play the wife for the sake of her father and not lose herself to the role but she would have to manage.

Curiously, she reached out to touch the back of his hand. Its warmth startled her, sending a surge of elemental longing through her. How she wished he was the husband she could trust and rely upon, one she could express her love for without hesitation.

Wistful thoughts lulled her caution. She let her fingertips follow along the firm swells of arm and shoulder. How soundly he was made, she thought admiringly, lean and well muscled just like one of their robust stallions. No wonder her father was adamant on his choice. She couldn't recall a finer specimen of manly strength. Her hand stroked downward, over hip, flank and thigh defined so attractively in the fitted stockinette trousers. Her practiced examination could find no fault. He was no weak-hocked hobby horse. Her attention was drawn back to his superb features. Lightly she touched his cheek then was tempted to the curves of his mouth. She gave a slight gasp when he pressed a kiss to her fingertips. She glanced up to find the sultry eyes open and intent. His lips bowed upward beneath her hand and she jerked it away.

"Did you want to see my teeth?" he asked in husky humor.

Rosalind flushed and searched for an acceptable excuse. She could find none. "I beg your pardon," she stammered. "I didn't mean to wake you."

"No?" he argued in amusement. Then his mood deepened and warmed to match his smoldering stare. "Come to me, my Circe, and see what manner of beast you've made me."

His large hand impelled her forward. She could have struggled but she didn't. The rumble of passion in his words undid her. They came together for a lengthy kiss, expressing desire so rich and urgent both were left breathless. Lips moist and pulsing from the unexpected union, Rosalind withdrew to eye him warily. Her own wants made her complaint a low, throaty murmur.

"What manner of beast are you that you can so bewitch me?" A reluctant hand was drawn to the dark gold hair. He captured it lightly and brought it to his lips for a damp kiss. "One you could easily tame if you would but try," he promised. Rosalind took her hand from him and regarded his reposed but not relaxed figure with a doubtful purse of her lips. She shook her head. "Such a dangerous task, my lord beast. I fear I would be devoured."

"Or do you fear you would enjoy it too much?"

"Yes," she answered softly with a sincerity that took him off guard. Slowly, she leaned forward to test his claim. Her lips moved in a cautious inquiry over the inviting part of his, tasting the potent sweetness he offered with the tip of her tongue. Her palms came up to hold his face between them while her exploring kisses mapped out the ridge of his cheekbones, the bridge of his nose, and the tender swell of his eyelids. When they settled once more upon his pliant mouth his moan of contentment gave her a chill of satisfaction. She looked deep into the heavy-lidded docile gaze and wondered, "Are you tame now?"

With a low growl, Geoffrey tossed her on her back and was quickly above her to warn gruffly, "You can never take all the wildness from the beast. That's what makes it a beast."

His open mouth dropped down on hers for a hungry feast, plunging her into a dark swirl of desires. Her fingers clenched in his hair as she countered his probing kisses with equal fervor, fencing with his tongue and sucking in his hurried breaths. When they parted, both realized something far beyond their control had passed between them in those urgent seconds.

"Do you want me to go, Roz?"

The rather hoarsely spoken question forced Rosalind from her enraptured trance. She glanced about as if realizing for the first time where they were. A reluctant protest was made half-heartedly.

"But what if we're discovered? Jessup sometimes forgets to knock."

Geoffrey's laugh cut her short, making her flush. "That a man and wife bed down together is not news that will shake the household. It's been known to happen before between married couples other than us."

His teasing only deepened her embarrassment. Afraid of losing the comfortable bed and willing wife, Geoffrey had a moment of inspiration. He traversed the bed on hands and knees, drawing the curtains to form an intimate tent of privacy about them. He paused to raise an expectant brow.

Smiling softly, Rosalind turned back the covers and patted the inviting space next to her.

The first intrusion into the room went unnoticed by the

sleeping pair. Camilla regarded the closed bedcurtains in puzzlement, but her question received a blunt answer when her gaze fell on the clothing Geoffrey had tossed carelessly to the floor.

Breathing in quiet hisses, Lady Dunstan crossed to the foot of the bed to carefully part the drapery. Her teeth ground in frustration at the sight of the golden head sharing the pillows with her stepdaughter's. Worse was the way his arm lay casually across her bared shoulders, keeping her close to his side. The scene smacked of peaceful intimacy and Camilla could have happily slain them both in their blissful conjugal slumber. She let the curtain fall to conceal the damning picture of consummated vows and slipped unnoticed from the room.

The second visit wasn't as stealthy. Geoffrey grumbled and tried to thrust away the hand that shook his arm. When it persisted, he looked up in bleary annoyance.

"Geoff, get up. There is a messenger below for you," Henri said in an urgent undervoice.

"Tell him to come back later," he mumbled. "Or why don't you take the message for me. Do one or the other but leave me be."

"Geoff, he won't leave the note with anyone but you. It's from Duchess du Pailieter."

"Lisette?" Curiosity moved him to sit up and put on the clothes Henri passed him. "But why?"

"I don't know. You'd best hurry."

After he'd gone ahead, Geoffrey lingered a moment, looking down on the serene face of the woman who had loved him so well and completely. He experienced a tightening in his chest as if something had lodged there to cause him discomfort. Lightly, his fingertips touched to the softly flushed cheek and his want to tarry made him sigh before following his brother.

Rosalind opened her eyes and frowned. She lay silent and thoughtful for a long time, mulling over what she'd heard. Though they had spoken in French, she understood a woman's name and the undercurrent of uneasiness. Lisette. Someone from Paris? What was Geoffrey to this woman that would tear him from her bed and warm compliance? Did she want to know?

Chapter Fifteen

When Jessup responded to Geoffrey's knock, he felt a bitter rush of disappointment sweep away his confidence. He couldn't keep the irony from his tone.

"Is her ladyship indisposed this morning?"

"Come in, my lord" came a call from behind the somber-faced maid. She stepped aside to grant him reluctant entry then hurried to Rosalind's side. She was sitting at her dressing table with half her heavy hair pinned up and the rest spilling in a shiny cloud about her shoulder. "I beg your indulgence for a moment. Jessup is almost finished."

Geoffrey moved about the room feeling restless in a lady's boudoir when his presence served no purpose. Rosalind's jewelry case lay open atop one of the satinwood tables and his attention was captured while he quickly totaled up the worth of the brilliant stones. Then a small frown puckered his brow.

"Where are the pearls I gave you?"

"They need to be restrung, my lord," Rosalind answered calmly. "A bit of an accident. Was it good news or bad?"

His avaricious gaze was pulled from the treasure box. "What?"

"Your message this morning."

"Oh." Geoffrey continued his pacing. "Not good, I'm afraid. My belongings have been delayed at least another month in France."

"Yes, that is discouraging." Her eyes followed him in the mirror and reflected her own distrust of that statement. Of course, it could be the truth but she doubted that a duchess named Lisette had anything to do with his stranded furnishings.

"How is your father?"

"He passed the night comfortably."

"And you? How did you pass the night?" His eyes met hers in the glass. Hers didn't waver.

"Most comfortably, thank you."

"I'm glad."

The charged undercurrent that sizzled beneath their polite words went unnoticed by Jessup as she finished winding up the last strand of hair. Geoffrey took her place at Rosalind's back.

Her shoulders tensed as his palms rested upon them but she didn't move away. The gentle kneading of his fingers brought an expectant shiver.

"It was a most enjoyable night for me as well. The first of many, I hope."

His hands slipped lower, dipping down to appreciate the bared tops of her breasts above the square neckline of her gown. She caught them before they could transgress farther and held them away. It was an act of modesty not rejection and Geoffrey's confidence soared.

"The doctor advised my father to return to London to see his own physician. He'll have better attention there. I would like to accompany him."

"Of course," Geoffrey was quick to agree. He kept the strength of his relief from showing too prominently in his expression. "When will we leave?"

"As soon as Father can travel. I'm sure you'll be glad to get back to the city."

The hint of melancholy in her voice brought him down on one knee beside her stool so their eyes were even. The caress of his hand eased the uncertainty in her eyes. "I was becoming rather fond of this place."

His kiss was as gentle as his touch and when he came away, her gaze was vulnerable and pleading in contrast to the rapid rush of her breathing. When he leaned forward again, her fingers pressed to his lips to stay him.

"Chilton, please. My feelings are in such confusion about you. Please don't make them more so."

His lips brushed her hand and he said against it, "I will follow your lead, my precious Circe."

Her fingers slid along the line of his jaw in helpless longing. He was too enchantingly fair with the broad, bewitching smile and slanted eyes that could charm and fascinate so easily. She was enticed forward to feel the warm magic of his kiss and to sample the silken luxury of his spun-gold hair. His contented response made the spell complete.

"Oh, Geoffrey, I wish I could resist you," she moaned against the cushion of his lips.

"No. No, you don't."

"Oh, dear. Please excuse me."

Two pair of startled eyes flashed to Camilla, Rosalind's bright with embarrassment and Geoffrey's dark with annoyance as he stood.

"Dunstan wants to see you both. Forgive me for the intru-

149

sion." Her stare stabbed at the viscount in silent challenge. Then, she was all sweet compassion as she took up Rosalind's arm for a heartening squeeze and led her down the hall. Geoffrey followed more slowly.

Lord Dunstan's room was dark and forbidding to Rosalind, who ventured with the utmost reluctance to the side of the great bed. She was grateful for Camilla's presence but it was Geoffrey she reached back for. He took up her hand in unquestioning reassurance. Though she hadn't said as much, he knew the rift between father and daughter concerned him and he was anxious to see it healed.

"Come nearer, Lindy," rasped the shadowed figure beneath the mountain of covers. "Is Chilton with you?"

"Yes, my lord."

"Camilla, you may leave us."

His wife balked at the dismissal but had no choice in it. She closed the door and leaned close to the small crack she'd purposefully let remain.

"How do you feel, sir? You are looking more up to snuff."

"Nonsense," he grumbled in response to Chilton's amiable lie. "I look dreadful, I know, but I do feel better. What I need to know is how things fare with you."

Geoffrey turned a quizzing glance toward Rosalind and she stammered hurriedly, "They are fine, my lord." To emphasize that, she made a display of their hands locked together. "Chilton and I will be accompanying you to London."

The bedridden man looked pleased and nodded his satisfaction. "I am glad you got your differences settled. It's good to know I will have someone capable to tend my affairs while I recover from this inconvenience. Will you see to things, Chilton?"

"You know I will, sir."

"Good. Very good. Leave me now. I would like to rest."

Rosalind bit her lips as her father seemed to sink into the pillows like a helplessly feeble invalid. The sight of him at less than his full vital strength brought a saddened ache to her breast. Men like James Dunstan weren't meant to be helpless. They should be taken down in their prime so as not to suffer the indignity to being powerless. She bent and pressed a tearful kiss on his cheek.

"I am so sorry, Papa," she whispered unevenly.

"It's forgotten, my girl, and I do love you even if I am remiss in showing it. I shall try to do better."

She sniffed miserably. "And I love you. Rest now. We'll speak later."

Goffrey took her gently by the shoulders and steered her out into the empty hall. There, she sagged against the solid comfort of his chest.

"Oh, Geoffrey, what have I done? I know he'd rather be dead than in such condition."

He held her tight and gave her a firm shake. "You're wrong. He'll recover and be himself again."

"I was so afraid. He may not have been the best father but he is my father."

"I know."

Rosalind collected herself determinedly and stepped away. Very quietly, she said, "Thank you for staying by me."

"Where else would I be?" He touched her cheek briefly. Then his expression clouded. "What differences did he speak of?"

She cast her eyes down in an awkward sweep. "It's nothing, my lord. It's settled now. Father wants us together and I owe that to him."

"But it's not what you want?" His question was intense and unavoidable. "Roz, answer me."

"I don't trust you, Geoffrey, and I don't trust myself with you." Her dark eyes told of that turmoil in the single, searching entreaty. She started to reach out to him, to touch the broad chest that had afforded her such a secure haven, then thought better of it. Her hand fell away and with one last anguished look, she hurried down the wide sweep of stairs.

"Give up the notion, Chilton," purred a silken voice from behind him. He turned to meet the mocking blue eyes. "She's an insecure child. She thinks like one and behaves like one. She'll never believe in you. You're too much of a man, too dangerous, too male for her goosehearted nature."

"I think you mistake your stepdaughter, madam."

Camilla's laugh was scornful. "Oh, I think not. I've listened to her fearful palpitations for nearly two years. I know how her mind works and I know exactly what she thinks of you. She tells me everything, you know."

Geoffrey could barely contain his disgust. "Yes, your motherly advice was a great comfort to her. Every maid should hear such an earful of rubbish on her wedding eve."

"The silly twit was in a positive quake."

"No longer." Geoffrey loosed a slow, well-satisfied smile to taunt her. "We dispelled those misconceptions."

Camilla's pouty lips thinned into an unpleasant line and she crooned her venom in a sweet voice. "So she has no fear of the

151

marriage bed. The question remains of who she'll share it with. Do you know what she was discussing with Dunstan when he had his seizure?" Seeing the wary stance of her opponent, she pressed on with a vinegary smile. "She was demanding he find a way to set you aside so she could wed Everard."

Geoffrey refused to let her see what a telling blow she'd delivered. With a confident bluff, he said, "I have nothing to fear from Everard."

"You may fascinate for the moment but Lindy prefers things that are safe. Everard is safe and familiar and I intend to see she finds that more and more attractive."

Geoffrey's sudden movement brought a look of alarm to the deceivingly pretty face. He seized her arm and jerked her up close to the intimidating strength of his body. "Stay away from Rosalind," he warned in a low rumble. "Stay away or I will tell her the truth about her loving stepmother."

Camilla's momentary fear melded into a desirous exhilaration. She fairly trembled in his grasp with an eagerness to know more of the fiery passions from him. Reading of her interest in the feverish blue eyes, Geoffrey pushed her away roughly.

"Tell her," Camilla taunted. "Tell her and see which of us she believes. Consider my offer again, Chilton, before you find yourself out without a penny."

She brushed past him with an icy smile. He let her go. He wasn't fool enough to doubt her words. Rosalind held the cunning woman in the highest esteem. If he were to expose her false friendship, she would most likely call him liar. Confronting the clever Camilla was not the way. He had to lessen Rosalind's dependence on the woman by replacing her as confidante. Camilla was determined to make it an all-out battle for the fortune. Geoffrey didn't mind the fight but he refused to let Rosalind become a casualty of it. She was the center of the struggle. She would be the innocent ground they fought upon. Whether it was to her liking or not, Rosalind had a champion in Geoffrey Chilton.

Geoffrey pulled his large trunk from the cupboard and tossed it onto the bed next to the dozing figure of his brother. Henri gave a start and rubbed his eyes in question.

"We're going to London, Hank. Get your belongings together."

Henri was up with a quick smile then grew cautious. He could no longer take "we" for granted. "You and me or you and your new family?"

Geoffrey didn't pause to placate the surly jibe. "This will

152

serve our purpose. I have to get to London and now. I needn't fumble for an excuse."

"When are you expecting Lisette?"

The bright head gave a shake. "The note didn't say."

"What does she want? She is the last of your *affaires des amours* I would have expected to pursue you across an ocean. How did she find us?"

"I don't know. The note only said she would get word to me when she arrives and that it was urgent." Geoffrey's tone was crisp. He said nothing to his brother of his worries. Just as he had kept his first meeting with Rosalind at the inn a secret from him, he wouldn't share this dread. If Lisette could find him, so could others.

Observing the tension in the younger man, Henri guessed at its cause. "You and the Duchess are not intimate friends, are you?"

The deep blue eyes flew up reproachfully. "No."

"Why are you in such straits that your drab wife find out then?"

Geoffrey resumed his packing, flinging the garments indiscriminately into the trunk. "I don't need any extra difficulties with Rosalind just now."

Henri laughed shortly. "What I last observed hinted at no difficulties."

"Rosalind is no simple chit. She has a good mind and a very suspicious one. One or two tosses beneath the sheets are not going to woo her. I have to get her to trust me. I am very close to having everything I want. I can't make any mistakes now."

"And what is it you want?" Henri asked plainly. He took the stack of starched shirts from Geoffrey's hands in order to command his full attention.

"What I've always wanted."

The Frenchman gave him a pensive stare. Geoffrey seemed the same, full of frenetic energy and unintentional disregard for all but his purpose. But he was different, too. He had suspected it, but seeing him console the teary Lady Chilton, brought it all too clear. "I am afraid I no longer know what that is, *mon frère*, or how it concerns me."

The frosty tone didn't quite conceal the anxiety behind the words and Geoffrey was nonplussed. Impulsively, he hugged his brother in a tight embrace and spoke low and convincingly. "I want the best for us, Hank, the best of everything. It's going to be just as we promised ourselves. Nothing will get in the way of that. I promise. I give you my pledge on my love for our

153

parents and my love for you. If you've any doubts that I can maintain this charade, say so and we'll go today, now, if you like. I have to know you trust me. I have to know you support me. Do you, Hank?"

Henri held him back by the shoulders and gauged his expression of desperate sincerity. "And if I was to say we go, would you walk away from the fortune and the woman?"

"Yes."

Henri should have believed him. He had no reason not to, yet a vague deep warning continued to give him pause. "All right, Geoff. I will trust you. Remember, the danger is not here but here." He tapped his temple then his chest. "Harden your heart for what you must do or have it broken. Remember the rules. Don't fool yourself into thinking no one will be hurt. Just see that it isn't you."

Geoffrey considered that warning as their coach traveled to London. It cooled his attitude toward the woman at his side, making him view her as a means to an end. He forced his concentration to linger on the opulent luxury of the coach, on the wealth of stones that adorned the slender neck, on the richness of the silk that draped shapely knees, hugged a firm waist, and caressed the full swell of generous breasts. Swallowing hard, he looked out the window to study the countryside instead. Estimating the treasures within the confines of the coach was too dangerous. He forced himself to remember Henri's challenge. He had to stay aloof and unattached, but the difficulty of both was taxing. Rosalind's cautious distance helped but failed to fully ease his chafing desires. He took a deep breath and made himself think of the past, of the miseries that had brought Henri and him to England to ply their lucrative games with London's elite. So much was at stake. His happiness was not a priority, for it wasn't something he often considered. Comfort and wealth meant happiness to him. It was a physical rather than a mental condition and he would continue to view it as such. Yet . . . His eyes strayed once again to the silken knees and an unfamiliar tug moved his untried heart. No, he told himself firmly. Better not to think of such things. He looked back out the window with an angry fierceness.

The earl's weakened condition forced them to travel more slowly, necessitating an overnight stay at an inn where Geoffrey's convictions were further tried. An unusual flow of guests limited the beds available and Lord and Lady Chilton were assigned a single, though elegant room.

Determined to relieve as much temptation as possible, Geoffrey remained in the cheery neighboring pub until a late hour, hoisting countless mugs as he counted the slow passage of time. When he finally wove his way to his room, he hoped weariness and the lack of sobriety would grant him a quick, merciful slumber. Not so.

Rosalind wasn't in bed, asleep, as he'd hoped. She stood at the mullioned window where her figure was torturously outlined in the nightdress she wore. Nor did she assail him with shrewish questions concerning his whereabouts or the hour. Instead, she asked softly, "Is all well with you, my lord?"

Don't be so kind to me, he wanted to shout at her. Don't look so damned desirable. Don't treat me as though I'm worthy of your concern.

"I'm fine," he mumbled thickly and steered a path to the narrow settee. It was a safe distance from the bed and he collapsed upon its yielding cushions with a small groan. He prayed consciousness would leave him immediately, however, his awareness lingered to taunt him with visions of Rosalind moving about the room. She bent over to toss back the comforter, presenting him with a tormenting curve of buttocks and hips. He squeezed his eyes closed and swallowed. The sound of her plumping the pillows coaxed them open.

"Come to bed, my lord. You look all in."

With a moan, he let himself sprawl out on the cushions. Nothing could make him endure the night on those inviting sheets with the woman he wasn't supposed to care for. He would take what rest he could find on the celibate sofa.

"Chilton, you can't sleep there. You'll be in knots by morning."

He feared parts of him were already in knots and paining him most severely. He made a miserable sound when she crouched beside him.

"Geoffrey, get up and come to bed," she urged. She gripped his shoulders and sat him up. The sudden change in position wrought an urgent distress in his stomach.

"I feel most unwell," he muttered faintly. "Must have been something I ate."

"More likely it's how much you drank," she corrected, not unkindly. She put a hand to his forehead. The warm touch upon his clammy brow made him toss his head to one side in denial.

"No, please," he groaned then pressed his lips together. The turmoil in his belly was growing harder to ignore and so was

155

her tender attention.

"Are you going to be ill, my lord?"

He began to shake his head but the joggling movement made him nod quickly. Deftly she provided an empty basin for the indelicate retreat of the night's spirits. While she disposed of it, he leaned back, eyes closed in an anguish of humiliation. The damp cloth she lay on his dappled forehead made him sigh with relief.

"Better?"

"Umm."

"If I undress you, do you think you could help me get you to bed?"

His eyes popped open in dismay. "Call Henri. He can see to me."

Ignoring his mortified plea, Rosalind knelt to tug off his boots. "There's no need to trouble him so late. I can do it. You'll feel better once you lie down."

"I want to die," he said in earnest.

"I don't think you will so you'll have to make the best of it." She leaned him forward and slipped off his coat and waistcoat. "Living is a suitable punishment for such foolish overindulgence."

He was afraid she was right. He sat helpless and embarrassed while she unbuttoned his shirt. Her touch was more than efficient as she skimmed the linen from the impressive chest and shoulders. He hoped she wouldn't note the quickening of his pulse beneath the gliding caress.

"I'm sorry," he mumbled. "I don't handle strong drink very well."

"And I don't handle heavy drunkards very well, either. You'll have to help me."

With her arm about his middle and a shoulder for support, Rosalind wrestled him from the low settee. He moved awkwardly at her side, his steps uncoordinated and shaky. She sat him on the bed as easily as possible, then went to turn down the light.

As he watched her traverse the room, Geoffrey's jumbled thoughts went back to a brave maid tending the man who intruded into her life. Had she known how much he would upset her world, she probably wouldn't have taken him in that night. Emotions rose to choke off his intentions and played rough upon his heart.

"I love you, Rosalind."

She turned at the low, indistinct muttering and asked,

"What was that, my lord?"

But he had sagged to the mattress, the admission already forgotten. Smiling, she went to him and pulled the covers about him. He drifted for several minutes then the dip of the mattress made him draw a quick breath. He held it painfully as she leaned over him to touch her palm to his cheek.

"Are you all right, Chilton? Is there anything I can do for you?"

He wanted nothing more than to lay his pounding head upon her soft bosom and have her hold him through the hours until dawn. He wanted to confess the misery that weighed on his conscience and to pour out the confusion of his feelings. He wanted to trust her with the truth of what he'd done and what he was. But fearing the looseness of his tongue and thoughts, all he could manage was a low groan. He rolled onto his side, away from her gentle touch and empathetic gaze but still he couldn't escape her nearness. Her slender arm slipped over the ridge of his ribs and her palm rubbed the smooth plane of his chest. He lay still, scarcely daring to breathe.

"Geoffrey?"

He didn't answer the low, hopeful call. His eyes squeezed shut when he heard her resigned sigh.

"Good night," she whispered.

Her lips pressed a small kiss between his shoulderblades. She might well have plunged a knife straight to his heart. He let his breath out in a shaky rattle and tried to summon sleep.

It seemed he had just closed his eyes when low voices teased them open. The brightness of the morning made him regret the action. Squinting in misery, he peered at the two women in the process of Rosalind's toilet. The sight of his wife in thin, lace-edged drawers and chemise made him forget the ache in his head in deference to another. He was careful to lie inert when Jessup scowled in his direction and was frankly relieved when the topaz velvet gown clothed the too-inviting form. Then he was able to relax and revel in his own discomfort.

Jessup's exit brought Henri in. He bade a courteous good morning to Rosalind then cocked at brow at the figure on the bed.

"He was most unwell last evening," Rosalind explained softly. "I know you must wake him but I beg you go gently."

"Yes, my lady. Indeed, I will."

Henri strode to the bed and tore down the covers. Geoffrey seemed to shrivel as bare skin was assaulted by the cool day.

"*Bonjour,* my lord. Time to set aside your lazy slumber,"

157

Henri said cheerfuly, disregarding the murderous, reddened eyes. "You look frightfully green. What sort of malady struck you down?"

"Oh, do shut up, Hank. My head is fairly splitting without having to endure your razor wit."

Geoffrey managed to sit up. Aware he was clad in only the immodest trousers and of the attention they drew from his wife's covert stare, he drew the comforter around him in an awkward shyness.

Unaware of his discomfort when confronted by both wife and brother, Rosalind brought a basin of cool water and sat beside him on the bed. She wrung out a cloth and touched it to his poorly colored face.

"Here, this will make you feel better," she soothed.

"Don't fuss over me, madam," he growled in surly temper and shoved her hand aside. "You only make matters worse."

Seeing her undeserved distress at the cruelly cutting words, Henri stepped in to say casually, "Excuse me, my lady." He lifted her up and took the wet cloth from her. "His lordship needs truly gentle handling this morning."

With the basin in one hand, Henri caught the back of Geoffrey's neck with the other and pushed his face into the tin of cold water. Bubbles of surprise burst in an excited froth before the Frenchman saw fit to bring him up, sputtering and blinking.

"There. An old remedy, but I've always found it works quite well," Henri pronounced. He slapped a towel briskly across the wet face. "Now, I'm sure he'd like to thank you for your kind care of him during his bout of illness. Wouldn't you, my lord?"

Blotting the moisture up, he mumbled, "Indeed, my lady. I am most grateful and apologize for my churlishness. Please forgive me." The chagrined mood didn't extend to his valet at whom he gave a sullen glower.

Hiding her smile, Rosalind said, "Yes, of course." She cast a timid glance at the usually reserved manservant and felt a sudden surge of comaraderie. "I'll leave you in good hands, my lord. I will see you downstairs."

"If I survive that long" came his muffled grumble.

Henri opened the door for her and gave a courtly bow. His severe manner softened toward her as he whispered a confident aside. "I will see he does, madame. Never fear."

She put a hand on his dapper sleeve. "Thank you, Henri."

His bow was stiff but the dark eyes warmed reluctantly to her gentle tone.

Chapter Sixteen

Lord Dunstan was settled comfortably into the Berkeley Square home amid much fuss from family and staff. Aside from exhaustion, he weathered the trip well but was grateful to be in his own bed. His personal physician spent a lengthy time with him then called his son-in-law into the parlor for a private word.

"How is he?" Geoffrey asked solemnly.

"He will recover from this attack as he has the others but each has taken a toll. He's not a young man and his heart is far from sound. If someone could make him see that, it would give him time he will waste otherwise."

"He's had other seizures? I wasn't aware of that."

"No one is, not even Lady Dunstan. He insisted it be kept quiet. I'm telling you in strictest confidence. He needs to be persuaded to slow down and to have some of the burden taken from him. Perhaps he would let you assume part of it. His biggest concern is that his daughter be cared for and you've seen to that."

"How serious is his condition?"

"Serious. Do not mistake that. His heart could go at any time. I've told him he's running on stubbornness alone these last years."

Geoffrey frowned. "And what can we do to give him more years?"

"I don't know that you can give him even one. Keep him from any agitation. Get him to stop pushing himself. I trust you will keep this to yourself."

"Yes, of course," he said in preoccupation. He was thinking of Rosalind who sat at her father's bedside not knowing he had rushed her to marriage to cushion the blow of his own death. He was thinking of what his desertion would do to the precarious state of his health and of how Rosalind would cope alone.

His features were understandably grave when Rosalind caught his arm after the doctor had gone. Her frightened eyes searched his desperately.

"What is it, Geoffrey? Is the news bad? Please tell me."

He forced a convincing smile and patted her hand. "My mind was on something else. I didn't mean to worry you. Your father will be fine. I plan to see he doesn't overtax himself and together we can assure he believes we are happy as man and wife. That's what he wishes most of all."

"Then we'll see that's what he believes," she agreed somberly.

And so they set up convincing housekeeping, making a public show as a contented couple while they kept to their own rooms in private. There was no adjoining door to tempt them to trespass and no offers to encourage it.

Rosalind was confused by the sudden cooling of Geoffrey's ardor. Where once it seemed she couldn't turn a corner without confronting his suggestive smile, she now had to seek him out. When together as a family, he was much the same, an incorrigible flirt and roguish tease, but when they were alone, he was carefully remote. While his inoffensive manner put her at ease, she missed the aggressive fire of his pursuit and wondered what caused it to lapse. Now that he had the distraction of London, had he grown tired of her? She might have accused him of it except he spent the majority of his time seeing to her father's interests. He lingered at his bedside during the morning hours discussing strategies then followed them through in the afternoons. His devotion was admirable yet she couldn't help but feel threatened, as though the business was consuming him as it had her father, stealing him away from her.

While Geoffrey had little time for Rosalind, his thoughts were rarely far from her. Keeping his distance was the hardest thing he'd ever done when all he could think of was the pleasures he denied himself. However, his purpose was proving successful. She was more relaxed with him. She seemed to enjoy their companionable time together and even initiated the meetings. She was beginning to trust him again. He had to tell himself it was worth the lonely nights he lay in restless solitude. She didn't encourage any intimacy between them so he restrained himself from demanding it.

He was aware, as well, of Henri's gauging stare. Since the incident at the inn, the Frenchman had ceased his baiting of Rosalind to him. He kept his opinions to himself and Geoffrey fidgeted unhappily in that silence. He knew he was being watched for signs of weakness and was determined to betray none. But there were weaknesses aplenty. He was captivated by Dunstan's world. The involvement in the earl's many ventures was invigorating, provoking him to careful thought and studied attention. His fondness and admiration for Dunstan grew daily. He was stimulated by the channeling of his usually idle energies and excited to see profits grow out of his own ideas. Dunstan made no secret of his respect for the younger man and was content to let him step into the role he once dreamed of having a son fill.

Geoffrey delighted in the weeks of dealings and entertainments on Dunstan's carte blanche. He felt useful, important, accepted. An empty space within him was filled and he would have been content if not for two very real threats, Camilla and Everard.

Like a careful predator, Camilla was patient, waiting and watching for the best time to spring. Her bright eyes followed Geoffrey in a fever of malicious desire, pouting lips eager for the taste of his kiss or his blood. She stayed away from Rosalind, her days occupied with Dunstan, but Geoffrey wasn't fooled into thinking she had given up her schemes.

The spiteful warning about Everard plagued him, for the young lord was rarely absent. Upon returning home, Rosalind found Everard a constant visitor. He escorted her gallantly to outings in the park and to the theater and attended her in the gardens with his ever-present book of verse. Geoffrey didn't really question the integrity of their meetings yet the nagging knowledge that she would set him aside to wed the limpid-eyed poet was a continual affront.

He was particularly aggrieved on finding Everard's ancient laudaulet at their doorstep when he awoke, then again at noon and a third time at seven. He prowled the front room, attention drawn to the parted drapes until the laudaulet returned. He paused at the window to see the lanky lord hand down his wife. They were laughing together. Her glove remained familiarly on his arm while they talked easily for several minutes. Geoffrey felt something unknown and unpleasant roil within him at the sight.

Rosalind handed her cloak to the waiting footman and started toward the stairs when a low voice startled her.

"Good evening, my lady."

She turned to see Geoffrey lounging against the door to the parlor. The casual pose struck her as affected for there was no languor in his manner. If anything, he was tense and keenly alert.

"My lord, did you wish to see me?"

His smoky eyes drooped heavily as he drawled, "That would be rather difficult considering your schedule. Where were you off to this evening?"

The deceiving silkiness of his voice made her defenses rise. Her reply was guarded. "I went to see Sarah Siddons at Covent Gardens. She is leaving the stage and I wanted to hear her one last time. She is quite marvelous. Do you know of her?"

"No," he clipped out. His attitude was becoming a mockery of his posture. "But I suppose Everard is a great fan."

"He and I have seen her perform several times."

"How good of him to see to your amusements."

"Yes, it is."

Geoffrey straightened and Rosalind retreated a step. She didn't know why his odd mood should be so intimidating.

"If you wanted to go to the Gardens to see this person, you should have asked me. I would have been happy to have taken you. Or was it the company you preferred?"

He sounded piqued and frankly jealous, Rosalind realized in some surprise. While that notion pleased her, his surly manner did not. She made her reply frosty.

"Nate and I have enjoyed each other's company for many years. Are you taking sudden exception to that, my lord?"

"Should I?"

"You are behaving quite boorishly, Chilton. If you are asking if I am compromising you with Everard, say so plainly."

"Are you?" he demanded tightly. He knew he was acting wrongfully in his accusations, but the question tumbled out on a wave of insecure doubt. Rosalind glared at him, dark eyes so cold the chill went clear to the bone. She refused to answer and with a regal disdain, turned to mount the stairs. He gripped her wrist in another foolish response to his frustration and she froze.

"Take your hand from me, sir," she said in wintery accents.

Geoffrey released her instantly and she ascended the steps without a backward glance.

He traversed the halls, anger growing apace with the grumble of the weather outside. His temper wasn't provoked by Rosalind or Everard but at his own situation that held him helpless. He knew he had no right or reason to command his wife to heel yet every moment she spent with

Everard felt like a betrayal. He was at a loss with his possessive tendencies and with the woman he couldn't control with a smile or a word. Why he should suffer such cruel pangs of desolation, he didn't know. He continued to chafe and bemoan his circumstance until faced with its cause once more.

Rosalind had changed into the baggy trousers and billowing shirt. Her hair was drawn up under a boy's cap. In the darkness, she would easily pass for a youth.

"Where are you going dressed like that?" Geoffrey wanted to know.

"I often ride at night," she said in brief explanation. She strode around him, tugging on her gloves as if he was dismissed from her mind.

"Not tonight, you aren't. It's going to storm and I won't have my wife traipsing about after hours like some senseless hoyden."

She leveled him a challenging stare then continued down the stairs. He fell into step beside her. "Why this sudden censure of my actions?" she complained in irritation. "First, you cast aspersions on Everard and now you think to chastise me for my behavior. You, sir, are not my father." She marched out into the brisk night with an independent toss of her head. She hadn't gone far when he jerked her up roughly.

"I am your husband."

She threw off his hand and argued, "In name only, my lord. Do not forget that. You overstep yourself, sir. This arrangement is for appearances only."

"And how does it appear when you are linked to Everard at every turn of the head?"

His querulous tone rallied a withering scorn. "It appears I have a kind and good friend who cares for me more than my fortune."

"Really? You think his motive is so pure? Don't you think he would eagerly step into my shoes to have his hands on that fortune or do you believe he'd be content just to have them on you?"

"You are odious," she exclaimed furiously. When she tried to whirl away, he caught her up in a desperate embrace, holding her to his chest while she struggled to be free of him.

"Is it Everard you wish to be wed to instead of me?" he demanded in a husky voice. "Is it, Roz? Would you rather have him than me? Tell me."

She slapped him. The strength of it set him back, an unsteady hand raised to the side of his mouth. His eyes were oddly blank and shiny for a long moment. Whatever else she would have said to him was detained by a sudden downpour of chilling rain. They ran, hands over their heads to the dry sanctuary of the stables. The short dash had drenched them through and left them shivering in the musty shelter. They stood apart, wary of each other yet unable to escape while the torrent raged around them.

Trembling in the damp, clinging shirt, Rosalind cast a sullen glance at Geoffrey's profile. He stood, arms hugged about himself, staring out into the rainy night. His rapid breathing and stiff stance spoke of his agitation. The sight of his swelling lip softened her temper with a liberal twinge of guilt.

"I'm sorry. I've never struck anyone before. You provoke me to an extreme."

"I deserved it," he said tonelessly. Everything about him was distant and strangely withdrawn.

"I am sorry."

She reached up to touch the bruise and was startled by the abruptness of his reaction. He lurched to the side, hands flying up to cross protectively over his face as if expecting another blow. When it didn't come, they dropped to clutch his shoulders in an insulating gesture. He shied away from her puzzled stare. What she had seen in his face so mismatched the situation she couldn't help but wonder what had stirred him to such a defensive panic. It had to be more than the ugly scene that passed between them.

Hoping to calm his unsettling mood, Rosalind said quietly, "I didn't mean to distress you by seeing so much of Nathaniel."

"I don't want to speak of this now," he replied gruffly. He wouldn't look at her.

"I won't see him again if you'd prefer I didn't."

That made his eyes cant toward her but his words were still stilted. "And what would that signify? It would be no answer.

"What answer do you wish to hear? That I'd rather my hours be spent with you?"

"Only if it was true" was his soft response.

"It is, Geoffrey," she claimed with an equal hush.

He didn't move as her hand rose slowly to mesh in his wet

hair. He stiffened beneath the lips that touched to his, gently searching. Undaunted, Rosalind held to him, kept from the closeness of his body by the barrier of his crossed arms yet sharing the dampness.

"I love you, Geoffrey."

A hard tremor rode through him, then he told her hoarsely, "I wish to God you didn't."

Before she could question the harsh sentiment, his arms unwound and curled about her. She was captivated by the urgent hunger of his mouth. His hands roved restlessly over her in a hurried possession, pausing to caress the firm thrust of her breasts against the cloying fabric, then lowering to cup her trousered bottom.

"Oh, Roz, how I've wanted to hear that," he confessed with a yearning breathlessness. "I've wanted you so." His grip tightened, pulling her closer so she would know the evidence of that claim.

"You have me now, my lord," she whispered against his parted lips.

Wordlessly, he took her down to a clean smelling bed of straw in one of the empty stalls. There on that fragrant pallet, they exchanged more kisses and eager touches until there was no thought of returning to the house to continue in proper surroundings. Damp clothing was shed and chilled flesh warmed by a purposeful friction. The rustle of hay, quickening breaths, and soft, feminine cries mingled with the nickering and stomping of the horses, then all fell into the natural silence of the night.

Wrapped in a woolen blanket, Rosalind dozed contentedly upon the solid plane of Geoffrey's chest and listened to the steady drum of his heart echo the more vigorous cadence of the rain.

"Warm enough?"

She nodded.

"Do you want to go back inside?"

She shook her head and let her palm wander in small circles over the light furring of his belly. She never wanted to leave the comfortable nest they'd found or the strong arms that held her close. In the aftermath of their loving, it was hard to imagine that there might exist differences between them or doubts of the rightness of their being together. For nothing felt as complete and perfect as lying with Geoffrey Chilton. She sighed happily as his lips brushed her hair.

Risking the loss of their tranquil mood, Rosalind reached up to touch the corner of his mouth where it still appeared tender. Geoffrey didn't flinch away. Instead, he pressed a light kiss to her fingers.

"I didn't mean to hurt you," she said quietly.

"It's forgotten and hopefully so is our quarrel."

"But I made you so very upset."

His arms formed a tight band about her. His voice was soft and remote. "It wasn't you, precious one. It was something else, something remembered that is best forgot. The memory surprised me is all."

"Memory of what, Geoffrey?"

"Of what's past and buried long ago. I would prefer it stay there." When he felt her draw another questioning breath, he added, "Please, Roz."

They were silent for some minutes, only the spattering of the rain and occasional restlessness of the horses intruding on their thoughts. Finally, Rosalind rolled onto her stomach to study him in the darkness.

"You're not truly jealous of Everard, are you?"

"Only of the time you spend with him. It's my fault, I know. I've been neglectful. Your father's kept me running with his work. And then, I'm never quite sure if you'll welcome my company."

"You make me sound very uncharitable toward you. But then I have been, haven't I?" His silence was her answer. "You've done so much for my father. You've given him back his strength and hope. He thinks of you like a son, you know."

"You've no idea how that pleases me. I've the greatest respect for him. And for his daughter. This is the kind of family I've always wanted to belong to."

The subdued wistfulness of his words provoked her curiosity. "What of your family, Geoffrey? I've never heard you speak of them."

"Would you? Surely you've heard the rumors." His bitterness wasn't directed at her but it made her frown nonetheless.

"I am not a gossip monger, my lord. I would prefer to hear from you than from unqualified whisperers. Unless you don't wish me to know the truth."

"The truth?" His laugh was short and brittle. "The truth is, Giles Chilton was a gamester and a drunkard. My mother

166

had to keep to her rooms under the pretext of ill-health to hide the marks he put on her face. I was afraid of him and I hated him. I was glad when we left England and I was glad to hear he was dead. It's not the kind of past one is proud of."

"Oh, Geoffrey, forgive my insensitive prying," she cried in quiet empathy.

His embrace strengthened, crushing her against the taut line of his body. "It's all right. I don't mind you knowing. I've put it behind me. My years in France hold many good memories and those are the ones I hold to when I think of family."

"Is your mother still there?"

"She and my stepfather died years ago. I have no ties left in France. I had hoped to make new ones here."

Rosalind stretched up to kiss him tenderly. Her words were rich with a gentle passion. "Will you be part of my family, Geoffrey?"

She heard him suck in a startled breath. After a pause, he asked huskily, "Is that truly what you want?"

"It's what I've wanted since our first meeting," she admitted shyly. Hopeful tears clung bright and fragilely to her lashes.

Geoffrey's large hands trapped her face between them, bringing her up for a fiery kiss. Then the gesture deepened from thankful to a provocative craving that had nothing to do with gratitude.

Rosalind let him sweep her up in the tempest of his desire and for the night she had no doubts that she had made the right choice.

She woke sometime later, unsure of where she was in the darkness until the sweet scent of straw and the firm contours of Geoffrey's form oriented her. It was his low moanings that pulled her from slumber. His breathing was rapid, rasping harshly in the quiet of the stable. When she touched his tossing head, she realized he was yet asleep.

"No, please," he murmured in his troubled dream. "Please don't."

"Geoffrey?"

When her hand brushed his cold cheek, his response was more violent than it had been before. With a fearful cry, he rolled away, arms protecting his head and knees pulling up in a defensive knot.

"Oh, dear," she said to herself, dismayed and uncertain.

Instinctively, she hugged to the hunched shoulders, willing him to take comfort from her. "Geoffrey, it's Rosalind. Wake up. It's all right. Wake up."

The desperate sounds stopped, and for a moment he stayed in his curled position, breath shivering fitfully from him. Abruptly, he turned to cling to her, damp cheek resting on her bosom. His voice was oddly pitched, like a child imitating a man.

"I won't let him hurt you, Mama," he vowed fiercely.

"Geoffrey, it's Rosalind."

Her words were wasted, for he slowly, soundlessly relaxed into a deeper plane of peaceful sleep and whatever had tormented him, fact or fiction, lay forgotten. The hurried tempo of his breathing slowed to a warm caress upon her skin. She continued to hold him, stroking the golden hair in a comforting rhythm long after his urgent grasp had slackened. She frowned into the darkness, cursing the father that could bring his son such tortured dreams. She only prayed they were just that, just dreams.

In the early glow of morning, the cobbled mews behind the terraced Georgian house became a bustle of ostlers and boys as they saw to the grooming of the horses and unloaded the wagons from the farms and fields of Surrey and Middlesex that brought in fresh fodder and hay bales. Amid all this industry, no one dared look surprised to see Lord and Lady Chilton emerge rather sheepishly from one of the stalls, brushing straw from rumpled clothing. Polite good mornings were rendered with eyes lowered. No one smiled until the mussed couple made a dignified retreat to the house. Then the sniggering and ribald laughter burbled up to last intermittently throughout the day, conjecture increasing with every colorful telling.

Chapter Seventeen

Henri's fine brows arched in pointed speculation as Geoffrey slipped into the room. He couldn't keep the smile from intruding into his words as he murmured, *"Bonjour, mon ami.* I am not sure I wish to know how you found yourself in such a state. One would think you spent the night, how you say, rolling in the hay? Who is she, this temptress of the barns?"

Geoffrey bestowed an annoying, bland smile upon him and began to shed his wrinkled clothes. His off-key whistling only provoked Henri further. He came closer to pluck several shafts of straw from the bronze hair. His nose twitched at the familiar perfume. His astonishment was monumental.

"You spent the night in the stables with the proper Lady Dunstan?"

"Chilton," he was corrected rather crisply. "We were caught in the rain and found a warm spot to wait it out."

"Hmm," Henri commented. His brother's growing color didn't pass unnoticed. He continued to scrutinize the other's distracted movements as he dressed. He was familiar with the air of edgy excitement and nervous sidelong glances and waited for Geoffrey to speak his mind.

"Hank, what would you say to staying here permanently?"

"How permanently?" The question was blunt.

Geoffrey evaded his direct stare. He lingered at his dressertop, fingering the fine fabric of his coat, the glittering diamond stickpin and cufflinks, the supple gloves — all trappings of wealth and success. His answer was very quiet. "Forever."

Henri took a long breath. "I was afraid that was what you meant." He began to pace, thoughts spinning while the dark blue eyes followed his agitated movements. "We should have left when I first suspected. Every day you stay with these people, the harder it is to leave."

"But I no longer want to leave."

That simple statement made the Frenchman turn on him in a high temper. "But you must. It was never part of the plan to remain. You cannot stay."

"Why?" he challenged. "Everything I want is here. Every-

169

thing I need, I have. Why should I want to leave?"

"Because it is all a lie, Geoff. All just a game. You've forgotten that. You are not the rich Lord Chilton who could marry into *bon ton*. Remember who you are."

"But I am Lord Chilton and will remain so."

"You cannot. Geoffrey, Geoffrey, why can't you see the dangers? You are confused. You've been seduced by the taste of this life and by the wiles of that woman. You have had the most spectacular women in France at your disposal, yet you shun their favors to take this plain, insipid spinster to bed with you. It is crazy. She has you soft in the head. Why this *affaire du coeur* and not the others? What is this woman to you?"

Geoffrey spoke softly but without apology. "The others were the wives of other men. Rosalind is my wife."

Henri gave him a hard shake. "No, she isn't. It is a title, not a fact. It was not meant to be permanent. You know that. She and her life do not belong to you."

"Why? Because you don't wish it to be so?" He flung off the hands that gripped his shoulders and stalked to the windows. He didn't want to listen to the words that knotted his stomach and filled him with a breathless panic. At the same time, he knew he should. He stiffened rebelliously when Henri came to embrace him in tolerant affection.

"Because it cannot be so," he explained with gentle simplicity. "Geoff, *mon ami, mon frère,* I love you. You are my brother. Don't you know that I would do anything to see you happy. Believe me when I tell you this will not."

"But I want it to," he argued with a desperate sigh. "Hank, it's all I've ever wanted. A good woman, a fine family, a place to belong, the money to make all things possible for us both. Why shouldn't I have those things?"

"You should. You will. But not here. Not with these people."

Geoffrey moved away from him in a restless frustration. He felt trapped and torn and sought a way to escape his predicament without having to surrender anything. "I know it started as just another scheme to easy riches. I never meant for it to be any different than the other times. I didn't want to involve myself, Hank. I truly didn't. But the part became so easy, so comfortable, so right and now it's not a part at all. I know you have no liking for Rosalind or love for the rich. I know you have cause to distrust and hate them. So do I. If the role is too difficult for you, I will understand if you wish to return to France. I would miss you, of course, and would probably fall prey to disaster without you to see me through my foolishness."

"That you would," Henri agreed in exasperation. He smiled thinly and shook his head. "You are trying to wiggle out of our conversation, my friend, and I cannot let you." Geoffrey's petulant scowl condemned him. "Is it the money that so charms you or the woman?"

"Both."

"Geoff, are you in love with her?"

His expression hardened into a guarded pout. "And if I am, what is the harm of it?"

"Because you have never loved before, perhaps you do not know. An *affaire d'amour* is no simple thing. You risk your heart recklessly, *mon frère*. She is going to break it. She is going to hurt you and that I do not want to see."

"Rosalind loves me," he protested. Henri's gentle tone had him alarmed, knowing he was trying to cushion a killing stroke.

"She loves Lord Chilton. That is not you. To these people, rank is everything. Will she be so generous with her love when she discovers what a *mésalliance* you have tricked her into?"

Geoffrey bristled at the term "bad match" and was angered by his fear that it applied. "She need never know that I am not who I pretend to be."

"She will find out. The ocean between France and England grows ever smaller. You will not be isolated for long. What happens when someone like Lisette speaks to your lady or someone who knows us exposes our relationship? It will happen, Geoff and then what will you do? You will lose all, the money, and your love. Leave her now and take the money, then, at least you'll have something."

"No. No, I won't. I won't run from this."

"You had better run, run far and fast."

"We'll go to the country and live there." He seized on that solution with the strength of someone drowning.

"What of her family? They will know the truth. Do you think that pretty viper will not rush to tell your lady the news? Is her father one to accept a marriage below rank? Would he will his fortune to one such as you? Is that what you want for Rosalind—scandal, shame, disinheritance?

Better her to hate you and go on with her life than to have you ruin it. You think on that, Geoff and while you do, read this. Perhaps it will convince you of how close your past is on your heels."

Geoffrey took the folded note with a chill of dread. The animation left his features as he read it. He sat in heavy defeat on the bed and moaned, "What am I to do? What can I do, Hank? Do I have to lose it all? Is there no way it can be salvaged? Please help me think of something."

Moved to pity by the desperate misery in the uplifted eyes, Henri shrugged. "I know of only one way. Go to her, Geoff. Tell her all and trust her to accept you for who and what you are."

Geoffrey recoiled from that stark suggestion and cried, "I can't. Don't you see? She'd know it was all lies and never believe the truth. I can't tell her now, not yet. I have to have time, time to make her love me so much she won't mind the rest."

Henri looked doubtful.

"I need time to make myself invaluable to her father so he won't cut me out. Help me get that time, Hank. Do you care enough to take that risk with me?"

"Cela va sans dire, mon cher," Henri said wearily. "That goes without saying. What would you have me do?"

On discovering Geoffrey had gone out for the morning, Rosalind decided to use the time until his return to make long overdue visits. Even the prospect of several dull teas couldn't dampen her mood. When her coachman had the effrontery to snicker under the pretext of clearing his throat, she gave him her most dazzling smile. She didn't care who knew of her scandalous rendezvous with her lover/husband, the desirable and impulsive Lord Chilton. Let them all gossip and cluck. She was proud to have a handsome husband who wanted her enough to choose such a clandestine meeting.

She found herself smiling in a most preoccupied fashion throughout the formal calls, forcing her hostesses to repeat themselves on more than on occasion. She didn't mind them thinking her feather-headed. She just couldn't regulate her mind to concentrate on the latest on-dits when her ears were tingling with the remembered timbre of Geoffrey's voice.

Nothing seemed important except returning to the warm arms for another night of love. Or afternoon, she thought boldly.

Her obligations met, Rosalind was eager to return home. The leisurely drive took them through Grosvenor Square. Fondly, she looked to the vacant townhouse and was surprised to see a strange coach in front. She called for her driver to stop several houses away and waited curiously to see who would alight. Her uncomfortable feelings of unworthy spying disappeared when a heavily veiled woman was handed down to be met at the door by her husband. Geoffrey accepted her hand and turned her into the foyer, closing the door to the astounded stare of his wife.

As evenly as she could, Rosalind instructed the driver to continue, murmuring that she'd forgotten the drapery maker was working on the renovations in her husband's home that morning. She sat pale and stiff until they reached Charles Street, then retired to her room. As she bent to pick up a chaff of straw from the carpet, her stunned thoughts began to work, sluggishly at first, then with increasing upset. The ideas that tumbled through her turmoiled mind were distressing. Had Geoffrey been carrying on an assignation in the Square while supposedly about her father's work? How long had he been entertaining the furtive woman? Had he been planning it even while he made such impassioned love to her? The doubts and mistrust swarmed over her in a merciless attack.

A brisk knock preceded Camilla's arrival. Her effervescent mood was quickly curtailed by the tragic set of her stepdaughter's features. At her solicitous prompting, Rosalind found herself pouring out her woeful fears.

"Have you any idea who the woman was?"

"None. It's no one I've seen. Oh, Cammy, I was so hopeful that all would be well between us. How can I trust him and not my own eyes? I shall just have to wait until he arrives to confront him with what I've seen. Perhaps he will have a simple explanation."

"And if so, how will he view you and your suspicions?"

Rosalind paused to consider that. "Do you think he'd accuse me of spying on him?"

"At best, you would appear foolish and green-eyed. Why not wait to see if he comes to you with his reason first. For now, don't worry. Trust Chilton and give him a chance to

173

prove himself to you."

Rosalind gave her a thankful hug and cried, "Oh, Cammy, what would I do without you? You are so wise."

Camilla patted her shoulder and smiled serenely. Her brilliant eyes gleamed with the beginnings of a clever plot. Her trusting stepdaughter had given her the means to have Geoffrey Chilton.

Unaware his greeting of the veiled woman had been witnessed, Geoffrey guided the duchess into the parlor. Her chuckle was low and gently chiding.

"I cannot say much for your abode, *Monsieur* Girard."

"It is temporary, madame. You wished to see me. Why?"

"So direct. I like that about you." The netting lifted to reveal hauntingly lovely features. Her smile was bittersweet. "So much I liked about you but that would not have brought me across that vile Channel. I've come for the necklace."

Geoffrey recovered from his astonishment with a practiced ease. "I no longer have it, Lisette."

The merry brown eyes hardened with the unwelcomed news but her poise was unshakable. "Get it for me, Geoffrey. I do not know what trickery you are involved in. I did not come to judge you or myself for my past mistake. You were charming, amusing, and oh, so pretty to look at and I, being a silly woman, was easily moved by your sad tale, which was probably sheer fiction. In a moment of folly, I gave you what was not mine to give and now I need it back. Immediately."

"As I've said, I don't have it and I don't know who does."

"Find out." The words were spoken sharply, then the fair duchess recanted. Her gloved hand lay against the smooth cheek. "I came myself because I did not wish to trust my mission to fools who would handle it clumsily. I could have sent men who would be, shall we say, most unpleasant with you. Do not make me deal harshly with you. I enjoyed our past friendship and would not want you to remember me unkindly. I am a desperate woman, Geoffrey. You see, the necklace was a gift from my husband. Now, he wants to see me wear it at an important dinner. I will not bore you with the particulars other than to say if I am not wearing the rubies, my marriage is in grave danger. I may be frivolous with my affections, but I have no intention of losing my husband or my position over an unfortunate infatuation with a wily fraud."

Geoffrey took her hand and kissed it gallantly. His smile was remorseless but not unsympathetic. "Madame, you know me as a *chevalier d'industrie* one who lives by his wits. I regret your circumstances, but I am not one to champion them. I, too, have to protect myself. I cannot get involved in this matter."

"But you are involved, *Monsieur* Girard, or Chilton or whatever you go by. My misfortune will be shared if you do not help me escape it. I do not like to threaten my friends. Let's just say the rubies would be an acceptable exchange for my silence. I understand you have been quite creative with your past in order to marry well. You would not want my congratulations to become condolences to your new bride."

Geoffrey's reply was very quiet. "When do you need it?"

"As soon as it can be arranged. I will contact you." She paused to regard the golden Englishman with a softening gaze. She had desired him once and was still prone to. His failure to become her lover had distressed her more than his clever ploy with the necklace. He was a vital, fascinating man and she wondered over the woman he had married. And was envious. She dropped her veil in place to conceal a wistful smile. She couldn't afford to underestimate him a second time.

"Do not frown so, Geoffrey," she coaxed. "I have no wish to intrude into your carefully laid plans. Provide me with what I seek and I won't trouble you again."

His smile was unconvinced. He knew he already had trouble and was reminded of it when Rosalind ventured into his room for the first time in the early evening. He and Henri had been busy with their desperate schemes and looked to her in no little surprise.

"Good evening, my lady," Geoffrey murmured in a low, warm greeting, wanting to make her welcome where she hadn't dared come before.

Henri never fully realized how awry plans had gone until he viewed them together. An excitement simmered between them, shy, awkward, eager, and yet with an intensity that sizzled. Volumes were wordlessly exchanged when their eyes affixed, expressing deep, private intimacies that excluded him completely. He had never seen his coolly confident brother so vulnerable before a woman and knew with a certainty that he would never willingly leave the woman who had charmed the elusive charmer.

175

"Excuse me," he pronounced stiffly. "Call me when you've a need of me, my lord."

"What? Oh, yes. Of course." Geoffrey didn't notice when he bowed his way out. His stare was lost in the somber circles that could share such feeling yet remain maddeningly detached. Like now. With a courtly elegance, he lifted her hand to place a leisurely kiss upon it. When he would progress to the softness of her lips, she eluded him with a subtle turn of her head so his mouth grazed her cheek. He covered his disappointment by making that chaste gesture a titillating caress. He could gauge Rosalind's response by the sudden quickening of her breath and wondered why she pretended to be unmoved. He longed to catch her up in his arms and entice her toward the beckoning pleasures of his bed; however, her preoccupied manner hinted she had more than matters of the flesh on her mind. He cooled his passion with difficulty and waited for her to proceed.

Rosalind had never felt more uncomfortable with him than within his thoroughly masculine lair. The furnishings, his belongings, his presence were all intimidatingly male and therefore threatening. She refused to let her timid gaze touch on the bed for fear his would follow and consider it an encouragement. She knew better than to trust her enfeebled will to resist if he became determined. She was, therefore, careful to deny any reference to the attraction that lay submerged between them.

"How was your day, my lord?" she began quietly.

Attuned to her restless avoidance of what was uppermost in both their thoughts, Geoffrey responded with equal civility. "Prosperous. I ran several errands for your father that occupied my morning. And you?"

She phrased her words with the utmost care, wanting to give him every opportunity to confide in her. "I visited several acquaintances. My travels took me through Grosvenor Square. Have you given up your plans to renovate your townhouse there?"

Rosalind turned to look at him, her inquiring stare containing an urgent plea. If he would just trust her with the truth, she could forgive him almost anything. She had asked him into her life and heart with an open invitation to share all she had. All he had to do was be honest with her and she would embrace him with an unquestioning devotion. If he was truly willing to start anew, she would forgive and forget

176

the past. But it had to start with his next words and she prayed they would tell her what she already knew.

Geoffrey smiled, dimples creasing his lean cheeks and slanting his dusky eyes with a glimmer of boyishness. He was so handsome, so desirable, and so false.

"I hadn't thought about it. I've been so involved with your father's doings, I'd quite forgotten my own plans. I haven't even been by since before our wedding. I suppose I should attend to it. It seems wasteful for such elegant rooms to go to unappreciated."

"Yes, doesn't it," she agreed in a conversational tone. She turned away, unable to look at the beloved features with the smooth lie still upon them. Surprisingly, she wasn't angry with him for the deceit or with herself for wanting to believe in him. What she felt was a crushing sense of hopelessness and defeat. She had no more questions for him. He had answered them all very neatly with that insincere smile. The only uncertainty that remained was how she would deal with that knowledge.

Rosalind gave a start when warm hands fell upon her shoulders. Her eyes squeezed shut to deny the delicious ripple of expectancy that simple contact awoke.

"It aggrieves me to say so but I have an appointment this evening and must be getting ready. Unless," he added silkily, "you would rather I canceled it."

The seditious kneading hands moved down her arms until they enmeshed with hers. Rosalind's hands were ice.

" 'Twould serve no purpose, my lord. I am to be out this evening as well."

Geoffrey's grip tightened unknowingly. "Oh? Off somewhere with Everard?"

"No. Camilla has asked me to join her for the evening. She deserves some time away from the sickroom, the poor, devoted dear."

"Yes, a veritable angel," he remarked blandly. He was far from pleased. Of the two, he preferred the company of his rival to his competitor. At least, Everard could be expected to play fair.

Rosalind withdrew her hands and stepped away from the dangerous heat of his body. Her voice was faint but decisive. "I must be hurrying, myself. Good night, Chilton."

"Until later, Roz?"

She couldn't meet his intensely hopeful gaze. "I think not,

my lord," she murmured and quickly exited the room.

Camilla was delighted with Rosalind's change of heart concerning the rout given by Countess Bertram. Dunstan insisted they go, claiming he'd had enough fuss and would prefer to sleep without the ever-watchful eyes upon him. For once, Rosalind was looking forward to the taxing mob. She wanted to loose herself and her thoughts in the milling congestion.

The gates to the exclusive Hanover Square were opened to emit the steady flow of carriage traffic. The Bertrams resided at a prestigious address on George Street. Their rambling home looked down from the upper end of the Square, providing a glorious view of the soaring spire and portico of St. George's Church. Seeing it gave Rosalind a nostalgic yearning for the life she had thought to begin at its rails. She dismissed such fancies with a forceful breath and entered the crush on the encouraging loop of Camilla's arm.

Like all such affairs, it was noisy, crowded, and hot. The constant shift and clamor made it impossible to conduct a decent conversation and for that, Rosalind was thankful. She was swept along in her stepmother's flighty social flutter until all the important figures of *bon ton* had been greeted save their hostess. Rosalind was worn and weary from the commotion and had Camilla's promise that they would leave as soon as they said their proper fare-thee-wells to the countess.

Odette Bertram was a refined, classically lovely woman. Her pale skin, thin nose, and haughty expression made Rosalind think of an immobile work of fine statuary. The self-possessed countess had rarely been moved to look down from the lofty heights of her Mount Olympus to acknowledge the existence of the plainly mortal daughter of James Dunstan. She made Rosalind uncomfortably aware of her own gracelessness with each carefully affected gesture. Like a goddess, she expected worship and was all too conscious that the unexceptional woman held her in disapproving disdain for all her grand airs. Censure was not something she tolerated well and it was with pleasure that she greeted the dour critic, considering the identity of her escort. Her slender fingers made a possessive claim on the fine cloth of Lord Chilton's sleeve.

Rosalind didn't know how she managed to get through the moment. Everything inside her seemed to freeze and knot all at once like a painful cramping ache. With a composure drawn from a strength she hadn't known she possessed, she made a polite speech to the smugly smiling countess and addressed her husband with a civility that betrayed no surprise or displeasure. Her poise contained what could have become the source of embarrassing speculation as if practiced in excusing a blatant indiscretion. She bade them both a cordial good evening and urged the smirking Camilla into a graceful retreat.

Geoffrey watched her go, heart sinking for the pain he knew lay behind the admirable facade of acceptance. He longed to race after her, to hold her tight and explain away the accusation he knew she harbored unfairly. He wanted to convince her that his actions were nothing more than a part he had played often and well, and was far removed from the place he held for her. But he could do none of those things. Time was short and he couldn't afford the luxury of easing her abused feelings. He couldn't desert his role and retain his credibility, and the role was all important. He could only hope that she would understand and forgive him. Or at least not hate him quite as much as her brief, unveiled glance had revealed.

With a nonchalant smile, Geoffrey turned to the woman on his arm and suggested they try the buffet table.

Chapter Eighteen

Geoffrey was miserably caught in the fine web of lies he'd spun. Each desperate turn only ensnared him tighter instead of providing an escape. Time was his greatest enemy, either passing too slow or too fast. He wanted to hurry it so he could resume his life with Rosalind. He wanted to stretch it to give him the needed opportunities to do what he must. He wanted to still it so the past couldn't catch him and the unknowns of the future couldn't destroy him. Yet time continued at its own pace, indifferent to his wants, trapping him in growing frustration at his inability to change it.

Since the night in Hanover Square, his relationship with Rosalind took a drastic turn. Any footholds he'd managed to claim on her rocky precipice were sheered away to present an insurmountable face. She'd met his clumsily offered apology with a rigid countenance that betrayed no anger or hurt then brushed him aside as if it meant nothing. And that was how she continued to treat him, as if he was no longer of any importance to her. There were no bitter words, no teary scenes. Nothing. As if she'd cut him out of existence. She treated him with an emotionless tolerance, as if resigned to his presence and determined to endure it gracefully. Any attempt by him to reestablish the closeness was handled with a stiff, formal rejection, the way one would deal with a stranger. As much as he would have liked to press against those barriers of apathy, his own conscience restrained him. How could he go to her and beg a second chance when still embroiled in the mess he'd made for himself? All he could do was chafe in the chill of her indifference and chance that she would have some feeling left for him when the matter was at an end.

However, the matter of the necklace wasn't so easily settled. Odette Bertram was coolly coy. While she encouraged his simmering attentions in public, she refused to meet with him in private where he could broach the subject of the rubies. She kept him in anxious attendance while tension-wracked weeks went by. He was certain each meeting was maliciously reported to his wife by a well-pleased Camilla though Rosalind never acknowledged the gossip. With each day, he expected word from the duchess telling him her patience was at an end, and beneath that sharp sword of Damocles, he searched for a way to conquer the teasing countess and return to his wife.

As he moped over his desperate situation, Henri passed him a folded note. Geoffrey let it lie unopened upon his lap for a long moment, then lifted it with a fatalistic resolve. He read the brief disclosure and gave a heavy sigh.

"I have until week's end," he relayed flatly. "It's a small comfort to know the date of a death sentence."

"Come, come. It's not as bad as all that. You still have four days," Henri said optimistically. He looked at his own reflection in the Hessians he was polishing and pursed his lips. "There is something I think you should know."

The hesitant statement brought Geoffrey's head up in alarm. "What?"

"I sold the necklace to Bertram as I said and we both assumed he'd give it to his wife. Bertram has a mistress as well, a rather prominent lady by the name of Wellsley. Perhaps he gave the rubies to her instead."

Geoffrey stared at him then dropped back on the bed with a tortured groan. "What else could possibly go amiss? I may well have wasted these past weeks wooing the wrong lady. It is too much. I give up. Pack our things. Vienna's dullness is just what I need."

Henri gave a narrow smile and continued to buff the glossy leather while his brother stared listlessly at the canopy in a picture of disheartenment. Then the dark blue eyes began to slant thoughtfully. Geoffrey rolled onto his stomach, expression animated by a sudden decision.

"Hank, fetch me some paper. It's time I settled this. I'll send invitations to the masquerade at Vauxhall to both ladies, and by evening's end I'll have the necklace from one of them."

Henri's brows soared at the ambitious plan. "Both in one night?"

Desperate times call for desperate measures.

"I wasn't aware you knew the Lady Wellsley."

"I don't, but she'll want to know me."

Henri smiled at the handsome man's casual conceit, knowing he was right. The only woman he had ever had difficulty charming was the only one he wanted.

Masquerade night at Vauxhall was always a lively scene. Decorous manners were often hidden, as well as identities when masks and dominoes were worn. The dashing blades used the affair to fall out of line and flirt outrageously with any lady who offered encouragement and even the chaperoned misses behaved with vivacious impropriety. It was also the choice of those who preferred to meet in secret, whether they be young star-crossed lovers or wayward wives who disappeared before the midnight unmasking.

The two brothers arrived on the twilight paths with very different purposes. Henri was eager to romance the society lovelies with the concealing black silk domino to span the barriers of rank. Geoffrey was tense and determined to make a success of his two concurrent trysts. They parted ways on the crowded walk and Geoffrey went to meet his first assignation in a leafy arbor.

The Countess Bertram was icily elegant in pale blue silk. She greeted Geoffrey with a languid offer of equally chilled champagne. For several minutes they exchanged a regimented discussion, then he excused himself on a vague pretext to see if his other companion had arrived.

Lady Annabella Wellsley was as far removed from the aristocratic countess as her fine champagne to the gin punch that awaited him at his second rendezvous. Bella, as she preferred to be called, was jovial and voluptuously well rounded, with a tousled mass of red hair and lively dark eyes. Her mismatched marriage of convenience to the staunch Thornton Wellsley was often compared to that of the Prince Regent and his flamboyant Caroline. She was similarly frank about her sensuous nature and the attractive viscount had more than her interest aroused. When Geoffrey took her fleshy hand, she used it to draw him close to the overly fragrant folds of her cloak.

"Good evening, my lord," she said breathily. "Imagine my surprise to receive your invite, as we're practically strangers. That's a situation we must remedy soon, don't you agree?" With contrived innocence, she managed to brush her ample bosom against him. He smiled widely to offset his hurried retreat then gulped down the punch he held.

"I do, indeed, my lady," he said silkily.

Her finger traced the outline of his mouth as she wet her

own lips. "Why waste time?"

"We needn't," he murmured.

For the next few moments, he struggled to seem willing without letting her aggressive amorousness overwhelm him. Had it not been for the occasional passersby, he feared she would have him straddled on the ground. For a well-bred lady, Bella Wellsley was very little of either. Gasping for air and fending off her too familiar hands, Geoffrey pried himself from her smothering embrace and placated her for a moment with a cup of the potent punch. Before she could launch another assault on his virtue, he rushed ahead with his plan.

"How lovely you look this evening, Bella."

"You think so?" she bubbled. "I never thought you noticed me before, though I've had my eye on you for some time." She gave a naughty chuckle and he had to nimbly side-step her playful fingers.

"I'm flattered, but I must return the compliment. I was captivated by you at the quadrille ball at the Cowpers'. I remember thinking how rubies would become you."

"A horrible squeeze, wasn't it? Rubies? I was wearing purple that night," she recalled with a doubtful frown.

His smile was quick and persuasive. "Rubies for the fire of your hair and your passionate nature."

"How pretty you talk," she oozed excitedly.

"And how pretty you would look to me with only the flash and heat of bloodred stones about your neck."

She shivered at the warm touch of his fingers against her throat. "What an intriguing idea. We shall have to do without the rubies. I don't own any. Will garnets do?"

She didn't have them. That realization sent Geoffrey's thoughts spinning ahead until he'd nearly forgotten his lusty companion. Her bold intrusion within the silken folds of his cloak startled him back into the present.

"Bella, could you possibly excuse me for a few minutes? There is someone I must speak to, then the rest of the night is ours." His eyes drooped with simmering promise and her breath expelled noisily.

"Don't keep me waiting long, my lord, or my ardor may cool beneath the lull of too much punch."

Geoffrey doubted that a bath of the hearty drink could quench her heated thirst. He granted her a lengthy kiss and had to wriggle away before she was too caught up to let him

183

escape. Once free, he breathed a grateful sigh and hurried to straighten his disheveled appearance before joining a rather peevish countess Bertram. She regarded him coolly through the slits in her mask as if reevaluating the course of the evening. Geoffrey knew of only one way to calm her temper without making complex excuses.

The countess leaned back from his very thorough kiss very much appeased. Her hand remained lightly on his sleeve.

"Chilton, what is that odd smell?"

"Smell?" Geoffrey scrambled to catch her meaning then remembered the odor of gardenias that floated about the other woman. "Oh. I bumped into some ill-bred chit who fairly reeked of the stuff. Awful, isn't it?"

"Nearly as bad as the taste of whatever you've been drinking."

"That was pushed upon me by one of Dunstan's associates. I couldn't very well refuse him. Here. This will make it better." He took a huge swallow of the champagne and smiled bravely as it collided with the sloshing contents of his stomach.

Coyly, the lady leaned forward to test his claim and sighed. "Yes, much better."

Feeling confident on the familiar stage, Geoffrey prepared to begin the well-practiced tale he had plied throughout France. Using the necklace had been his idea. Like the ring, it had belonged to his mother, yet he hated it as much as he cherished the circle Rosalind wore. He schemed to make his own and Henri's way by turning the fiery stone through the hands of countless faithless wives. Henri would sell the necklace to the husband and Geoffrey would woo it back from the wife. It had proved unfailing and was not a totally dishonest way to earn money. They did nothing illegal. It wasn't stealing. Geoffrey didn't trouble himself with the moral shades of the question when swaying a wayward wife with his easy flattering charm and encouraging kisses that would go no farther unbeknowst to them. The well-warmed women fell eager prey to Geoffrey's inventive story of how he'd been obliged to sell his mother's precious heirloom only to find he couldn't live with himself. He would offer a paltry sum, swearing he would somehow manage the rest to secure the treasured piece. With that earnest plea, the right inflection on a heavy sigh, and the desperate glimmering in his beseeching eyes, the overwhelmed lady was moved to make him a gift of the necklace. It was a deceiving piece of manipulation, but Geoffrey suffered no pangs from it. If the ladies had been true to their husbands, they wouldn't have been gulled by his smooth ploy. In his mind, they were deserving of the lesson.

"My lovely Odette, your beauty would be enough to draw me to you, but I must confess another reason."

The countess's fingers rubbed over the back of his hand. "Oh? Pray tell what that might be."

"I've a particular attachment to a piece of jewelry your husband purchased for you recently. You see, the rubies belonged to my mother and—"

The dark eyes snapped to attention. "Rubies? Did you say rubies? Purchased by Ivo? When?" Her tone was brittle.

"Several months ago." Geoffrey feared he had lost some of his sharpness with the slogging of too many spirits. He paused then rushed on to correct his error. "Perhaps I've misspoken myself. Perhaps it was meant for a gift and—"

"Our anniversary was two weeks ago."

"I must have made some mistake," he stammered hastily but the cold, angry eyes looked right through him. Her fingers tightened into talons on his arm.

"The mistake wasn't yours. Her birthday was last month. To me, he gives a string of indifferent pearls. Her, he bestows with rubies." Her voice grew strident before she realized he was staring at her through very round eyes. Pulling together her dignified poise in deference to her companion, she drew herself up regally and dismissed Geoffrey with a curt aside. "I fear I must cut our evening short, Chilton. I have matters to attend to at home."

Geoffrey didn't pause to watch the furious countess sweep away. He rushed back to the eager arms of Bella Wellsley for the answers he had to have.

The voracious lady's appetite hadn't lessened in his absence. After a long, reacquainting kiss, the forward Bella suggested they take a stroll. Hoping it would be of no great distance to tax his none too steady senses, Geoffrey let her take him in arm and steer him along the crowded walk. When he saw where she was leading, he nearly balked. Wise or not, he drew a deep breath and accompanied her into the maze of shadows.

When she turned into his arms, he knew a moment of complete, panicked loss. There was no checking the redhead's urgent passions. Her kisses were devouring and her tugging hands, impatiently persistent. Clothing askew and mask lost in the tussle, Geoffrey lurched out of the intimate embrace to pant a bit raggedly. He felt a kinship to a maid struggling to retain her virginity at the hands of a determined suitor. He thought of the many times he had pursued Rosalind thusly and was sorely ashamed.

Bella Wellsley regarded the plainly reluctant and nervous viscount with an amused expression. Her chuckle was good-natured. "If it had not been for your note, I would think an alliance with me was the last thing on earth you desired. I have never come close to raping a man, yet I feel it would come to that if this continues. Why did you ask me to meet with you, Lord Chilton?"

Geoffrey had recovered his breath and his composure enough to adopt a contrite voice. "I beg you not to take offense, my lady. Were I free to enjoy your charms, you would not find me hesitant. Even so, you tax my restraint to the limit."

"Nicely said, my lord. I am flattered though disbelieving."

"It's not you, pray believe me. I find myself unable to go contrary to the vows I spoke not so long ago. It makes you no less attractive, just me unfortunately old fashioned. It was not my intention to insult you."

The woman's smile was sadly wistful as she put a hand to his flaming cheek. "Nor have you. If his lordship had similar notions, I would not be accosting strange men in darkened bushes. I should beg your pardon." She sighed then gave him an amiable pat. "Now, my lord, tell me why you sought me out."

Geoffrey relaxed his pose and said candidly, "I'm searching for a ruby necklace. I was led to believe you might have received it from an—admirer."

"I see. So that was at the bottom of all your sweet talk." She was pleased to exact a deep flush. His lordship was most beguiling when contrite. "I did receive such a gift."

Geoffrey gave a thankful sigh but her next words preempted it.

"Unfortunately, a bad turn at the cards prompted me to sell it. I couldn't go to my husband to cover my debts. He would have been most disagreeable. The necklace was sold, you see, so I do no longer have it."

Trying not to let his dismay overcome him in his precarious state, he asked, "Whom did you sell it to?"

"A very discreet broker I've dealt with before. I could give you his name if you like."

"I would be most grateful."

"Indeed?" Her hopeful pout won her a most rewarding kiss. She lingered upon the inviting shirtfront to indulge in a moment of regret, then stood away to admire the handsome lord. "Your lady is very fortunate. If ever you should have a change of convictions, I would be most glad to hear of it."

He cupped her cheek in a gentle palm. "You would be the first to know of it, madam. You are a gracious lady."

Bearing the name of the pawnbroker, Geoffrey steered the resigned lady from the dark passages on his arm. Confident once more and fueled by an intoxicated joy, he brushed a thankful kiss on the masked cheek then was coaxed to ply the wanting lips. As he came away, a silly smile lingering on his face, he confronted a pair of strickened eyes. He squinted to focus his unsure attention on the figure in a rose silk domino then sucked in a horrified gasp when the loo mask was pushed up by unsteady hands to reveal his wife's ashen features. They exchanged a long, stunned look, then she spoke hoarsely to her lean companion.

"Take me home, Nate."

Before he could gracelessly untangle himself from Lady Wellsley, the rose domino had disappeared. He hurried in pursuit, but the darkness and his own hazy condition frustrated his search. He scanned the sea of anonymity until a shimmer of rose silk caught his eye. He lost no time in pulling the startled figure aside.

"I cannot let you go until you realize how much I love you," he vowed huskily and proceeded to ravage the astounded lips with a possessive passion. He was too lost in his own desires to note the strangeness of the shy response. It wasn't until his hands slipped within the cloak to handle the pliant figure that his eyes snapped open. The slight, willowy contours weren't those of his wife. Impatiently, he pushed up the mask to reveal the enraptured face of a total unknown.

"I beg your pardon," he mumbled in acute embarrassment. "I seem to have mistaken you for another."

"That's quite all right," the dreamy-eyed miss assured him in a failing voice. She followed the hurried retreat of the quixotic figure in the swirling black cloak and gave a tremorous sigh. Her friends would never believe her retelling of the

187

encounter, but she vowed not to miss another masquerade night.

Rosalind stiffened when she heard the front door open to admit her husband. She had been waiting in the darkened parlor after shooing a solicitous Everard away. Now that the moment was at hand, she had a cowardly desire to sneak off to bed unseen. She had no idea what to say and feared when the confrontation came she would be without voice. From the same well of strength that served her on the night of the Bertrams' rout, a steeling calm crept over her.

Since that night, she had become a stranger to herself, one of unshakable poise and cool forebearance of any emotion. She expected to be crushed by the knowledge of Geoffrey's faithlessness but she hadn't been. She would have believed the insincerity of the tenderness they shared on a rainy eve would destroy her yet it hadn't. Oddly, it had little effect on her at all. Nothing did. She withdrew into a close protective shell of numbness that refused to acknowledge any hurt. She moved by rote through the days doing what she felt she must, not out of any need but because it was expected of her. Her marriage was just another part of that disassociated life she once thought to lead. None of it was real so it couldn't affect her.

She thought she had come to terms with her lot. She was married to a man who didn't love her, who had bedded her in hopes of increasing his fortune, who openly courted other women. As unpleasant as it all was, it wasn't particularly shocking or unheard of. Like other wronged wives, she would be expected to be ignorant or tolerant of any Other Interest her husband might have, with no recourse other than to accept it with as much grace as possible. It would have been easier if her foolish heart didn't hang in the balance. She thought she had successfully dulled it to any further hurt until seeing him exit the Dark Walk on the arm of his rumpled and bruised-lipped lover. The whispers had been bad enough. The evidence was excruciating. She had fled, unable to control her feelings. Now, she had to hold a tight rein on them. Her pride could not bear his pity least he be moved by her distress to act charitably. She preferred his callousness to that.

Attention caught by her movement, Geoffrey stopped in

the doorway. He stood simply looking at her, making no move to approach. How weary he seemed, she thought fleetingly. Weary and rueful. Thankfully, he didn't launch into some repentant speech or try to sway her with convenient excuses. He met her eyes directly and spoke with a somber quiet.

"It was never my intention to see you hurt. Knowing how much I respect you, you must believe that."

Rosalind tried to reply, but the words dammed up in a choking knot in her throat. Struggling to dislodge them brought an unwelcome burning to her eyes. Tears were the last thing she wanted.

Heavily, he continued. "I know how it appears to you now. I cannot expect you to trust me and I won't ask it of you. I beg you not to judge me too harshly, at least not yet, not until you know all."

"Is there more?" The question escaped in a trembling cry. She bit her lip to retain the bitter sobs that would follow if unchecked.

"Roz, I never meant for this to happen."

A pathetic attempt at a smile wavered on her lips. "I see. Am I to forgive you then?"

His passionate outburst startled her somewhat. "I wish to God I could be certain you would."

"You don't need my forgiveness, my lord," she contended with a good deal more tartness. Though her eyes shimmered, the vulnerable tears refused to fall. The cool civility was beginning to slip back into place as an effective means of defense. That subtle, very purposeful withdrawal brought him several steps into the room.

"How very wrong you are about that."

The lower octave of his voice made Rosalind cautious. She knew too well the persuasive power he used against her better judgment. "It seems I have been wrong about a great many things."

The bitter turn of her phrase wounded him deeply, causing his convictions to fail him. In sudden desperation, Geoffrey found himself begging for her pardon. "Roz, let me explain what you saw. If you'd listen, perhaps you'd realize things are not what they seem."

She recoiled from that, a contemptuous look battling the dampness in her stare. Her voice was barely controlled. "Please spare me that, at least. Don't insult me by trying to justify yourself. I am not a simpleton, even though admittedly a fool. Nor do I suffer from failing vision."

Her eyes squeezed shut to close out the expression on his face. She turned away as a mournful sound escaped her. He would have gone to her then and taken her in his arms had it not been for an untimely intrusion.

"Yes, what is it?" he snapped at the apologetic footman.

"A Count Bertram here to see you, my lord."

Geoffrey nearly groaned in frustration. He cast a glance at his wife's rigid form, torn by the need to comfort her and the necessity at hand. With a savage sigh, he said, "Very well. I will speak to him in the book room."

"Very good, my lord," the servant murmured as he bowed out of the room.

Geoffrey looked back to Rosalind indecisively. What good could he do to dispel her mood in a few moments? He feared years would not be time enough to heal the damage that had been done between them. Without a word, he left her to her silent dignity to meet with his unexpected guest.

When the severe-countenanced Bertram exited after only a few words were exchanged, Henri entered the library to be met by his brother's oddly humored smile. He paused, not knowing what to make of it. "Have you found the necklace, Geoff?"

Geoffrey waved a distracted hand. "Oh, yes, that is, I know where to look. A pawnbroker has it."

"When do we see him?" he urged, puzzled by the colorless tone and alarmed by the crooked, meaningless smile.

"Tomorrow, if it still matters by then."

"Geoff?"

"You see, it may not signify at all by then. Bertram found himself compromised and affronted to the point of being obliged to call me out. I could well be dead by morning. That would solve everything, wouldn't it?"

Chapter Nineteen

As it was, Geoffrey was the only one to get a good night's sleep. He was almost cheerful when Henri came to ready him. The Frenchman's handsome features were sharpened with consternation though he tried not to display his emotion.

"Is this necessary, *mon frère?*" he argued with feigned disinterest. "To risk one's life over such trivialities is nonsense."

"An *affaire d'honneur* usually is" was the casual reply. *"Cherchez la femme.* And usually over a woman."

"But these women are nothing to you. Cry off, Geoff. Who would care?"

"It's already a *fait accompli.* It's too late. Perhaps if I am wounded, Rosalind will be moved to compassion." He seemed pleased with that notion.

"Idiot. She will hardly be flattered that you could be maimed or killed over a dalliance with another woman. She's probably hoping you'll be done in for your indiscretion."

Geoffrey pouted at his reflection as he adjusted his cravat. "More than likely. Do you think she knows of it?"

"The entire house, with the exception of the old lord, knew last night. It is all the talk below stairs. I cannot imagine her maid did not speak of it to her. Or the other one." He meant Camilla, of course.

"Yet she didn't come to me," he mused to himself. That she would be so indifferent when his death might be assured shortly after the sun rose was more wounding that the thought of Bertram's bullet. "Shall we go?"

When he turned, Henri seized him up to place sound kisses on either cheek. Geoffrey blushed as he always did at that emotional French gesture and offered a heartening smile.

"Don't worry, Hank," he said flippantly. "I've no plan to die this morning."

That may not be your plan, but what of Bertram's?" his brother stated with a return to his proper aloofness.

"I'll have to convince him. Come. I don't wish to be late and aggravate him even more."

191

As he followed Geoffrey's hurried descent of the half-darkened stairs with a more sober tread, Henri was called aside by a low voice. He was surprised to see Lady Chilton, clad in her morning wrapper, gesture to him from her doorway. When he approached, he noted how drawn and pale she looked, as if, like himself, she had found no sleep during the long night. She hesitated for an awkward moment then spoke with a quiet determination.

"I don't want him to come to harm over this matter, Henri. Please see to it."

Her cold hand was taken up for an admiring kiss, then pressed between two larger ones until their warmth was shared. It was unbecomingly bold behavior for a servant, but Rosalind took courage and comfort from the brief exchange. She said nothing more, releasing him to tend his lordship, to see to his welfare when she, because of circumstance, could not.

The ground was still wet with dew and icy slick on the grassy field where a grim Bertram and his second waited. He had purposely chosen a remote spot well outside London as if distance alone could prevent the eminent scandal. He extended a stiff greeting to the uncommonly jovial Lord Chilton who arrived punctually with his manservant in attendance. Chilton's high spirits continued as he was offered a choice of well matched pistols. He selected one casually and weighed it in his hand.

"I prefer blades, myself. That's the custom in France. Pistols are so indelicate and brutal."

"Let's get on with it," Bertram growled. He was growing unnerved by the banal banter. Only an imbecile would be so animated when facing the threat of death. Or one certain of his own victory. Despite the cool breeze, Bertram began to sweat.

"I am not a man of violence," Geoffrey continued. "I always prefer reason, but if that fails, one does what one must." He sighted down the long barrel with a practiced eye. "Nicely balanced," he mused. He pointed the muzzle upward, then in one smooth deadly movement, brought it down to the side at arm's length and fired without seeming to aim. A distant branch snapped cleanly. Geoffrey gave a broad smile and handed the piece to Henri. "Reload for me the way I like it."

Bertram was a bit pasty yet still determined. "I am no fan of violence myself, Chilton, but am compelled to demand satisfaction."

"Oh, I quite understand," the viscount agreed pleasantly. "I must have cost you a great deal of distress and discomfort with my loose tongue. I am excessively sorry, of course, but will comply honorably if you feel bloodshed is the only solution." He took the primed pistol from his second and this time, gave it a thorough examination. He sighed resignedly and his amiability ended. "Whenever you're ready, sir," he said grimly.

"I can see no other way around it," Bertram went on rather hurriedly. "It's nothing personal, just a matter of inconvenience where my wife is concerned."

"What would it take to soothe her aggrieved disposition?" Geoffrey asked with a subtle shrewdness.

"She showed particular interest in an emerald tiara at Senchal's," he recounted.

Geoffrey adopted his most accommodating smile. "Since neither of us has a real desire to do the other harm, I suggest an alternative to recompense you for my blunder. If a certain tiara was delivered to Hanover Square this afternoon, would your honor be met?"

Bertram pretended to give the matter careful thought, but Geoffrey could tell by his easier breaths that he had already decided. Magnanimously, he said, "I am satisfied." With that, he returned to his coach, not only appeased but alive and richer for it.

Henri expelled a heavy breath and shook his head. "Is there no one you cannot sway if you've a mind to?"

Geoffrey's response was pensive. The precariousness of the past few minutes he'd already put behind him as his thoughts sped onward. Facing Bertram's aim was the least of his many concerns. "Only one, my friend. We've some stops to make, but first, I want to go home."

He didn't need to explain his reasonings. She was waiting in the front hall. Her eyes flew over him in a quick assessment, as if to assure that he was whole and leaking nothing vital. Then, very coolly, she turned and went upstairs with a graceful decorum.

The proper rebuff told him her concern would not lend itself to forgiveness and Geoffrey was despondent. He climbed heavily after her in the darkest despair, never expecting to find her waiting on the landing. Without a sound, she came into his arms, clinging to him with a shivery desperation for what seemed an eternity. Then, still without a word, she stepped away and was gone. Geoffrey had to let her go. He deserved no more than the noncommittal embrace. Even that was a great show of benevolence considering the reasons he had given her to despise him. It was enough to hold to, to give him hope that he could yet reclaim her love. But not yet, not until the matter of the necklace was settled.

Hamlet, the jeweler, operated a shop in Cranbourn Alley. It was to him the desperate turned with pledges of inherited silver or wives' jewels for loans of extra cash. And to him Bella Wellsley had sold the ruby necklace.

The jeweler assessed the anxious-looking noble with a practiced stare. He knew all the blades who played deep and beyond their means, but this was an unfamiliar face. He waited patiently to be approached.

"Perhaps you can help me. I am looking for a piece of jewelry for my wife. A necklace. One with teardrop-shaped rubies set in gold and diamonds. I understand from a certain lady that you handled it for her recently. I would like to buy it. Name your price."

The jeweler smiled helpfully. "That I would if I still had it."

"You mean you don't?" The handsome face fell.

"Sold it this morning. A pretty piece it was, too."

"To whom?"

The sharp tone put the broker on the defensive. "I am sorry, sir. That is confidential. Is there something else?"

Geoffrey took a deep breath to control his frustration and smiled easily. "Yes. Show me something in amethysts."

He pretended interest in the display of several necklaces and chose one randomly. As he set up an account, he asked the now more congenial man, "The ruby necklace you sold is very important to me and my family. It was an heirloom. Could you just this once breach your rule and tell me who bought it?"

"Couldn't even if I wanted to. The lady came in heavily veiled. She asked for it direct just like you did."

Frowning slightly, Geoffrey took the wrapped necklace

and said a preoccupied thank-you.

As she readied for her evening at the opera, Rosalind discovered a tissue-wrapped box upon her dressing table. Finding no attached card, she opened the gift and stared in some bewilderment at the fashionable necklace of silver and coolly elegant amethysts. She lifted it out to admire the way the light shimmered in the faceted stones then frowned. It was from Geoffrey, of course. Only he knew of the new gown that had been delivered for her to wear this evening and what a superb match it would be to the jewels she held. Since he hadn't seen fit to give it in person, she could only guess at his motive. A peace offering? A bribe to soothe a guilty conscience? The furrows deepened in her expression. Did he think she would be so easily bought? She set it back in the box and tried not to think of it or him.

Garbed in the sleek, high-waisted gown of lavender taffeta, Rosalind sat restlessly as Jessup wound up her hair. Her eyes kept straying to the box. With a feigned nonchalance, she lifted out the necklace and let it lie against her throat. It felt so cold. Or perhaps it was her own skin beneath it.

"What a lovely piece, my lady," Jessup said innocently. "Will you wear it tonight?"

Rosalind looked at the stones and considered the symbol they would become if she wore them. "I think not." She returned them to the box and tucked it inside a drawer. Her evening would be difficult enough without the sparkling reminder of her husband's misconduct about her neck, tightening like a noose as the night wore on.

As it was, Rosalind bore the evening with admirable credit. There were whispers and looks, but she ignored them with a proud indifference. It would not do to let the society gossips feed off her misfortune. Since she was not shunned by the proper figures in their exclusive boxes, she assumed little of the incident had been made public. The rumors might flicker, but without facts to fuel the flame, they would soon die down. She wished the same was true of her own feelings.

Everard brought her home in a very pensive mood. He'd been a quiet companion all evening though she had paid small heed to it while so involved in her own troubled thoughts. When he saw her inside, he stayed her in the hall.

Her small hand was clutched between his. She looked up at him, a bit startled by his intensity.

"Rosalind, do you remember a vow I spoke to you on your way to the altar? I promised to be there for you if things went awry with Chilton. I want you to know that I meant that. Speak the words and I will take you away with me."

Rosalind stood transfixed. Before she could respond to the incredible speech, a cool voice intruded.

"A very kind offer, but why would she want to do that?"

They turned to the indolent figure of the viscount lounging in the door to the book room. His features were set in lines of wry amusement; however, the darkness of his slanting eyes bespoke nothing of humor. They were hard and well guarded. Rosalind stiffened beneath that bold possessive stare. Hew dare he make such a jealous claim on her? she fumed indignantly. She looked to Nathaniel with a fond politeness.

"Thank you for the pleasant evening, Nate, and for your treasured friendship." She squeezed his hands and stretched up to place a gentle kiss on his cheek. Without a glance at the narrow-eyed lord, she retired to her room.

Geoffrey's eyes traveled from the erect figure of his wife as it disappeared above to the surprisingly hostile Everard. "Come share a glass of port with me, Everard," he offered civilly.

The lanky young man grew even more disapproving. "I do not want to drink with you, sir."

Geoffrey's pretense of hospitality fell away. "And I do not want you to overstep yourself with my wife."

"It's not I who will take the steps. You are a fool, Chilton. Rosalind deserves better. I would not treat her so poorly were she my wife."

The judgmental speech made Geoffrey bristle. His reply was coldly cutting. "But she is not. She is mine."

"For now, my lord. Good evening."

Geoffrey frowned after him, annoyed by his presumptuousness and, deeper than that, afraid. The man's final lofty phrase had struck an uneasy chord in him, one that he couldn't toss aside as casually as he had in the past. A low chuckle disturbed him even more.

Camilla stepped from her vantage point in the front parlor where she had been listening in smug interest to the exchange. She approached the surly viscount with a sugary smile. "Such a withering reproof from the mild Everard. Really, Chilton, it seems everyone is set on thwarting your clever plans."

He scowled at the pretty, taunting face and said, "I am not interested in your observations, madam."

"Very well, but you might take an interest in those of your much aggrieved lady. A jilted wife, an eager and ever-present suitor." She pursed her lips in speculation. "It's enough to make you wonder. I know of several fine ladies who've born the babes of their lovers. They had less reason to stray than your precious Rosalind."

"Be thankful for your sex, madam. Had it been otherwise, I might be obliged to close that vile mouth of yours."

"Oh, I am very thankful and I believe you would be as well. Stop the pretense, Chilton. You know I am the one you desire." She leaned toward him, red lips ripe and inviting. Geoffrey's response was cruelly blunt.

"You delude yourself, madam. I've no interest in the type of spider that devours its mate."

The lilt of her laughter followed him up the stairs and her words lingered to provoke undo suspicion. Against his better judgment, he found himself intruding on his wife's toilet.

Cool dark eyes rose to regard him in the glass. Rosalind made no effort to face him as Jessup continued to take down her long, glossy hair.

"My lord, you wanted something?"

"Yes. I do." His tone was low and dangerously pitched. He stared pointedly at his lady's maid, but the loyal Jessup remained at her station.

"It is late, Chilton. It can wait until a decent hour." The curt accents made no attempt at civility.

"I think not," he disagreed softly. He began to prowl the room, aware of the cautious stare that followed him in the mirror. "I can wait."

Unwilling to continue to the more intimate details of her disrobing beneath his close scrutiny, Rosalind held up a hand. "Leave me, Jessup. I will call when I'm ready for you to finish." When the obedient servant took her leave, she turned on the stool to confront the restless figure of her husband. "Well? What is it that makes you interrupt where you are not welcome?"

"Am I truly welcomed anywhere by you?"

Rosalind ignored the sullen question and waited with an

imperious arch of one dark brow.

"The necklace I gave you would have suited your gown. Why aren't you wearing it?"

"Because it didn't suit me" was the chilly reply.

"You seem to have a penchant for disliking my gifts. Is my taste so abhorrent to you?"

"Only the reasons for them, sir. If that satisfies your curiosity, please leave me so I can ready for bed."

His smoky eyes slid toward the downy surface of her comforter then back, growing sultry with intent. "I can maid you myself," he offered silkily. His hand strayed to the bare slope of her shoulder to brush aside the cap of her sleeve and was met by a sharp slap across the knuckles. Her voice was just as stinging.

"No, thank you, my lord."

The wide mouth thinned with displeasure. His tone was smoothly contrary to the roil of emotions that churned inside. Those feelings of slight and injury were pushing him into areas he knew a wise man wouldn't tread. He didn't feel particularly wise at the moment. He was angry and he wanted to be assured that all his unwarranted doubts were just that.

"That was quite a bold speech from Everard. Does he have cause to make such an invitation to my wife?"

Rosalind's posture grew rigid. Her dark eyes stood out in brilliant relief against the pale alabaster of her skin. "Are you asking if I have encouraged Everard's friendship? Then, yes, I am guilty. If you wonder about more than that, you must phrase yourself more clearly."

"Are you going to run off with him or become his mistress?" That was clear enough and fiercely said.

"No. That would be quite impossible." Her frosty stare gave him no comfort.

"Is that the truth, madam?"

Rosalind's laugh was brittle. She stood to face him, tensed posture full of defiant outrage. "How droll that you should question me on fidelity. Believe what you will, sir."

A startled gasp escaped her as his large hands circled her arms like imprisoning steel cuffs. "You said you loved me. Is that still true or have your affections turned to another?"

That he would dare demand such a thing of her considering what he had put her through made Rosalind's fury seeth out of control. No longer was she coolly detached. Her words

198

rumbled with the passion of her anger. "You have shown no interest in my feelings to date, so why concern yourself with where I choose to bestow them?"

"Because I need to know that you still care for me."

"You don't *need* anything from me, not my companionship nor my love. You have found ample substitutes for both. The only thing you *need* of me is the fortune that I can bring you. Well, you won't have it so you might as well leave me now as later and spare us both the unpleasantness."

Her words struck so close to the mark that he was stunned into releasing her. Once freed, she thought only to escape his presence and fled the room in an agitated rustle of taffeta. She was halfway down the stairs when he called out to her, diverting her attention for a moment.

"Roz, wait. I'm not going to leave you."

As if she could believe him! Tears blinded her as she turned to continue her rapid flight. Through the watery blur of her grief, she misjudged a step. A jolt of agony shot through her foot, numbing her to the bumps as she tumbled in an awkward cartwheel of petticoats down the remaining stairs. Her head cleared slowly, coming to focus on a pair of worried blue eyes.

"My God, Roz, are you all right?" he insisted in a panicked voice.

"My ankle," she managed to moan.

Gentle hands plied the already swelling limb, making her cry out in distress. Still, it was a tender touch, one she had felt before, an eternity ago.

"Not broken, thank heavens. What a crazy thing to do. You might have broken your stubborn neck. Can you stand if I assist you?"

She sat up slowly and a new fear came to her eyes. "Geoffrey, call our physician. Have him come immediately."

The uncertain fright in her tone made him blanch in apprehension. "What is it? Are you in some other pain?"

"No. Just please fetch him for me. Please, Geoffrey." Tears began to pencil down her very pale cheeks.

"Of course, my precious love," he murmured huskily. He scooped her up and cradled her close to his chest to bear her back up to her room. His sharp call brought Jessup to attend her so he could race for the physician.

* * *

The pink of dawn warmed the pale walls of her room and shone with a deep molten splendor on the head bowed by her bedside. He had been there all night, her hand clenched tightly between his. She had seen him in the brief snatches of wakefulness during a fitful slumber. He was in such concentrated thought that she was able to observe him for some time before he noticed she was awake. How tired and serious he looked, and older without the devil-may-care energy to animate his appearance. But still so wonderously fair. Her heart felt a pain to rival that in her ankle.

The dark dusky eyes rose with a startled flicker. "Oh, good morning. Were you able to manage some rest."

"Some. More than you, it would seem. You didn't need to remain, my lord." She said that softly, kindly.

He didn't answer right away. His stare was intense, locking into hers in an unwavering probe as if trying to puzzle out something of great importance.

"How are you feeling?" His voice was low and oddly pitched, as if life had left it and the words were an effort for him.

"Sore all over. What did the doctor say?" She waited for his reply, her gaze searching his anxiously.

"That you'd be sore all over. Your ankle took quite a twist. He said not to try it for several days then to go very slowly." He paused as if there was more, then lapsed into an awkward silence.

"Is that all he said?" Rosalind prompted nervously.

Geoffrey came off the chair with a sudden violence and stalked across the room. The hands clenched behind his back kneaded together fiercely. He turned to regard her incomprehensibly, features working in agitation. Rosalind shrank from that dark accusing look, fearing its consequence. She trembled at his vehement demand.

"Why didn't you tell me about the child, Rosalind?"

It was her turn to fall silent as her eyes quickly lowered. Her face was as colorless as the bed linens.

"Well, madam? The doctor said you are at least three months gone. You had to have known of it. What reason can you give for not telling me of it? Why would you think I didn't have the right to know you are carrying my child?"

When she failed to respond, a slow, incredulous look crept over his face until his expression was blanked with a queer mix of hurt and outrage. Camilla's words provoked a thought so terrible, he could barely voice it.

"Unless it isn't mine."

The dark eyes flashed up, at first injured then plainly, furious. "How dare you suggest such a thing? If the child wasn't yours, I wouldn't be so distressed." That took him aback like a briskly delivered slap. "Are you satisfied now? Now will you leave me alone? You've done what you were paid to do. A pity you will have to wait six more months before you and my father can boast of your virility. Take your wait somewhere else, my lord. I do not wish your greedy eyes upon my belly in hopes of convincing this child to be a son. A cruel justice it would be to all if it proves a female child to spite you. Go away. My physical pain causes suffering enough."

Her head turned on the lacy bank of pillows and her eyes closed on the offensive sight of him. Thusly dismissed, Geoffrey hesitated for a moment, seeking some way to make amends. Finding none that would excuse his countless blunders, he quietly left the room.

One look at his grave features brought Henri up from his chair in an anxious start. "Geoff, what has happened? Is it your lady? Has something gone amiss?"

Had the circumstances been other than they were, Geoffrey might have been amused by the cynical Frenchman's show of concern, but there was no place in his heavy heart for humor.

"Only everything, Henri," he exaggerated in a fit of depression. "It seems you will be an uncle after the first of the year."

"But, *mon frère,* that is splendid news. It is what you wanted, *non?* A male child will bring you all you desire."

Geoffrey gave a wan smile.

"Why are you not pleased?"

"Should I be pleased that she hates me and hates the child she carries because it is mine?"

"Surely that is not so."

"You didn't hear her words or see the way she looked at me. What good is all I want at the cost of what I desire most?" He dropped with dramatic dejection upon the bed and heaved a futile sigh. "What could be worse?"

"Perhaps, this."

Miserable blue eyes slanted over to view the folded note his brother held. With a feeble moan, he pulled a pillow over

201

his head and cried in muffled despair, "No more, Hank. Spare me, please. I don't want to know what it says."

"It's from the duchess."

His hands came up to hold the pillow down more tightly. "Don't read it. I'm too tired to think and too unhappy to cope. Take care of it for me, Hank. Tell her you couldn't find me. Tell her I've gone to the country for the next ten years. Tell her I died of a broken heart. Tell her anything, but give me a few hours to sleep. Please, Hank."

Henri smiled fondly upon the prone figure and said easily, "I will see to it for you. It can wait another day." When there was no response, he called softly, "Geoff?"

His brother was asleep.

Carefully, Henri drew a coverlet over him. "Rest easy, *mon cher.*"

While Geoffrey slept, Rosalind lay in the next room brooding over her own troubles. Now that he knew of her condition, how would things change between them? Her hand rested protectively on the flat plane where life flourished as yet undetected. Her own confusion prevented her from answering his entitled question. How could she admit that she had stayed silent because she feared once he knew he'd accomplished his task, he would see no need for further contact with her? As much as she despised his motives and distrusted his reasons, she continued to yearn for his closeness. His stirring kisses could make her forget all. Beneath his sensuous touch, she could be free to express the love she had to hide deep within the misery of her soul. She upbraided herself for using the concealing silence to ensure his attention. Then, she forgave the trickery when in his arms.

Now that he knew of her deceit, he was free to spend his time with his various Interests while she was safely set aside to incubate his fortune. Even unfairly won, his insincere desire was better than the casual indifference she anticipated from him now that his part of the bargain was done. She cursed the fertility of her body for ending his charade of devotion, yet she could not hate the babe he had planted within her. How could she but love that part of him?

Teary eyes fastened on her still-flat middle, she wondered if that tiny life would yield son or daughter. She lay back with a sigh, not knowing which to pray for.

Chapter Twenty

After a long day and night of undisturbed discomfort and boredom, Rosalind awoke to a brilliant morning and a room overflowing with flowers. The fragrant scent from the pallet of blooms was deliciously heady and gave her spirits an immediate lift. Her smile remained even upon the experimental appearance of her husband. Seeing her lightened countenance, his hesitancy was washed away with a wide, dimpling grin.

"So you like them. I saw no use in giving you jewelry you could disregard in a box when these would be so much harder to ignore."

Her smile faltered slightly at the reminder but her words were gracious. "Thank you, my lord. Your thoughtfulness has cheered me considerably."

He was encouraged. "Then indulge me further. I thought you might enjoy escaping this confining room to breakfast with me in the garden. It's warm and very inviting outside."

His dusky eyes were warm and inviting as well and Rosalind found herself willing to be convinced. "Give me a moment to dress, my lord."

"Nonsense. Just throw on a wrapper. Everything's getting cold."

With his charming smile to urge her, Rosalind sat up and slipped into the robe he extended. Before she could think to object, he scooped her carefully from the bedcovers and bore her easily as she blushed in surprise downstairs and out into the temperate morning.

As he had promised, an elaborate meal for two had been arranged al fresco with more of the delicate blossoms adorning the table. She couldn't help but be delighted. They dined mostly in silence, each testing the other's mood. Geoffrey finally ventured into the volatile subject that was upon their minds.

"Have you told your father yet?"

Rosalind's pleasure in the morning began to fade. "No."

"Don't you think he has the right to know?"

She responded with a tart sarcasm. "Why, so he can gloat and pat you on the back?"

"No, because he's your father. Rosalind, please. I don't wish to upset you or provoke a fight but there are things that must be discussed between us."

His quiet and serious attitude tempered her hostility, but she couldn't quite control the brittle emotion the topic and his presence inspired. "What things, my lord?"

Geoffrey looked uncomfortably away, pretending to study the tropiary with concentrated interest. His words were even and paced as though they'd been carefully rehearsed. "I accept the feelings you have for me. I've earned your contempt and deserve to be scorned. I will not argue that. What I ask—no, what I beg of you, is that you not let your hatred of me extend to the child you carry. It is blameless and cannot be held responsible for the many sins of its father. Rosalind, promise me that you'll love our child. Every child needs to be loved by its parents. Every child."

Rosalind waited, hoping he would turn so she could see what strange emotions worked upon his features. When he did not, she laid a hand lightly over his.

"You have my promise."

The breath left him in short, uneven catches. His fingers curled about her hand and he lifted it to the unexpected dampness of his cheek. "Thank you, my lady. You are a kind and generous woman and I am very, very honored to share this new life with you."

He kissed her hand quickly, then released it as if he feared offending her. Her touch returned to his cheek to gently encourage him to look her way. Their glances mingled in a poignant search until called away by a regretful intrusion.

"*Pardonnez-moi,* my lord, but you have a visitor in the front room. Perhaps you would allow me to attend her ladyship while you see to your guest."

"Thank you, Henri," Geoffrey acknowledged reluctantly. "Forgive me for leaving you like this, Rosalind. May we speak later?"

She nodded to the somberly hopeful question and he was less uncertain about being called away. She watched him go, her heart laid bare in that wistful gaze until she remembered she was not alone. Her attention swiveled to the carefully averted face of Geoffrey's valet. She studied him for a long moment as if for the first time. Under that lengthy stare, the dark, eyes rose and they regarded each other steadily, cautiously, as if equals.

Henri Girard had always puzzled her. He was an arrestingly handsome man with fine, perfect features framed by a strongly squared jaw. She had heard the upstairs maids sighing over him and his enticing foreign manner. It was that manner that bewildered her. He was very correct and properly haughty and unfailingly courteous yet completely without humility. His groveling acquiesence bordered on mockery and his chiseled mouth seemed to twitch with an amused smirk. He had a way of fixing his dark, liquid eyes with an unseemly directness. No servant would dare be so bold. When he and Geoffrey were together, his attitude was almost casual and Geoffrey responded in kind. She hadn't forgotten the way he had taken her hand on the morning of the duel, nor could she ignore the candor in his unwavering stare.

"Will you have a cup of tea with me, Henri?"

"No, thank you, madame," he replied primly.

She continued her perusal and he didn't drop his eyes. "Henri, you have been with his lordship for a long time, have you not?"

"Since his arrival in Paris, madame."

"And how long ago was that?"

"Over twenty years."

"And you are very close."

"Madame?" The dark eyes narrowed suspiciously and his reserve increased to a formal stiffness.

"You are more than a servant. Geoffrey treats you more as a friend."

"*Oui*," madame. His lordship has been very generous with his good nature."

She began to smile. The Frenchman was fencing with her, using his polite vagueness to parry her questions. "And you, Henri, do you consider him your friend?"

The pose dropped for the briefest instant as he said, "I would lay down my life for him and he wouldn't have to ask it of me." Just as quickly, he realized he'd revealed too much and the artificial posture returned.

Feeling she'd won a small concession from the guarded steward, Rosalind relaxed her own reserve. "I'm very glad he has someone like you to see to him."

Her sincere words made Henri's affected stance loosen and he gauged the woman he had held a degree above contempt with a new awareness. He could see what had drawn Geoffrey—the toughness, the intelligence, the gentle biting wit wrapped up in the confines of an uncertain shyness. And though he didn't like believing it, he thought his brother had chosen his wife amazingly well, with or without the added attraction of her wealth.

Rosalind toyed with her teaspoon, then asked, "Did his lordship talk to you of his life in England?"

Henri's expression abruptly closed. His reply was frigid. "I believe he would prefer to forget it, madame." Was there a subtle warning in the dark eyes?

"Was it as bad as that then? His father must have been a dreadful man to have so terrified a child."

Henri gave her a sharp look, wondering what Geoffrey had told her to give her such insight. He offered no comment, not realizing the tightening of his fine lips was statement enough.

"It must have been awful to force his mother to flee the country," she mused somberly.

"It was to save her life and Geoff—his lordship's, and none to soon, it was. I have been too outspoken. You should hear of these things from him not me."

"I'm grateful he found happiness in France. He speaks most lovingly of his family there."

Henri's eyes lowered and he was silent.

The sun had slipped behind a curtain of clouds and Rosalind shivered in the absence of its warmth. "I should like to go in now. If you would let me use your shoulder, I think I can manage."

Henri assisted her up and let her cling to him for balance while she tottered on one leg. She overestimated her own tolerance of her injury and cried out in hurt when applying the slightest weight. Gallantly, Henri lifted her into his arms.

"I believe this the more practical solution, madame. Where do you wish to go?"

She instructed him to take her to her room. With her arms looped loosely about his neck, she surrendered to

206

the awkward position with the best possible grace. As they passed the doors to the parlor on their way to the stairs, two voices could be heard exchanging rapid words in French. One was Geoffrey's, the other a woman's. From over Henri's shoulder, she could see the woman's profile as she argued with her husband who wasn't visible through the gap in the doors. The heavy veil made her certain it was the same woman from Grosvenor Square. How could he be so callous as to invite his mistress to her own home? She turned away, a small sound of distress catching in her throat.

"I'm sorry. Have I hurt you?" her bearer asked quickly. She shook her head, not trusting her voice to support the claim.

"Are you in much pain, madame?" he asked solicitously.

"Nearly more than I can bear" was her faint reply.

"Shall I send for your physician?"

"No. I shall have to learn to bear it on my own. I will manage, thank you."

"Yes, madame."

He laid her carefully upon the bed and went so far as to arrange the covers about her. He lingered for a moment as if he wanted to say more.

"Thank you, Henri. You've been very kind." She made herself smile at Geoffrey's man despite her unhappiness and was nonplussed when he bowed in a courtly fashion over her hand.

"And Madame is very brave," he murmured before making a prompt exit.

Rosalind's wish to mope in silence was foiled by a rap on her door. In her surprise, she found no objection to her father's entrance. James Dunstan had been slowly regaining his strength, enabling him to sit up in a chair for extended periods, but she was unaware that he could walk about. He came to her bedside slowly, hesitant gait aided by a dark walnut cane. He looked winded but had a smile to share with his daughter.

"How do you feel, Rosalind? It seemed unfair to have both of us abed."

"Should you be up, Papa?"

"No fussing, girl. I hear enough of that from your stepmother. I came to bestow a bit of that mother-henning on you, if you'd allow it."

He waited hopefully for her response. Rosalind could never remember him waiting on her before and it quite confused her. Everything about him seemed different, as if the slowing effect of his infirmity had crept into other aspects of his life to temper his brash urgency to dominate all before him. Oddly, he appeared content with it and, for a change, with her.

"Sit down, Papa. I've something to tell you."

In the room below, the meeting there was far from as successful.

"A week, Lisette," Geoffrey was imploring. "I need that long. I've found the necklace, but the owner will not be returning to London for another week. I can get it for you then. It's out of my hands. Surely you must see that."

The duchess patted his hand soothingly as if to dismiss her earlier words. They had been dark with shadowed threat. "Of course, I do. You may have your week but no more. I am booking passage out of England. I expect the rubies to sail with me or we both sink together. *N'est-ce pas?*"

"Yes," he said flatly. "You've made yourself very clear."

He was brooding dejectedly when Henri arrived on the heels of the Frenchwoman's departure. "One week," he moaned heavily in answer to the probing gaze. "I've managed to put her off that long, but then what? When I don't have the necklace for her, she'll go to Rosalind and all will be ruined."

"I think you fail to give your lady enough credit, *mon ami.*"

Geoffrey shot him a doubtful look, his spirits too low to accept the frail hope. "It wouldn't matter. Her father would toss me out. His ideas of breeding wouldn't allow someone like me in their exclusive stable. No, I can't risk being found out. If only there was time, I could have the damned thing copied even if the cost would bury me. I see no way out of this corner, Hank. Perhaps it's time to put mistakes behind and do as you've been suggesting all along."

"You would desert her after filling her with your child?"

Henri's tone was so condemning, Geoffrey winced. "What choice do I have? Things will only worsen. I

208

cannot bear the unfair hurt I've caused her to endure thus far. How can I expect her to weather more? Better that I leave her now."

"You could learn something of courage from your lady, Geoff," his older brother chided. "She would not abandon you so."

Geoffrey stared at the uncharitable visage and frowned. "I don't understand this sudden sympathy for Rosalind. You've never cared for her by half."

"Do you?"

"Do I what?"

"Care for her. The truth, Geoff. I need to know if you are serious. None of your fancy speeches. Do you want to stay with this woman, to make your life and family with her? Would you be content to keep her even if the fortune doesn't accompany her? Think hard and answer me truthfully."

Geoffrey studied his hands for a long moment then said softly, "Yes."

Henri tipped his head up so he could look into his eyes. "Again."

"Yes."

"*Très bien.*" He gave Geoffrey's chin an encouraging chuck then rubbed his own thoughtfully. "A week is not much time so we must get busy. I will see if I can discover more from the jeweler and will have the house-maids ask their acquaintances if any of their mistresses has a new ruby necklace. You, *mon frère,* see to your wife. I believe she saw you with Lisette and is not as indifferent as she'd like you to believe. She loves you, Geoff. Do not take that for granted. Even a woman in love can be a dangerous creature when slighted. Clip her claws before you feel the cut of them."

Geoffrey puzzled over the reserved Frenchman's change of heart and asked the reason for it. Henri raised a refined brow and explained simply, "Because I think she will provide me with an exceptional niece or nephew. And she will make you less of an *enfant gâté.*"

"Who is spoiled?" was the pouty challenge.

Henri laughed, his case proven.

The earl was overjoyed by the news of his impending

grandchild. It seemed to magically restore much of his vigor and, despite Camilla's objections, he refused to return to his sickroom to idle away another day. To show his pleasure with Geoffrey, he gave the viscount his choice of any of the fine horses from his excellent stock. Geoffrey was too much of a gentleman to seem less than enthused. Better was the transfer of one of his shipping companies into his son-in-law's name. For Rosalind, at Camilla's urging, he began arrangements for a lavish affair so he could make his announcement to all the high members of ton in grand, if indelicate style. Little did he realize how this proud gesture alarmed and embarrassed his daughter. He couldn't believe she would not delight in the spectacle, especially after Camilla assured him it was so. Stacks of elaborately penned invitations were dispatched and Camilla gathered the staff for her precise instructions. She meant for the event to be the talk of the Season. Thusly involved, she granted Dunstan a much appreciated lull from her pampering and he was able to venture back to his business.

Geoffrey viewed the approaching date of the gala with as much apprehension as his wife. Friday, he thought glumly. How appropriate that the eve of his ruin be a night of unrivaled celebration, a sort of last fling in the world of plenty. A proper send-off it would be. Henri's diligent pursuit of the necklace had yielded no clue and it was his fatalistic belief that it had vanished along with all his hopes and ambitions. He spent the last of his privileged evenings in urgent sociability, sharing games and posing languidly at White's with Brummell and his blue-and-brass entourage. The days, he used to gently court his wife.

Rosalind was wary yet enticed by the viscount's determined suit. Each day heralded an abundance of fresh flowers, exotic ices, and sugar plums from Gunther's, novels from Hatchard's, and her husband's amiable company. Always polite and proper, he saw unfailingly to her amusement whether it be a morning in the sunny garden listening to his crooning rendition of Byron or an excursion in Hyde Park at his inexpert handling of the reins. His tender consideration lulled her suspicions and she began to anticipate their time together, grateful for the distraction it served to her worries over the upcoming event. The only time Geoffrey left her was during Nathaniel Everard's visits. He absented himself without complaint, never rekindling the volatile discussion that precipitated her accident.

And as she received his gentlemanly attention, Rosalind couldn't help but wish he'd be less so. His careful, inoffensive handling made her yearn for a more impassioned touch. In such close company, she was ever reminded of how splendid their few times together had been. Geoffrey Chilton still held her in a fascination of longing and excited desire. Though he played the perfect companion, she was acutely aware of him as a man, a man she desperately wanted for all the cautions her mind would insist upon. She bore his name and would bear his child. How could she pretend he wasn't a part of her? Her heart ached for the chance to forgive him and take him back into her arms, yet her pride could not condone such a step without concessions from him.

As she watched him daily, her eyes avidly poring over his elegant form and pleasing face, a want to jealously possess him proved a constant torment. Knowing he'd been with others and perhaps still sought them out, should have discouraged her, yet she found her dependence all the stronger for it. She was obsessed with winning his love and singular devotion and frustrated by her inability to have either. Had she been pretty or clever like her vivacious stepmother, she would have had reason to hope. As it was, as plain dreary Rosalind Dunstan Chilton, how could she think to keep her vital husband's interest from straying? She had seen how he affected women and knew how he devastated her. What could make him avoid the eager temptations ever at hand to attend his unexceptional wife?

Her unhappy broodings made his actions suspect. Why was he being so kind to her? Was it guilt that demanded his attention or could he be genuinely fond of her? Were his mannered affections tempered by a fear of offending her or a sign of his disinterest? Now that she was with child, did he consider that part of their relationship at an end or had his passions only been feigned to further his fortune? She wanted to believe he had taken some pleasure from their nights together. She needed to know he had desired her, if not enough to remain faithful, then at least enough to want her on occasion. She hated her willingness to be used in that manner, on a whim, at his casual inclination. However, her feelings could not be suppressed by force of will or painful realities. Nor could she seek relief of them elsewhere. In her position, it would have been fashionable to take a lover. Rosalind dismissed that solution. What purpose would her own infidelity serve? She neither courted revenge nor the complications involved in a frivolous affair. And quite simply, she wanted no one save her husband.

Had she been able to read his thoughts, Rosalind's mind would have been at ease. While Geoffrey lounged beside her in the sun, his eyes strayed from the text he read to follow along the silken line of her figure, wondering how she would react if he were to cast the tepid verse aside and bury his face in her bountiful bosom. While they exchanged conversation, he scanned the luscious softness of her lips, savoring the memory of their sweet compliance. When he transported her in his arms, the feel of her inviting curves inspired a heated anxiety that only the sharpest rein could curb. He had to tell himself that she didn't desire his affection and most likely would resist any overture that suggested intimacy. He'd shattered her fragile trust, and winning it back required a delicate approach. He couldn't afford a rutting passion to destroy the tentative acceptance he'd managed to earn. Still, he had little confidence that the shallow relationship would survive the truths the duchess meant to tell. Even if Rosalind could forgive him the lie, she would never accept the facts of his past.

Knowing he would possibly have no other time alone with her, Geoffrey intruded upon the final minutes of his wife's toilet. The large, apprehensive eyes sought his in the glass and the fearful look abated. Her smile was faltering but warm with welcome.

"Wait a moment, Chilton. I am almost finished here. I am counting on the strength of your arm to get me downstairs tonight."

Knowing she didn't refer to her injury but to her anxiousness over the gathering company below, he murmured, "I'm at your service, my lady."

He lingered at her request, trying to remain unobtrusive beneath Jessup's quelling gaze. When Rosalind finally turned to him, Geoffrey was dazzled. He couldn't compare her to the flawless beauty of her stepmother, for they were so different there could be no fair likening. Camilla was all surface perfection. Rosalind's attraction ran deep. The ebony-haired lovely could turn the eye and provoke lusty thoughts, but she lacked the earthy complexity it took to become ingrained with subtle permanence upon the heart. Camilla would amuse for the moment; Rosalind would fascinate for a lifetime.

"You look magnificent," he judged with a low sincerity which fused her cheeks becomingly. Her hand rose uncertainly to the plunging scoop of the décolleté gown. The ruby satin glowed hotly next to the rosy warmth of her skin. She had been surprised that her father would have such a voluptuous creation made for her, its curving lines so frankly displaying her figure and the neckline immodest to the point of escaping decency by a scant border of ivory lace. The smoky eyes drank in that teasing near exposure with candid appreciation until she felt scorched by his gaze.

Alarmed by his perusal, Rosalind turned to the mirror in dismay. Now that he had called attention to it, she wasn't sure she dared wear the gown in public. The fitted bodice squeezed her breasts upward to create a precarious swell of creamy flesh. An incautious move would convince them to spill forth in deference to gravity. Her thoughts were busy devising a means to save her modesty, perhaps with a shawl or lacy tucker, when Geoffrey's hand lay lightly upon her shoulder. Her heart gave a nervous tremble though she tried to remain aloof.

"I wish this night was over," she said vehemently, hoping to distract him.

Geoffrey's fingers tightened until she winced in discomfort. "Don't hurry it, precious one. I should like it to last forever."

The husky insistence in his voice made her shy from him uneasily. He was suddenly too intense, too disturbingly male. To cover her disquieting awareness of him, she began to chatter rapidly.

"Papa's going to make some grand announcement to embarrass me for the rest of my days. He has no consideration for my feelings. He expects me to bear up like Cammy does. I wish I had a pinch of her poise to sustain

213

me. I am such a timid goose."

"Nonsense," Geoffrey stated firmly. He caught her hand and pressed it. "Camilla could do with some of your character." Before she could disagree, he said, "Besides, I've discouraged your father from making a speech. News of your condition will be spread decorously through the gossip mill. So you see, you've no reason to fall into hysterics."

"I do not have hysterics."

Her staunch decree made him smile, remembering a feisty chit who had boldly snared his affection on first meeting. "I forgot. Forgive me. This is your evening, Rosalind, in your honor. You will be at my side, carrying my child and both things make me so very proud and so very fortunate."

Her breath drew in sharply as her hand rose to his lips. They brushed across it lightly. He paused when her fingers closed convulsively about his. Slowly, he turned her hand to kiss her lacy palm then her wrist where it was left bare by the wispy fingerless gloves. Her blood raced beneath that touch. His eyes lifted to her in question, seeking the cause of this sudden panic. Dare he hope it was the same that made his pulses thunder? Her eyes were dark and dilated, drawing him into their deep, drowning pools. They began to slowly close as he leaned toward her until the touch of his lips sealed them tightly.

Their kiss was awkward and experimental, yet when Geoffrey would pull away in uncertainty, Rosalind's arms curled about his neck to encourage his unconditional return. She met him with an unrestrained urgency that would deny their guests below in favor of the celebration she longed to host between them. She whispered his name with a sighing expectancy as his mouth blazed a heated trail from her avid lips to the fragrant valley of her breasts. Her hands caught in the dark gold of his hair to mesh and tangle in impatient desire. A moan of breathy ecstasy escaped her as his hands pushed her straining bosom even higher so he could rub his face upon the luscious, rounded curves of scented satin.

And when his greedy mouth rose to take hers once again, its reckless reception drove him to disregard time and place in lieu of the promising temptation of her parted lips. With a purposeful step, they were at the edge of the bed, then tumbling back upon it. Satin crunched in sensual invitation and Geoffrey's hands were hot in their hurried caress of her thighs.

"Rosalind, I'd like a word with you."

"It's Papa," she squeaked in maidenly alarm against her husband's determined kiss.

"Maybe he'll go away," Geoffrey panted hopefully and proceeded to steal her breath with a plunging kiss.

A brusk knock shattered that illusion. Rosalind retrieved his exploring hands and pushed him aside so she could sit up. Much of her struggle to resist him was halfhearted, for even as she fended off his insistent embrace, she continued to meet his urgent mouth.

"Geoffrey, stop," she whispered unconvincingly between the ardent exchanges.

"Is that what you want?"

"No," she murmured and indulged in another lengthy union of breath and tongues. Resolutely, she vied for leverage, hands bracing against the hard muscle and racing pulse of his chest. "But we must. Papa—our guests—"

"Let's send them all away. Roz, I need you now."

The rough rumble of passion made her groan in frustrated desire and necessity. She succumbed to another long moment beneath his persuasive touch.

"Rosalind, are you all right?" came the anxious voice on the other side of the door.

"A moment please, Papa," she called out and ducked under Geoffrey's arm to free herself from him.

They regarded each other with an open need to know the fulfillment of what they'd started. Rosalind's hand fitted against his flushed cheek. "Promise that we'll take this up at the evening's end," she beseeched huskily.

"It will be a very short evening. I anticipate you tiring early and I, being a thoughtful husband, will see you to bed." His lips pressed hotly to her palm.

"I am fatigued already."

His head dipped down. Determinedly, she evaded the much desired taste of him and gave him a forceful shove. "Don't make this more difficult than it is."

With an aggravated sigh, Geoffrey went to the window. He threw open the sash and gulped in the stabilizing night air while Rosalind tidied her appearance.

"Come in, Papa."

215

Dunstan looked from his daughter's heavy eyes and puffy mouth to the rigid stance of his son-in-law and raised a suspect brow. He would never be discourteous enough to suggest the two of them were involved in unseemly behavior while a hundred guests waited below. It was satisfaction enough to know they were getting on better. He was glad to dismiss the murmurs Camilla offered that they were on the outs.

"How lovely you look," he said fondly, cupping Rosalind's chin in his hand. "Nothing becomes a woman like motherhood. It was so with your mother."

Though the remark made her heart clutch happily, Camilla brushed it and him aside with a "Dunstan, pray do not be so indelicate." She hadn't missed the couple's tosled appearance either and it strained their countenance.

"This is a special night," he continued, undaunted. "I've been given a treasured gift and it deserves one in return."

Rosalind took the flat box with a bemused smile. A reward for granting him eternity, she thought wryly. However, she was in no mood to deny him his triumph especially when Geoffrey came to stand at her shoulder. Just the heat of his presence was enough to stir all sorts of wicked thoughts of how they would spend the rest of their evening. She opened the lid and exclaimed softly. That awed sound was echoed more hoarsely behind her.

From its bed of rich black velvet, Rosalind lifted the exquisite work of gold, diamonds and rubies. The gold and fiery gems formed an intricate mesh from which the bloodred stones dripped in stunning elegance.

"Camilla said you'd admired them on Lady Wellsley and insisted I get them for you," her father explained proudly.

"I don't recall seeing it before but it is truly spectacular. Thank you. I shall wear them tonight. Chilton, would you fasten it on for me?"

Geoffrey took the dazzling necklace she extended and lay it about her throat. How suddenly cold his hands were.

Camilla watched his expression in smug amusement. "I thought it a proper gift considering its background. But then, Chilton can tell you better than I, can't you, my lord?"

Rosalind swiveled to look up at him. His eyes were

216

fixed on the stones with a flat, expressionless stare. His voice was oddly strained, almost a whisper. "They're called the Ruby Tears," he said softly. "They were a gift to my mother from my father. I didn't expect to see the necklace again." He lifted his gaze to Camilla, reading the malicious mirth in her expresssion. Who had she talked to? Lady Wellsley? More likely either Lord or Lady Bertram. He had heard whispers that the courtly lord showed an interest in Dunstan's youthful wife. She knew how surprised he would be and savored the awkwardness of his position.

"Of course," Rosalind said, holding up her hand. "It's a match for the ring."

"It was supposed to be."

The terseness of his reply made her look to him sharply. His manner was strange, angry. More secrets? she wondered with a faint frown. She touched the necklace, curious as to why he didn't revere it like he did the ring.

"Shall we go down to join our party?" Dunstan suggested. He held out his arm for his daughter, offering his support and his favored patronage. She took it with a cautious smile.

Behind them, Camilla extended her hand. "Will you do me the honor of your escort, Chilton?" she cooed.

With wooden formality, he placed her gloved fingers in the crook of his elbow and led her to the celebration.

Chapter Twenty-one

Rosalind's evening of sultry promise faded upon her arrival at the gala in her honor. Amid all the exclusive guests, only two stood out in her mind, the Countess Odette Bertram and Lady Annabella Wellsley. Both greeted her with a cool civility, much too refined to behave otherwise before such elite company. In the presence of her husband's lovers, she could hardly feel at ease. She wondered if he was disturbed by the awkwardness of the situation as he met each lady with indifferent courtliness. Beneath the carefully maintained facade, a tension simmered between the countess and him whereas Lady Wellsley was decidedly coquettish. Bertram himself exchanged a short howdy-do and Rosalind writhed miserably in the center of all the illicit intrigue.

Ankle still too tender to attempt more than a graceless hobble, Rosalind was confined to a comfortable settee. While she received congratulations and well wishes, Geoffrey stood behind her like a rigid sentinel, his cool fingers resting on the slope of her shoulders. She could feel his tenseness through that light touch. Gone were the persistent caresses and silkily veiled intimacies, and she wondered unhappily which of the ladies distracted him. Affixing a frozen smile, she vowed to survive the evening, though with each solicitous inquiry about her health, her mood sunk lower. How could she pretend a happy pride in her condition when her husband's virility was scattered about the female company with such a casual affront? Finally, she could endure no more of the private pain. Alone, she could bear it, but here on public display, it was nearly impossible. She couldn't pretend it didn't matter. Each time one of the infamous ladies circulated near her, a hot anger arose. It wasn't logical that she would wish to tear out their hair as if they were solely responsible for her husband's deceit. Yet it was easier to vent her frustrated hurt on them than to turn it upon the object of her ill-fated love. Though Geoffrey was far from innocent, she steadfastly sought to protect him from her own enraged feelings. Those strong, unfounded instincts served to confuse her more. If only she could harden her heart or serenely accept his infidelities.

She stood, and Geoffrey's hand was instantly at her elbow. She couldn't bring herself to look at him. "I'm very weary. I should like to go upstairs," she said in a constricted undervoice.

Wordlessly, he lent his arm and helped her to the door where she graciously thanked her parent for his well-meaning gesture. He was not at fault, at least not directly, for her present woes. She extended her cheek for his kiss and was given a gentle hug as well.

"I am very pleased with you, Daughter," Dunstan said gruffly, uncomfortable with the display of his emotion. "You have given me a son I can be proud of and an heir to complete me. I am a happy man."

When she gazed up at him, her dark eyes swam and glistened as brilliantly as the stones about her neck. "That's all I've ever wanted to do, to make you proud. Good night, Papa."

As they ascended the stairs, leaving the noisy revelry behind them, Rosalind leaned heavily on the supporting arm, depending on its guidance to lead her through the shimmering haze of her unshed tears. Geoffrey left her briefly in the upper hall to speak to Henri. The Frenchman's dark eyes flashed up to her then dropped quickly away. His features were grim as he nodded to the viscount's hastily spoken words. Was it his task to arrange a rendezvous with one of his master's lovers, she wondered dispiritedly as he hurried below.

Once within her room, Geoffrey dismissed Jessup, saying he would maid his wife himself. Rosalind offered no protest. She limped awkwardly to the window to gaze out into the indifferent night. Geoffrey hesitated in the room's center, held by a curious battle of emotions as he viewed the silent figure. The room was lit solely by the golden aura of firelight which drenched her bright gown with a glow akin to living flame. He knew he should concentrate on retrieving the necklace yet his eyes lingered over the elusive woman. He had felt her cool withdrawal from him and was eager to coax back the warmth they had shared earlier. That tempting challenge pushed aside the urgency of his purpose to one of longer standing. He checked his pocket watch. There was ample time to secure both.

He felt Rosalind tremble when his hands slid up her arms to the fair, silken luxury of her shoulders. He bent to brush his lips along that smooth expanse until her stilted voice checked him.

"I do not wish to keep you from your pleasure, my lord."

His reply was husky. "Thank you."

Rosalind gasped as his mouth pressed hotly to her throat. Her resolve wavered beneath the leap of her impassioned pulse. Then she said more firmly, "I know you've other matters on your mind. Please feel free to attend them."

His startled eyes rose to their reflection in the dark pane. "Oh? And you know what they are, madam?"

"Not by name, sir. I do not know your preference, only your inclinations."

Rosalind was decidedly stiff beneath the leisurely massage of his strong fingers. She studied her own taut features in the glass. His were too beguilingly fair for her frail will.

"And how am I inclined?"

"Do not mock me, my lord." She shrugged away from his touch and faltered across the room to seek the warmth of the fire instead of a more seductive heat. "You have played your part admirably this evening, but the pretense need not extend to my chambers. Pray do not keep your lady waiting."

Geoffrey stared at her rigid back with open astonishment. He'd no notion her thoughts worked in that direction. Softly, he said, "I fear I have neglected her unforgivably. It's time I made amends."

"Who do you go to, Geoffrey?" came her involuntary cry. It was followed by a tormented moan. "No, don't tell me. I know too much already. Just go to her and spare me the details."

"But you should know of them," he insisted. "The woman I'm spending the evening with plagues my every thought. The time I'm away from her weighs heavy and whenever she's near, I can scarce control my need to have her. Every morsel of affection she spares me only feeds my hunger. She is my *raison d'être*, my true *affaire du coeur*. The thought of a future without her is too terrible to consider. If only the deeds of times past didn't conspire to keep us apart."

Rosalind stared into the flames. It was all too cruel, yet she had to know more. Her heart was breaking as he spoke such feeling for another. Faintly, she asked, "Is she married?"

"To an incredible fool of a man who doesn't deserve his good fortune."

Her grief trembled in her words. "You sound as though you love her." Her eyes squeezed shut in agony at his candid reply.

"I do."

Firelight reflected in the jewellike wetness upon her cheeks. She drew a deep, resigned breath, realizing she could no longer keep what she never possessed. "Go to her then with my blessing."

There was a moment's silence then he said quietly, "I'm glad you approve."

Rosalind's startlement escaped in a choked-off cry as she was abruptly turned to meet the full measure of his powerful form. Her teary eyes flew up in amazement and remained open in sheer stupefaction during his lengthy, claiming kiss. When he stepped back, her breath spilled out in a series of shaky sobs. It was his turn to stand in uncertain surprise when she pushed at him and whirled away. His soothing grip brought the quaking line of her shoulders back against his chest as she was shaken by silent weeping.

"Roz—"

"No, Geoffrey, please," she beseeched in a faltering voice. "Please don't torture me like this. Don't ask me to have faith in fantasy. Be merciful enough to let me suffer the truth."

"The truth, Roz? I've told you the truth."

"No," she wailed. "I know the truth. I've seen it with my own eyes."

He pulled her tighter into the circle of his arms where she sagged pitifully, her strength deserting her. Her tears fell more rapidly as his kisses scattered over her crown of glossy plaits and against her temples.

"Believe what's in your heart," he urged, "not what your

eyes and ears have told you. Believe in the love that bound us together from that first meeting."

"It was a lie! It was all a lie!"

"No. Not the way we feel for each other."

"Stop it, Geoffrey. No more. You have what you wanted. There's no need to hurt me so."

"I never meant to hurt you. You're what I want, Rosalind. Don't torture me with your indifference."

Her head fell back weakly against his shoulder as her eyes closed in a futile struggle to halt the flood of dampness that streaked her face. "I wish I was indifferent. I wish I didn't care that you share the pleasures that should be mine alone with others. I wish the image of you lying with them wasn't branded upon my heart betwixt the lies you've had me believe. I wish I could hate you but I cannot. I love you. I want you to be mine. You were supposed to be mine."

"Oh, Roz, please forgive me, not for what you think I've done but for what I failed to do. If I had told you, you'd know I could never betray the vows of our marriage. Trust me just enough to keep loving me. You're all I want, precious one. Don't deny me the generosity of your heart because of the wrongs you believe me guilty of. Love me, Roz. Just love me."

His hurried kisses brushed the wetness from her cheeks as he turned her toward him then settled upon the slack compliance of her lips. His mouth was sensually insistent in its movement, testing her willingness and enticing a response. Crushed to his chest, the straining bodice of her gown realized the limitations of its meager capacity and surrendered the captive peaks from their lacy confines. Geoffrey's mouth dipped down to seize those grateful refugees in a ravishing imprisonment of first one then the other.

Rosalind's hands rose to his waist, then to broad shoulders, then to the lure of hair bronzed to molten glory in the firelight. Her shaky sobs had quickened to a tempo of reluctant rapture. How could she deny the surges of desperate desire he stirred beneath the tease of his lips and the tantalizing flicker of his tongue. She had no protest as the barrier of her gown was removed between them. It sighed wistfully to the floor. He lifted her from the vivid pool and sat her on the edge of the bed while he knelt to

222

remove her slippers and clocked stockings. The lacy pantaloons proved an easily breached fortification and with all he saw, conquered, Geoffrey laid her back upon the fluffy comforter. The necklace was the last to leave her, finding a place on her bedside table.

While she watched him shed the layers of his elegant evening wear, Rosalind felt the bitterness return to choke her. She lay passive as he joined her on the bed. His kisses left her unresisting mouth to tenderly touch upon the bruises sustained in her fall, gently caressing the mars on her ribs, hips and thighs. From there, they made a shockingly thorough exploration of her form on the journey back up to the waiting part of her lips. The rippling sensations his bold travels awoke had her shivering with the intensity of her desire. He was understandably surprised by her renewed weeping.

"Is this what you do with your mistresses? Do you make love to them the way you do with me? Do you—"

His hand halted the outpouring of anguished words, sealing them in as it clamped firmly over her mouth. Her tears fell hot and wet upon it.

"No," he told her with rough emotion. "I've never given myself so completely, not to anyone but you. Can't you understand? Can't you believe? I am yours. I've shared none of what I am with any other, nor do I wish to. I have no mistresses, no lovers. The reason I was with those women has nothing to do with what we share. It was nothing personal. Nothing intimate. Nothing that reflects upon how much I want to be with you, loving you, having you." His impassioned words dropped off with a sigh. "You don't believe me."

Above his silencing hand, her dark, liquid eyes rolled away in misery.

"Roz, I love you."

Her eyes squeezed shut as her body gave a hard shudder. The gesture called him liar with a force more wounding than any words.

"I do," he said again, more softly this time. A lingering caress backed that ardent claim. "After tonight, I mean to spend the rest of our lives proving that to you. Even if it takes years, I'm going to make you believe me. I'm a persuasive man and nearly as stubborn as you. God joined us in spirit, our child in body, and now I plan to see to the union of heart and soul."

His hand left her mouth, replaced by the insistent demand of his own. When the union he spoke of was accomplished, he felt her placid resignation falter and fade as the passionate woman within her was lured to life. She strained upward to return his potent kisses and to meet each powerful stroke that claimed her as his alone. There was no place in that exquisitely personal moment for doubts of recriminations and Rosalind gave herself wholly to the pursuit of the burgeoning pleasures quickened between them.

Geoffrey concentrated on her satisfaction, wanting to complete her every need and fervent wish. He worked to bring each sensation to a harmonious peak until they crested in a shivery crescendo. Only then did he give full attention to his own part in their intimate duet. The finale was soaring, lyrical splendor, leaving the whisper of its soft melody upon his soul as they lay together, silent and replete. When Rosalind finally stirred, he greeted her with a sweetly poignant kiss.

"Can you still think I care nothing for you?" he challenged gently.

Rosalind looked deep into the dark blue eyes, so sultry and steeped in sincerity. The thoroughness of his loving took the sting of irony from her tone but not its sadness. "Does it matter what I think, my lord? You've proven you can sway my staunchest argument. I've no defense against your considerable charm. It proves you are an admirable lover."

He gave a frustrated groan and rolled onto his back where he frowned handsomely at the canopy. "You are the most maddening woman. I don't want to charm your passions alone. I want you to love me."

She sighed heavily and admitted, "I do love you, Geoffrey."

"You make it sound like some unpleasant curse affixed upon you. Can you find no joy in loving me?"

"I have enjoyed your loving very much" was her noncommittal reply.

"That's not what I meant," he growled in annoyance. He came up on his elbow to face her guarded expression. "I want you to be happy with me as your husband."

"You are my husband, my lord. Isn't that answer

enough?"

"No."

His petulant air made her smile. She touched her forefinger to his wide, pouting mouth and said with rueful chiding, "So greedy, my ambitious lord. You have yet to learn the art of compromise. You cannot have all your way."

He caught her hand and kissed its palm with a commanding certainty. "Yes, I can and I will have it all. I'm going to be worthy of your love and your trust. I will make you happy, in bed and out." Her delightful blush prompted him to steal a hard, determined taste of her soft lips. He lingered above her, weight supported on elbows placed at either side of her head. His gaze was intense and compelling and Rosalind felt her resistance slip. His fingers toyed with the wispy strands of hair that curled against her temples. "You accuse me of being a charmer yet underestimate yourself. You've taunted me most cruelly with your proper indignation. I don't deserve it, Roz. You're the only one to tame me and yours is the only lead I follow. Rein me in if you fear I stray, but I beg you, don't let me go. I love—"

Her palm silenced him then rubbed the taut plane of his cheek. His eyes sparked and simmered. She cried out as he caught the fleshy part of her hand between sharp teeth then laved the same spot with a sensual swirl of his tongue. Her finers twined in the burnished hair and brought him down to the eager part of her lips. Her own desperate hunger for him made her break away, panting and frightened. His broad, confident smile quieted her fears and enticed her back for more of the delicious warmth his mouth offered. And for more of the exacting delights of his body.

While Rosalind slept against him in sated contentment, Geoffrey let his gaze shift to the night table where the rubies glowed with seducing brilliance. With them safely delivered, his secrets would be secured and he could make good on his promises. In the morning, he could invent a reason for their disappearance, one that would placate his wife and silence the scheming Camilla.

Carefully, he slipped his arm out from under the dark, heavy head. Rosalind murmured softly but didn't stir. He gathered up his hurriedly discarded clothing and dressed in the faint light from the dying fire. Purposefully, he didn't look to the unmoving figure nestled amid the tempting covers. Leaving her was difficult enough without the contemptible reason for it.

"Forgive me, Roz. I do this for us," he told himself to pardon the unseemly act in his own mind.

Had his gaze turned toward the bed, he would have seen startled dark eyes open to witness the furtive hand closing on the bright jewels. They gave a damning blood-like glitter until secreted in the pocket of his tail-coat. Rosalind pretended sleep until she heard the door close softly behind him.

"Lying beast," she swore in a fierce mutter as a quick search affirmed the necklace was gone. Anger mastered her hurt. She tossed off the offensively warm covers and hobbled to her cupboard to pull a robe about herself. With all the stealth she could manage, she limped along the dark upper hall. Geoffrey hadn't returned to his room. A light from below directed her ungainly pursuit. Slowly, she crept down the stairs, keeping to the shadows. The entry hall was empty in the lateness of the hour, diligently cleaned after the last departing guest had gone. A strip of brightness shone from beneath the parlor door.

Mustering her abused pride, Rosalind reached for the door handle then froze. She could hear voices from within, speaking in rapid French. Geoffrey's sounded urgent. The woman sounded pleased.

Cautiously, she eased the handle down to muffle its click and created enough of a gap between the doors for her to spy on the unwelcome scene. The woman was the same mysterious one from the two earlier rendezvous. She had to bite her lip to keep from crying out in fury and dismay when Geoffrey passed her a handful of brilliant stones. The woman gave a low, grateful exclamation and stretched up to kiss her husband fully and familiarly upon the mouth.

She had seen enough. Insides trembling with shock and rage, Rosalind stood away from the door. Her fluttering heart could not stand the strain of a confrontation here before one of his many mistresses. With a painful awkwardness, she ran to the stairs and pulled herself upward with the aid of the smooth balustrade. Her sudden tears were not caused by the agony from her twisted limb but rather from the wrenching of a tortured heart. She paused in the upper hall, clinging weakly to the rail and weeping softly as her ankle threatened to give out. She couldn't return to her room, to the bed where he had made love and false promises to her. There was only one other place, one other sanctuary she knew of and she sought that trusted council as she had many times before. She was greeted with the same open arms and tender heart as always and poured out her grief in a purging torrent.

And when her bitter tears found an end, Rosalind listened to the gentle yet firm words of advice, not seeing the gloating smile that hovered about the lips that spoke them.

The necklace returned and the ugliness of his past successfully hidden, Geoffrey's only thought was to slip in beside the warm figure of his wife to hold her until dawn. He frowned upon finding the empty bed and cool sheets. After waiting several minutes in hopes that she would appear, he finally went to his own room where the hours passed in unsettled speculation.

Morning brought answers more unpleasant than he could have imagined. The door to Rosalind's chamber stood open for the influx of porters carrying out her bags. He watched for a long, apprehensive minute then wound his way inside about the the trunk and band boxes.

Rosalind and Camilla were sipping tea amid the chaos, the former dressed soberly for travel.

"What goes on here, madam?"

Rosalind's dark eyes lifted. Her gaze pierced through him with a stabbing chill then grew remote. She took another sip from her steadily held cup before granting him an answer.

"I've decided to go to the country for my lying in. The air is much healthier there and the tranquility will be good for the child."

"When did you decide this?" he asked and stepped aside to allow a clucking Jessup to direct the other servants as to what to take up.

"Last night, my lord" was her cool response.

"Without consulting me?" His eyes went in alarm to the empty cupboards from which her gowns had already been removed. The connotation of that hollow space quickened an uncertain dread.

227

"I knew you would want the best for my father's heir." Her stare was carefully detached though the pinch around her eyes and lips betrayed her displeasure. What had happened, he wondered in a sudden panic. Why was she abandoning him? Camilla's sly smile hinted at a partial answer. He could see her cunning touch in the abrupt turnabout. He could only guess that Rosalind had seen the departing duchess and had drawn an unfortunate conclusion. He would have to talk fast to make amends.

"Rosalind, may I have a private word with you?" he requested urgently.

"Dear Chilton, there is no time for sentimental good-byes," Camilla said with a sweet satisfaction. "Come, Lindy. Dunstan will want to see you off."

Rosalind began to follow her out when Geoffrey seized her hand, bringing it up to his lips. His breath was quick and shallow upon it. He sought her eyes in an intense entreaty.

"Roz, don't leave me," he asked in an unsteady undervoice. "Let me come with you."

For a moment, her eyes softened with a misty hesitation. Then, with a forceful blink, the dark, hard shine returned. She pulled her hand away. Her tone was brittle with meaning.

"Don't fret, Chilton. I'm leaving you in good hands, I know. My father needs you here. You've already done your part in breeding this child. The rest I can manage by myself. I will send you notice after the birth so you will know whether to start spending my fortune or to pack your bags. Good-bye, my lord."

She walked past him with unfaltering dignity, trapping him awkwardly in the confines of appearance before the servants that forbade him from making an impassioned scene. As he regarded her departing figure, he made one last, desperate attempt to stay her.

"Roz?"

She paused reluctantly in the hall then after a moment, turned to him in question.

"I love you."

That was the last thing she wished to hear from him; a final, unforgivable lie. Her lips compressed into a tight, pained line. Without an acknowledgment, she continued her determined course.

Geoffrey stood unmoving in a daze of disbelief. She was really going. The last of her luggage was carried out, leaving him in the empty, lifeless room. He heard her on the stairs, speaking with Camilla in low tones. The impulse to rush after her was nearly overwhelming, but he controlled it, realizing it was too late, at least, for the moment. Slowly, he walked to one of the large windows overlooking the bustle in the drive below where a line of conveyances waited. There, Rosalind and Camilla exchanged a fond embrace and the younger woman stepped up into her chaise.

Geoffrey's palm slapped against the glass in a futile gesture.

"Geoff?"

"She's leaving me, Hank," he mourned softly as he leaned his forehead to the cool pane that separated him from his beloved. "What am I going to do? I've made such a muddle of it all."

Henri pressed the rigid shoulders. "Go after her. Tell her everything. She loves you. She'll understand what you've had to do and will forgive you."

"No," he moaned, head rolling from side to side. "No, she won't. She might forgive the lies in time, but the truth, never."

Below, the caravan pulled away in a stately procession. Geoffrey made a quiet sound of wordless misery as his hand slid down the pane to fall heavily at his side.

Chapter Twenty-two

The serenity of the country estate was a balm to Rosalind's injured heart. The calm, quiet days flowed one to the next in the unhurried sameness she thrived upon. There was Jessup and Pettigrew for company and the pleasure of long, undisturbed rides that would soon know an end when the progression of her state made them imprudent. Then, she would walk, blessed with fine health and a vigorously stirring babe. She might have forgotten all about the life she left in London had it not been for the melancholy she felt in the sitting room and the letters from Camilla.

At first, the rambling pages made no mention of Geoffrey. The lines were filled with news of her father and the latest Mayfair on-dits. She wrote detailed volumes concerning Czar Alexander and King Frederick of Prussia's visit in June, relaying a malicious delight in their slight of the Prince Regent. In July, there were elaborate descriptions of the fete in honor of Wellington. She made the special hall built at Carlton House by Nash sound very pompous yet delightful and admitted to staying until six in the morning. In August, she highlighted the celebration for the masses in Hyde Park. She declared it was an extravagant, tasteless display then went on to depict most happily the many wonders concluding with the fireworks finale that filled the sky with a blaze of new stars and left an aftermath of burnt ruin. She made all sound like good fun and Rosalind was thankful she could enjoy it on the written page rather than in person. Unless, of course, she had Geoffrey to enjoy it with. She was certain he had indulged in the spectacles without minding her absence.

When Rosalind finally grew brave enough to inquire after her husband, Camilla's tactfully veiled statements made her heartbreak worsen. It was more from what was left unsaid than anything she pointed out in the vague phrases meant to protect yet inform her of his continued behavior unfettered by a wife in residence. She imaged what Camilla was careful not to say. Lord Chilton was enjoying his freedom. She was grateful for the solitude that allowed her to mope and lapse into teary intervals without explanation.

She tried not to think of Geoffrey by concentrating on his child. She spent contented hours readying the nursery for the new year's arrival, and focusing on that event gave her the strength to overlook the rest. She already loved the babe that rounded her belly and slowed her steps. She would love it in lieu of its father and raise it here in the country alone. Rosalind had no desire to return to London again. That was where Geoffrey was. The distance was necessary, for even across the miles, she longed for him with an irrational disregard for how he had sullied their relationship with his numerous affairs. She feared she would be helpless to resist him even now if he came to her. But he wouldn't come. He was too busy with the Mayfair distractions to think of the drawn-out isolation of rolling hills and a solitary wife. It was better that he stayed away so she could pretend to be satisfied with her rural seclusion.

The monotony was considerably brightened by the arrival of the Everards en route to their own estate. True to their reputation for tactless invasion, the bunch of them took up residence, bedeviling the small staff with constant demands and filling her with a welcome annoyance. She was truly grateful for Nathaniel's presence. His stable friendship lightened her dragging spirits even though it was a daily effort to entertain him with a smiling countenance. A consummate gentleman, he would never hint that she was less than happy. And he never mentioned her estranged husband.

The long hot days of summer gave way gracefully to the cool of fall and Rosalind gave up the pretense of any grace at all as she rested her plump form in the gardens listening to Nathaniel recite verse. It was almost as though he was her husband and father of the child and she could tell by his often wistful glances that he wished it was so. And so, the days passed uneventfully.

Not so the days in London. With the crush of visiting royalty and special events, the scene was one of constant preparation for one thing or another. Dinners lasted until dawn, blurring time and place into an endless social whirlgig. Once, Geoffrey would have fed on such frivolous fun to channel his boundless energy. Now, the more he saw of London, the less he liked it.

After living the life of a bon vivant in Paris, he found the English stuffy and impossibly hypocritical. The hub of ton spent their time dwelling meticulously on the unimportant, such as the proper texture of one's snuff or the number of folds in the cravat while ignoring the grave social shifts around them. They were lax with their coin and behind an impeccable front, with their morals, as well. The surface Eden concealed a Sodom and Gomorrah right up to the doors of Carlton House. He grew bored and restless in the shallow glitter of prominence, of trading idle conceits with the dandyish men and eluding the suggestive eyes of their proper wives. More and more of his time was spent on the city's southside, sitting comfortably in a crowded tavern in the preferred company of his brother.

Living in Charles Street without Rosalind was the most taxing of all. There, he was constantly reminded of her and wary of the conniving Camilla. The only thing that relieved his days was working beside his father-in-law. His respect for the man grew apace with his desire to emulate him. Dunstan reciprocated, bringing Geoffrey deeper and deeper into the handling of his investitures. Geoffrey was a natural in his world, smooth, charming, clever, and not above a degree of unscrupulousness. A better son he could not have spawned of his own blood.

Dunstan was unaware of the friction between his wife and son-in-law. He never saw the way the fair Camilla followed the younger man with desirous eyes or heard the sparring undercurrent in their table talk. She had grown even more blatant as the autumn months stretched out drearily, for when France's new king, Louis XVIII, returned to Paris, half of London's fashionable rank followed, leaving her excluded and testy. She vented her frustration by baiting Geoffrey with sexual overtures and taunts about his wife. She was in high form during one such dinner in early October, having that day returned from a luncheon where she listened secondhand once again to the worldly delights of the Continent.

"I was speaking to Lucinda Coxwilliam this afternoon. She just returned from Paris with the most interesting tales."

Geoffrey continued his meal in noncommittal silence, preparing for another dull recitation. Even abroad, the British flocked together, dining at the Café des Anglais on the Boulevard des Italiens on English beefsteak and potatoes, going to balls at the British Embassy or attending soirees held by Lady Oxford in her hotel on the rue de Clichy. They never did anything adventurous or singular, preferring the familiar to experiencing the delights of the foreign culture.

Seeing his waning interest, Camilla leaned upon the table with a predatory air. "It seems she took a French lover. Her Monsieur Roget was quite familiar with all the important families. Odd that when she asked about you, he could recall no one by your name or that of your French family. Nor could anyone else."

Geoffrey's eyes lifted slowly from his plate. His spine knew a strange prickling. "Not so odd," he remarked blandly. "The aristocracy was unsettled during the Revolution. A whole new set evolved from that."

"And why was it that yours did not?" she prodded with silky intensity, aware that Dunstan had paused to take note.

"Because they were beheaded," he said with a brutal clarity.

"Oh," she murmured in genuine horror, very much taken aback.

"Would you like the details, madam?" he asked tightly, causing her to pale in alarm.

"Let's talk of something else," Dunstan suggested forcefully. "This is not subject matter for the table."

"Please forgive me," Geoffrey mumbled, his challenging glare dropping in compliance.

It took Camilla only a moment to recover before launching a new attack. "I received a letter from Lindy in today's post." Geoffrey's rekindled interest gave her a sharp turn, yet she enjoyed dangling the news, knowing he'd had no communication from her. "It seems your grandchild is becoming quite apparent, my lord."

"How does she feel?" Dunstan asked eagerly. "Not troubled by any ills, I trust."

"She says she feels wonderful, largely, I suspect, to the company. Everard has been visiting for some weeks and you know how well they get on." She smiled innocently in the face of Geoffrey's hard, brilliant stare. Let him cut his teeth on that news for a time, she thought vindictively. She waited until after their meal to catch him alone so she could twist the knife of that knowledge a little deeper.

"Isn't it nice that Rosalind has dear Nate to keep her company while she believes you to be whoring your way through London."

Geoffrey's eyes were cold, bared steel. "I hardly think I have to worry as my wife is six months gone with child."

Camilla purred poisonously, "Yes, but isn't it strange that she should ask Everard and not you to attend her, unless of course the child's parentage is in question."

"It's not," he snapped, but his defensive pose betrayed him.

"Perhaps. Then again, they may be planning their future for after the child comes. Do you think you'll be included in it, dear Chilton?"

Her tinkling laugh followed his retreat to his room where Henri found him pacing restlessly in a too frequent agitation. His suggestion that they go in search of some entertainment was met with an indifferent shrug. Henri was hard-pressed to understand his brother's edgy hostility of late but knew of its cause. He said nothing as their hired hack carried them across Westminster Bridge to the Black Hind Tavern in Southwark. There, instead of finding some calm, Geoffrey's nervous energy increased to a shaky high-spiritedness that had Henri curious. Usually, Geoffrey would partake in his slight limit of alcohol then obligingly fall asleep while Henri partnered up with a willing petti-coat. Though his pleasing face drew much attention from the loose-mannered ladies who frequented the noisy public bar, Geoffrey politely discouraged their invitations. Until this night. A buxom brunette cast him a hopeful lure and was quick to respond to the wide, dimpling grin. As the night progressed, she found herself seated on his knee with his hand beneath her skirts upon the plump white flesh of her own.

Henri was so bemused by his brother's bold manner that he nearly neglected the warm creature cozied up beside him. Geoffrey was an accomplished flirt, but he had never seen him so aggressive with a woman, even one of such questionable caliber. It was unnatural, as was his high color and glittery eyes. The roguish Frenchman was the last one to protest a mild *affaire d'amour*, yet knowing his brother's feelings on them, he was beginning to think he should, especially when his stepbrother buried his face in the pillowy breasts then kissed the nameless woman with a scorching passion. He was convinced of it when the dusky eyes settled on the coarse face with a feverish glow of devotion. It was the way he looked at Rosalind.

Henri ordered more drinks for the ladies and urged, "Excuse us for a moment, mademoiselles." He gripped Geoffrey by the arm and towed him into a private nook to demand, "What are you doing, *mon ami?*"

"Enjoying myself" was the defensive retort.

"Enjoy yourself any more and you'll be puking in the gutter with your pockets emptied and an aching conscience."

Geoffrey scowled sullenly at that probable portrait and grumbled, "Why shouldn't I live down to her expectations while she is testing my replacement."

"You talk nonsense," Henri stated simply. "Geoff, if you want to crawl under the sheets with that woman, you don't need my blessing. All I ask is that you realize why and for whom. If you're doing it to hurt Rosalind, it will only break your heart later. If you just need a woman, we'll get a fine room and settle in for the night. What do you want to do?"

"I don't want to think about it or her right now," he cried angrily. He was coiled so tight with nervous tension, his hand shook with it as it threaded through his hair. "I just don't want to think about anything."

Henri bowed to that and let him return to the table with no further lecture. Geoffrey stood for a moment looking down into the woman's unfamiliar face, then leaned down to kiss her with a gentle consideration. She stared up at him in awed silence. He smiled and wedged a gold coin between her ample breasts.

"Good night, my lady," he said softly, then turned to Henri. "Enjoy your evening. I think I'll walk and clear my head."

"It's a long stretch, Geoff," Henri warned.

"And hopefully very cold." He put a hand on his brother's shoulder and ambled out into the cool night air.

After several blocks, he began a tuneless whistle. The exercise felt good, releasing his frustrations in a more positive activity. The vigorous pace worked out the knotted anxieties. Slowly, he was able to conquer them both and he considered the evening's events. The threat of his background in France, the mention of his parents' death, the hint of his wife's infidelity had pushed him into an uncomfortable corner just as Henri warned it would. His efforts to ignore the problems had brought him to the brink of shame. He had to think about them, each in turn without relying on impulsiveness or luck. The long walk would give him the opportunity. He had worked hard toward becoming the kind of man he thought Rosalind ought to have yet had nearly lost it all in a moment of foolish weakness. He couldn't afford to falter, not in any way if he was to be deserving of her.

Thinking of Rosalind brought back the keen ache of need and loneliness he knew one night with a stranger wouldn't have eased. She was the only cure for the misery he felt and she was so far away. And with Everard. His steps quickened as he envisioned the soulful-eyed poet mooning over her in the gardens of Dunstan Manor where he had once courted her favor. Had he fallen completely from it now? He had to know yet couldn't bring himself to invade her privacy without cause. And he had no cause until this moment.

"Bon soir, Monsieur Jenoit."

The oily voice from the past spoken at his elbow when he'd prayed never to hear it again gave Geoffrey a vicious turn. He didn't bother to turn to see if the cadaverous man was the same as he'd remembered. He bolted.

"Don't let him escape. He's faster than a whore's virtue," the man he knew as La Belette called after him in French.

Geoffrey dodged a shadowy shape but was caught up by the back of his coat. Frantically, he twisted and wriggled, trying to slip out of it and had nearly succeeded when a beefy fist connected with a solid stunning force. He dropped to the dirty street on elbows and knees, head spinning in a fog of pain. His arms crossed reflexively over his head, leaving his ribs unprotected for the jarring kick from a heavy, scuffed boot. He struggled to contain the low, whining sound that wanted to escape in response to the flood of remembered terrors. It was far from his first beating and instincts long forgotten helped him escape the worst of it. Finally, he was hauled to unsteady feet and thrust facefirst against a gritty brick wall. Winded, hurt, and panicked beyond clear thought, he remained pressed to the rough stones until turned to face La Belette.

The name "the weasel" was earned partly because of his furtive manner and partially due to the sharp, ferret-like features. La Belette grinned at the not so handsome Geoffrey Jenoit and brandished a small, wicked knife.

"Surprised to see me? Why is that, I wonder? You are a slippery one, Monsieur Jenoit. Perhaps I should skin you so you would be easier to hold onto."

Geoffrey sucked in a quick breath as the narrow blade scored his neck beneath his clenched jaw. His eyes shone white in the darkness as he searched the side streets for a way to flee these relentless ghouls from his past. Belette was a nightmare from the sewers of Paris any sane man would tremble before and he was no exception. He wasn't afraid that Belette would kill him. The little man could think of much more unpleasant things. The fear was worse than the pain, swamping, paralyzing, yet they were intertwined, one with the other. The throbbing ache in his face began a thunder of uncontrolled panic and confusion of time and place. He bit his lip to check the want to repeat the useless pleas a frightened boy had cried so many years ago. They would be wasted on Belette just as they had been before. His belly felt as though it was filled with shards of ice.

"Where's your pretty brother? We wouldn't want him to miss the fun, now would we?"

The mention of Henri sliced through the numbing fog of past horrors to bring him to the present with a waking jerk. He blinked and stared at the shadowy outline of his assailants. They weren't going to hurt him. They needed something from him. He was driven by a similar need, of protecting his brother.

"He's in Paris. He didn't come with me," Geoffrey bluffed in a bold if quavering voice. He swallowed hard to gain control of it. "What do you want?"

"What, he asks." Belette laughed thinly. "The money and the necklace."

The damned necklace again. An odd-sounding chuckle faltered from his lips. What irony. It would yet be his undoing. "Too late, Belette. It was claimed months ago. It's around the neck of a duchess in France."

"Is there any reason I should spare yours then?"

237

"The money."

"Oh, yes. I haven't forgotten. Pay me and perhaps I will let you live to cheat others."

"That's nearly £40,000. I haven't that kind of money." The warm feel of his own blood beneath the encouraging prick of the knife prompted him to add, "But I can get it."

Belette gave a ferral smile. "Of course you can."

"I left everything behind. Surely you gained something from the sale of it, at least £15,000."

"Expenses and interest, you understand."

Geoffrey closed his eyes. His breath was coming much too fast. He had to think. They called him Jenoit. Did that mean they had found him by chance? If they didn't know the name he was using, perhaps he could escape them yet. His gaze came up and centered over Belette's shoulder. Loudly, he cried, "Henri, don't shoot."

As attention turned from him, Geoffrey ducked under Belette's arm and ran. Hearing the shouted oaths and threats behind him, he dashed out onto a well-lighted section of street and barely avoided being struck down by a carriage. Panting, he waited for it to pass then swung up on the rear attendant's step to hunch down in the shadow of the coach. Belette's angry curse echoed down the dark streets to follow his rapid escape from danger and he didn't stop shaking until he saw the lights of Berkeley Square ahead.

A fond concern prompted Henri to check in on his brother, but the state of the room held him with a quickening of alarm. Trunks had been pulled out and stuffed full of clothes. Geoffrey's coat lay discarded on the floor. It was soiled and torn. The water in the basin was discolored and the towels beside it stained the same dark, vital hue. Now worried with cause, he crossed to the bed. Geoffrey lay curled tight upon it, still dressed, with his back to him. The tense posture denied the possibility that he was sleeping, yet he didn't move when Henri called out to him.

"Geoff? Are you all right? What's happened here?"

Geoffrey flinched away from the inquiring hand on his arm with a hoarse cry of "No!" and drew up into a more protective knot. The low, desperate sounds he made provoked a frown on the older man's face and a dark suspicion. He gripped the forearms that crossed over Geoffrey face and rolled him onto his back, then pulled them down, having to struggle to do so.

"*Mon Dieu,* Geoff! What happened? Who did this to you?" When he reached up to touch the ugly welt on his cheekbone, Geoffrey shied away as if the gesture contained a further threat. Seeing him cringe beneath a raised hand, took Henri back over the years and, unconsciously, he spoke in the same quiet, soothing tone he'd used then to wake a troubled boy from his nightmares. "Geoff, it's all right. It's Henri. Open your eyes, *mon frère*. I'm here and I'll see that no one hurts you."

The blue eyes came open cautiously. With a wordless relief, he sat up and hugged his brother about the neck. The stranglelike hold and the runaway breathing both lessened almost immediately and before Henri could return the desperate embrace, Geoffrey had pushed away and was off the bed in a fever of agitation. He began to poke in the loose ends so he could close his trunks securely.

"Pack. We're leaving tonight," he said urgently.

"Leaving for where? Geoff, what is this sudden madness?"

"We're going to the country, to the manor."

"Who's hurt you?" Henri asked quietly of the frenzied figure.

"I fell" was his almost angry lie. He glared at the silent Frenchman as if daring him to argue it. When he didn't, Geoffrey gave a guilty flush and turned away to gather his toiletries in a sweeping armload. "You don't have to come along," he threw out tightly over his shoulder. Then he seemed to sag, the shivery breaths returning. "Come with me, Hank," he asked huskily without meeting his eyes.

"Give me a moment to gather my things."

A brief note was left for the Dunstans and the loaded-down chaise sped from the mews shortly after four in the morning. In the coach's dark interior, Henri observed the huddled figure on the opposing seat with a deepening sense of foreboding. Something was very wrong and it was unlike Geoffrey not to trust him with his troubles. His talent was for getting into difficulties, not for getting himself out of them. That's what he depended on his older brother for.

The mark beneath Geoffrey's averted eye had grown ugly, swelling and purpling with the promise of a mighty ache. Someone had struck him, terrified him, and sent him running, not to Rosalind but from London and the dangers he wouldn't speak of. Henri had seen the look on his face before, once when he and his mother came to live at his father's house and again at the execution of their parents. Something or someone had shaken him badly to send him scuttling back into the dark recesses of remembered terror. A fierce fury toward whoever had hurt him mounted, tempered by a protectiveness that held him silent. He would discover the truth of it and someone would pay dearly. He had made a promise to a frightened, battered boy over twenty years ago and he wouldn't break it now.

Geoffrey was the only family Henri had. He accepted him without question of shared blood even before their parents had married. The nervous, desperately cheerful boy had inspired deep fraternal instincts and time had anchored them firmly. During those first few months, Geoffrey became his constant shadow, eager to please and gain the approval of the older boy. Henri had been flattered and was quick to give his protection to the little Englishman. In time, Geoffrey's bruised body and spirit began to heal. The frequent night terror lessened and he no longer cowered at a raised hand or voice. Finally, he took his first confident step out of that long shadow to stand at Henri's side and there he had stayed. From then on, the cocky self-reliance couldn't be curbed in the daring, often foolhardy boy. Henri was forced to be his frequent champion with the neighboring children who took offense to his brash manner. Geoffrey was bold with his tongue but no taunt or provocation could make him take up his fists. Only Henri knew it had nothing to do with bravery or lack of it. That aversion remained even to adulthood. Geoffrey would face down anyone with a weapon but physical violence ruined him. His audacious charm got him out of most situations and his older brother, the rest. Henri had never seen anyone so determinedly grasping for objects as most would for affection. Geoffrey was content with his possessions and stingy with deep feeling. But because he loved him even for his faults, Henri indulged him and rescued him from his impulsiveness a countless number of times. While he grumbled over his lack of independence, Henri would never think to abandon his flighty, irresponsible brother. And he wouldn't now even if Geoffrey didn't ask for his help. He would be there because he promised he always would be.

Geoffrey could feel the questioning stare and guiltily refused to meet it. He knew Henri wasn't fooled by his feeble attempt to appear calm. His brother would be wondering what sort of scrape he'd gotten himself into and would be waiting for the particulars. Nothing would be easier than to turn over the entire disaster. Henri was incredibly capable, as coolly calculating as he himself was clever and spontaneous. Between them, a solution was certain. However, he couldn't turn to his brother with this latest dilemma. He had gone to La Belette against Henri's advice, then had allied with him in an ill-fated scheme that had collapsed just ahead of their flight from Paris. He had thought himself safe until meeting the two men on the road to London. And now Belette himself had come and his ill-advised plans caught up to him. And because of the secrets kept from him, Geoffrey couldn't ask his brother to save him without telling him all. Aside from the fact that he would be furious, it would place him in similar jeopardy, and that he wouldn't risk. He would have to stay a step ahead of the persistent weasel until Rosalind's legacy paid off and going into hiding was the best way to do it.

Geoffrey closed his eyes and let his head rest against the back of the seat. Though weary and frayed, he didn't expect to find sleep. The side of his face and his ribs pained him and his mind ached with fatigue and worry. What a dreadful night it had been, full of nasty, unexpected turns. He hadn't considered what he would do if Rosalind refused to take him in. But of course she would. Seeing her would be just what he needed to calm his agitation and right his thinking. His thoughts leapt ahead in anticipation. He hadn't realized how lonely he had been during the months of their separation until their reunion was hours away. Now, he could clearly define his dissatisfaction with all around him. It hadn't pleased him because it hadn't included Rosalind. He was assaulted by memories of her nervous laugh, of her wry smile and somber eyes, of the silken feel of her skin— He checked those images, reminding himself that she was six months pregnant. With his child. A strange, shivery sensation slid through him, filled with pride and warmth and expectancy. Things would work themselves out. After all, their future was now permanently bonded into the special being she carried. That wasn't something she would dismiss lightly, not like—others.

Rosalind, the child, the Dunstan inheritance; those were the things he would concentrate upon. He had no reason to panic yet.

Just the same, his eyes opened to stare out at the passing black countryside and sleep was an apprehensive stranger.

Chapter Twenty-three

Rosalind turned with a welcoming smile, expecting Everard's to be the step she heard. Her features froze and became the color of the linen shawl draped about her shoulders. As she drew a sharp gasp of the cool fall air, her heart seemed to stop then resume with a crazy erratic flutter that returned the high blush to her cheeks. She had to swallow quickly to find a high, reedy voice.

"My lord, you surprised me. I wasn't aware you'd arrived."

"Am I welcomed, then?" he asked with a husky confidence. When she didn't reply, he advanced into the gazebo where she had been reading with her feet propped on a pillow. The breeze ruffled her sculpted coif, leaving loose tendrils to float about her uplifted face with a waifish charm. Heedless of the warning in the dark eyes, Geoffrey was drawn by the sight of soft, perfect lips parted in unwitting invitation. He bent to taste them, but her head turned purposefully to offer a cool cheek instead. He made the gesture brief and stood away. Attuned to her guarded mood, he smiled blandly, hopes of a joyous reunion effectively dashed.

"How fine you look, madam. Are you well?"

"Yes. Life here suits me very well." Her remark was pointed and he was not dense enough to miss its barb.

"You aren't happy to see me."

"I was not expecting you," she countered in precise evasion. She was not happy to have him appear so suddenly and throw her staid existence on its end with resurgences of powerful and painful emotion. She was unsettled, confused, overwhelmed but not exactly unhappy.

"Forgive me for not writing ahead to ask your permission for a visit." His tone was peevish. This was not the reception he envisioned.

"As well you didn't. I would have encouraged you to remain in London."

Geoffrey grinned disarmingly. "Very bluntly put, dear wife. Absence has not warmed your heart or lessened the sting of your wit."

"You'll find little has changed, my lord."

Her tart rejoinder was followed by an intruding voice. "Instead of our usual tea, Lindy, today I thought we might try—"

Nathaniel Everard's sentence died on his lips as he viewed Lord Chilton with startlement then with thinly veiled displeasure. He set the tray he carried beside Rosalind and politely extended a hand.

Geoffrey took it reluctantly. His insides gave a sickened turn at the cozily domestic scene presented him of Everard faithfully doting on his wife in an obvious afternoon routine. Camilla's intimations chewed on his jealous heart as he adopted a fixed smile.

"Good to see you again, Everard. How kind of you to look after my wife in my absence."

"It was no trouble, sir. Indeed, quite the pleasure." The level stare was to make him feel the interloper.

Geoffrey stiffened in well-controlled outrage. The incredible impertinence of the man. With rigid formality, he bowed and stated, "I'll leave you to your obvious pleasure then. I should like to settle in. It's been a fatiguing journey. I trust my room is still available."

Rosalind flushed darkly and said, "It is." Her eyes shot daggers at his insinuation.

"Please excuse me then."

Seeing Rosalind's apparent distress as Chilton stalked away, Everard bent down solicitously to capture her hand. "Are you all right, Lindy? If his presence upsets you, I shall send him away."

Rosalind gave an unkind laugh. "Don't be absurd, Nate. He is my husband. He has a right to come as he pleases."

"And to trample your heart as he pleases?"

The hand was withdrawn with a frosty warning. "You overstep yourself, sir."

"Forgive me, Lindy," he rushed on, emboldened to speak his mind. "I have no liking for a man who shows you so little consideration. I cannot bear to see you so in the blue."

"Then perhaps you should go."

Everard was no fool. He kept his opinions on Chilton to himself. To have her defend the unworthy cur to him was

244

most disturbing, yet he didn't want her hospitality withdrawn. Just when things had been progressing so nicely.

"It grows too cool out here, Nate. I should like to go in now."

Geoffrey was unprepared for a dinner with the Everards in attendance. Chappingham he knew only slightly and he had been introduced to the quiet Lady Everard at Alvanly's. The four girls ranging from schoolroom to marketable age were noisy and unexceptional. They ogled him with unbecoming candor. The dowager gave him a brief glance, for he was outside the field of her severely limited vision. She tapped Nathaniel on the wrist to demand stridently, "I thought you said Rosalind's rakish husband was here. Well, where is he? Not off chasing some chambermaid while we starve for want of dinner, I trust."

Geoffrey contained his grin with difficulty at the sight of Nathaniel's crimson face. Before her grandson floundered for the correct words, he crossed the room and lifted a birdlike hand.

"Good evening, madam. A thousand pardons for keeping you waiting. What an ungrateful host you must think me."

The old woman gave a cackle of amusement and used his hand to draw him closer. "Chilton, you say? Yes, I can see it now. You resemble him greatly. A fine looking pup, that Nigel."

"No, madam. Nigel is my uncle. Giles was my father."

The cloudy eyes narrowed, never leaving his face. "Oh, that one," she pronounced stiffly. "I trust you do not resemble him, young man."

A bony finger touched the bruise on his cheek. Geoffrey drew back sharply. His reply was a bit strained. "No, madam, I do not."

The grizzled head nodded. "See that you don't. I preferred Nigel. Charming young man. Your mother was a lovely girl, I recall. Is she well?"

"She is no longer living, madam."

"Did he break more than her spirit then?" the old woman asked softly. She refused to relinquish his hand, though Geoffrey was anxious to escape her.

"She was a victim of France's Revolution."

Rosalind had witnessed only the last part of their conversation. She came forward using her hands to gently free Geoffrey's, then patted the dowager's arm while he reeled back in an effort to recoup his composure.

"Come, Mother Everard. It's time to dine. I've had the cook prepare salmon for you."

"With white sauce?" she crowed gleefully. "It quite devastates my digestion but it's so wickedly rich. You quite spoil me, child."

With the bent figure leaning upon her arm, Rosalind reached out to touch Geoffrey's sleeve. He looked so remote and distracted. "Will you join us, my lord?"

Her soft inquiry woke him from his moody thoughts and he gave a faint smile. Gallantly, he escorted them both to the table.

The lengthy meal was a torturous trial. Geoffrey sat silent and excluded, watching the comfortable hubbub about him with sinking spirits. While the Everard men argued amiably, Rosalind kept a tight rein on the lively girls with a fond tolerance. He felt as though he was observing a completed family, one which held no place for him. He had been wrong to assume so much, to confidently believe she would embrace his return. She seemed not to have missed him in the slightest, too absorbed with the close-knit structure of the Everard clan. Watching her easy manner and frequent laugh, he could believe her better off in their midst rather than bedeviled by his presence. Perhaps it had all been a mistake, a not uncorrectable one.

Rosalind was puzzled by his odd quiet. She had never seen him look so downcast and her instinct was to comfort him despite all the rigid reprisals she spoke to herself. The last thing she wanted to do was involve herself with Geoffrey Chilton again. She was grateful when he excused himself immediately after the last course but found herself anxious to plead her own good nights and follow him up.

Unable to let herself go to him, Rosalind took a place on the settee in the room that joined theirs together, willing him to seek her out. He didn't keep her waiting long. They eyed each other cautiously, then he crossed to the warmth of the fire.

"Is this still considered neutral ground?" he asked in wry humor.

"I've no wish to fight with you, my lord. Especially when your defenses are at such a low."

246

"How charitable of you, madam." His back was to her as he fingered the delicate figurines on the mantelpiece. Rosalind's eyes lingered over him from the molten gold of his hair across the breadth of his shoulders to lean waist and hips and down the long line of his legs. The sight created an uncomfortable stir for one in her position. Her thoughts were most unbecoming to a mother-to-be. Oblivious to her heated appraisal, Geoffrey said generously, "How good of the Everards to keep company with you. You seem very content among them."

"Nate is an old friend. I've spent many a holiday with his family. They can be trying at times but having them here has made the time pass quickly."

"It was wise of you to invite them, then."

"Oh, they didn't come at my summons. Camilla suggested they stay for a time. She knows how fond I am of Everard."

"Indeed she does. I shall have to thank her for her foresight." He set one of the Dresdens down abruptly. Still, he didn't face her.

"I'm sorry the dowager distressed you with her questions, my lord. She could not know you were sore on the subject. I will speak with her."

"No. There's no need," he said quickly. "Her questions weren't out of step, but to censor them would be. I reacted badly out of fatigue. It won't happen again. I did not mean to put you to the blush in front of your guests."

Rosalind frowned. How strangely he was acting, all stiff and proper. How unlike the brash, conceited viscount who had so captivated her. Her own wariness was lulled by the puzzle of his manner. While he would pretend a languid calm, she could feel the tension and restlessness within him. It could be explained by fatigue or the unsettled relationship between them, but she didn't think so.

"Why are you here, my lord?"

"It's warmer than in my room," he said with purposeful misunderstanding.

"I mean here instead of London."

"Not to put you out, madam, I assure you. If you would prefer not to house me, say so. You have never been one to mince words with me. Do you wish me to leave?"

"You are being quite silly, Chilton. This is your home as well."

His fingertips brushed along the carved mantelpiece in a slow caress. "Yes, it is," he remarked somewhat vaguely. He gave a heavy sigh, shoulders slumping with the weight of it.

"You look tired, my lord. Come and sit by me."

He greeted the kind offer with a suspect frown. He did look weary, his eyes dulled by it and features etched with it. He came to her with a slow, mistrusting step, but the promising comfort of the cushions lured him down beside her. His keen energy ebbed as he settled himself and Rosalind was moved by a tender sympathy.

"Geoffrey, what's wrong?"

His alertness snapped up in a defensive pose and was hidden behind a mocking smile. "I travel through the night to see my wife, the mother of my child after three long months to find her playing house with an old lover and not at all pleased to see me and she asks what's wrong. I would laugh if it weren't such an effort."

Rosalind looked chagrined but not convinced. "Are you all right, my lord? What happened to your face?" she persisted. He flinched away when she attempted to touch the painfully discolored cheek.

"I wasn't caught by a jealous husband, if that's what you're thinking. Are you concerned, dear wife? Such concern might have warranted at least one brief note in three months time." His querulous tone succeeded in drawing her off. Her chilly attitude returned.

"I didn't think you had the time or the interest to read of my mundane activities."

"Why else do you think I came?"

"Why, indeed, my lord?"

He stared down at his glossy boots, his mouth pulled in a sullen pout. "You carry my child, madam. Surely you can understand why that might interest me."

Her laugh was brittle. "Of course, for the money. Fear not, Chilton, I have guarded your investment well."

"Damn it, woman, that isn't the reason," he snapped. The harshness of his words made her pale and draw back. His eyes closed and unsteady fingers rubbed his temples. "Forgive me, Rosalind, I am not myself tonight."

She relaxed gradually and stared at his fine profile. "The child is healthy, my lord. Surely Cammy told you as much. Or didn't you ask?"

"She told me a great many things, more than I wanted to know."

The cryptic words brought a furrow to Rosalind's brow, but when he turned to her, she arranged her features in a careful mask of indifference.

"I hadn't expected you to look so desirable," he began huskily. Then his lips gave an amused quirk. "Or so delightfully round."

She flushed at his bold statements. Her hands went self-consciously to the prominent swell of her middle to be joined by one of his. At her quick look, he withdrew it tentatively.

"May I?"

She guided his palm to the ripening fullness and held it there. Obligingly, the life within her dealt him a hearty kick. His hand jerked back and he stared at her stomach in round-eyed amazement. Slowly, a wide grin spread, then was stilled. He bent to press a kiss upon that expanded girth and let his head rest there with a shaky sigh.

Rosalind sat very still, startled by his nearness and by the poignant gesture. Cautiously, she put a hand atop his golden head. His body relaxed beneath that accepting touch.

"Let me stay, Roz," he murmured thickly. "Please don't hate me enough to wish me gone."

She hesitated, then said simply, "I don't hate you."

His breath expelled noisily and his eyes closed. "Then can I hope that you still—"

Her fingers covered his mouth then, when he lay silent, stroked leisurely up his cheek. He made a soft sound and brought his boots up on the seat. She continued to caress his face and silken hair long after his lips parted slackly in sleep. His weight was uncomfortable yet so pleasantly familiar. Her quiet mood freed a slow current of emotion that twined and lapped against the sterner fortress of her heart. She hadn't wanted him to come, yet she couldn't turn him away. What a miserable trap he held her in.

"Would you like me to move him, madame? He must be quite heavy for you."

She looked up in a moment of alarm, then smiled softly. "Hello, Henri. No. Leave him. He's all right."

"As you wish, madame." His gaze fell upon his brother's peaceful countenance with a bittersweet realization that he had sought her out for comforting. He began a stilted bow when her question checked him.

"Henri, has something happened? Is he in some sort of trouble?"

"I cannot say, madame."

"Henri, please. I don't expect particulars or for you to betray a confidence. I just need to set my mind at ease. Is Geoffrey all right?"

Her sincerely worried eyes and the gentle way her hand rubbed along the still cheek gave Henri pause. His rigid posture loosened. "As far as I know, my lady. He has said nothing to the contrary."

Rosalind gave a breath of relief, then smiled somewhat shyly at the elegant manservant. "Thank you, Henri."

"Bon soir, madame."

Rosalind stirred and curled into the circle of warmth that spread such a sense of contented comfort through her. She dozed for several long minutes until the unsettling edge of awareness made her eyes spring open in dismay.

The room was dark and for a moment as unfamiliar as the sound of quiet breathing beside her. When she tried to sit up, a heavy weight across her chest frustrated her awkward momentum. There was a soft mutter of disturbance and the possessive arm tightened. Her head rolled to the side, wide eyes regarding the man next to her in bewildered outrage. Her abrupt movement made the heavy blue eyes open to observe her with like startlement. Then he smiled widely, with infinite pleasure.

"Hello. Is it morning?"

"What are you doing here?" she cried. Her struggle to remove his arm was ineffective.

"I was sleeping. This is my bed, is it not?"

"Then what am I doing in it?"

"You were sleeping, too. Unfortunately, that was all circumstances would allow."

She scowled at his amusement and demanded, "How did I get here?"

"I brought you. You looked so uncomfortable in the other room. I thought you'd prefer to lie down."

"I have my own bed for that."

"Yes, but I didn't think you'd appreciate waking to find

me in your bed."

His logic left her agog. "And you thought I'd prefer this?"

"You weren't awake to ask."

"Let me up this instant. I don't wish to be here." Her indignant squirming brought her up flush against him. Though she was still wearing her simple shift, he, obviously, wore nothing. The contact was searing, stunning her protest into a silent lapse. The hands she had raised to push against his chest were enthralled by the warm stretch of skin over hard muscle. No! her will cried, don't weaken. If he wanted you, why was he in London playing the libertine? She forced her voice to remain strong. "No, my lord. Not again. I will not have you back."

He crushed her close in a convulsive embrace, holding her tight against the protesting thunder of his heart. His voice was hushed and faint with panic. "You can't mean that. You don't mean that. You love me. We love each other."

"It's not enough, Geoffrey. It won't take between us. We both know it."

"I know no such thing," he cried in low pitched anguish. "I need you, Roz."

"You don't need me, my lord. We've been through this before."

He released her abruptly and sat up, clutching the covers that tented over his knees. His features became a study of fierce sullenness. "Fine. Put an end to it then. If you don't want me, divorce me. Do it now because I don't think I could bear it after the child is born. I'll stay out of your life and you can be free to remarry. Everard will treat you well, far better than I have."

"Freedom will suit you, too, my lord. I fear you were not made to tend one woman. It will be better for us both this way."

The deep blue eyes came up in amazement. "Do you really mean to divorce me?" he asked in blank disbelief.

"It was your solution."

His handsome features puckered in dismay. "Well, I wouldn't have suggested it if I thought you would do it."

Rosalind sighed and regarded him sadly. "What else can I do? It hurts too much to be with you. I can't believe you'd ever change. Each time I hope, you disappoint me. I do love you, but I have to let you go. I'll see you get an ample settlement—"

"No!" It escaped him in a pain-filled wail. Geoffrey's arms looped about her and his head fell upon her knees. "Don't leave me, Roz. Please. I don't want the money. I want you and our child. Don't leave me. I love you so much."

To her horror, Rosalind realized he'd broken off into low weeping. The last of her resistance crumbled as she put a hand upon his head. "Oh, Geoff, what am I to do with you? Is it my lot to be forever welcoming you back when you tire of the arms of your mistresses?"

"There's been no one, Roz," he muttered hoarsely. "Only you."

She said nothing. She had heard it from him before and how many more times? Her hands soothed over his rumpled hair and the sleek angles of his shoulders and the pride of belonging to him clogged her reasonings. He felt so good. Nothing had ever felt so good and so right, so why did it always go so wrong?

"What do you expect from me, Geoffrey? What is it you want? A dull little wife who asks no questions and is satisfied with the tidbits left over from your grander feasts? Those scraps don't satisfy me. When I sit down to a meal, I want to enjoy it all, every bite, every taste. I want no one eating from my plate or stealing samples when my back is turned. I want no more of that. If you want to stay, you'll belong only to me. My lead will be very short and will brook no nonsense. If the clover isn't sweet enough for you in these pastures, you're free to go, but I won't take you back. I may be a fool for giving you this chance. You don't deserve it. I don't trust you. I don't believe a word you say. I suspect your motives. But I love you, Geoffrey. I love you enough to be the fool just one more time, but it will be the last time."

"Just love me, Roz. Love me and don't let me go," he urged with a husky fervence. "I won't fail you. I will make you happy. We needn't go back to London. We can stay here, the two of us . . . the three of us. When the babe is older, we can travel. Whatever you like. Whatever makes you happy. Just don't leave me."

Her palm crooked under his chin, lifting his head. Her fingers caressed the taut planes of his face and tested the firm luxury of his mouth. "So beguilingly fair," she mused reflectively. "I want to believe you, yet do I dare?" She smiled softly as he pressed a kiss to her hand. The warm tingle of desire spread throughout her every nerve and fiber. "Perhaps it doesn't matter just now."

She bent down to consider the pliant charms of his lips, cradling his face between her hands while she explored the generous contours at her leisure. His eyes stayed closed and his breath shivered in slow, poorly controlled pants. When those tempting kisses traveled down to the smooth heat of his chest, unsteady hands caught her shoulders and held her away.

"No more, Roz. I haven't that kind of strength. Three months has been an impossibly long time and the thought of three more will drive me to madness if you continue with this."

Rosalind was about to question his claim of long-standing chastity with a tart disclaimer but was silent. He looked so genuinely uncomfortable that she wondered if he was telling the truth. Was the only injustice done that of her harkening to the maligning whisperers? That idea made her tremble with sudden conviction.

"Geoffrey, make love to me."

He recoiled from the suggestion with wide-eyed uncertainty and a soft cry of, "I can't. I mean, I shouldn't. With the child and all. I don't want to hurt you. It—it wouldn't be proper."

Rosalind laughed at him. "Is this the man who would bed me in a fish pond or in an open carriage in Hyde Park? Can this be the same randy Lord Chilton speaking of propriety to me, the virgin bride?"

"Don't tease me, Rosalind," he grumbled with an endearing blush. "I don't know about such things. You're the only married woman I've ever lain with, let alone one plump with child."

She stared at him for a moment, gauging his seemingly impossible statement. Then her arms were about his neck, bringing her full breasts up against him in an agonizing enticement. Her kisses rushed along the side of his hot face and through the silken hair. Her whispers were a warm, sweet breeze in his ear.

"Love me, Geoffrey, this once, tonight. I want you so. Make it special enough to carry us through these next long months of being near yet so terribly apart. Love me so I can bear holding you without having you. Lay with me tonight so I might know that you are truly mine. Oh, Geoff, please love me."

He took her down to the mattress where he kissed her with an urgent passion. Then that eager hunger quieted, becoming so gentle, she received it with teary emotion. He took her with a slow, loving consideration, trembling with the difficulty of restraint. Somehow, that made the strength of her fulfillment that much greater. It was a closeness she refused to surrender as they lay together in contented silence, his arms cuddling her close to the affirming thunder of his heart. She smiled as his lips brushed her forehead and let the heavy peace lull her to sleep, secure that he loved her.

Geoffrey reveled in the bliss of lethargy, his body exquisitely languid and his plaguing worries at bay. Things were far from settled between them, but this was a satisfactory beginning. He had won his place at her side, and for now that was all important. The fateful brush with past terror in London seemed distant and removed from the beautiful love he had made to his wife. He felt untouchable, safe, secure; all emotions encouraged by the naive notion that the past was once again past. He didn't want to consider its ugly consequence just as he wanted to deny the persistent aches that still plagued his body. Rosalind had the strength to carry him to the future he desired, that of family and affluence. He would be Lord Chilton, the man she loved and never again Geoffrey Girard or Geoffrey Jenoit or Geoffrey of no sir name. Unwittingly, he had discovered the means to make all possible and the love to make all complete. And he would do anything to keep both. He would have all.

Chapter Twenty-four

Even with houseguests as impossible as the Everards, Geoffrey marveled at the efficient manner in which Rosalind maintained a semblance of calm. Watching her, he was amazed by the transformation from the shy, easily quelled Miss Dunstan to the authoritative figure of Lady Chilton. Where once she'd been anxious to leave details to others, she excelled in keeping a firm hand on matters from the kitchen to housekeeping. No longer did she hide herself in the stables. She had become, in every aspect, the lady of the manor. He delighted in the glow of confidence he saw in her and the respect he'd always held knew full merit. Glumly, he attributed that strengthening of character to the many hurts he'd dealt her. He had forced her to find the resources within herself to go on. And go on she would, with or without him. He was determined to make that "with."

Making a comfortable place for himself in his wife's regimented new life was Geoffrey's first concern. His position as lover would have to be postponed for several months despite its rewarding success of the night before. With that tender moment to sustain him, he would weather the rocky wait rather than risk any harm to wife or child. His talent as charming escort was wasted in the isolated countryside, for there were no routs or fancy balls to squire her to. The ever-present and underfoot Everards seemed to fill her need for companionship to overflowing. That left him a rather unsettled outsider and that was not where he was content to remain.

While he pondered on a solution, Geoffrey leaned upon the paddock gate in the crisp October morning. A smile softened his wide mouth as he watched the leggy black colt gallop about with unbridled energy. He put out his hand and the shell-like ears cocked forward at the sound of his off-pitch whistle. The velvety muzzle stretched out until warm air blew on the open palm. Then, with a sudden distrustful snort, the foal skittered away, defiant hooves kicking out in bold independence. Geoffrey chuckled in appreciation.

"He reminds me much of you, my lord."

He looked about to find Rosalind settled beside him. The cool breeze brought a comely flush to her cheeks. Her smile was easy, exciting a sudden shiver within him. She radiated a happiness that had his heart in hopeful cartwheels.

"Why is that?"

The dark eyes appraised Tamburlaine. "He's a pretty little thing, all spunk and fire, wild yet touchingly sweet. For all his mischief, there's no meanness. He'll grow to be a fine animal."

Geoffrey looked bemused. "And that's how you see me?"

Her glance was bashful. "Yes."

He was pleased by the observation. Dimples creased his cheeks beguilingly as he looked to the spirited colt. They stood together at the gate in a moment of silent communion. Abruptly, her hand touched his.

"Would you like him, Geoffrey? I think the two of you would suit. Papa did give you your choice from our stables and I don't believe you've made one."

He looked flattered, then nonplussed. He eyed the colt as it cantered about the perimeter of the fence and chewed his lip. A frown began to cloud his features. "What would I do with such an animal?"

"You ride, don't, you?" At his silence, she gave a surprised laugh. "You don't, do you? How very odd. But then I'd forgotten. You're quite afraid of horses, aren't you?"

"Me afraid of these stupid four-legged demons? Deathly." He tried to make it a joke but there was a tension to him that affirmed his words.

"Have you never tried?"

"My father tried to teach me when I was a child. I fear I was a poor student."

Something in his tone made her bristle in his defense. Perhaps it was the vulnerable self-deprecation that weighed softly upon the words. "Are you sure it wasn't a poor teacher?"

Geoffrey shrugged. "Whatever. It doesn't matter now."

"Would you let me teach you, later, I mean, after the child is born? Or Pettigrew could get you started. He taught me. He's really very patient for all his gruffness. I think you two would get on if you tried."

His smile was kind but unenthused by her suggestions. "I don't think he'd care to tutor me and though I appreciate your offer, I think I'll stay with my own two feet."

"If that's what you want," she said softly. She reached out to stroke the colt's glossy hide as it passed close then jerked back to avoid a frisky nip. Her swat sent it gallivanting away and earned a laugh from Geoffrey.

"Is that how you plan to deal with me as well?"

"When you're impertinent, yes," she replied archly.

His smile faded as the warmth moved up into his eyes. Rosalind took a tentative breath as his large hand molded to the sweet curve of her cheek.

"I'm very happy to be here with you."

The caress of his voice made her uncomfortably aware of him and of the night they'd spent together. In her nervousness, her retort was cynical. "For how long, my flighty lord?"

"For as long as you'll let me stay" was his undaunted answer. "And you, my practical lady, are you content to have me?"

The dark eyes grew heavy with meaning. "Having you has always been an extreme pleasure."

They exchanged speaking gazes until a call of greeting broke through their concentration. As Everard grew closer, Rosalind stepped away from the tender claim of her husband's touch with a deep, disconcerted flush and Geoffrey let her withdraw with an irritated frown.

"Good morning, Chilton. Lindy, are you ready for your ride?"

Rosalind looked flustered, her eyes darting up to the handsome scowling features of the man beside her. There was so much promise to what had begun between them, but perhaps it was already too late to recapture it.

Seeing her hesitate, Nathaniel was quick to take her elbow in a gentle encouragement. "Come, Lindy. The horses are hitched and ready. Excuse us, won't you, Chilton. Invite you along but there's only room for two."

The dark blue eyes slanted in wry amusement. His reply was stiff but civil. "But of course. Enjoy your outing."

Rosalind cast him a helpless glance before her eager escort hurried her off. Geoffrey watched her go. His expression was tight with displeasure. A sudden hard nudge between his shoulderblades distracted his piercing glare. He smiled and rubbed the questing nose that pushed toward him. When his gaze returned to the figures of his wife and his subtle rival, his mouth pursed thoughtfully.

"Do you suggest I go after them, *mon petit cheval?* I think not this time, but you are right. Something must be done. Time for a little *gros bon sens;* a little horse sense, eh, my friend?"

The colt gave his coat sleeve a playful bite. Geoffrey chuckled and gave the satiny nose a fond pat.

"I quite agree."

Nathaniel Everard advanced into the spacious hall somewhat puzzled by the unexpected summons. The sight that greeted him made him pull up short, his timid heart plummeting to his boots in uncertain dread.

"Ah, Everard. Join me."

Reluctance plain in his halting steps, Nathaniel crossed the parquet tiles to where Geoffrey Chilton stood in his shirtsleeves sporting a huge grin, a glass of wine, and a razor-sharp saber. His manservant was lounging indolently against a table, the sword's mate dangling from his hand. From the liberal dappling of perspiration and faint breathlessness of both men, they had obviously been involved in a rigorous fencing exercise. Geoffrey took a long swallow from his glass and wiped his rolled shirtsleeve across his sweat-slicked face. The smoky eyes were overly bright from exertion and a disquieting excitement. Everything about the viscount disturbed the sensitive poet. He was suddenly too virile, too aggressive, too threatening, like a hungry, stalking beast. Even his smile was intimidating.

"Do you fence, Everard? I was taking in some sport and thought perhaps you would like to cross swords with me. I tend to get lazy if I don't indulge in some vigorous activity. Come, it will be amusing."

Everard responded to the wolfish grin and glittering eyes with a rather weak smile. "I'm afraid I have no talent for the art. My father saw no need for me to cultivate the capacity for violence."

The viscount arched a languid brow, his wide, sensual mouth twisting in a poorly restrained smirk. "Really? In

258

France, it is a game for children and the sport of men. Parisians are a passionate lot. They settle everything with a blade. Using one well is as necessary as having one's trousers done before going out in public. The French will duel over any slight, but mostly they quarrel over women. If a man looks at a French noble's wife, it is cause enough to draw steel. I've seen many an innocent man fall in the Bois de Boulogne for a harmless flirtation. I myself have never seen fit to call anyone out. But then, I was not married at the time."

The arc of deadly steel came up to bisect Geoffrey's face. The tip of his tongue traced lightly over his bottom lip as his brilliant gaze caressed the curved blade. He brought it down with a quick slice that made the other jump nervously.

"Being a gentle soul, I suppose you see no value in the *affaire d'honneur*. I would rather avoid it myself unless unforgivably provoked. I don't think Rosalind would intentionally tempt a man to his death. She's much too sensible. And besides, she is too in love with me to lead another astray. I am a fortunate man. But then, I am putting you to the blush with the particulars of my marriage." He drained his glass and tossed it to Henri. The intense eyes focused on the blanching Everard, and the languid ease was abruptly dismissed from his pose. He snapped his fingers, then deftly caught Henri's saber in his left hand. Using the two swords together, he plucked a bunch of freshly cut flowers from their vase and gave them a toss in the air. They fell in a fine confetti after the scissorlike flourishes of the twin blades slashed them to pieces.

"I am as jealous as any man who possesses a woman he loves. I wouldn't hesitate to do the same to anyone who threatened my happiness." His toe scuffed the colorful petals, then he was all congenial smiles. With a careless disregard, he flipped one of the sabers, catching it by the blade so he could extend it toward Everard. "Take it. I'll show you a few moves. You need have no fear that you'll come to harm. After all, I have no reason to wish you harm."

Everard looked from the sword to the mangled flowers then into the bright dazzling stare of the smiling viscount. It took a ridiculous effort to swallow and to keep his voice from shaking as badly as his knees. "Thank you, but I must decline. I have a rather urgent matter to attend to."

"Oh, too bad. Maybe another time. I'm always willing to give a lesson to someone deserving." The blade was reversed in his hand a second time with a casualness that was frightening, at least to the anxious Nathaniel.

Geoffrey smiled at his hurried retreat then turned to his brother. Henri had to react quickly to catch the reckless return of his weapon.

"Stand me to a few more rounds, Hank," he challenged cheerfully. "This country life will make me dreadfully fat."

Their swordplay was interrupted some minutes later by a sharp voice.

"Chilton!"

Distracted, he glanced toward his wife then ducked the fierce slice of Henri's blade. He countered with an agile attack that ended with the Frenchman disarmed and admitting defeat with a sullen chagrin. He handed Henri his saber and crossed to where Rosalind waited, her features a study of displeasure. Without letting him catch his breath, she began a harsh inquisition.

"What did you say to Nate? He came to me shaking like a *blanc-manger*, mumbling some nonsense about having to leave right away. If you put him off with some bullying arrogance, I'll never forgive you. I've told you there is no romance between Everard and me, that we are just old friends, yet you insist upon moaning about like a wronged man. If you have dared—"

He had listened patiently to her tirade to this point, then, grinning broadly, drew her up to the sweaty heat of his body and seized her lips in a masterful kiss. Rosalind's fists struck him once, then again, then opened so her hands could glide up over the curve of his shoulders. When he would lean away, smugly satisfied, she pursued the generous part of his mouth and enticed him down for a deeper exchange. Her fingers curled in the wet hair at the nape of his neck and were reluctant to release him.

"After that, could you believe I'd fear another man taking you from me?" he teased huskily. His large hands rubbed her shoulders, then lingered down her arms as if he didn't want to stop touching her. "Look at me. Do you find anything lacking that would make you seek another? You didn't lead me to believe so last night."

Blushing, she cast a quick glance to Henri who was idly

examining his boot heels, then let her gaze scorch over the splendid figure before her. No, she could find no fault. Lord Chilton was every well-defined inch a man. The sight of him, his skin flushed with a sheen of perspiration and damp shirt delineating the powerful contours of his torso, made her deliciously warm and anxious. The want to feel the slick heat of him unencumbered in her arms and to taste the moist delight of his mouth upon her own made her look away self-consciously. His knuckles brushed her highly colored cheek to bring her gaze up.

"In answer to your question, all I did was invite Everard to join me in a little sport. He declined. More fond of exercising his brain than his brawn, I gather. I was the perfect host. My voice never raised, nor did my temper. I swear to you, Roz, not once did I try to bully him. After all, I know how much you enjoy his company."

Rosalind gave him a long, critical stare. He seemed completely innocent, deep eyes wide and guileless and smile, harmless. Her lips pursed suspiciously as she pointed to the tattered bouquet.

"What happened there?"

"I was testing the edge of the blades. Everard seemed quite impressed," he remarked blandly.

"I'm certain he was." Her mouth quirked in a reproachful smile, sure the timid Nathaniel had envisioned his entrails so filleted. Yet how could she kindle ire at such a picture of boyish blamelessness? Mischievous but not mean, she was reminded. "You are incorrigible, sir," she pronounced to show him she was neither fooled nor upset. He responded to her mood eagerly.

"When are our houseguests leaving?" he asked a trifle too enthusiastically.

"The way Nate was scurrying, they'll be down the drive before I have a chance to say good-bye. Shame on you, Chilton."

"Are you very angry with me?" His tone was winningly subdued.

"Yes, very." However, the way her fingertips brushed the back of his hand took the sting from her words. "A perfect host would dress himself properly to see them off."

"With pleasure, my lady." His grin was disarming as he brought her hand to his lips. When he released it, she gave him a gentle swat that made his smile that much wider.

Lord and Lady Chilton stood together on the steps of Dunstan Manor to witness the departure of their guests. Even the sulky Nathaniel had to admit what a fine couple they made. The elegant viscount kept his wife tucked into his side with a possessive hand upon her shoulder. Beside him, Rosalind seemed content to remain. Her countenance glowed when the deep blue eyes lowered to collect a shy smile. Her hand rested lightly against his stylish waistcoat. In that quickly exchanged glance, Everard learned all. Here were two people in love. Rosalind would be safe with her rather brash husband, he told himself, grateful for the excuse to withdraw his protection. He had seen beyond the wide smile and amiable words and did not want to provoke Geoffrey Chilton. Seeing his devotion to his burgeoning wife, he wondered if the accounts of his notoriety were exaggerated by Rosalind's stepmother. The matter was out of his hands. He was looking forward to the quiet of their own shabby estate. And when they returned to London, he would begin suit with an eligible lady of fortune. Rosalind Chilton was not going to be available.

The great house fell into an odd silence after the Everards were gone. Yet with all the empty space, Rosalind felt crowded, alone within the same walls as Geoffrey. Though she didn't see him for the rest of the day, the aura of his presence seemed to surround her. It was an uncomfortable and at the same time exhilarating feeling. She warned herself to be on her guard against his stealthy charm. He'd been able to steal her sensibilities from the first with a show of dimpled cheeks and was no less vulnerable now. She had taken a stand to hold him to his promises and if she let herself be swayed from it, she could never command his respect, or indeed, her own. She wouldn't be taken lightly or for granted again. She was his wife, the mother of his child and he claimed to want nothing beyond. She would see and it was not going to be easy to convince her. Or was it?

Geoffrey wasted no time in wooing her. A clattering of silver brought her curiously into the sitting room after dressing for dinner. There she found an intimate meal for two being laid out before the fire. From his opposite doorway, Geoffrey launched his attack with a slow, inviting smile. Her barriers began to crumble. Determinedly, she called forth reinforcements to counter the subtle sensuality he used as a weapon. Her fingers clutched the richly colored skirt of her gown. The brilliant hue never failed to stiffen her with remembered injury. It was the color of rubies.

Geoffrey abandoned his languorous pose and crossed to collect his dinner companion. He executed a handsome bow and lifted her hand.

"Good evening, Lady Chilton. I thought you might enjoy a quiet repast after suffering so many boisterous ones during the past weeks."

Rosalind smiled cynically. His tone was as smoothly textured as her sumptuous silk gown. That made him extremely dangerous. "How thoughtful, my lord," she said noncommittally as he led her to the small table. After seating her, his hands took liberties with the soft expanse of skin along her arms and shoulders. It was all she could do not to tremble. Very dangerous indeed, she reminded herself.

They dined mostly in silence and he was right—it was wonderfully appreciated. Rosalind hadn't realized how the Everards had worn on her. The peaceful moment was as gratefully received as the company. The dusky stare studied her in a confident assessment over the tender pieces of ham and roast beef. He viewed her like some confection he was saving for dessert. She wasn't sure she minded.

When the dishes were cleared away, his insistently intimate manner grew more apparent. The knowledge that they were alone in the great house, without distraction or the need for convention fueled his determined courtliness. The heated enticement of his gaze and compelling strength of his nearness brought up her desperate defenses. With no minions to support her, the battle was entirely in her hands and she was afraid surrender was imminent and unconditional.

Restless under his caressing stare, she moved to the window. It was cooler there, the fierce October winds seeping through the inefficient panes. The chill felt reviving after the stifling heat of the fire burning in the grate and in her veins. Both could use a little temperance if she was to be comfortable.

"How beautiful you look tonight, my precious one," he began in a sultry siege upon her will.

Lest her defiant pose fall with shameless ease, Rosalind

263

turned to the offensive with a careful sortie. She had listened to his beseeching vows of renewed faithfulness. Now, she would test their strength.

"It's the gown. It's always been my favorite. I should be wearing my rubies. How stunning they would look. I'll send Jessup for them."

"No, he objected, then relaxed with a smile. "You look perfect as you are."

She returned his smile tartly, then drove her attack forward without mercy. "I must wear them tonight. I overlooked them in my case. Perhaps Jessup put them somewhere for safekeeping. She knows how I treasure the necklace."

Geoffrey was very still. Rosalind could imagine the frantic scramble of his thoughts. What would he tell her? Some elaborate lie, or would he stand silent? She felt no guilt in watching him squirm . . . well, only very little.

Admiringly, he didn't create a quick story and had the decency to look mortally afraid, if only for an instant. He turned away from her. She didn't need to see his face to read his mood. His stance was rigid, his shoulders a taut line of tension. His answer didn't come glibly.

"Jessup doesn't have it and neither do you any longer," he told her quietly.

"How could you know that, my lord?"

His shoulders rose and fell with the mighty effort of his next breath. "Because I took it from you the night before you left London."

"Why would you do such a thing, Geoffrey?" She waited, wondering if she was a fool for hoping he would tell of his gift to his lover. Did she really want to hear the details? Could she bear the knowledge from his own lips? She realized her mistake in bringing up the matter. She didn't want to know. She wanted to pretend none of it had ever happened so her pride wouldn't demand she retaliate. She didn't want his answer to end the fragile truce between them. And in a way, it didn't.

"I needed the money, Roz. I was in a tight pinch and could find no other way."

"If you needed to stave off creditors, why didn't you go to Papa—or come to me?"

His laugh was short. "And have you crying that I'd married you for your money all over again? No, thank you. I

264

prefer to be tagged a wretch than a beggar. I saw a chance to take care of two miseries at once and didn't consider the consequences."

"Two? What was the other one?"

"The necklace. That damned necklace. I hate the sight of it and even more so around your neck."

Rosalind was taken aback by the odd turn his apology had taken. Now, he was the aggrieved party and very angry. "Geoffrey, I don't understand. I thought it was a match to your mother's ring."

"Not a match, a copy, and a vile one at that," he said harshly. He began to pace in agitation, almost forgetting the original cause of their confrontation, as, in fact, had she. "Seeing you wear it and knowing its place in my family was too offensive. I couldn't bear the reminder. I know what I did was wrong and I beg your pardon. I don't expect you to understand or forgive me. I stole from you. There is no excuse. I should have been the one to leave, not Everard. At least he was honorable."

His restless traversing brought him to her side, where he plucked in fierce distraction at the heavy drapery cord. She regarded his taut profile for a long moment as a decision warred in the battleground between head and heart. Finally, the fighting within her stopped and acceptance gave her voice an unwavering control.

"What's mine is yours, Geoffrey. That foundation was laid on the day we spoke our vows. The necklace belonged to your family and was rightfully more yours than mine. Had you asked, I would have given it freely. Yet, you didn't."

The generous mouth thinned as his features tightened into a severe relief of shadows. He wouldn't look at her. He couldn't stand to see contempt in the same velvety eyes that had once glowed with love.

"Will you tell me what secret the necklace holds?"

The golden head shook sharply. "No."

"Then I don't understand and I can't forgive, but, Geoff, I'd like to forget."

He turned to her uncertainly, even flinching slightly as her arms circled him and her head lay over the startled pumping of his heart. His surprise-leadened arms rose to gather her more closely still.

"Where does this leave us then?" he asked softly.

265

"Looking forward, never back. We have our first child coming. The future holds too much to be fettered by the past. I want you in that future, Geoffrey Chilton, not Nathaniel or endless years of spinsterish solitude. I want you, my vexing and oh-so-handsome lord and I shall never tire of wanting you."

She tipped back her head and his lowered so their lips could meet in an unhurried affirmation of what stirred within their hearts. As Rosalind's hands rose to cup his face between them, Geoffrey grew aware of a more prominent stirring. In unsettled reluctance, he held her away.

"I'd better say good night to you now," he said gruffly. When her fingertips touched his compressed lips, his eyes darkened in discomfort. "Good night, my lady," he repeated staunchly. He took her hand and bowed over it formally, then nearly fled the room. Rosalind smiled after him, her hands resting on the plump curve of her waistline.

"Good night, my lord. For now," she said softly.

Chapter Twenty-five

Over the next two months, a pleasant rhythm was adopted at Dunstan Manor. With only the lord and lady in residence, formality was relaxed and comfort the mode. Though Rosalind watched him anxiously, Geoffrey showed no signs of growing restless with the leisurely pace or with her company, which he rarely abandoned. Their days were spent in long carriage rides until the bumpy conditions and her own increasing one ended the jaunts in favor of walking. Rosalind insisted it didn't overtire her and that it couldn't be but good for the child. When the winds grew sharp, she would huddle inside Geoffrey's voluminous great coat while they strolled. The warmth of his nearness was more than an equal to the weather.

She found her husband a fascinating companion. He was ever charming and always amusing with anecdotes from his years in France. She couldn't help but notice for all his stories, none went deeper than the superficial. He was as much a mystery as ever. He spoke of the nobles' life with a searing humor, as if he secretly scorned it. That was another puzzle, his contempt for that which he courted so aggressively. He was a continuous contradiction in all but his devotion to her.

Geoffrey treated her with a tender deference. As her girth grew larger and her step cumbersome, he was ever solicitous. He handed her carefully up and down the stairs and out of the treacherous sinking cushions and provided a nightly massage to her aching neck and back and swollen feet. For all his pampering and gentle care, there were times after their quiet dinner while nestled on the sitting-room settee when he would turn to her with sudden urgent kisses that made her feel desirable rather than maternal. When the heated demands of his mouth escalated to tantalizing touch, the babe would stir with untimely vigor to set him back with profuse apology and reddened countenance. Chagrined at being unable to control his lusting for a

267

woman so obviously with child, he would beg her leave and stomp about in the cold night air until his ardor sufficiently cooled.

Henri was another puzzle she sought to solve. While he was faultlessly correct in her presence, with Geoffrey he was casual to the point of insolence. When she had come upon him in the middle of seducing a giggling maid in the upper hall, he had given her a mocking bow yet voiced no apology nor released his hold about the girl's slender waist. When she confronted Geoffrey rather prudishly with his valet's bold behavior, he had grinned and murmured he would ask him to be more discreet. Ask, not tell. Provoked by his indifference, she had called Henri in to dress him down stiffly. He bore her lecture stoically. Appeased, she began to march away, then turned to catch the two of them mimicking her severity with naughty-boy smirks. Indignantly, she refused to join Geoffrey for dinner, preferring to pout in her room until loneliness and the ridiculousness of it made her recant. She found the two of them in their shirtsleeves splitting a bottle of wine and a saddle of mutton. Their feet came immediately off the table as Rosalind joined them without comment. The three of them dined together and thereafter, Henri's rather unorthodox position in the household was never questioned again. Rosalind accepted him as Geoffrey did, unconditionally, and was pleased to find he possessed a droll, sharp humor when coaxed to give his opinions. Somehow, she guessed that by earning Henri's approval, odd as it seemed to her, she was that much closer to Geoffrey.

Camilla's letters came with the weekly post. They were entertaining bits of gossip containing little substance so Rosalind was sometimes remiss in opening them right away. A particularly thin missive lay forgotten overnight which only heightened her guilty horror when she scanned it after breakfast.

Geoffrey's eyes settled on his wife's face over the rim of his teacup. His frown grew apace with her pallor until worry made him demand to know what was wrong.

Rosalind set down the single sheet. Her misty eyes lifted in a daze. It was a moment before she could master speech. "It's Papa. He's suffered another seizure. Cammy says the doctor gives little hope of a full recovery. I must leave at once."

Geoffrey scooped up the note and read through it quickly. The news was indeed grim, telling of partial paralysis and loss of speech. He recalled the promise he had made to keep the truth of his condition a secret. That oath seared his conscience as he looked after the ungainly retreat of his wife. He caught up to her on the stairs, tempering her rush with a cautioning hand on her arm. She clung to him gratefully, already winded, yet she rebelled against his gentle words.

"I know how worried you must be, Roz, but I can't let you go. The child is due next month. You can't afford to risk such a long, upsetting journey."

Knowing he was right didn't please her. She had been so healthy throughout her pregnancy that to be held helpless by it at such a crucial time was unfair and frustrating. "But I must," she cried irrationally. "He's my father. What if he doesn't recover? I'd never forgive myself for not being there."

They had reached the hall and Geoffrey turned her into the circle of his arms. "It's too dangerous, precious one. You must consider the child you carry. Your father would be the first to discourage you from the trip. I know what it's like to be powerless when a loved one is suffering. Believe me, I do understand. If I could help you, I would."

Rosalind brightened. "You go," she suggested suddenly. "You go in my stead. Please, Geoffrey. I would feel so much better."

Geoffrey hesitated, hoping the dismay that froze his insides wasn't betrayed on his features. A journey to London was the last thing he wished to take. He couldn't be certain the danger was no longer there. He didn't want to bet his life on it.

Then he looked into the moist, velvety eyes that lifted so trustingly to him and he heard himself saying, "I'll go."

While he packed a single bag, Geoffrey was aware of Henri's probing gaze. He didn't want to meet it, leery of the questions that he didn't want to answer, yet when the final catch was secured, he could find no excuse.

Henri only needed a sample of his brother's furtive glance to demand, "What is it, Geoff?"

"I've grown quite fond of the earl. This isn't a pleasant trip to make."

Henri wasn't taken in. He began to frown and, inexplica-

269

bly, to worry. The quick, anxious movements hinted at something more, something more visceral than concern, something like fear that could bring a sweat on a cool December morning.

"It's not Dunstan. It's London," he guessed shrewdly. The reaction was subtle but conclusive. "I didn't press you when we left but I must now. What trouble are you in, Geoff? Don't bother to spin some pretty lie. I know you too well. We've been one step ahead of fate too many times for me not to know the look behind your eyes. What's put it there? What are you keeping from me, *mon frère?*"

Geoffrey looked into the somber, dark eyes and nearly faltered. Then his pride stiffened his resolve. He was no longer a boy who could depend on an older brother to wage his wars and expel his fears. He had a child on the way and a wife who looked up at him through eyes warm with trust.

In a low voice, in accents calm and firm, Geoffrey replied, "It is nothing for you to worry over, Hank. I owe some money, a paltry sum, really. I plan to sell everything expendable and get myself right again. It was my doing, my foolishness, so I'll see to it myself."

Henri stood silent for a long moment. He didn't know how to respond. He was used to the role of parent, stern, chastising, yet ever helpful. It was a role Geoffrey always encouraged with his childlike desperation and nervous panic in the throes of his reckless deeds. This sudden, mature self-sufficiency rocked him. He found himself oddly reluctant to let go of the little brother he had always sheltered and protected.

"If that's what you want, Geoff."

Geoffrey smiled and gave a certain nod. He paused, wondering how to phrase his next request without firing Henri's suspicions all over. Finally, he said quietly, "If some mishap should befall me, I want you to take care of Rosalind. Remember, you're her baby's uncle."

The handsome features tightened, but his answer was reassuring. "I'll see to my *belle-soeur* and you see to yourself."

Geoffrey started to take his extended hand, then with a sheepish grin, wiped the dampness from his palm on his trouserleg before grasping it. Henri used the fond clasp to pull his brother into an embrace.

"How dangerous is this, Geoff?" he insisted quietly when he felt the other's tension.

"Dangerous enough" was the gruff reply.

"Let me come with you, *mon cher.*"

"Not this time, Hank." Geoffrey pushed away with a grim smile. "I shan't be gone long. I can't be late for the birth of my first child."

"See that you're not."

Henri released him as if under protest, but the dark eyes shone with a proud respect. That single glance was more heartening to Geoffrey than any other encouragement could have been. He surrendered his heavy portmanteau to his quasi-manservant with a quick grin.

Rosalind greeted him in the hall with an awkward hug over the massive obstruction of her belly. He held to her tightly, breathing in the poignantly familiar scent of her and delighting in the soft catch of her breath as if she restrained a sob. He brushed a kiss upon her temple and forced himself to let her go.

"Don't be gone long, my lord," she said huskily.

His response was gently teasing. "You sound as though you shall miss me."

"Nonsense," she returned saucily, but her moist gaze countered that claim. She looped her arm through the gallantly crooked elbow and walked down the stairs with him. She held him up in the front hall with an unvoiced reluctance. She was sending him to London, the city of temptation and past deceptions. She was sending him alone to where his lovers waited, enticingly slim and eager, to fulfill the needs he'd abstained from with her. How inviting they would seem after being cloistered with a plump, often grumpy wife for three months. Would he resist the easy availability of all he had enjoyed before? Would he want to?

Something in her closed expression or in the pinch of her fingers on his supporting arm must have clued him to her turmoil. He cupped her cheek with a warm palm as his thumb lightly rubbed over soft, wistfully parted lips.

"I'll be back as soon as I can. I'll be thinking of you and our baby every second I'm away. Don't let the anxious little creature arrive in my absence. I'll try to return within the week unless your father has pressing matters for me to see to. I'll send word either way so you won't worry. I shall miss you, Lady Chilton."

He bent forward and touched his lips to hers in sweet promise. When he began to straighten, her hands rose to capture his face between them and hasten his return for an urgent kiss. That long, impassioned exchange chased the doubts from her mind.

"I love you, Geoffrey," she whispered against his desirous mouth. She felt his smile and her spirits rose buoyantly.

"Good." He cleared his throat so his passion wouldn't roughen his words and told her, "Henri will take care of you. You rest and don't worry over anything."

"Tell my father I would have come if I could."

"I'm sure he knows that, but I'll tell him anyway."

"Tell him his grandson is impatient to see him."

Geoffrey grinned and touched one hand lovingly to the heavy middle and the other to her cheek. Afraid to test his will any further, he took up his bag and opened the front door. The chill of the day was bracing. His chaise waited and one of the footmen hurried to take his bag. He glanced back once to the sight of the two he loved most in the world and prayed he would have no delays in returning to them quickly. Raising a hand, he turned and stepped into the coach.

The house on Charles Street was unnaturally quiet, giving Geoffrey a sense of foreboding. He was welcomed in a hushed voice by one of the servants and directed upstairs. The upper halls befitted the silence of mourning. Geoffrey's Hessians echoed with unseemly vigor along the polished wood floors. The sound brought up the nodding head of the woman seated in the sitting room next to Dunstan's. She regarded him through tired, fatigue-circled eyes, then gave a soft acknowledging cry.

"Oh, Geoffrey," she called in heavy anguish as she came out of the chair that had held her both day and night. Her arms went tightly about his middle as her dark head sought the comfort of his shoulder. Her genuine emotions of relief and upset made it easy for him to hold her in a gesture of compassion. "I'm so glad to see you," she continued faintly. "I don't think I could have managed much longer alone. Is Lindy with you?" She stepped back and cast a weary glance over his shoulder.

"No. It wasn't safe for her to make the trip. I came with her best wishes for her father. How is he?"

Camilla ran a distracted hand through the untidy tendrils that brushed her lovely face. "Better, I think, but far from fine. He can speak, but his words are difficult to understand and that makes him impatient. He's such a proud man. His right arm and leg are useless. He gets so angry when I try to help him. I'm so worn out I don't know what to do." She looked it, too. He had never seen her appear less than flawless, yet, somehow, her mussed look made her even more alluring with its hint of a vulnerable nature.

"May I see him?"

"He'll welcome seeing you. Oh, Geoffrey, thank you for coming."

"While I'm with him, why don't you lie down and take your mind off everything. I'll see to it all."

The gentle suggestion brought a surprising dampness to the bright blue eyes. She clutched his hand gratefully. How good it was to have his strength to lean on. Slowly, her tired eyes lingered over him. And how good it was to have him here, alone.

Geoffrey stepped into the darkened bedroom. It smelt stale like sickness and death. Determinedly, he crossed to the window and threw open the heavy drapes so the crystaline December sunshine would scatter the shadowy depression. He schooled his features so his reaction to Dunstan's wasted appearance wouldn't be evident when he turned to the sunken figure on the bed.

"Good day, my lord. I'm here to walk in your shoes till you can fill them again. What can I do?"

For the next few days, Geoffrey was busy securing Dunstan's interests from those who'd thought to take advantage of him. They learned quickly that his son-in-law was more than competent, but, in his own way, as shrewd a businessman as his predecessor. Though gratified by his successes, Geoffrey was eager to finish his work so he could return to where his thoughts strayed. He smiled when he considered how he had changed, he who always ran with the bit in his teeth now content to be tethered. Along with the anxiousness to return to his wife lurked a fear of what was in London, the threat of his past and the lovely temptress who watched him with plotting eyes across the supper table each night.

Once she had Geoffrey to intercede with Dunstan, Camilla's vivacious charm was quick to return. Geoffrey

273

was surprised by how deeply she seemed to care for her ailing husband. She spent hours at his side, reading or just chattering and was quick to fluff a pillow or cater to any whim. He was suspect of such devotion, reminded of her friendship with Rosalind that she turned so cruelly to her advantage. Even when she was on her best behavior, he refused to relax his guard. The beautiful lady was too unpredictable and too dangerous.

As they dined together, Geoffrey insisting on the formal dining room instead of the intimate setting of her sitting room that she had suggested, he announced casually, "I'll be returning to the manor in several days."

The vivid blue eyes flashed up to fasten on his. "You can't."

Geoffrey raised a languid brow. "I beg your pardon?"

Camilla licked her lips nervously, then presented a sweetly entreating face. "But, Chilton, I cannot manage alone. I know nothing of his lordship's business."

"That's why, with his permission, I've engaged a very capable man to see to it until he can himself. So you see, everything will be taken care of."

She chewed her petulant lip for a moment under his cool regard. When she spoke, her tone was peevish and purely selfish. "But what about me? I need you here."

"For what purpose, my dear *belle-mère?*"

"Because I am bored. I have no one to talk to, no one to make me feel alive. Even your contempt is more invigorating than most men's suit. Everyone is either in Paris or lingering in that horrid Vienna. I'm the only one who can't escape. All I have is you and I will not let you desert me."

He smiled ruefully and said, "Madam, it is not my place to entertain you."

"But you have and you do," she insisted. She tried to capture his hand, but he made it unavailable. With a helpless sigh, she exclaimed, "You must stay. You simply must."

"I have a wife to return to, in case you've forgotten, and a child due to be born."

"Wife," she sneered scornfully. "How can you speak of that drab, colorless figure with any affection. What can she possibly offer that I cannot give in greater abundance?"

"Her love," he said bluntly.

"Lud, what a fool you've become." She laughed. The music of it was discordant. "What is love when wealth is in the balance? Together, we could have it all, Geoffrey, everything we've dreamed of, the fine clothes, the elaborate parties, jewels, respect, travel, pink champagne by the buckets." The sudden shimmer of his eyes made her smile tauntingly. "Of course you want it. It's all that matters, having it all."

Geoffrey swallowed the choking taste of his avarice and told her, "I already have it all."

"And if her child is a girl, what then?" Camilla jeered. "Are you prepared to live on an allowance, counting your shillings, wearing last season's styles? Do you want to live in dull obscurity in that dreary country house with only Lindy's plain face to view day after day?"

"And hopefully year after year. You've no idea, do you, of what it's like to care for someone, to care enough to do without?"

"Why should I? Dunstan gives me everything."

"And how do you repay him?"

Her delicate features tightened. "I've done nothing to be ashamed of. I never fooled James, not for a minute. He's always known I married him for the money and it doesn't bother him. All he wanted was a pretty companion, not a soulmate. I am what he asked for. And I do care."

"And what of Rosalind?"

"Don't blame me for her gullibility," she said in a crisp defense. "She was eager to believe what she saw and I took advantage of it—just as you did. So who is more to blame, my self-righteous lord?"

Geoffrey was silent for a moment, hating it that she was right. What an unscrupled pair they were. "I think I shall leave tomorrow," he said flatly as he dropped his napkin to his plate. "Excuse me, Lady Dunstan. I have arrangements to make." He pushed away from the table while she glared in thinly guised fury.

"You're not the only one who has arrangements to make. I would have protected you, Geoffrey, but not any longer." He didn't pause to question her odd words but began to walk away. She shouted after him, "I'll make you sorry, *Lord* Chilton. You'll regret the choice you've made."

"I already regret many of them. Good night, my lady."

He found no peace from her as he stood at his window, watching a cold dismal rain fall in the slumbering winter gardens. How much more dreary his own spirit. He had to tell Rosalind the truth. He turned from the speckled glass and began a restless pacing. She wouldn't forgive him. He'd already pushed her to her limits but he couldn't go on keeping to the lie, living each day under the threat of exposure. She would be hurt, but how much more so if she heard it from damning lips such as Camilla's. He tried to convince himself that if she truly loved him, the past wouldn't matter, but his lying to her about it was another thing all together.

While he moralized and fretted over his limited options, he was unaware that many of them were being taken from him as a furtive message was sent from the house on Charles Street to a scurrilous tavern. At least he was until a poorly penned note was brought to him. He broke the crude seal and read the short summons. There would be no more running from the past.

Chapter Twenty-six

Located at the end of Charles Street where it became a rutted lane, the Red Lion was crowded with coachmen and grooms from the nearby Berkeley mews. The secluded and well-kept pub with its low-ceilinged rooms and intimate nooks had long been a favorite of the below-stair residents of the great houses and it was a rare night when its tables weren't full, even on one as damp and miserable as the one that brought Geoffrey Chilton to it.

A single figure in a dripping great coat drew no undo attention as he wove between the tables to be quickly flanked by two burly men. They escorted him into the shadowed rear of the large room where a sharp-faced man awaited.

"How nice of you to come out on such a night," the ferral man said with false sincerity. He poured a second mug of what he was drinking and pushed it toward the discreetly garbed man.

"How did you find me?"

"Simple, my greedy friend. We followed your line of creditors right to your door. You have predictable habits." The smug smirk faded into razor-sharp grimness. "Now, to business."

Having no great want to linger, Geoffrey asked tersely, "How much to leave me alone and to disappear and forget I exist?"

"I think £60,000 would cause that memory loss."

The figure was staggering, but Geoffrey didn't haggle. He wanted the matter behind him and his mind worked quickly to find a way. "I can get you five, maybe six by day after tomorrow."

"And give you time to disappear again? I think not."

"Don't be a fool. Do you think I carry that kind of blunt about in my pockets?"

The cutting tone set La Belette back with a narrowed look. He would deal with his impertinence after he had the

277

money. "When can I expect the rest?"

Geoffrey sketched out the terms of Dunstan's inheritance, omitting the risk of chance on the baby's sex. No need to make them more nervous than they already were, he thought prudently. "Watch for the announcement of the birth. I'll contact you as soon as the money is turned into my trust."

"We'll contact you, Jenoit or Chilton, whichever you like. Never fear, we shan't be far away. And I want £15,000 delivered to me tomorrow evening."

Geoffrey gaped at him. "That's impossible."

"You've always managed the impossible before. Don't make us come looking for you or I may decide your life is a better payment than your money."

After running all the way back to the house, Geoffrey was soaked and shivering with nerves as well as cold as he tore through his room, tossing everything of value onto the bed. A quick tally left his total far short. Mentally, he listed all he could think of: curricle, the pair of bays, the landau—no, that wasn't paid for yet. Why not? he thought and included it anyway. Not enough. Figures swirled in his head. Not enough. Frantically, he crossed to Rosalind's room and methodically searched through it. He allowed himself a tremulous smile when he opened a drawer in her dressing table. Carelessly, he pitched the vibrant stones onto its top until they glittered together, diamonds, amethysts, topazes. He scooped them into an indifferent handful, then stopped. His breath hissed jaggedly into the stillness of the room. He stared down at the sparkling trickle of gems that trailed from his grasping fingers and gave a low cry of disgust.

"What can I be thinking?" he moaned aloud. "Oh, Roz, forgive me for even considering it."

He let the jewels drop back into the drawer and shut it quickly before his desperate mood could convince him otherwise. Angry with himself but no less anxious, he stepped into the hall.

"You're very restless tonight, my lord."

Camilla Dunstan created a picture no man could look away from easily. Why she wore a wrapper was inconceivable. It was a sheer cloud of pale blue gossamer. The gown it sought coyly to conceal and reveal was a web of fragile lace. The backlight from her open bedroom door shone through it with an intriguing play of tempting shadow. She had the face of a sweet angel and the body of a shameless devil.

"Come, Geoffrey. Join me for a glass and we'll talk about your troubles."

The honied voice lured him across the hall to where he knew he shouldn't go but couldn't keep himself from. Her boudoir was a fantasy of frothy pink gauzes and the scent of roses. While he stood awkwardly at the door, Camilla floated away to pour a glass of amber liquor. His eyes followed the fluid feminine motion as she knew they would. She brought him the glass and coaxed it gently into his unsteady hand.

"What troubles you, my lord? I would offer my help, if I can," she purred invitingly.

Senses dulled by the sensual play of peek-a-boo lace and drugged by heavy panic, he heard himself confide, "I need to raise some money. At least £10,000."

The petal-soft lips curved in a sultry smile. "I can help you, Geoffrey. We can consider it a personal loan. Shall we discuss the terms?"

He was tired, frustrated, cornered. It was so easy to listen to her offer of salvation, so enjoyable lingering over her pleasing features and perfect form, so comforting having her hands slide up the lapels of his coat to warmly cup his damp, half frozen face. Her lips were warm and encouraging as well, moving slowly upon his to entice an apt response. The diaphanous robe filtered to the floor at the persuasion of his roving hands. She leaned into the hard strength of his body, reveling in it the way she knew he did hers. It had been so long, his passions moaned seditiously. She was offering things he needed, an answer to all in such an agreeable package. He would have his money and the comfort of ending his long-frustrated celibacy. It was all so tempting and his will trembled with self-serving weakness. She knew him well. They were alike.

His breath had deepened and grown quick, she assumed with passion. Camilla let her eyes close, pliable in the large, strong hands. Her words were throaty with the promise of satisfaction.

"I knew it would be like this with us," she breathed against his parted lips. "I always knew you'd be mine."

The smug, hungry words and the eager quest of her

hands inside his coat brought Geoffrey's wavering thoughts into sharp, painful focus. My God, here he was being so noble about not stealing his wife's jewels when he was ready to take from her what she valued the most.

Camilla was round-eyed with astonishment when she found herself pushed firmly away. It took her a moment to control her galloping passions.

"Forgive me, madam. I have trespassed where I had no right to be," he said stiffly.

"But it is right," she protested, molding her supple figure to him only to be shaken off abruptly.

"No, nothing about this is right," he said, backing away. His eyes were dark and unreadable.

"What about your money?" she demanded.

"You ask for too much interest" was his soft reply. He executed a formal bow in parting and escaped the silken trap that would have destroyed him.

The next rainy afternoon found Geoffrey stripped of all possessions and still nearly £10,000 shy of what he needed to have. Too deep with the moneylenders to go there, he was left with the unsavory task of trying to borrow from an acquaintance. The pickings were as thin as Camilla had forewarned, most of the wealthy out of town. Geoffrey scanned White's elegant interior, dismayed to find so few dandies in house. He managed to draw Brummell aside to confide his difficulties. The Beau nodded with cool sympathy but was no help to his cause.

"You've caught me at an awkward time, Chilton, being quite strapped myself. If the tables show me the face of fortune perhaps I can be more generous tomorrow." He quizzed his peer's hastily wrought cravat with a displeased eye. "Really, Chilton, an empty pocket is no excuse to go about untidy. It really won't do."

Geoffrey managed a tight smile at the pompous criticism and thanked him graciously for the offer even though the sentiments would be too late. He wasted hours directing the same plea to countless others to much the same result, profuse apologies but no assistance. Darkness was settling about him with a chilling warning as he walked aimlessly toward Berkeley Square. He braved the cold drizzle with hunched shoulders because he didn't have the cost of a hack. His future was as unpromising as the desolate night fast approaching with its fateful hour. In a heavy gloom, he considered the options left him. He could meet La Belette with the £5,000 in his pockets. The most pleasant end to that meeting would be his death. To attempt to placate him with such a paltry sum would be suicide. Better not to go at all, he concluded spiritlessly. If he didn't appear, he would have to run. That meant leaving all behind him, fleeing not only London but the country altogether. Without Rosalind, for how could he take her? How could he explain? Bad enough to be waiting like some greedy predator for the birth of her child to yield him the expected carrion of wealth to buy him out of his debts. It was like stealing, stealing from the precious cache of Rosalind's trust. Was there no way to resolve the demands of his past without dealing her an unfair hurt? Perhaps it would better serve them all, Rosalind, her father, Henri, if he just took a fateful step into the all-solving currents of the River Thames.

He continued along beneath his black, hovering cloud of dire consequence when a hail from a slowing coach drew his dejected attention.

"Lord Chilton, can that be you out in this infamous weather? Let me offer you a ride."

He accepted the invitation, settling across from the vivacious redhead with careful deference to his sodden attire. Though he apologized for it, Bella Wellsley could find no fault in his appearance. Some men would look wilted and drowned after such a soak, but Lord Chilton managed to appear even more attractive with the sleek helmet of damp hair and rain-slicked features. The musky, pungent smells of wet wool and crisp, fresh rain mixed in a surprisingly heady fragrance that was basic and very male. Lady Wellsley breathed it in with an excited awareness of the man she longed to savor like that compelling scent. Knowing she never would only made the enticing bouquet more rare and desirable. She could hope for no more than friendship, but she could yet dream.

Smiling wistfully at her own thoughts, Bella asked, "What forces you out on such a disagreeable eve? Can I offer you more than a dry place out of the storm?"

"That will have to suffice, my lady, and I am most grateful for it," he said with a poor imitation of his usual amiability.

"What more do you seek?" she asked, encouraging his

confidence with a familiar hand upon his knee. "You never know from which direction providence falls. It could be from mine."

"It has before," he agreed halfheartedly as if he didn't dare hope. He looked into the florid face to find an earnest expectancy. For all her bold manners, Bella Wellsley was sincerely generous. Even if she had an insufficient purse, she wouldn't be stingy with some much-needed compassion. "I need a selfless benefactor with an easy bankroll to fall into my lap."

"Though your lap offers intriguing possibilities, would you settle for an opposing seat?"

He drew a quick breath. "I need £10,000, tonight."

"Is that all?" she dismissed with a casual wave of her hand.

"I need it without conditions," he added quietly.

"I would ask for one small one," she bartered coyly as her thick lashes fluttered over the gleam in her eyes.

"Madam?"

"One of your delightful kisses, no more, no less."

A smile teased about the morose set of his lips then broke into his dazzling grin. "Done, madam."

Impatiently, Lady Wellsley thumped the roof of her coach and called for her driver to see her to her house. She then sat back, smug and well pleased with the small concession she'd won. "It will be my pleasure entirely, Lord Chilton."

Chapter Twenty-seven

"You're cheating. You must be cheating. Have you told me all of the rules to this game?"

The sulky demand drew Geoffrey to the door of the sitting room with a deepening frown, wondering who his wife could be entertaining at such an hour. When he peered within, it was dispelled, an amused grin taking its place. Rosalind and Henri sat before the fire, she on the settee, bare toes peeping from beneath a shawl and he cross-legged on the floor in his shirtsleeves. Rosalind was examining the cards spread on the table between them with a petulant scowl. For a moment, he was content to absorb the scene of his wife and brother passing the time in each other's amiable company. It created a sense of permanence, of security, of family that swelled within him, pushing aside the shadows of his harrowing time in London. This was reality, solid, good, fortifying, and the warmth of his love for the two of them restored him.

"He does cheat. Terribly."

Two sets of dark eyes flashed about in surprise. Two spontaneous smiles greeted him and never had he felt more welcome, more at home.

"Good evening, my lord. I wasn't aware you would return tonight." How faint and breathless her voice sounded, as if she was experiencing the same crush within her chest as he.

"So I gather. I hope you weren't playing him for money. We'll be paupers for sure."

Henri looked up as Geoffrey's fingertips rested lightly on his shoulder. They exchanged a speaking gaze that conveyed all without a word. It said all was well and thanked him for seeing to his wife, then excused him from the task, eager to resume the role himself.

"You dishonor me, my lord, to suggest I find your generous compensation so lacking that I must fleece your wife in your absence. If you will forgive me, Lady Chilton, I will see to his lordship's unpacking." He rose with a stiff propriety, the consummate servant once more until he slid Rosalind a conspiratorial wink. She withheld her smile with hard won decorum until alone with her husband. Then, he had all her attention.

Geoffrey hung back, lingering by the fireplace with an awkward nonchalance. His smile was strained and his eyes shifting. "I trust Henri kept you amused while I was away," he said casually.

"It was kind of you to lend me his services. He is most unusual as a servant, but quite delightful as a companion." She, too, spoke in a nervous stilted tone. She feared if she did not, her longing would pour forth with unseemly abandon. His distance helped her retain her control. If he was closer, she couldn't have resisted the need to touch him. As it was, looking was temptation enough. And she looked, long and thoroughly, detailing every treasured expanse her eyes traversed in their urgent summation. She didn't want to reveal her mood until certain of his. His guarded stance gave no clues.

"You sound as though you missed me not at all."

The slight pout on his sensual mouth undid her. With a shaky breath, she extended her hand to his unyielding figure. "Come and see how much," she coaxed softly.

When he took her hand in hesitant fingers, she began to struggle up, prompting him to exclaim, "Pray stay seated, madam. Let me come down to you."

And he did, on bended knee before her. His tentative grasp tightened, drawing her hand up to his lips. They had barely brushed the warm skin when he said hurriedly, "You've no idea how I've wanted to be here with you."

The husky emotion in his voice shook Rosalind mightily, rattling her calm and freeing her own desperate desires. Her reply was equally rough. "Oh, I think I do, my lord."

They came together in an eager embrace, lips seeking and finding each other's. Any nagging insecurities Rosalind might have felt during his absence were swept away by the insistent demands of his impatient kisses. She felt weak and all at once powerful beneath the impassioned onslaught. As his mouth moved hungrily upon hers, his hands began a restless caressing, gliding over her flushed cheeks, plying the tumbled weight of her hair, rubbing the smooth flesh of her shoulders as they encouraged her down on the plump arm of the settee. Only when his avid lips left hers to plunder the luscious swell of her breasts did the haze of desire clear enough for her to say his name in a warning protest.

"Geoffrey, Geoffrey, you race too recklessly down a road that is too short. Slow yourself, my lord, lest you take a tumble."

With a frustrated groan, he let his head lie heavily upon the inviting cushion of her bosom. His breath rushed in panting shivers against her bare skin. It was enough to make her want to writhe in her own discomfort.

"Forgive me, my lord, for being helpless to relieve your torment," she murmured regretfully as her fingers threaded through the burnished luxury of his hair.

He begged, "No, forgive me. You must think me singularly coarse to behave like such a rutting beast."

He couldn't see the smile that softened her features with a gentle pleasure. Her words were hushed. "I think I am equally to blame, for I want you most shamefully."

The smoky blue eyes rose in amazement. "Truly?"

Her fingertips grazed his warm cheek and settled upon his mobile mouth. "Truly, my lord."

Their gazes interacted for a long moment of tender telling, then his dusky eyes drifted shut as his kisses nibbled the ends of her fingers. The intent of that gentlemanly gesture soon became anything but as the tempting taste of her led him back to the sweetness of her receptive lips. She sighed in the rapture of the moment, wanting to lose herself there, to be the lover he needed and she wanted to be for him. Then a mindful kick beneath her ribs reminded her that the time was wrong for such indulgent play. With a moan of effort, she twisted to one side and pressed her palms to his chest.

"Perhaps we should just talk," she suggested with an uncomfortable desperation. He straightened immediately and made an affected show of smoothing his attire. When he responded, his voice was strained.

"Yes, that would be more productive." His quick grin relieved the stiffness of his phrase. "And safer," he added ruefully.

They regarded each other with rather shy smiles until a quiet sense of contentment settled between them. To keep her thoughts from the sensuous curve of his mouth and the wide plane of his chest she wished to free from the confines of his correct clothing, Rosalind asked conscientiously, "How is my father?"

Grateful for the sober topic to distract his unrequited lusting, Geoffrey told her how he had left things. He made his tone optimistic to lighten the creases that mapped her brow, then paused. He looked deep into the dark, serious eyes, noting the strength and intelligence there, and unwilling to insult either, he told her the truth of her father's condition. Though her expression puckered in concern, she accepted the grim news bravely.

"I feared it was something like that," she said in a small voice.

Geoffrey took up her hands. He couldn't believe how badly he suffered her distress. "I shouldn't have kept it from you, Roz. I was wrong to think I was sparing you."

There was no hint of blame in the misty stare. "As soon as I'm able to travel with the baby, we must return to London."

Geoffrey's insides recoiled in a massive shudder. Return to London. Panic surged up. He forced his answer to be coolly noncommittal. "Perhaps by then, he will be well enough to visit us here."

Rosalind responded not to his statement but to the sudden dampness of his nearly painful grip on her hands. "Geoffrey, is there something else? Something you haven't told me?"

His smile came with quick insincerity to match the unthinking denial. "No. I'm tired, is all. It's been a long day."

"Of course," she murmured in a tender concern that savaged his heart. "I'll let you retire. We can talk more in the morning."

With his aiding hand on her elbow, Rosalind stood with ungainly difficulty. His glance followed the slender hands that rested atop the full-blown contour of her middle. Mind still dulled, he blurted thoughtlessly, "Why, Roz, you're huge! Are you going to gift me with a child or a pony?"

Devastated, she gave a self-conscious wail and fled with surprising agility into her room. Only when the door slammed did Geoffrey realize his incredible faux pas. Nonplussed, he hurried to make amends.

Rosalind was curled atop her bed, weeping in soulful

286

misery. The gentle hand upon her shoulder caused her lamentations to raise an octave. She shrugged it off and refused to respond to her name. Carefully, she was gathered into an embrace she couldn't escape as he settled on the bed and drew her back to him.

"Don't cry, precious one," he soothed. "I spoke foolishly, in jest, not to hurt you."

"B-but it's true. I am huge and ugly and clumsy. I w-waddle when I walk. I can't get out of a chair and I look like a puffed-up toad. No wonder the sight of me offends you so."

He laughed. He couldn't help it. The sound rolled out in anxious amusement as he struggled to hold her still.

"Don't make sport of me," she cried in tearful fury. "This is your fault, after all."

"Oh, Roz," he began, choking back his inappropriate chuckle. "I delight in looking at you. You are the most beautiful woman in the world to me. It's my jealous desire that makes me foolish. I chafe for every moment our selfish child keeps you from me. My thoughts are scrambled with the want to have you, even now. When this babe arrives, I plan to keep you long abed."

Rosalind rolled toward him, the effort far from graceful. Her palm pressed to his face. "Good," she told him simply with a directness that made him blink. Then he smiled that broad, smug, very male smile of satisfaction. With his arm draped about her, he nestled deeper into the bedcovers. He looked to her with hopeful eyes.

"May I stay here with you tonight?"

Rosalind was surprised by his softly spoken request and alarmed by the effect his proximity had on her. Yes, she wanted him in her bed but not to snuggle against for companionable warmth. Face flushing uneasily, she said, "Oh, Chilton, really I don't think that would be wise."

"I promise not to make things difficult."

"How can you help it? Geoffrey, I—"

"Please, Roz. I need to be with you, to be close to you. Don't send me away."

The anxious plea made her frown. "What's wrong? Please tell me?"

She felt him withdraw on a shakily pulled breath followed by an unconvincing, "Nothing. I missed you is all and it's too soon to part. Let me stay. I won't disturb you."

Rosalind made a doubtful sound but relented. "Be warned. I am very restless these days."

"You won't bother me," he assured her and sat up to quickly tug off his boots. His coat and shirt followed them to the floor, but when he reached for the flap of his trousers, she stayed him with a nervous objection.

"Let's not tempt fate too cruelly."

Geoffrey shrugged and tunneled into the bulky nest of covers. Modestly, she turned down the light before slipping on her nightdress. When she got into bed, Geoffrey's warmth and nearness created an immediate threat. But what an inviting danger. Not appeased by an impartial distance, he rolled over so her gently curved back fit the contours of his chest and his thighs hugged her buttocks. One outstretched arm pillowed both their heads while the other framed her thick middle. She had just begun to relax her misgivings and enjoy the closeness when the seemingly unintentional brush of his fingers made the peak of her breast spring to startled attention.

"Geoffrey," she hissed in warning.

"Excuse me," he muttered into the fragrant mass of her hair and his hand curled laxly about the abundant orb.

"Oh!" she exclaimed in a confusion of helpless desire when she felt the obvious exception to his languorous pose. "Geoff, this was a mistake."

"No mistake," he crooned to pacify her. "I can't help that. It's your fault for not being a huge, ugly toad." He felt the reverberation of her silent laughter and ventured a gentle squeeze.

"Good night, my lord beast."

"*Bon nuit,* my Circe."

Remarkably, she did sleep well, her first good rest in many weeks, lulled by the warmth, presence, and love of her husband. After tending her crowded bladder, she scurried beneath the snug blankets and wondered over the slumbering figure she shared them with. He was beautiful in sleep, all flushed, boyish innocence and at peace. It drew a sharp contrast to the subtle edginess he'd been trying to disguise. Another secret? she pondered. Another lie? She didn't want to know. All she knew was that she couldn't be without him again. All her bold words were so much huff compared to the emptiness of her soul when he was gone from her. Nothing could detract from the way

288

her heart had leapt on hearing his voice or from the way her skin tingled in anticipation of his touch. She could no longer deny Geoffrey Chilton's place in her life. How he got there no longer mattered. What was important was that he stay.

"I love you, Geoffrey," she said quietly as she indulged herself with the hot, heavy, satin feel of his chest. He made a soft, complacent noise. Happily, she cuddled up to him with a possessive satisfaction and closed her eyes.

It was late that morning when they breakfasted in the sitting room where they had enjoyed many selfsame hours. Over tea and hot breads, Rosalind opened the stack of mail left at her elbow, devoting only snatches of her attention to it. She couldn't keep her gaze from the oddly domestic sight of her husband. He hunched over his tea cup, eyes drooping in a reluctance to recognize the hour. In his rumpled shirtsleeves, cheeks sporting a neglectful stubble and golden hair tousled like windblown shafts of rich, ripened wheat, he had never looked better to her. There was a deep sense of security in feeling comfortable enough to not have to look one's best. The fact that he was at ease in his untidy state was an extreme compliment.

Rosalind was halfway through the note in her hand before it caught her full notice. With a jolt of cold abruptness, her eyes flew to the first line and moved along each subtly damning word with growing horror. She couldn't breathe. The connotations the letter contained seemed to wrap themselves about her chest and squeeze with a constriction likened to the one that crushed her heart.

"Roz?"

The dark, swimming eyes wavered up dully to view him as if profoundly perplexed. She stood. A fluttering gesture of one hand spilled the pile of letters to the floor. In a small, quavering voice, she murmured, "Please excuse me, my lord," and hurried from the room.

Fearing she'd received some dreadful news on her father's health, Geoffrey snatched up the page. It was from Charles Street, but it didn't concern Dunstan. It was about him. By the time Henri stepped in to question his lady's lumbering flight, he was livid.

"Damn her," he swore fiercely. "Damn her to hell."

Henri was taken aback. Geoffrey rarely cursed and he never looked as angry as he now appeared to be. He picked up the crumpled page Geoffrey hurled to the table-top and smoothed it out. The text was a clever twist of fact and fiction. The tactful slurs mentioned Geoffrey in the company of Another Interest, of them being seen going into her residence while her husband was Not At Home, failing to return to Charles Street until the Next Morning. Brief, truthful, and suggestive and enough to shred all the budding hopes of a future.

"Not true, I assume?"

Geoffrey shook his head vehemently. He tore his hair in frustration, then let clenched fist fall to his sides. "I'm not going to let her do this to us," he vowed determinedly and ran after his wife.

Rosalind waited in the front room, stiffening when she heard his approach. She turned to him slowly, the closed set of her features bringing him up short. He hesitated, wetting his lips uncertainly.

"Will you listen to me?"

"Why?"

"Because I don't want you to mistake what you just read." He began to advance into the room, caution tempering his steps.

"Is that what I've done? Made a mistake? A rather monumental one, I would think." Her sarcasm was biting. Before he could come close enough to comfort her with the treacherous availability of his strong arms, she took several steps of retreat, placing the chaise between them.

"Lady Wellsley lent me money. That's all. I was in her house no more than five minutes. I swear to you."

"You must have been in a great hurry," she sneered. "And the rest of the night?"

"At a place called the Red Lion. I had to meet a man there to pay my debts."

Rosalind considered this. Her dark eyes shimmered with hurt and distrust. She could envision the titian haired Bella Wellsley kissing him at Vauxhall and the credibility of his tale crumbled. "So the generous lady lent you money. You had to secure this loan in the middle of the night in the absence of her husband when you could have drawn a draft on your account in the morning. Please, Chilton. Be more imaginative."

"I have no account," he claimed tersely. "I have no money. Not a shilling."

Rosalind frowned. "But the townhouse, your fine clothes, the jewels—"

"All on credit, a credit line a mile long and as deep as a grave. I couldn't let you know I had no fortune of my own. You would never have married a pauper."

Her mind reeled in confusion. "But your inheritance, the house on Grosvenor Square?"

His laugh was as bitter as hers had been. "My father threw away all our money on his vices. I borrowed the house. I've never met my uncle. I don't even know if he's alive. It was all a pretense to impress you. So you see, I had to have the money that night and Bella was kind enough to stake me."

"I see." She was very pale and he feared she saw very little at all. He waited, future hinged on her next words. When they came, the harshness was brutal. "So after telling me that all I believed about you is a lie, you ask that I trust you in this."

"Yes."

The hopefully offered monosyllable triggered a flare of hot emotion and violent fury. She leaned across the chaise and dealt him a fierce slap.

"You bastard," she shrieked as he stumbled back, hands covering the lower half of his face and eyes squeezed shut. She rounded the lounger to pursue the attack. "Lying, whoring, deceitful bastard." When her arm drew back to deliver another blow, Henri stepped in to seize it with a firm, restraining grasp. She twisted in his inexcusable embrace, furious to think he would handle her in such a fashion.

"If you seek a liar, madame, look no further than your dear stepmother," he told her bluntly.

"Cammy?" she gasped incredulously. "Nonsense. She's my friend. What reason would she have?"

"Thousands of them plus one you've been blind to."

She stared at him blankly.

"Revenge on your husband for refusing her bribe and her bed."

It was too awful, too insane. Rosalind shook her head in a daze and looked up through wild, disbelieving eyes at the strange, aggressive Frenchman. "No."

"She tried to seduce the man you married with a share of her wealth and the pleasures of her body if he didn't sleep with you and beget an heir to upset her."

"Hank, enough," Geoffrey said softly. Rosalind's horrified look had shaken him back to his senses. He reached out a hand to touch her cheek but she shrank away, rejecting it and him. "Roz, I have never been unfaithful to you. I've spent these last months working to earn your trust. Can it be so fragile as to shatter with a nasty whisper from one who has gulled you from the start? You said you love me. Believe me. I've told you the truth. All of it."

"All of it?" she challenged hoarsely. "Then swear to me, Geoffrey. Swear there are no more lies between us."

His mouth opened to make the claim, then slowly closed. His unhappy silence spoke all too clearly. With a sob, she turned her face into Henri's coat. His arm rose reluctantly to prop the sagging figure.

Geoffrey's lips thinned in impotent anger, anger at her for not having faith and at himself for making it impossible for her to. The sound of her weeping, so raw, as if her heart had broken, tore the heart from him as well. In a low, throbbing voice, he told her, "I can't go on with this anymore. I've tried in every way possible to convince you that I love you. I've sworn up and down that I've never broken our vows. I've done all I know how to please you and still you doubt me. She told me you would, that you would take her word over mine. If I mean so little to you, I see no point in going on. You're never going to accept me, no matter what I do or say. I concede to your wrongful convictions. I never really had a chance, did I?" He paused, hoping she would protest. When none came from the sobbing woman he spread his hands wide in defeat. "I guess there's nothing more to say."

By the time Rosalind had control of her tears, she turned to find him gone.

"Geoffrey?" Her voice quivered. She took a hurried step forward and nearly collapsed as a wrenching pain tore through her belly. With one hand clutching her middle, the other flung back in a desperate grasping. It was taken up in a quick rescue. "The baby," she managed to cry.

"Geoff!" Henri called out to the empty hall as he eased the doubled up figure to the floor.

Chapter Twenty-eight

It was bitterly cold. In his haste to escape the house, Geoffrey had forgotten his state of undress. The biting wind cut through his linen shirt to sting his flesh as unmercifully as his wife's mistrust. His slippered feet were soon wet and frozen from breaking through the thin crustlike glaze atop the puddled ground. He was shivering fitfully by the time he entered the warm, stuffy confines of the stables. The smells he'd once thought abhorrent seemed welcoming now.

He found himself leaning on the door of one of the immaculate stalls to mope in helpless misery. A sudden encouraging nudge brought a feeble smile. His hand stroked idly down the glossy coat while the usually frisky colt was content to stand at the gate in an amiable mood.

"What suggestions do you have, *mon ami?* Perhaps you could make a better case than I. I'm convinced I'm two legs shy of her affection. Perhaps you could lend me some of your horse sense. I seem shy of that, too." The velvety nose prodded his ribs as if in sympathy.

"You think I should go back inside? How can I? More words will not change things. She's told me she won't have me back, yet how can I go? It's all the fault of that spiteful woman. I should have just lain with her. That's what Hank would have done. If Rosalind really cared, she wouldn't have believed the maligning words."

The colt gave a snort in judgment of his pettish words. Geoffrey gave a wry smile and sighed.

"You're right. I've no one to blame but myself. I should have told her the truth the moment I realized I loved her. What am I to do now, my friend? Set up housekeeping in here with you? What advice can you give me?"

"While they make good listeners, they seldom have answers for you."

Geoffrey started with an embarrassed flush and turned to the burly Pettigrew who was observing him with a bemused smile.

"As for sharing his stall, my quarters aren't much bigger but they're a sight more accommodating. I have a bottle of something that might warm you up and improve your mood."

Puzzled by the unexpected offer, Geoffrey shrugged and followed the stocky head groom to the neat apartment over the stables. His was Spartanly furnished yet pleasant and inviting with the baking heat of a small stove. Geoffrey sat on a lumpy chair and wrapped himself in the folds of the colorful knit throw Pettigrew supplied. He laid his sodden footwear on the hearth and stretched his cold bare toes toward the fire. The prickly sensation comforted him as did the mug of strong spirits he was given. His physical complaints met, he looked curiously to his host, wondering at the invitation and sudden hospitality.

Pettigrew leaned against the back of an opposing chair and stared pensively into his mug. He spoke carefully, respectfully, a man of few words.

"I've known Miss Lindy since she was a babe and acted the father to her when her own was too busy, so you might say I have an interest in seeing her happy. God's truth, I had little liking for you when you came here all full of yourself, strutting and cocky. Told myself Miss Lindy didn't need another to pin her heart to and be left in the lurch. Figured you was after the money like the rest and didn't care a whit for the lady. Goes to show I ain't got much sense, either."

Geoffrey said nothing, sipping from his drink in a relaxed silence.

"Told myself all along that some smart buck would be bright enough to see beneath the surface to what she really was. I watched her grow up, hiding out here from the world in her trousers where she could control her life like the reins in her hands. I've seen her hold down a stallion wild enough to make my best men pale then go all goose-livered over the thought of having tea with some silly matron. What she needed was a man who could see the fire inside that winter, a man who could stoke the coals and coax a flame. She needed a man to show her

294

the world and how to conquer it. I didn't think that'd be you. But I was wrong."

Geoffrey frowned as his mug was refilled. "Perhaps you were righter than you knew."

"Only if you prove me to be," he countered. "That woman in the house ain't the same skittish girl she was before you came. You must have taught her something."

Geoffrey drained his cup. The liquor calmed him and loosened his tongue before this unlikely ally. "How could I teach her security and trust when I courted her with a lie? She has no faith in me."

"No?" Pettigrew laughed until Geoffrey scowled at him, failing to find the humor. He explained as if it was all too simple. "That colt she gave you—"

"Tamburlaine?"

"That foal was going to be her pride and delight. She fussed over that mare like she was kin. Her ambitions for that foal were endless. She gave him to you, into your trust and care. Do you have any idea what a gesture that was?"

"Apparently not," he admitted softly.

"She trusts you," the rough-hewn man stated with a certainty. "She might be afraid to believe in that trust, but it's there."

Geoffrey was slow to believe himself. How could she trust him when he himself did not? Had he been hiding behind his secrets to avoid a commitment? Did he nurture her mistrust so he would have an excuse to slip out of the entanglement if things went awry? Did he play the games out of habit or necessity? He'd been doing the right things, but his reasons had been confused. He had never intended to steal her fortune. He'd wanted to steal her heart, the way she had his.

"Would you teach me to ride?" he asked abruptly.

"You ain't dressed for it, my lord. Come talk to me later and I'll fit you out proper so you can keep up with your lady."

With an optimistic smile, Geoffrey lifted his cup for another filling. While he listened to Pettigrew ramble on fondly about Rosalind as a child and finally dozed into a contented sleep on the lull of the liquor, he had no idea of the frantic happenings in the house or how desperately Rosalind called his name.

As she moaned it a second time, Henri stood to go after him, but she caught his hand tightly.

"No, please don't leave me," Rosalind begged in an anguish of fright and pain. When he knelt down, she clutched his hand in a panic as the swamping waves of hurt overwhelmed her. When they ebbed, she found enough breath to weep, "It's too soon. It's not time for the baby to come. Oh, dear God, don't let anything happen to this baby."

Holding her hand in one, Henri used the other to slowly stroke along her pale, taut face. The movement was gentle and reassuring, as was his tone. "I won't let you lose Geoff's child. I know little of babies but I do know they come in their own time. Relax, my lady, and when you're up to it, I'll carry you upstairs."

Distracted by his tender manner, Rosalind looked up intently into the dark eyes. "Who are you?" she asked softly.

He didn't need her to explain the question. He answered simply. "Geoff is my brother."

She looked satisfied with that and asked no more of him. Instead, she breathed noisily into the next twisting pain. It wasn't as severe or as long and, afterward, she managed a brave smile. "Take me up, Hank, or I fear I'll have this babe right here on the floor."

She used his name the way Geoffrey did and felt natural in doing so. When he lifted her up, her arms looped about his neck with no awkward shyness. Accepting him as family was easier than seeing him as a servant. He was Geoffrey's brother, no, probably his stepbrother so he was hers as well, to her thinking. It was one secret she wasn't distressed to discover, for it fit so well in place to settle her past confusion.

Once in her bed, with Henri held at her side, there was a moment of panic as her condition was made known. No midwife had been secured as her time was thought to be weeks away. A flustered Jessup rushed to see if anyone on the meager staff knew how to deliver a child while Rosalind regarded her newfound relation with an amused smile.

"Are you prepared to birth this babe?"

The dark eyes widened in mock horror. "Please, madame. I would prefer you to wait for someone more qualified. Let us talk of something else. What are you going to name this child?"

"James," she said firmly. After a moment, she asked, "What was your father's name?"

"Etienne."

"What is that in English?"

"Steven." His brows knit in puzzlement.

"James Steven Chilton."

For a moment, he looked boyishly pleased, even a bit shiny-eyed, then he said formally, *"Merci beaucoup,* madame. You do my family a great honor. And if the child is a girl?"

Rosalind recoiled from that idea, shaking her head with denying vehemence. "It can't be. It's a boy, a son for Geoffrey and an heir for my father."

"You've no way of knowing for certain."

"I do know," she claimed fervently with a desperate belief. "This child is a boy. It has to be or Geoffrey's going to leave me. If he hasn't already." Her head turned on the pillow in an effort to hide the weakness of her fears, but a warm, persuasive touch brought her back.

"He won't leave you, Rosalind. Geoff loves you. You're the only one he's loved since — since our parents were killed."

The tightening spasms began again and she was eager to be preoccupied. "How did they meet, Henri? In France?"

"In Paris. My father owned a modest chateau outside the city. My mother had died after a long illness and he engaged Madame Chilton to care for our home and to teach me English. Her son was eight and I, almost sixteen. She was destitute, fleeing a bad marriage in England. My father fell in love with her at once."

"You said they fled to save their lives. The viscount abused them?"

"Oui, madame," he answered faintly. The vivid memory of the little boy with the huge blank eyes and bruised body and soul choked his words back. He skipped ahead in his story with stilted purpose. "We took them in and loved them like family until they became part of ours. They were married the day news of Chilton's death reached us and we were happy until Citizen Robespierre and his greedy whore, Madame Guillotine, stole it from

us."

"How did they die?" she asked in a hushed voice.

"My father was housing aristocrats fleeing the judgment of the New Order. To save his wife and children, one of the men Papa sheltered gave up his name and he and my *belle-mère* were arrested. They shared the same fate as the wealthy."

Rosalind cried out   horror. "But Geoffrey's mother was English."

"She slept with a Frenchman and that was enough. They would have taken Geoff, too, and me if we had been there. Friends warned us away. It was too late to save them so we saved ourselves."

He was staring straight ahead, out of the realm of the tastefully decorated room to a loud, unruly mob pushing close to cheer as the Revolution claimed its victims. His features were as stoic as they had been then as he watched first his father then his stepmother mount the stairs to their quick brutal deaths. He was there because he hadn't wanted them to die alone. Geoffrey had come because he couldn't stop him. His father had gone bravely, without a sound, and his courage was an inspiration. Isadora Chilton Girard had wept with a quiet dignity that broke her son's resolve. Henri had held him tight in the folds of his cloak to hide his weakness from the frenzied crowd. The rumble of the heavy blade racing downward, the solid thud and moment of morbid silence before the bloodthirsty yells still rang in his mind as did his brother's wail of pain and grief. And when they had huddled together on a cobbled back street, Geoffrey distraught and clinging to him for direction, he had vowed to protect him and to revenge the loss he wept for in the privacy of his heart.

The sudden crush of his fingers brought him back to the elegant bedroom. His gaze lowered to the woman who held to him dependently, as Geoffrey had. She was one of the rich and privileged he had sworn to hate and he had wanted to. Yet when Geoffrey had entrusted him with her care, he had made her family. She was looking at him, too, her eyes damp with a sympathy that overshadowed her own pain. She guided his hand up to the softness of her cheek and pressed it there.

"They were brave to risk so much even for the deserv-

298

ing. You must be very proud."

"As I am of you for what you have and will endure."

She knew he was not speaking of the birth. Gently, she touched his hand to her lips. "He has us both to love him now. Perhaps together, we can erase the agony of the past."

He had begun to smile when Jessup returned with several maids, declaring one had delivered all six of her own children plus nine grandchildren. They shooed his lordship's valet out with clucks of disapproval but not before he told her confidently, "I'll bring him to you."

She smiled and surrendered herself to the efficient hands of the women.

It was nearly dark when Geoffrey reentered the house still shivering from the chilling dash across the huge yard. He found a tense Henri awaiting him in the foyer. One look at his set features made his heart lurch.

"What is it, Hank? Is it Roz?"

"Go to her, Geoff. She needs you."

He took the stairs two at a time, his anxiety giving him a swiftness to match the race of his blood. He found Rosalind banked on her pillows, attended by a group of chattering females. They dispersed quickly when he crossed the room. When Rosalind's dark head turned toward him, he was rooted to the spot. His gaze took in the reddened puffy eyes that looked to him so grievously and to the telling flatness of her abdomen beneath her defensive hands. Before he could speak, she said hoarsely, "Oh, Geoffrey, I'm so sorry. Please forgive me."

Then the words wouldn't come. He stared at her incomprehensively until her head rolled away. The sound of her soft weeping shocked him back to life. His own eyes overflowed with a rush of impossible knowledge. "Dear God, Roz, have we lost our child?"

A strange, unfamiliar noise coaxed down the hands that had covered his twisted features so he could stare in amazement at the small bundle Jessup held.

Rosalind's eyes slid to watch him, the dread of the moment nearly suffocating her as he peered wondrously at the tiny babe.

"Lord Chilton, your daughter," Jessup announced proudly.

For a moment, Geoffrey was still, then his face split

with a spontaneous grin. There was no forced pretense in that joyous expression and Rosalind tendered a faint hope that the pleasure would last when he considered the consequences of the child's sex. He was distracted for a long while by the wriggling blankets, then remembered the woman who bore him the fragile delight. When he turned to her, Jessup withdrew tactfully.

Geoffrey sat on the edge of the bed and brought her slack hand to his lips. "Well done, madam," he murmured softly. "Is all well with you?"

"I am tired, my lord, but otherwise, fine." Her answer seemed an effort. Her features were etched with the weariness she bespoke. She kept her eyes lowered to the level plane of her coverlet, missing the devotion in his gaze.

"She's a beautiful child, Rosalind. I wish I had been here."

That brought up her somewhat resentful glance. It touched his briefly, saying sullenly, "But you weren't," then dropped away. With a milder sentiment, she said, "I should like to rest now, my lord."

Very gently, his palm cupped her cheek. When his mouth lowered to hers, she ducked her head so his kiss fell upon her forehead. Pricked by her slight, he contented himself by holding her until she objected to that as well. She drew away and rolled her head to one side, her eyes closing to dismiss him.

Geoffrey wandered about the sitting room feeling moody and excluded from the events around him. Finally, Rosalind's teary apology made sense to him. She had given him a daughter, not the son and heir that would assure his fortune. Had she thought he wouldn't want the babe if no bankroll came attached? That hurt him no little bit, especially to think that it was almost true. He despised himself for harboring a whisper of crushed expectation. What kind of man did that make him? One who was shallow and greedy enough to resent the sweet child he'd been blessed with? Surely that wasn't true. His conscience rebelled against the idea. True, he had lost a desperately needed inheritance but he wouldn't pin that disappointment on his wife or child.

Henri interrupted his brooding with two glasses and a bottle of precious French brandy. Geoffrey took the proffered glass with a faint smile and it was generously filled.

300

Their glasses clinked in a silent toast and each drank deeply. Henri followed him across the hall to the nursery where the woman hired to be nanny was laying the sleeping baby in her bassinet. Looking down on the helpless infant made the two men puff with an unfamiliar swell of masculine pride and virility. Henri placed a congratulatory hand on his brother's shoulder.

"Beautiful, isn't she?" Geoffrey said in a mindful whisper.

Henri agreed to be polite, assuming he suffered from the fond blindness that affected new parents. Personally, he saw nothing attractive about the wizened creature that slept with such fierce concentration.

"You've a fine daughter," he said sincerely. "What did you name her?"

The blue eyes came up in an embarrassed surprise. "I don't know. I forgot to ask."

"Her mother named her Isadora," the nanny supplied.

Geoffrey's breath caught as a knot of unexpected emotion lodged in his throat to choke off any words and bring a sudden burning to his eyes. He tried to swallow it but that only made it constrict more painfully. Henri's arm encircled him in an easy embrace and for a long moment he depended on its support as his world wavered.

"I'll be right next door, my lord. Call if you be needing me," the woman said quietly and withdrew.

"Geoff?"

"I'm all right, Hank," he said roughly as the back of his hand made a swipe across his eyes. "I'd just like to stay here alone for a time."

Once by himself, Geoffrey sat in the rocker next to the frilly basket and watched the baby sleep. Isadora. She had named her after his mother. The stinging returned and he made no effort knock the wetness from his cheeks. He was at a loss with his mood of buoyant joy tempered with poignant sadness. He let the confusion in his heart spill forth in soundless, uncertain tears while he adored his precious daughter. She brought him no fortune, at least that he could grasp, yet he loved her without regret or reservation. His only misery was that he had nothing to give her, no fine name or proud heritage. That would come from her mother. What, indeed, could

301

he give? What kind of father could he be when he knew nothing of the state except the brutality of the one he'd known and the abandonment of the one he didn't. Etienne Girard had been kind but he hadn't been free with his love as he was with his own son and his mother. The fear of failing shook through him until he was weak with it. Rosalind's child deserved better, just as she did and he felt he was cheating them most cruelly.

Too uncomfortable and weary for sleep, Rosalind slipped on a robe and shuffled to the nursery. Even though it felt like a dream, the aches of her body told her the baby had indeed arrived.

The room was lit by a single lamp. That faint glow gleamed with muted brilliance on the golden head bent in sleep. Rosalind paused, startled and nonplussed to find him there, then a small, satisfied warmth misted her eyes. She walked quietly by him to pick up the squirming, thoroughly wet child and in the process of changing her, woke Geoffrey to the sound of impatient wails. He straightened in the chair with a perplexed frown, then his features lightened at the sight of mother and child.

"I'm sorry if she woke you, my lord. She's hungry," Rosalind apologized. She flushed uncomfortably, wondering how she was going to ask him to leave so she could see to her feeding.

"Would you like to sit here?" He was up quickly, offering the chair, but made no move to go when she took it. Instead, he crossed to the window to stare out into the night. Rosalind glanced at him uneasily until the child's noisy rutting demanded her attention.

From his stance at the window, Geoffrey observed the reflection of his wife nursing their child with a wistful longing. He felt barred from that intimate scene and chafed at his position of uselessness. With her creamy breast bared to the suckling babe, Rosalind looked serene and Madonna-like, yet he was stirred by an inappropriate and oddly jealous desire. Ashamed of his lustful thoughts, he forced himself to concentrate on the shiny blank panes.

Rosalind watched him as well with careful glimpses. Once she felt confident in her role of nourishing mother, she gave her silent, lingering husband more consideration.

"I named her Isadora," she told him quietly so as not to disturb the nearly sleeping child.

"I know."

The noncommittal response told her less than nothing. "Is that all right with you?"

He nodded slightly, his back still to her.

Provoked by his uncharacteristic brevity, she continued more stiffly. "I am sorry if I failed you and my father. I wish I could have given you a son."

That brought him about. His expression was tight with displeasure. She guessed it rightly aimed at her but not for the same reason.

In a harsh, strained voice, Geoffrey said, "If you are suggesting that I would trade my daughter for your father's fortune, you are wrong. Don't apologize to me for giving me this beautiful child."

Rosalind's eyes dropped with a guilty glimmer to the wispy golden head, so like her father's. Before she could speak, he came to kneel beside the chair contritely.

"Forgive me, Roz. You've every reason to doubt me. Please believe that I'm not in the least disappointed with either of you." The curve of his palm guided her head up and, over the slumbering figure of their child, he kissed her, gently, sweetly to affirm his claim. When he leaned back, she regarded him intently with an unreadable gaze.

"Breakfast with me in the morning, my lord. We've much to discuss."

With that faint encouragement, he bent forward to kiss the downy head, then his wife's cheek before retiring.

Chapter Twenty-nine

Baby Doree had breakfasted and fallen to a satisfied sleep before her father joined her mother. Seated at their small table in the sitting room, Rosalind offered him a smile and Geoffrey was momentarily put off. She was garbed in a clingy wrapper of sapphire-colored silk, his wedding pearls looped gracefully about her throat. He thought no woman who'd just born a child had a right to look so alluring. His long-denied passions gave a disquieting rumble as his gaze measured the snug fit of her bodice.

"Good morning, Chilton. What are you hungry for?"

The innocent, or perhaps not so innocent, question fused his cheeks a deep crimson. He ceased his ogling and quickly took his seat. "Whatever you're having is fine," he managed a bit huskily.

They dined silently, each casting tentative looks at the other as if to test the marital waters before plunging in.

"Are you badly in debt?" Rosalind began cautiously. She blushed at her boldness but hurried on. "If you are, I can manage £10,000 maybe £15,000. Will that be enough?"

How could he look into her hopeful eyes and tell her he needed three times that? How could he admit his debts could well be fatal? He had no right to place such a burden on her, especially now, when she had the baby to think of.

His smile was grateful as he gently declined. "I don't want your money, Rosalind."

"But if what you said before was no exaggeration, you're quite penniless."

He winced at her lack of tact. "Just so, madam."

"I have an annual allowance of £20,000. It has always been generous for me but will you be able to support yourself on it as well?"

"I'm not going to game it away or make extravagant purchases, if that's what you're asking."

She flushed at his abrupt retort and murmured softly in her own defense, "It wasn't. I only meant if you did not think it would suffice, I could petition Papa for an increase. Forgive me, for I have no idea what costs you might have."

"Pray don't go to your father," he cried in deep mortification. "I admit to being an incorrigible spendthrift, but I will be content to let you hold the pursestrings. It is your purse, after all."

"It's ours, Geoffrey. I know this is excessively disagreeable to you, but I need to know these things."

He looked chagrined and muttered that this was so.

Rosalind took in his discomfort with little sympathy. She was thinking of the elaborate charade he had mastered to win her hand. Or had he been after any eligible heiress? That made her brow pucker. She could excuse his motive if it had been one of love but not of indifferent greed. Which had it been for her fair husband?

Shifting beneath her probing stare, Geoffrey summoned his poise and courage to ask, "Knowing what you do, is it your wish to have me still?"

Her silence was ominous. When she spoke, her cool tone didn't assure him. "You are the father of my child, Chilton. How could I cast you out?"

She said nothing of her own feelings, he noted unhappily and he didn't feel confident enough to press her for the answer he wanted to hear. At least she wasn't showing him the road. As long as they shared the same roof, there was the possibility that they would eventually share more.

He had no time to brood as Henri entered the room bearing an armload of exquisite, out-of-season white roses. Rosalind exclaimed in delight when he handed them to her so she could breathe the delicate fragrance.

"Oh, they're lovely. Geoffrey, thank you." When Geoffrey looked comically blank, Henri interposed smoothly, "His lordship had them delivered specially for you, Lady Chilton, in gratitude for the fine child you presented him with."

Wishing he had thought to do so, Geoffrey gave his brother an appreciative glance, then smiled at his beaming wife. Her brimming eyes rose to his and he swallowed the guilty taste that thankful gaze caused him. "You deserved them, Rosalind, and more could I get it for you," he vowed gallantly.

Her gaze simmered, then dropped to the bouquet. "What I want, I have, my lord," she told him simply. "Henri, would you have one of the maids put these in water for me?"

He took the bundle with a formal bow. "Of course, Madame Chilton."

Her hand lay on his sleeve for an instant. Her eyes told him she knew the gesture was his and spoke of her pleasure. "His lordship is lucky to have such a devoted servant. Thank you, Henri."

Betraying no hint of the smile that warmed his dark eyes, he bowed again before withdrawing.

Puzzling over her secretive smile, Geoffrey wondered where to begin in his plan to court his wife all over again.

He had little chance for any romancing during the next weeks. The baby demanded much of Rosalind's time, leaving him idle and restless. A cool note of congratulations came from Charles Street bringing a strained look to her face. She could feel her father's disappointment in Camilla's carefully penned words. Duly chastised for her failure to produce an heir, she never mentioned a return to London and Geoffrey had his own reasons to be thankful.

Those reasons weighed heavily on his mind, making him as nervous as one condemned and sleepless with worry. The only time he felt a reprieve was when he held his tiny daughter. When the squirming infant was in his arms, there was no room in his swelling chest for fears. Her presence further confused his relationship with Rosalind. His feelings for her were a mix of attraction and reserve as he viewed her as unapproachably maternal and painfully desirable. Whenever he sought time alone with her, she was called away by the impatient wails or too tired to give him much notice. He paced and chafed in his solitary room, never dreaming that on the other side of the sitting room, she was moved by like frustrations.

As February dawned with unseasonably warm temperatures, Rosalind left Doree in the care of her nurse sunning in the gardens while she went to the stables in search of her husband. She found him lounging against the rail of the paddock, watching his leggy colt gallop about. His gaze seemed distant and preoccupied as it often did of late, and she hesitated in her approach. She must have made some sound, for he turned and welcomed her with a smile.

"Good morning, my lord. A fine day for testing the clover."

He stared at her, befuddled by her teasing statement, but she ignored his look to lean on the rail beside him. She was fetching garbed in royal blue and a deeper hued waistlength Spencer. Its stand-up collar of soft velvet brushed her flushed cheeks. Bare headed in deference to the warmth of the day, her glossy tresses were wound up in a full, flattering coif. The day was not the only thing growing warm as he looked away with uncomfortable determination.

Rosalind wasn't about to let him gain control of his quickening passions. She let her hand rest casually on his shoulder, delighting in the way his muscles contracted beneath her touch. Her fingers traveled leisurely down the fine fabric to the cut-away waist of his coat. From there, they stole inside, close to the heat of his body. As her palm rubbed along the curve of his ribs, she felt him draw a deep, shaky breath and he turned to her in cautious question. His eyes were deep and smoky with uncertain desire. In tempting response, her face lifted toward aim.

"Aren't you going to kiss me, Geoffrey?" she coaxed in a sultry tone.

Stiffly, he bent to give her a chaste sample then withdrew. His breath was coming fast, as hurried as his insistent needs. Yet he hesitated.

"Geoffrey, I said kiss me." Her chiding voice was accompanied by the circle of her arms about his neck. When they tightened, her body molded to the taut line of his, the invitation clear and very basic.

With a low rumble of want, Geoffrey seized her upturned face between his hands. Mindless of where they stood, his mouth came down upon hers, open and carelessly eager to fill his hungry demands. She was just as eager to satisfy. The tip of her wanton tongue stroked over the luxurious contour of his lips then plunged between them to exact an impatient groan. He mirrored the tantalizing gesture with an agonizing thoroughness until she

307

clung to him, panting lightly.

"Oh, Geoff," she moaned desperately. "Hold me, touch me, love me."

The words coursed like consuming fire through his coiled and aching loins. The sensations were potent and powerful, surging hotly upward to bind his heart and sear his mind. His hands tightened unconsciously to still their trembling. He tried to speak but found his mouth suddenly dry. He made another attempt. The words were hoarse and raw with emotion.

"This isn't the best place to make such a suggestion. Shall we go inside?"

Her gaze burned up into his as she wet her lips in a provocative manner. "Lead the way, my lord."

With her hand tucked possessively in the bend of his arm, Geoffrey started rather hurriedly toward the house. His fierce annoyance at the servant who interrupted them was stilled at the apologetically delivered words.

"Lord Chilton, there is a French gentleman from London to see you."

Geoffrey loosened Rosalind's grasp and kissed the back of her fingers gently. His voice was hushed. "Go upstairs and await me. I shan't be long."

"Geoffrey?"

"Go on, Roz," he urged, giving her a slight push.

Something in his shadowed gaze made her reluctant to leave him, but he was adamant. Containing her prickling of dread, she did as asked.

Her bedroom window overlooked the garden and in her restless pacing, Rosalind noticed the large, unfamiliar figure of a man lingering amid the dormant beds. He held Doree in an easy cradle of one arm while the nurse looked on. While she watched, her intrigue grew as Geoffrey approached. Her intent to simply appreciate his manly form shifted to a puzzled speculation as he crossed to the big, smiling man and took the contented baby from him. Doree began a distressed fussing as she was crushed with unintentional vigor to her father's chest. He handed the child to the nurse and hurried them away.

Rosalind frowned as she watched the two men talk. The stranger was relaxed. Geoffrey was gesturing in agitation. He looked angry and appeared to be shouting. The man she had thought a stranger began to look oddly familiar. When her memory placed him, she ran through the sitting room and called to Henri who was stacking Geoffrey's shirts away. He followed the worried Lady Chilton to the window.

"Henri, do you know that man?" she asked, then added urgently, "The truth, please."

"No. I don't know his face. Should I?"

"I thought you might. He's French and Geoffrey knows him."

Henri looked more closely but shook his head.

"I've seen him once before," Rosalind told him. "On the night I met your brother."

"In London?"

"No, before that, at an inn." Henri looked surprised. Had Geoffrey kept the details of their meeting from him? "Geoffrey had me hide him from two Frenchmen. That man was one of them. I'm sure of it. He said he'd won money from them, but I think he's the one who owes. Henri, I fear he's in terrible debt but he's too proud to ask for my help. He won't talk of it to me. Please, please see if you can find out what's wrong. I can't help him unless I know."

The mysterious visitor had gone and within several minutes, Geoffrey came to a stop in the doorway. He seemed disturbed to find them both together at the window and was uneasy under their twin stares. Gruffly, he said, "Hank, pack my things. I'm leaving for London and want to be off as soon as possible."

"Henri, have the chaise brought around," Rosalind instructed calmly. "And have Jessup ready my bags and the baby."

Geoffrey turned to her with ill-concealed upset. "You're not going, madam."

She arched a quizzing brow. "Of course I am. Doree and I are fit to travel and I would like to see my family."

"Do it another time," he snapped. He glanced at Henri, who hadn't moved, and said curtly, "Must I repeat myself?"

"No, my lord," the Frenchman drawled, giving an exaggerated bow before retiring from the room.

Rosalind remained where she was. Her expression had

taken on a stubborn edge that he couldn't appreciate under the circumstances. "I'm coming with you, Geoffrey."

His generous mouth thinned in displeasure and she was a bit intimidated by how furious he looked. "Do not argue with me, madam. I said no."

"Then name a reason why you don't wish me along," she challenged.

"Damn it, woman, I don't need to give you reasons. He instantly regretted the harsh words yet couldn't call them back. He reminded himself that he was protecting more than her feelings.

Rosalind's eyes brightened with hurt and an even greater rebellion. She knew he was in some desperate trouble and was anxious to be rid of her, and, contrarily, she refused to be put off. If he wouldn't let her help, she would be there to lend him support. Whether he liked it or not.

"I don't mean to defy you, my lord, but since you can name no reason, I am going to London. You can refuse to let me ride with you but that will not prevent me from following in a separate coach."

"This is not a game, Roz."

"Then tell me what it is."

Her earnest entreaty backed him into an uncomfortable corner. To fight his way out, he chose a cold, sneering attack. "Is it that you don't trust me, dear wife? Do you fear I rush to the arms and bed of some *amourette?*"

He hurt her and her dark eyes shone with it yet still she would not back down. "Think what you will, sir."

He fairly seethed with frustration. His hands clenched at his sides to keep them from shaking her. Helpless to forbid her without giving cause, he said cruelly in hopes of dissuading her, "Come if you must. Satisfy your doubts, but I resent your spying upon me and will not have you dogging my steps. Is that understood?"

Rosalind nodded stiffly. She was very pale yet grimly pleased to have won a place at his side. Without further contention, she went to see to her belongings.

Shoulders slumped in resignation, Geoffrey turned into his own room where Henri was folding his coats with a crisp efficiency. He didn't look up. Geoffrey watched him, chewing his lip. He was at a loss as how to approach him for help. He hadn't wanted to. He'd thought he could deal with it alone, but when La Belette's messanger greeted, him with his child in his arms, reality hit him with an unfair, crippling blow. How foolish he'd been. He'd closed his eyes and left all to fate, a fate that had blessed him with a daughter but not a reprieve. That La Belette would reach him at the manor stripped away his naive sense of security and left him vulnerable. And very afraid. His mind was agonizingly blank and his insides churned frantically, yet how could he in good conscience embroil his brother in the consequences of his own poor, greedy judgment?

Henri took the decision from him, asking shortly, "How much do you owe?"

"£50,000."

The elegant shoulders grew rigid as Henri paused, then he resumed the packing more briskly. "Impossible. You can't have spent so much since we've been in London."

"I owe £8,000 in London. The £50,000 is a debt of long standing."

Geoffrey took a prudent step back as the dark eyes rose. "From where and to whom?" he demanded. The low, level tone didn't mislead the younger man.

"From Paris," he mumbled.

"Paris." An ugly suspicion tightened the handsome features. But surely Geoff wouldn't be so stupid or so bold . . . He looked into the deep blue eyes that could fire with such brilliance and lack of caution and he knew. "You said you paid him, Geoff. The total was nowhere near that. I gave you the money and you told me you paid him."

In carefully measured accents, he said, "I was involved with him in another matter. I knew you wouldn't approve so I—I didn't mention it. There were other expenses—the passage out of France, favors I owed, clothes. I got you that case of champagne, remember? It was gone so fast. I never thought he'd come after us. Then I was sure I could pay him with the inheritance. Now, I've a shared allowance of £20,000 and he's going to kill me when I tell him so."

"I ought to do it for him," Henri exploded. He flung the coat he'd been aligning across the room and began to pace while Geoffrey watched him in silence. "Fool! Imbecile! How could you do it? How could you believe you would

311

get away at La Belette's expense? You're always reaching for things out of your grasp. You think because you're quick and clever, you'll be able to stretch just a bit farther, but it doesn't always happen like that. Luck and a pretty smile will not impress these men. La Belette would kill you over a shilling and you take him for a fortune. You always think there's more. Well, you had it all and you've thrown it away because of your reckless greed. Damn you. If that woman or child suffers for it, I swear I'll have no part of you."

"I never thought—"

"You never think," Henri railed, spinning to face him. His rage was monumental. "Your brain stops at your pockets. How could you take a wife and beget a child knowing this would catch you? How could you be so selfish and thoughtless?"

His clenched fist rose in frustrated anger. The sudden gesture rocked Geoffrey back on his heels. He made a soft, panicked sound as his eyes squeezed tightly shut. For a long minute, he didn't breathe. The light touch of his brother's hand against the side of his face and neck made him flinch and his breath spilled out in uneven rushes. His words were gravelly.

"They hurt me, Hank. If they harm Roz or Doree, I—" A sudden hitch fractured his sentiment.

Henri drew him briefly, crushingly to his shoulder and promised fiercely, "They won't." Then he gave him a rough push away and began to pace and think.

Geoffrey straightened, swallowing the dizzying fear and his pride as he looked to the Frenchman. "Hank, help me. I don't know what to do. I love them so much."

"Would Rosalind give you the money?"

"She doesn't have it," he answered quietly, ashamed that he had already considered it. He was feeling very small and very desperate.

"Fifty thousand pounds! Oh, Geoff, it's so much."

"I know."

"He's waiting for you?"

"In London."

"You cannot go."

"But—"

"He'll kill you, Geoff and perhaps your family as well

312

just for principle. He's not going to like hearing you're not going to pay him."

"And I certainly don't like telling him."

"I'll go. I'll think of some way to put him off. You wait at Charles Street and keep your family safe."

"You're my family, Hank."

"I can take care of myself. If he won't be put off, I may have to kill him. That would put an end to it." He said that coldly, eyes as hard and expressionless as they had been when watching his father die. He'd sworn an oath that day and bound it in his father's blood.

"Thank you, Henri," Geoffrey said softly, not knowing what else to say.

"Il n'y a pas de quoi."

And so he wouldn't speak of it again. For himself, he wouldn't have allowed the risk but the image of his baby daughter in the hands of La Belette's murderer held him silent, and he remained so as the chaise wheeled toward London.

Rosalind sat across from the tight-lipped stranger, fretting over his manner and its cause. She wanted to sit beside him, to share her warmth and her love, to support him in whatever trouble furrowed his brow, but his aloofness asked nothing of her and the presence of the baby's nurse kept her from any overtures. She hadn't thought about the reunion with her father or how her meeting would fare with his wife. Her attention was too involved in the remote figure who hadn't spared her a glance. Was he still angry with her? Would he be unforgiving toward her for pushing her away where he didn't want her to be? To have her loving husband of scant hours before snatched away in lieu of the man who ignored her now was frustrating, and frightening. It didn't matter that he was annoyed with her or that she wasn't wanted. If he was in danger, and she sensed he was, she had to be with him. They were a family and their place was together.

The arrival of Lord and Lady Chilton and their firstborn took Charles Street by surprise. While Rosalind saw the baby settled and her appetite appeased, Geoffrey went to the large suite of rooms where he found Camilla Dunstan outside her husband's door.

"Chilton, how good to see you," she crooned, caught up

in the sudden desirous heat he evoked within her. "Dare I hope you are alone?"

Geoffrey's tone was cutting. "I need to speak to Dunstan."

Camilla's eyes narrowed as she took in his poorly guised anxiety. "He's sleeping. You may talk to me."

"I'll wait."

"If it's of a financial nature then I am the one to speak to. I control the family's money now. And I want to thank you for that."

Begging money from Dunstan was men's business, disagreeable but honorable. Making such an arrangement with her would have nothing to do with honor. He stood in silence, staring at the cool, smug beauty. If what she said was true, that would place him at her unscrupled mercy.

"You do need money, don't you?" she continued. Her fingertips traced along the bottom edge of his waistcoat. "One hears things, like your rush to dispose of your belongings. I offered my help before. I'm still willing to be generous, with my purse . . . and other things." Her body swayed close. Her slender hand stroked down his well-made thigh in lingering appreciation. As it returned on a more intimate upward trek, he stepped back with a contemptuous glare.

"Madam, you have absolutely nothing I want."

Camilla sucked in her cheeks in doubting amusement. "We shall see."

"Tell Dunstan when he awakes that I wish to see him."

"Of course, my lord," she promised with a saucy smile. "Keep my offer in mind, Chilton. You'll find it most rewarding."

"In what way, Cammy?"

They both turned to Rosalind, who had just entered the room. Camilla stepped quickly to embrace her but the somber dark eyes looked over her shoulder to Geoffrey. There was no accusation in the glance, just a question. He evaded it by stalking past them.

"Oh, Lindy, how well you look. One would scarcely guess you'd had a child."

Rosalind regarded her stepmother coolly. Henri's warnings would never allow her to see the pretty woman the same way again. The charged scene she had come upon

314

only furthered his words.

"I should like to see my father."

"He's resting. He hasn't been well the last few days. Influenza, I think. I'm sure he'll want to see you the moment he wakes."

How affectedly cheerful she sounded, Rosalind thought. The thin veneer of amiability was beginning to show a fine webbing of cracks and she was upset by it. She didn't want to choose between Geoffrey and this woman who had offered her friendship and acceptance. She murmured some banal words and escaped from the picture she didn't wish to see forming in place of the welcoming idyll.

She found Geoffrey in the nursery. He was seated with Doree sprawled upon his chest. Her tiny fists were kneading his shirtfront. His hands were huge and engulfing as they gently held the baby to him in an almost desperate clasp. His head was lowered so he didn't notice her right away. His nakedly poignant expression lodged a hard knot of emotion beneath her breast.

"Geoffrey?"

His head jerked up and he began to reflexively jostle the startled child to calm her.

"Are you all right?"

"I just wanted to spend some time with my daughter." His tone was defensive. He looked quickly down at his placated child to avoid her questioning eyes. "What you heard between Camilla and me—I—"

"I don't care about that," she interjected firmly. She knelt down beside the chair, her hands clutching his arm. "I want to know what's wrong. I want you to talk to me."

"There's nothing to say."

The flippant tone made her fingers tighten. "Geoffrey, please. You can tell me anything, anything at all. I love you. Please let me help you."

The golden head shook. "I can't, Roz. I can't talk of it now."

"When? When, Geoffrey? Will you never trust me?" she cried in distress.

"I can't afford to trust anything right now, not even your love. I asked you not to come."

Tears sparkled on the fringe of her lashes. "I had to," she whispered. She laid her cheek upon his sleeve, her eyes closing tightly. She gave a shaky sigh as his hand touched lightly on her silken hair. The gesture was quickly withdrawn and when she glanced up, his expression was unreadable. "I'm here for you, Geoffrey, no matter what," she claimed with a gruff tenacity. Her palm pressed to his cheek before she stood and left him to his preferred silence.

The following day passed in long, uneventful hours with no summons from Dunstan or word from Henri. Geoffrey kept to his room, walking the floor, a jumble of raw nerves and half-realized fears. A dozen times, he thought of calling to Rosalind, of going to her just to have her in his arms and to have the comfort of her undeserved love. His anxiousness held him away. He was so tense and nervous, she would never believe nothing was amiss and he couldn't bear to speak another lie to her. The ones before were torture enough.

So he paced in his self-imposed isolation and tried not to be consumed by his worries. Henri wouldn't fail him. He never had. His brother always managed to right his tipping world and set it on path again. If he could trust and depend on one person, it was Henri Girard.

And then a parcel was delivered by unidentified courier just as the sky darkened into early evening and an angry frozen rain began to fall. And when he opened it, everything crumbled.

Chapter Thirty

"Geoffrey?"

Rosalind tapped on the door then opened it. The mysterious package lured her with a fateful curiosity. She was certain it had something to do with his odd behavior. The room was dark. She wasn't sure he was within until she reached for the lamp.

"Leave it off."

The hushed gravelly words came too late to keep the light from flooding the bedroom. From his seat by the window, Geoffrey squinted and turned his head away from the piercing brightness.

"Leave me alone, Roz" came the same husky voice. It drew her to him with its quality of hoarse despair.

"I can't, my lord. I have to know what's troubling you and I won't leave until you tell me."

His head shook in a jerky denial. Still, he wouldn't look at her. Clutched to his chest much in the same manner he had held their daughter earlier was a single dark garment. From the crude wrapping at his feet, she assumed it was the content of the package.

"What is this?" Rosalind asked softly. He resisted briefly but let her take the coat from him. It was a man's coat, too narrow to be his. As she examined it, she found twin holes, front and back, liberally surrounded by brown, crusted stains. Her insides gave an abrupt shudder. "Geoffrey, where's Henri?"

He looked up then, not really seeing her through eyes dazed and tragically lost.

Rosalind's words were sharp with her own mounting fears. "Geoff, where's your brother? Tell me!"

That brought a dull focus to his gaze. He blinked in surprise and mumbled, "How did you know?"

"He told me," she explained impatiently. "Just tell me where he is."

The darkened eyes grew bright and glittery. In a small

317

voice, he said, "I think he's dead."

Her hand touched quickly to his lips. "Don't say that. He's not," she insisted with a calming forcefulness.

Geoffrey took a deep, uneven breath, but he didn't look convinced. He pushed himself from the chair and moved about in a choppy agitation. "It's my fault," he said punishingly. "I let him go. I always let him fight for me. I never considered he'd lose. I never thought—" His words broke off and he gave a strained little laugh. His gaze settled on the collection of priceless figurines that had so fascinated his avaricious nature. He lifted one and rested it in his palm, weighing the prestige of having it and all the rest against the sacrifice he'd wordlessly asked his brother to make so he could keep them. With an aimless violence, he hurled the piece at the wall where it shattered into meaningless fragments.

"Oh God," he moaned. "I'm sorry, Hank. I had it all turned around." He sucked in a fortifying breath and expelled it angrily. When he turned, his expression was sharp and purposeful. "I need a carriage, Roz."

"Tell me what I can do."

"Do?" He looked confused then adamant. "I don't want you involved in this."

"I am involved," she argued. "He's my family, too. Tell me where he is and how we can get him back."

Geoffrey's fingertips brushed her cheek wonderingly, then he said with the return of his control, "The note named a place." When he mentioned it, she nodded.

"I know where it is. It's outside of London. We could be there in an hour."

"I can't let you go," he said quietly.

"You can't risk going without me. You'd never be able to handle the reins. The roads are all ice. You'd be in the first ditch. Am I right that we can't involve anyone else in this affair?"

Geoffrey gave a heavy sigh. She made too much sense. He nodded.

"Since I am involved, will you tell me in what?"

He raked a hand through his hair and said disparagingly, "In a stupid scheme of my own making. I owe a great deal of money to some very desperate fellows. Henri meant to bargain for more time. Apparently, they were in no mood to wait." His stare took on a hard glitter. She'd seen that look before, in the dark eyes of Henri Girard, and it frightened her. "They're holding him until full payment is made."

"Do you have the money?"

"I'll get it."

That flat phrase gave her another uneasy turn, but she let it go unchallenged. "When do you want to leave?"

"Get things ready in the stables. I'll meet you there."

Rosalind nodded. She started out only to have her hand caught up tightly. She looked into the solemn blue eyes and felt a shiver steal through her.

"I've made some unwise choices but marrying you was not one of them," he told her with a quiet candor, then released her. She gave him a tight smile and hurried off.

Camilla Dunstan regarded the man at her bedroom door with a slow, sultry smile. She held it open, then closed it behind him.

"I need £50,000, he announced without a preamble. "I need it tonight. Do you have that much."

She contained her surprise with a cool "Of course."

"The same terms as before?" he asked with resigned grimness and began to unbutton his waistcoat.

Camilla's eyes dilated and her breath quickened as she watched the determined movement. Then, she stayed his hand almost regretfully. "Have you been with Rosalind since the birth of the child?"

"What the hell business is that of yours?" he burst out incredulously.

"Just answer."

"No," he snapped out. "I haven't."

Camilla wet her pouty lips and smiled. Her fingers traced the curve of his severe mouth. She wasn't offended when he jerked back. "As desirable as I find you, Chilton, there is something I want more."

"Name it, madam."

Rosalind edged back into the shadows as a large dark shape loomed out of the night. When the dimmed lantern gleamed against deep gold, she stepped out quickly to join him.

Geoffrey noted his wife's appearance with a wry appreciation. She was wearing trousers and an ill-fitting coat

319

that hid her hands and, with the collar up, most of her face. Beneath a low-crowned hat, her eyes were bright and capable.

"Did you get the money?"

"Yes," he answered tersely and was glad she said nothing more. She had hitched a pair to a light curricle that would afford them speed and not hamper the horses on the slick roads. Its disadvantage was that it was open.

"It's the only conveyance we have that isn't crested," Rosalind explained as she hopped up to take the reins. "I thought you'd prefer discretion over comfort."

He nodded and settled beside her, praising his fortune for having such a wife and praying their efforts wouldn't be for naught.

The roads were treacherous. Only Rosalind's expert handling kept them from overturning or sliding into ditches as they sped from London onto narrow, less traveled roads. The heavy sleet was punishing and made visibility negligible yet they arrived at the decrepit coaching house without mishap.

When they turned into the muddied yard, Geoffrey spoke for the first time since leaving Berkeley Square. "Wait here, Roz."

"In this weather?" she cried. "I'm going with you. At least it will be dry inside."

"And dangerous," he warned. "They may no longer be satisfied with just the money."

Rosalind met his stare boldly. "More the reason that I should be along."

His mouth thinned unhappily as he agreed. He couldn't leave her alone in the nasty evening at such a place. At least with him, he could offer some protection.

Together they entered the squalid bar area where their passing drew idle attention. Rosalind hung close to Geoffrey's side, keeping her head ducked so she would be taken for a youth rather than a woman. Before they had traversed the smoky room, two large men positioned themselves on either side of them. She swallowed hard in recognizing them. One of them spoke curtly to Geoffrey in French and gestured that they follow to a dingy room at the rear of the second floor. One of the men proceeded them inside and the other flanked them.

"Good evening, Chilton. Nice of you to be so prompt."

La Belette rose from his rickety chair. Geoffrey's glance touched on him then darted to the still figure sprawled on the unmade bed in the room's deep shadows. It was difficult to look away.

"Have you the money?"

"You'll have it as soon as I know my brother's all right."

La Belette made a generous gesture for him to see for himself.

"Roz, see to Henri," Geoffrey instructed quietly in English.

She skirted the two within the room and sat on the edge of the bed. There was so much blood. The sheets were stiff with it. She reached a tentative hand to the colorless cheek. It was so cold, she nearly cried out. Please don't make me have to tell him his brother is dead, she wished fervently. She touched the side of his neck and waited an agonizing moment.

"He's alive," she called in weak relief.

The sound of her voice created a stir as it identified her gender. She met the newly interested looks with a fierce glare.

"Your money," Geoffrey sneered to draw them off his wife. He tossed a bulky bag to the floor. Belette motioned for his man to retrieve it, then rifled through the notes with an avarice pleasure. "Our account is settled, Belette."

The ferral eyes gleamed coldly. "I think not. You have cost me much time and effort. When my men let you slip away that first time, I had to come all the way over here to this drab country to settle things myself. I cannot let others think I will allow such liberties. Then no one would take me seriously. You and your brother will serve as examples. I have not yet decided if you will survive it."

Geoffrey's arms were pinned from behind, but before he could struggle, a cold command was spoken.

"Let him go."

Geoffrey was no less surprised than the others to see the oddly garbed woman bracing a huge pistol in both hands. It might have even been amusing except for the humorless steel of her gaze. He shrugged out of the imprisoning grasp and asked, "Do you know how to use that thing?"

"I shoot almost as well as I ride," she said coolly.

"Famous." He grinned and in French proudly announced, "Gentleman, my wife." He moved by them, careful not to come between them and the steadily held gun and went to bend over Henri. The blood stunned him, the cool flesh terrified him. "Hank?" There was no response.

In one smooth move, Geoffrey turned and struck Belette hard enough to send him staggering. Rosalind's pistol rose to keep the other two at bay while her husband caught up the Frenchman and pummeled him with a fierce vengeance. A rage that had lain silent and repressed for too many years burst forth through the clenched fists. He struck out blindly for all the times he had feared to. Then he held the sagging figure up by the lapels and warned with deadly intent, "If my brother dies, I'll follow you into hell itself. Take your money and go back to Paris. Don't you ever come near my family again. Do you hear?"

La Belette stumbled into the waiting hands of his men. Touching a handkerchief to his split lip, he snatched up the money and mumbled awkwardly, "Don't worry. Nothing could lure me back to this cursed place." He pushed free of the supporting hands and marched from the room with his men.

Rosalind lowered the heavy pistol with a shaky sigh. She didn't have the courage to tell Geoffrey that in her rush earlier that evening, she'd forgotten to load it. Her knees trembled inside the billowing trousers as she gave thanks that her brazen bluff hadn't been challenged.

Geoffrey rubbed his scraped knuckles. His hand ached but it was a splendid pain. He'd never struck anyone before and felt a satisfying sense of accomplishment in having come to Henri's defense this time. Thinking of his brother brought him back to the edge of the bed where the gnawing dread returned. Rosalind reached in front of him to open the badly stained shirt. A crude, dirty bandage wrapped the bullet wound beneath his shoulder. Though the bleeding had stemmed, there was abundant evidence that it had bled, quite extensively.

"Will he be all right?" Geoffrey asked faintly.

"I'm no doctor, my lord."

"Then let's get him to one," he urged impatiently.

"I'm no doctor," she continued softly, "but I know he's too weak to be taken out in this weather. We'd be wiser to wait until morning and hire a conveyance to see us back to London. Besides, I'd feel safer not sharing the same darkness with your friends."

"They're not my friends," he snapped, then gave an apologetic sigh. He seized the hand that pressed his and held it tight. "That was quite a stroke thinking to bring a gun."

And forgetting to load it, she thought wryly as she accepted his praise. "I also thought to bring some extra money. Let's see if we can buy some comforts in this frightful place."

By dropping several notes, the manager was pursuaded to grant them a larger room, one with a working fireplace and windows that didn't leak. A few additional pieces induced his charitable conscience to help Geoffrey carry the wounded man to it. The shift jarred Henri to a vague, restless awareness. His eyes flickered and finally stayed open long enough to focus on a familiar face.

"Geoff," he whispered hoarsely. His fingers curled loosely about the hand that held his. "Sorry I failed you."

Geoffrey's composure faltered. He pressed the cold hand to his cheek and cried, "Forgive me, Hank. No more schemes. Never again. If you'd been killed—"

"I'll hold you to that," Henri whispered.

Geoffrey gave a ghost of a smile and gently laid down the slack hand as his brother's eyes closed. "Never again," he repeated.

With Henri resting more easily, Rosalind saw to her husband's and her own comforts. A hearty bottle of port was brought in as well as several downy quilts that she stretched out before the crackling fire. She encouraged Geoffrey to shed his wet outerwear and did the same only to discover her shirt was unpleasantly damp and cloying. While Geoffrey was pouring their wine, she slipped it off and snuggled into the inviting drape of a comforter. When she reached for her glass, it slid free of her shoulder, exposing the gleaming slope to his suddenly intent gaze.

Geoffrey sipped the bolstering wine and let his eyes wander the swaddled figure beside him. The teasing glimpse had fired an insistent purpose, to ease his own tension and to spite a damnable bargain he'd been forced to make. Without a word, he set his glass aside and closed the distance between them. Her eyes came up, startled but not objecting as his large hands swept the covering from her bared skin. She sat very still as his stare roamed slowly over the full, taut breasts. He guided her to the coverlets with the pressure of his kiss, but it was all too brief, a prelude to the ritual of creation.

Rosalind was unprepared for his abrupt possession. There was no tender preamble of touch or words and she cried out softly in hurt and surprise. She clung to the hard, flexing line of his shoulders more in defense then desire, trying to find some point in his fast, furious movements to join in, to share with him. But it was as though he sought no response, as though he wanted none. His lovemaking was urgent, even desperate, not driven by love or lust or even pleasure though all existed on the periphery. It was an elemental mating of a simple, primal purpose, that of creating life.

His thrusts were deep and sure, reaching for her very womb with no thought to gentleness until he reached a shuddering conclusion. His breath shivered forcefully against her cheek for several long minutes, but he never relaxed the tension of his body to enjoy the comfortable yielding of hers.

Still deep inside, he raised up so he could command her uncertain gaze and said, no, demanded, "Take what I've given you and make a son. Make me a son, Rosalind."

Then he withdrew from her as roughly as he had come and sat apart to stare into the fire. Slowly, Rosalind gathered her scattered wits from their confusion and went to him, to lean against the sweaty heat of his back. His flesh seemed to shift in complaint and then, more obviously, he sidled uncomfortably until she ended the contact.

Hurt and bewildered by his brusque and now aloof manner, Rosalind retreated to the protective cocoon of her covers and rolled away from him. She couldn't explain her feelings of unhappy fright and he, apparently, was insensitive to them so she closed her eyes in her isolated huddle and willed herself to sleep.

Geoffrey stared at the brilliant flames until his eyes ached with the unfocused concentration. Cautiously, he let them cant to the undistinguishable figure of his wife. Though he could see nothing but the top of her head, he could tell by the even sound of her breathing that she was no longer awake. He let the taut bind of his emotions go and trembled as they shook through him. He hadn't wanted it to be that way, so impersonal that he knew he'd bruised her feelings. He'd wanted to lavish her with all the love in his heart, to linger sweetly over each gentle curve and inviting hollow, yet he knew the pain would be all the greater then.

Camilla's support exacted a heavy toll, one he found nearly impossible to bear and to consider had his brother's life not been in the balance. Her terms had been shrewd and coldly rational and he suffered over the agony of prolonging his payment. Finally, he made himself comply, urging his reluctant body to quietly dress and his more reluctant heart to sever ties that twined about his soul.

He didn't touch Rosalind. He didn't dare. That would have been too hard. Instead, he looked down on the pale, refined features of his brother and friend and sighed in anguish.

"You'll call me coward for doing it this way. You know me better than anyone else and I could never say good-bye to you." He took up the limp hand, then realized his mistake. The link was already too solidly forged without the added complications. He replaced the heavy hand on the bed. "Rosalind will take care of you, *mon frère*. And you see to her for me and to little Isadora."

There was more he wanted to say, but forming the words was too difficult with his heart crowding his throat. He bent down and brushed an unembarrassed kiss on either rough cheek.

"Good-bye, Hank."

"Geoff?"

The dark eyes opened hazily to the sunlit room, finding nothing familiar in it. Had he dreamed the vaguely re-called words? He tried to sit up and a shaft of agony lanced through his chest. With a groan, he writhed in misery until the punishment subsided to a warning throb.

There was a rustling at the foot of the bed. He raised his head cautiously to confront a pair of round brown eyes peering over the footboard. He blinked in confusion.

"Good morning," Rosalind murmured, nervously aware of her lack of dress as she crouched out of sight.

" 'Morning," he returned in a raspy whisper. "What are you doing down there?"

Rosalind flushed and was flustered. When he attempted to lift up a little higher, she gave a squeak of modest alarm. "No, no, you lie back. I'll be but a moment."

There were a series of scuffling sounds and, finally, Rosalind stood in her boyish garb. Still blushing, she came to place a hand on his feverish forehead.

"Is Geoff here?"

Her eyes made a quick assessment. "He was. I don't see him. He must have gone down to arrange for a carriage to take us back to London. How do you feel?"

"Like hell is leasing the inside of my chest. Begging your pardon."

She gave him a small smile. "You rest a moment. I'm going below to see if all is ready. Hopefully, he's managed some breakfast as well."

What she found was far different. Instead of her husband, she found a brief note left with the manager, who grumbled about being woken in the middle of the night to play messenger. When she returned to the bedroom, pale and worried, she met Henri's grim expression.

"He's gone, isn't he?" he asked softly. "I thought I had dreamed it."

"I feel as though I still am. He took a northbound coach an hour ago. I don't understand. He left a note, but it's in French."

Henri took it gingerly. He had managed to sit up and was weaving perilously. His features grew even more pinched. "He says good-bye and that it's for the best and that—and that he loves us both." The paper dropped from his fingers. "He's blaming himself for this mess, as well he should. I'd better go after him." His intentions far surpassed his strength and there was no question of him actually standing. He leaned against Rosalind, sucking air and struggling not to faint.

"First, we get you to London and to a doctor, then I'll go after him. If only I knew where to look," she added anxiously.

"I think I know."

Their arrival on Charles Street left the servants agog, Rosalind in her mannish clothing supporting her husband's valet, who seemed drenched in gore. She nonplussed them further by insisting he be placed in his lordship's bed and treated with the benefits of an honored guest. As the footmen made ready to carry him upstairs, Rosalind pressed an impulsive kiss to his cheek.

"I'll bring him back, Hank," she promised.

He nodded and let his consciousness wane.

Rosalind paused only long enough to change her clothes, still electing trousers, and to relieve her burdened breasts to a very eager baby who had not cared for the hastily found substitute the night before. Forced to relax while her daughter lingered over her meal, Rosalind found time to reflect on the curious happenings. Looking down at the small figure she held, Geoffrey's words came back to her.

"Make me a son, Rosalind."

Why would he want to fill her with his child if he knew well he was going to desert her? Why would he insist on a son if he wasn't to be a part of the inheritance? He loved her. He adored Isadora. So why would he flee when it seemed the worst of their troubles had been challenged and met? More puzzling was the fact that he would leave his gravely wounded brother before certain of his survival.

She lay the sleeping child in her bed and smiled upon the innocent features that were so familiar. "I'll bring your daddy home, Doree."

Munching on a heel of fresh bread that would do for breakfast, Rosalind strode through the house on her way to the stables. She didn't have time to chat with her stepmother but her words drew her up short.

"You're on a fool's mission, Lindy. He's gone and for the best of all."

She stared at the other woman for a long moment, unpleasant notions coming to life in the pit of her belly. "What do you know of this, Cammy?"

"I know he doesn't plan to come back to you. He told me as much when he came for money."

Rosalind was taken aback by the cool disclosure. "You gave it to him?"

"It's the money he wanted. When you failed to give him a son, you lost him. Do you think a man like that would live on your paltry allowance when he was after a king's fortune? Did you actually think it was you he was interested in?" Her chiming laugh was incredibly cruel.

327

"You've seen the last of your fortune-hunting Chilton."

Rosalind met the maliciously merry eyes with a cold, smiling countenance. It was Camilla's turn to be startled by this frightening embodiment of Lord Dunstan. "I wouldn't be too quick to gloat, madam. Geoffrey may have already left his heir with me."

Camilla grew rigid and pale. "Impossible."

"Having experienced motherhood, I know well how it is accomplished. Now, excuse me. I'm going to fetch my husband."

Camilla hurried after her, alarmed that the meek girl had evolved into such a commanding rival. She had seriously underestimated the threat. She flung her final barbs, hoping to forestall her determination. "You don't know what he is, Rosalind. He made his living in France by swindling wealthy women. He's made a joke of you. You'll be the laughingstock of all London. You're making a fool of yourself over a man your father bought for you."

Rosalind turned to confront the ugly words with an icy demeanor. Camilla drew back, intimidated by the steely composure and sneering smile.

"I don't care what he is. My father bought him for my husband and he has always given me the best of everything. Too bad he couldn't choose so well for himself."

She spun on her heel and marched regally to the stables.

Chapter Thirty-one

To catch the northbound coach, Rosalind pushed her black stallion to its limits. Pericles's long, mile-eating strides carried her across the frozen back roads in a direct course that intercepted the heavier livery on a deserted stretch. The driver drew up on the reins, cursing the boldness of highwaymen that would strike in the light of day.

"Stand easy," she called in a roughened voice to protect her identity. "I have an urgent message for one of your passengers. Lord Chilton, step down."

Geoffrey's surprise was monumental as he recognized the figure in the swirling cloak yet he schooled his features to betray none of his thoughts as he approached the rider.

"What do you want, madam?" he asked with an annoyed indifference that made her bravery quell in brief uncertainty. "Pray do not make things more uncomfortable by creating a scene on the roadside. Was my note unclear? I believe I said my good-byes."

Rosalind didn't waver beneath the cold, dusky stare. Her voice was low and firm. "Why did you marry me?"

"For your father's money," he replied with a blunt lack of hesitation. He saw her wince and her tender lips tremble, yet her next question was just as evenly said. "Is that your reason for leaving me, as well?"

Geoffrey drew a deep breath of the frigid air, hoping it would brace him. What it did was bring everything into a crisp focus, centering on the woman who looked down at him through such expectant eyes, the woman who had steadied his unbalanced world with her quiet show of strength and had stolen his heart with her unqualified passion. He tried to say the harsh words that would drive her away but he found himself lost in her consuming

329

stare. "No. It was because I love you, Roz," he told her helplessly.

Without a sound, she put a hand down to him and freed a stirrup so he could swing up behind her. She nodded to the coach driver and urged the horse ahead.

They traveled at an easy canter. Rosalind was well warmed and exhilarated by the arms that circled her and the hard thighs that pressed tight to her own. When he realized they had not turned toward London, Geoffrey asked their destination.

"Where Henri said I'd find you. We'd never make London by nightfall. We'll have to start off again in the morning."

Geoffrey fell silent. She could feel his sudden tension through the knotting of his muscles and, when the distant manor appeared, in the abrupt hoarseness of his breathing.

The rolling lands had long since fallen to auction but the house remained in a tragic state of disrepair. Most of the mullioned windows had been broken by adventurous children or idle vandals who made temporary homes in the sprawling rooms. It looked tired, sagging, forgotten. Except by one.

"No, Roz. I can't," he said in a hurried panic. "I don't want to be here."

"But wasn't this where you were coming? Isn't this your family's home?"

"It's where I was born, but it's not my home," he clarified in a gravelly hush. "Please, just turn about. Now."

But Rosalind reined in the spent horse in the overgrown yard. A drizzle of rain had begun to preface the mounting darkness of angry, swollen clouds. "There's nowhere else. Pericles has to rest. He'd never carry us both to the nearest inn. I don't want to spend another night in this beastly weather." She swung a graceful leg over the pommel and slid to the ground. She waited, then put a hand on Geoffrey's knee. He gave a jerk, his attention leaving the house in her favor. "Let's go in before we're drenched clear through."

With the horse tethered beneath a leaning porch, they entered the house. It had been gutted and left to waste by time and neglect. The huge, high-ceilinged rooms spoke of one time elegance, but all that had sadly faded. Rosalind wandered through the maze of rooms in a melancholy fascination with a very silent Geoffrey close on her heels. The only chamber that was weathertight was a cavernous drawing room. While Geoffrey stood in its center, she collected an assortment of kindling to lie in the crumbling hearth. After several attempts a small flame was coaxed forth, but with a promising heat came a billowing of thick choking smoke.

"Here. Let me." Geoffrey reached by her to open the flue and fanned the sooty clouds until a sufficient draw sucked them up the ancient chimney. She coughed and huddled close to his unyielding form until the chill began to abate. The flames cast a mellow glow amid deepening shadows. When she looked up at Geoffrey, she saw his gaze riveted to a crooked oil painting that hung above the mantel. It was a full portrait of a woman. The vibrant colors were dulled by soil and age, but more tragic was the vicious scoring that defaced the canvas, shredding it so the identity of the figure was destroyed.

Rosalind's attention was called to the woman's hand. She reached up to rub away the dust. The ring was unmistakable. It was the one she wore.

"It's your mother, isn't it? What an awful thing for someone to do to such a lovely painting."

"He did it," Geoffrey said tonelessly, then turned away without explanation. The fire didn't help. The chill of the past seeped deep into his bones with shivers of memory and emotion. Since he couldn't bear to look within, he went to gaze out into the impersonal darkness.

Rosalind looked from the mutilated portrait to the withdrawn figure at the window, just beginning to realize what the return was costing him. For more than twenty years, the nightmare within these walls had taunted him. A strange wrinkle in time seemed to shrink him to the eight-year-old boy who had stood in the same spot watching a near deranged figure flail at the likeness of his mother with an iron from the fire. And then that seething drunkard had turned to glare at him through wild, reddened eyes.

Geoffrey gave a sharp start when Rosalind touched his arm. "Come sit by the fire, my lord. It's cold here and you're shaking. Let's warm one another."

He let himself be led back below the tattered painting and obligingly joined his Garrick with hers to make a pallet for them to sit upon. When Rosalind curled into his side, his arms went around her instinctively. Hers stole inside his coat.

"How's Henri?" he asked to break the odd silence.

"He may not want to give up your bed when you return. Perhaps you will be forced to share mine." Her tone implied no regret.

He cleared his throat awkwardly. "I didn't expect you to come after me."

"I've no plan to let you go, my lord," she warned in fond humor.

"Roz, there's so much you don't know."

She shrugged off his dire cautionings. "What? That you've no fortune? That you and your brother supported yourselves off rich women? That you married me to get my inheritance? That to save Henri's life, you promised Camilla you'd leave me so there would be no heir to threaten her?"

Geoffrey looked dumbfounded. "She admitted to that?"

Rosalind laughed. It was a soft, almost admiring sound. "Oh, no. She's too clever for that. Too clever for her own purposes."

"Knowing all that, you still want me?"

"All I need to hear is that you love me and that you'll be faithful to me."

Geoffrey turned away from the earnest gaze and shook his head.

"Do I ask too much?"

The small voice tore through him mercilessly. "You don't ask enough. Roz, you're worth a dozen of me. I have nothing. I've lied to you since we met. I've done nothing but hurt you."

"You're the man I love," she said, as if that equaled all the rest. "You married me, you taught me love and respect, you gave me a child, you stepped in to save my father's businesses. You're family, Geoff, you and Henri, and I don't care what you were before."

"But you don't know what I was or what I still am. Or rather what I'm not. I'm not the son of Giles Chilton."

"But—I don't understand."

His eyes lifted to the shadowed portrait and he gave a grim smile. "Oh, my mother was married to him, but he didn't father me. She never told me who did that honor, just that he had given her that necklace, the Ruby Tears. I often wondered what kind of a man would give such an extravagant gift then not care that the woman he gave it to had to live with such an animal. Or that he'd let his own son grow up in the shadow of such a man. I grew up hating my absent father almost as much as the one who gave up claim to me. So, you see, I'm not a penniless lord. Ton is full of them. I'm a penniless bastard and that is hardly the same thing. No one is going to open their drawing rooms to me or to my heirs."

"As if it mattered to me," she chided gently. "I was never looking for a title. I was looking for a man. And I found one, the one I wanted."

"You can't be serious."

"You were willing to stay with me knowing my fortune was lost to you and dare presume I would shun you for not having an old, stuffy name. What's wrong with Girard?"

"Nothing except it's not mine to claim. Henri's father never gave me leave to it. I'm still Chilton, for lack of anything else."

"Then it will suit us just fine," she pronounced, putting an end to it. Her palms began to rub against the fine linen of his shirt, one following the ridge of his spine and the other crossing the flat plane of his stomach. He felt good. She closed her eyes, her head resting on his shoulder, and concentrated on the unique feel of him.

"And your father?" he demanded tersely. He was too overwrought to notice the sensual movement of her hands, yet his body responded, his back arching and his breath quickening.

"I don't care what he thinks. After all, he courted you more aggressively than you did me so he's partly to blame for us being together."

"And are we? Together?"

"Not as together as I'd like to be." Her head turned so she could taste the warm flesh of his neck. His pulse leaped beneath the nibble of her lips. She had succeeded in working his shirt free of his trousers. The texture of bare skin was much more satisfying than the concealing fabric. When her hand dropped to the taut gloving of stockinette over his uncontrolled arousal, he pushed her away with an anxious cry. "Not here, for God's sake," he said in hoarse denial. "Not in this house."

"Why not?" she countered softly. "It's only walls, floor, and ceiling. There's nothing here anymore, nothing that can harm you."

"You don't know that," he argued tightly. "You don't know anything. You don't know what it was like in this house, the fear and the hurt."

Her hand turned his face toward her and her mouth was upon his, moving firmly, intently, the way he had taught her. His breath left him in a quiet sigh, all his tension expelled with it. His eyes stayed shut until her fingers wove through the flame-drenched gold of his hair. The gaze they shared was expressive — tender, compelling, needful and completing.

In a voice so low and husky, it rumbled, Rosalind said, "Geoffrey, give me a son."

She awoke some time close to dawn, warmed by the low fire yet missing a more immediate heat. A quick scan told her Geoffrey wasn't in the room. The presence of his waistcoat and outerwear reassured her that he hadn't strayed far. She dressed quickly and padded barefoot across the cold floors in a room-to-room search. She found him in the upper hall, leaning in an open doorway. She couldn't guess at what he saw as he stared into the empty room. He gave a violent start when she touched his shoulder.

"It's only me. Are you all right?"

He shook his head. "No. I keep thinking if I blow the dust away, it will all be here the way it was."

"But it won't be. It's all gone. They're gone."

He shook his head again, more vehemently. "No. They're here." He touched his temple, then his chest.

"And here." His arm began to swing aimlessly, his knuckles thumping the doorjamb in a quiet rhythm, gently tapping. "You know, it's funny. The happiest day of my life was when he told me he wasn't my father. It was the day we left for France, the day he ruined the portrait. All those years I wondered why he didn't love me, how he could hurt me. He'd known from my conception that I wasn't his and my mother would never tell him a name, no matter what he did. I wanted to make him stop, but I was so afraid."

"Geoffrey, you were just a child," she insisted softly.

The tapping grew louder, his knuckles bumping the wood.

"I'm not a child now and I'm still afraid. I used to dream that my real father would come for Mama and me and take us away, but he never did. All we had was that damned necklace and each other. This place was beautiful then, full of fine things, even more splendid than your homes. I used to love the things in this house. It was safer than to care for the people in it."

The rapping became more vigorous.

"We escaped to France without a shilling. We had to leave everything behind. She was too proud to take any of it but not too proud to work for our keep."

"Henri told me how his father took you in."

"Did he? France was like waking from a nightmare. Girard was very bourgeois. My mother fascinated him because she was of quality. He made a good home for us. There were no pretty things, but there was Henri and he was my family. His father wanted to be one of the rich and titled and was eager to mingle with them by helping them escape the purging. He wanted to be like them and he had his initiation in blood. When I saw him die, all I could think was how I wished it was my father instead of Henri's. I wanted to see him die and delight in it. I wished it could have been my hand that took his life instead of his own carelessness. I hated him. I do hate him. He hurt me and he still hurts me."

His hand had closed into a fist and the tapping became a pounding hard enough to tear flesh. Rosalind seized it to halt the impotent violence, then brought the skinned knuckles to her lips.

"He's dead, Geoffrey. He's being punished for what he did to you."

"It's not enough. He turned to her abruptly. His eyes were bright, almost feverish. "Take me home, Roz. Take me with you to our home."

She embraced him with a small sound of relief, holding to him until his hands came up slowly to rub her shoulders. Then she was able to stand away. "Let's go home." He gave her a faint smile and urged, "You get the horse ready. I'll be right there."

His tone was strange, making her reluctant to leave him and relieved when he joined her in the puddled yard. Wordlessly, he settled on the stallion behind her. As she was about to rein the horse around, a faint orange glow glimmering on the fragments of window glass made her hesitate then cry out in alarm. Before she could react, Geoffrey's heels dug fiercely into their mount, sending it into an urgent gallop. They were a distance away before she finally gained control and turned back. By then, the flames were racing along the old wood, devouring it with an increasing, purifying hunger.

Geoffrey gave a grim smile of satisfaction. He told her simply, "I'm burning the bridges to my past."

Rosalind had no reply. She nudged Pericles toward the road to London.

Tired and disheveled, they returned to Charles Street, drawing many a curious stare in passing. Some would swear they saw Rosalind Chilton sitting astride a horse dressed like a man, for wasn't that her personable husband doubling behind the hoydenish figure? Murmurs began and eyebrows raised and in surprising time, the whispers reached the elegant Lady Dunstan at her afternoon tea. With a gay laugh, she disclaimed the rumors but hurried off as soon as it was prudent. She found her stepdaughter in the parlor sipping tea, an image of propriety in a white muslin shift.

"How could you parade yourself through town in that outrageous attire? Have you any idea of the on-dit you stirred?"

Rosalind arched a fine brow and coolly observed the

other's flushed countenance. "Good afternoon, dear step-mother. Was it my attire or the fact that I was not alone that has you so put out?"

Camilla drew a sharp breath. That part of the story she hadn't heard. "Chilton came back with you?"

"Of course, he did. Do sit down, Camilla. You look overly warm."

Warm didn't touch on the hot fury she felt. How dare he break his bargain and return with his dowdy wife? She frantically sought a way to shore up the crumbling house of comfort and affluence she'd built about herself. She leveled a cold, undisguised glare at the poised woman.

"You're forgetting the fee I paid him. He took £50,000 from me. I demand he stand to the terms. If you want him so badly, go with him, but he will go. I will see I am rewarded. The money is mine by right."

Rosalind set down her cup with a disconcerting calm but her dark eyes hinted at a submerged storm brewing. "We shall see. I never wanted the fortune, but you have made me reconsider. I think it would be better served in the hands of my husband until my children come of age."

"Your husband is a nameless schemer who deserves nothing but this family's contempt."

"Shall we see who is held contemptible?"

Pale with anger and a growing insecurity, Camilla followed her up the stairs to Lord Dunstan's suite. The unlikely sound of a child's delighted squeal came from within. Rosalind paused, momentarily overcome by the sight of her gruff father playing with the squirming, giggling infant who lay beside him on the bed. With an emotional smile, she crossed to press a kiss on the firm cheek.

"Hello, Papa."

"A fine child you have here," he said proudly. His voice held a trace of a slur but not of infirmity. "Reminds me of you when you were a babe." He stopped waggling his fingers above the waving arms and regarded the two women. There was no mistaking the tension. He made a motion to the nanny. "It's time for this little one's nap. She can visit me later. Or perhaps I will come visit her.

Am I to assume more will follow this engaging little creature?" He leveled a stare at his daughter, who met it without a blush.

"Many more," Rosalind assured him promptly.

"Good. I made no mistake about Chilton. Fine stock, that one."

Rosalind intercepted Camilla's denouncement saying, "Perhaps you did, Papa, but it isn't a mistake I regret."

"Daughter?" The stern lines strengthened his features.

"You once said you wouldn't care if I wed a lamp-lighter as long as you had heirs. Would you accept an untitled penniless pretender as well?"

Dunstan frowned in confusion. "Are you saying that Chilton—"

"Has no legitimate claim to that title. But I love him, Papa and will have no other. It will be his sons who succeed you, fine, lusty sons to carry on your name."

Seeing the thoughtful furrow of his brow, Camilla stepped in to cry, "You cannot accept such deceit. Our name will be ruined. The man has already stolen £50,000 from me. Would you let him take our honor as well?"

"What's this?" Dunstan growled. He looked to his daughter to demand an explanation.

"I will make good his debts," she declared with a willful resolution, which was pleasing to him in itself. "I don't care if I have to sell everything I own starting in the stables. Everything is expendable except this ring I wear. If I have to buy my husband back, I will."

"No, you won't."

Rosalind turned to Geoffrey, who had entered the room silently. Her gaze was warm and entreating, offering him all he could wish for.

"No, Roz," he repeated. "You won't sacrifice your belongings for me. I won't allow it. I will pay for my own mistakes. I accepted your stepmother's loan and the terms she named and will abide by them. As soon as Henri can travel, we return to France. You can go or stay as you choose. I wouldn't blame you if you preferred to remain, but I would want you and Doree with me."

Her eyes conveyed the answer with an open candor

and he responded to it with a smile.

"Nonsense," Dunstan roared. "I won't hear of it. I want my grandchildren here with me."

"They belong where their father is, Papa," she corrected softly as her gaze adored the handsome face of Geoffrey Chilton. "As I do."

"Chilton, I won't allow you to ignore your responsibilities here," the earl ordered.

An indolent brow arched. "To what and to whom, sir?"

"To me and my holdings."

"I was not aware they were my obligation."

"They are if you wish to have them. I won't give them to you. You have to work for them, even if you are my only son."

Geoffrey blinked. "I don't understand."

But Camilla was afraid she did, all too well. "You can't," she vowed shrilly. "What of the agreement, the year condition? What of the money he owes me?"

Her petulant claims were silenced with a quelling glance. Then Dunstan settled back, looking smug and contented. "The conditions were set to provoke my daughter into marrying and producing children and I am well pleased with the result of both. I've already had the papers drawn. Since he is not accountable for the use of his own funds, there will be no more discussion of it."

Camilla had grown very pale. Her bright eyes flashed between her husband and the couple who had snatched away the wealth she coveted. Desperately, she said, "But he's a bastard of no consequence." Geoffrey flinched at that and Rosalind's glare was murderous. She hurried on. "Our name will be ruined, Dunstan. Your reputation will suffer and so will our social standing. Our friends won't deal with him. You're making a terrible error."

"I've made them before," he answered curtly. "As for our reputation, if nothing leaves this room, who will know of it? If the matter is handled discreetly, the secret is kept." His meaningful stare touched on his wife. To Geoffrey, he said, "It wouldn't matter to me if you were a groomsman. You please my daughter and you serve me well. I ask for nothing more. If there is a scandal, we will survive it as a family. Now, I want a word with

Camilla, if you'll excuse us. We have some things to set-tle between us."

Camilla stood mute and visibly trembled. Rosalind felt no sympathy as she closed the door. She turned to her own husband with a smile.

"Welcome home, my lord."

Chapter Thirty-two

The large house on Charles Street was thrown open to receive a parade of elegant guests. It was the first rout officially hosted by Lord and Lady Chilton. Fans of his and critics of hers were eager to be amused or find fault with the affair and anxious to be summoned to the Georgian manor. Dunstan was no entertainer and invitations to his home were few and select. They anticipated the enjoyment of his fine liquors and buffets as well as the company of his lovely young wife. While the former were superb, the later was oddly disappointing.

The charming Lord Chilton met each arrival with a personal greeting and an ample quantity of his engaging smile. In turn, he passed them to his wife and even the most severe judge was favorably stunned. Lady Chilton dazzled the beholder. Surely Rosalind Dunstan, the shy sparrow and this graceful dove, were not one in the same? This gracious woman welcomed each guest with an extended hand, direct smile, and no trace of a reticent manner. While not a perfect beauty, she was comely, her complexion warmly blushed, lips finding no difficulty in the repeated smiles and dark eyes lively with unfeigned contentment. She was handsomely garbed as well in sequinned tulle that accented the unusual diamond collar about her slender throat. She touched the horseshoe-shaped pendant often in a gesture more loving than nervous.

Placated by the gentile manner of Lady Chilton, the company, especially the ladies, were intrigued by the Dunstans houseguest. Henri Girard was introduced as Chilton's brother and though he seemed somewhat familiar of face to several in attendance, none could place him. He was smoothly continental with an exaggerated manner and richly accented voice. Those who hadn't made the coveted trek to Paris were eager to corner him for his opinions. His casual disdain for all but his *famille* created all the more interest in courting his favor in what he would cynically call typical English fashion. Only Nathaniel Everard seemed nonplussed by his inclusion, but his disconcertion was quickly managed when his dear Lindy took him aside for a quiet word.

Camilla Dunstan, the perpetual social moth, made a brief appearance. To say she was wan was to be kind. She spoke brief words to a few close friends then retired. It was quickly circulated that her husband was moving her to their Gothic country manor for the remainder of the Season. Modest speculation that she might be on the increase was ended by her stepdaughter who cited a sudden frailty of her health as the reason. There were murmurs that she would be missed and the explanation went unquestioned. Dunstan's recovery added to the easy acceptance. He, too, made himself available but excused himself early, pleading fatigue. The night clearly belonged to the Chiltons.

Only his deliciously foreign brother commanded a greater female following than Geoffrey Chilton. Rosalind eyed the flirtations with a judicious calm until the approach of the flamboyant Bella Wellsley. The buxom redhead stood toe-to-toe with her husband, her majestic bosom brushing his elegant shirtfront each time she heaved an expressive breath, which was often. Geoffrey smiled down at her, taking no offense in her outrageous behavior or ever dreaming anyone else would until a firm, discreet swat was delivered to the well-fitted seat of his trousers.

While he recovered from his surprise, Rosalind took up his arm and greeted the florid woman with admirable poise. The bit jerked from his teeth by her commanding tug on the reins, Geoffrey regarded his wife with a duly chastised pout, then was quick to make amends.

"Lady Wellsley, have you met my brother, Henri? I have a suspicion that you would get on quite well."

For Geoffrey Chilton, the evening was an unqualified success. He felt comfortable in his role as host in a house he now considered home. He was proud of the woman who circulated through the crowd with an easy, natural charm. His gaze warmed as it followed her and was rewarded when, as if she felt his caress, she lifted her eyes to him. They exchanged a long, speaking glance before her attention was called away. He was pleased as well by the quick acceptance of his brother into ton's tight circle. He smiled when he imagined Henri's tart comments on the evening and looked forward to hearing them later that night over a shared toast.

He was still smiling as his roving gaze scanned the company then froze with a shock so profound, he feared his heart had stopped. It resumed to a pace so erratic, his chest ached in containing its frantic lurches. Blindly, he pushed his way through the crowd, mindless of the startled looks his stumbling flight evoked. His only thought was to escape.

Henri stepped into the darkened book room and closed the door behind him.

"Geoff?"

The figure at the window didn't acknowledge him. Cautiously, he drew nearer and said his name again. Geoffrey was leaning against the cool glass, palms pressed to it and his rapid breath fogging the black pane. A light touch on his shoulder set off a series of fierce tremors.

"Mon Dieu, Geoff? What is it?"

In the tones of a panicked madman, his brother gasped, "I saw him, Hank. I did. I did. Oh, my God, my God. I have to get out of here. Get me away from here."

Truly alarmed, Henri gripped him firmly. "Who? Who's here?"

"My father" came the incredulous moan.

"Geoff, that's nonsense. He's dead."

With a jerky shake of his head, the large, darkened eyes opened. "No. I saw him. He came in just now. He's wearing a red cloak. I saw him, Hank."

"Geoffrey? Henri? What's going on here?"

Henri held up a staying hand to the woman who slipped into the room. "Rosalind, a man just came in. You won't know him. He's in a red cloak. Find out who he is."

"I know who he is," Geoffrey groaned in faint protest.
"You must be mistaken. Go on, Rosalind."

She was absent for several minutes, during which Geoffrey managed a precarious calm. His wife's dazed look started the shallow breaths once again.

"He gave his name as Nigel Chilton, ninth earl of Harlech. Geoffrey, are you all right? What on earth's happened?"

Uncle, not father. It took a moment for his fractured thoughts to grasp that knowledge. Of course there would be a resemblance, but he'd never expected it to be so unnatural and disturbing. He clung gratefully to the woman who came to embrace him, focusing on the very real contact to thrust away the ghosts of the past.

"Here, Geoff. Drink this."

Henri filled his hand with a hearty dose of more material spirits. He gulped down the glassful and was able to control the mad careening of the past few minutes. With a steadying breath, he stepped back from Rosalind and looked anxiously toward the door.

"Why would he come here?" he wondered aloud.

"Does he know the truth about your parentage?" Rosalind asked softly.

"I don't know. If he does, he could destroy everything. He could denounce me before all London. Roz, I can't have you humiliated like that. If I were to leave now—"

Her hand pressed to his mouth. "I'm not afraid of anything he might say. Let's hear it from him first, then we can act on it together. My lord?"

He secured the hand that wore his ring and kissed it. "Yours is the cooler head, madam. We shall do as you suggest. Henri, find my uncle and bring him here."

While they waited, Rosalind drew his hand to her cheek. Her gaze held him. "I love you, Geoffrey. Whatever he says will not change that. I married you not for a name but for a man I could not live without."

"I thought it was because I had good teeth and the ability to breed virile sons upon you."

She responded to his strained humor with a tight hug. "That remains to be seen, my lord," she teased in return.

The levity was short-lived as the noise of the crowded

assembly intruded when the doors opened. Rosalind was struck by the resemblance, not to a man she'd never seen but to the one beside her as Henri ushered in a tall, distinguished man. She puzzled over it in silence.

Lord Nigel Chilton stood looking long and emotionally at the younger man. Finally, he crossed with arms outstretched. "Geoffrey, I've anxiously awaited this meeting."

Geoffrey retreated in a guarded fashion. The features were too familiar, too like for him to feel comfortable. He extended a reserved hand. "Good evening, sir. I was not aware you were in town."

"I've just arrived in the country. I beg your pardon for crashing your affair but I could not wait until morning."

"For what, my lord?"

"To meet you, finally. Your mother had taken you from England while I was abroad. If only she'd waited." He gave a heavy sigh and a look of great sadness weighted his expression. "Her passing was a tragic thing."

Geoffrey had no comment. His next words were rudely blunted. "Why are you here, sir?"

"This should be shared in private."

Geoffrey's hands touched the two who stood near him. "This is my wife, Rosalind, and my brother, Henri. They may hear anything you have to say to me."

"Brother?" Chilton looked confused.

"Henri Girard. Geoffrey's stepbrother," Henri explained with a stiff bow. His fingertips rested lightly between the tensed shoulder blades in unspoken support.

"And your wife," the elder lord mused softly. "Then this should go to her."

Rosalind took the tissued parcel with an uncertain thank you. She looked up for Geoffrey's approving nod before opening it. She felt his sharp recoil even as she gasped. Henri, too, sucked in a startled breath as he peered into the box. They were as beautiful as the first time she'd seen them, the fateful Ruby Tears. She closed the box with a snap and waited for Geoffrey to tell her what to do with the unexpected gift.

"Where did you get this?" he asked in a taut voice.

"From a woman in Paris. I was fortunate enough to see her wearing them at an inaugural. I had been searching for such a sign for fifteen years."

"A sign of what, sir?" he demanded stiffly.

"Of your trail, the one I had lost and found a dozen times. She told me you were here and so I came."

Rosalind clutched her husband's arm. A vague suspicion began to grow as she looked between the two. Geoffrey was still unaware of what she guessed to be the reason for the visit. She wanted to cushion the blow but knew she couldn't prevent it. Henri intercepted her urgent glance and frowned until understanding brought an unwelcome scowl.

Then the truth was revealed with all its hidden connotations and nothing could make that knowledge any easier to bear.

"You see, I had that necklace made for your mother."

Geoffrey shook his head in a daze. "No. My father gave it to her."

"I did, not Giles."

"No," he repeated, slow to grasp the nuances of what he said, then unwilling to accept what he'd heard.

"Geoffrey—" The hand he placed on the other's arm was thrown off with a fierce rejection. He went on determinedly. "She called them the Ruby Tears because they were a symbol of misspoken love."

"You and my mother—I don't believe it." He turned away and grasped his brother's arm for balance. Everything was teetering. He squeezed his eyes shut and let Henri steady him. His features screwed up as if in some terrible agony as he tried to shut out the rest of the words.

"Isadora was very unhappy in her marriage to my brother. I was in the Army at the time and home for the holidays. She confided her misery to me and though we never planned or wanted it, we had a brief love affair. I was called back to duty and she refused to leave Giles. The necklace was my parting gift. She wrote me one letter to say she was content in her marriage and had borne a son. I took every foreign assignment I could to delay coming home and when I did, she had already taken you to France."

Geoffrey wobbled on his feet, the years of anguish too

346

bitter to be shed as simple tears. They dammed up hotly in his throat making his words rough and hoarse. "Why didn't you come for me? Why did you leave us with him? If you were my father, why didn't you care?"

Chilton reached out but Henri discouraged him from making contact by firmly staying his hand. He sighed heavily and mourned, "Because I didn't know. I didn't know you were my son. She didn't tell me. I never knew how bad things were or I would have come. I knew Giles had a temper, but he loved Isadora. I never guessed his drink and jealousy would push him so far."

"And when did you know?" Geoffrey asked in a hushed tone as he studied the ceiling.

"Not until years later. Giles was dying. I went to see him at his house. He told me that Isadora's child wasn't his own and then I knew. I came to look for you, but by then, France was in turmoil. I found out that your mother had died, but you were difficult to trace. It was providence that I saw the necklace, providence that brought me here."

Geoffrey revolved slowly, his expression wary of further hurt or disappointment. "Why? To what purpose after all this time?"

"So I could claim you as my son and heir."

There was a short, bitter laugh. "It's a bit late for that, wouldn't you say? I have a family now, one I love dearly."

"But I have no one. You're all I have, Geoffrey, and that's been little more than an elusive dream for so many years."

"That's not my doing," he cried angrily. "Where were you when I needed you, when I prayed you would come? You show up now just when my life has some meaning and demand I welcome you. Well, I don't. I don't want you here. You've come too late." With that, he stalked from the room.

Rosalind bestowed a smile on the disheartened man and asked, "Have you a place to stay, my lord?"

"My people are readying my townhouse," he said heavily.

"Geoffrey will be by to see you tomorrow."

"I think not, my lady."

Rosalind smiled again. "I know my husband, Lord Chilton. He will see you there. Henri will see you out." She delayed the Frenchman to ask in a low aside, "See that our guests are politely discouraged from remaining."

"I'll pass the word that the wine has run out. That should send them home."

She pressed his hand then hurried to find her husband. He was standing in the cool, darkened garden where she had once tearily asked if he planned to have mistresses. She had no such questions now. He held her hands tightly when they slipped about his middle.

"You think I'm wrong, don't you?" he accused softly, without rancor.

Laying her cheek against his straight back, she hugged him and said, "No, Geoffrey, but we do see things differently. You see the savior who never came to rescue you, I see a lonely man trying to reclaim a past he was cheated of."

"Should I just open my arms and heart to him and say, 'Hello, Papa'? I can't, Roz. How could you expect me to?"

"I don't. I don't think he does, either."

"Then what does he want?"

"To know you, Geoffrey, to try and forget the lost years with a new start. Is that so much?"

"I can't forget," he cried out at the darkness. His fingers crushed hers painfully.

"But wouldn't you like to put it all behind you? In truth wouldn't you like to be Lord Chilton? Perhaps you could help each other."

He shook his head then said almost sadly, "It's too late. My family is complete. I have you and Doree. I have your father's respect and I think of him almost as a father. I have Henri. My heart has been regimented carefully for those I love and trust and I want to let no one else in."

"Are you saying there is no more space, even a small tiny one?"

The quality of her voice made him turn in the circle of her arms. His eyes were wide and searching. "Roz, what are you telling me?"

348

She gave a secretive smile that touched the very quick of him. "That soon your virility in breeding sons may no longer be in question."

He caught her up to his chest, easing the excited embrace only long enough to seek her tender lips. Their shared kiss was rich with a joyful yearning. His mouth slid away to graze her warm cheek and fasten urgently above the circlet of diamonds.

In a breathy voice of caution, Rosalind cried, "Please, my lord. Not here in the primroses while our guests await within."

Geoffrey was not dissuaded by the mild protest. "Give Henri a moment to chase them all away, then we can indulge ourselves wherever we choose. He's very capable."

"Let's choose somewhere indoors. It grows chilly out here."

That persuaded him to see her to the house where the servants were busy cleaning the already emptied rooms. Geoffrey stopped one of the workers.

"Where is my brother?"

"He went to escort a Lady Wellsley home, my lord" was the bland reply.

The devilish eyes slanted to his wife as he whispered confidently, "I told you they would get on."

Rosalind smiled generously, pleased that Annabella Wellsley would find someone to get on well with other than the man at her side. With his hand tucked happily in the crook of her elbow, she gave a slight tug. "Shall we retire and leave them to their work?"

The smoldering gaze was her answer. "After you, Madam Chilton."

Nigel Chilton was sipping tea and reading a recent journal. There was so much to catch up on in this, his native country. He had already sent an entourage to his country home to ready it for his arrival. There seemed no reason to linger in London. He had no acquaintances here to renew and apparently little else to hold him.

The townhouse had been swept clear of its dust sheets and gleamed with efficient care. He had mused over the stack of books in the front room, assuming them to be Geoffrey's. He was pleased by the wide range of material. The boy seemed ambitious as well as intelligent. A shame that would be all he would ever know about him. He sighed and set aside the paper. Perhaps he would leave today. Why fall into melancholy by remaining?

His butler cleared his throat softly to command attention before announcing, "You have visitors, my lord."

"Who is it, Timmons? I've no wish to entertain this morning."

"Good morning, my lord" came a soft voice.

Chilton smiled at the woman he would have been pleased to accept as his daughter-in-law. His smile wavered slightly as emotion tugged his heart. His eyes misted as they beheld the sparkle of rubies that proudly circled Rosalind's neck. It wasn't until he stood that he saw she was not alone. With a knowing smile, Rosalind reached back her hand for the familiar crush of warm fingers.

The two men regarded each other for a long, awkward moment. Then the silence of endless years was broken.

"Hello, Papa."

350

Lauren Giddings loves to hear from her readers. You can write to her c/o Zebra Books, 475 Park Avenue South, New York, New York 10016.

Cat Sitter
Among the
Pigeons

ALSO BY BLAIZE CLEMENT

Cat Sitter Among the Pigeons

A Dixie Hemingway Mystery

BLAIZE CLEMENT

St. Martin's Paperbacks

This is a work of fiction. All of the characters, organizations, and events portrayed in this novel are either products of the author's imagination or are used fictitiously.

CAT SITTER AMONG THE PIGEONS

Copyright © 2010 by Blaize Clement.
Excerpt from *The Cat Sitter's Pajamas* copyright © 2011 by Blaize Clement.

For information address St. Martin's Press, 175 Fifth Avenue, New York, NY 10010.

Library of Congress Catalog Card Number: 2010037537

ISBN: 978-1-250-06309-0

Minotaur hardcover edition / January 2011
St. Martin's Paperbacks edition / December 2011

St. Martin's Paperbacks are published by St. Martin's Press, 175 Fifth Avenue, New York, NY 10010.

P1

Acknowledgments

The idea for this book was planted during a dinner conversation with Jason Jeremiah about drag racing. Thanks, Jason!

I owe a larger debt of gratitude to Pulitzer winner David Bradley, who taught me everything I know about the craft of writing. I've written several million words since David's MFA seminars at Temple University, but I still hear his voice in my head every time I write something that should be tossed out. Thanks, David.

I try to pass along everything I learned from David to the "Thursday Group"—Greg Jorgensen, Madeline Mora-Sumonte, Jane Phelan, and Linda Bailey—who meet around my dining table every week. I'm supposedly the workshop leader, but they teach me and enrich my work and my life in ways too numerous to count.

So does Marcia Markland, my patient and compassionate editor at Thomas Dunne. Thank you, Marcia! Many thanks, too, to the production department at St. Martin's Press who carefully and respectfully transform my manuscripts into finished books, to the distribution reps who see that bookstores have the books, and to all the overworked and underpaid booksellers who loyally display, recommend, and promote Dixie Hemingway.

And a huge thank you to Al Zuckerman, the über-agent at Writer's House whose wit and wisdom always astonish me.

To my family, who have endured a terrible year with grace, humor, and courage, thank you for being you.

And to readers who send me their own stories, you kept me writing through a time of grief. Thank you for your support.

If you are alone you belong entirely to yourself.
If you are accompanied by even one companion
you belong only half to yourself.

—Leonardo da Vinci

1

I read somewhere that if two quantum particles come into contact with each other—like if they happen to bump shoulders in the dairy aisle of a subatomic supermarket—they will be forever joined in some mysterious way that nobody completely understands. No matter how far apart they travel, what happens to one will affect the other. Not only that, but they will retain some eerie form of ineffable communication, passing information back and forth over time and space.

Ruby and I were a bit like those weird particles. From the moment I opened the door and saw her standing there holding her baby, we had a strong connection that neither of us particularly wanted. It was just there, an inevitable force we couldn't resist.

I met Ruby the first morning I was at her grandfather's house. Her grandfather was Mr. Stern, a name which fit him remarkably well. Slim, silver-haired, and ramrod straight, Mr. Stern had ripped his bicep playing tennis. He was not the sort of man to make a fuss about a torn muscle, but his doctor had insisted that he rest his arm in a sling until it healed. That's where I came in. Mr. Stern lived with a big orange American Shorthair named Cheddar, so he had asked me to help twice a day with cat-care things that required two hands. When he asked and I agreed, neither of us had known that Ruby was on her way with her baby. We hadn't known how much exquisite pain we'd both suffer in the following days, either. Not muscle pain, but heartache.

I'm Dixie Hemingway, no relation to you-know-who. I'm a pet sitter on Siesta Key, a semitropical barrier island off Sarasota, Florida. Until almost four years ago, I was a sworn deputy with the Sarasota County Sheriff's Department. Carried a gun. Had awards for being a crack shot. Went to crime scenes with the easy self-confidence that comes with training and experience. Had faith. Faith that I could handle anything that came along because I was solid, I was tough, I had my act together, I was on top of things. When I looked at myself in the mirror, I had calm, fearless eyes. Then my world exploded into an infinity of sharp-edged fragments and I've never had those fearless eyes again.

But on that Thursday morning in mid-September when I met Mr. Stern and Ruby for the first time, I had dragged myself out of a cold, dark pit of despair. I wasn't hollow anymore. I enjoyed life again. I had even thawed out enough to take the risk of loving again. I was actually happy. Maybe all that happiness was the reason I got careless and ended up in big trouble.

I usually make a preliminary visit to meet pet clients and provide their humans with written proof that I am both bonded and insured. The humans and I discuss my duties and fees, and we sign a contract. But since Mr. Stern had something of an emergency, my first trip to his house was also my first day on the job.

He lived on the north end of Siesta Key on one of the older streets where, during the mass hysteria that hit southwest Florida's real estate market, nice houses originally valued at two hundred thousand had sold as teardowns to be replaced with multimillion-dollar colossals.

Mr. Stern's house was a modest one-level stucco painted a deep shade of cobalt blue. In most places in the world, a cobalt house would probably seem a bit much, but on Siesta Key, where houses nestle behind a thick growth of dark greens and reds and golds, it seemed just the way God intended houses to look. It sat too close to an ostentatious wealth-flaunting house on one side, with another overblown house on the other side that had a huge untended lawn. The lawn sported a bank foreclosure sign—a not-so-subtle reminder that the real estate boom was over and that the value of anything depends on human whim, not on any intrinsic worth.

Slim as a spike of sea oats, Mr. Stern had neatly combed thin gray hair, bushy eyebrows above fierce blue eyes, and a spine so straight he didn't need to tell me he was a military veteran. He told me anyway. He also told me that he was not the kind of man to waste his time on a cat, and that the only reason he had one was that his granddaughter had left her cat at his house and now he was stuck with it. He told me this while he gently cradled Cheddar, the cat, in the crook of his good arm.

American Shorthairs are uniquely American cats.

Their ancestors came to this country along with the first settlers. They were excellent mousers—the Shorthairs, not the colonials—and they were noted for their beautiful faces and sweet dispositions. Something you can't say for sure about the first settlers.

Cheddar didn't seem the least bit offended by the way Mr. Stern talked about his disdain for cats. In fact, his lips seemed to stretch toward his ears in a secret smile, and he occasionally looked at me and blinked a few times, very slowly, sort of a cat's way of saying, *Between you and me, everything he says is hooey.*

Having made it clear that he was a no-nonsense kind of man, Mr. Stern gave me a quick tour of the house. Lots of dark leather, dark wood, paintings in heavy gilt frames, photographs scattered here and there, a book-lined library that smelled faintly of mildewed paper and pipe tobacco. Except for a sunny bedroom with flower-printed wallpaper and a net-sided crib rolled into one corner, the house was what you'd expect of a cultured gentleman who rarely had houseguests.

In the dining room, Mr. Stern opened a pair of french doors with a *ta-da!* gesture toward a large bricked courtyard. "This is our favorite place."

I could see why. Stucco walls rose a good fifteen feet high, with flowering vines spilling down their faces. Butterflies and ruby-throated hummingbirds zoomed around coral honeysuckle, Carolina jasmine, flame vine, and trumpet vine. The perimeter was a thick tangle of sweet viburnum, orange jasmine, golden dewdrop, yellow elder, firebush, and bottlebrush. A rock-lined pond held center stage, three of its sides edged with asters, milkweed, goldenrod, lobelia, and verbena, while a smooth sheet of water slid over an artfully tumbled stack of black rocks at its back. Inside the pond, several orange fish the size of a man's forearm languidly swam among water lilies and green aquatic plants.

Cheddar twisted out of Mr. Stern's hold and leaped to the terrace floor, where he made a beeline to the edge of the pond and peered at the koi with the rapt intensity of a woman gazing at a sale rack of Jimmy Choos.

I said, "This is lovely."

Mr. Stern nodded proudly. "Those gaps between the rocks make the waterfall something of a musical instrument. I can change the tone by changing the force of the water. I can make it murmur or gurgle or roar, just by turning a dial. At night, colored lights inside those openings dim or brighten on different timers. Sometimes Cheddar and I sit out here until midnight listening to the waterfall and watching the light show."

Ordinarily, when a man talks like that, he's referring to himself and a spouse or a lover. I found it both sad and sweet that Mr. Stern was a closet romantic who turned a stern face to the world but shared his sensitive side with a cat.

The churning sound of wings overhead caused us to look up at an osprey circling above us. It was eyeing the koi the same way Cheddar did, but with greater possibility of catching one. Ospreys are also called fish hawks, and they can swoop from the air and grab a fish out of water in a flash. As I watched the osprey, I saw a dark-haired young woman looking down from the upstairs window of the house next door. She turned her head as if something had distracted her, and in the next instant disappeared. Another woman appeared. The second woman was older, with the sleek, expertly cut hair of a professional businesswoman. When she saw me, her face took on a look of shock, and then changed to venomous fury. A second passed, and she jerked the drapes together and left me staring at shiny white drapery lining.

The hot air in the courtyard bounced from the bricked floor and climbed my bare legs, but a chill had moved in to sit on my shoulders. As unlikely as it seemed, the older woman's animosity had seemed personal and directed straight at me.

The osprey made another circle overhead, hovered atop the wall a moment, then extended its long stick legs for a landing. But the instant its toes touched trumpet vine, it lifted and flew away.

Mr. Stern smiled. "Those birds are smart. There's coiled razor ribbon along the top of that wall. You can't see it because it's hidden under the flowers, but that osprey sensed the danger."

The osprey's shadow had caused the koi to sense danger too. They had all disappeared under rocks and lily pads. The koi were smart to hide. In the garden paradise Mr. Stern had created, life and death teetered on a fine balance.

If I had been gifted with the ability to see into the future and know that Ruby was at that moment coming to bring danger to all of us, I would have followed the lead of the osprey and the koi. I would have hidden out of sight until the danger passed, or I would have left the place entirely and never come back. But I'm not psychic, and even though the next-door neighbor's wicked glare had been unnerving, I wasn't afraid of her.

At least not yet.

2

Mr. Stern scooped Cheddar up with his good arm, and I followed them inside. I opened my mouth to ask Mr. Stern if he knew the women next door, and then snapped it shut. A cardinal rule for people who work in other people's houses is to refrain from asking nosy questions about them or their neighbors.

Mr. Stern said, "Cheddar likes a coddled egg with his breakfast. Do you know how to coddle an egg?"

I said, "While I'm coddling an egg for Cheddar, how about I soft-boil one for you?" It isn't part of my job to take care of humans, but something about Mr. Stern's combination of tough irascibility and secret sensitivity reminded me of my grandfather, a man I'd loved with all my heart.

He said, "Make it three for me, and leave one in long enough to hard cook it. I'll have it later for lunch."

While I served Cheddar's coddled egg, Mr. Stern got out a plate for himself and sat down at the kitchen bar.

I said, "Would you like me to make coffee and toast to go with your egg?"

"I don't need to be babied, Ms. Hemingway." He pointed at a small flat-screen TV on the kitchen wall. "If you'll turn on the TV, I'll watch the news."

I found the remote, turned it on, and handed the remote to Mr. Stern, who was using his good hand to slap at his pockets. "Blast! I left my glasses in the library. Would you get them for me?"

I sprinted to the library to look for his glasses and found them on a campaign chest in front of a small sofa. As I snatched them up, the doorbell rang.

Mr. Stern yelled, "Would you get that? Whoever it is, tell them I don't want any."

I loped to the front door and pulled it open, ready to be polite but not welcoming.

A young woman wearing huge dark glasses and a baseball cap pulled low over blond hair stood so close to the door the suction of it opening almost pulled her inside. In skinny jeans and a loose white shirt, high heels made her an inch or two taller than me. She had a baby in a pink Onesie balanced on one forearm, a large duffel bag hanging from a shoulder, a diaper bag dangling from the other shoulder, and the hand that steadied the baby against her chest held a big pouchy leather handbag. She was looking furtively over her shoulder at a taxi pulling out of the driveway. I got the impression she was afraid somebody would see it.

Everything about her seemed oddly familiar, but I had no idea who she was.

She swung her head at me and did the same quick *I know you, no I don't* reflex that I'd done.

She said, "Who are *you*?" Without waiting for an

answer, she surged forward as if she had every right to come in.

From the kitchen, Mr. Stern yelled, "Who was it?"

The young woman called, "It's me, Granddad."

Footsteps sounded, and I could almost feel his grim disapproval before he came into the foyer with Cheddar at his heels.

His voice was frosty. "What are you doing here, Ruby?"

For a moment, the planes of her face sagged, and then she took on the hopeful look of a child who thinks she might get a different response if she asks one more time for something she's always been denied. She dropped the duffel bag on the floor and removed her dark glasses. Without them, she looked even younger than she had before, barely in her twenties. That's when I recognized her. She looked like me. Not the current me, but the me of ten years ago. She also looked desperately unhappy.

Maybe it was because I remembered what it was like to be that unhappy, or maybe it was because she reminded me of my own outgrown self, but I felt her misery like a barbed shaft hurled at my chest.

Cheddar trotted to her duffel bag and sniffed it. We all watched him as if he might do something wise that would resolve this awkward moment.

The woman said, "I don't have anyplace else to go, Granddad."

"Why don't you go to your so-called husband? Or did Zack kick you out for some other drag-race grouper?"

If he hadn't sounded so contemptuous, I would have found it amusing for him to confuse a fish with a celebrity

hanger-on. But there was nothing funny about his cold-
ness.

The woman didn't seem to notice his slip, but her hopeful look disappeared. "Please, Granddad. We won't be any
trouble."

He made a sputtering sound and waved his good arm
at her, which frightened the baby and made Cheddar
climb atop the duffel bag and stare fixedly at him. The baby
howled in that immediate, no-leading-up-to-it way that
babies do, and Mr. Stern seemed shocked at the amount
of noise coming from such a small form. This was something he couldn't control. The young woman looked as if
she might cry too, and began to jiggle the baby as if jos-
tling her would shut her up.

I'm a complete fool about babies. I can't be around one
without wanting to cuddle it, and the sound of a baby crying makes me react like Pavlov's dog salivating at the sound
of a bell. Without even asking for permission, I stepped
forward and took her. I held her close so she would feel
safe, murmuring softly against her bobbly head, and patted her back in the two-one heartbeat rhythm that babies
listen to in the womb. I had soothed Christy that way
when she was a baby, and for a moment I lost myself in the
scent of innocence and the touch of tender skin brushing
the side of my neck like magnolia petals. As if she recognized an experienced hand, she stopped shrieking and regarded me solemnly with wide pansy eyes.

The woman said, "Her name is Opal."

"Pretty name."

"It was my grandmother's."

A grimace of old grief twisted Mr. Stern's face. "You can stay, I guess. But nobody's going to pick up clothes you throw on the floor. And you know I like things clean."

As she reached to take the baby from me, she said, "I haven't thrown my clothes on the floor since I was thirteen, Granddad."

The baby's bottom lip puckered as if she were thinking of crying again. The woman said, "I need to change her and feed her."

Mr. Stern said, "Your old room is just like you left it."

If she found anything contradictory about Mr. Stern acting like the curmudgeon of the year one minute and then in the next minute saying he'd kept her old room unchanged, she didn't show it. Bending to grab the duffel bag, she gently edged Cheddar off it and clattered down the hall with Opal's head bobbing above her shoulder. Cheddar galloped after them.

Mr. Stern and I regarded each other with solemn faces. He said, "That's my granddaughter, Ruby. She claims she's married to a drag racer named Zack. Maybe she is, I don't know."

I said, "The granddaughter who left Cheddar with you?"

"The only granddaughter I have."

I said, "Now that she's here, I don't suppose you'll be needing me."

He snorted. "Ruby's not the kind you can depend on. I want you to keep coming."

Acutely aware of the emotions in the house, I hurried to clean Cheddar's litter box. It was in a guest bathroom across the hall from the flower-sprigged bedroom, and while I washed the box and spritzed it with a mix of water and hydrogen peroxide, I could hear Ruby's soft voice murmuring to the baby. She sounded the way I remembered sounding when Christy was a baby—the voice of a young mother absolutely besotted with her infant.

When I finished with Cheddar's litter box and headed down the hall, I glanced through the open bedroom door. Ruby had rolled the crib from the corner so it stood in front of glass sliders open to a little sunshine-filled patio. Opal and Cheddar were both in the crib. Cheddar's nose was touching Opal's chin, and Opal was laughing with the soft sound of a baby duckling. Ruby's face was naked with love. Mr. Stern had said Ruby wasn't reliable, but a woman who takes time to play with her baby and is gentle with pets goes to the top of my list of trustworthy people.

I stopped in the doorway. "That's a great crib."

It was, too. Of obvious Scandinavian design—those cold climes must create minds with a keen regard for common sense and practicality—it had a steel frame on large casters. With solid padded ends and what looked like fine fishnet stretched tightly in steel-framed drop-down sides, it combined all the advantages of a regular wooden crib without the dangers of slats or loose-fitting mesh. I was impressed that designers had made such progress in the six years since I had bought a crib.

Ruby looked up and smiled. "It was mine when I was a baby. Actually, my mother slept in it when *she* was a baby. I don't think they make them anymore." She seemed amazed at the idea of a piece of furniture holding up for three generations.

Lifting Cheddar from the crib, she set him on the floor. "Sorry, Cheddar, but it's time for Opal's nap."

Shorthairs are probably Taoists. They accept what *is*, without making a fuss about it. Shorthairs don't have legs made for high-jumping like Abyssinians or Russian Blues, so Cheddar watched Ruby raise the crib side, calculated the odds of leaping over the top rail, and yawned—the kitty equivalent of a shoulder shrug. As if sleeping under Opal's crib had been his plan all along, he oozed under it and curled himself on the floor. I'll bet cat doctors never see an American Shorthair with high blood pressure.

I wiggled my fingers at Ruby and Opal in a mock good-bye wave, and left them. I found Mr. Stern in the library. He wasn't reading or watching TV, just sitting on the sofa staring straight ahead. A grouping of framed black-and-white snapshots was on the wall behind him, all of young men in military uniform. One of them, a tall man with fierce eyes, was apparently their commanding officer. He looked like a much younger version of Mr. Stern, and for a second I wondered if he was a son. Then I noticed a framed banner bearing a red American eagle and inscribed: *The 281st Engineer Combat Battalion, 1944,* and I realized it was Mr. Stern himself. It reminded me that we can never imagine the histories of people we meet, the challenges they've faced, the losses they've known.

He said, "I guess Cheddar remembers Ruby." He sounded sad, as if he felt abandoned.

Trying to make my voice tiptoe, I said, "Cats love being with babies."

He seemed to brighten at the idea that he'd been rejected in favor of the baby instead of Ruby. As for me, a job I'd expected to be neatly delineated had become frayed around the edges by a host of complex emotions emanating from Mr. Stern and his granddaughter.

I said, "I'll be back this afternoon."

As if he'd heard a bugle call, Mr. Stern got to his feet and stood ramrod straight. He walked to the door with me, followed me outside, and watched me get in my Bronco. I gave him my most fetching smile and waved at him like somebody on a parade float. He nodded sternly, like a general acknowledging the presence of inferiors, then scurried around to the back of the car and began whirling his good arm in come-on-back motions.

I groaned. Mr. Stern was turning out to be one of those men who believes every woman with wheels needs a man to tell her how to turn them. Which sort of explained some of the tension between him and Ruby. But, okay, what the heck. It wouldn't cost me anything to let him think he was a big manly man helping a helpless female back her car out of his driveway.

Ordinarily, I would have used my rearview mirror to see if anything was behind me, but with Mr. Stern back there vigorously miming me to back straight out, I sort of felt obliged to swivel my head around and pretend to watch him. But as I looked over my shoulder I saw the young woman at the next-door house again. This time she was at a front window, and I could see her features. She was plump and plain, and something about her seemed indistinct and faded, like old sepia photographs of immigrants arriving in this country at the turn of the century. I kept looking at her until a palm tree blocked my view, and then I remembered Mr. Stern, who was in the street whirling his arm.

He was a nimble man, I'll give him that. He jumped out of the way at the right moment and back-walked along the curb, circling his arm to signal me to turn the wheel. The only problem was that he was directing me to turn in the wrong direction.

So, okay, no big deal. I pulled into the street pointed the wrong way.

I gave Mr. Stern another parade-queen wave and drove off in the wrong direction past the vacant house with the foreclosed sign. In my rearview mirror, I saw him head back toward his open front door. I also saw a long black limo pull away from the curb half a block behind me. Nothing unusual about a limo on the street. People in Siesta Key's upscale neighborhoods take limos to the airport all the time. There wasn't even anything alarming about the way the car stayed the same distance behind me. The street wasn't made for passing, so we both drove along at a steady speed.

I had intended to turn on a side street and work my way back to a main thoroughfare, but residential streets are short on the Key, and this one had no side streets. It ended in a cul de sac, where I made a U-turn. The limo driver made the same turn, and I felt a moment of camaraderie with him, both of us caught by surprise by a dead-end street. As I passed Mr. Stern's house, I looked toward the windows of the house where I'd seen the young woman, but all I saw was the glare of sunlight bouncing off glass.

That's all I could see of the windows of the limo that followed close behind me, too, because the limo's windows were tinted dark. To tell the truth, I didn't wonder about who was in that limo. My mind had drifted to

Ruby and her unhappiness, to Opal, who was one of the cutest babies I'd ever seen, and to Mr. Stern, who presented a cold face to the world but took his cat into the courtyard at night to watch light play on his waterfall.

I reminded myself that every family has its own drama, and that whatever Mr. Stern's family's drama was, it didn't involve me. No matter how much I felt Ruby's misery, no matter how cute her baby was, and no matter how much I thought Mr. Stern's stiffness was a cover-up for a soft heart, it wasn't any of my business. I was strictly a cat sitter, nothing more.

At the corner of Higel Avenue, I stopped for a break in a gaggle of cars tearing past in both directions. Then I spun right, gunned the Bronco south, and lost sight of the limo in my rearview mirror. Instead, a giant insect with long yellow antennae and a black-and-yellow-striped body hovered just behind me. The insect was atop a dark green van, which made me stop thinking about Ruby and Mr. Stern and try to decide whether the bug was an advertisement for a taxidermist or an exterminator.

Later, I would wonder how I could have been so easily distracted. My only excuse was that I'd had a man in my life—again—for about six weeks, and I still wasn't used to it.

3

Having a man in your life after you've lost the habit is like being hit by a persistent case of embarrassing hiccups. Jerky little blips happen in the midst of things that ought to be smooth and automatic. Like at the supermarket, you have a startled moment when you wonder if you should buy six peaches instead of three—in case he should be at your place one night and want a peach while you have one—but you don't even know if he *likes* peaches, so you stand there in front of the peaches like a total idiot asking yourself how it could be that you don't know if the man you love likes peaches. Or like when you get out of the shower, you make sure you hang your towel with the ends even in case he goes in your bathroom and judges you for hanging your towel crooked. Or like you're not sure just how the whole relationship is going to go, or how you want it to go. It's enough to make you batty, just thinking about it.

Which is what I was doing as I turned off Higel to Ocean and drove to the Village Diner where I go every morning after I've finished with all my pet-sitting duties. By that time it was close to ten o'clock. I'd been up since four, without caffeine or food, and I was ready for breakfast and a long nap.

That's my excuse. I was a woman in love, and I was hungry and tired. So when I pulled into the shelled parking area at the side of the diner, I didn't pay much attention to the black limo that purred to a stop close beside me. Like I said, Siesta Key is a prime vacation spot for well-heeled tourists, so limos are almost as numerous as egrets or herons. But when I opened the Bronco door and slid out, the limo's back door on my side opened too, which boxed me in. I did a mental shrug. As every year-round resident on the Key knows very well, some tourists are so rude and pushy that we would cheerfully toss them into the Gulf if it weren't for the fact that they keep our economy going.

Friendly as a Chamber of Commerce volunteer, I closed the Bronco door and waited for the limo's backseat occupant to get out and close the limo door so I could move forward. In the next instant, a large man in a ski mask lunged from the limo's front passenger seat and another masked man popped from the backseat. In about two nanoseconds they had my mouth covered, my limbs pinned, and me stuffed in the cavernous backseat of their car. Even in the shocked midst of it happening, while I kicked and grunted and squealed and tried to wrest myself free, part of my mind coolly appraised their expertise. These guys were pros.

The doors closed and the limo backed out of the lot and drove down Ocean at a normal speed. Both men had got into the back with me, so the driver was alone in the front. He kept his face turned forward so all I could see was the back of his head. One of the men in the back put a strip of tape over my mouth, and they had my wrists and ankles bound together before we got to Higel. As the car turned left, they pulled a black hood over my head.

Even with a hood over my head, I could tell they followed the dogleg on Higel to Siesta Drive and over the north bridge to the mainland. For a few seconds, I made angry noises. But they were a waste of energy, so I shut up and tried to pay attention to anything I could use later to identify the men. There wasn't much. The men in the back stayed silent, and so did the driver.

After the time it would take to get to the Tamiami Trail, the limo stopped, waited, and turned left. We were headed north, which led to Sarasota Bay and the marina. If they planned to put me on a boat, that would be the place to do it. North led to Sarasota's downtown streets, too, but I doubted they had shops or theaters or restaurants on their minds.

They could also turn off Tamiami onto the fixed-span bridge that leads to Bird Key, St. Armands Key, Lido Key, Longboat Key, and Anna Maria Island. Rich people live on those keys, so if some rich person had hired these goons to kidnap me, they might be taking me to the rich person's house. But I couldn't think of a single person, rich or otherwise, who would want to kidnap me.

We didn't turn off Tamiami Trail, just kept going straight ahead. My mind raced with possibilities of where we could be headed. I doubted it would be the Ringling Museum of Art, or the Ringling College of Art and Design, or the Sarasota Airport. The car kept moving and after a while I stopped trying to guess where we were going. Instead, I started wondering how long it would be before somebody realized I had been kidnapped. That was depressing because it would probably be hours.

That's one of the problems with living alone and having a weird schedule. I get up every morning at four A.M. Most days it's ten o'clock before I have contact with any being who doesn't have fur and four legs. Then I stop at the Village Diner for breakfast. Everybody knows me there, and they would notice if I didn't come in. Tanisha, the cook, always knows the minute I enter, and by the time Judy, the waitress, has my coffee on my regular table, Tanisha is already cooking my usual two eggs over easy with extra-crispy fried potatoes and a biscuit. But every now and then something comes up and I don't have breakfast there, so neither Judy nor Tanisha would think of me as a missing person if I didn't show up. They wouldn't call the cops and say they thought I'd been kidnapped.

But both of them took breaks, both of them left the diner to go home when their shifts ended. If they saw my Bronco in the parking lot, they'd wonder why it was there and I wasn't. At least they would if they recognized the Bronco as mine. I wasn't sure they would. I knew Judy and Tanisha as well as I knew anybody, but I didn't know what kind of car either of them drove. I saw them only at the diner, not driving their cars, and that's the same way they saw me. Heck, for all I knew, my Bronco could sit in that lot for two or three days without attracting any attention.

Michael, my brother, would miss me, but not for a

while. He and his life partner, Paco, live in the Gulf-side frame house where Michael and I grew up with our grandparents. I live next to them in an apartment above our four-slot carport. Michael is a fireman with the Sarasota Fire Department, so he works a twenty-four/forty-eight shift, meaning he's on duty twenty-four hours, then off forty-eight. He had gone on duty that morning at eight o'clock, so he wouldn't be home until the next morning. Paco is an undercover officer with the Sarasota County Sheriff's Department. His hours are erratic and never announced, so he might or might not come home and wonder where I was.

And then there was Guidry, a homicide detective with the Sarasota County Sheriff's Department. Guidry, with his calm gray eyes and beaky nose and a face that looks stern until you notice little white smile lines etched around his eyes. Guidry, who made my heart clatter when he was near, but who wasn't near on any regular basis because neither of us was ready yet for any kind of routine. We were more spontaneous. At least we told each other and ourselves that we were, but somehow spontaneous had added up to a lot of evenings together and a few mornings, which made us both skittish as feral cats wanting and fearing at the same time.

If Guidry called and I didn't answer, he would think I was busy grooming a cat or cleaning a litter box. If he called again and I didn't answer, he might think I was gathering information from a new client or that I was in the middle of busy traffic. But if I didn't call him back, he'd think something was wrong. Even then, he wouldn't consider that I'd been kidnapped. I mean, who gets kidnapped?

Children of wealthy parents. Heads of big multinational corporations. Big drug dealers by their rivals. Third-world politicians. Cat sitters don't get kidnapped.

The limo made a right turn, but I had lost track of where we were. All I knew was that we were quite a way north of Sarasota. After what I judged to be two or three miles, we turned left again. I could hear the whine of car tires and feel the vibration of rolling over highway joints so I guessed we had turned onto Highway 301. After several more miles, we turned right again, and went straight far enough to have crossed I-75 before we made a left, two more rights, and then a left onto a road that threw gravel onto the underside of the limo.

Another left turn, and the limo stopped. I heard electronic beeps like a control board being punched, then a sound like metal dragging on pavement, and the limo moved forward for a short distance and stopped.

One of the men pulled the hood from my head. "Okay, girlie, we're here."

I looked out the window at a smooth paved area where a jet sat in front of a gleaming white metal hangar. I don't know much about planes, but I knew this one was large for a private jet. An area of artfully planted trees and flowering shrubs separated the hangar from a rambling low-slung stucco house. The hangar looked almost like a regular freestanding garage, except it was big enough for a good-sized plane.

A tall, wide-shouldered man walked from the hangar like Donald Trump getting ready to fire somebody. He was middle-aged, gray-streaked hair combed straight back from a receding hairline, ice-blue eyes, a long face that might have been good-looking without the surly scowl.

The driver put down his electric window and grinned. "Hey, Tuck. I got her. Followed her from the old man's house."

The man leaned to look in at me, and the two masked men holding my arms tightened their grip and sort of tilted me toward the window for viewing. I did my best not to look scared when I glowered at him.

His eyes raked over my face a couple of times. His mouth twisted, and for a moment he looked frightened. Then arrogance took over again. "That's not her!"

The driver half turned to look at me. "You sure?"

"Of course I'm sure! Good God, I'm surrounded by morons and idiots!"

He fixed his cold eyes on me. "Ma'am, I want you to know I had nothing to do with this. I don't know anything about whatever these men are up to."

Turning his fury back to the driver, he said, "Take care of this, Vern!"

"Take care like—"

"No, fool! I mean fix it! With nobody getting hurt! Understand?"

Behind him, some other men had stepped from the hangar to try to get a glimpse of the wrong woman in the limo's backseat. I had a feeling I would be a lot better off with them than with Vern, so I made some more loud squealing noises, but nobody offered to take the tape off my mouth.

In a voice of hurt dignity and self-righteous demand, Vern said, "What do you want me to do with her?"

"It's your screwup, you figure it out! And don't come back here until you've got more sense!"

He went inside the hangar, sliding bay doors descended, and the interior was hidden from our view. Vern waited until the doors thudded onto the pavement with a sound of utter finality. Then, in a fury, he started the car, made a screeching K-turn, and sped through the open gate. I couldn't see them, but I was sure the gate doors closed behind us. I wondered if the man would change the code for opening the gate.

The men in the backseat released their hold on me. One of them turned his head toward me and spoke through the slit in his mask.

"I guess we made a mistake." He sounded hopeful, as if he thought I might forget the whole thing.

The other one said, "Vern, what're you going to do with her?"

I wanted to know that myself.

They hadn't replaced my hood, and in the driver's dash mirror I could see Vern's piggy little eyes darting back and forth with the effort of thinking what to do with me. I was pretty sure whatever he came up with wouldn't be anything I'd like.

His eyes met mine in the mirror. "It's just your word against ours, lady. If you tell anybody, we'll say you lied."

I nodded, trying to look humble, which took an effort. I also tried to look scared, which was no effort at all.

We retraced our route, first along the graveled one-lane road with its twists and turns, then down some streets where the lots were at least an acre, some of them with a horse or two cropping grass. I knew we were on the outskirts of some small town, but the area wasn't familiar. It didn't seem to me that Vern had a route in mind, but was driving aimlessly hoping for inspiration.

We finally approached an I-75 intersection where service stations and fast food places clustered in a traveler's stop. Vern pulled into a vacant parking lot behind a Friendly's restaurant. With the motor idling, he turned to me.

"Okay, now this is what's going to happen. We're going to untie you and let you out here, and we're going to drive away. You're going to face the other way until we're gone, then you're going to go in Friendly's and call a cab and you're going to go back where we got you. And you're going to keep your mouth shut about this whole business. *Comprende*?"

I nodded, trying to memorize his face while he talked. He had a long upper lip that covered his top teeth. His lowers were smoker's teeth, dark at the roots, with magenta gums. When he spoke his lower teeth were bared, making him look like a bulldog. "If you say one word, we'll come after you and next time it won't be for a pleasure ride. You got it?"

I nodded again. Faster.

He said, "Okay, untie her."

Untying really meant cutting through the duct tape they'd wrapped around my wrists and ankles. Duct tape is useless for taping ducts, but it comes in handy for kidnapping people.

I could see the men's eyes behind their ski masks. They looked embarrassed and scared. They must have been a lot smarter than Vern, who didn't look the least bit embarrassed. Like every loser in the world, Vern was feeling sorry for himself.

I didn't make any sudden moves. I was docile as a Ragdoll cat. When they'd got the tape off my ankles and wrists, Vern handed me a fifty-dollar bill.

"You can use this for cab fare."

One of the other men grunted approval, and they opened the car door and moved aside so I could climb out. As soon as I was upright on the pavement, the limo door closed and the car zoomed out of the lot. Even if I'd disobeyed orders and turned around to look at the limo's tags, it was gone before I managed to force my body to stop trembling.

Gingerly, I lifted a corner of the duct tape and carefully peeled it off my mouth. It felt as if some of my lip went with it, but it didn't bleed. Holding the tape between thumb and finger, I held it away from me and walked around to the front entrance of the restaurant. A family came out before I got there, and the father held the door for me. I thanked him and walked directly to the ladies' room at the back.

As I'd hoped, a paper towel dispenser was on the wall beside the row of sinks. The towels were the smooth brown kind that are useless to dry your hands on, but perfect for preserving latent fingerprints on a strip of duct tape. I pulled a towel out, folded it loosely around the tape, and tucked it in one of the pockets of my cargo shorts. Then I leaned on the counter and shook for a while. Adrenaline does that to you. After I'd got myself more or less composed, I used the facilities, washed my hands and face, and examined my puffy lips in the mirror. Women who want lips like Angelina Jolie should forget about collagen shots and just rip some duct tape off their mouths every few days.

The only thing left to do was pull my cellphone from a pocket and call Guidry.

4

I didn't go into a lot of detail, just told Guidry I'd been grabbed by some guys in a limo and driven somewhere near Bradenton and put out at Friendly's.

He said, "Are you all right?"

I said I was, and he told me he'd be there in thirty minutes.

I left the ladies' room and went to sit at a table by the window. Adrenaline shakes from my harrowing experience had morphed into hunger shakes from going a lot of hours without eating. When a waitress brought a menu, I asked for immediate coffee. She not only brought me a full mug but stood by ready to give me a refill.

I winced when the hot coffee stung my lips, and the waitress looked distressed.

I said, "My lips are chapped."

She nodded, but I could tell she knew they were more than chapped. I thought about explaining that I'd lost a layer of lip skin when I ripped tape off them, but decided against it. Instead, I ordered a cheeseburger and extra-crispy fries.

The waitress must have realized I was so hungry I might start gnawing on the table, because she said, "It'll just take a few minutes. We're not real busy yet."

She topped off my coffee and scurried to turn in my order. I sat looking out the window reviewing all that had happened. Some woman had been the target of a kidnapping, but the kidnappers had been so dumb they'd nabbed me instead. It didn't take a lot of imagination to know the intended woman had been Ruby. Vern had said, "I followed her from the old man's house," which had to mean Mr. Stern's. Furthermore, even though I was a good ten years older, Ruby and I were both pale-skinned blondes, both about five-foot-three, both about a size six.

I had seen Vern's face and could identify him if I saw him again. The other two men had worn ski masks that hid their faces, but they had not worn gloves and I may have got good latents from the duct tape they'd put on my mouth.

Latent prints are only valuable if they match prints on file in IAFIS, the Integrated Automated Fingerprint Identification System maintained by the FBI. The file contains millions of prints taken from criminals, people fingerprinted in conjunction with job applications, and a large percentage of military officers and enlisted personnel, especially those taken after 2000. If the guys who'd bound and gagged me in the limo didn't have criminal records, had never worked for an employer who required fingerprints, or had not served in the U.S. military, their latents wouldn't help identify them.

While I thought about all that, the waitress brought my cheeseburger and fries. She poured another cup of coffee, hovered a moment as if she were afraid I might stuff the entire burger in my mouth at one time and choke to death, then gave me a motherly smile and left me alone.

The burger was good, with honest yellow mustard, a square of American cheese, tomato, lettuce, and a slice of onion that brought tears to my eyes just to smell it. Being as I had a man in my life and had to consider my breath, I removed the onion slice.

Mustard and salt burned my raw lips, but I finally got the hang of pulling my lips back so only my teeth touched the food. I've seen horses do that. Maybe their lips are tender too. The waitress refilled my coffee mug after I polished off the last fry. I cradled the mug with both hands and thought some more until I saw Guidry walking toward me.

Most homicide detectives wear polyester suits with drip-dry short-sleeved shirts and scuffed brown lace-ups. They wear ties either too wide or too narrow for the current style, and the buttons on their shirts are always straining against ten pounds put on since the shirt was new. Guidry wears cool unlined linen jackets with linen trousers that don't match. The jackets hang from his shoulders in a way that makes you know they were made by some Italian with an attitude. The sleeves are pushed up his bronzed forearms. The trousers are wrinkled just enough to make you think of fibers spun from grains that grew under Egyptian suns. His shirts are knit, probably of silk or some threads spun by insects I don't even know about. His bare feet are shoved into woven leather sandals. Good leather, not that cheap cardboard-like stuff.

He does not wear ties, but lets his shirts lie open at his throat. His throat has a little hollow between the bones that my lips fit into perfectly. It smells of clean skin and honesty.

He looked calm as ever, but the lines around his lips seemed deeper and his gray eyes were stormy. He slid into a chair opposite me and studied my face.

He said, "Are you really okay?"

I nodded. "They put a hood over my head and wrapped duct tape around my wrists and ankles, but they didn't hurt me."

"Your mouth is swollen."

"They put tape on my mouth too. I saved the tape for prints."

"You know who they were?"

"There were three of them. The driver's name was Vern. Caucasian, about forty, broad shoulders. I didn't see him standing up, but he looked tall in the seat. The other two were also Caucasian, medium height, medium weight, wore ski masks. I heard one of them speak, but there wasn't anything distinctive about his voice."

"What'd he say?"

"He said, 'I guess we made a mistake.'"

Guidry raised a *no-shit!* eyebrow.

I said, "They meant to kidnap a different woman."

"What different woman?"

"I'm pretty sure they thought I was a woman named Ruby. She's the granddaughter of a man who has a cat I'm helping him with. He tore his bicep muscle. The man, not the cat. The cat is a big orange Shorthair named Cheddar. The man's name is Mr. Stern."

Guidry's gray eyes took on the bleak look he gets when I talk about animals.

I said, "They took me to a man named Tuck. He has a big hangar next to his house, with a landing strip for a private jet. Tuck walked out to the limo and I think he was expecting me. Vern said, 'I got her,' but when Tuck saw my face he said, 'That's not her!' He was mad at Vern, and told him to take care of me without anybody getting hurt. He apologized to me, said he hadn't had anything to do with it and didn't know anything about it, but I think he did."

"Where were you when they grabbed you?"

"The Village Diner parking lot. They drove in and parked right beside me."

"They'd been following you?"

I hesitated, embarrassed to admit I hadn't been paying attention. "A limo like theirs was behind me earlier, but traffic got between us on Higel. I didn't see them back there when I turned on Ocean, but they must have been."

"Where were you earlier, when you saw them behind you?"

I told him where Mr. Stern lived. "The limo was a couple of houses down the street when I left Mr. Stern. It pulled behind me and stayed on my tail until I turned on Higel. Vern told Tuck he'd followed me from 'the old man's house,' as if they both knew who 'the old man' was. I think he meant Mr. Stern's house."

I touched my sore lips. "Ruby doesn't live there, but she has a bedroom with a crib in it so she must have spent a lot of time with Mr. Stern. She's been gone someplace, but she came back this morning while I was there. Ruby's at least ten years younger than me, but we look a lot alike.

She has an adorable baby named Opal. She's about four months old."

Guidry got the same expression he got when I talked about pets. "You know Ruby's last name?"

I shook my head. "Mr. Stern said she might or might not be married to a drag racer named Zack. He seemed to think Ruby might have lied about being married to him."

"Zack Carlyle?"

The way he said the name made it sound as if Zack Carlyle was somebody famous. I guess he could tell from my blank face that I'd never heard the name before.

He said, "This guy Tuck, was his place east of Seventy-five?"

I nodded. "It's that super wealthy area where all the homes have private landing strips and hangars."

"Tuck is probably Kantor Tucker. Richer than God, flies his own big jet, has lots of important contacts."

I'd never heard of him, either. Once again, I realized that I was ignorant about a lot more things than I was smart about. I hate when that happens.

Guidry looked down at me and quirked the corner of his mouth. "So Vern and his boys drove you here and let you out?"

"Vern gave me fifty dollars for cab fare."

"Vern's all heart."

"I ate a cheeseburger and I'm going to use Vern's fifty to pay for it. You want one?"

He grinned and refused, his smile a white flash that never fails to make my toes tingle.

With tax, my hamburger and coffee were a little over ten dollars. I left the rest of the fifty for the waitress.

5

On the way back to Sarasota, Guidry and I were both quiet. I don't know what Guidry was thinking, but I was thinking that once my kidnapping was reported, it would be a matter of public record. Which meant that local reporters who troll police reports for news would see it. Which meant that my private life would be displayed for the world to see. Again.

In my mind, I played out two options and their consequences. I could report that I'd been kidnapped and go through the law-enforcement process of identifying Vern and his cohorts, or I could keep quiet about the whole thing.

If I could identify Vern from mug shots, and *if* the latent prints on the tape weren't too smudged, and *if* IAFIS had matching prints in their files, the cops could identify the man who had taped my mouth. Those were important *ifs*, because the tape was the only proof I had that the kidnapping had actually happened. If the tape had no usable latent prints, it wouldn't be proof at all.

If Vern and his goons were brought to trial, I knew how it would go. Their lawyers would argue the kidnapping hadn't happened, that even if it had, I hadn't been hurt, hadn't been taken across state lines, hadn't been raped, hadn't been threatened with a gun or a knife. They would say it wasn't really kidnapping because nobody had made ransom demands. They'd claim they had simply taken me for a short ride as a harmless prank. They'd pull self-righteous faces and claim that as soon as Vern had realized it wasn't funny to me, he'd let me go with money for cab fare.

A smart lawyer would make me look like a whining neurotic who took herself far too seriously. Even if a jury believed I'd been taken by force, the penalty probably wouldn't be very severe.

And then there was wealthy Kantor Tucker, who would surely deny that he'd ever seen me. He was a man in the public eye, and if I said I'd been kidnapped and taken to him, the media would have a field day playing with the fact that Vern had grabbed me for Tucker and Tucker had refused me. On top of everything else, I would look like a kidnap rejectee.

I said, "I'm not going to report it."

Guidry gave me a quick sideways look. "You have to put an end to that fear, Dixie."

"Easy for you to say. You aren't the one who got pilloried by the press."

I sounded bitter and self-pitying, which bothered me more than memories of seeing myself on TV lunging at a woman reporter at Todd and Christy's funeral. My face had been twisted in a murderous rage, and if Michael and

Paco hadn't grabbed me, I probably would have choked the woman right there on camera. She had stuck a mike in my face and asked me how it felt to lose my husband and child in such a senseless way, and I'd gone mad-dog crazy. The next time I'd made the news was when I killed a man. That time I was a heroine, but the slimy feeling I'd had when I saw my name in headlines had been as bad as the first time I'd seen it. I didn't want to see it again. Didn't want to read: PET SITTER KIDNAPPED.

But I knew what Guidry was thinking: my reason for keeping quiet about a crime shouldn't be solely to avoid publicity. If I didn't report it, criminals would have gotten away with treating a woman like an object to be carted around at their whim. They might feel so invincible they'd commit some other crime against some other woman, and next time they might not stop at nabbing her off the street.

With a defensive whine to my voice, I said, "If I thought bringing charges against them would send them to jail or get them a hefty fine, it would be different."

Guidry didn't respond, but I could see by the way his lips firmed that he didn't believe either of those penalties would happen. One of the paradoxes of living in a democracy governed by laws is that laws sometimes work in favor of law-breakers more than law-keepers. I don't like that, but I also wouldn't like living in a country where some dictator made the rules.

We rode awhile longer in silence, then Guidry said the words I should have expected, but hadn't. "Dixie, I'm a sworn officer of the law. I have to report any crime I have knowledge of."

For a moment, I felt betrayed, even though I knew he was right. For another moment, I wished I'd used Vern's money to pay a cab and kept the whole incident a secret. But I knew that would have been wrong, too. I didn't want my relationship with Guidry to include secrets. Secrets may start out as little cracks between two people, but they end up as chasms a mile wide.

I scootched forward on the seat and dug my Keds into the floor, knowing that Guidry would drive me straight to the sheriff's office on Ringling Boulevard, where I would look at mug shots of known criminals who matched Vern's description.

That's exactly what he did, too. The problem with people with ethics is that they have ethics all the time, even when it's inconvenient. So I reported the crime, handed over the duct tape I'd peeled from my lips, and spent two hours looking at mug shots that did not include any face I recognized as Vern's.

When the investigators were done with me, Guidry drove me to my Bronco in the Village Diner's parking lot. After he parked and turned off the engine, he turned in his seat and slid an arm around my shoulder.

"That wasn't so bad, was it?"

"That wasn't what I dread, and you know it."

He rubbed his thumb against my shoulder bone. "Look, it's bad enough that you may get some embarrassing mention in the press. But if it happens, deal with it then. You're reacting to something that hasn't even happened yet."

At times like that I always wish I chewed bubble gum. If I did, I could blow a big round balloon and pop it right in somebody's face every time they were right and I was wrong. Since I couldn't do that, I just stuck out my lower lip a little bit like a two-year-old.

Guidry patted my shoulder like I was a puppy. "I'll follow you home. Check out your apartment, make sure everything is okay."

I gave him a cool look. "This morning, a man directed me when I backed out of his driveway. It was a straight driveway."

"Are you saying I'm a control freak like him?"

I leaned forward and kissed his cheek. "I'm saying I'm a big girl, and I don't need you to follow me home. At least not to check out my apartment."

He took a deep breath. "If you see that limo again, get the tag number."

"I will."

"And be careful when you go home."

"I will."

He pulled me close and kissed my sore lips so lightly it was like being touched by a butterfly's wing. But a good kisser can put a lot of passion into the tenderest of kisses, and Guidry is an excellent kisser. Oh, yes, he is. So good that I may have staggered a little bit when I slid out of his car and got into my own. I hoped he didn't notice. I mean, I have my pride.

He waited until I started the Bronco and drove out of the lot, then followed me as far as Midnight Pass Road where I turned south. He tooted his horn goodbye and turned north. I drove home with a goofy grin on my face. Somehow the kiss had made the morning's unpleasantness not seem so bad anymore.

I sure as heck didn't look forward to the media finding out about it. I didn't feel optimistic about Vern and his buddies being punished for kidnapping me, either. But it had been cowardly of me to even consider keeping it a secret and I was glad Guidry had pushed for what was right.

Furthermore, even though I hadn't seen Vern's face in the mug shots, I knew it would take deputies handling the investigation about two nanoseconds to find out who Vern was. I had no idea what would happen after that, but I knew at least two deputies—Guidry and Paco—who would take an extremely personal interest in the investigation.

Guidry wouldn't be part of the investigating team because he was homicide, and Paco wouldn't be part of it because he did drug busts and undercover surveillance, but they would both pay close attention. Female logic made me see that kind of male protectiveness as a good thing, not at all like Guidry's offer to follow me home or like Mr. Stern directing me out of a straight-shot driveway.

Like a hunting dog finding all kinds of tantalizing scents in the woods to explore, I let my mind trot down several trails. Vern hadn't struck me as the kind of man who was trusted to make independent decisions, so I doubted he had just happened to see me leaving Mr. Stern's house and decided to grab me. If I was right, somebody had ordered him to take me to Kantor Tucker. But who? Tucker had no way of knowing I was at Mr. Stern's, so it wouldn't have been him. And certainly Mr. Stern wouldn't have called Vern and told him to follow me and kidnap me.

I thought about the woman who had looked down at me with such venom from her second-story window. Her face had held outraged anger, as if she'd had personal animosity toward me. Could she have mistaken me for Ruby and called Vern to grab me? If so, why had she wanted Ruby kidnapped and taken to Kantor Tucker?

The biggest question of all, of course, was what would have happened to Ruby if Vern had got her instead of me.

Whatever the answer was to those questions, I had to let Ruby know that somebody meant her harm. And as soon as I did, I would be stepping into somebody else's life, something I had vowed not to do again. But sometimes you have to speak up, especially if it might be a life-or-death situation for another person. In this case, I had a strong feeling that it definitely was a matter of life or death.

6

Sunlight, humidity, and sandy sea breezes have softened all the hard edges on Siesta Key. Petals of hibiscus blossoms are indistinct at their edges, palm fronds are faintly fringed at their borders. Even the thorns on the bougainvillea have a vagueness at their tips as if they might decide to turn soft if the idea pleased them. All over the island the lines are sinuous, undulating, ambiguous.

The Key is eight miles long, north to south. We are bordered on the west by the Gulf of Mexico and on the east by Roberts Bay and Little Sarasota Bay. We have some of the finest beaches in the world, some of the wealthiest part-time celebrity residents in the world, and a steady current of sun-dazzled tourists. We also have every shorebird and songbird you can think of, manatees, dolphins, the occasional shark, and semitropical foliage that would smother us in a minute if we didn't keep it trimmed back. The Key is where I was born and where I will die. If I moved someplace else, I wouldn't be me.

Midnight Pass Road cuts a north–south line through the center, with short meandering residential lanes leading east and west. Siesta Beach and Crescent Beach, where the sand is like cool powdered sugar, are on the western Gulf side. Turtle Beach, where the sand is more gray and dense and is a favorite place for people who like to collect shells, is at the extreme southern end.

I live on the south end of the Key on the Gulf side, at the end of a twisty shelled road lined with oaks, pines, palms, and sea grape. Colonies of parakeets live in the treetops, squirrels make their homes in the trunks, and rabbits nibble at the vegetation on the ground. Every time I make the final curve in the lane and see the sun-glittered sea lapping at the shoreline, my heart does a little jig of gratitude for my grandfather's good fortune to stumble on our little curved piece of beachfront paradise back in the thirties.

He had been traveling through Florida on business, land in Florida was dirt cheap, and he had known then and there that he'd found his true home. He and my grandmother bought a two-story frame house from the Sears, Roebuck catalogue, set it facing the Gulf, and raised my mother there. Later, after my father had died and my mother had left us, my brother and I went to live in that house with our grandparents. I was nine, Michael was eleven. When our grandparents died, Michael and his partner, Paco, moved into the house. Almost four years ago, after my husband and little girl were killed, I came back to live in the apartment above the carport. The house and the apartment are like a lot of native Floridians, old and weathered, but strong and sheltering.

I parked in my slot in the carport and stepped into the

brooding torpor peculiar to early afternoon on the coast. During those hours, when the lasering sun seems to draw closer, the sea's hot breath wilts everything in its path and seabirds and songbirds desert the beach for siestas. Even rippling waves lower their heads to conserve energy.

As I went up the stairs to my apartment, I used my remote to raise metal hurricane shutters that cover the entry doors. The shutters were halfway to their soffit when I got to the top of the steps, and I could see Ella Fitzgerald peering at me through the glass in the french doors. Ella is a true calico Persian mix, meaning she's mostly Persian and her coat has distinct blocks of vivid red, white, and black. Ella got her name from the little scatting noises she makes. She had originally been a gift to me, but in no time she had given her heart to Michael and Paco. A lot of females do that when they meet Michael and Paco. Fat lot of good it does them.

A long covered porch runs the length of my apartment. It has two ceiling fans, a hammock strung in one corner, and a glass-topped iron table and two chairs. The roof provides shade, but at noon the porch is almost as hot as the rest of the Key. I unlocked the door and stepped into air-conditioned coolness.

Ella twined around my ankles and said, "Thrripp!"

I picked her up and kissed her nose. "I'm sorry I'm late. I got kidnapped."

She looked deeply into my eyes and blinked slowly. She did it twice, which in cat language means *I love you.* I blinked back at her in the same language, even though I knew she would drop me like a hot lizard if she had to choose between me and Michael or Paco.

Ella officially lives with them, but we don't like to leave her alone any more than we have to, so whichever man is last to leave the house in the morning brings Ella to my apartment. When I come home, she and I take a siesta together and she sits with me while I do clerical duties that go along with a pet-sitting business.

My entire apartment is the same neutral creamy white that my grandfather put on it when he built it for visiting relatives. I guess it seems spartan to other people, but it suits me just fine. The living room has a love seat and club chair covered in dark green linen printed with red and yellow flowers. My grandmother bought the set for her little personal parlor that she'd created with the intention of finding privacy from the rest of us, but I don't think she ever sat on it much. There's also a coffee table and a couple of side tables with lamps. No pictures on the walls. No houseplants. No doodads sitting around.

A one-person bar separates the living room from the kitchen, which is about the size of the postage stamps of some developing countries. A window over the sink looks out at the driveway and its trees.

My bedroom is to the left of the living room. It's only big enough for a single bed pushed against the wall, a nightstand, and a dresser. Photos of Todd and Christy sit on the dresser, and I always pause to touch them when I come home. Todd was thirty-two when he was killed, Christy was three.

I grieved so deeply when they died that I will never be the same person again. Grief is about the loss of yourself as much as the loss of a loved one. The person you were when you were with the other is gone forever. You'll never be exactly the same with anybody else, laugh at the same jokes, share the same private memories. The special facet of yourself they brought out is dimmed or erased forever. I have created a new self without Todd and Christy, but they continue to live somewhere in my mind, healthy and laughing. I suppose they always will.

A door in the bedroom leads to a hall where a stacked washer and dryer sit in an alcove. To the left of the alcove is a small bathroom. To the right is a large closet big enough for clothes on one side and a desk on the other. I take care of my pet-sitting business at the desk, so half of my closet—about thirty-six square feet—qualifies as an office for tax-reporting purposes. I'll bet that gives some IRS guy a big laugh.

I put Ella on my bed, and on the way to the bathroom peeled off my clothes, including my Keds, and put them in the washer. In the shower, I shampooed my hair and stood a long time under a warm spray in case Vern and his goons had shed any of their skin cells on me. Just the thought made my skin quiver.

Out of the shower, I patted myself mostly dry, pulled a comb through my wet hair, brushed my teeth, smoothed on some conditioner, and slicked some Vaseline on my sore lips. My mouth looked like the pouting lips of weird dark-water fish I've seen on the Discovery Channel. Naked, I padded to the hall, added my damp towel to the clothes in the washer, threw in detergent, and turned the thing on. Then I climbed into bed and let the washer's sounds of filling and sloshing and spinning make a homely symphony while Ella and I slept.

When I woke, the kidnapping incident seemed like a

dream. Not a nice dream, but not a nightmare either. On a scale of one to ten, compared to the worst experiences of my life, it didn't even rate a two or three. More like a one-plus. Except for the niggling question of what the connection was between Vern and Tucker and Ruby, I was totally over it.

To convince myself of how over it I was, I focused on my mundane routine as if it were a meditation practice. I made myself a cup of tea, then I flipped the switch on my CD player and listened to Tommy Castro doing "Let's Give Love a Try" while I tossed wet laundry into the dryer and got dressed. With Ella sitting on my desk, I entered morning visits in my client record. The music changed to Eric Clapton's blues. Ella flexed the tip of her tail to the beat. After I finished the office work, I took Ella down to the redwood deck between the house and my apartment, put her on a table my grandfather built, and groomed her. I had just finished going over her with a brush to make her coat shine when Guidry's dark Blazer rounded the curve of the lane. He parked beside the carport and walked to the deck, where he and Ella gave each other appraising looks.

I was all set to kiss him, or at least hug, but he had a removed look that told me he was having some kind of internal debate.

He said, "Ah . . . I have to tell you something. I would have told you earlier, but it didn't seem like the right time."

I felt a prickle of alarm. When somebody is reluctant to tell you something, it's usually bad news.

I said, "Is Michael okay? Paco?"

He looked surprised. "It's not anything like that."

I felt myself blush. "Sorry, I guess I'm still jumpy."

He colored a bit himself, and seemed sorry he'd said anything. When he spoke, I suspected he'd dredged up something to say that didn't have anything to do with what he'd originally intended to say.

"I checked the records. Ruby and Zack Carlyle were married eighteen months ago."

The air seemed to have thinned around us. One of the advantages of having an alcoholic mother is that children get a sixth sense that tells them when they're being lied to. Guidry wasn't exactly lying, but I didn't believe he had come to talk about Ruby's marriage. He'd had some other intent and then changed his mind.

That's one of the problems inherent in a new relationship, when both people have scars from former unions. You have to step carefully, be constantly mindful of where you stand and where you want to go.

Taking the safe route, I pretended to believe Guidry had truly come only to tell me that Ruby was married to a race car driver. "So they're really married."

"There are no records of a divorce."

"Any other kinds of records?"

"He's clean, but the investigators will want to talk to Zack about your kidnapping."

From the grim sound of his voice, I got the impression that Guidry took my kidnapping personally, as if it had been a gauntlet thrown down for him. I suppose it's a guy thing to feel that everything that happens to your woman might be a challenge to your masculinity.

I said, "I don't think Zack had anything to do with me being kidnapped."

"You can't be sure of that. The guy who kidnapped you thought you were Zack's wife."

Well, yeah, there was that.

Ella turned her head and looked at me with something of alarm in her eyes.

All of a sudden the memory of Vern's angry eyes came barreling at me, and I felt my fear again, remembered how my heart had pounded, remembered how scary it had been to have my head covered and my mouth taped shut, how frightened I'd been when I didn't know what was going on, who my captors were, what they planned for me. Even if Zack Carlyle's involvement was totally tangential, he was involved through Ruby, and his part couldn't be ignored.

I must have zoned out for a moment remembering the morning, because Guidry caught my attention with a light tap on my shoulder. He leaned to kiss my cheek and said, "See you later."

Ella and I watched him walk to his Blazer and drive away. I don't know what Ella was thinking, but I was wondering *Later like when?*

That's the thing about men. They're not specific. They come to your house intending to tell you something important, but then they change their mind and talk about something else. They leave you dangling with indefinite words like *later* and *sometime* and *see you*. They really are the most exasperating other sex in the world.

7

When it was time to make afternoon pet rounds, I put Ella in Michael's kitchen and headed for my first stop. Always, mornings and afternoons, that's at Tom Hale's condo in the Sea Breeze on Midnight Pass Road. Tom's a CPA who has been in a wheelchair since a wall of wooden doors fell on him at a home improvement store, so I go twice a day and run with his greyhound, Billy Elliot. In exchange, Tom handles my taxes and anything having to do with money.

I parked in the big lot in front of the condo and took the elevator to Tom's place. He and Billy Elliot were watching *Oprah* on TV. It must have been a show about physical fitness because Oprah was watching a man on a metal contraption hoist himself upwards, like chinning. His arms were shaking from the strain, but he kept doing it, over and over. Except for his middle-aged body, he looked like a kid showing off for a girl. Oprah looked slightly bored. She's probably used to men showing off for her.

Tom switched off the TV and watched me snap Billy's

leash on his collar. Tom has a mop of curly black hair and wears round Harry Potter glasses. He's like a cute poodle you want to pet on the head.

He said, "How're you holding up in the heat?"

I would have told him that the heat wasn't as bad as being kidnapped, but Billy Elliot whuffed to remind me that I was there to run with him, not to chat with Tom, so I led Billy out to the elevator in the hall. Downstairs, we went out to the parking lot where cars park in an oval around a central green spot. The track between parking spaces and the center makes a perfect running track for me and Billy. Like the kind of track I imagined all race cars sped around on.

Contrary to their reputation, some greyhounds don't enjoy running at all. They'd rather sit and watch TV. But not Billy Elliot. Billy Elliot likes running better than anything in the world. He doesn't run because he's a greyhound, he runs because he's like those people who get up early every morning and run two or three miles just for the fun of it. I don't understand those people, but I'm sure Billy does.

After he'd peed on every tree trunk he thought needed peeing on, Billy led me onto the track and we set off. Billy is considerate. He always begins slowly so my muscles can get warmed up before he really takes off. But about halfway around the track, he speeds up. By the time we've made two rounds of the track I feel like a lab rat trying to stay upright on a moving conveyor set too fast. At the condo entrance, I pulled Billy to a stop and leaned over and panted with my hands on my knees. A grandmotherly woman came from the building carrying a white

Lhasa Apso with Cindy Lou Who hair tied with a pink ribbon on top of its head.

The woman stopped. "Are you all right?"

I wheezed, "Just out of breath."

She walked on toward her parked car while the Lhasa looked over her shoulder at me. Before she got into her car, the woman called, "Awfully hot to be running."

I nodded and flapped my hand to say thanks for the tip, while Billy pranced around me, grinning. When we went inside and got into the mirrored elevator, my face was still beet red. Billy was still grinning and wagging his tail in doggy joy.

In Tom's apartment, I went in the kitchen where he was at the table typing on a slim laptop computer. Personally, I'm not a computer person. I'm probably the only living person in the western hemisphere without a Web site or an e-mail address. My life is complicated enough without adding all that electronic crap to it, so I don't blog, Twitter, Facebook, YouTube, Google, or text-message. But every now and then, when I want to take advantage of the availability of instant information, I impose on friends who are computer savvy. People like Tom.

I got myself a glass, filled it with water from the tap, and rested my back against the countertop edge while I drank it.

I said, "If I gave you an address, could you find the person who lives there?"

With his fingertips poised above the keys, he looked at me over the top of his glasses. "What's the address?"

I gave him the house next door to Mr. Stern, the one

where I'd seen two women looking out the window. In about two nanoseconds, he had the owner's name.

"Myra Kreigle."

I went still, with the same kind of *something's-not-right* feeling that comes just before you realize you've stepped into thong bikinis wrong so the crotch part is riding on your hip. I had asked about the address because I wanted to know who had looked down at me with such fury from the house next door to Mr. Stern. Now that I knew she was Myra Kreigle, the way she'd looked at me seemed even more peculiar.

Tom said, "You know who Myra Kreigle is?"

"Sure, the big flipper."

In Sarasota, *big flippers* once meant the appendages loggerhead turtles use to propel themselves onto the beach every year to lay eggs. Now it means somebody who fraudulently drove up real estate prices and fueled southwest Florida's economic meltdown.

Tom said, "Worse than that. Myra Kreigle was a big flipper with an REIT Ponzi scheme."

I vaguely remembered skimming over newspaper headlines when Myra Kreigle was indicted for fraud in connection to her real estate investment company. A vivacious, attractive woman in her fifties, Myra's photo had usually been in the paper in connection to her investment seminars or because she'd donated money to a charity or an arts association. I had been surprised to learn of her dark side, but since I didn't travel in Myra's social circle, she had only been a name to me, not a real person.

Tom said, "She's used up all her trial postponements.

They've already selected the jury, and her hearing starts Monday."

I hadn't even known a trial date had been set. I wondered if the young woman I'd seen at Myra's window was her daughter. If she was, having a notorious liar for a mother would explain why she looked so unhappy. My mother had been a liar too, so I could relate.

I said, "Can you tell me in twenty words or less exactly what Myra did?"

"It'll take more than twenty words, but I'll condense it as much as possible. You know how flipping works, right?"

"Somebody buys a house at its real value, then gets an appraiser to inflate the value. He does a bogus sale to an accomplice at that inflated price. The accomplice gets a mortgage, a banker who knows what's going on lends the money and gets a bonus, and the accomplice either passes the money he borrowed to the seller or they split it. Then the buyer walks away and lets the house be foreclosed on."

"That's how small flippers worked. Big flippers formed a bunch of post-office-box companies or limited partnerships and sold the same property back and forth between them with ever bigger appraisals, larger mortgages, more profits. Myra Kreigle bought and sold hundreds of properties that way. That in itself was a crime, but Myra had formed a real estate investment trust, otherwise known as an REIT, through which she suckered investors by telling them they would get double-digit returns if they gave her money to invest in real estate. About two thousand people fell for that, but it was a scam."

Any time people talk about big money, I always feel like my eyeballs are rotating. Maybe they really were, because Tom grinned and began to speak more slowly.

"A Ponzi scheme is when a lot of people invest in something too good to be true. The con pays the first investors from the money the later investors put in, so word spreads and more people rush to get in on a good deal. As long as new investors are pouring in money, it works. There's enough money to pay off people who ask for their profits, and the con running the scheme can live high on the hog on other people's money."

"So Myra never really invested in real estate?"

"Oh, she bought some mortgages, but most of them were high risk, and none of them paid back what she was promising her investors. The fraud was in sending her investors false monthly reports showing huge profits she claimed she'd made for them by brilliant real estate trades. Most people let their profits ride, but if somebody wanted to collect, she paid them from the investment money. She took in nearly two hundred million dollars that way. Her investors will never get their money back. I imagine most of it is socked away in offshore banks."

"I don't understand how she got away with it for so long."

He rolled his eyes. "If pigeons are getting fed, they aren't picky about who's feeding them."

I nodded, but I still didn't see how intelligent people could be fooled so easily.

Tom said, "Ponzi schemes are called *affinity* crimes because the criminal preys on his own people. Fundamentalists hoodwink fundamentalists, New Agers manipulate

New Agers, Catholics scam fellow Catholics. Myra went after her own kind."

Myra's own kind were the cream of Sarasota's society, the smart set who ordered three-hundred-dollar wine when they lunched at Zoria's. Smugly confident, they were the beautiful people who traveled the world, went to all the classy parties, had their photos in the society pages. Myra had smiled, beguiled, sucked the fat right off their sucker bones, and left them gasping for air like stranded fish. When they went down, they took with them all the little people who had cleaned their houses, landscaped their lawns, taught their children, and sold them goods.

Tom continued to tap keys on his computer and peer at his screen. Some people can multitask like that. Personally, I have difficulty talking and walking at the same time. His fingers raised from the keyboard and he leaned toward the screen to read something he'd pulled up. He wrinkled his lips like he'd bit into moldy cheese, and closed his laptop.

"It'll take a decade before our economy gets back to normal. Myra Kreigle should be in jail now, and if that Tucker guy hadn't put up a two-million-dollar bond for her, she would be."

The short hairs on the back of my neck stood up.

"Kantor Tucker?"

"That's the one. Everybody else thought she was a flight risk, but Tucker is a close friend and put up the money. He can't protect her forever, though. State investigators have a solid case against her. Several counts of securities fraud, mail fraud, wire fraud, and money laundering fraud. Unless something happens to make the case fall through, she'll serve several years in a white-collar-crime prison."

I finished off the glass of water and filled it again. "Some guys kidnapped me this morning and took me to Kantor Tucker."

Now I had Tom's complete attention. "Somebody *kidnapped* you?"

"They grabbed me outside the Village Diner and drove me east of Seventy-five where Tucker has a place. Big spread with a landing strip and a hangar beside his house. The guys who took me to him thought I was somebody else. When they found out I wasn't who they thought I was, they took me to a Friendly's and put me out. I called Guidry and he came and got me. I reported it. I don't want the publicity, and I can't prove they did it, but Guidry made me report it."

"Good God, Dixie."

"I know. I looked at mug shots at the sheriff's office but I didn't see the driver of the limo. His name is Vern."

"That's all you've got? The guy's first name?"

"They put tape on my mouth, and I saved the tape. It may have latent prints on it. I gave it to the investigators."

"Is that why your mouth is puffy?"

"Is it still puffy?"

"I thought maybe you and Guidry had been playing rough kissy-face."

I took another drink of water. "Some of my lip skin stayed on the tape when I ripped it off."

His hand rose to his own lips as if he needed to confirm they were in one piece. "Who did they think you were?"

I shrugged. "They didn't say anybody's name." Strictly speaking, that was true.

"Do you think grabbing you had something to do with Myra Kreigle?"

"Not really. Probably just a coincidence that the limo was in front of her house when I left the house next door."

I tried to sound convincing, but Tom knows me well enough to know when I'm not being totally honest.

I got busy emptying my water glass and putting it in the dishwasher. When I left, Tom and Billy Elliot watched me leave with identical wrinkled brows. Billy Elliot was probably pondering how long it would be before he and I ran again. Tom was probably wondering what Myra Kreigle had to do with me being kidnapped.

So was I.

8

Myra Kreigle and her kind weren't the first real estate swindlers in Sarasota's history. As Sarasota became fashionable during the 1920s, the town was flooded with land speculators who sent property values skyrocketing. Fortune hunters razed orange groves for subdivisions, but left without completing them. People bought property in the morning and sold it for a profit that same afternoon. But in September of 1926, a destructive hurricane ended the real estate boom. The Great Depression struck next, when businesses went broke and tourism slowed to a trickle.

By the 1950s, land was selling again, but not to speculators. In a period of sane and responsible growth, shopping centers, housing developments, schools, churches, and condos went up, all intended for families and retirees seeking a pleasant life. Sarasota would not see another overwrought speculator-fueled boom until Myra Kreigle and her cohorts saw the opportunity to cheat people through fraudulent real estate deals. When I thought of what my grandfather would have had to say about Myra Kreigle, I had to grin. He was a man who could be persuaded to suffer fools, but not thieves. More than likely, he and Mr. Stern would have enjoyed each other's company.

I pulled into Mr. Stern's driveway that afternoon around the time retirees in Florida start crowding into restaurants for the Early Bird Specials. As I started up the walk, a three-woman cleaning crew came out the front door lugging a vacuum cleaner and a plastic basket holding supplies. The woman carrying the vacuum was young and obese and weeping. The other two were thin and older, and were murmuring comforting words to her. They passed by me with barely a look. I suspected that Mr. Stern had said something that had hurt the crying woman's feelings.

Ruby opened the door with Opal balanced on her forearm. Mr. Stern stood behind her with Cheddar cradled in his good arm. They seemed to be in the middle of an argument.

Mr. Stern said, "If American GIs had stopped work every time they got upset, we'd all be speaking German."

Ruby said, "She lost a baby last month. She got upset when she saw Opal."

As if she understood what her mother had said, Opal's bottom lip trembled and she wept for a minute. Ruby jiggled her and Opal hushed and closed her eyes. She probably thought it was the only way to stop being jiggled. I forced my arms to stay at my sides and not reach for her.

Mr. Stern said, "How do you know she lost a baby? Did she waste more time telling you about it?"

"I'll finish the vacuuming, Granddad."

Mr. Stern snorted and stalked off toward the kitchen. Exasperated, Ruby rolled her eyes and walked toward her bedroom, while Opal's round eyes stared at me over Ruby's shoulder.

I followed Mr. Stern to the kitchen where he took a seat at the bar and watched me shake dry food into Cheddar's bowl.

He said, "Cheddar takes a chicken liver in his dinner. There's a tub of them in the refrigerator. Don't heat it. Just put it on top of the food."

The contrast between the consideration Mr. Stern showed Cheddar and the lack of consideration he showed human beings was striking, but not shocking. Pets bring out the hidden goodness in the most hardened hearts, even if it's only in tiny amounts.

I dropped a chicken liver in Cheddar's dish, and Mr. Stern gave a nod of approval. Cheddar jumped on the food and gobbled it up while I washed his water bowl and filled it with fresh water. Mr. Stern's gaze drifted toward a wine rack at the end of the kitchen counter.

I said, "Hard to use a corkscrew with one hand. Shall I open a bottle of wine for you?"

"A Shiraz would be nice."

I opened a bottle of wine while Mr. Stern got himself a wineglass. I poured wine in his glass and left the bottle open in case he wanted more. Cheddar had finished his supper and was licking his paws, so I washed Cheddar's food bowl and dried it while Mr. Stern sipped wine. Of the three occupants of the kitchen, Cheddar was the only one studiously not mentioning Ruby or Opal.

I got my grooming supplies and opened the french doors in the dining room. Cheddar came and stood on the threshold, half in and half out, peering into the garden as if he'd never seen it before.

I scooped him up, closed the door, and sat down in one of the deck chairs by the koi pond. Shorthairs don't need daily combing, but they enjoy it and it helps keep loose hair from shedding on the furniture. I took out my slicker brush and combed his throat with the short strokes cats love, careful not to let the bristles dig into his skin, then quickly moved over his entire body. Cheddar gave an annoyed swish of his tail, so I went back to his throat to soothe him.

Mr. Stern came out holding a plastic cup filled with koi food. Stone-faced, he leaned over the pond and sprinkled food on the water's surface as koi came swarming to the spot. He watched them gulp the floating food for a moment before he sat down in a deck chair.

He said, "Koi don't have stomachs so they can't eat much at one time. If they do, they'll die."

Cheddar and I watched a yellow butterfly sail over Mr. Stern's head, then flit to a mound of lobelia.

He said, "Filtration is even more important than food. Koi can live for weeks without eating, but they'll die in an hour in bad water."

Cheddar jumped from my lap to the brick floor, then into Mr. Stern's lap. Mr. Stern's hand rose in automatic response and stroked Cheddar's back. Cheddar reared on his back legs and put his front paws on Mr. Stern's shoulders, nosing his chin and purring loudly. Mr. Stern's lips threatened to smile.

Looking into Cheddar's eyes, he said, "My daughter died when Ruby was in high school. Ovarian cancer. She was only forty. Beryl was her name. After that, Ruby lived with my wife and me, but I couldn't control her. Drugs, bad crowd, all that. My wife died a year after Beryl. Broken heart, I think."

Cheddar stretched his neck and ran the tip of his tongue across Mr. Stern's chin. Mr. Stern smiled and bent to rub his nose against Cheddar's forehead. Speaking directly to Cheddar, he said, "Ruby started hanging out with the witch next door. The two of them got thick as thieves. Ruby moved out, didn't go to college, I didn't see much of her. I don't know how she came to be mixed up with that race car fellow, but she married him. At least she said she did, I never was sure if she was telling the truth."

Cheddar tipped his head and rubbed the top of it against the underside of Mr. Stern's chin. Mr. Stern's lips pinched into a straight line as if he regretted letting Cheddar know how painful his thoughts were. "She came home when the baby was just a few weeks old. I don't know if she left him or he left her. That's when she brought Cheddar."

I told myself to get up and walk away. I told myself I shouldn't be listening to a man's personal anguish, but my feet were rooted to the courtyard floor.

Still looking at Cheddar, he said, "She didn't stay long. One day she just took Opal and went away. I don't know where she's been. I called that Zack fellow but he claimed he didn't know where she was either."

I said, "What about Ruby's father?"

My voice seemed to startle him. "He was killed in Iraq."

His voice quivered, and he turned his head away. Apparently, Mr. Stern felt he had lost a son as well as a wife and daughter.

I gathered my grooming supplies and stood up. It was time for me to go. The situation in this house was laced with legal, emotional, and familial complications that were way over my head. Ruby and Mr. Stern needed a good lawyer and a good family therapist, not the unavailing sympathy of a pet sitter.

I said, "Is there anything else I can do for you before I leave?"

He shook his head, and I left quickly. We both pretended he didn't have tears in his eyes.

9

In the kitchen, Ruby stood holding Opal and turning side to side. New parents always seem to think babies want to be jiggled or rocked or swayed. I'll bet if they asked the babies, most of them would vote to stay still.

She said, "Opal's teething, I think. She was awake most of the night."

I went to the refrigerator and pushed the lever to release an ice cube into my hand, then folded the ice into a corner of a clean dish towel and smashed it with a cutting board.

I held out my arms and Ruby handed Opal to me as if she'd been waiting for me to work some kind of magic. With Opal cuddled close against my chest, I offered her the cold towel and her swollen gums seized on it like a baby bird grabbing a fat worm from its mother's beak.

I brushed the downy blond sprouts on Opal's head and breathed in the irresistible scent of clean baby skin. "When my little girl was teething, she liked to chew on cold things like this. A damp washcloth left in the freezer will work too."

Ruby grinned at the way Opal was gnawing on the towel. "How old is your little girl?"

I felt the familiar reluctance to answer, coupled with an unwillingness to deny my child's truth. "She was killed when she was three."

"Oh, God. How did you stand it?"

"For a long time, I didn't. I went crazy for a while. My husband was killed at the same time. It was almost four years ago. An old man hit the accelerator instead of the brake and crashed into them. It happened in a Publix parking lot, and for two years I couldn't buy groceries at that store."

Ruby's eyes glistened. "I don't think I could go on living if anything happened to Opal. I never knew how much you can *love* until I had her. It's not like any other kind of love, not like loving a man or loving your parents or your friends. It's like this little demanding person is your *breath,* and you'd die without it."

Every time I talked to Ruby, I liked her more.

As if she understood that her mother was talking about her, Opal gave me a shy, gummy smile. There's nothing in the world like a baby's smile to make you feel better about the human race. Babies don't smile to manipulate or ingratiate, they just smile because they come with a reservoir of smiles inside them and they pass them out with bounteous generosity. Opal's smile made my heart expand. She truly was an adorable baby, and I wanted to hold her in my arms forever.

I said, "She has beautiful eyes."

"She has Zack's eyes. That dark blue that's almost purple, and those long thick eyelashes."

She reached for Opal, and Opal's arms immediately turned toward the person she trusted most in all the world. I felt a momentary pain that I would never again see that look of absolute trust in my own child's eyes.

Ruby said, "Granddad thinks Zack is low-life, but he doesn't understand drag racing. Of course, Granddad thinks I'm low-life, too."

"Actions speak louder than words. Your granddad left Opal's crib set up in your old bedroom. That cancels out a lot of what he says."

She half smiled. "I guess it does. I can't remember Granddad ever telling me he loved me. I doubt he ever told my mother or grandmother he loved them, either, but I know he did. I think he just never learned how to show love, you know? That's why I got Cheddar for him."

"I thought Cheddar was your cat."

She shook her head. "I told Granddad he was, but I got Cheddar at the Cat Depot so he could love something he couldn't boss around."

I grinned. "From what I've seen, Cheddar has trained him very well."

"I lived with him and Granna after my mom died, and it was awful. If I was ten minutes late coming home, he acted like I'd been out whoring or shooting up heroin. If I didn't get all As on my report card, he carried on like I was destined to live in a Dumpster. After Granna died, it got worse. If it hadn't been for the woman next door, I would have gone crazy. Myra was the only person who believed in me, the only one who offered me a hand. Granddad never has forgiven her for it."

Carefully, I said, "I saw a woman looking out the window next door when I was here this morning. Mr. Stern and I were in the courtyard and she was watching us."

Ruby's face tightened. "That's Myra Kreigle. I'm sure you know who she is. I worked for Myra, and I'm a witness in her trial. I don't want her to know I'm here."

"But she's the woman who was good to you?"

"She was good to me *then*. People can be good and bad, you know? Nobody's all bad."

I remembered the venomous hatred on Myra's face as she looked down at me, and wasn't sure I could believe Myra had a good side.

I said, "There were two women, actually. A young one and an older one. Does Myra have a daughter?"

She shook her head. "I was the closest thing she's ever had to a daughter, and I didn't last."

Opal whimpered, and I handed over the towel with the cold, wet corner. But it had lost its appeal, so Ruby put her bent forefinger in Opal's mouth to gum.

Ruby said, "When I was a senior in high school, Myra started paying me to solicit rich men. Not solicit like a hooker, but circulate at her investment parties, talk to them, make them feel like they were big important hotshots, like I was really blown away by a man with so much money. I would put my hand on their arm, you know, lean in to show some cleavage, tell them how Myra was making a lot of money for other men, make it sound like I was more impressed with those other men because they were making so much more money. And then I'd ask them why they weren't letting Myra make them richer too, and offer to get them into her hottest investments. Most of them fell all over themselves getting in. It was funny, really, to see them scramble to impress me. Like they thought they were buying me when they gave Myra money."

"Did you know how she made her money?"

She looked away. "Not at first. I still don't know exactly how she did it, but over time she got careless about talking in front of me and I picked up little clues that her investment deal wasn't what she claimed."

She took a deep breath. "A lot of investors got money back, more than they'd put in. Every time a new person put money in, there was more money to pay out to the ones who wanted to collect their profits."

"And the more you hustled them, the more new people invested."

"Something like that."

Opal whimpered and moved from Ruby's finger to gnaw on her collarbone.

She said, "Until a few months ago, I'd never even heard the term *Ponzi scheme*. All I knew was that Myra paid me good money to go to her seminars and flirt with old rich men. I never slept with any of them, I never went out with any of them. Well, I did go out with some of them, but not anybody serious except Zack. I would have gone out with him even if he hadn't put money in Myra's investment trust."

Okay, now I was beginning to get the picture. Zack was one of the pigeons Ruby had enticed into Myra's trap.

"Did you ever tell Zack that Myra's investment was a scam?"

"Myra promised me he would get all his money back. She guaranteed it."

Feeling as if a boulder was balanced on my shoulders, I said, "Ruby, it isn't any of my business, but does the DA who's prosecuting Myra Kreigle know where you are?"

Sounding proud, she said, "I've been meeting with him for several weeks, telling him what I heard, what I saw. He came to see me before he filed charges against Myra, and then he found me a place to stay so she couldn't get at me. We worked out a plea bargain deal. I'll tell what I know about Myra's business, especially where she put the money, and I won't be charged with helping her."

The look in her eyes was as trusting and naïve as Opal's.

I already knew the answer, but I had to ask the question. "Does Zack know you've been cooperating with the DA?"

"Zack thinks I was part of Myra's deal. He thinks I lied to him, that I only married him for his money." With a firming of her jaw, she said, "I guess he'll sing a different tune after he hears me testify."

I had a bad taste in my mouth. Ruby was half streetwise sucker-bait and half babe in the woods. And her woods were filled with cruel traps. Myra had used her to entice men to invest in her phony scheme, the DA had used her to build a case against Myra, and she believed with all her twenty-year-old heart that Zack would know she truly loved him when he heard her turn state's witness against Myra. I could almost see the vision she had of Zack swooping her up in his arms and striding out of the courtroom like Richard Gere in *An Officer and a*

Gentleman while the audience cheered and Myra was hauled off to jail.

I said, "Do you know somebody named Vern? Or a man named Kantor Tucker?"

For a moment, I could see a family resemblance to Mr. Stern in the cool wariness on her face. "Why did you ask me that?"

"This morning when I left here, three men in a limo followed me to my next stop and grabbed me. They bound my ankles and wrists, put tape on my mouth and a hood over my head, and took me to a man named Kantor Tucker. The driver of the limo was a man named Vern. He told Tucker he'd seen me leaving here. I believe he thought I was you."

Ruby had gone pale. She closed her eyes and lowered her forehead on the top of Opal's head as if seeking strength.

She said, "Vern is Tuck's muscle. Sometimes he works for Myra."

"I'm older than you, but we look a lot alike. Same height, same size, same coloring. When Myra saw me in the courtyard with your grandfather, she must have thought you had returned. She probably called Vern and told him to grab you and take you to Tucker."

For an instant, Ruby tilted slightly to the side like a blighted tree. Fear or guilt or shame made her speech slurred. "How did you get away from him?"

"When Tucker got a look at me, he said, 'That's not her!' and sent Vern away. Vern didn't hurt me, and he gave me cab fare when he let me out. But they must be watching for you."

The french doors opened and Mr. Stern came inside carrying Cheddar. He stopped when he saw Ruby and me in the kitchen. He must have been able to read our faces and know something had just passed between us, but we turned to him with false smiles, and the moment passed.

Mr. Stern seemed more relaxed, perhaps because Cheddar was sending him love purrs. Or perhaps because he had unloaded some of his pain in the courtyard. Whatever the reason, he let me leave without directing me out of the driveway.

At least he and Cheddar had benefited from my visit. But Opal's gums were still sore and swollen, and I'd given Ruby reason to be frightened.

As for me, I was also frightened. Not for myself, but for Ruby. Now I was sure that Vern had thought I was Ruby when he grabbed me. And I was afraid I knew the answer to the question of what would have happened to Ruby if he'd got her instead of me.

The only bright spot I could find in the dark cloud that seemed to be hovering over Ruby and Opal was that the people who had sent Vern to kidnap Ruby would surely know by now that I'd told her they'd got me instead. They would expect her to be on guard now, which should discourage them from trying anything again.

That's what I tried to make myself believe. Every now and then I succeeded.

10

On the way home, I shared the street with bikers in skin-hugging Lycra shorts and shiny skull-protecting helmets. On the sidewalks, Roller-blading parents maneuvered baby strollers between kids trying to ollie on skateboards. In front of me, a tourist couple in a too-clean red Jeep surveyed the world with self-conscious smiles. His shorts were crisp khaki, his knit shirt was white, and his pale legs wore telltale black socks with sneakers. Her shorts were iron-creased yellow linen, her shirt was floral, and she wore a new straw boater with a rhinestone band.

At the firehouse where Beach Road intersects with Midnight Pass, two firefighters were in the driveway polishing a fire truck's chrome, while another firefighter was on the lawn tossing a Frisbee to a Doberman. The fireman tossing the Frisbee was my brother, Michael. The Doberman was Reggie, a courageous dog whose humans had been brutally murdered the year before. Reggie and I had saved each other from similar fates, and when

Michael and his fellow firefighters learned that Reggie had been left homeless, they'd taken him in as the official firehouse dog. Reggie had settled into the firehouse routine as if he'd been training all his life to live with a bunch of big burly guys who played with him and fed him and occasionally jumped into long pants and boots and drove off in a screaming red truck.

When I pulled into the drive behind the fire truck, men and dog all turned their heads with identical expressions—a mixture of hopeful anticipation of pleasant diversion and annoyance at having their fun interrupted. When they saw it was me, they all smiled, and Reggie wagged his stump of a tail. Maybe some of the men did too, I couldn't tell.

I slid out of the Bronco and Reggie ran to kiss my knees while Michael strolled to meet me with his face creased in a big grin. Like Paco, Michael is the kind of man who causes otherwise intelligent women to go weak-kneed with basic lust. He's blond and blue-eyed and his solid muscle is so bulky that he automatically swivels sideways going through doors. He's a firefighter the way our father was, a guy other firemen know they can depend on no matter how bad the situation is. He's also the kindest, most gentle man in the universe, and my best friend.

He glanced at my swollen lips, blushed, and looked away, obviously jumping to Tom Hale's conclusion that I'd been kissing too hard.

I said, "I thought I'd drop off a new tug-toy for Reggie."

One of the guys polishing the truck said, "Good! Reggie goes through those things fast."

I went around to the back of the Bronco and pulled two of the toys from a box of pet toys I keep back there. Mostly the toys aren't purchased, but mundane things dogs or cats like to play with. Dogs especially like braided tug-toys that are dirt cheap and dead easy to make from strips of flannel. I buy red plaid flannel blankets from Walmart—pets seem to like bright colors best—and cut them into strips about five inches wide and a yard long. Then I tie three strips together at their ends and tightly braid them. When the braided end is knotted, it makes a perfect toy for a dog to carry around or for a game of tug-of-war with a human. Since it's flannel, the tug-toy doesn't fray and leave strings lying around, and when the dog destroys it, you can make another one in no time from the same blanket.

I tossed a fresh tug-toy to Reggie, who immediately trotted off like a conquering hero with it gripped in his jaws.

As if they'd had the same thought at the same time, the other two firemen zipped to the truck's cab and pulled out a metal box.

Michael said, "We have something cool to show you."

The three men surrounded me while Michael opened the box. "It's an oxygen mask for animals. Somebody donated one for every fire truck in Sarasota County. It'll fit over an animal snout as small as a kitten's or as big as a Great Dane's. Uses the same oxygen tanks that EMTs use for humans."

Reverently, as if it were something holy, I touched the mask with a fingertip. When a house is burning, pets may die of smoke inhalation because they crawl into small spaces in an attempt to escape the heat. The new oxygen masks would undoubtedly save pets' lives.

I said, "Wow."

The men nodded solemnly, and replaced the box in the truck. They carried it as if it were the ark of the covenant.

I said, "Somebody donated masks to every fire truck?"

With one voice, the men said the woman's name. They spoke it with the same reverence they'd shown the mask. For a moment we were all still with the knowledge that any fool can cause deaths, but only the very special cause life.

Reggie ran up to Michael with the tug-toy dangling from his mouth and whuffed, a clear announcement that he'd been patient with human conversation long enough, and that it was time to get on with the important things in life, like playing. I gave the top of his head a quick smooch, and did the same to Michael's cheek.

I said, "I'll see you tomorrow."

"I may fill in tomorrow for one of the other guys. His kids want to go to Disney World before school starts, and it's the only weekend his wife can get off. We're taking turns, so tomorrow may be my day."

That's part of a fireman's life, doing double shifts occasionally for a buddy. Sometimes it means more sleepless hours fighting fires and sometimes it's merely another twenty-four hours of boredom. For Michael, it means cooking three more meals at work instead of at home. For Paco and me, it means the firefighters get the good stuff and we have to fend for ourselves.

Michael is the cook in our family. Since he was four and

I was two and our mother went off on a bender while our dad was on duty at the firehouse, Michael has assumed that it was his duty to feed me. He's also the cook at the firehouse. No matter where Michael is, he's the cook. He cooks the way poets write, with passion and tender ruthlessness. Paco and I eat the way poetry lovers read, savoring every nuance down to our very souls.

I got home just as the setting sun stained the sky crimson. Paco was on the deck with Ella in his arms, both of them watching the sun hover below a low wisp of cloud cover. Paco is tall, slim in the places a man should be slim, and broad in the places a man should be broad, like a triangle. He's Greek-American, but with his dark hair and eyes and olive skin he can pass for Caribbean, Middle Eastern, or Hispanic. Since he works undercover for SIB—Sarasota County's Special Investigative Bureau— the ability to look like a lot of different races and nationalities comes in handy. But Paco isn't just a pretty face who can infiltrate criminal organizations in disguise, he's also smarter than about ninety-nine percent of the people in the world. Sometimes he's so smart he's scary. But most important of all is that he loves my brother, and by extension, me. Paco and I are family.

I hurried across the sand between the carport and the deck to join him and Ella. They both gave me a quick look, then turned their attention back to the sunset. Our sunsets are the most spectacular in the world, so most people on Siesta Key can be found outside every evening watching the sun slip beneath the sea. It's always the same, but always different, and we don't want to miss any of its variations.

Tonight the pulsing edges of the sun were tinted burgundy as if they had gotten bruised on the way down. In the sun's glow, an undulating rose-hued highway stretched across the silver water to our beach like a red carpet of invitation. For a long moment, the sun hung lazily above the water as if it had forgotten it was supposed to drop below the horizon. A V of seabirds flew across the sun's face and, startled and embarrassed, it slid into the sea.

We watched the radiant sky a few more minutes, and then the spell broke.

Paco said, "Red sky at night, sailor's delight."

I nodded as if he'd just said something sage and wise, even though Paco isn't a sailor and neither am I. We just like to pull up old bits of almanac wisdom like red sunsets foretelling dry weather.

Paco said, "I heard you made some new friends today, kidnappers and such."

I said, "That would be a guy named Vern."

"What are you doing for dinner?"

That was another new thing about my PG—post-Guidry—status. Before Guidry became a significant part of my life, Paco and I had always taken it for granted that we would share dinner on the nights Michael was at the firehouse and we were both home. When Michael was home, we took it for granted that he would cook for us and that the three of us would sit down together and eat what he cooked.

But now in my PG status, Paco didn't know if I had plans to be with Guidry so he was unaccustomedly tentative with me. And since I was torn between wanting to be with Guidry and feeling defensive about the want, I tried to sound as if I had never even considered the possibility of dinner with him. The truth was that he hadn't mentioned it, and neither had I. We were both so new to this couple thing that we hadn't settled into any routine yet. I hoped we never would. I hoped we would, and soon. I was a mess.

I said, "I don't have any plans. Do you?"

"How do you feel about Mexican?"

"*Me gusto* Mexican. Give me fifteen minutes to shower and change."

Leaving Paco and Ella on the deck, I loped off to wash away cat hair and dog spit.

Being the world's fastest shower-taker, I was dressed in a denim miniskirt and white scoop-neck knit top within my promised time. I'd even pulled my hair into a knot at the back of my head with some long hairs hanging out to look fetchingly artless, and slicked some lip gloss on my tender lips. Big gold hoop earrings and high-heeled mules gave me just the right balance between slutty and stylish, and got me an approvingly raised eyebrow from Paco.

We didn't talk about my kidnapping until we were at El Toro Bravo, our favorite mom-and-pop Mexican place on Stickney Point. We opted for an outside table, accepted cold mugs of beer, crispy fried tortilla chips, salsa and guacamole from the waitress, and ordered platters of our favorite things smothered in chili, cheese, and extra jalapeños.

While we waited, Paco said, "Okay, tell me."

I gave him the CliffsNotes version. "Three guys in a limo grabbed me in the parking lot at the Village Diner. Two guys in ski masks rode with me in the back, the driver didn't have a mask. They bound my wrists and ankles with duct tape and put a hood over my head. They took me east of I-Seventy-five to that wealthy area where everybody's house has its own private landing strip and hangar. A man called Tuck came to the car and the driver said, 'I got her,' meaning me. Tuck looked in at me and said, 'That's not her.' Vern was the driver's name. Dumb as a stump, and mean. Tuck told Vern to fix the problem, also meaning me. So Vern drove me to Friendly's on Sixty-four and put me out in the parking lot. He told me he would deny anything happened if I reported it, and that I'd be in big trouble."

Paco dipped a tortilla chip in the guacamole and studied it as if he might find insight in it. "Guidry made you report it, didn't he?"

"He said as an officer of the law he had to report it. Now there'll be stuff in the newspaper about me again."

He gave a dismissive wave of the tortilla. "I wouldn't worry about it. Some reports of criminal behavior are confidential. Especially if there's an ongoing investigation."

A weight lifted from my shoulders. "I went to the Ringling office and looked at mug shots. I didn't see any that looked like Vern, but I know who Vern thought I was."

The waitress came wearing padded mitts and carrying metal platters holding bubbling chili-drenched food. As she set the plates down, she said, "The plates are very hot. *Very* hot."

She always says that. Like idiots, Paco and I compulsively touched the plates anyway. We always do that. Then we jerked our hands away because, like the waitress had warned, those plates were plenty hot.

After we'd gone through the initial ritual of forking up bites so hot we had to fan our mouths and cool them with beer, Paco said, "Who did they think you were?"

I told him about Ruby, and how Ruby had worked for Myra Kreigle pulling rich men into her Ponzi scheme.

"She said Vern was Tucker's muscle, and that he sometimes works for Myra."

Paco blew on a forkful of enchilada. "Vern is Vernon Brogher. Vern's a relative of some sort to Tucker, cousin or something. Works as a bouncer in a strip joint on the north Trail, drives limos for movie stars who come for the Film Festival, generally moves around job to job. He's been in jail a few times for being drunk and disorderly, fighting in bars, that kind of thing. Word is that Vern sucks up to Tucker and Tucker throws him a bone now and then because he's a relative."

I had a mental image of Paco and Guidry standing over the desks of the deputies investigating my kidnapping and soaking up every bit of information.

I said, "What about the other men with Vern? The ones in the ski masks?"

"Last I heard, they hadn't got results back from IAFIS yet."

I said, "Ruby has a baby. Looks about four or five months old, a real cutie. Her name is Opal. Ruby is married to a race car driver named Zack."

Paco nodded. "Zack Carlyle."

What is it about men and race cars? I'd never heard of Zack Carlyle, but I had the feeling I could go stand in the middle of the street and say "Zack!" and every man for miles would know who he was.

I said, "I always thought a drag race was two hot rods on a downtown street illegally racing."

"Actually, it's very expensive gutted-up old cars driven by professional racers on a legal drag strip. Very short course, very fast cars. Zack Carlyle is a champion Pro Stock racer. His uncle is Webster Carlyle, who's sort of a drag race legend. Webster's retired, but I guess he was a big influence on Zack, bigger than his father anyway. The father owns an electrical supply company in Bradenton, and Zack works for him. From all accounts, the father isn't keen on his son spending so much money on a hobby like racing, but Zack makes most of it back in prize money, so I guess the dad can't complain too much. From all accounts, Zack's a solid, stand-up guy. He runs a camp for disadvantaged kids, and he's persuaded a lot of professional racers and other athletes to come out and work with them. They have a little racetrack, run kid-sized racers around it. The kids have fun and learn about timing, sportsmanship, things like that."

I took a sip of beer and parsed what Paco had just told me. Zack's father was a successful businessman, Zack was a successful athlete, and there probably was some tension between them. I wondered if Zack's father had approved of Ruby as a daughter-in-law.

I said, "Zack and Ruby are separated. Mr. Stern doesn't know if she left Zack or Zack left her, but she came home when Opal was just a few weeks old and then left again without telling Mr. Stern where she was going. According to Ruby, the DA had put her someplace where Myra and Tucker couldn't get at her. She and the DA worked out a plea bargain deal and she's going to testify against Myra."

Paco raised an eyebrow. "If Ruby knows where Myra stashed the money she stole, she could do a lot of damage to Myra. Which means Myra has several hundred million reasons to try to keep Ruby from testifying."

A beat went by. I wondered if Paco knew more than he was telling. I wondered if Ruby was as innocent as she'd seemed.

I said, "Zack thinks Ruby was in cahoots with Myra, but Ruby expects him to change his mind after she tells the truth in Myra's trial."

Paco looked skeptical. "Zack Carlyle's organization for kids put about a quarter of a million in Myra's real estate investment trust. He and the other athletes had big plans for expanding the kids' program. Myra sent out false monthly reports showing their original investment had doubled. The reports were all lies, of course, and their money is down the drain. If Ruby knew the reports were false and kept quiet, he has good reason to be mad at her."

I thought of Myra Kreigle's hate-filled face looking down at me, and decided not to mention it to Paco. "No matter how the trial goes, it won't change anything for all the people who've lost jobs and homes because of Myra."

"Dixie, don't get involved in this mess. White-collar criminals are just as violent as any other kind. They'll kill you just as quickly if you get in their way."

"I'm just taking care of Mr. Stern's cat. Now that Vern knows I'm not Ruby, he won't bother me again. He probably won't bother Ruby, either. He knows she'll be watching for him now."

"People like Vern and Tucker and Myra Kreigle have been hurting people since humans stood upright. The only way to be safe from them is to stay away from them."

"I promise I'm not involved."

As I said it, I saw Opal's trusting face. Adults can use common sense to keep themselves safe, but who will keep babies like Opal safe?

11

While Paco and I ate dinner, the sky had darkened to the color of a newborn baby's eyes, with a lackadaisical gathering of stars punching weak holes in its vault. As we rounded the last curve on the drive to our house, we caught the glint of thin moonlight bouncing off Guidry's Blazer parked beside the carport. Paco chuckled softly and waggled his eyebrows at me. I poked him in the side, but it was hard to look angry with my lips turned up at the corners. Paco parked in his space and we both climbed out of the car.

He said, " 'Night."

I said, "Thanks for dinner."

Neither of us looked up at my balcony where we both knew Guidry waited. Paco walked briskly to his kitchen door and disappeared inside. I climbed the stairs to my apartment. I did not run, I walked normally. Well, I may have taken them a little faster than usual, but I definitely didn't run.

In the shadowy darkness of my covered porch, Guidry

was almost invisible. With his hands folded over his chest and his legs crossed at the ankle, he was asleep in the hammock strung in the corner. It was a rare opportunity to memorize his face without him knowing, so I stood quietly looking down at him. Except for his chest rising and falling, he looked like a corpse. A very healthy, bronzed corpse.

Around us, the night spoke with the soft chirps of tree frogs, the questioning whistles of ospreys, and tremulous wails of tiny screech owls. The sea seemed to hold its breath waiting for the evening tide.

As if he sensed my presence, Guidry opened his eyes, smiled, and reached for me. I stretched out beside him, the hammock rolled, and we ended up in a tangle of arms and legs on the porch floor, my laughter smothered under his lips. I gave a fleeting thought to the Mexican food on my breath, and then forgot it.

The moon smiled, the tide chuckled, the stars drew closer to watch, and at the end of time our hearts lay bare under an infinite sky, no longer separate from time and space but melded at the limit of love.

Later, behind Guidry's sleeping shoulders in my narrow bed, I allowed my mind to acknowledge that my happiness had tears in it. Allowed myself to remember the weeks after Todd was killed, how I had inhaled his scent, pressed his shirts against my face, pushed the fabric close to my nose and sobbed. For a long time I hadn't been able to sleep without him beside me. Death removes the smells, the sounds, the feel of the other that gives them life, so I hadn't wanted to eat or bathe for fear I would lose the scent of him and have no more memories of him in my pores.

And now another man was in my bed, and I was inhaling him the way I had once inhaled Todd, and it was good and right that he was there. Pain was still with me, but there was more sweetness than pain. New love had come as quietly as cats' paws, silent as smoke or trickling sand. It had drifted into my consciousness when I least expected it, shoving out memory of old loves, lost loves, hopeless loves, wrong loves, betrayed loves, true love, all fading into the darkness of doesn't matter. This new love stood alone, marvelous and electric, always believed in but never expected. The lightning it created lit up the universe from eternity to infinity, and lit up my heart from edge to open.

I moved closer to Guidry and pressed my cheek against his bare back. In the night's space, the touch of his skin made me feel safe. I drifted to sleep knowing that moment was the only thing that mattered, the only truth I needed to hold fast.

12

My daily schedule is set so firmly that I could do it in my sleep. A time or two I may have. I roll out of bed when my alarm rings at four A.M., splash water on my face, brush my teeth, and pull my hair into a ponytail. Still half asleep, I drag on shorts and a T, lace up fresh white Keds—I can't stand yesterday's sweaty shoes—and head out to walk the dogs on my schedule. Dogs can't wait the way cats can, so they get first dibs. Next I call on the cats. Maybe an occasional rabbit, ferret, or guinea pig. No snakes. I refer all snake-sitting jobs to other people. Not that I have anything against critters without feet, but it creeps me out to drop little mice into yawning snakes' mouths.

Leaving a drowsy man in my bed is definitely not part of my routine, and it felt weird to do it. Even though I'm thirty-three years old and have every right to have a man in my bed any time I choose to, I sort of hoped this was the day Michael would pull an extra shift at the firehouse. Otherwise, he might have come home before Guidry left and know he'd spent the night. Michael respects my right to live my own life, but he's a bit of a Victorian prude where I'm concerned.

The sky was a stretch of dull blue felt, with a few pale dawdling stars. On the horizon, night had lifted her dark skirt a few inches to let in a shimmer of pale pink day. Along the shoreline, surf babies were tumbling while mother sea slept unaware. The air smelled of ocean and first beginnings, and dew diamonds turned trees and flowers into fairy fantasies. On the porch railing, a slumbering snowy egret trembled at my presence and opened his topaz eyes to monitor my intentions.

Moving slowly so as not to alarm him, I went down the stairs to my Bronco, shooed a sleeping pelican and a young egret from the hood, and got myself back into a professional mode. Spending the night with a man is a surefire way to make a woman's career go to dead bottom on her list of priorities.

Starting at the south end of the Key and working my way north, I did my usual run with Billy Elliot and the other dogs. Then I reversed direction and called on cat clients, which on that day included three mixed-breed cats who'd been left alone while their humans went on a cruise, a pair of Siamese who'd only been left for a day while their humans were at the hospital welcoming a new baby, and several single cats whose humans were away for reasons none of the cats thought were good enough.

As I was leaving the house of one of the single cats, I saw two women getting out of a van next door. They were taking cleaning supplies from the van, and one woman seemed to be having a personal fight with a rebellious vacuum hose. I was at my Bronco before I recognized them as the cleaning women I'd seen the day before at Mr. Stern's house. The woman who'd been crying wasn't with them. Since they worked for Mr. Stern and I worked for Mr. Stern, and since I was pretty sure that Mr. Stern had been rude to her, I sort of felt a sisterly compulsion to go speak to them, maybe try to smooth things over so they wouldn't think badly of our mutual employer. I caught up with them before they got to the front door, and they both turned to me with the annoyed looks people give missionaries out ringing doorbells.

I said, "Hi, I'm Dixie Hemingway. I'm taking care of Mr. Stern's cat while his arm heals. You clean for him, don't you?"

They both studied me for a moment, still waiting for a punch line that would cost them something. Finally the older one said, "I remember you. You were going in when we were leaving."

The other one said, "Everywhere we go people have cats. We vacuum up more cat hair than anything else. Ruins the motors. This here vacuum is almost brand-new and it's already running hard from all the cat hair."

I said, "I know your friend got upset because of the baby at Mr. Stern's house. I hope she's okay."

The older woman scowled. "We don't know because Doreen didn't show up this morning. We always meet in the Target parking lot, but she never showed. I called and called, but she didn't answer her phone, so I don't know what to think."

The other woman said, "Doreen had a baby a couple of months ago, but it only lived a few hours, and she's been real emotional ever since. Then her boyfriend left her, and that about put her over the edge."

The older woman shook her head. "She's better off without him, if you ask me. He never was any help to her, didn't even help with her doctor bills."

I began half-stepping backwards, wishing I hadn't started this conversation. "Well, I just wanted to say 'Hi,' you know, since we all work in the same house."

They stopped talking and stared at me, once again looking suspicious. Neither of them said goodbye, but watched me get in the Bronco and back out. I waved goodbye, but they didn't wave back. I did a silent groan, imagining them quitting their job with Mr. Stern and telling him it was because I'd followed them and spied on them.

For about the millionth time in my life, I had followed an impulsive urge to be friendly to a stranger who had reacted as if I were a CIA operative trying to frame them for a crime. I try not to follow those impulsive urges, but the wisdom of sailing on by is always more obvious after the fact than before it.

The sun was fully up and the morning's moisture had dried on every leaf by the time I got to Mr. Stern's house. When I rang the doorbell, Ruby let me in. Her skin looked dry and chapped, and she had blue shadows under her eyes.

She said, "I just put Opal down for a nap, thank God. She was awake half the night. Cheddar's in the bedroom with her." With a sudden conspiratorial grin, she said, "Come see!"

All her fatigue seemed to fly away as she skittered down the hallway ahead of me. She was like a teenager leading a girlfriend to see her latest secret, and I was reminded again of how young she was. With exaggerated stealth, she turned the bedroom doorknob and pulled the door open just enough for me to look inside the room.

When I peeked in, I grinned, too. Opal was sound asleep in her net-sided crib. Under the crib, Cheddar slept in a shallow cardboard box. The box was a bit too small for his entire body, so one of his paws flopped over the edge in boneless bliss.

Ruby said, "Is it okay to leave him there until Opal wakes up?"

I knew exactly how she felt. When you've finally got a baby to go to sleep, you don't want to do anything that might wake her.

I said, "If Cheddar lived in the wild, he would eat whenever he found food, not at some special hour."

She said, "Granddad's in the courtyard feeding the koi."

I wasn't sure whether she was merely relaying information or hoping I'd keep Cheddar's delayed breakfast a secret from Mr. Stern.

She followed me into the kitchen and watched me shake dry food into Cheddar's clean feeding dish. It would be ready for him whenever he and Opal finished their naps.

I got eggs from the refrigerator and put them in a pan. "Mr. Stern likes me to coddle an egg for Cheddar and boil a couple for him."

"It's nice of you to do that."

I covered the eggs with water and set them on a burner. The impulsive urge to tell her that I knew Mr. Stern was wrong to doubt that she was truly married to Zack Carlyle drifted across my cortex and then stopped itself before it came out my mouth. I'd already followed one impulsive urge to speak about something that day, two would be pushing it.

But my brain must have exercised all the control it could handle, because the next thing out of my mouth was even worse. "Ruby, was Kantor Tucker a partner in Myra's Ponzi scheme?"

"I don't know if he was a partner or just knew what Myra was doing and kept quiet."

"Now that you know how far they'll go to try to stop you from testifying, what are you going to do?"

The look she gave me was puzzled. "You mean kidnapping me?"

I resisted saying, "D'uh!" and nodded.

"Believe me, I already know how far they can go. Tuck had a guy cross him once and he flew him out over the Gulf and shoved him out of the plane. *That's* how far they'll go."

She said it flat-voiced, not like somebody repeating a terrible crime.

I said, "Are you sure of that?"

"I didn't see him do it, if that's what you mean, but he laughed with Myra about the guy being shark food. I don't think he was joking. If he thought he could get away with it, he'd feed me to the sharks too."

A cold snail moved up my spine leaving a slimy trail of dread. Ruby apparently had knowledge of other crimes besides fraud, knowledge that made her even more dangerous to Myra and Tucker.

"So what are you going to do at Myra's trial?"

"What I told the DA I'd do. I'll tell what I know."

Her young face was set in lines I'd seen on my own face too many times. Fierce courage mixed with the kind of faith that only comes from utter naivete. Sometimes that mixture moves mountains. Sometimes it creates an abyss that you walk into unaware.

I said, "What about Zack? Does he realize what's going on?"

She shook her head. "Zack's a Boy Scout. He believes the world is black and white, good and bad. He thinks I'm as bad as Myra. He wouldn't believe me if I told him the whole story."

A thin cry came from Ruby's bedroom, and we both froze. But it didn't continue. Opal had waked for a moment and cried, and then gone back to sleep. Babies do that, and Ruby and I gave each other relieved looks. Ruby was relieved because she was Opal's mother and attached to her in that mystical maternal way of all sensitive mothers. I was relieved because I felt too much of a connection to Ruby and Opal. Not just because Ruby and I looked alike, but because I *knew* her. Knew what it was to yearn for a lost mother, knew what it was to be too young or too dumb to intuitively recognize criminal behavior in someone I trusted. Knew what it was to fall head over heels in love with a good man and have his baby and be as close to it as to my own pulse beat.

The water on the eggs came to a boil, and I turned off the heat, set the timer for three minutes, and used a spoon to fish out Cheddar's egg.

I broke the coddled egg over the dry food in Cheddar's bowl and turned to face Ruby.

"Do you think Myra and Tuck will try anything else to stop you from testifying?"

"They might, but until the trial begins, I'm not leaving this house, not even to go in the courtyard. And if the doorbell rings, I'm not answering it unless I know who it is."

"A wise person once told me that white-collar criminals are as dangerous as any other criminals."

She met my eyes with a fearless directness. "Myra and Tuck would have me killed if they thought they could get away with it. But they can't. Besides, I've already given the DA enough information to convict Myra of every charge they've made against her."

Something about that line of reasoning seemed wrong, but while I searched for a response, the timer sounded and I hurried to lift Mr. Stern's eggs from the hot water.

Mr. Stern chose that moment to come in from the courtyard. With a disapproving look at Cheddar's food bowl, he said, "Where's Cheddar?"

Ruby said, "He's in my bedroom under Opal's crib. They're both sleeping."

He made a fitzing sound with his lips, not exactly a raspberry but close. I had the feeling his disapproval came more from jealousy than from concern about Cheddar's delayed breakfast.

As if he felt a need to reestablish his authority, he frowned at me. "Are you boiling eggs?"

"I just took them out."

"I'd like toast as well. Make it two. Buttered."

Ruby stared at Mr. Stern, and seemed to press her lips together to keep from speaking.

My own tongue probably got shorter because I had to bite it to keep from telling him that in the first place I wasn't his maid, and in the second place he was acting like a total butt. I scooped his eggs onto a plate and made his toast while he took a seat at the bar and watched me like a big brooding bird.

When I left him, my mind was stuck on the fact that Cheddar sleeping under Opal's crib was making Mr. Stern act like a jilted lover. For a man who claimed not to have any time to waste on a cat, his jealousy was a little bit funny. At least it would have been if he hadn't acted so snotty to Ruby. Of all the emotions human beings fall victim to, jealousy and possessiveness may be the most unattractive.

At the time, it didn't occur to me that it was Ruby, not Cheddar, who Mr. Stern believed had been stolen from him. Or that he resented that loss with a rancid hatred.

13

The tension at Mr. Stern's house hadn't changed the fact that I was empty as a koi without a stomach. Heading for the Village Diner for breakfast, I paid close attention to all the other cars on the street, especially the occasional limo. I didn't see anything suspicious. Even so, I sat a moment in the parking lot after I'd parked the Bronco just in case somebody was there planning to kidnap me.

I didn't intend to linger over breakfast. I wanted to get home and take a long nap and get wholly back into my own body. Having Guidry in my life was great, but I'd worked hard at arriving at a place where I was fairly content with who I was, and I didn't want anything about myself to change. It was another one of those boring versus comforting things.

Inside the diner, I waved at Tanisha on my way to the ladies' room. Tanisha's broad face dimpled when she saw me, and I knew she'd have my breakfast ready by the time I sat down in my regular booth. I liked that. I'm a lot more satisfied with life when it stays the same, day after day. Lots of people would find that boring, but I find it comforting.

Sure enough, after I'd washed up and got myself as presentable as possible in the ladies' room, Judy had a mug of coffee ready for me. Like Tanisha, Judy is a good friend I only know through the diner. Judy is tall and angular, with light brown hair that frizzes in the steam from Tanisha's kitchen, eyes that change from hazel to Weimaraner amber, and a sprinkle of copper freckles across her nose. She's cynical and snarky and loses her heart to men who hurt her. She was kind to me when I lost most of my mind after Todd and Christy were killed, and she was the first person to predict that Guidry and I would wind up together.

As I slid into the booth, she said, "Missed you yesterday."

I said, "Yeah, I got kidnapped."

She grinned and scooted off to pour somebody else some coffee. I am the kind of person whose life is so weird that people think I'm joking when I tell the truth about it. If I'd told her that I'd just come from a house where a woman was up to her eyebrows in a Ponzi scheme trial, she probably would have laughed her head off.

Judy had just returned with my breakfast when Guidry ambled down the aisle and slid into the seat opposite me. Judy stood aside and watched us, and I knew she could see us exchange the looks of people seeing each other for the first time after they've spent the night together. A look that combines a residue of pleasure, a hint of embarrassment at having let down all their defenses, and a frisson of excitement at the hope they'll repeat it.

Guidry said, "I'll have what she's having."

Deadpan, Judy said, "With bacon?"

He grinned. "Oh yeah, I forgot she never orders bacon."

Judy said, "She just steals it off other people's plates."

I shrugged because it was true. I love bacon beyond reason. If I get a choice of a last meal before I leave this planet, I'm going to order a BLT with extra-crispy bacon, no icky white bumps anywhere in it, no curled ends, no droopy middles. I rarely order bacon because it's bad for my health and for my waistline, but everybody knows that fat doesn't settle on you if you eat it from somebody else's plate.

Judy left a mug of coffee for Guidry and hurried away to turn in his order. He and I gave each other the self-conscious grins of two people who'd slept coiled together like strands of a rope.

I sipped coffee and looked at him through the steam.

"I talked to Ruby this morning while I was at Mr. Stern's house—he's her grandfather, has an orange cat named Cheddar, lives next door to Myra Kreigle—and she said she's not sure if Kantor Tucker was a full partner in Myra Kreigle's fake REIT or if he just kept quiet about it."

Guidry's gray eyes studied me for a moment, and I knew he was having an internal conversation with himself about the way complete strangers told me highly personal and private things. Since his job was to get information from people, it made him nuts that people blabbed everything they knew to me. Sometimes when I didn't even ask them.

He said, "Tucker and Myra Kreigle have been connected for several years, maybe lovers, maybe partners in crime, maybe just good friends. If she leaves the country before her trial, he'll lose the two million dollars he put up for her bond."

"He has a private plane at his house. Maybe he'll fly her out of the country."

He grinned. "Not likely. He'd be met and arrested wherever he landed, and his plane would be confiscated. But she may have transferred two million to him from one of her hidden offshore accounts, so he won't really lose anything if she bolts. But if Ruby's testimony places Tucker in Myra Kreigle's deal, it could be his undoing."

I had an uneasy feeling that Guidry was placating me, that he really had something else on his mind that he wanted to talk about, but couldn't get up the nerve to say it.

Judy came with Guidry's breakfast, topped off both our coffees, and zipped away without speaking. I took one of Guidry's rigid slices of bacon. For a few minutes we were quiet. I nibbled my bacon while Guidry ate.

He said, "I had a friend in New Orleans who was a drag racer like Zack Carlyle. At least he was until he got a detached retina from the jolt of decelerating too fast."

"You're kidding, right?"

"Some of those cars go faster than a space shuttle launch. They have to use parachutes to stop. You go from three hundred thirty miles an hour to a dead stop in less than twenty seconds, and it'll cause a drag up to five Gs. My friend did that and it caused his retina to detach. His wife said she would be the next thing to detach if he raced again, so he quit."

I said, "Ruby said Zack has dark blue eyes that are almost purple. The baby has his eyes."

I could tell Guidry didn't give a gnat's patootie about Zack's eyes. His mind had drifted someplace else. He finished eating, took a last gulp of coffee, put money on the table for Judy, and got to his feet.

He did that shoulder-tapping thing again. "See you later."

Judy came with her coffeepot and we watched him leave. I seemed to be watching his back a lot these days. Which wasn't bad, with those shoulders and the easy way he moved. But it still made me uneasy to see him leaving, as if every time was the last time I'd ever see him.

It occurred to me that whenever Guidry mentioned New Orleans, his voice took on a longing quality. Like a man speaking the name of a woman he'd once deeply loved and lost. Or a woman he'd once loved and wanted back.

I was still thinking about that when I headed for the Bronco, so engrossed in all the awful possibilities of the idea that I almost walked into Ethan Crane. Ethan is a tall, drop-dead gorgeous attorney with jet-black hair and dark eyes from Seminole ancestors. When I saw him in front of me, we did that self-conscious side-stepping dance that men and women do who were never lovers but once had the hots for each other. To tell the truth, we sort of still did, but we had both decided that somebody else was really more appropriate for us. Another attorney for

Ethan, another cop for me. I had met Ethan's new girl-friend, and he knew Guidry. We approved of the other's choice, but my hormones still stood up and applauded when they smelled Ethan, and from the way his eyes lit up when he saw me, I suspected certain parts of his anatomy were also standing up.

We stood in the glaring sun and bantered a little bit, nothing important, just the usual awkward small talk people do to try to cover up the fact that they really want to ask each other more important questions. Like *Do you miss me?* Like *Are you happy with somebody else?* Like *Do you ever regret your choice?* My answer would have been that I was happy with Guidry and I had no regrets, but I sort of hoped that Ethan sometimes regretted his.

When we said goodbye, I felt that odd exhilaration that comes with knowing you've spent time with a man who thinks you're desirable. Even if you don't want him, it's exciting to know he wants you.

At home, Paco's truck was gone, but Michael's car was in his slot. Instead of going straight upstairs, I walked across the sandy yard to the wooden deck and opened his kitchen door. When he and Paco had moved into our grandparents' house, they remodeled the kitchen to bring it into the twenty-first century. A butcher block eating island with a salad sink at one end stands where our grandmother's round pedestal table once took center stage, and Michael has added enough Sub-Zero built-in refrigerators to hold all the fruits and vegetables at any farmer's market, plus two or three steers.

When I walked in, he was leaning over a refrigerator

drawer forcing a stalk of celery to fit into a space already filled with other vegetables.

He looked over his shoulder at me. "Hey."

Ella Fitzgerald was on her assigned stool. She and the guys have an agreement—if she stays on the stool and doesn't beg for food, she can sit there and adore them. I smooched the top of her head.

I said, "I want you to hear this from me."

Michael straightened and looked down at me with eyes that had suddenly gone slitty. "Hear what?"

"Well, here's the thing, I'm here and I'm obviously okay. So it's not important, but it happened, and I know sooner or later you'll hear about it, so I just want to be the one to tell you."

His eyes got slittier. Ella sat up straighter and looked alarmed.

I said, "The thing is, yesterday morning a guy named Vern mistook me for a woman named Ruby and drove me out past Seventy-five to that stretch of big estates where everybody has a landing strip and a hangar. He took me to a man named Kantor Tucker, but as soon as Tucker saw me he knew I was the wrong woman. Vern drove me to Friendly's and gave me fifty dollars for a cab. I called Guidry and he came and got me. That's all there was to it."

"So Vern just asked you nicely to get in his car, and you did, and he drove you to a place where a stranger could get a look at you. Is that how it was?"

"Pretty much. I'm taking care of Ruby's grandfather's cat, and I guess Vern saw me leaving there and jumped to the conclusion that I was Ruby. She's a witness in Myra

Kreigle's trial. You know, the woman who ran the real estate Ponzi scheme. Ruby worked for her."

"What else?"

"That's it, truly. Except for the part about the two guys in Vern's limo who grabbed me and put a hood over my head. Vern drove while they taped my wrists and ankles, and put tape over my mouth. But they didn't hurt me, Michael. They overpowered me, but they didn't rough me up or anything."

Michael's lips weren't relaxed anymore, and a muscle worked in his jaw. "So what did Guidry do?"

"He made me report it. I went to the office on Ringling and looked at mug shots. I didn't see anybody that looked like Vern, but the guys investigating already know who he is. He works for Tucker, sort of a hanger-on. They don't know who the other men were, but the deputies have the tape that was put on my mouth. They're running latents from it through IAFIS to see if they get a match."

Michael walked around the butcher block island a few times, like a man on the deck of a ship that he can't get off of. Ella watched him with big round eyes.

"So what's going to happen now? Is Guidry taking care of this?"

Michael's tone said that if Guidry wasn't doing his job, Michael would.

I said, "Guidry's in homicide, so he's not part of the official investigation, but he's involved. So is Paco."

"Paco knows about this?"

"Yeah, we had dinner together last night and I told him."

He looked a little hurt, so I hurried to tell him about Ruby being married to Zack Carlyle.

He brightened. "Zack Carlyle? No kidding."

He said it as if Zack Carlyle went around wearing a red cape and leaping over tall buildings.

At least I'd got his mind off Vern kidnapping me.

Upstairs, Guidry had neatly made up my bed before he left. I found it sort of touching that he'd gone to the trouble. After a shower, a nap, and some time spent updating my client records, I cleaned my apartment. I got rid of every speck of dust, every smear on a mirror, every dull haze on anything chrome. I polished and disinfected and vacuumed until I was high on bleach and ammonia fumes. My brother handles stress by cooking. I handle it by cleaning the heck out of everything. My brain tells me that bad things can happen to people with clean apartments, but my Scandinavian genes tell me that cleanliness and order are as good as a horseshoe over the door. They protect you even if you don't believe in them.

As I put away the vacuum, I heard a peculiar tapping noise coming from my kitchen window. A female cardinal was obsessively flying at the glass and hitting it with her chest and beak while the male flew in anxious circles behind her. Cardinals do that sometimes during springtime nesting when one sees its reflection and thinks it's another bird invading its territory. But this was September, not a time of building nests, so the female's attack on her own image seemed out of the natural order of things. I wondered if the bird was afraid a rival female was on the periphery of her territory ready to move in. Whatever her reason, the cardinal attacked her own image with the intention of keeping a tight hold on what was her own. A noble purpose, perhaps, but she could kill herself.

I stood for a while and shooed her away. Every time I left the window, she came back to do her kamikaze dives at the glass. I taped paper to the glass, but it didn't stop her. I found a magazine picture of a glaring owl and taped it to the glass, but she wasn't fooled. While I dressed for afternoon rounds, the sound of her beak hitting the glass was like the relentless sound of a ticking clock. I had mental images of her beak splitting down its length and making it impossible for her to eat.

When it was time to leave my apartment to make afternoon rounds, I was acutely conscious that a bird was slowly committing suicide at my kitchen window. On the sandy shore, a few gulls, terns, and sandpipers braved the glaring sun to pick up microscopic nutrients from the lapping sea, their subdued cries like doleful omens. Driving slowly, so as not to disturb the songbirds and parakeets taking siestas in the trees lining the drive, I was all the way to Midnight Pass Road before I got myself under control. Nature has been getting along without my direction since the beginning of time. The cardinal would either give up her attacks on her reflection or she wouldn't. In either case, I had done all I could do to save her.

Nevertheless, I had a skitty feeling that the cardinal carried some sort of message for me, a woman-to-woman bit of wisdom. But I wasn't flinging myself against a hard surface that would hurt me, and I didn't believe that some other female was trying to steal my mate. At least I didn't know of one.

14

At Tom Hale's condo, Billy Elliot met me at the door with a big grin. Tom was in the kitchen with his laptop open on the table.

He yelled, "I want to show you something."

As if he wanted to make sure I stayed focused on my reason for being there, Billy Elliot walked close beside me to the kitchen. Tom pointed at a photograph on the computer screen.

"Is this the guy who kidnapped you?"

In a newspaper photo, Vern and Kantor Tucker stood in front of an airplane, Vern a little bit behind Tucker. They were both smiling, Tucker more broadly than Vern. The caption read, "Kantor Tucker at his aero-compound." An accompanying article identified the plane as a new Boeing 707, the latest addition to "Tuck" Tucker's private fleet of planes. There was no mention of Vern.

I said, "That's Vern."

Tom said, "Here's another picture." He clicked some

keys and the screen filled with a mug shot of Vern's bruised, sullen face.

He said, "This is from Indiana, a year or so ago. His name is Vernon Brogher. He was arrested after he slammed a guy's head into a wall in a bar. The guy had asked him to stop taking cellphone photos of the guy's girlfriend, and Vern nearly took the guy's head off. Literally."

"Is he a pilot?"

Tom snorted. "I don't imagine Vern is smart enough to fly a paper airplane, much less a jet."

"Ruby said he's Tucker's muscle."

"Does that mean he's Tucker's bodyguard or the man who beats up people for him?"

"With Vern's history, it probably means both. How'd you find those pictures?"

"If you spend enough time on the Internet, you can find anything, especially things of public record."

Billy Elliot leaned against my knees to remind me that time was passing. Tom watched me snap Billy's leash on his collar.

I said, "Do you know anything about drag racing? The professional kind?"

"You taking it up?"

"Ruby is married to Zack Carlyle. He's a drag racer. You know, one of those guys who race around on a track."

His face took on the look of a kid hearing about a really cool video game.

He said, "Drag racers don't go around on a track, Dixie. A drag race is a straight shot and it only lasts a little over four seconds. Two cars at a time race over and over, until one car has beat out all the others in its class."

I said, "Hunh." No matter what Tom told me, I kept imagining a line of cars tearing around an oval track. I couldn't wrap my mind around the idea of a straight race that lasted only four seconds.

Billy Elliot whuffed to remind me that I was there to run with him, not to chat with Tom, so I led Billy out to the elevator in the hall.

When we came back upstairs, I unsnapped Billy Elliot's leash and waved goodbye to Tom.

He said, "How'd you like to go to a drag race? You and Guidry, me and Jennie."

It seemed like every being in the world was either in a new relationship, like the humans I knew, or fighting to keep a relationship, like the self-destructive cardinal flying into my kitchen window. I guess some relationships bring serenity and some bring desperation.

Jennie was Tom's new girlfriend, and she had passed my test of worthiness by running on the beach with Billy Elliot. But I wasn't sure if Guidry and I were at a double-dating stage yet. Joining another twosome makes a different kind of statement than doing things alone as a couple. I wasn't sure what the statement was, but I didn't think we were ready to make it yet.

I said, "I'm sure Guidry would like to go to a drag race, but I don't think drag racing is my thing."

I didn't say it, but what I thought was that Zack Carlyle might be a name that men got excited about, but as far as I was concerned, he was a man who had failed the test of loyalty to his wife and baby.

Tom said, "It might not be a good idea anyway. Those guys who grabbed you may have something to do with drag racing, and men who kidnap women off the street aren't usually the kind of men who'd appreciate her following them. Especially if she's following them with a cop."

"They wouldn't know Guidry is a cop. He doesn't look like a cop."

Tom's eyes got a pitying look. "Dixie, even Billy Elliot could look at Guidry and know he's a cop. Cops look like cops. They can't help it. They have cop eyes and cop mouths, they move like cops. Believe me, you go to a race-track anywhere in the world with Guidry, and half the people there will take one look at him and remember pressing engagements elsewhere."

For the rest of the afternoon, I thought about what Tom had said. When I looked at Guidry, I didn't see a cop, but it was true that cops get a look in the eyes that people in other professions don't have. A watchful look. Not like rangers scanning the horizon for forest fires or like store detectives on the lookout for shoplifters. More like a three-hundred-sixty-degree awareness of everything going on around them even when they aren't looking directly at it. I had to admit that Guidry had that look. If we went to a racetrack where Vern and his buddies were, they might recognize the look. If they did, it might scare them enough to leave the county, which would be fine with me.

As I pulled into Mr. Stern's driveway, I instinctively looked upward at the Kreigle house next door. No face was in a window looking down at me. I hoped the sad young woman had gone someplace where she would be happier.

Inside the Stern house, a new tension rode on the air. Ruby was silent and grim, Mr. Stern was on the phone in the kitchen. Even Opal seemed to have pulled inside herself.

As I shook dry food into Cheddar's bowl, Mr. Stern spoke to Ruby as if they were mid-conversation. "You're a big girl, Ruby, and you know how to use the phone. You're not doomed to starve just because I've ordered food for myself."

She said, "I know that, Granddad. It just seems peculiar for a person to order dinner delivered without asking the other person in the house if she'd like something too."

"I guess I got so used to not seeing you or hearing from you that it just slipped my mind that you were here."

Ruby's eyes flooded and she left the kitchen with Opal hugged tightly to her chest.

I didn't speak. Just left Mr. Stern in the kitchen to sulk alone. I cleaned Cheddar's litter box while he ate, then went back to the kitchen and washed and dried his bowls. I put fresh water in his water bowl and left the kitchen with my lips squeezed shut. Mr. Stern had a waiting empty wineglass on the bar, but he didn't ask me to open a bottle of wine for him, and I didn't offer.

Outside Ruby's bedroom door, I tapped lightly and called her name. Her "Come in" was muffled, as if she'd had her face buried in a pillow. When I went in, she was sitting on the edge of the bed. Opal was in her crib watching the play of late sunshine on the wall.

I said, "This is my last stop for the day, and I'm going

home to have dinner with my brother and his partner. My brother is the best cook in the world. Would you and Opal like to join us?"

She looked so grateful that I had to avert my eyes so she wouldn't see the pity in them. "Do I need to change clothes?"

"Heck no, we're barefoot diners."

"I'll just put a clean Onesie on Opal."

I waited, thinking how young mothers may go out of the house looking like yesterday's warmed-up oatmeal, but they want their babies to always look cute.

Before we left, Ruby ducked into the kitchen. "I'm going out with Dixie for dinner, Granddad. Can I have a house key?"

Taken by surprise, he muttered something I couldn't hear, and when Ruby joined me at the front door she held a door key in her hand.

On the way to my place, neither of us spoke of the tension in Mr. Stern's house, or of the fact that he was treating her shabbily. Neither did we speak of Myra Kreigle, of the trial, or of Vern. Instead, we talked about people on the street, the clothes they wore, the clothes movie stars and celebrities wore, the shops in Sarasota where women could buy those kind of clothes. Trivial woman talk to avoid deep woman talk.

At home, Michael and Paco accepted a guest lugging a baby with graceful equanimity. Paco hurried to set an extra plate on the redwood table on the deck, and Michael made the kind of admiring noises at Opal that warm the cockles of a mother's heart. I left them on the deck to get acquainted while I zipped upstairs to shower and get into clean shorts and a T. When I came downstairs, Paco had Opal in his arms and Ruby was helping Michael carry food from the kitchen.

For a moment I felt as if I were looking at a slice of life preserved in the amber of time, with the baby being Christy, Ruby being me, and Todd a numinous presence somewhere in the shadows. The moment passed and we were just people getting acquainted—a woman who was a younger version of myself, a baby who was like my own child who had died, Michael and Paco who had always been there for me, and the wrenching memory of my beloved husband.

Ella did not share my bittersweet feelings. Ever since she had given Paco a scare by bounding into the trees while we ate, he had decreed that she would wear a light harness with a cotton leash looped around the leg of a lounge chair. She had come to tolerate that indignity, but she watched Michael and Paco fawning over the baby with the gimlet-eyed imperiousness of the Red Queen.

Dinner began with a cup of lentil soup with a squeeze of lemon to give it a lift. Michael whirred up a tiny bit in the blender for Opal and got a flirtatious flutter of eyelashes and a drooly smile. No matter how young or old, every female falls for Michael.

After the soup, Michael brought out poached Alaskan salmon with dill sauce, baby red potatoes, and a salad of cucumber, orange, and Florida avocado. Hot french bread and a crisp white wine made just the right finishing touch.

Over dinner, Michael and Paco and I kept the conversation moving, tossing topics around like beach volleyball players with the easy familiarity of people who know one another extremely well and speak a kind of code that doesn't have to be explained. We talked of inconsequential things—the weather, a funny scene Paco had witnessed on the street, Michael's buddy at the firehouse who had taken his family to Disney World.

"We're taking turns filling in for him," he told Ruby. "My day will be tomorrow."

Ruby didn't care what Michael's schedule was—why would she?—but Paco and I nodded like business executives noting a significant change in plan. I didn't know if Ruby was aware of how diligently we worked to avoid speaking of Myra Kreigle or her trial.

Dessert was big chunks of sweet watermelon, the real kind with black shiny seeds and honest flavor. Ruby let Opal gum a tiny bite, but she mostly drooled red juice on her Onesie, and the new experience of watermelon made her cry. Opal had enjoyed as much of new acquaintances as she could stand.

I said, "I think it's time to drive you home."

Ruby smiled. "If you don't mind. It's past Opal's bedtime."

While Ruby gathered up the diaper bag and said her thank-yous and goodnights to Michael, Paco slipped inside the house to put on shoes. He followed us to the carport and climbed into his dented truck. "I'll follow you."

His voice didn't leave any room for discussion, which made me realize that in addition to adding shoes to his attire, he'd probably also added a few loaded guns. I looked toward the deck, where Michael was busily gathering up leftovers and chatting with Ella. He and Paco had come to a decision they hadn't discussed with me, and the decision was that Paco would stick to us like glue and make sure nothing happened to Ruby on the way home.

If Ruby found it unusual to have an armed deputy riding on our bumper, she didn't mention it. At Mr. Stern's house, I pulled into the driveway and left the motor running while Ruby gathered her baby paraphernalia. Opal was fussy, but Ruby leaned across to hug me before she slid out of the car. "Thanks, Dixie. I appreciate that dinner more than you can ever know."

She slammed the car door closed and scurried toward the front door, with Paco close behind her. He waited until she had unlocked the door and disappeared inside, then glided past me to his truck. On the drive home, he stuck close to me, and it occurred to me that he was guarding me as carefully as he'd guarded Ruby. It was a disquieting thought.

Back home, I waved a thank-you to Paco and headed up my stairs while he ambled across the yard to his back door. I was inside my apartment before I realized he'd ambled with deliberate slowness to give me time to get inside. Another disquieting thought. I didn't believe I was in danger, but apparently Paco thought it was a possibility.

A wave of exhaustion hit me as I got ready for bed, and I crawled between the sheets with the kind of mind fog that comes from too much thinking. Even so, I was still thinking. I wondered how long it would take Ruby to recover from the trauma of the last several years of her life. From what Mr. Stern had said, Ruby's life had taken a sharp turn when she was in her early teens. Within two or three years, her mother had died a lingering death, her father had been killed in a war, her grandmother had died of heartache, and Ruby had been left with a grandfather who was incapable of showing affection. In her pain, she had turned to Myra Kreigle as a mother substitute. In her naivete, she had let Myra use her to defraud other people. With the same need for love that we all have, she had believed she had found it with a race car driver named Zack Carlyle. Zack had turned against her when he lost all the money he'd invested with Myra Kreigle, and Myra was willing to destroy Ruby to save herself.

I wondered what any individual's limit is. How much pain and loss can any of us absorb before we collapse? I knew what my own limit was, and I knew every person has his or her own limit. Ruby had taken more hard knocks than most women could take, even women a lot older, but I knew a moment would inevitably come when she couldn't take any more.

If I ran the world, every adult would get several time-outs from life. The time-outs would come about every twenty years, and each one would last five years. Five years to recover from school or marriage or parenthood or career or war or grief. Five years to cry or sleep or pray or stare at the wall. A roof and a bed would be provided, along with an unlimited supply of wholesome food, musical instruments, and books. No drugs, alcohol, or tobacco would be allowed. No therapists or religious proselytizers. At the end of five years, recovered lifers would swear an oath to give more thought to the four Fs—family, friends, food, and fun—than to career goals, achievements, possessions, status, or bank statements.

When sleep managed to shut up my thinking mind,

my dream mind took over and sent me to a gift shop so posh and out of my league that I was embarrassed to pollute it with my presence. I didn't have any choice, though. Under dream rules, I had to buy a gift for Guidry and I had to buy it at that particular shop.

I said, "I want to buy a gift for someone important to me."

As soon as the words left my lips, I felt my face flush. The female salesclerk, who looked like Myra Kreigle but was somebody else, gave me a pitying look.

"Would that be a male or female? Adult or child?"

My face got even hotter. I should have thought this out before I came in.

"Male," I said. "Adult."

"Aha," she said, as if I'd gone beyond her expectations. "Now, is this adult male a coworker, a family friend, a relative, or a lover?" The sneer in her voice implied that it was highly unlikely I had a lover.

Now my face was so hot I knew I had turned an unlovely magenta. I had to get this conversation under control. *My* control, and the way to do that seemed to call for pretending not to be Guidry's lover.

"More like a friend who might conceivably become a lover. Someday. Maybe."

She gave me a coolly appraising look and I knew she was wondering how anybody as incoherent as I had ever managed to meet a man like that. Meanwhile, my face had got flaming hot because I'd used the word *conceivably*, as in *conceive*, as in get pregnant not by asexual means.

She said, "Does he have any hobbies that you know of?"

Clearly, she doubted I knew a man well enough to

know if he had hobbies. I felt insulted, but the truth was that if Guidry had any hobbies, I didn't know what they were.

I said the only thing that came to mind. "He's from New Orleans."

She nodded, the way people encourage awkward children, but she disappeared without suggesting an appropriate gift. I was left feeling I'd missed the only opportunity I'd ever have to give something valuable to Guidry.

15

I woke the next morning feeling as if a weight had rolled off me while I slept. I still felt that Ruby and I were kindred spirits, but Ruby's load was her own to carry, not mine. The law of cause and effect creates strict boundaries in every person's life, and Ruby was experiencing the effects of her own decisions and actions. I could sympathize with her and be of help to her, but I knew I could not and should not interfere in her life. Furthermore, I was a pet sitter. My job was to empty Cheddar's litter box, not to imagine myself mother to Opal or big sister to Ruby. Mr. Stern was Ruby's grandfather, and even though he had behaved like a prize boob the day before, I believed he was a better man than he acted, and that he cared for Ruby and Opal. They would all be okay without my hand-wringing concern.

Going downstairs to the Bronco, I whisper-sang off-key, "You're entirely way too fine, entirely way too fine, get me all worked up like that, entirely way too fine, da-da-da-di-da, um-hunh." Lucinda Williams will never fear competition from me. The air had a salty, sandy, fishy Gulf smell, the fragrance of life. The sky was fleecy, with a thin disc of retreating moon hanging over a pewter sea. On the pale shoreline, as if to echo my whispered song, a sighing surf foamed scalloped designs onto the sand. A great blue heron asleep on the hood of my Bronco extracted his plumed head from under his wing when he heard my song, gave me a red-rimmed glare of indignation, stretched his wings to their full six-foot span, and flapped away with the muted sound of an avalanche. All in all, a normal, run-of-the-mill, predawn morning on the Key.

The rest of the morning was typical. The horizon pinked at the right time, glowed apricot on cue, and ever so subtly transmuted itself into a smooth pale blue canvas for the day's artistry. Gulls gathered into balletic groups to swoop and wheel against the sky's blue scrim, terns and egrets got busy picking up tasty morsels on the ground, songbirds trilled and chirped just because they felt like it. Billy Elliot and I did our regular run, and then I went house to house feeding cats, grooming cats, playing with cats. I was so efficient, so cheerful, so *good,* I could have been the star of a documentary about pet sitting.

Even Mr. Stern's sulkiness didn't faze me. When I got to his house, Ruby opened the door. She looked happier, and I hoped it was because she'd escaped stress for a little while the night before.

She rolled her eyes toward the kitchen in a sort of conspiratorial way to let me know that Mr. Stern could hear us. "Cheddar's with Opal again. He slept under the crib last night and he's been in the bedroom all morning. Opal looks for him when he's not there. It's funny how they've bonded."

I didn't imagine Mr. Stern thought it was funny. I had an image of him sitting alone in the dark courtyard, watching the play of light on the waterfall without Cheddar in his lap.

I bustled into the kitchen as if I didn't notice Mr. Stern's dour expression. He sat at his spot at the bar, waiting for me to arrive and boil his eggs, make his toast, pour him a cup of coffee from a pot heating on its pad on the counter. Mr. Stern was perfectly capable of boiling his own eggs, making his own toast, and pouring his own coffee. Jealousy of Cheddar's attachment to Opal had caused him to go infantile and demanding, traits he would have sneered at in anybody else.

Ruby drifted into the kitchen, poured herself a cup of coffee, and leaned against the counter to watch me cater to her grandfather's grouchy mood. I had the dance down pat: eggs in a pan, a pirouette to the sink for water on the eggs, another to set the pan on the stove. Two slices of bread in the toaster, set the darkness indicator, do an arabesque to the cupboard for the cat food, a plié to sprinkle dry food in the cat's bowl and set it on the floor. I felt so graceful and birdlike, it's a wonder I didn't break into canary song.

With Ruby and Mr. Stern as audience, I added Cheddar's coddled egg to his food, got out a plate for Mr. Stern, fished his soft-cooked eggs from the pan, and buttered his toast. But as I set Mr. Stern's breakfast on the bar, an uneasy awareness of something not right made me turn my head toward the bedroom wing. At the same moment, Ruby's head rose like a dog sniffing the air.

In the next instant we both whirled and ran.

Behind us, Mr. Stern shouted, "What is it? What's happening?"

I could smell it now, an acrid odor of smoke along with an oddly sweet scent.

I yelled, "Fire! Call nine-one-one!"

Down the hall, tongues of flame licked from under Ruby's closed bedroom door, and I could feel waves of heat emanating from it. Even with my mind in chaotic panic, I knew the intensity of that heat made no sense. It was too strong, too forceful, too driven. Heat of that magnitude could only be generated by a blaze that had been raging for a long time.

Ruby screamed and pushed past me to open the bedroom door. But before her clawing hand reached the knob, the door blew toward us as if it had been hit by a bomb. In its place was an impenetrable wall of raging fire.

Howling with panic, Ruby clambered over the door toward the roaring flames. I would have done the same if my baby had been on the other side of that wall of fire, but I caught her around the waist and pulled her back.

She twisted against me and beat at my hands. "Opal is in there!"

"We can't go through those flames! We'll have to go through the outside door!"

If she heard me, the words didn't register. Determined to go through fire to get to her baby, she clawed and kicked at me while I tried to drag her away from the doorway.

As if it had malevolent intelligence, the fire stood like a pillar from hell, its mighty force melting the paint on the door frame in cascading ripples that added a rubbery smell to the stench of smoldering wood.

Mr. Stern ran toward us, ineffectually yanking at his shoulder brace to try to free his injured arm.

I yelled, "Did you call nine-one-one?"

"Fire trucks are on their way!"

With one arm still immobile in its brace, he charged toward the flames with the same determination Ruby had.

I yelled, "You can't go in there, Mr. Stern!"

He stopped, but his rigid back said he was trying to figure out how best to dash through the flames and rescue his great-grandbaby. His carriage said he was a military man, he'd encountered fires before, he could handle this.

Fiery fingers reached through the doorway to stroke the wallpaper in the hall, and still he stood poised to run forward. Wild with terror, Ruby struggled against me like a feral creature. I could barely keep my hold on her. I couldn't fight them both. If Mr. Stern plunged into that furnace, I would not be able to stop him.

"Mr. Stern, please!"

With a shudder of broken acceptance, he turned toward me, reaching with his good arm to help me restrain Ruby. He meant to help, but the truth was that holding Ruby was definitely a two-handed job. Besides, I needed as much space as I could get, and he was in the way.

In my deputy voice, I shouted, "Stand aside, please!"

He looked shocked, then hurt, then nodded sad understanding. I had succeeded in reminding him that he was too old, too weak, and too useless to save either his great-grandbaby or his granddaughter. With a last sorrowful look at the inferno that had been Ruby's bedroom, he ran down the hall toward the kitchen.

"Mr. Stern, we have to get out of here!"

He yelled, "Not without Cheddar!"

I didn't have any breath left to argue with him. He had either forgotten that Cheddar had been in the bedroom with Opal, or he had slipped into denial.

My throat burned from the smoke, and my arms felt as if they were being pulled from their sockets. With my last shred of strength, I spun Ruby around so fast her feet left the floor. Kicking the air, she screamed and fought while I slogged her weight toward the front door. But I was no bigger or stronger than she, and I wasn't sure how much longer I could keep her from twisting away from me. If she did, she would die trying to save her baby.

The siren grew louder. Grimly holding on to Ruby, I floundered down the hall. At the front door, I shouted to Mr. Stern again, but got no answer. With one last burst of effort, I managed to hold Ruby with one arm and grab the doorknob and wrench it open with the other. Blessed fresh air hit my face, along with the sight of a fire truck pulling to the curb with uniformed firefighters spilling from it.

Michael was at the forefront, and as he ran up the driveway he looked so much like our father that I felt an out-of-time sense of history repeating itself. But our father had died saving a child's life, and I was sure the child in this house was already dead. No living being could survive the cauldron of fire that Ruby's bedroom had become.

Seeing me struggle with Ruby, he took her from me as if she were a rag doll and stood her on her feet. "Stay out of the house!"

Ruby's hair was wild, her face smudged with soot and smoke, her eyes all pupil, black and insane. "My baby's in there!"

Putting his face close to hers, Michael shouted, "Then don't get in the way while we put out the fire!"

She recoiled as if she'd been slapped, but her eyes focused and she didn't try to run back inside.

I said, "The fire's in a bedroom with an outside sliding door. There's a baby in the bedroom. Also a cat. And an elderly man in the kitchen. He's looking for the cat. He doesn't want to leave without him."

Other firefighters surged forward, and Michael barked information to them. "Outside slider to the bedroom where the fire is. Baby and cat in the bedroom, elderly man in the kitchen, irrational."

Within seconds, a fireman had gone in and brought Mr. Stern out the door, with orders to all of us to get as far away as possible. We huddled in a clump at the end of the driveway, staring wordlessly at the house. Ruby shook so violently that I put both arms around her and held her tightly, like swaddling an infant. Mr. Stern was pale as white marble, his eyes dry and staring as if he'd suffered a shock that left him unable to blink.

More sirens approached, more fire trucks jerked to a stop in front of the house, more firefighters appeared in their helmets and boots and uniforms. Two ambulances with EMTs came, along with a department car driven by a deputy fire chief. Across the street, neighbors had come outside to watch, clotted together as if to protect one another.

A woman ran across the street and put an arm around Ruby.

The woman said, "You shouldn't be this close, come across the street."

She and I half-carried Ruby while Mr. Stern followed like an obedient child. Other neighbors had spread quilts and pillows on the grass for people to sit on. My rational self was grateful for their kindness. My cynical self resented the way they seemed to prepare for an outdoor concert. My cynical self had misunderstood their intent. Instead of watching as if it were an entertaining event, the neighbors observed a solemn hush as if they were in church.

Ruby stared mutely for a while and then with an anguished howl toppled to the ground facedown. Wordlessly, women gathered beside her and stroked her back, their eyes meeting in silent pity above her devastated form. None of us could imagine a grief so shattering as Ruby felt. None of us could offer any solace or hope or comfort. All we could do was surround her with compassion. Mr. Stern sat alone, sending out waves of resistance that kept the neighbors away. I didn't approach him either. Every person grieves in his own way, and I respected Mr. Stern's right to suffer in solitude. He knew what had happened. He knew that there was no hope for either Opal or Cheddar.

I don't know how long we sat there. Time seemed to both speed up and slow to a crawl. I took it all in as if I were watching from a disincarnate distance.

After what seemed eons, Michael stepped from the front door cradling a small blanket-wrapped form in his arms.

16

A woman in the group said, "What's that fireman carrying? Is that a baby?"

Ruby scrambled to her feet. "Opal!"

Michael hurried to one of the ambulances where an EMT opened the back door.

With me close behind her, Ruby ran across the street and clutched Michael's sleeve. "My baby?"

He shook his head. "It's the cat."

He turned a corner of the blanket back to reveal Cheddar's limp form. He was not burned, but his eyes were closed and his mouth open, and I couldn't see any sign of breath.

Michael said, "I found him when I felt under the bed. At first I thought it was a stuffed toy."

Ruby turned to me with hope lighting her eyes. I knew what she was thinking: if Cheddar had escaped the flames, Opal might have too. But a cat can crawl under a bed when a room is afire. A four-month-old baby cannot.

Michael handed Cheddar to the EMT and ran back to

the house. The EMT climbed into the ambulance where a second EMT already had the pet oxygen mask ready to put over Cheddar's snout. When it was in place, Cheddar lay on the EMT's lap with a hose attached to an oxygen tank snaking over his limp body.

Across the street, Mr. Stern had managed to push himself up from the ground—not an easy feat with one arm in a sling. He moved toward us in jerky steps like a marionette whose strings needed adjusting. When he reached Ruby, he put his good arm around her shoulders. At his touch, Ruby sagged against his thin chest while he awkwardly patted her back.

One of the neighbor women ran to help Ruby back to her spot across the street.

Mr. Stern watched them go, then turned his attention to Cheddar. Only a fine tremor in his shoulders betrayed his despair.

I said, "Mr. Stern, the EMTs have a special oxygen mask for animals. They're using it on Cheddar."

"What about Opal?"

I had never heard him say the baby's name before.

"We don't know yet."

"So much *tzuris*," he muttered. "Such *tzuris*!"

I didn't know Yiddish, but the sound reflected the suffering and trouble around us.

Across the street, Ruby had folded to her knees and buried her face in her hands while neighbor women tried to comfort her. Watching them, I thought of the way Myra Kreigle had once mothered Ruby. I wondered if Myra was watching Ruby now from her second-story window.

After what seemed like an eon, the EMTs gave each

other tentative smiles. I hadn't seen a change in Cheddar, but the EMTs must have seen a twitch of his tail or a blink of his eye. Mr. Stern made a thin noise in his throat that told me he'd seen their smiles too. But that was all we had, that hint of possible success.

In a few minutes, we both saw the tip of Cheddar's tail lift, saw him paw at the oxygen mask, saw his eyes open. Mr. Stern's face crumpled into unashamed tears of joy.

A few more minutes, and they removed the oxygen mask and gently lifted Cheddar to his feet. He stood, stretched his tongue in a wide-mouthed yawn, then curled into a ball on the EMT's lap.

The second EMT stood up and spoke to Mr. Stern. "Sir, I think your cat's going to make it. He's breathing on his own, and he's able to stand up. We're going to take him to an animal clinic. You can ride with us, if you'd like."

Humbly, Mr. Stern said, "Thank you, young man." I'd never heard him be humble before.

I said, "I'll follow you in my car."

"No, you stay here with Ruby."

I didn't argue. Technically, my job was to help Mr. Stern take care of Cheddar, but I knew I would not be needed at the animal hospital. Ruby, on the other hand, needed all the help she could get.

I helped Mr. Stern into the ambulance and waited until it had driven away before I crossed the street to sit with Ruby.

Nobody spoke. We waited silently, staring fixedly at the house. One woman had her arm around Ruby's shoulders and I held Ruby's hand, but I doubted Ruby was aware of us.

A growling sound of an approaching muscle car intruded into the silence, the kind of sound you usually notice in the middle of the night and wonder who would be driving that fast at that hour. The sound made Ruby raise her head, and when the car sped to a stop in front of her, she got to her feet. The car was a sleek, black, low-slung foreign convertible that I didn't recognize. Two men were in it, one of them about as skinny and thin-skinned and blond as a Caucasian can get, with eyebrows and lashes so white they were almost invisible. He was young, mid-twenties, and looked like the kind of kid that hadn't dated much in high school because he'd been more interested in physics or math.

The other guy was the exact opposite, as broad and black and tall as an African-American man can get. About the same age as the white guy, his head was shaved, his muscles bulged in all directions, and he had a face that would frighten criminals on death row. He and the white guy looked like mismatched peas in a shiny foreign pod.

Ruby made a soft bleating sound and stretched her hand forward, while the white guy looked at her with so much pain and anguish that it hurt to watch.

17

With neighbors looking on in rapt silence, the narrow white guy got out of the car and looked across its hood at Ruby, his face a cage holding in roiling emotions. The black guy heaved an impatient sigh, threw open his door, lumbered to Ruby, and enveloped her in his arms. He looked even bigger standing up. Having a brother as big as Michael has made me accustomed to wide shoulders and chests, but this guy was twice as big as Michael.

A spasm of envy crossed the white guy's face, but he seemed more envious of the other guy's ability to show feelings than jealous that Ruby was holding on to him as if he were a savior.

I stood up and waited, like a guard ready to leap into some possible fray.

The white guy walked around the car and stood beside me. "I came as soon as I heard."

Up close, he looked like a young Tom Petty, with a kind

of tensile strength under tender vulnerability. His eyes were so dark blue they were almost violet.

Ruby turned a wrecked face to him. "They haven't found Opal yet."

The white guy winced, and the black guy spun Ruby into the white guy's arms. He did it the way someone would move a dish from the soapy water to the rinse water, as if it were the right time. And Ruby and the white guy held one another as if they accepted the black guy's wisdom without question. Ruby began to keen, her mouth muffled against the man's chest, while he rocked her back and forth the same way she had rocked Opal.

The black guy turned to me and gave me a dimpled smile that was the sweetest expression I've ever seen on anybody over the age of two.

He said, "How do, ma'am. I'm Cupcake Trillin."

Now I understood why he kept his features arranged in a mean scowl. With a smile that sweet, he'd probably been given the name Cupcake when he was a baby, and grew up having to protect himself because of it.

"Pleased to meet you, Cupcake. I'm Dixie Hemingway. I'm here to help take care of Ruby's grandfather's cat."

My hand disappeared in his, and for a second I could feel the thrum of raw power zinging into my palm. Cupcake was the kind of man you wanted on your side, not playing on the enemy's team.

As if he wanted to make sure everybody understood what he meant, Cupcake raised his voice. "That man with Ruby *where he belongs* is her husband, Zack."

Letting a beat go by for everybody to absorb the full

import of both his words and the emphasis he gave to some of them, he said, "What's the story here?"

He was asking me, not Ruby. Ruby was too lost in her husband's arms to hear anything Cupcake said.

"The fire started in Ruby's bedroom where the baby was taking a nap. It came up suddenly and hugely. Ruby tried to go through a wall of flames, but I stopped her. I had to fight her to keep her from going in."

His eyes were steady on me, intelligent eyes that seemed to understand the entire situation in its entirety. He seemed about to ask me another question, but stopped when he saw Michael come out the front door and head toward us. I knew from the way Michael walked that he did not have good news.

If Michael wondered who Zack and Cupcake were, he didn't show it. He simply stopped in front of Ruby and waited a second to give her a chance to prepare herself. His eyes were very sad.

Speaking directly to Ruby, he said, "We didn't find the baby. I'm sorry."

Ruby swayed toward him, eating his words as if they had tangible form.

He said, "The fire was mostly contained to one spot in front of the bedroom door."

She said, "I don't understand."

Zack said, "He means somebody set the fire and took the baby."

Her voice rose to a hysterical pitch. "Is that what you're saying? Somebody took Opal?"

"We can't make that assessment until the investigators

rule out the possibility that she climbed out of her crib and found a hiding place we didn't uncover."

As if each word took superhuman effort, Ruby said, "She's only four months old. She isn't crawling yet."

Michael already knew that. He had held Opal on his lap the night before and fed her lentil soup. He knew exactly what the situation was. But he was not in charge of the investigation and he could only speak of what he knew as a firefighter on the scene.

He said, "We're calling for searchers to look for her."

Zack said, "It was arson." He was making a statement, not asking a question.

As soon as he said it, I knew it was true. Now I understood what the strange sweet odor had been. Somebody had put some sort of flammable concentrate in front of the bedroom door and set fire to it. While it raged, Opal had been taken from her crib, carried out the side door, and the door closed, trapping Cheddar inside the room.

Michael said, "I can't make a call about arson. That's for the fire marshall."

Conflicting emotions moved across Ruby's face like a string of disparate clouds. I knew what she was feeling, because I felt it myself. Michael was offering the possibility that Opal was alive.

Heavy with fatigue and sadness, Michael looked down at her. "As I said, we'll continue to search the house and grounds for the baby. But if nobody else was in the house . . . and if she couldn't get out of her crib by herself . . ."

As if she had suddenly remembered something terribly important, Ruby whipped her head to stare at Myra Kreigle's house. Understanding dawned in her eyes, and in an instant her soft young face hardened into a concrete mask of enraged hatred.

Jerking from Zack's arms, she raced across the street to Myra's closed door. As she ran, she unleashed a hoarse shriek that trailed her like a bloody shroud. I recognized that howl. It was the sound of anguished rage I had made when I learned that Christy had been killed, the betrayed sound every bereaved mother has made since time began, the cry that echoes forever unto the outer reaches of infinity.

I ran after her. When I was halfway up Myra's front walk, Ruby began banging and kicking the front door. "Open the door! Open the door or I'll knock it down!"

The door swished open, and I stopped where I was. Myra was so intent on Ruby that she didn't seem to register that I was there. Perhaps she was so sure of herself that she didn't care.

I had seen newspaper photos of Myra, and I'd seen her face at the upstairs window, but this was the first time I'd had a chance to see her up close. She was an imposing figure. At least a head taller than Ruby, she was whippet thin, with smoothly coiffed raven hair and the stark white complexion that some dramatic brunettes have.

Ruby shouted, "What have you done with Opal? Where is she?"

Myra's crimson lips stretched in a saccharine smile, and I had a momentary flash of being eight years old and feeling terror in my heart as I watched Cruella de Vil's malicious red lips curve on a movie screen.

"Why, Ruby, dear! Whatever is the matter? Have you gotten careless and misplaced your baby?"

Ruby shrieked and charged at her, but Myra stepped back and Kantor Tucker slipped into her space. With both arms stiffened, he grabbed Ruby's wrists.

Kicking at him, Ruby shouted, "Where is Opal?"

He twisted her wrists and leaned to bring his face close to hers. In an automatic reflex, my toes flexed against the pavement to push myself forward to help her. But the oily sound of Tucker's voice stopped me.

"I always thought you were a smart girl, Ruby. But a smart girl doesn't tell lies about people who've been good to her. A smart girl knows people who've been good to her will be good to her baby, too. Unless she's not smart. Unless she repeats those lies. Then her baby might end up with the sharks. You understand me, Ruby?"

For a long moment, we were all frozen in place. Then I moved to stand at Ruby's side. I didn't know what I could do for her, but she was too vulnerable standing alone. Tucker didn't show any more awareness of my presence than Myra had. I had the feeling I truly didn't exist for them. Myra and Tucker had their own little universe, and their rule of it was absolute.

Staring intently into Tucker's eyes, Ruby had gone almost as pale as Myra.

Through lips gone white with fear and futile rage, she whispered, "I understand."

Tucker released her wrists and cupped her hands in both his own. "There's our good girl! And we take care of our own, Ruby. You know that. We take very good care of our own."

Ruby whimpered a helpless cry as Myra came back to stand beside Kantor. She looked down at Ruby with an expression that seemed genuinely sad.

She said, "I was the only one who was good to you, Ruby. The only one."

Weeping softly, Ruby choked, "Yes. Yes, you were."

"You have broken my heart."

"I'm sorry. I'm sorry."

"We won't speak of it again. But you must trust me. You see? That's what life is all about, two people trusting each other to do the right thing."

"I understand."

With a triumphant glance at me, Myra stepped away from the door and Kantor pulled it closed. Ruby buried her face in her hands and sobbed, but there was a shred of relief in her tears, like a beggar grateful for a crust not tainted by mold.

My mouth tasted of ashes. I wasn't sure what had just happened, but I knew it was something terrible. Perhaps more terrible than arson or kidnapping.

Once, when I was a deputy, I had been present when a man had to be cut from an overturned tanker transporting gasoline. The man's foot was crushed under tons of metal, the tanker was smoldering and threatening to explode at any minute. The only way to save the man had been to amputate his foot. The tanker blew up seconds after the man had been removed to safety, and his face had worn the same mixture of unbearable loss and resigned acceptance that I saw on Ruby.

Zack and Cupcake crossed the street, both looking confused and wary. They had seen what happened, but they hadn't been able to hear what was said.

Zack said, "Ruby, what's going on? Do you think that Kreigle woman has something to do with Opal being taken?"

Ruby raised her head and stood with her hands clasped together like someone in prayer. The despair in her eyes was like a bleeding wound. A few hours before, she had been a pretty young woman. Now she looked old and haggard.

She said, "Myra didn't have anything to do with it. I just went a little crazy for a minute. I was wrong."

I was amazed at how easily and convincingly she lied. I was also amazed that she was protecting Myra. From the look that Zack and Cupcake exchanged, I got the feeling they knew she lied and weren't at all surprised by how well she did it.

18

While Zack and Cupcake and I stared at Ruby, each of us processing this latest piece of an increasingly strange puzzle, two cars screeched to a halt at the curb. One was a black sedan driven by a gray-haired man I'd never seen before. The other was a green-and-white from the Sarasota County Sheriff's Department. Mr. Stern's house was no longer strictly a fire-fighter's problem. The fire marshall would investigate the arson, and the sheriff's department would investigate the crime of child abduction. The fact that arson had been a cover for kidnapping would require the two departments to join forces. Like trying to get the FBI and the CIA to work together, that would either be a positive thing that would bring a quicker solution to the crimes, or a complication that would throw a wrench into the smooth workings of both units.

Sergeant Woodrow Owens slammed out of the sheriff's car, moving faster than I'd ever seen him move. A tall, lanky African-American officer, Owens usually moves like swamp water and talks like his tongue is wallowing a mouthful of buttered grits. He also has one of the quickest minds in the universe. I know because he was my superior when I was a deputy.

Two other sheriff's cars arrived in quick succession, and Owens stopped to speak a few terse words to them. The white-haired man from the other car came to stand in front of Zack and Ruby like a flagpole. His eyes cut disapproving slashes into Zack.

He said, "Son, haven't you gone through enough because of this woman?"

Stiffly, Zack said, "Dad, the baby's been kidnapped."

The older man's voice dripped ice. "Ruby, I'm sorry about your baby. But that's how life works. You lie down with dogs, you get up with fleas."

Zack's pale face flamed. "She's not just Ruby's baby. She's mine too."

His father's lip lifted in a sneer. "I wouldn't be too sure of that."

Ruby whirled toward him. "No wonder Zack doesn't know how to be a father to Opal! You've done everything you could to keep us from being a family, and you succeeded! But don't you dare imply that Opal isn't Zack's baby!"

Stung, Zack said, "How could I be a father to Opal when you took her and left? What was I supposed to do when I didn't even know where you were?"

Zack's father looked pleased, but Cupcake's brow creased like a worried hound's.

Cupcake said, "Look, folks, let's stay focused. There's a

missing baby. All that other stuff can be straightened out later."

Zack looked chagrined. "Cupcake's right. We have to find Opal and bring her home."

His father said, "Stay out of it, son. Let the cops handle it. That's their job. And for all you know, Ruby may have set it up herself. It wouldn't be the first time she's pulled a dishonest trick."

I expected Ruby to explode, but she merely gave her father-in-law an anguished look.

The knob of Adam's apple quivered in Zack's skinny neck, as if his voice had to climb over it to be heard. "Dad, I think it would be best if you left now. I understand how you feel, but I have to make some decisions and I need to make them without your help. Please."

The older man looked shocked, and I had the feeling he rarely heard Zack speak so forcefully. He contemplated his son as if he were a defective piece of merchandise. "We all know the kind of decisions you make without my help."

Zack stood straighter. "Dad, I'm asking you to leave. Please."

With an exasperated huff, Mr. Carlyle spun toward his car, turning back halfway there to say, "Just don't let yourself be pussy-whipped, boy."

Zack's face burned, and Cupcake's frown deepened. Ruby seemed too preoccupied with inner pain to notice the latest volley of scorn from her father-in-law.

Deputies began stringing crime scene tape around the yard, and Sergeant Owens headed toward Mr. Stern's front door. He saw me and stopped.

"Hell, Dixie, what are you doing here?"

"I'm taking care of a cat for Mr. Stern. He's the owner of the house. Has a torn bicep muscle."

His eyes raked my sooty clothes. "Were you in the fire?"

"A little bit, but I'm okay."

With a nod toward Ruby, I said, "This is Mr. Stern's granddaughter, Ruby Carlyle. She's the mother of the kidnapped baby. And this is the baby's father, Zack Carlyle."

A light glinted in his eyes. "Zack Carlyle." He rolled the name over his tongue like a connoisseur of fine wine tasting something rare and wonderful. I decided it was official. Every man in the world knew about Zack Carlyle.

He said, "Who was present when the fire started?"

I said, "I was here. Mr. Stern was here, and Ruby was here. Mr. Stern's cat suffered smoke inhalation, and the EMTs saved him. Mr. Stern has gone with the EMTs to take the cat to an animal hospital."

Zack said, "My friend and I heard about the fire on the news and came straight here."

Owens said, "The baby's disappearance was on the news?"

"No, just the fire. The house is next door to Myra Kreigle. That makes the fire newsworthy, I guess."

Owens didn't ask who Myra Kreigle was. Everybody in Sarasota knew what Myra had done.

To Ruby, he said, "Ma'am, do you know anybody who might have kidnapped your baby?"

She raised her head and spoke clearly. "I think it may

have been a cleaning woman who was here yesterday. She cried when she saw Opal, and the other women with her said she'd lost a baby a few months ago. She's the only person I can think of who would steal Opal."

I was stunned. Both at the logic of what she'd said, and at the ease with which she'd said it. But I had to admire the brilliance of the lie. The cleaning woman was a perfect suspect. Mothers who've recently lost their own babies can become so irrational in their grief that they take somebody else's baby. For a second, I even considered the possibility that the cleaning woman had actually stolen Opal. But only for a second. As soon as I remembered Tuck's chilling words to Ruby, I discounted the possibility of anybody other than one of his goons sneaking into the bedroom and snatching Opal from her crib. This wasn't about stealing a baby, it was about people with more power and money than the entire state making sure that Ruby didn't testify in Myra's trial.

Ruby looked at me with pleading eyes. I thought of Paco saying that white-collar criminals would kill as quickly as any other criminal. I thought of Tucker's plane, and of Ruby saying Tucker had flown a man over the Gulf and shoved his body out to be eaten by sharks. I thought of Tucker's slimy innuendo when he'd spoken to Ruby, the veiled threat that Opal might meet the same fate unless Ruby cooperated.

I said, "I talked to those cleaning women this morning. They were working at a house next door to one of my clients, but they said Doreen hadn't shown up for work today. That's her name, Doreen. She's obese. If you put out a bulletin to watch for a woman like that with a baby, add obesity to the description. About my height, but easily over two hundred pounds. Depression does that, you know. Puts on pounds. The other women said Doreen's boyfriend had left her after her baby died."

Ruby shot me a look of pure gratitude.

Owens grimaced. "He must be a stellar guy. Do either of you know the woman's last name?"

Ruby said, "You'll have to ask Granddad."

"Okay, I need to go inside the house for a minute and speak to the deputies in there. Mr. and Mrs. Carlyle, I'll need to get more information from you."

He looked a question at Cupcake, who shrugged his massive shoulders. "I'm just here as Zack's friend."

"Your name?"

"Cupcake Trillin."

"Sorry, I didn't recognize you."

I looked hard at Cupcake. Apparently he was somebody I should recognize, but I didn't.

Owens said, "Mr. and Mrs. Carlyle, would you mind going downtown to the Ringling office and talking there? It'll be more comfortable than standing out in the yard."

For a minute there was a discussion of who would ride in which car, since Zack's car only held two people, with a final decision that Cupcake would ride with Sergeant Owens to the station and wait.

Owens said, "I have to talk to the deputies inside for a minute, and then I'll lead you folks to the station. Dixie, don't leave. I want to talk to you, too."

He meant for me to hang around in the yard until he was ready for me. Former deputies don't get invited to sit in chairs and drink coffee at the sheriff's office. We get interviewed in driveways, on sidewalks, and in the drive-through lane at Taco Bell.

I didn't look forward to being interviewed anywhere. There were too many weird things going on, too many knotted personal relationships, too much sadness.

19

Sergeant Owens went into the house, leaving me and Cupcake to watch Zack guide Ruby across the street and help her into his car.

Cupcake said, "You know what's going on here?"

Maybe it was because he was so big, or maybe it was his sweet smile, but I trusted Cupcake.

I said, "I know Ruby is supposed to testify in Myra Kreigle's trial. I know her testimony will send Myra to prison for a long time. I know Myra will go to any lengths to keep that testimony out of court."

Cupcake exhaled, a sigh that came out like a warm wind. "That's what I'm thinking too. That old witch had somebody take that baby to shut Ruby up."

"I think I know who took her. A man named Vern. He grabbed me yesterday and took me to Kantor Tucker. He thought I was Ruby."

Cupcake studied me. "You do look like Ruby."

"Ruby and I thought that would be the end of it. We never dreamed they'd get to her through Opal."

"She should have been with Zack. He's her husband. He should have been watching over her."

"Ruby says Zack believes she tricked him. Is that true?"

He sighed again. "I don't know if that boy knows what he believes anymore. His dad has him all twisted up. He feeds him a lot of crap about how Ruby can't be trusted and how she's a two-timing slut, but it's not true. Ruby's a good girl. She got in with the wrong people, but she didn't know what they were until it was too late."

Sergeant Owens came out the front door, and Cupcake hurried to dig a crumpled card from his pants pocket and hand it to me. "We need to help those kids."

I didn't know if he meant Ruby and Zack or the underprivileged kids he and Zack wanted to help.

Sergeant Owens and I watched Cupcake lumber across the yard to the sheriff's car and crawl into the passenger seat. I sneaked a look at his card but all it said was *Cupcake Trillin,* with a phone number.

Owens said, "You know who that is?"

Without giving me a chance to admit I didn't, he said, "Inside linebacker for the Bucs. He's like a granite mountain."

"Hunh." Being more or less sports illiterate, I didn't know what an inside linebacker was, but I tried to look as if I did.

Owens said, "What do you know about Ruby Carlyle?"

"She used to work for Myra Kreigle, and she's a witness in Myra's trial."

"Okay."

"Ruby's job was to lure rich men into Myra's Ponzi

scheme. That's how she met Zack Carlyle. They were married about eighteen months ago. He and some other athletes had started a foundation to help needy kids. Thanks to Ruby's influence, the foundation invested heavily in Myra Kreigle's phony REIT. I'm not sure how much Ruby knew of what was really going on, but Myra promised her Zack wouldn't lose any money. He lost it all, and now he believes Ruby was as guilty as Myra. Thinks she married him for his money."

Owens raised a bony finger and scratched his cheek a few times, as if he were tabulating suspects.

"Dixie, from what you've seen, do you think there's any chance the mother could be involved in the baby's disappearance? Maybe she's trying to get attention from Zack Carlyle, or maybe she's planning to claim she's too distraught to testify in the Kreigle trial? Maybe this whole thing is a scam, like Kreigle's Ponzi deal. Wouldn't be the first time she's put on a phony act."

He sounded like Zack's father, which made me snap at him. "I haven't seen anything that would make me think that."

That was the absolute truth. I had not seen a thing to make me believe Ruby would engineer a fake kidnapping of her baby. But a good actor can fool anybody, including police officers, judges, juries, and me. Ruby was a good actress, good enough to make old rich men feel young and virile in her presence, good enough to cause them to invest millions of dollars in a phony real estate investment trust. She might have fooled me too, but I didn't believe her love for Opal was faked.

I said, "Yesterday morning a man named Vern Brogher

mistook me for Ruby and strong-armed me into his limo. He took me to see a man named Kantor Tucker. He's the man who put up two million dollars' bond for Myra Kreigle. He has a place out east of Seventy-five where people have airstrips alongside their driveways. When Tucker saw that I wasn't Ruby, he sent Vern away. Vern took me to a Friendly's and put me out. Ruby said Vern was Tucker's muscle, and that he also worked for Myra. Vern may have taken Ruby's baby."

"What about the obese cleaning woman?"

An edge to his voice made me think he was suspicious of the story of the cleaning woman.

I said, "There really is a cleaning woman, and she was truly upset when she saw Opal. And it's true that the women who work with her say she lost a baby a few weeks ago, and that her boyfriend left her."

"But you think the kidnapper may be that Vern guy?"

In my memory, I heard Ruby talking about Tuck shoving a man out of his plane over the Gulf. And I heard Tucker's threatening voice say that Opal could become shark food. Ruby was afraid to accuse Vern because she was afraid Tuck and Myra would kill Opal if she did. I was afraid of that too.

I said, "All I know is that Myra Kreigle's trial begins Monday, and if Ruby testifies about what Myra did with the money she took from people, Myra may spend the rest of her life in jail. If Ruby thought Vern had kidnapped her baby to keep her quiet, she might decide not to tell what she knows. Myra would get a shorter prison sentence, and the stolen money would still be there waiting when she got out."

He looked skeptical, and I didn't blame him. A criminal investigation can't run on speculation and vague hunches.

"That's an interesting theory, Dixie. You have anything except intuition to back it up?"

I clenched my jaws on words that begged to be said: *I heard Tucker tell Ruby that Opal might become shark food if Ruby said bad things about her friends.* I had no right to say those words. Like Ruby, I had to choose between telling the truth and saving Opal's life.

Owens said, "We'll put out an Amber Alert right away, and we'll notify public transportation services to be on the lookout for an obese Caucasian woman with a four-month-old baby."

"That ought to narrow down the field."

Ignoring the sarcasm, he gave me a half salute and strode off to join Cupcake in the car. Dully, I watched them drive away, watched Zack and Ruby pull in behind to follow them to the sheriff's office.

Except for a lone deputy car, my Bronco was the only vehicle left. Firefighters were putting equipment back into their trucks and driving away. Across the street, neighbors were retrieving their quilts and pillows from the grass and returning to their own homes.

The fire marshall's investigating team hadn't yet arrived, and I knew the deputy inside was mostly biding time until they showed up. I had no reason to stay, but I couldn't make my feet move. I felt as if I were an impostor in my own body, somebody who looked like me and talked like me but was a total stranger to me. When I'd agreed with Ruby that the cleaning woman might have kidnapped Opal, I had helped implicate an innocent woman in a crime. It didn't help that I knew she would be found innocent. I had violated every principle I held dear.

But I wanted to save Opal, and I believed Tucker could get away with murdering a baby without ever being called to account for it. He was that powerful, he was that amoral. If he and Myra were accused, he might dispose of Opal just to be rid of the evidence.

The sun was mid-heaven now, way past my breakfast time. But I was too grimy and sad to eat. The only thing I could do was go to my apartment, my quiet refuge away from insanity and greed, away from twisted people who could justify stealing a baby in order to force its mother to lie to a jury.

A car door slammed shut in Myra's driveway, and I turned to see a black Mercedes back to the street and drive away. Seconds later, a red BMW backed rapidly from Myra's garage to the street, it turned with squealing brakes, and roared away. Myra and Tucker had both left her house.

I turned and looked at Myra's house. The young woman I'd seen at the window might be in there alone. Or she might have Opal with her. Vern might have come down the side of the vacant house into Mr. Stern's side yard, sneaked into Ruby's bedroom, set the fire, grabbed Opal from her crib, and left the same way he'd come, circling behind Mr. Stern's walled garden to the back of Myra's yard and into her house without anybody seeing him. Opal might have been inside the house while Myra and Tucker talked to Ruby at the front door. If that were true, Opal could be inside Myra's house right that moment, and Myra and Tucker were gone.

The young woman I'd seen at Myra's window had looked gentle and kind. Defenseless, even. I was an ex-deputy. I had gone to police academy. I was not gentle and kind. If that soft young woman was alone in Myra's house with Opal, I could go in and easily take the baby away from her.

After I had the baby, I would call Sergeant Owens and he would make sure the baby was put in a safe place. Ruby would be able to tell the truth, and Myra and Tucker would spend the rest of their lives in prison. Most important of all, Ruby and Opal would be safe.

I didn't see a single flaw in my reasoning. That's how far gone I was.

20

A modest corridor of lawn separated Mr. Stern's walled courtyard from Myra Kreigle's driveway. I circled the end of the wall separating the lots and looked down the side of Myra's house. Flower beds ran alongside the house's foundation, and a gravel walk between the beds and the driveway was edged with begonias. The walk led to a side door. That side door beckoned me.

I took the crunching graveled walk to the side door. Anybody watching would have seen me moving at a normal speed, not running like a thief. At the door, my hand tried the doorknob. Myra must have been in too much of a hurry to lock it when she left, because it turned. I pushed the door open and stepped into a spacious laundry room with side-by-side washer and dryer and cupboards above.

I moved into the kitchen where a window above the sink let in midday sunshine. Even gliding through as quickly as I did, I appreciated the way the kitchen managed to look both contemporary and antique. Dark wood floors, granite countertops, glossy dark cabinets that reached to the ceiling, and a pale green stove with French Provincial legs and a hooded top. The stove pretended to be vintage, but was undoubtedly a reproduction that had cost an obscene amount of money. A wide baker's cabinet stood at an angle in a corner, either a genuine antique or a very good reproduction. I doubted that Myra ever pulled out its work table and kneaded dough or rolled pie crusts on it. It was strictly for show, like everything else in Myra's life.

The living room was equally charming, with Oriental rugs and paintings that looked as if a decorator had chosen them to match the color scheme. Staying well back from wide windows veiled in sheer curtains, I took in a ceiling with pecky-cypress beams. The brick on the fireplace looked old. Myra had probably robbed it from some medieval castle.

Scuttling through the living room as fast as I could, I raced through a slew of richly decorated downstairs rooms, then took heart-pine stairs to the second floor. The house was shadowy and quiet, the way an empty house would be. But I didn't believe the house was empty. I believed a young Latin American woman was in it. Perhaps willingly, perhaps as a prisoner.

Careful not to let the soles of my Keds squeak on the wooden floors, I walked as quickly as I could down a central hall with doors on each side, some closed, some open. I sped down the hall looking first into every open door, then retraced my steps to check the rooms with closed doors. It was deathly quiet, and a nugget of doubt began to work its way into my brain. Maybe I'd been wrong, maybe the young woman I'd seen wasn't here.

One closed door led to a bedroom in which a satin dressing gown was tossed over the foot of the bed, and the scent of expensive perfume hung in the air. I guessed it was Myra's, but I didn't take time to investigate. Another door led to a guest room with a king-size bed, gender-free maroon bedspread, a long dresser, and two club chairs. It smelled of furniture polish, and had a private bath with rolled stacks of maroon towels. Another led to a no-frills bedroom with a beige tailored spread on a double bed. The bedspread was rumpled, as if something had been moved around on it, and the wooden floor had the kind of detritus that falls out of opened purses or luggage—tiny shreds of tissue, bits of foil from chewing gum wrappers, a broken rubber band. This bedroom also had a private bath. The towels were white and not as plush as the maroon ones. A damp washcloth had been carefully folded over the lip of the sink.

In my imagination, I saw the young dark-haired woman pack a cheap suitcase she'd laid on the bed, saw her wash her face and hands, saw her take time to fold her washcloth before she hurried from the room. She hadn't had time to smooth the bedspread or pick up what the luggage had shed when she'd opened it.

I had been wrong about the young woman being in the house, and I had to get out before Myra returned. Downstairs, I skittered through the living room and into the kitchen. At the side door, I reached to turn the knob. The crunch of approaching footsteps on the gravel path made me jerk my hand away.

Like a cornered rat, I ran back into the kitchen, my eyes darting back and forth for any hiding spot. The side doorknob rattled, and I dived for the lower doors on the baker's cabinet. The angels that protect idiots must have been with me, because that base section was empty and big enough for me to wedge myself into. I pulled the doors closed and held my breath while footsteps clattered from the laundry room.

Of all the pin-headed, numb-nutted, dumb-assed things I'd ever done, this one was the star on the tree. My chin dug into my knees, my fingers gripped my tight-folded legs, and I didn't dare take a good breath for fear the person who'd just come in would hear me. If I sneezed or coughed, I was done for.

Four feet away from my hiding place, Myra's voice said, "Tuck? Where are you? Why aren't you answering your cell?"

She waited a beat and then grew more shrill. "Vern scared Angelina and she ran away. Went out on the highway and some woman picked her up and brought her to a bodega on Clark Road. You have to drive her back there. Call me as soon as you get this."

A softer voice said, "I will not stay in house with that man." She spoke with an accent, and with a Latin rhythm.

With daggers in every word, Myra said, "Angelina, do you remember what I told you would happen to your mother if you broke your promise?"

"That man say if I don't do what he wants, he will give me to those alligators. Big alligators, both sides of the road."

Myra muttered, "Son of a bitch."

A cell phone beeped, and Myra snarled an answer. "Tuck, you've got to take control of that damned man! He stayed in the house with Angelina and threatened her."

A pause, and then, "What do you mean, you can't take her back? You have to! I can't take the time to drive forty miles to that house! I have a million things to do before the trial starts."

Another pause, and Myra made a groaning sound of pure fury. I imagined she had bared her teeth.

Silence stretched, and Myra heaved an exaggerated sigh. "All right, I'll drive her! But you have to take care of Vern!"

Another silence. "Okay. Okay. When your meeting is over, call me."

She must have closed her phone, because her next words were to Angelina. "Mr. Tucker says for you to be a good girl and keep your promise so nothing bad will happen to your mother. I'll drive you back to the house, and you must not leave again."

"I not stay in house with that man."

"Mr. Tucker promises the man won't bother you again."

Angelina made mumbling noises of reluctant assent.

Cowering in my tight quarters, I listened to Myra's high heels clicking to the side door along with Angelina's soft padding. The door opened and closed.

I waited until I was sure they weren't coming back, then eased my cramped self out of the baker's cabinet and limped to the side door. When I stuck my head out, I didn't see anybody. I slipped out the door, pulled it closed, and sauntered to the Bronco as nonchalantly as I could manage. The deputy's car was still at the curb. The neighborhood looked the same. The only thing that had changed was me.

In the Bronco, a surge of adrenaline caused me to grip

the steering wheel and tremble for a while. When the shakes passed, I started the motor and drove away in a state of euphoric frustration. I had learned some valuable information, but I wasn't sure what it was.

Neither Myra nor Angelina had mentioned a baby. But I would have bet my entire collection of white Keds that Vern had taken Opal and Angelina to a house somewhere forty miles away where Vern had scared Angelina so much she'd run away. If I was right, she had left Opal alone with Vern.

With my head pounding from exhaustion, stress, and hunger, I headed home, where the carport looked bleakly empty and the shorebirds walking along the edge of the surf seemed sad and dispirited. In my bathroom, I was shocked when I saw my reflection in the mirror. My skin was streaked with a greasy film of gray smoke, my eyes were red-rimmed and pink-veined, and my hair clung to my scalp in heavy dull strands. I not only felt like hell, I looked like hell.

Peeling off my smoke-stinking clothes, I stuffed them in the washer. Cupcake's wrinkled card fluttered to the floor, and I retrieved it and put it in my bag. Just knowing it had been in Cupcake's big warm hand gave the card a peculiar kind of power I wanted to hold on to.

As I got into a hot shower, I heard my cell phone's distinctive ring reserved for Michael, Paco, or Guidry. I let it ring. I was too tired and too nasty to talk to anybody. As blessed hot water sluiced over my skin and hair and washed away the odor and fatigue, I realized that I was still shaking. Fine tremors seemed to be emanating from my bones, traveling through my flesh and jittering my skin in a combination of adrenaline, exhaustion, fear, and shame.

When I was sure I was free of the stench and grime from smoke, I stepped out of the shower, toweled off, and pulled a shaky comb through my hair. Walking like a feeble old woman, I shuffled to my bed and crawled under the covers, already halfway into the oblivion of sleep.

I dreamed I was in some cavernous place where shadowy forms moved around me. I knew they carried important information, but none of them would come close so I could find out what it was. When I chased them, they dissolved, and when I stood still and begged them to come to me, they turned into hard boulders that couldn't move.

A banging at my french doors pulled me from the dream. Guidry was on the porch yelling my name. I groaned. There are times in a relationship when you are ecstatic to see the other person, and there are times when you just want to be left the hell alone.

Louder, Guidry yelled, "Dixie?"

I groaned again and slid out of bed. I was halfway to the door when I remembered I was stark naked, so I detoured to the closet and grabbed a sleepshirt. Not that Guidry hadn't seen me naked before, but answering the door wearing nothing but skin seemed just wrong. Decently covered, I yanked open the french doors. In the next instant, Guidry was holding me close and I was blubbering all over his nice linen jacket.

He said, "Owens called me and told me about the fire."

I sobbed, "They took Opal."

"The baby?"

I rubbed my face up and down against his chest. "Uh-huh."

"Who? Who took her?"

I opened my mouth to answer him, and the little male secretary in my brain who zips around opening file drawers to retrieve information when I need it came to a screeching halt. Whirling to a specific filing cabinet, he whipped out a file marked "Officers of the Law Are Required to Report All Crimes of Which They Have Knowledge."

Once again, I was faced with the partnered-person's dilemma. I had good reason to believe that Vern had taken Opal and put her in a house forty miles away. But I had to choose between gut instinct, which was to share my awful secret with Guidry, and the knowledge that his integrity as an officer of the law would compel him to take actions that might lead to Opal's death.

Pulling away from him, I wiped away tears with both hands. It gave me an excuse not to look up at Guidry.

"It may have been Vern. Or it could have been a cleaning woman who was at the Stern house yesterday."

My little brain secretary smiled and replaced the file.

"Owens said the fire was arson."

"That's what Michael said, too. He saved Cheddar."

"Cheddar?"

"Mr. Stern's cat. Cheddar was in the bedroom with Opal, and he hid under the bed. Michael found him and brought him out to the EMTs and they gave him oxygen. He's at the animal hospital now, but they think he's going to be okay."

Guidry smoothed my damp hair back from my forehead. "What about you? Are you going to be okay?"

I burst into sobs again. Stood there and bawled like a two-year-old. "I'm hungry, and Michael's at the firehouse and I don't have anything to eat."

Guidry chuckled and pulled me into his arms again. "Tell you what, I'll cook dinner for you tonight at my place."

I wailed, "I'm not crying because I'm hungry."

"I know."

"I didn't know you could cook."

"You still don't. It's only a theory."

He squeezed me in a hug, kissed the top of my head, and released me. "You need to sleep. I'll see you tonight."

Crying, hiccuping, and sniffling, I watched him walk across my porch. I watched him go down the stairs until his head disappeared from view. Then I pulled the french doors closed, pushed the button to lower the folding metal hurricane shutters, and shuffled back to bed, sobbing all the way. I was still crying when I fell asleep. Maybe I even cried while I slept.

21

My nap lasted only about fifteen minutes, way too short, and I woke feeling headachy and depressed. The headache was a no-food-since-last-night dullness. The depression was a crushing weight made from worry about what was happening to Opal, wondering where Vern had taken Opal, and guilt from being partially responsible for the sheriff's office including in its list of suspects an innocent cleaning woman already torn by grief over losing a baby.

I padded to the kitchen and put on water for tea. I thought about going downstairs to Michael's kitchen and raiding his refrigerator, but I couldn't dredge up energy for more than pouring water over tea bags. While I drank a cup of under-brewed tea, I wondered how long it would take Sergeant Owens to remove the cleaning woman from his suspects.

When I couldn't stand it any more, I pulled out my cellphone and dialed his number. It was engraved in my memory from my days as a deputy.

When Sergeant Owens answered, I said, "This is Dixie. I just wondered if you'd got any leads about the kidnapped baby."

He sounded surprised. Not at my curiosity, but that I'd called him.

Carefully, as if he didn't want to hurt my feelings, Owens said, "I know you're concerned about the baby, Dixie. We all are. But it may take time to find her. We've put out an Amber Alert, and we have people searching the neighborhood. We also have the cleaning woman's full name. Doreen Antone. We've tracked down her address, but nobody's home and her car's gone. We've talked to Doreen's boyfriend, and he said she might have gone to her sister's in Alabama. He's thick as a board, doesn't know where the sister lives, like what town, but he knows Doreen is from Alabama and that she has a sister there. We've alerted airports and bus stations and put out an APB to be on the lookout for an overweight young Caucasian woman with a four-month-old baby. We're checking high school records, DMV records, everything we can. We'll find her."

My chest felt as if a trapped eagle were inside flapping its wings against my heart in a desperate search for truth that would lead to freedom. But the terrible truth was that Myra and Tucker had more money than all the law enforcement agencies in the country. Money is power, and Myra and Tucker were ruthless in their use of it. If I told Sergeant Owens that following Doreen Antone was a useless expenditure of department energy and money, I'd have to tell him the truth about Opal being held in a house forty miles away. That could lead to Tucker learning he was a suspect. If he did, Opal could be dead and disposed of in an hour. I couldn't jeopardize Opal's safety by telling Owens the truth. Like Ruby, I had to swallow my honor and accept the unacceptable.

I thanked Owens, apologized for taking his time, and rang off with more worry and remorse than I'd felt before I called. Knowing about Ruby's tacit agreement with Tucker and Myra had given me the ability to see the future with an awful clarity. At Myra's trial, Ruby wouldn't remember a single offshore account where Myra had stashed millions in stolen money. In exchange, Kantor Tucker would keep his part of the agreement and fly Opal and Angelina to another part of the country where they would be discreetly installed in a nice house and given a plausible cover story. Angelina would be supplied with all the papers necessary to pose as Opal's mother, and nobody would suspect that Opal had been kidnapped. In ten years or fifteen or twenty, whenever Myra was released from prison, she and Tucker would collect the offshore accounts. If Ruby was out of jail by that time, they might permit her to be reunited with Opal, but Opal's love and allegiance would be to the woman who had raised her.

Now here's the thing about secrets: Like the Big Bad Wolf, secrets have big jagged teeth and strong jaws. Kept inside, they use their sharp teeth to tear off big chunks of your tender innards, gnashing your flesh in their spring-trap jaws and ripping you to shreds. Secrets have to be told to *somebody,* just not to somebody who will repeat them or who will be personally affected by them. Somebody like a trusted psychotherapist, maybe, or a spiritual guide. I didn't know any psychotherapists or spiritual guides, but I knew Cora Mathers, and I felt a sudden urge to get to her as fast as possible. In a feverish rush, I pulled on clothes, grabbed my keys and bag, and hurried out my front door.

I took the north bridge to Tamiami Trail, followed it around the marina where tall sailboats were anchored, and then a few blocks to Bayfront Village, an upscale retirement condo on the bay. A uniformed parking attendant rushed out to open my Bronco's door, and double glass doors sighed open to let me pass into the big lobby. Handsome elderly people stood around in groups making dates to play tennis or golf or to go to the opera or the museum or a movie. I don't know why it is, but rich old people seem to have more fun than young people, rich or poor. Maybe it's because old people who are rich had to be luckier or smarter than other people to get rich in the first place, so they use the same luck and smarts to enjoy old age.

I headed for the elevators, and from her place behind a big French provincial desk, the concierge waved and picked up her house phone to let Cora know I was coming. She knew that Cora always wanted to see me, so I didn't have to wait for permission.

Cora is in her late eighties, but she's the youngest person I know. Cora and her granddaughter started out poor, but her granddaughter made a lot of money in ways that Cora has never suspected, and she bought Cora a posh apartment in the Bayfront Village. The granddaughter was murdered while she was a client of mine a few years back, and Cora and I became close friends. She's not at all like my own grandmother was, but she has sort of taken her place. I'm not at all like her granddaughter either, but in many ways I've taken her place. Which I guess proves that friendships don't depend on any of the things we think they do, they just happen when two people like each other a lot.

On the sixth floor, Cora's door was already open and she had stuck her head out to watch for me. Cora is roughly the size of an undernourished middle-school child, with thin freckled arms and legs and white hair so thin and wispy her pink scalp shines through. When she saw me step out of the elevator, she waved her entire arm up and down like a highway flagman, as if she thought I wouldn't know which door was hers if she didn't signal.

Before I got to the door, she said, "You knew I was baking bread, didn't you? I'll bet you smelled it all the way across town."

I could smell it now, and the scent drew me forward like the odor of cream to a kitten. Cora has an old bread-making machine that was a gift from her granddaughter, and by a secret recipe that she won't divulge, she makes decadent chocolate bread in it.

I gave Cora a hug—carefully, because I'm always afraid I'll crush her—and followed her into her pink and turquoise apartment. It's a lovely apartment, pink marble floors, paler pink walls, turquoise and rose linen covers on sofa and chairs, and a terrace beyond a glass wall through which she has a magnificent view of the bay.

The odor of hot chocolate bread made me walk with lifted nose like a hound first getting a scent of something to chase.

Cora said, "I just took it out, so it's piping hot."

Habit made Cora take a seat at a small skirted table between the living area and a tiny one-person kitchen while I assembled our tea tray. Cora's teakettle is always on, so it only took a minute to pour hot water over tea bags in a Brown Betty pot, get cups and saucers from the cupboard, butter from the refrigerator, and add the hot round loaf of chocolate bread. I put the tray on the table and took the other chair. Cora watched me lay everything out and pour two cups of tea.

We each tore off two fist-sized hunks of bread from the loaf—Cora insists that it can't be sliced like ordinary bread—and slathered them with butter. Cora's chocolate bread is dark, dense, and studded with morsels of semi-sweet chocolate that have not fully melted but instead gently ooze from their centers. Angels in heaven probably have Cora's chocolate bread with tea every afternoon. If God's on their good side, they may invite him to join them. I ate half my chunk before I said a word. Partly because it was so good, and partly because I couldn't get the words out.

Cora said, "You look like you've been wrung dry. What's wrong?"

I don't know how she does it, but she always knows.

I sipped tea and put my cup back in its saucer. "A baby I know has been kidnapped. She's about four months old. Her name is Opal, and she's beautiful. I'm sure I know who took her, but if I tell, it could cause her to be killed."

Cora tilted her head toward the light coming in from the glass sliders at the back of her living room so that the fine lines that etched her skin seemed to shimmer.

"You're sure you know?"

I took a bite of bread and chewed while I tried to figure out a way to tell Cora how I knew that Myra and Tucker had sent Vern to kidnap Opal.

I said, "It's too complicated to go into all the details, but I overheard a phone conversation. There's a man and woman who hired another man to take the baby. They did it because the baby's mother knows things about them that can get them sent to prison for a long time. If she keeps quiet, they'll take good care of her baby, but she'll go to prison. If she tells what she knows, she won't go to prison, but they'll kill her baby."

Cora laced her fingers together on the table. "It would take a very low person to kill a baby."

"They're that low. They're about as low as a human being can get."

"You don't think you might have misunderstood what you heard?"

I shook my head. "I heard enough to convince me. The baby's mother has known them a long time and she says the man has flown his plane out over the Gulf and shoved people out. She thinks he'll do that to the baby if she talks."

"My goodness."

"I don't know what to do. I'm afraid to tell what I know, and afraid not to tell."

She took a sip of tea, her hooded blue eyes watching me.

She said, "Losing a baby is the worst thing that can ever happen to a person. You don't ever get over it. You can think you've moved away from the hurt, but every time you hear about some other baby being lost, you feel like it's happening to you all over again."

My breath caught in my chest as if a hand had grabbed my throat, and in the next instant my face was buried in my hands and I was sobbing again, not about Opal but because my baby had been crushed to death in an insane accident in a supermarket parking lot. Cora did not get up and comfort me. She was too smart for that. She waited me out. And because I knew she was strong enough to wait me out, I didn't try to dam my flood of tears but let them flow until they slowed to a trickle and stopped.

When I took my hands from my face, Cora handed me a stack of paper napkins. I mopped my cheeks and gave her a tremulous smile. "I didn't expect to do that."

She said, "Oh, you'll always do that. It'll catch you when you're not even thinking about your child. It's been over forty years since my daughter died and left me her baby to raise, but sometimes it hits me all over again that she's gone, and I'm just laid low. I don't guess it will ever stop, that awful pain. It just goes into hiding for long stretches."

I said, "The baby's mother is very young, and she already has a lot of heartache, and now this goon has kidnapped her baby. It's just not fair."

"I don't know why people are always surprised that life isn't fair. It never has been, never will be. You can't do anything about that."

"I guess not."

Cora said, "Well, you have to find that baby and bring her home. Her mother's not going to be able to help you much. Women aren't much good at getting things done when they're scared and grieving. Men are better at that.

Seems like they can turn all their grief into action. Go bomb something, shoot somebody, start a fistfight, bust up a saloon. Half the time they make it worse, but at least they can move. At least they can do *something*."

I said, "The baby's father is a race car driver."

Cora's pale blue eyes lit with some old memory. "Race car drivers are good at taking action. They're good at breaking hearts, too. If I was you, I'd get the dad to help you get that baby back. See if he's got the gumption to do something besides break a woman's heart."

From the acid in her voice, I thought it was a safe guess that Cora's heart had once been broken by a race car driver.

I said, "I don't know the father very well."

She shrugged. "You can fix that."

As usual, Cora had oversimplified a complex situation that she knew nothing about. But for some fool reason I felt as if a huge load had been lifted from me. I even felt as if she'd given me a solution of sorts. All I had to do was figure out how to put it into action.

I put away our tea things and kissed the top of Cora's feathery head.

I said, "Thank you. For the bread, for the tea, for listening to me."

She patted my hand. "You're a good girl, Dixie. You just have to stay strong."

As I rode down in the elevator, I told myself Cora was absolutely right. I needed to stay strong. And maybe, just maybe, Zack Carlyle was the person who would help me find Opal.

Before the elevator came to a stop on the lobby level, I

had pulled out Cupcake's card. By the time the valet brought my car to me, I had called Cupcake and asked to meet with him. He seemed to have been expecting my call. We agreed to meet in thirty minutes at the Daiquiri Deck on Siesta Key. When I rang off, I almost felt as if I'd accomplished something.

22

A favorite meeting place for both locals and tourists, the Daiquiri Deck is a raised veranda restaurant on Ocean Boulevard. Partly a young people's pick-up joint, partly a viewing platform to watch passing foot traffic, and partly just a place to get tasty food and drinks, the Deck is the spot where everybody who comes to the Key eventually ends up.

I took an umbrella table where I could watch for Cupcake, ordered an iced tea, and scanned the menu while I waited. Cora's chocolate bread had helped, but I needed more food in me before I left for afternoon pet rounds. I asked for an order of buffalo shrimp with bleu cheese sauce, and had just dunked a crispy fried shrimp into a bowl of sauce when Cupcake appeared at the top of the steps. Zack was with him, looking suspicious and un-happy.

I waved at them and took a bit of pleasure from the way men's heads turned to watch them walk to me. I had been invisible before, but now every male on the Deck looked at me with new appreciation. Not because I had suddenly become a guy magnet, but because I knew Zack and Cupcake. One or two men actually stopped Cupcake and Zack to ask for autographs, and the others gazed at them with such shining eyes you would have thought the hottest chick on the planet had arrived.

Cupcake and Zack pulled out chairs and sat down without speaking to me. Not in an unfriendly way, just all business. Cupcake eyed my buffalo shrimp and beckoned to a waitress. "Bring two more orders of that, and a Corona on draft. Zack, what do you want?"

Zack looked startled. "Um, I'll have a Corona too."

The waitress scurried away, and Cupcake watched me lay a shrimp tail on my plate.

"You don't eat the tails?"

"I just use the tails as handles."

"Where I come from, people think the tails are the best part."

I opened my mouth to ask him where that might be, but Zack interrupted us.

"Why did you call?"

He sounded like a man who'd been tricked into making an appearance before, only to discover that somebody had merely wanted to be seen with him.

I said, "Zack, I just want to help you find Opal."

Zack fell silent, as if listening to some other voices inside his own head. I guessed some of the voices belonged to his father. A beat passed, and he spoke as if he'd been contemplating speech for a long time.

"It's hard to know what to do, you know? When to give a woman what she wants, and when to be a man and hang tough."

Cupcake visibly tensed.

I said, "Maybe being a man *is* giving a woman what she wants."

Zack moved his lower jaw back and forth as if he needed to line up his teeth.

"Before she died, my mom had to prop her head up with her hand. For two or three years she went around with one hand on the back of her head holding it up. She even drove like that. You'd see her going past, one hand on the steering wheel and one hand holding up her head." He stared into the hot sky. "My dad didn't do a thing to stop her. Not one thing."

"Was there a medical problem that made your mother's neck weak?"

"Nah, she just wanted Dad's attention."

He seemed to be comparing himself to the kind of husband his father had been and finding himself superior. I wondered if he thought Ruby's involvement with Myra had been like his mother's weak neck. Maybe he believed he'd been more of a man because he'd turned against Ruby because she'd worked for Myra.

His lips tightened into a mirthless smile. "The Thanksgiving before she died, she asked Dad if he couldn't say something nice about the big dinner she'd cooked. He said he didn't intend to thank her just for doing her job."

It occurred to me that he was a younger version of Mr. Stern, which was probably why Ruby had been drawn to him. She was familiar with men who couldn't show emotion or give affection.

I said, "Every woman in the world wants attention and praise from her husband, Zack. And by the way, Ruby didn't marry you for your money. She truly loved you."

Zack looked shocked and suspicious, as if he'd caught me trying to put one over on him.

Cupcake heaved a sigh that seemed to have a lot of history with Zack's distrust of women behind it. "When you called, you said you had information. What is it?"

"I think I know who took Opal. And I think we can put our heads together and figure out where she is."

Zack's blue-purple eyes almost disappeared in a skeptical squint. "If you know something, you should tell the cops."

"I'm afraid telling what I know could make matters worse."

I wiped my shrimpy hands on a napkin and leaned forward. I gave them a quick rundown of how Vern had kidnapped me the day before and taken me to Kantor Tucker's place. I told them I believed Myra had seen me in Mr. Stern's courtyard and ordered Vern to grab me. I told them about the young woman I'd seen at Myra's window.

The waitress came bearing beer and two orders of buffalo shrimp. She put a plate in front of each man, but Zack pushed his across the table to Cupcake. Deftly, Cupcake transferred all the shrimp to one plate and handed the empty to the waitress.

As soon as she left us, Cupcake circled a finger the size of a bratwurst for me to go on with my story.

"This morning, after everybody left Mr. Stern's house, I saw both Tucker and Myra leave. I thought the young woman might be in the house with Opal. It was stupid, I know, but I went into Myra's house looking for Opal."

Zack looked disapproving, Cupcake put a whole shrimp in his mouth and beamed at me.

Zack said, "So you like to involve yourself in the affairs of well-known people, is that it? Think you'd like to see your name in the newspaper?"

I felt heat rising to my face. "My name has been in the newspaper several times, Zack, and I hated it. Once was when my husband and child were killed. I know the pain of losing a child, and I hope you and Ruby never feel that pain."

Zack looked chastened.

I said, "Just for the record, I was a deputy for several years."

Cupcake raised a plate-sized hand. "Dixie, there's something you should know too, just for the record. The arson investigators found some nitrous oxide canisters in the bedroom where the fire was. They questioned Zack about them."

"I don't understand."

Zack's voice was bitter. "Pro Modified racers use nitrous oxide to supercharge their engines. I don't do Pro Modified racing, I'm Pro Stock, but whoever started that fire tried to implicate me with those canisters."

I said, "There was a weird sweet smell along with the smoke."

"That would have been the nitrous oxide. It's not flammable itself, but it intensifies fire."

"I don't imagine the kind of people who kidnap babies and set fire to their bedrooms would get all moral when it came to leaving false evidence behind."

"You're right. Sorry to act like an ass. Go on with your story."

I could see why Ruby had fallen for him. He had a problem with expressing emotion, but he made up for it with integrity.

I said, "I went all through Myra's house, but it was empty. I can't be sure, but it looked like somebody had packed a suitcase in one of the bedrooms. Before I could leave, Myra came home with a young Hispanic woman named Angelina. I hid, and I heard enough to know that Angelina had run away from a house where Vern had taken her. He had frightened her so badly that she'd gone out on a highway where a woman picked her up and took her to a bodega on Clark Road. She had called Myra to come get her. Myra was furious at her, and called Tucker to tell him he had to drive Angelina back to where she'd been. She got even more furious when Tucker told her she'd have to do it herself. She said she didn't have time to drive forty miles to deliver Angelina. She had no choice, though, so she promised Angelina that Vern wouldn't bother her again, and they left. That's where Opal is, forty miles away."

Both men stared at me.

Cupcake said, "Forty miles in which direction? In which house?"

Zack said, "This isn't information, it's gossip."

I said, "Think about it. Angelina said there were lots of alligators on the road, on both sides."

Dryly, Cupcake said, "Well, that narrows it down to about every road in Florida."

"Not really. She sounded like the alligators were very close to the road, the way they are along Highway Seventy-two where it goes through Myakka State Park. The alligators along that stretch of road are huge. They'd scare anybody walking along the shoulder."

Cupcake dipped two shrimp at one time into runny bleu cheese. "I don't think there *is* a shoulder on that stretch."

"That's what I'm talking about."

Zack said, "Have you told this to the officer handling the investigation?"

I studied his face, looking for a sign that would tell me he had the imagination to think in a non-linear, non-rote, non-lockstep way. The only thing I saw was a young man dazed by shock and misery.

I said, "If either of you repeat what I'm going to tell you, I'll deny that I ever said it."

Their necks straightened and their eyes widened. Cupcake even stopped eating.

"You know when Myra and Tucker spoke to Ruby this morning? And how Ruby told you she'd been wrong to think Myra had anything to do with the kidnapping? Well, she lied. I heard what Myra and Tucker said to her. They didn't exactly spell it out, but they made it plain that Opal would be kept safe if Ruby zipped her lips at Myra's trial. But if Ruby tells the truth about where Myra put all the money she stole from investors, Opal will be thrown to sharks."

A spasm of pain flickered across Zack's face. He took a long, shuddering breath, his jaws clamped together so hard that his lean cheek muscles quivered.

I said, "If this were a TV show, I'd go tell the investigators and they'd arrest Myra and Tucker, find Opal, and bring her home. But this is the real world, and Tucker is richer than the state of Florida. He probably owns a crooked cop in every county. The minute Tucker becomes a person of interest in Opal's disappearance, one of his informers will call him and warn him. He could dispose of Opal's little body in a million different ways, one of which could be tossing her to alligators in one of those swamps in Myakka Park."

Zack said, "What do you have in mind?"

"First, we have to find out where they're hiding her. Then we have to go in and get her."

A look passed between Cupcake and Zack, one of those *Are-you-thinking-what-I'm-thinking?* looks that old friends do.

Cupcake said, "Chainsaw's."

Zack nodded. "If anywhere, that would be the place."

While I tried to figure out what the heck they were talking about, Zack seemed to go inside himself and wrestle with an inner demon. After a long moment, he looked from Cupcake to me with a stern young face. "Ordinarily, I'd say we had to play it by the book, not play vigilante and take the law into our own hands. But not this time. This time my baby's life is on the line, not some principle."

Cupcake gave Zack a dimpled smile. "Atta boy."

I said, "Who's Chainsaw?"

Cupcake said, "It's a what, not a who. Dive on the edge of Bradenton where lowlifes like baby-kidnappers hang out. Somebody there may know something."

In one fluid motion, Zack stood up and tossed money on the table. "Let's go."

I said, "I'll follow you." No way in hell was I going to let them go without me.

Zack was moving toward the steps to the sidewalk as if the decision to act had galvanized him. Cupcake and I hurried after him.

Cupcake said, "You got a cap or something? Somebody in that place might recognize you."

I had already had the same thought. If Vern or one of the guys who'd kidnapped me hung out at the bar, they'd spot me at once.

I said, "It's in my truck. Also some dark shades."

On the sidewalk, Zack and Cupcake rushed to Zack's convertible and I loped off to my Bronco. Zack waited to pull away from the curb until there was a gap in traffic big enough to let me swing into the street behind him. You can tell a lot about a person by the way they handle being the lead car in a two-car convoy. Whether they're thoughtless or aware, whether they're able to gauge their speed so both cars end up on the same side of a red traffic light, whether they weave in and out of traffic or stay in the same lane. Zack was a good leader. My respect for him was climbing, but I still wished he would be his own man and not let his father push him around.

Chainsaw's turned out to be a squat building in one of Florida's few remaining old fishing villages on Cortez Road, a narrow street connecting Anna Maria Island to the mainland. Grill net bans have mostly put commercial fishermen out of business, but nostalgia and stubbornness have kept a few areas free of high-rises and hotels. Chainsaw's was in one of those moldy places. It sat at one end of an almost abandoned strip center. A Goodwill store was at the other end.

Neither looked as if they were frequented by people living the good life.

23

I parked next to Zack's car in an odd-shaped graveled lot full of potholes deep enough to lose a child in. I rummaged in the Bronco's glove box and dragged out an old black cap with a big bill and a fishing lure embroidered on the front. It had originally belonged to Michael, and it had been in my car long enough to acquire a patina of aged dust. With my ponytail coiled under it and the cap pulled low over a big pair of dark glasses, I felt sufficiently disguised to pass under Vern's nose without being recognized.

Crossing the uneven lot toward Chainsaw's entrance felt as distasteful and dangerous as slogging across the river Styx. To add to the feeling, Chainsaw's entrance was flanked by a row of humanoid figures crudely carved from driftwood. Every head was identical, with round maniacal eyes like sixteenth-century gargoyles. A tattoo parlor next door to Chainsaw's had a big red NO DRUNKS! sign on the front door, but the sign looked as if it was accustomed to being ignored.

Inside, it was so dark that we had to wait a moment to let our eyes get accustomed to the change from bright sunshine. Considering the early afternoon hour, the place was surprisingly crowded. Shadowy masculine figures that looked a lot like the driftwood carvings slumped on bar stools, other men hunched over tables centered by dim lights inside thick red shades. A few heads turned to look our way, but mostly the men seemed too absorbed in their own bored resentment. Florida fishermen have long memories, and they'll never reconcile to being ruined to further tourism and development.

When we could see, we followed a waitress way too old for the loose tank top that revealed sagging bare breasts in front and a mermaid tattooed across her back. She showed us to a table, took our orders, and weaved her way through tables and drunks coming from the men's room. We sat back and scanned the room, not certain who we were looking for, but hoping we would recognize him if he was there. The men at the bar were silent, drinking bottled beer and staring at the wall covered by faded photographs of fishermen and their boats.

To one side of us, a drunken middle-aged man and woman were deep into sloppy pre-coital grins and slurred innuendos they believed were clever. He probably had a wife somewhere at work, but for the moment he was caught in the illusion of being free and desirable. They pushed back their chairs and left as the waitress brought our beers.

With practiced disdain, she watched the couple maneuver through the door with their arms around each other's waists. "Between you and me, that woman's days for making money with her body should have ended about ten years ago. Now she's got it all held together with them elastic underthings, those whatcha-call-'em, Stanks."

I said, "Spanx."

She set our beers down with sharp clicks.

"You go around pushing things out and pulling things in that nature don't mean to line up like that, it's the same thing as lying to God and think he don't know no better."

I said, "You got that right."

"You ain't from around here, are you?"

"Not since I was real little. My daddy was a fisherman. I'm just passing through, wanted to stop here for old times' sake."

"Not many fishermen come here anymore. Mostly just a bunch of scum."

She arched a meaningful eyebrow at a man at a table behind us, and I swiveled in my chair to get a better look at him. Caucasian, wide shoulders, big hands. He could have been one of the men who helped Vern kidnap me, but then so could most of the other men in the downrun bar.

The waitress leaned down and lowered her voice. "If that creep bothers you, you let me know."

Somebody hollered for a refill, and she swished away with her back muscles rippling so the mermaid tattoo undulated.

The creep she'd singled out had an empty pitcher of beer on his table and a half-filled mug. From his flush-faced, loose-lipped scowl, he looked as if he'd already emptied several pitchers.

Cupcake straightened in his seat and yelled loud enough for everybody in the bar to hear. "Hey, sweetheart, my buddy over here's running low. Bring him a fresh pitcher!"

The waitress whirled and stared at Cupcake, then looked at me as if I'd betrayed her. I shrugged and rolled my eyes, a woman-to-woman message that said I wasn't to be held responsible for the dumb things any man did. She did the same eye-roll, and in a minute plopped down a full pitcher of beer at the next table. The man looked up at her stupidly, too drunk to realize what was going on.

In a nanosecond, Cupcake had scooted his chair across the grimy floor to the man's table. "Drink's on me, buddy! We gotta stick together."

A little bit of drool moistened the corners of the man's lips when he grinned. "Schtick together!"

Cupcake said, "Yes sir, me and my other buddy here have been where you are. We know what it's like to be out of work, no paycheck. Man, it's rough! Now we're in the money, we help out our buddies."

The man squinted and frowned. "I ain't out of work. Got a good job."

Zack stood up, dragged his chair to the man's table, and sat down as delicately as a Sunday school teacher. "It's okay, friend. Nothing to be ashamed about. Lots of good men out of work right now."

Red-faced, the man sat as upright as he could manage. "Nah, nah, I'm telling you, man, I got a good job. Big job. Hell, my boss owns this place!"

Zack said, "This bar?"

"No, man! This whole place! All of it!"

His voice heavy with sarcasm, Cupcake said, "You saying you work for Jeb Bush or somebody like that?"

"I'm saying Jeb Bush probably works for my boss."

Cupcake drawled, "But you can't tell us your boss's name, right? We just have to take your word for it."

"Kantor Tucker! That's who I work for! You know who that is? He's big, man. Got a plane bigger than the President's, more money than God. He says jump, everybody else says, 'How high?'"

Zack and Cupcake exchanged the kind of grins adults show when a small child tells a big bragging lie.

Cupcake said, "Friend, I was born in the morning, but not *this* morning. I don't believe you work for Kantor Tucker. If you did, you'd be swilling beer at the Ritz, not emptying pitchers in this dump."

The man blinked as if Cupcake had made a good point in a debate. "I never said I worked *directly* for Kantor Tucker. Not *directly* directly. I work for the man that's Tuck's right-hand man. That's what his friends call him, Tuck."

Zack sloshed beer into the man's mug. "So you work for a bigshot who works for Tucker. We apologize for thinking you weren't important. It must be something to work for a man smart enough to be Kantor Tucker's right-hand man."

The man managed a sneering grin while he took a long pull from his mug, but not without letting beer run down his chin. "He ain't all that smart. And he won't be a bigshot long. To tell the truth, Vern's too dumb to breathe on his own. If I didn't point him in the right direction, he'd screw

up everything he does. Like the other day we were supposed to pick up a woman and take her to Tuck. You know
what Vern did? He got the wrong woman! Can you beat
that? The wrong damn woman! Tuck was some steamed."

I froze in my chair for a second, then relaxed. The guy
was so drunk he wouldn't have recognized me if I'd ripped
off my cap and glasses and danced on his table.

Carefully, Zack said, "I guess old Vern shaped up after
pulling that stunt."

"Nah, he didn't change a bit. Dumb shit got his ass in
a wringer for sure today."

Cupcake pulled his lips back in a fake smile. "What'd
he do, grab another wrong woman?"

The drunk leaned forward in a conspiratorial hunch.
"See, Tuck sent us to get a kid for a friend of his. I don't
know the whole story but I think the friend was tired of
paying child support to his ex-wife so Tuck was helping
him out."

For a second, the inanity of what he was saying seemed
to seep into some of his brain cells, and his head lifted a
fraction as if he might be about to think.

Zack intercepted the urge with a laugh. "Man, I wish I
could have somebody take my kid away from my ex-wife
so I wouldn't have to pay the gold-digging bitch any more
money."

The drunk's chest swelled with pride. "Well, Vern
couldn't have done it without me. See, Vern has this big-
ass limo he uses to drive celebrities and people like that
around, so he parked it behind a vacant house next door
to where the kid's mother lived. He sneaked in the side
door of the woman's house and planted some nitrous ox-

ide to make it look like this race car driver did it. Somebody Tuck has a grudge against, I guess. Anyway, while Vern grabbed the kid and set off a big fire in the room, I went down an alley to another house and got this Mexican woman Tuck had hired to take care of the kid. I led her to the limo, Vern came with the kid, and we took off."

Cupcake said, "Sounds like it went off okay. Where's the screw-up in that?"

The drunk looked as if he might cry at the enormity of Vern's mistake. "We were supposed to leave them in a house, the woman and the kid, but when we got there Vern got horny and put some moves on the woman and she ran away. Just ran out the front door and disappeared in the woods." He slumped in his chair, shaking his head at the memory.

My hands were clenched into such hard fists that my knuckles were frozen in place.

Cupcake poured more beer into the man's mug. "She take the kid with her?"

"Nah, she left it with us. Vern was all for us leaving it there in the house, but when I told him the woman was probably calling Tuck right then, he got scared. He was already in deep shit with Tuck, and Tuck ain't the kind of man to mess around with. So Vern left the kid with me and took off in the limo to look for the woman."

Cupcake said, "So you and the kid were alone in the house?"

"See, that's what I was thinking. I'm in the house with a kid we stole, and Vern's out driving up and down country roads, and the Mexican woman's out there somewhere, and what if cops come looking for the kid? They're going to think I'm the one that took it, and they ain't gonna believe all I did was walk a babysitter to a car, you know? So I got the hell out of there. Walked down Gator Trail to the highway to Arcadia, got a bus to Bradenton, got a cab to bring me here. I don't want to be anywhere around when they find that kid."

I felt a thrill of optimism. We practically had an address!

At some unspoken accord, Zack and Cupcake stood. With Cupcake frowning and towering over him, Zack looked like a skinny kid standing up to the town bully. They tossed a handful of bills on the drunk's table, and then some on mine.

Cupcake said, "Good luck, old buddy."

The drunk grinned at them in sloppy gratitude. They had made him feel important. For a few minutes he had forgotten that he was one of the world's losers, a piece of slag at the bottom of society's barrel. He had enough beer in him to turn his brain to mush and enough ego-stroking from Cupcake and Zack to make him completely ignore the fact that they'd left me alone while they talked to him.

I waved goodbye to the waitress and we got out as fast as possible. Outside, we grinned at one another like happy hounds.

I said, "Arcadia is forty miles from here."

Cupcake said, "Highway Seventy-two goes to Arcadia. Right through the alligator swamps."

Zack said, "We can look for Gator Trail on the map."

If any of us considered that Gator Trail might run for miles and have a hundred houses on it, we ignored the thought. Neither did we let ourselves think of the probable tangle of back sand roads, falling-in houses, and rusty squatter campers around Arcadia. Or the bleak image of a four-month-old baby left alone in an empty house. Or, if Vern had returned, under the care of a man known to be both a kidnapper and attempted rapist.

If we had let ourselves think of those things, hopelessness would have swallowed us entirely. Every minute that passed lessened the probability of finding Opal, and we were elated to have *any* landmark to go by.

Zack said, "Shouldn't go in daylight where they'd see us."

I said, "We'll have to be very discreet. And very careful."

Cupcake said, "She means don't tell your old man what we're doing."

Zack grimaced. "Don't worry."

I said, "What time?"

They both looked at their watches—big silver things with lots of little dials on their faces that probably told the time in every capital of the world, along with the humidity and temperature.

Zack said, "The sun sets early now."

It was true, and my inner coward shivered at the thought of driving through alligators in the dark. It's scary enough to be close to alligators when the sun's shining on them. I sure as heck didn't want to be with them at night.

Zack and Cupcake exchanged a look. Zack said, "We have some things to line up. Phone calls to make, things like that, and it may take some time."

"Phone calls?"

"Nothing about this. It's okay."

I didn't believe him. I thought he was planning something he didn't want me to know about, and that Cupcake knew what it was and approved. But if I said anything more, he might cut me out of the trip altogether. He was, after all, Opal's father and Ruby's husband. I was merely a pet sitter with a personal attachment to his wife and baby.

Zack said, "We'll leave no later than eight." For a skinny kid, he was surprisingly decisive.

We agreed that I would meet them at Zack's place, and we all got into our vehicles and went off to our respective responsibilities.

Personally, I drove off with my blood singing. I was taking action to find Opal. Her father was taking action. A strong athlete was taking action. We weren't passive, we weren't letting Myra Kreigle and Kantor Tucker get away with kidnapping Opal.

I was halfway to Tom Hale's condo for my first afternoon pet visit before I remembered that Guidry planned to make dinner for me that night.

That's another glitch in having a man in your life. As soon as you're a couple instead of a single, you have to coordinate schedules, arrange meeting times and places, get your life organized around an *us* instead of a *me*. Sometimes that's comfortable and nice. Sometimes it's a royal pain in the kazoo. I loved having Guidry in my life, but little pieces of myself seemed to have floated off when I wasn't looking. I needed to pull them back in.

24

Morning or afternoon, I usually spend a good half hour at each pet's house, so that seven or eight pet calls take at least four hours. Add to that travel time and the extra time some calls need because a dog needs extra cheering up or a cat requires some premium cuddling, and it can take five hours. But that afternoon I cut all the visits short.

Tom Hale was working at his kitchen table when I arrived at his condo, and only waved hello. I was glad, because I didn't want to take any chances of slipping up and telling him what I was going to do when I finished afternoon rounds. Billy Elliot had to be content with only one lap around the parking lot. He seemed a little puzzled, but wagged his tail in forgiveness when I told him I had to go look for a missing baby. That's the neat thing about pets. You can trust them to keep your secrets.

All the other clients were cats. Every cat got petted and given fresh food and water. Every litter box got cleaned. But that was it. No cuddling, no games of chase-the-ball or leap-for-the-peacock-feather. It was strictly a no-frills afternoon. I explained the reason to each cat, and I solemnly promised that I would make it up to them on the next visit. Each one listened to me with the royally benign tolerance that only a cat can bestow on a human.

After the last pet visit, I swung by Mr. Stern's house, where a van was parked at the curb. It looked innocuous, but I was sure it was manned by an officer monitoring phone calls. If no ransom demand was made within the first twenty-four hours of Opal's kidnapping, the sheriff's department would call in the FBI. I was sure nobody would call to ask for money. Opal's kidnappers didn't want money, they wanted silence.

I still considered myself on the job for Cheddar, so I called the Victim's Assistance Unit of the sheriff's department for the name of the hotel where they'd taken Mr. Stern and Ruby. Whenever a crime or fire leaves a family homeless, Victim's Assistance puts them up in a hotel, gives them emotional support, and makes arrangements for whatever they need. At the hotel, the desk clerk rang their suite and got permission for me to go up to see them.

Ruby opened the door to the suite and stepped aside to let me in. Behind her, voices murmured on a TV.

She said, "Granddad's gone back to the animal hospital to be with Cheddar."

"Is he okay?"

"Granddad or Cheddar?"

"Both."

"The vet says Cheddar could go home tonight if he had a home to go to. Granddad's sad and worried."

On the TV, the volume rose for breaking news. "Zack

Carlyle's kidnapped baby still hasn't been found. Police have issued an appeal to people in Florida and Alabama to be on the lookout for a woman named Doreen Antone. She is believed to be traveling north toward Alabama. Her sister in Alabama says she has not heard from her and does not believe she would kidnap a baby. Antone's parents also say kidnapping is not something their daughter would do."

A quick clip of a harried-looking older couple flashed on the screen, with the woman saying, "We raised our daughters right. Doreen wouldn't do nothing like that."

They were replaced by a photograph of Opal, and then a grainy snapshot of the cleaning woman when she was much younger and slimmer.

The announcer pressed on. "Antone's former boyfriend, Billy Clyde Ray, has told investigators that Antone had been depressed since giving birth to a stillborn infant six weeks ago. Ray says he has not seen Antone for over a month and does not know anything about the baby's kidnapping. He is considered a person of interest in the case, but the sheriff's office stressed that Ray is not a suspect, merely one who might have important information."

Ruby stared woodenly at the set. If she was offended that Opal was identified as "Zack Carlyle's baby," she didn't show it. I whirled to the TV set and turned it off.

"Ruby, are you sure you're doing the right thing?"

For a second, she seemed to consider pretending not to know what I meant, then dropped it.

"I was a fool to think I could go up against Myra and Tuck."

"But you can't let them—"

"I have to. I'll have a terrible case of amnesia at Myra's trial. I won't be able to remember a single detail of what I saw while I worked for her. I won't remember anything about Tuck being involved in her business. I won't remember a name or a date or an offshore account. I won't remember a thing."

"And then?"

"Then I'll go to prison and Opal will live. She'll even live well. While I'm in prison, she'll have a nice home with a kind person to take care of her. She'll be well fed and healthy."

I had to make an effort to make my mouth work. "How can you be sure of that?"

"I know Myra. She's a piranha when it comes to money or business deals, but she was like a mother to me when I needed one, and it wasn't an act. She'll make sure Opal gets good care."

I couldn't think of a thing to say. As much as it broke her heart, Ruby had analyzed the situation with cold logic, and she'd made the only decision that would save her baby's life. And I knew she had the terrible and wondrous strength to follow through with it.

I said, "Ruby, the other woman I saw in Myra's house looked like a kind, caring woman."

She licked dry lips. "You think she's the one they got to take care of Opal?"

"I think it's possible."

The hope in her eyes was pitiful. "And she seemed kind?"

"She did."

Stumbling backward, she sank to the edge of the hotel bed.

Even though I knew it might not be true, I wanted to tell her that her husband and I were going with Cupcake to rescue Opal. Instead, I said, "You're a strong woman, Ruby. You'll get through this."

Ruby closed her eyes and rolled onto the bed with her back to me. I touched her ankle lightly and left her. There was nothing else for either of us to say.

The sun was about three hours higher in the sky than usual when I got home. Paco's truck was in the carport and Ella wasn't in my apartment. Michael wouldn't be home until the next morning.

As soon as I was inside my apartment, I called Guidry.

"Could we do supper early? I'm really beat, and I need to go to bed early."

He didn't exactly jump at the idea, but he agreed. I told him I'd be at his place in an hour, and stepped into a hard-driving warm shower. I let the spray unsnarl some of the kinks in my muscles. I shampooed my hair and shaved my legs. I used a buffing thing on my heels and elbows to make my skin silky smooth. That's another thing about having a man in your life. You make sure nothing will snag on any of your corners. Besides, I might get killed that night, and I didn't want to leave life with stubble on my legs.

With a quick slide of lip gloss and a touch of blush, I hurried to my closet-office, pushed stuff around, and chose a short khaki skirt and a crisp white shirt. With a cool raffia belt and the shirt sleeves rolled partway up, I looked casual but a little dressed up. I added a string of pearls to

peep from under the shirt, a couple of slim silver brace-
lets, and stepped into linen espadrilles with tall heels. If I
say so myself, I looked damn good.

I'd never been to his house before, but I knew Guidry
lived in a small stucco bungalow a stone's throw from Siesta Key's business district. The yard had the look of being
cared for by efficient professionals who trimmed with
more haste than love. A small front porch needed sweeping, and a spiderweb stretched across the front door in a
sure giveaway that Guidry entered and exited the house
through a door in the attached garage.

I rang the bell. Guidry opened the door with the web
hanging between us like an unreliable lifeline. He swat-
ted it away, and I stepped inside.

The house had the same easy elegance Guidry has: polished concrete floors the color of old copper, a wall of
books, black leather furniture, Mission-style tables, big
plush pillows in rough textured fabric, standing swing-
arm architect lamps, and a sound system playing soft jazz.
No window coverings except wooden louvered shutters.
Pure Guidry.

The only surprise was that Guidry wore jeans and a
T-shirt. The jeans were plain worn Levi's and the T-shirt
was ordinary white cotton. Seeing him in faded jeans
was like seeing him naked, only I'd already seen him naked and he'd looked as elegant without clothes as he did
in designer linen. Jeans were something else. Jeans erased
an invisible line that had been drawn between us. Jeans
said he was on my team.

We stood and looked at each other for a long moment,
then came together like two magnets drawn by forces

preordained. Have I mentioned that Guidry is a great kisser?

Oh, yes, he is.

When we finally came up for air, he rubbed his thumb across my jawline and smiled down at me. I'm always shocked at those moments of seeing him vulnerable. Shocked and a little scared. I don't want another person's happiness in my hands. It's too much responsibility. I might fail.

I said, "What brought on this urge to cook?"

"I know how much you like to eat, so I thought I'd better start feeding you. Besides, I want to talk to you about something."

There it was again, that something he wanted to talk to me about. I caught a glint of apprehension in his eyes that scared me. Whatever he wanted to talk to me about was something he dreaded.

"Is it about Opal?"

"Who?"

"The baby that was kidnapped."

"No, nothing like that."

"Then what?"

"Later. First we have to cook."

We?

I followed him into a kitchen that was bigger than mine, but looked the same—a room where not much cooking got done. On the countertop, he had assembled a stack of lasagna noodles, some cheese, some cans of tomatoes and sauce, and several jars of seasonings. My brother would have looked at that collection and felt the thrill of challenge, a zippy bubble in the blood that comes from delight. I looked at it and saw tomato spatters, pasta paste, cheese gunk, a huge mess to clean up.

For a few seconds, we stood staring at all the ingredients, suddenly awkward as two people who'd somehow landed on the moon at the same time.

Guidry said, "I've never asked, but do you cook?"

"Of course I cook."

"What?"

"Are you going deaf?"

"I meant what do you cook."

I felt a little panicky. I boil eggs. I scramble eggs. I heat soup. I make salads, both green and tuna. I can even make pancakes from scratch. But with a brother who's not only a great cook but loves to feed everybody he knows, I've never been *called* to cook much.

I said, "What were you planning?"

He looked as if he'd caught my panic. "Ah, I got this stuff for lasagna. You like lasagna?"

"Sure."

"My mother makes it with sweet Italian sausage and ground turkey, so I got some. Also some ricotta cheese, parmesan cheese, and mozzarella cheese."

He waved a hand at the assemblage on the counter. "I got lots of stuff."

I had a sudden image of him calling his mother in New Orleans and asking her how to make lasagna. I doubted he had ever made it in his life. I doubted he had ever even *watched* anybody make it. That made two of us.

I took a deep, measured breath. I smiled. "You have wine?"

"Good Chianti."

"Okay then. Let's do this."

I felt a surge of confidence. We were going to be okay, Guidry and I. We were going to make dinner together. We were going to work smoothly together the way happily married couples do. We were going to join our talents and our energies and produce something wonderful.

It's a wonder bluebirds didn't pick up the dish towels and fly around the kitchen with them. Or that rose petals didn't drift from the ceiling and settle on my shoulders. I was that goofy.

25

Twenty minutes later, the sweet Italian sausage was sizzling in a big pot on the stove and Guidry no longer looked like a way fine homicide detective. He looked like a man with a shiny forehead and a T-shirt with a meat-juice stain across the chest. Personally, I was chopping onions at the narrow counter beside the sink while holding a bleeding finger well away from the knife blade. I had wrapped a paper towel around my nicked fingertip to soak up the blood, but it was still a little oozy. I suspected I'd smeared blood on my face when I wiped away onion-chopping tears. And all the time I chopped and wept, my mind kept going to Opal, with quick awful glimpses of terrible things that could be happening to her.

Guidry was equally subdued. No easy banter like the kind in Michael's kitchen while he cooked. We worked like convicts in a prison kitchen.

While the sausage fried, Guidry consulted scrawled directions—I'd been right, he'd called his mother—and then brought all the jars of spices to the counter where I worked.

He said, "I was supposed to get fresh basil, and I got dried."

With my eyes streaming tears from the onions, I looked up at him and forced my hand not to wipe at my face. "I think dried would be okay."

"Yeah, but how much? What's the dried equivalent of a half cup of chopped basil?"

It was downright pathetic that he thought I'd know that.

A burning odor caught our attention, and we turned to see billows of dark smoke rising from the big pan where the sausage fried. Guidry swore and ran to jerk the pan from the heat while I ran around opening cupboard doors. I think I left some blood smears on some of them.

He said, "What are you doing?"

"Looking for a fire extinguisher."

"It's not a fire, it's just smoke."

I wrapped a clean paper towel around my bleeding fingertip and came and stood beside him. We looked at blackened links of sausage in the skillet. The oil they'd been burning in was black too.

I said, "I think you're supposed to take the casings off the sausage before you fry it."

"You sure?"

"That's what Michael does. Then while it fries he sort of mashes it around to break it up."

"Well, we can't use this burned stuff. Do you suppose the sausage part is vital?"

We looked at the package of uncooked ground turkey

waiting on the countertop. At the rate we were going, it would be midnight before we got all those layers of noodles and cheese and meat stacked in a pan. It might be even later before we managed to make a decent sauce. I had appointments I couldn't do later. I pushed my folded shirtsleeves higher on my arms. Somehow both sleeves had acquired black marks. Also some mystery stains that might or might not be my own blood.

I said, "I don't think cooking lasagna is our thing."

Guidry had burned a finger. The burn looked as if it would soon blister. He blew on it and looked glum.

He said, "Let's do what we should have done in the first place. You call the pizza place while I clean up this mess. We'll talk in the living room."

I gave him a grateful smile, but behind my smile I was scared. He wanted to talk about something important, and I was afraid of what he wanted to say. He'd said it wasn't about Opal, but I couldn't think of anything else that would make his eyes get that wary look, like he didn't want to tell me something that had to be told.

While Guidry made clean-up noises in the kitchen, I phoned for pizza, antipasti, and cannoli in the living room. I found Guidry's bathroom, which was almost tragically clean and neat. Recessed lighting, round marble sinks with shiny chrome faucets arched so tall you could wash a dog under them. Not that Guidry ever would. Thick brown towels so plush that after I splashed water on my face and washed away onion and smoke damage, I patted myself dry with a tissue from a sleek brown box on the counter.

I resisted an impulse to slide open wide mirrored

doors on a medicine cabinet and look for Band-Aids. Just because we were a couple didn't give me the right to snoop. Well, it sort of did, but my finger had pretty much stopped bleeding, and I didn't want Guidry to think I'd been in his medicine cabinet. I made a neat wrapper out of toilet paper and went back to the living room.

Two glasses of red wine sat on the big square coffee table. Candles were lit and the lamps were turned low. Soft jazz cooed from hidden speakers. I took a deep breath, slipped out of my shoes, and settled into the corner of one of the matching sofas.

Guidry brought a stack of plates to put on the coffee table, along with enough paper napkins to blot up the BP Gulf oil spill. He had cleaned up too, dried the sheen on his forehead, changed into a fresh T-shirt. He took a chair kitty-cornered from me, toed off his leather sandals, and put his feet on the coffee table. He had elegant feet. Long and slim, with smooth toenails. I wondered if he got pedicures.

I lifted my own pink-nailed feet onto the coffee table and raised my glass of wine to make a toast.

He said, "What happened to your finger?"

"I just nipped it a little bit while I was chopping onions."

"You want a Band-Aid?"

"No, it's fine."

I held my glass up again. "Here's to ordering pizza!"

He grinned and raised his own glass. "Amen!"

We sipped wine, we smiled at each other, we waited for the doorbell to ring with the pizza. And whatever Guidry wanted to tell me slinked around us with a sly grin on its sneaky face.

The pizza delivery came while we were still on our first glasses of wine. Guidry padded barefoot to the door, paid the guy, and came back balancing some big bags atop a huge flat pizza box.

He said, "What'd you do, order one of everything?"

I shrugged. "I worked up an appetite chopping those onions."

He spread it all out on the coffee table and for a few minutes we were too busy organizing stuff on our plates to talk. Then for a few more minutes we were too busy chewing and swallowing. In spite of myself, my scatty mind went to Ruby and Mr. Stern, caromed to Opal, then looped to Zack and his uptight father. While I'd watched Ruby and Zack together that afternoon, it had been obvious they loved each other. Zack was wrong not to trust Ruby, and Ruby had been wrong to take Opal and leave him.

I said, "Ruby and Zack are both good people. They're just young. They don't know yet how precious every moment is. If they had played their lives differently, they could have made a good home for Opal."

Guidry put his slice of pizza on his plate and leaned forward to set it on the coffee table. He took a sip of wine and studied my face.

He said, "You'd like to have another baby, wouldn't you?"

I was so shocked that I had to remove my feet from the coffee table and sit up straight to stare at him. "Why do you think that?"

"Well, for one thing, we weren't talking about the Carlyles. And for another, when you talk about babies, you get a look."

"I do not."

His eyes were sad. "No kidding, Dixie, would you like to have another baby? We've never talked about it, and we should."

I suddenly felt the same way I'd felt several weeks before—when I'd jumped into the bay to save a woman and been under water longer than I could hold my breath. In that watery blackness, I had felt blind, clawing panic, and that's what I felt now. I had only recently got over irrational guilt for replacing my dead husband. I certainly wasn't prepared to talk about replacing my dead child.

I slammed my plate on the coffee table and stomped to the bathroom, where I stood panting in front of the mirror over the sink. Staring at my flushed face and blazing eyes, I had one of those out-of-context memories that carry important messages. This one was about the first crack I had seen in my parents' marriage. I had been about five, and I remembered watching my mother dress for a Bruce Springsteen concert in Tampa. She had worn a skirt so short her legs seemed to go on forever, and she and my dad had argued about it. He thought it was too revealing and she thought he was a prude. They were still arguing when they came home hours later, and from my bed I'd heard my dad say he'd lost all respect for my mother when she took off her panties and offered them to Springsteen. The Boss hadn't taken them, and my dad said that showed how inappropriate she'd been.

The memory had surfaced off and on all my life, the way childhood memories of quarreling parents will, but now for the first time I saw it from an adult woman's perspective. Viewed that way, I imagined my mother had felt so humiliated at being rejected by Springsteen that she couldn't forgive my father for witnessing it. Somehow that insight helped me calm down and look at my own situation from an adult's perspective.

I didn't feel humiliated by Guidry's question. I even recognized that it was a reasonable question for a man to ask. But it had stirred up emotions and memories that I wasn't yet ready to visit, and I wished he hadn't asked it. Guidry had no children, and now I wondered if that was because of circumstance or design. I wished I didn't wonder that, because it might change something between us if I found out he didn't want children. I truly hadn't considered having another baby, but some day I *might*, and I wished he hadn't forced me to consider it.

I slid open a mirrored door on his medicine cabinet and found a box of Band-Aids. His razor was on a shelf, and some shaving cream. I didn't look at anything else. I put a Band-Aid on my finger, replaced the box, and stood a few more minutes to be sure I could talk without weeping or losing my cool.

I must have stayed in the bathroom a long time, because when I went back to the living room, Guidry was asleep on the sofa. He felt me beside him and opened his eyes. He held out his hand and I sat down next to him.

He said, "I was insensitive. I'm sorry."

When a man already knows what he's done wrong, there's not much to say.

"I'm just not ready for it yet."

"That's what made it insensitive. I'm sorry."

Maybe it was because I didn't want to talk about babies as a possibility for myself. Or maybe it was because I just wanted to deflect attention from myself. Whatever, I wasn't able to talk about babies in general without talking about Opal in particular. I decided I couldn't keep the secret about Myra and Tucker being behind Opal's kidnapping away from Guidry.

I said, "If we're going to have an honest relationship, we have to share what's going on in our lives."

Guidry looked contrite. "Dixie, I've been offered a job with the New Orleans Police Department."

"*What?*"

"I'm sorry I haven't told you. It just never seemed like the right time."

I heard a tinny ringing in my ears. "What are you going to do?"

"It's a good offer. I'd head up the homicide division. I'd be a part of rebuilding my city."

The buzzing in my ears got louder, with replays of every conversation Guidry and I had ever had about New Orleans. His family lived there, he'd grown up there, his roots were there. It was his passionate love for the city that had pushed me over the edge into falling in love with him.

I sat on his black leather sofa and looked at all the Italian food on the coffee table. I was sorry I'd ordered so much. Sorry I'd mentioned Opal. Sorry the evening was ending dark and bent as a stubbed-out cigarette.

I said, "You've already decided to take it, haven't you?"

"I wanted to talk to you first."

It was a lie. He may have *wanted* to talk to me before he made the decision, but the decision had probably been made at the moment the offer was proffered. New Orleans was as much a part of Guidry as Siesta Key was a part of me.

We stared into each other's eyes with all our unspoken fears and hopes exposed like naked corpses.

Guidry said, "The city is struggling to recapture its soul. A lot of its heart and talent and love and laughter left with the people who were driven out of flooded homes. Artists and musicians and cooks, generations of families. They want to come back, but a lot of them don't have anything to come back *to*. I want to help rebuild. Not just neighborhoods, but the police department too. New Orleans law enforcement officers tolerated corruption too long. But when the levees broke, crooked cops ran like rats. Now that the department is free of them, they're starting over with a clean slate."

His voice slowed to a trickle. "I guess what it comes down to is that my awareness of belonging to something larger than myself is rooted in memories of growing up in New Orleans. Those memories call to me."

I completely understood because the same memories of Sarasota called to me.

Woodenly, I slipped my shoes on and stood up. "I have to go home. I can't talk now."

He rose too, and touched my arm. "We could make it work, Dixie."

He meant marriage, living together in New Orleans, making a life together there.

I said, "I can't think now."

He leaned down and kissed my forehead. Tenderly, the way people kiss a dead person at a memorial service.

"I love you, Dixie."

I touched my open palm to the side of his face. "I know you do."

26

I drove home on autopilot, feeling light-headed and weird, caught between a future that could be completely different than the one I'd always imagined, and a past that would always be a part of who I was.

I was shocked at the idea of Guidry moving away, shocked at how I'd reacted when he'd told me. When Todd and I were together, I would have followed him to another continent. Why was I so disturbed at the idea of moving to New Orleans with Guidry?

I didn't think it was because I loved Guidry less. It was more that I loved me more. I'd worked too hard at learning to be at home in the person I was to abandon that person. And I wasn't sure I'd still be me if I moved away from the Key, where I was a part of every grain of sand on the beaches. I had to decide how far love can stretch, how much it can remold you and reshape you and leave you glad you've changed.

If I went to New Orleans, I'd be somebody else, and there was no guarantee I'd be comfortable as somebody else. If I ended up hating the person I became after I went with Guidry to New Orleans, I'd no longer love him either. And I knew, with a terrible awareness, that Guidry feared the same thing was happening to him, that he was losing himself away from his beloved New Orleans. If he did, he would lose his love for me.

There was another factor that I'd never considered until this evening, but now I had to look at it. When my little girl died, a part of me had died with her. I'd never expected to have another baby. I hadn't wanted another baby. But now that Guidry had forced the issue, I felt the idea nibbling at the edges of my mind, and I wasn't sure I wanted to push it away.

Guidry had been right when he said we'd never discussed the possibility of us having babies together. Now it seemed strange that we hadn't. Even stranger was that I had no idea why Guidry and his ex-wife hadn't had children. I should have known something that important. I should have asked if their childlessness had been by choice. More specifically, whose choice? If Guidry didn't want children, I should know that. Not that I wanted to have a baby, but someday I *might*.

I thought about Ruby and Zack, and how their love had become diseased by bitterness and distrust. Had they chosen to have Opal, or had she come as a fortunate accident? If Ruby went to prison and Opal was spirited away to live someplace with Angelina, Ruby and Zack would never have a second chance to create a family. They would suffer the loss, but Opal would suffer more.

In an ideal world—one in which I made all the rules—everybody's drinking water would contain birth control chemicals. Consenting adults could screw around all they wanted to. They could fall in love, out of love, break people's hearts and have their own hearts broken. They could spend all their money, gamble it away, or stuff it down a rat hole. They could live as selfishly as they wanted for as long as they wanted.

But if a couple decided to have children, they would have to pass rigorous tests of character and kindness and good humor. They would have to prove they were responsible people with the ability to provide a good home, medical care, and education for a child. They would also have to agree to stay together for the rest of their lives, and swear that if something went wrong in their relationship they'd damn well fix it. Only then would I issue the antidote to the birth control chemicals.

Turning down the drive to my apartment jerked me back to reality. I didn't run the world, I wasn't married or pregnant and might never be again, and any decision I made about moving with Guidry to New Orleans would have to be made later.

At home, I was glad that Paco was inside the house with Ella. If I hurried, I might be able to leave for the trip to Arcadia without lying about where I was going. Upstairs in my apartment, I hurried to change clothes. I kept the lace underwear on. If I got killed trying to rescue Opal, at least I'd look good when people viewed my body. But when it came to outerwear, I chose tough. Faded jeans, a hooded black T, and a pair of sturdy boots.

I chose tough for accessories too. I got them from the secret drawer built into my bed's wooden frame. The drawer was custom designed to hold my guns—some that had once belonged to Todd and some that had been my own off-duty guns. Always cleaned, oiled, and ready for use, they lie in special niches inside the drawer. I'm qualified on all of them, but my favorite is a sweet five-shot J-frame .38. With its black rubber grip, stainless steel barrel and cylinder, it's lightweight and easy to slip into a pocket. No safety levers to think about, no magazines to fail. It was the perfect weapon for the night's mission.

I picked the revolver out of its niche, slid it into the back of my jeans, and pushed a couple of filled speed loaders into my pockets. Then, fully armed with lipstick, lace underwear, and revolver, I headed out to meet Zack and Cupcake.

Every civilized person knows that violence of any kind is the ultimate admission of failure. Whether it's between individuals or between nations, it points to a level of ignorance or stupidity or laziness too profound to resolve grievances with words or compromise. But if I had to shoot somebody in order to save Opal, I wouldn't hesitate for a nanosecond.

Zack's property—his home and adjacent race shop—was on the southeast side of Sarasota county, one of the few spreads still immune to developers and gated communities. A flush of twilight still lingered on the western horizon when I arrived at a gate blocking the entrance to Zack's tree-thick property. The gate was wrought iron, with a design of a race car worked into the bars. Through the gate, I could see a neat frame house set under oaks and pines, with a green lawn that looked as if somebody gave it careful attention.

A double-decker transport van sat beyond the house on an immaculate paved area in front of a long, low building with an open front. The building looked somewhat like an automotive repair shop, with tools and auto parts hanging on the back wall, a row of new tires along the side, and a pit in the center with a rack for lifting a car overhead. There were also several things I didn't recognize, like a couple of metal frames that looked as if they'd been designed to fit inside a gutted car. A black Chevy Camaro with rusty spots on its fenders was angled on the pavement in front of the garage's open bay doors. Several other vintage cars were parked to the side.

I rolled to the ubiquitous security station, pressed a button, and waited for a human voice to ask my business. In this case, the human voice was gruff and male.

I said, "I'm Dixie Hemingway."

The voice became gruffer. "Wait for the gate to open."

The gate parted, and I rolled into a parking lot that quickly filled with a throng of men.

Zack came to my window. "Some of my friends have come to help."

One by one, men with grim faces stepped forward to shake my hand through the car window. They looked at me hard in the eyes, as if they were taking my measure.

Cupcake stood to the side watching them.

With all that testosterone, an argument was bound to start. Zack and Cupcake immediately got into a debate over which car we should use, while the other guys offered grunts of agreement or dissent.

Zack wanted to drive one of his race cars because it was faster. Half the other men thought that was a good idea. But Cupcake argued that he and I should ride in the same car with Zack, and Zack's car only held one person. I didn't understand why it only held one person, but if that was its limit, Cupcake was obviously right.

Raising my voice over the male ones, I said, "My Bronco sits high and has plenty of room."

A dozen heads tilted down to look at me, a dozen pairs of eyes registered surprised respect that I had an opinion.

Zack said, "No speed."

Cupcake said, "Don't need speed, bro."

With a broad dimpled grin at me, he lumbered to the Bronco, wriggled his bulk into the backseat, and leaned back like a maharaja waiting for his elephant to carry him where he wanted to go.

Zack turned to the other men. "Okay, stay connected. I'll keep you informed. When it's time, we'll put the plan into action. You know what to do."

I didn't know what their plan was, but there were immediate nods, back-slapping, and words of agreement. The men walked off to cars parked beside Zack's home race shop. Those cars didn't look like they'd make it to the end of the block. But men got inside them—one man to a car—started growling engines, and sat waiting for Zack to lead the way.

I saw Zack's father looking out the front window of the house. He did not look happy.

As Zack got into the front passenger seat of the Bronco and belted up, I noticed that he wore a wireless phone clip on his right ear.

I said, "Would one of you like to tell me what's going on?"

Zack did a rolling motion with his hand. "We'll fill you in on the way."

I didn't have an option. I could go under Zack's terms or not at all. When I turned the ignition key, Zack watched my hand as if he doubted I had sense enough to drive. I goosed the Bronco a little bit to give it a macho sound, and we sailed through Zack's gate.

On Clark Road out of Sarasota, I looked at Zack's profile and wondered what was going through his mind. Athletes have always been a mystery to me, and drag racers were an even bigger mystery. I was beginning to realize that drag racers have to be more calculating and deliberate than other athletes. They're more in competition with themselves than with other racers, and speed is only one component of the competition. The rest is about timing and fuel and precision, things that take intense focus.

I looked over my shoulder to see if the other cars were close behind us, but Cupcake took up so much space that I couldn't see out the back window. He smiled at me when I looked back. He really did have the sweetest smile I'd ever seen.

Outside Sarasota, Clark Road becomes State Road 72, a stark two-lane highway edged by pines and oaks dripping gray moss like old men's beards. The highway runs due east to Arcadia, the only incorporated community in DeSoto County. Arcadia is a town of survivors. On Thanksgiving Day in 1905, it was destroyed by a fire that started in a livery stable. A century later, on Friday, August 13, 2004, the city was almost destroyed again by Hurricane Charley. Arcadia still depends primarily on agriculture for its economy, but it has reinvented itself as a tourist attraction for antiques lovers. People drive from miles around on Sundays just to eat a good country breakfast at one of their restaurants and shop in their antiques stores.

Along the highway, bridges span boggy swamps where giant alligators stretch themselves as if posing for tourist photos. Fields of cabbage palms harbor rattlesnakes. Orange groves and fields of ragweed are neighbors to fenced pastures where heat-tolerant Senepol cattle raise their smooth polled heads to look at passing cars. Turkey vultures circle fresh carcasses of small deer or wild pigs struck by speeding trucks. An occasional mailbox atop a post marks a dirt lane twisting to an old Florida world that will soon be extinct.

I drove with both hands on the wheel, careful around frequent twists in the road, imagining how terrifying it would have been for Angelina to hitchhike along this gator-edged highway. Large alligators are awesome animals. They consume anything that comes close to them. Tourists who underestimate their speed or ferocity have been known to lose a family pet to them.

When we were halfway to Arcadia, Zack said, "I looked up Gator Trail on the Internet. It intersects State Road Seventy-two a few miles this side of Arcadia. Just before Horse Creek."

He sounded as if everybody in Florida knew where Horse Creek was. Maybe they did and I was the only one who didn't.

I said, "Uh-huh."

In my rearview mirror, I could see headlights from a line of cars snaking behind us.

We ate up a few more miles and Zack spoke again. "About two years ago, some coyotes crammed a bunch of illegals inside a refrigerator truck and smuggled them into Florida. They dumped them in a house somewhere outside Arcadia and left them. Men, women, and children. They were all half dead from dehydration. Some of them died."

Cupcake said, "People shouldn't be treated like that."

Zack said, "The thing is, Myra Kreigle owned that house. I remember it because Ruby and I had just started dating, and Myra's name caught my attention. The police talked to her, but she claimed she didn't know anything about any smuggling. The police believed her, but now I wonder if she was in on the whole thing."

I said, "Do you remember where the house was?"

"Some place outside town."

Arcadia is edged by makeshift communities of tin-roof shacks and old mobile homes on dirt roads. As if he realized the futility of looking for Opal in any of those places, Zack went silent and still.

I said, "You promised to tell me why your friends are going with us. And let me just say, for the record, that I think it's a bad idea. We'll attract too much attention."

From the backseat, Cupcake said, "Tell her, bro."

Zack seemed to try to collect his thoughts. I had the feeling that racing came a lot easier to him than speech.

He said, "They're just coming along in case we need them. You know, safety in numbers, that kind of thing."

I could almost feel Cupcake's eyes roll at the way Zack had evaded the question. Zack didn't want to share his plan with me, and that was that.

I said, "We're getting close to Arcadia. Watch for Gator Trail."

Almost immediately, Cupcake said, "There's Horse Creek!"

A neat white rectangle low to the ground announced that Horse Creek lay directly ahead. Before we got to it, another well-painted sign at a blacktopped road announced Gator Trail. It seemed as if the entire universe had entered into a conspiracy to help us find Opal. First we'd got information about where Vern had left Opal, now there were signs to direct us. How much better could it get?

I made a sharp turn onto Gator Trail, amazed at how fortunate we were. I was sure we had lucked out, big time.

Somewhere, a donkey probably laughed.

27

As I turned onto Gator Trail, Zack mumbled something into his headset, and instead of turning with us, the line of cars behind us went straight over Horse Creek. In the side mirror, I watched their taillights pull to the shoulder and park half hidden under the trees.

I refused to ask why they weren't following us to the house. I supposed Zack had given them instructions. I supposed he and his racer friends had arrived at some kind of plan that seemed logical to them. Something told me I might be happier not knowing that plan.

Faint light from a rind of moon carved shallow pools in Gator Trail's unlit, single-lane blacktop. Our headlights cut a tunnel between a dark tangle of scrub pines, oat grass, conifers, mossy oaks, and palmettos on each side of the road.

Cupcake gestured toward the black silhouettes. "Wild hogs live in there. They come out at night to forage. During the day they dig holes to sleep in." He sounded as if his skin crawled at the thought.

I didn't want to think about those feral hogs. As ferocious as alligators, wild hogs are not choosy about what kind of flesh they eat.

After a mile or two, the road made a sharp right, but my headlights caught something on the left that made me stop, back up, and turn the Bronco left.

A decades-old sign almost hidden by brambles and tall weeds announced the entrance to Empire Estates. A second sign warned: NO TRESPASSING! RESIDENTS AND GUESTS ONLY!

The sign had been formed by wooden blue letters nailed to a white board, but the blue paint had crazed like old china, and the letters hung at dipsy angles. Beyond the sign, our headlights picked up the gleam of a white sand road so encroached upon by trees and underbrush that it was narrow as a cart trail. Once the entrance to a luxury retirement community, the broken sign and silver road were all that was left of failed hopes.

Cupcake said, "Somebody's been stuck."

Ahead on the road, tires had eaten deeply into sand and left two long furrows. The humped ridges reminded me of the way loggerhead turtles throw up piles of sand while they dig their nests. But we were a long way from loggerhead nesting grounds, and a different kind of reptile had made those furrows. Most likely, he had done it in a black limo with tinted windows.

Zack said, "Heavy car, too much speed for sand."

Cupcake said, "Locals would know better."

"Yup."

An explosion of light and an impatient honking sound made us all jerk and look out the rear window at a tall pickup. The truck's engine thrummed with the impatient energy of a motor prepared to roll over anything in its path. Praying the truck wasn't driven by one of Tucker's goons, I leaned out my window to get a look at the driver. It was a woman, and she looked like she was on her last nerve.

In half a nanosecond, I was out of the Bronco and trotting to the pickup. The woman had her window rolled down and an elbow resting on the frame.

I said, "Gosh, I'm sorry! I didn't see you back here! The thing is, I'm not even sure I'm on the right road, and when I saw how somebody had got stuck in the sand, I was afraid to go on."

She didn't smile, but the hard look in her eyes softened. "Yeah, some fool got stuck there. Big old black limo with a numb-nuts driver."

I said, "Oh God, I'll bet that was my crazy old uncle's driver. That's who I'm looking for. He's my mother's brother, and she's worried about him."

She perked up at the thought of my crazy old uncle. "He lives around here?"

"Well, that's the thing. He lives in Tampa, but he owns a house around here somewhere—I think it's on this road, but I'm not sure. He's rich as all get out, has a big black limo and a driver, more money than good sense, to tell the truth. Anyway, he told my mother he was going to come stay in his house down here for a few days. He's probably all right, but I promised my mother I'd check on him."

The woman took her elbow off the window frame to get down to dissing my crazy uncle.

"Only one house it could be. You go about a mile and then turn at the first right. It's about a half mile down. Mailbox at the road, but the house is behind trees. Nobody lives there, but every now and then you'll see several cars there. I always figured something hinky was going on in there, gambling or women or something. But we don't stick our noses in other people's business out here, you know?"

I looked at the bleak landscape of tall weeds and overgrown trees. "Doesn't look like many people live out here."

"Only a few of us. Most are mobile homes or RVs. We all know each other, watch out for each other. But that house is one nobody knows about."

I could tell she couldn't wait to spread the news about my rich uncle and his eccentric ways.

I said, "You think I can drive through that sand and not get stuck?"

"You just got to be careful, is all. Don't hit it hard."

"Actually, I think I'll skip it. If his limo driver was here this morning, then my uncle's fine. I'll get out of your way now."

I sprinted back to the Bronco and pulled it back to the main road so the woman could drive through the Empire Estates entrance. She tooted her horn and waved at me as she drove past. At the rutted sand, she slowed to a crawl and eased her way through.

Zack said, "What?"

"She said a black limo got stuck in the sand. Also said there's only one house where nobody lives full-time. Sometimes cars are parked there, but most of the time it's empty. She told me how to get there."

Zack twisted his torso around to look at Cupcake. They exchanged some kind of silent communication that made them both solemnly nod their heads.

Zack fingered the phone speaker attached to his ear and spoke quietly. "We're on the road to the house. Stand by."

Turning to me, Zack said, "Dixie, after we talked to you, Cupcake and the other guys agreed on what we'd do if we found out for sure that Opal was here in a house."

"What's your plan?"

"I'll explain it later. Let's drive on."

Everybody wanted to wait until later to tell me important things. I hate later.

I said, "You're not afraid we'll get stuck too?"

He shook his head. "Different tires, different weight, different driver."

We rolled on, straining to see ahead, our tires gnawing their way through the ruts Vern's limo had left. The road got more narrow and uneven, with deep holes dug by rain and time. We bumped along until we came to a side road with a rotting sign that gave a street name we couldn't read. There were no houses on the road. Evidently, the Empire Estates hadn't sold well. At another intersection, we drove to the end of yet another lurching sandy road. The car's motor hummed in concert with the whine of mosquitos rising from the surrounding palmettos and sawgrass.

After about a mile, the road made a right angle. Another

quarter mile, and Zack's forefinger pointed toward a copse of trees ahead. "A house is in there. Pull over."

I couldn't see it, and from Cupcake's silence I didn't think he could either. But a metal gate ran across a driveway that one could assume led to a house, so I pulled to the road's edge and parked. I could barely make out a chain running from a gatepost to the top of the gate, but I knew people rarely lock gate padlocks. Too much trouble for the owners to get out of their cars and unlock the things every time they go through, so the chains only serve as notice that the place is off-limits. If you drive in, you could be shot for trespassing. If you sneak in like we intended, you could be shot and displayed on a metal spike as a warning to others.

We sat panting like stressed dogs for a moment, then Zack pushed his door open and slid out of the car. I leaned to grab my 4-C-cell flashlight from the space between the front seats, touched the .38 at the back of my jeans to reassure myself it was still there, and got out too.

With flashlight and gun, those two "weapons of opportunity" that no cop is ever without, I felt as if I were back in uniform. Hit somebody on the head with a gun barrel, that's using a "weapon of opportunity." Hit them with the handle of a flashlight, that's another "weapon of opportunity." With the woods full of feral hogs and other swine, I figured I needed all the weapons of opportunity I could lay my hands on.

Cupcake got out last, squeezing his bulk through the opening like an enormous baby being born of a Bronco. We stood a moment beside a ditch that ran beside the road, getting our bearings and letting our feet get accustomed to the lay of the land before we moved forward. On the other side of the ditch, a swath of sawgrass lay silvered by wan moonlight. Beyond the sawgrass, a dark morass of trees and shrubs led to the spot where Zack thought he'd seen a house. As I looked across the ditch, I made out the dark outline of a vulture in a skeletal cypress tree. It may have been my imagination, but it seemed to me that the bird turned its head and looked at me.

Speaking low, Zack said, "When we get there, we'll go to the front door and engage whoever's inside while you go around to the back door. You'll go in and look for Opal. When you find her, you'll bring her out and get in the car. When we see you, we'll leave."

"That's your plan?"

He nodded solemnly, his head bobbing like a shadow puppet against the muzzy night. "The other guys will cover our backs."

I stifled a nervous giggle. He had left out so many moves that it was almost funny, except I knew very well what those moves were going to be, and it wasn't at all funny.

Cupcake leaned forward and spoke close to my ear. "If you want me to, I'll go inside with you. Just in case you need muscle."

That made me actually sputter a laugh that sounded like the bark of a teacup chihuahua puppy. Zack was a Boy Scout with a keen mind for electronics and motors and speed ratios and probably a lot of things I didn't know diddly about. Cupcake was a mountain with a sweet smile and dainty feet who could stop other mountains carrying footballs. But when it came to rescuing Opal, they were babes in the woods. In a few minutes I would be confronting hardened criminals, and all I had for backup were two innocent children.

I said, "I have my gun."

Zack said, "You won't need that."

Cupcake said, "Nah, we won't need no bullets."

From the tone of their voices I knew they were thinking I was a female on the verge of hysteria.

Zack pointed into the thick growth beside the road. "Okay."

Zack and Cupcake crossed the ditch and melted into the shadows under the trees, and I followed them. Cupcake led the way, his massive bulk pushing through palmetto fronds like the prow of a boat winding through mangroves. I walked in his footsteps, close enough to his broad back to avoid being hit by swishing fronds, and Zack brought up the rear, plodding stolidly through swarms of mosquitos and veils of spiderwebs. Every now and then one of us would catch a toe on an exposed root and stumble with whispered curses.

Above us, the tree canopy was so thick it blotted out every glint of night light. Below us, our shuffling feet stirred composted leaves that gave off a dank odor of mold and mildew mixed with animal urine. We moved through a timeless place that would have been cheerless even in bright sunshine. In the darkness, it seemed downright sepulchral.

After what I judged to be about the length of a football field, Cupcake stopped, held his left forearm out to the side, and waggled his fist. The movement must have been some sort of code for Zack, because he touched my shoulder and mimed for me to veer right and come up at the rear of the house.

This was apparently the moment when Zack and Cupcake expected me to slip into the house and grab Opal while they chatted up her kidnapper at the front door. It was a stupid plan, but for the moment it was the only plan we had.

Zack and Cupcake angled to the left and continued parallel to the road, while I tried to guide myself in a kind of arc that would take me to the back door of a house I still hadn't seen. I wasn't even positive Zack had seen it. For all I knew, all that lay ahead was more of what we were in.

Without Cupcake's back to shield me, I walked with one hand raised to touch tree trunks and hanging palm fronds before I stumbled into them. With every step, I prayed my booted toes didn't disturb a rattlesnake's sleep or catch the attention of a marauding wild hog. To my left, the trees along the road had thinned to a narrow strip, but I didn't see any sign of Zack or Cupcake.

After a century or two, I spotted a weak light glinting through a narrow gap in the curtain of trees. Cautiously, I navigated a shallow ditch and continued forward through undergrowth and low branches.

The dark rectangle of a tall house emerged in such sudden relief that it startled me. Like a lot of Florida real estate gone to seed, the house had probably been built as a summer getaway with living quarters upstairs and a screened "Florida room" downstairs. Its redwood siding was blackened by mildew and mold, and in the screened lower half, where somebody had once planned to hold neighborhood get-togethers, a few lawn chairs sat at awkward angles. Upstairs, a dull light shone through a small square of opaque glass—most likely a bathroom window—but I didn't see any movement behind it.

In its dark isolation, the house had the appearance of a melancholy memory of things best forgotten. As my eyes adjusted to its shape, I made out the outline of a compact sports car parked on a depressed graveled area to my left. It appeared to be red, probably a BMW. The last time I'd seen a car like that, it had been leaving Myra's house.

A twig cracked with the sound of a pistol shot. It could have been Zack or Cupcake who stepped on it. Or a lookout guarding the house readying his gun to empty into me. Or an owl peering down to see what fool thing a human was doing.

Around me, the night had gone silent, the way it does when an intruder causes nature to hold its breath. No tree frog chirps, no screech owl cries, not even whirrs of insect wings. As if it bore witness, the night waited for the house to divulge its secrets. Cautiously, I moved to the back of the BMW and dropped to my knees. From that angle, I could make out the rectangular frame of a door set in the screened lower half of the house.

A blurred silhouette moved behind the opaque glass of the upstairs window, and then the window went black. The shadow behind the glass was adult-sized, but it could have been male or female. In a minute heavy footsteps thudded down invisible stairs, and a man-shaped shadow moved through the gloom behind the screen. I had hoped it was Angelina, and a nasty taste of disappointment burned my throat when the door opened and an unmistakable man stepped out, furtively catching the screen door before it slapped shut. He was broad-shouldered, muscular, looked as if he could defend himself in a fight. He could have been Vern. Or he could have been one of the men with Vern when I was kidnapped. Or he could have been an innocent man who lived in this house and had no connection to Vern at all.

He walked a few feet away from the house and lit a cigarette. In the flare of the lighter I caught a momentary glimpse of his features. Not enough to identify him, but enough to see that he was Caucasian and clean-shaven. He smoked in concentrated drags, pulling on the cigarette as if he wanted to reduce its length in a hurry. I couldn't see any sign of a weapon, but that didn't mean he wasn't armed.

My heart pounded so loud I was afraid he would hear it. I wondered if Cupcake and Zack were watching the man too, or if they were at the front door of the house. As naïve as they'd seemed about the dangers in what we were doing, I could imagine them drawing straws to see who would knock.

A muffled wailing noise sounded from inside the house, and the man spun as if the noise frightened him. Flipping his cigarette to the ground, he jerked open the screen door and charged through, letting it slap shut with a sharp cracking sound. The man's dark outline melded with the blackness inside the screened enclosure, and in a minute the dull crying sound stopped as abruptly as it had started.

My mind ticked off all the possible sources of the oddly muted sound. It could have been a cat mewing. It could have been the sound of an electronic alarm of some kind. But I believed it had been a crying baby. I believed it had been Opal. Not Opal crying in a baby's normal cry, but in a way that had been strangely baffled. My mind backed away from images of all the possibilities for that dulled sound, along with reasons the crying had stopped so abruptly. I clung to the hope that Angelina was in the house, and that she had rushed to pick Opal up and give her a bottle. The chances of that being true seemed fewer every second.

The red BMW was an unexpected worry. Myra wasn't the only person in the world who drove that model, but its presence seemed too coincidental. Myra had left Sarasota in a car that looked like this one to bring Angelina to this house. If her car was here, that had to mean she was here as well. But why would Myra be upstairs in that unlit house with the man who had come downstairs?

A nagging voice in my head suggested that the BMW belonged to the man who had tossed away his cigarette when he heard his baby cry. His wife might be working in town while he watched their child, and Opal and Angelina might be miles away in another house.

28

Something wide loomed at my side and set my heart chuddering.

Cupcake's hoarse whisper cut through the darkness. "Is that you, Dixie?"

My own whisper sounded too much like a bobcat's hiss. "Yes! Where's Zack?"

"In front. A limo's hidden in the yard."

For a moment I felt elated at the presence of a limo, because it had to mean that Vern was in the house. Unless it was somebody else's limo. In the next moment, the futility of what we were doing suddenly came in waves. Our entire trip was insane. We were insane. We had strung together a theory based on a story told by a drunken braggart at a bar, then leaped to follow directions from a woman who might have been having fun with visiting yahoos, and set off into dark woods where we could get shot by a limo-driving homeowner who heard us blundering around his property.

So low my words were more exhaled than spoken, I said, "I'm not sure Opal is in there."

I could hear Cupcake's breathing. He probably used up as much oxygen in one breath as most people take in ten. When he spoke, it was in the same exhaled whisper I'd used. "We're not sure it's *not* her, either."

I couldn't argue with his logic, and for a moment I argued our case to an imaginary judge with a robotic voice. I admitted that even though any thinking person could have driven a fleet of trucks through the big holes in our evidence, we weren't entirely off the wall in thinking Opal was inside that house. We weren't hundred percent kooks, only maybe seventy-five percent. But as I told the imaginary judge, if everybody waited until they were positive before they took risks, no babies would ever get rescued.

The imaginary judge was not impressed. He reminded me that if my evidence was sound enough to justify my hiding in the darkness with a loaded gun stuck in the waistband of my jeans, it was sound enough to notify the local law enforcement office. The imaginary judge got specific. He suggested that I call Sergeant Owens and fill him in on all the information Zack, Cupcake, and I had collected. He stressed that Owens could then pass the evidence on to the FBI agents when they joined the case so that county, state, and federal agencies could team up and come streaming to our side.

The imaginary judge must have read too many action comic books or seen too many episodes of *CSI*, because his idea of how the law worked was laughably unrealistic. Following his advice would mean losing critical time

trying to convince disbelieving law enforcement professionals that a leading citizen of vast wealth was behind
the kidnapping of a baby, and that the baby was being
held in a remote house outside a little town forty miles
from the kidnap site. Even if we succeeded in convincing
them, vital time would be lost while various agencies
sparred over who had jurisdiction. After that was settled,
a search warrant would have to be issued for an address
we didn't have, something that could take several hours.
And while we waited for the wheels of justice to make
their agonizingly slow turns, the likelihood was high that
word would leak to Kantor Tucker. If that happened,
Opal would be disposed of before anybody went looking
for her.

We had no choice but to save her. Furthermore, Zack's
idea of going to the front door and distracting the kidnapper while I went in the back and got Opal no longer
seemed so squirrelly.

Hunkered beside me, Cupcake seemed to realize I'd
come to a decision. "Now?"

I took a deep breath and nodded. "Let's do it."

I'm not sure what I expected him to do, but it wasn't
what he did. Still squatting on his heels, he lifted his head
and whistled. Not a referee kind of whistle, but a long,
quivering, mournful trill like a screech owl makes, starting low, rising to a tremulous wail, and abruptly ending.
An answering cry came from the darkness at the front of
the house. Hearing one screech owl's eerie cry in the dark
woods is enough to make rational people look over their
shoulders for ghosts. Hearing two raises the hairs on the
back of your neck.

Cupcake grinned, his white teeth flashing like the Cheshire cat's smile.

In the next instant, a loud pounding cut through the darkness, a sound like a heavy stick hammering against a front door.

At the same time, a man's drunken voice yelled, "Hey, Clyde! Open up! It's me, Leon! Clyde? I know you're in there! Open up! Hoo-ya! Hey, Clyde! You hear me, Clyde?"

It took a minute for me to realize the drunk at the front door was Zack.

The house remained dark and silent.

The pounding got louder and Zack's voice raised to a sharp-edged roar that half the county could probably hear. "Come on, Clyde! I got women coming! Open the door! Women are behind me, good-looking women! They wanta meet you, you old dog! It's Leon, dude! We gonna party! We gonna party hardy! Woo-ha!"

Cupcake touched my shoulder. "Let's roll."

For such a large man, Cupcake moved across the sandy yard with surprising speed. With me behind his elbow, he went through the screened door and moved directly to the wall-hugging stairway to the upper floor. With my flashlight's barrel resting on my shoulder, I gripped it by the bulb end and followed Cupcake to the second level.

The open doorway to the second-floor living space made a black rectangle against a dark gray interior. Cupcake took one side of the opening and I took the other, both of us angling our heads into the space to look into a large open room. Windows were open for ventilation, but what little air drifted in was heavy and humid.

A man stood at a window facing the road. The window had venetian blinds and the man had pulled one slat up to peer through. Downstairs at the front door, Zack continued to make a loud racket. In the night's stillness, the noise could be heard for miles. The man apparently knew that, because his entire body jittered with increasing nervousness.

Cupcake eased his bulk around the door facing and flattened himself against the wall. I followed his lead, pressing my back against the wall beside the door. So the whites of my eyes wouldn't give me away, I tilted my head back and lowered my eyelids to look through thin slits. I was afraid Cupcake wouldn't know to do that, but he had the same chin-up profile. Probably learned in Indian Guides or Boy Scouts how to slip through darkness. He must have also learned how to sneak up on a man listening to a drunk's yelling, because he melted into the shadows and moved toward the front window.

I heard no baby sounds, smelled no baby scents. Their absence was alarming. Perhaps the cry I'd heard earlier hadn't been Opal after all. Or perhaps it had been and she had been permanently silenced.

Thrashing, clattering, grunting sounds at the front window told me that Cupcake had reached the man and taken him by surprise. I couldn't see the fight, but I recognized the sickening sound of fists hitting bare skin, and the hoarse choking sound of somebody's breath cut off by a squeezing hand or by the edge of a stiffened palm hitting a hyoid bone. Cupcake was bigger, but the other man was obviously familiar with dirty fighting. Downstairs, where Zack couldn't hear the fight, the yelling and pounding continued.

I had to have light to find Opal. With my big flashlight still resting on my shoulder so it pointed down, I thumbed the switch to make a wide circle of light. The room's dark periphery where Cupcake and the man fought was now a lighter shade of black.

I moved the light along the wall to my right, where a double bed with a mussed yellow chenille bedspread was shoved against the wall. In the center of the room was a sagging sofa, a reclining chair with white stuffing spilling through cracks in the fake leather upholstery, a card table, and some folding chairs. No crib, no playpen, no sign of a baby.

In the far corner beyond the bed, an apartment-sized range and refrigerator made a kitchen area, along with an abbreviated countertop with a sink. A gathered plastic skirt hid the pipes under the sink. A door was ajar at the edge of the kitchen area. I imagined the door led to a bathroom, but I'd have to pass through the fighting men to get to it. Sweeping my light slowly around the room to illumine every inch, I scanned the room with mounting panic. When I moved the light across the spot where Cupcake and the man continued to thrash and grunt, I saw two straight chairs pushed against the wall behind them. Myra Kreigle was in one, Angelina in the other. Both women were bound and gagged, with duct tape over their mouths like Vern and his goons had put over mine. Myra's eyes were furious and demanding. Angelina's were terrified and pleading.

I had to make a decision, and I had to make it fast. The women's presence meant the plans Myra and Tucker had made had gone terribly wrong. The man fighting Cupcake was stuck with Myra as a hostage and Angelina as a witness to a host of crimes. If Vern's buddies were outside watching Zack, they knew Cupcake and I were inside, and any second might find them up the stairs and holding guns on us. We could end up as trussed and helpless as Myra and Angelina.

To get to the bathroom door and look behind it, I'd have to pass through the fight. To get to Angelina and set her free—setting Myra free was not an option—I'd also have to pass through the fight.

In the nanosecond that I weighed choices, my light caught Cupcake's eyes and caused him to stumble backward against the venetian blinds. In the bright light, his nose streamed blood, and his eyes had the astonished look of a Goliath realizing that a smaller man might best him. Taking advantage of Cupcake's momentary loss of balance, the other man's hand dipped toward his ankle in a move that made me spring forward. My flashlight's handle made a satisfying crack on the back of his head, and he sagged to his knees.

Cupcake surged upright and gave me a dimpled grin. "You got some jiggy moves, girl."

I pulled my .38 from the back of my jeans and pointed it at the man's head.

It was Vern. He recognized me at the same time I recognized him.

Dazed, he sputtered, "Who? Wha . . . ?"

I said, "Cupcake, he has a gun in an ankle holster. Get it. He may have a knife too, so pat him down."

The look Cupcake gave me was probably the look a man in a bar gets when he realizes the woman he's been flirting with is his sister in a wig.

Vern was even more confused. "Who the hell are you?"

I said, "Long story, Vern. Where's the baby?"

His swelling eyes took on a sly look. "What baby?"

I spun away from him and pushed open the door to a miniscule bathroom. No tub, just a metal shower enclosure. No baby inside it.

Zack had stopped yelling, which either meant he had seen the light behind the blinds or that somebody had grabbed him and silenced him.

I ran to Angelina and grabbed an end of tape covering her mouth. I said, "Sorry, but I have to do this."

Tears sprang to her eyes when I ripped the tape off her lips. I knew exactly how she felt.

I said, "Where's the baby?"

She began to weep in earnest. "I do not know! I hear baby cry, but is dark and I do not see!"

Behind the tape on her mouth, Myra made a guttural sound of demand and jerked her head and shoulders side to side.

I said, "Cupcake, you got a knife?"

He grunted and moved to Angelina's chair. While he cut through the tape holding her hands and feet, I turned back to Vern. He was getting his wits back, no longer swaying with dizziness.

I put the barrel of my revolver against his temple. "Here's the deal, Vern. As far as I'm concerned, men who harm babies should be strung up by their gonads and left to turn slowly in the wind. I could do that. Or I could kill you and save somebody else the trouble. If I kill you, the cops will pin it on the guy you left here today with the baby. They'll think he waited until you came back and then he shot you in the head. So if you have any interest in staying alive, tell me where the baby is, and I'll think about letting you keep breathing."

The thing about making threats to low-life people is that they only believe you if you really mean what you say. At that moment, I meant every word. I don't know if I would have carried out the threat, but when I said it I thought I would. I wanted to do Vern serious harm, and he knew it.

He licked his lips. He shifted his eyes back and forth. His Adam's apple bobbled.

He said, "Under the bed."

Behind him, Cupcake was helping Angelina stand, and she was stamping her feet to get life back into them. Myra squealed with fury and flashed her dark eyes. The bitch expected us to rescue her, set her free, have compassion for her. Tough titty.

I ran to the bed, dropped to the floor, and raised the ratty chenille bedspread to peer under it. All I saw among the dust bunnies and dead spiders was a small cedar chest, the kind southern women store their woolen sweaters in. With my heart pounding, I dragged the box out and opened it.

Surrounded by a putrid odor of old urine, Opal lay atop a skimpy bed of rumpled T-shirts. Her eyes were closed and her breath was so shallow I was afraid at first that she was dead. Tenderly, I scooped her up and clutched her to my chest. Then I stood up and ran down the stairs and outside. I was almost to the front of the house when I heard Cupcake's thundering footsteps and Angelina's whimpers behind me.

Zack materialized out of the gloom, his pale face grim and rigid.

I said, "I have Opal!" I didn't add that she was sleeping with a stillness that could only come from drugs.

He said, "Come on!" If he noticed Angelina, he didn't say anything.

With Angelina's soft cries and Cupcake's heaving breath behind us, we raced across the sandy yard, floundered across the ditch, and thrashed through weeds like rogue elephants on a rampage. At the road, we ran like hell. Or at least Zack and I did. Angelina was slow and Cupcake hung back to steady her. Halfway to the Bronco, he flung Angelina over his shoulder like a sack of flour.

A crack of rifle fire sounded behind us. I hollered, "Fan out! Serpentine!"

Zack said, "What?"

Cupcake wheezed, "Zigzag!"

As we reached the Bronco, I heard a car engine start. I was sure Vern didn't intend to chase us in his heavy limo, but Myra's car was light and available.

Zack yelled, "I'll drive!"

No argument from me. I said, "Keys are in the ignition!"

Setting Angelina on her feet and slinging open the back door so she could crawl inside, Cupcake wrenched open the front passenger door, helped me maneuver in with Opal in my arms, then flung himself in the back. Angelina's face was wet with tears, but she looked relieved.

Zack started the engine and moved the car slowly forward. Headlights flashed behind us. Zack turned on our own lights and goosed the Bronco through the sand as fast as he dared. More rifle shots sounded.

Cupcake said, "I sure hope he's a bad shot."

I said, "If he hits us it'll be pure dumb luck. But it might be a good idea for you and Angelina to hunker down so your heads aren't sticking up."

Zack said, "You do that too. You and Opal."

I slid to the edge of the seat so I wasn't such a good target. Nobody spoke the fact that Zack's head was sticking up in clear outline. Preoccupied with driving and muttering instructions to his friends on the highway, he probably didn't even think about it.

29

We made it down the bumpy sand road to Gator Trail without being shot. Vern drove too fast and too erratically to get off a hit. He even managed to get stuck for a minute in the same furrows he'd made with his limo. Vern was a perfect example of a man who never learned from his past mistakes.

Zack drove carefully until we turned onto Gator Trail, and then it seemed to me that we were going faster than my Bronco was meant to go. But Zack held the wheel with such a sure touch that I decided we must not be going as fast as I thought. Then I looked at the speedometer and realized we were going even faster. Cars must recognize the touch of an expert driver and pull out all their reserves.

Vern slewed onto Gator Trail behind us, and fired off another couple of shots. The idiot must have thought he was in a movie. At the juncture with State Road 72, Zack slowed to let Vern get closer, and then at the last moment cut the Bronco hard to the left. As he did, a line of clunker cars appeared out of the darkness to form an L-shaped barrier that forced Vern to make a sharp turn to the right.

Tires screamed. Metal screeched. The BMW slewed, slammed broadside into the railing over Horse Creek, lifted on one side for a moment, and then rolled over the railing.

I said, "Vern went into the water."

Zack said, "Too bad."

Cupcake sighed. "Pull over, man."

Zack grimaced, but he edged the car to the side of the road and stopped. Cupcake hauled himself out of the backseat, hiked back to the bridge, and disappeared down the embankment toward the water. Angelina whimpered under her breath. I imagined she feared that Cupcake would bring Vern back to ride with us, but I didn't have the energy to reassure her. The other drivers had gathered on the bridge to look over the broken railing. The men on the bridge were silent.

While we waited, I pulled my cellphone from my jeans pocket and dialed Sergeant Owens. When he answered, I spoke tersely.

"I'm in DeSoto County with Zack Carlyle. We have his kidnapped baby. We found her in a house where Vern Brogher was holding her. He also had Myra Kreigle and another woman bound and gagged in chairs. We left Myra in the house. The other woman is with us. She's a witness to several crimes. Vern Brogher has had an accident in which his car rolled into Horse Creek. Cupcake Trillin has gone into the river to rescue him. Zack and I are going to take the baby to her mother at the Charter Hotel on Midnight Pass Road. I'd appreciate it if you'd have a physician meet us there and examine the baby. She seems healthy, but I think she's been drugged."

Several beats went by.

Sergeant Owens said, "Horse Creek. Charter Hotel. I'll get on it right away." Owens has never been what you'd call an effusive man.

I ended the call and shoved the phone back into my pocket. I patted Opal on the back. I hummed a little tune close to her ear. Her breath was warm on my neck.

The Bronco's engine rumbled under the hood as if it objected to sitting still. Zack looked as if he had the same objection. After several minutes, one of the men on the bridge trotted to us and leaned through Zack's window.

"Cupcake fished the son of a bitch out. He's alive. Cupcake's holding him until the cops come. We'll wait for them. You go on."

Zack said, "Thanks, man. For everything."

He revved the engine and pulled back to the highway.

For some reason known only to babies, Opal chose that moment to wake up. Still groggy from whatever Vern had given her, she pulled her head back from my chest and gave me a goofy grin.

Softly, I said, "Hey, Opal."

As if she understood that she was out of danger, she gurgled a half-laugh.

Zack turned his head and stared at her as if the sound shocked him. Then he laughed too, a rollicking sound of pure joy.

30

Halfway back to Sarasota, we met several speeding green-and-whites from the sheriff's department. Their sirens were blaring, and I knew they hoped to get to Horse Creek before deputies from DeSoto County arrived there. A little farther on, we met TV vans with uplink dishes sprouting from their roofs like mushrooms. The reporters inside were probably salivating like blood-hounds at the idea of filming the arrest of the man who had kidnapped a famous race car driver's baby, only to be saved from drowning by a famous inside linebacker for the Bucs. I still didn't know what an inside linebacker was, but Cupcake was a man I was proud to know.

Opal drifted back to sleep, waking every few minutes with more alert awareness. She smelled to high heaven, and she was so wet that she'd soaked through my sweat-shirt. When we got to Sarasota's outskirts, I pointed to a strip center where a 7-Eleven was open.

"We need to get diapers for Opal."

Zack looked surprised, as if the idea of diapers was

alien to him, but he pulled into the lot and cut the engine.

I said, "Get the Size Two kind. I think they'll fit. And get a box of wet wipes too."

"You want *me* to get them?"

"Yeah, Zack. You're her father."

A smile flitted across his face. "How about baby food? Should I get something for her to eat?"

"Good idea. Maybe some strained fruit. We can go for other stuff later."

From the backseat, Angelina said, "I get it."

She had her hand on the door handle, ready to jump out. I pushed the child-lock gizmo on my door to make it impossible for the back door to open.

I said, "Zack, hurry."

He must have understood that Angelina intended to run away, because he slid out of the car, slammed the door closed, and went into the 7-Eleven at a fast clip.

I said, "Sorry, Angelina, but you have to stay with us. You must talk to the police, tell them everything you know."

Wide-eyed with fear, she said, "Mr. Tucker will kill my mother."

"Mr. Tucker is going to jail, Angelina. He won't hurt you or your mother. But you have to tell what you know about him and about Myra Kreigle."

"That man at the house."

"Him too. The man's name is Vern. They're all going to jail, Angelina."

She didn't trust a word I said, and continued to push against the door as if sheer force would make it open.

Inside the 7-Eleven, Zack was talking to the cashier and gesturing toward the car. The cashier looked through the glass at us, then hurried from behind the counter and led Zack behind an aisle. In a moment they hurried out, both of them carrying items in their arms. From the enthusiasm of the cashier, I figured he must have known who Zack was. I was sure of it when I saw Zack hand him cash and then write something on a slip of paper. I guess famous people can't even buy diapers without leaving autographs.

Back in the car, Zack looked quickly at Angelina, then handed me a package of diapers and a plastic bag holding a clutter of baby food jars and a box of baby wipes. As he backed the car from the parking place, Angelina moaned with despair.

By the time I got Opal cleaned and changed, my nose was wrinkled and Zack looked as if he might barf at the odor.

After I stuffed the soiled diaper in the plastic grocery bag, he said, "Holy shit!"

I laughed. "Just normal baby shit, Zack. Find an open Dumpster and I'll throw it away."

"Do they all smell like that?"

"Just when they haven't been changed for twelve hours. Opal always smells sweet and clean. She has a good mother."

"You think I'm a real horse's ass, don't you?"

"I don't know what kind of ass you are. All I know is that a baby needs both parents."

"Ruby left me. She took our baby and left."

I couldn't argue with that.

I said, "I'm just guessing here, but did your father have anything to do with her leaving?"

He took so long to answer that even Angelina stopped whimpering to hear what he had to say.

"Dad never trusted her."

"How many women would you say your dad *does* trust?"

He took even longer to answer that. "I can't think of any."

"Zack, was your mom a good woman?"

"She never said a mean thing about any human being. Never did a mean thing in her life."

"But your dad didn't trust her."

He sighed. "Okay."

We rode silently down Clark Road, crossed Tamiami Trail where Clark Road becomes Stickney Point Road, and rolled over the drawbridge to Siesta Key. At Midnight Pass Road, Zack turned toward the Charter Hotel. I wanted to ask him what he planned to do about Ruby, but I kept quiet. Opal was wide awake now, lying on my lap looking around with eyes so dark blue they were almost violet.

Zack said, "My mom's eyes were like Opal's."

I didn't remind him that he had the same eyes. It was possible that he'd always been so focused on electronics and speed that he'd never taken a good look at himself in the mirror.

When we pulled into the Charter Hotel parking lot, we saw several sheriff's cars, an ambulance, and a few ubiquitous panel trucks from TV stations. Angelina moaned again. She apparently thought all the attention was for herself.

Zack pulled under the hotel portico, where a uniformed bellman stepped forward. "Sorry, sir. You can't park here. We're expecting somebody the police are meeting."

Zack's eyes narrowed. "I believe we're the somebody. Tell the cops to keep the reporters away while we get out of the car."

"I can't park it for you, sir. We don't have the insurance to cover valet parking."

It was such an inane non sequitur that Zack tilted his head back to look under his eyelids at the man. "Maybe you can get one of the cops to park it."

As he spoke, a uniformed deputy tapped on my window, and I turned my head to see Deputy Jesse Morgan peering in at me. Morgan is the Key's only sworn deputy. He and I have had occasion to meet over dead bodies enough times for him to believe that I have a dark cloud over my head. I was happy that this time was different.

I lowered my window, smiled at him, and tilted my chin toward Opal.

He said, "Ms. Hemingway," but he looked past me at Zack. From the excited gleam in his eyes, I almost expected him to ask for an autograph like the 7-Eleven guy.

I said, "Officer Morgan, this is the baby that was kidnapped this morning. We're taking her to her mother here in the hotel, and we'd appreciate it if you'd keep the reporters away from us."

"We'll do our best, but you know how it goes."

I knew that journalists were allowed anywhere in the public viewpoint, as a sidewalk or street or right of way, and they could take photos from any of those places. A business or a hotel open to the public is considered a public place, but hotel lobbies and hallways are gray areas, sometimes considered private and sometimes public, depending on the nature of the crime committed there. Since most journalists operate under the philosophy that it's better to be chased away than to be denied permission, I expected a volley of shouted questions to surround us when we left the car.

I said, "The woman in the backseat is a witness to several crimes. She is also a flight risk. She's frightened, and with good reason."

Morgan leaned down to look at Angelina. "Yes, ma'am."

He straightened and beckoned to a cluster of deputies at the edge of the portico. They trotted over, Morgan gave them quick orders, and when I released the child-lock control, they opened the back door and took Angelina into custody. They were gentle, but very firm. As they led her away, she looked over her shoulder at me with anguished reproach. Clearly, she didn't trust me any more than she trusted Myra.

The waiting journalists had only given the Bronco a passing glance. They must have expected Zack to arrive alone, zooming in like Batman with his baby on his back. They clearly hadn't expected a dusty SUV with a man and woman in the front and another woman in the back. But when a covey of journalists saw uniformed officers lead Angelina to a sheriff's car, they turned toward us like vultures sniffing carrion.

At the same moment, through the glass wall of the hotel lobby, I saw Ruby burst from one of the elevators. Her arms were already outstretched to hold her baby. I knew if she came outside she would be surrounded by a cacophony of bright lights, shoving reporters, and shouted questions. Zack saw her too, and had the same reaction as I did.

Simultaneously, we opened our car doors and ran toward the hotel entrance. Startled by the movement, Opal began to shriek, and I pulled her close to shield her from the lights and noise. We loped across the marbled lobby and met Ruby in the middle.

She was luminous and wild. I think if anybody had tried to stop her, she would have torn them to bits with her hands. I put Opal into her arms and Zack rushed to put his arm around them both. Behind us, Morgan and some other deputies arranged themselves in a meager phalanx in front of the entrance doors.

With Zack half-pushing, half-pulling Ruby, we ran across the lobby to the bank of elevators.

As we stepped into the elevator, I heard Morgan shout to the reporters. "Get a grip, people! You are not allowed to follow anybody to their hotel room. You are not allowed to wait outside their hotel room. If you want to camp out here in the parking lot, that's your business, but if any one of you tries to infringe on a hotel guest's rights, you'll be arrested."

I was impressed. I'd never seen Morgan so decisive.

Opal was still howling, and Ruby was crying while she tried to examine her for bruises or cuts.

I said, "She doesn't seem to be hurt."

Ruby wailed, "Why is she so *filthy*?"

Zack and I exchanged a look, remembering how much filthier she had been before we got clean diapers for her.

I said, "Did the sheriff's office send a physician?"

"He's in the suite with Granddad."

Zack stiffened. "Your grandfather's with you?"

She shot him a hostile glare. "He's an old man, Zack. His house almost burned to the ground this morning. Where else would he be?"

Zack seemed about to make a snappy retort, then crimped his lips into a straight line. I had the feeling they had argued about Ruby's grandfather and Zack's father so many times they had a repertoire of one-liners they could spit out on cue. I wished Cupcake were there to sweeten their practiced sourness.

When we got out at Ruby's floor, I saw Mr. Stern standing in the hall like a sentinel. Zack's jaw hardened when he saw him, the look of a young warrior preparing himself for battle against an older, more seasoned combatant.

But instead of taking a snarky attitude, Mr. Stern held his hand out to Zack. His eyes were fierce, but not with anger. As if she recognized him, Opal's cries subsided to droning hiccups.

Mr. Stern said, "Young man, let me be the first to tell you how much I admire what you did. That took guts. Real guts like most men your age don't have anymore. It's a privilege to shake your hand."

Abashed, Zack said, "Thank you, sir. But I didn't do it alone."

"A good offense takes teamwork, son! And only leaders who've proven themselves get smooth cooperation from their troops. It speaks well of you that you had people willing to help you."

Ruby and I rounded our eyes at each other. Mr. Stern had either undergone a profound change, or he'd been locked up and some other old man was impersonating him.

A chubby man in a sweatshirt with a stethoscope dangling from his neck came to the door.

"Bring the baby inside, please."

Ruby tightened her grip on Opal. "She seems fine. I think she just needs a bath."

"You can bathe her as soon as I check her."

We all trooped into the hotel suite and watched as the doctor took Opal and laid her on the bed. She began to cry, and so did Ruby.

The doctor removed Opal's grimy clothes, listened to her heart, looked into her nose and ears, examined her bottom, searched for bruises or scratches on her arms and legs, palpated her tummy, ran his hand over her skull, and pronounced her undamaged.

As Ruby snatched her and held her close, the doctor said, "How long has she gone without nourishment?"

We all looked at each other and shrugged. Only Vern or Angelina or Myra would know the answer to that, but we doubted she had been fed.

Zack said, "We can pick up whatever she needs on the way home."

Over Opal's head, Ruby looked a question at him.

A crimson flush climbed Zack's pale neck and crept to his hairline. "We'll all be going home *where we belong.*" I wondered if he had picked up the line from Cupcake.

Turning to Mr. Stern, he said, "We can pick up your cat from the hospital, too."

For a second, Mr. Stern's entire face smiled. Then he looked at Ruby and Opal, and grew sober. "You young people need some time alone. Away from old men and cats and everybody else." He flashed a look at me, and I felt my own face heat.

I said, "Until you can move back into your own home, I think we can find a hotel that will allow you and Cheddar to share a room."

"Tomorrow," he said. "This day's had enough."

So had we all.

In a quick flurry of hugs and handshakes, Ruby and Zack hurried out to the hallway. I stayed a second to tell Mr. Stern that I would find him a new hotel the next morning, and then followed them. We were all dragging with fatigue and relief.

On the way to Zack's house, we stopped at a Walmart where Ruby ran in to scoop up everything she could find that Opal might ever conceivably need. Zack and I sat in the car with Opal and waited. Opal was fussy, every minute more wide awake from whatever Vern had used to drug her—the doctor had guessed paregoric. Part of me was furious that she'd been drugged, another part was grateful. I hoped her trauma had been lessened by being asleep for most of her ordeal.

Before Ruby returned to us, Zack made several phone calls, the first to Cupcake.

"Opal's okay, bro." A pause, then, "I'm taking them home right now. Ruby's in the Walmart buying stuff for the baby, then we'll go home." Another pause, and a husky, "Thanks for everything, buddy."

As he dialed the next number, he glanced at me. "Cupcake says the cops took Vern to jail. Also Myra."

Before I could answer, his phone connection clicked.

"Dad, it's me. I'm on my way home with Ruby and our baby. I'd like you to be gone when we get there."

I heard gruff squawking sounds, and Zack sighed.

"Go home where you belong, Dad. Stay in your own house, not mine. I'm bringing my family home and we're going to stay there together, the three of us. If you disrespect my wishes on this, you won't see me again. Ever."

He looked out his window and saw Ruby tearing across the parking lot with several large shopping bags hanging from her arms and shoulders.

He said, "I have to give my wife a hand now, Dad. Goodbye."

In a flash, he was out of the car and helping stow bags into the backseat. Before Ruby climbed into the passenger seat beside me, he leaned down like a skinny comma and kissed her cheek. Ruby was trembling so much when she got in that she fumbled getting the seat belt to latch. I handed Opal to her and drove off smiling. One of the nicest surprises about life is that sometimes impossible things happen.

31

Zack, Cupcake, and I sat in the back row of the courtroom during Ruby's swearing-in. Opal slept on Zack's shoulder, and he made sure that Ruby had a clear view of their daughter from the witness stand.

The bailiff held out a Bible for Ruby to place her left hand on, told her to raise her right hand, and asked the question we've all heard a million times on TV shows. "Do you swear to tell the truth, the whole truth, and nothing but the truth, so help you God?"

Standing straight and steady, Ruby swept her gaze over Myra and her team of defense attorneys, and then gave a tremulous smile to Zack. "I do."

The jig was up for Myra, and she knew it. Myra occupied a straight-backed wooden chair at the defendant's table. The chair looked uncomfortable. Myra looked cadaverous, pasty white and hollow-eyed.

Denied bond, Tuck was in jail and would be tried separately for his part in her Ponzi operation. After Ruby's testimony, he would spend as many years in prison as Myra.

Vern hadn't had anything to do with their Ponzi scheme, but he was in jail charged with kidnapping, illegal imprisonment, attempted murder, and an assortment of lesser crimes. He had been denied bond, and he would be in prison for a long time. To Mr. Stern's delight, one of the most damning pieces of evidence against Vern had been the presence of orange cat hairs on Vern's limo seat. DNA testing found the orange hairs had come from Cheddar, proof that Vern had picked up cat hairs when he lifted Opal from the crib where Cheddar had been allowed to visit while Ruby was in the room.

I didn't stay for Ruby's entire testimony. I had cats to groom and feed, and anyway the testimony would be dry and boring once it moved to the minutiae of money transfers and contracts and taxes and foreign bank accounts. Boring to me, anyway. Tom Hale would have found it juicy and riveting.

Mr. Stern and Cheddar were happily together at the Bide-A-Tide Villas on Turtle Beach. Cheddar had a screened lanai to watch shorebirds leaving tracks in the sand, and Mr. Stern had a row of history books about Florida that excited him as much as the birds excited Cheddar. Workmen were busy at Mr. Stern's house putting in new wallboard and floors in Ruby's bedroom, painting, replacing furniture, and getting rid of the odor of smoke throughout the house. I stopped by the Bide-A-Tide twice a day to give him a hand with Cheddar, and I went to the house once a day to feed the koi. Without Mr. Stern and Cheddar to give it life, the courtyard seemed strangely empty.

Sometimes when I was tossing fish food on the pond

for the koi, I had an eerie feeling that eyes were looking down at me from Myra's house, but the house was empty. Angelina had been questioned at length, and her answers had helped law enforcement officers connect the dots in several cases against Kantor Tucker. Like flying a man who was in the country illegally over the Gulf and shoving him out. The man could not be reported missing because he didn't legally exist, but Angelina knew his widow, and the widow could give dates and times that corresponded to a body that had washed up on Anna Maria Island.

As for me, I was in purgatory. Or hell. Or some weird place between lives like the Tibetan *bardo*.

People who aren't true to themselves are lost to everybody else as well. An easy thing to know, but a hard thing to do. In my imagination, I tried to place myself in a city where I breathed the odor of chicory coffee and beignets instead of sea air. I tried to imagine what it would be like to live in a place where jazz was the subliminal background sound instead of the sigh of surf and cries of seagulls.

All that was easy. It was even easy to imagine myself feeling joy in seeing Guidry's city through his eyes, getting to know his family, creating a home for us. The only problem was, I couldn't imagine doing it forever. A few weeks, maybe. A month or two. But I knew as sure as I knew the back of my own hand that I would wake up one morning and *need* the sounds and smells I'd known all my life. I would need them the same way I needed air. Without them, my soul would shrivel.

My mind desperately raced looking for compromise.

But I always ran up against the hard wall of knowing that compromise isn't possible when it comes to *needs*—the unique basics essential to a person's happiness. Needs can't be bartered or denied without something intrinsic to the soul dying. *Wants,* on the other hand, are just the things that make life more pleasant. They're like gravy on your mashed potatoes. Not essential, but nice to have. They can be compromised all over the place, but only after your basic needs are met.

And the hard truth is that while someone who loved me could give me some of my *wants*, the only person who could meet my *needs* was me.

The trick was to tell the difference between needs and wants.

When the levees holding back the sea outside New Orleans broke, the city suffered devastation unlike any this country has ever experienced. When artists, musicians, writers, culinary wizards, and ordinary citizens were driven away by the floods, New Orleans lost part of its soul. For Guidry, the urge to go home and be a part of recovering the city's soul was a *need,* not simply something that would add to his enjoyment of life. That need was something only he could define, and only he could meet. Loving him meant that I wouldn't try to stand in his way.

Myra Kreigle and her sort had caused financial ruin for a lot of hardworking people on Siesta Key, but I couldn't honestly say that I felt the Key needed me for its survival. With me or without me, Siesta Key would continue to be a beautiful place where gentle people walked the beach every morning, where they marked turtle and plover nests to keep them safe, where they rescued wounded manatees and seabirds.

The truth was that I needed the Key a lot more than it needed me. I needed its sand beneath my feet, needed to breathe its sea air, needed to hear the cries of seabirds and share space with tropical vegetation. Without them, I would not be me.

The truth was that while I greatly *wanted* Guidry's touch, his keen intellect, his loyalty, and his love, I would continue to be myself without them.

It was that truth that broke my heart.

Read on for an excerpt from

THE CAT SITTER'S
PAJAMAS

the next Dixie Hemingway mystery from Blaize Clement,
available in hardcover from Minotaur Books!

W hen you live in a resort area, every third person you meet on the street may be somebody famous. Here in Sarasota, which probably has more famous personalities per capita than any other city in the world, you might sit beside Toby and Itzhak Perlman in a movie theater or see Stephen King in Circle Books on St. Armand's Key. We locals stay cool about it. We don't run up to them and gush like yokels. We just dip our heads in silent respect and hope they notice how generous we are to grant them privacy. If we should become friends with one of them, the way I did with Cupcake Trillin and his wife, Jancey, we don't go around bragging about it. We treat them like any other friend, but we're always aware that fate has given them an extra allotment of talent or looks or determination that the rest of us don't have.

I'm Dixie Hemingway, no relation to you-know-who, that other famous Floridian. I live on Siesta Key, which is one of the semi-tropical barrier islands off Sarasota—the others being Casey, Bird, Lido, St. Armand's, and

Longboat. Connected by two drawbridges, Siesta is the closest to the mainland, and in most respects it's like a small town. People gather for sand-sculpting contests, Fourth of July fireworks, and Christmas tree lighting. They run with their dogs on the beach, walk to the post office inside Davidson Drugs, gossip over coffee at one of our gourmet coffee shops. So far, we've been able to keep chain stores off the island, and we're proud that all our businesses are locally owned. Except in "season," when snowbirds come, the Key is home to about seven thousand people. During season, we swell to about twenty-four thousand, and traffic and tempers get a little quicker.

I live here for the same reason so many famous people have second or third or maybe eighth homes here—because it's a paradise of riotous colors, balmy sea breezes, cool talcum-sand beaches, and every songbird and seabird you can think of. Snowy egrets walk around in our parking lots, great blue herons stand vigil on people's lawns, and if we look up we see the silhouette of frigate birds flying above the clouds like ships without a home.

My only claims to fame are that once I went totally bonkers while TV cameras rolled, and later I killed a man. I was a sheriff's deputy when I went crazy, but I didn't kill anybody until after I'd got myself more or less together and become a pet sitter. Pet sitting is a lot more dangerous than people think.

Cupcake Trillin's fame came from being an immovable inside linebacker for the Tampa Buccaneers. He's the size of a walk-in closet, and has one of the tenderest hearts in the universe. He and I became friends when we rescued the baby of his best friend.

He and Jancey had left their two cats, Elvis and Lucy, in my care while they spent a two-week vacation in Parma, Italy. For Jancey, it was a long-planned chance to learn to make authentic Italian dishes. For Cupcake, it was a last-minute change of plans—he'd been widely reported to be attending a private meeting of fellow athletes who sponsored a camp for disadvantaged kids—but a welcome opportunity to get personal with honest-to-God prosciutto and Parmesan cheese.

The Trillins lived on the south end of the Key in an exclusive gated community called Hidden Shores. Since the famous and rich are always on guard against intruders, the main difference between Hidden Shores and a maximum security prison is that it costs big bucks to be confined in Hidden Shores. In addition to a security gate, a tall stucco wall hung with riotous bougainvillea and trumpet vine surrounds the area. Those pretty flowers conceal coiled razor ribbon.

Cupcake and Jancey had been in Italy a week on the Tuesday morning when their lives and mine took a sudden turn. It was early, with a few horsetail clouds fanning a mango sky, when I drove up to the Hidden Shores gatehouse. I punched in my temporary security code and watched the gate slide open. In our humid climate, most entry gates are built of aluminum, but this one had been powder-coated to look like wrought-iron. A good seven feet tall, it had sharp spikes at the top to discourage anybody rash enough to think about climbing it. As it opened, I kept one eye on the rear-view mirror in case a robber or serial killer tried to whip around my Bronco and race through ahead of me—places like Hidden Shores are guaranteed to make anybody paranoid.

A human is usually at the gate, but at that hour the gate was unmanned. I guess the security people figure robbers work nine to five. As I pulled through the opened gate, my name, the time, and the date were electronically recorded at a security company's office. More than likely, my photo was snapped by a hidden camera.

In the Trillins' driveway, I took a moment to flip open my notebook to remind myself of my temporary house code number, then hustled up the path to the front door. I was humming under my breath when I punched in my code. I think I was still humming when I turned the doorknob and pushed the door open. But the instant I stepped into the foyer I froze.

Houses have signature odors as distinctive as a human's individual scent. I couldn't have accurately described the unique breath of the Trillins' house, but I knew it well enough to detect a change in it.

At about the same instant I realized an intruder was in the house, a willowy woman with skim-milky skin stepped from the living room into the foyer. Her long titian hair was lit by subtle hues that only occur on very small children and women with expensive colorists. She wore bright scarlet lipstick, and her fingernails and toenails were the same bright red. Except for an oversized, brightly printed man's shirt hanging unbuttoned from her narrow shoulders, she was naked.

I tried not to look, but it's not every day you run into a naked woman with a Brazilian wax job in the shape of a valentine heart. The pubic heart was red like her hair, which made the old naughty doggerel run through my head: *mix another batch and dye your snatch to match!*

She gave me a gracious, hostessy smile and extended a limp hand as if she expected me to cross the foyer and shake it.

In a husky, seductive voice, she said, "I'm Briana."

Under the terms of my contract with my clients, I make it clear that I need the names of all the people who have permission to come in while they're gone. Otherwise, if I find anybody in the house, I'll take them as unlawful intruders and act accordingly.

I said, "I can't let you stay here without the owner's permission."

Her smile grew more serene. "You don't understand. I'm Cupcake's wife."

I said, "That will come as a surprise to the wife with him right now."

Her eyes clouded in momentary confusion. "Excuse me?"

My throat tightened. The woman seemed to really believe what she'd said.

From somewhere in the house, a faint noise sounded— the click a refrigerator door makes when it's surreptitiously closed, maybe, or the *snick!* from unlocking a glass slider to a lanai.

Without another word, I stepped backward and pulled the door shut behind me. Outside, I took out my cellphone to call the cops, and then hesitated. Ordinary people can have intruders in their house and it never makes the papers. But Cupcake was famous, and reporters would salivate at a report of a naked woman in his house while he and his wife were away.

Instead of dialing 911, I called Cupcake.

Cupcake answered with a note of concern in his voice. "Dixie?"

For some reason, I was surprised that caller ID worked all the way across the Atlantic.

I said, "There's a woman in your house. She says her name is Briana. I think somebody else may be in there too."

Cupcake said, "Oh, *ma-a-a-an*." He sounded like a kid learning his ballgame has been called off.

He lowered the phone to yell at his wife. "Jancey, it's Dixie. There's another woman. This one broke into the house."

Jancey took the phone. "She's in our *house*?"

I said, "I'm afraid so."

Cupcake said something too muffled for me to hear, and Jancey quit talking to me to talk to him.

"Are you kidding me? She's in our *house*, Cupcake! In our shower! Sleeping in our bed! And you want to *protect* her?"

I grinned. Cupcake's tender heart sometimes forces Jancey to play the heavy.

There were some more muffled sounds, probably Cupcake wresting the phone from her.

He said, "Those women that stalk us have to be some kind of sick. I feel sorry for them."

Jancey yelled, "They stalk Cupcake, not me!"

Cupcake sighed. "Call the police, but try to get them to commit her or put her in a hospital or something."

I said, "She acted like she knew you. Do you know anybody named Briana?"

"Never heard of her."

Jancey got on the phone again. "Dixie, get that woman out of my house. Are the cats okay?"

"I haven't seen them yet. I came outside to call you as soon as she told me she was Cupcake's wife."

"She said *what*? Oh my God!"

I could have slapped myself for telling her that. What woman wants to hear that another woman is going around claiming her husband? But it was done, and I couldn't take it back. At least I hadn't told about the woman being naked, or about the huge shirt she'd worn. I was pretty sure the shirt was one of Cupcake's.

I hurried to tell Jancey I would have the woman taken away, got off the line, and called 911.

"I'm a pet sitter, and I just walked in on an intruder in a client's house. A woman. She seemed mentally disturbed and should be handled with care. There may be another person in the house as well."

I gave the address, but when the dispatcher asked for the homeowner's name, I tried to distract her.

"It's a gated community. Whoever comes will have to use a code to get in. I guess they could use mine."

Crisply, the dispatcher said, "No problem, ma'am. We have our own code. A deputy will be there shortly."

I grinned and shut off the phone. I knew about the bar code affixed to the side of every Sarasota County emergency and law enforcement vehicle. As the vehicle approaches the gate, an electronic reader scans the code and automatically opens the gate.

I also knew that reporters with police scanners listened to 911 calls. I doubted that any of them knew Cupcake's address, and I didn't think they'd go to the effort of looking up the address I'd given the dispatcher. At least I hoped they wouldn't. I hoped they'd yawn and wait for something juicier than a cat sitter calling about an intruder. If the stars were in the right alignment for Cupcake, the woman in his house would be hustled off without the world ever knowing she'd been there.

I waited in the Bronco, imagining Briana inside the house wondering why I was still there. Or maybe she wasn't. She had seemed so spaced-out that she might have forgotten me as soon as I left. Cupcake was right, the woman was mentally ill. Jancey was probably right, too. The woman had probably been in their bed and in their shower.

Deputy Jesse Morgan and an unsworn female deputy from the Community Policing unit arrived in separate cars, both parking behind me in the driveway and walking toward me with the near-swagger that uniforms give both men and women. I didn't know the woman, but Morgan and I had met a few times in situations I didn't want to remember. I was never sure if he thought I was a total kook, or if he thought I just had really bad luck.

Morgan is one of Siesta Key's sworn deputies, meaning he carries a gun. He's lean, with sharp cheekbones and knuckles, and hair trimmed so short as to be almost nonexistent. He wears dark mirrored shades that hide any emotion in his eyes, but one ear sports a small diamond stud. I'm not sure what that diamond says, but it's about the only thing about Morgan that indicates a personal life outside the sheriff's department. The Key has so little true crime that most of our law enforcement is done by the unsworn deputies of the Community Policing unit, like the woman with him. Community Police officers wear dark green shorts and white knit shirts. Except for a gun, their belts bristle with the same equipment used by the sworn deputies.

Morgan greeted me with the half-hearted enthusiasm with which a dog greets a vet wearing rubber gloves and holding a syringe. Civil, but pretty sure he's not going to like what's coming. He introduced Deputy Clara Beene and she and I did a brief handshake. Beene seemed more intrigued by the house and grounds than in me, so I figured she had never heard of me. Like I said, my fame is very limited.

I said, "I'm taking care of two cats that live here. When I went in, I found a woman in the house. She claimed to be the wife of the owner, but I know she's not. I think somebody else was in there, too. I came out and called the owners. They don't know who the woman is. They think she must be mentally disturbed, and they asked for her to be committed to a hospital or something instead of put in jail."

Morgan tilted his head to peer down at me. If I'd been able to see his eyes, I imagine they would have had a sharp glint in them. We both knew how hard it is for law enforcement officers to do anything constructive about law-breakers who are mentally ill. Under Florida law, a cop who believes a person is about to commit suicide or kill somebody can initiate the Baker Act that involuntarily commits a person for testing. The commitment period lasts only seventy-two hours, and unless two psychiatrists petition the court to extend the commitment time for involuntary treatment, the person is released.

I doubted that Briana would be considered an imminent threat to herself or anybody else. More likely, she would be considered an extreme neurotic with a delusional crush on a famous athlete.

Without commenting on what he thought about trying to get Briana hospitalized, Morgan flipped open his notebook and clicked his pen. "What made you think somebody else was in the house with the woman?"

"Just a noise I heard. Like maybe somebody unlocking the lanai slider. It could have been something else."

"But you didn't see anybody else."

"No, it was just a little clicking noise."

"What's the homeowner's name?"

"Trillin."

He lowered his pen and angled his head at me. "*Cupcake* Trillin?"

"I hope we can keep this out of the news."

His jawbone jutted out a bit, like he'd just bit down hard on his back teeth. "I'll just put 'Trillin' as the owner's name. You ever see the woman inside before?"

"No. She said her name was Briana."

"Briana who?"

Beene, the Community Policing woman said, "She just goes by Briana. That one name. She's a famous model."

Morgan and I turned to look at her, and she shrugged. "I watch *Entertainment Tonight*."

Morgan's nostrils flared slightly like it might be against department policy to watch shows like that.

"So?"

"So she's here in Sarasota. I heard it on the news."

Beene looked from Morgan to me. "You must have heard of her. She was all over the news last year. You know, she's the model that caused a big stink at the fashion show in Milan."

Morgan and I shook our heads. I might have heard about somebody in a cat show who'd made the news, but fashion shows were out of my world.

As if he had heard all he could stand about fashion models, Morgan put his pen and pad away and took a deep breath. With Beene a step behind him, he strode manfully to the door and rapped on it.

He yelled, "Sarasota Sheriff's Department!"

The door didn't open. No sound came from inside.

Morgan waited a few seconds, then knocked and shouted again. Nobody answered.

I felt a little shiver of guilty relief. Briana and whoever had been in the house with her had probably slipped out the back door while I watched the front door. Maybe they were halfway to Tampa by now. Maybe they would never come back. Maybe Briana had learned her lesson and would stop stalking Cupcake.

Morgan turned to look at me as if it were my fault nobody had answered the door.

"You got a key?"

"I have a security code."

"Please use it."

Feeling important under their gaze, I stepped forward and punched in my special number. The lock clicked and I turned the knob and opened the door. Morgan motioned me aside, and he and Beene went in the house.

Once again, intuition or subliminal cues made the hairs on the back of my neck stand up, as if trouble was barreling toward me.

I said, "Don't let the cats out."

My sixth sense was right about trouble coming, but it wasn't two runaway cats . . .

El delito
de la
limonada

El delito de la limonada

escrito por
Jacqueline Davies

Houghton Mifflin Harcourt
Boston   Nueva York

Houghton Mifflin Books for Children es un sello editorial de
Houghton Mifflin Harcourt Publishing Company.

hmhco.com

El texto de este libro está en tipografía Guardi.
Las ilustraciones se realizaron con pluma y tinta.

Catálogo Biblioteca del Congreso. Fecha de publicación
Davies, Jacqueline, 1962—
El delito de la limonada / escrito por Jacqueline Davies.
p. cm.
Resumen: Cuando desaparece dinero del bolsillo de Evan, alumno de cuarto
grado, todos piensan que lo robó Scott, su irritante compañero de clase. La
hermanita de Evan organiza un juicio, en el que hace participar a toda la clase,
para probar qué ocurrió en realidad.
1. Juicios—Ficción. 2. Comportamiento—Ficción. 3. Hermanos y hermanas—
Ficción. 4. Escuelas—Ficción. 5. Perdón—Ficción.] I. Título.
PZ7.D29392Le 2011 [Fic]—dc22 2010015231

ISBN: 978-1-328-59444-0 Spanish hardcover
ISBN: 978-1-328-60608-2 Spanish paperback
ISBN: 978-0-547-27967-1 English hardcover
ISBN: 978-0-547-72237-5 English paperback

Printed in the United States of America

DOC 10 9 8 7 6 5 4 3 2 1

4500748438

Para C. Ryan Joyce

in loco parentis para muchos...
y para una persona en especial

AGRADECIMIENTOS

Muchas gracias a las buenas personas que ayudaron a guiar este libro: Tracey Adams, Mary Atkinson, Henry Davies, Mae Davies, Tracey Fern, Jennifer Jacobson, Sarah Lamstein, Carol Peacock y Dana Walrath. Un agradecimiento especial para Ann Rider, quien supo cuándo empujar y cuándo detenerse, y luego volver a empujar nuevamente.

Índice

Capítulo 1
Fraude

fraude, s. El delito de engañar a alguien para lograr un rédito personal o económico; persona que simula ser algo que no es.

—¡No es justo! —dijo Jessie. Señaló las cuatro galletas con chips de chocolate que su hermano, Evan, estaba metiendo en una bolsa Ziploc. Estaban parados en la cocina, casi listos para ir a la escuela, el cuarto día de cuarto grado para ambos, ahora que los dos estaban en la misma clase.

—Bueno —dijo Evan, mientras sacaba una galleta y volvía a ponerla en el frasco de galletas—. Tres para ti. Tres para mí. ¿Contenta?

—No se trata de estar contenta —dijo Jessie—. Se trata de lo que es justo.

—Como quieras. Me voy. —Evan se colgó la mochila en el hombro y luego desapareció por las escaleras que llevan al garaje.

Jessie fue hasta la ventana de la sala de estar y observó mientras su hermano pedaleaba la bicicleta en la calle. Ella todavía no tenía permiso para montar en bici por lo que no podía ir en bici a la escuela si no la acompañaba uno de los padres. Era uno de los problemas de saltarse el tercer grado y de ser la más pequeña de cuarto grado. Todos los demás de su clase podían ir a la escuela en bicicleta, pero ella todavía tenía que ir caminando.

Jessie fue hasta el refrigerador y tachó otro día del calendario de almuerzos. El almuerzo del día era Hamburguesa de pollo. No era su favorito, pero estaba bien. Con el dedo, marcó cada día que restaba de la semana y leyó en voz alta el plato principal: Hot dog deli (*asco*), *Nuggets* de pollo con dip, Tacos de tortilla suave y, el viernes, su favorito: Palitos de pan francés glaseados de canela.

El espacio del sábado estaba vacío, pero alguien había escrito con marcador rojo:

Jessie se puso las manos en las caderas. ¿Quién lo había hecho? Probablemente uno de los amigos de Evan. Adam o Paul. Desordenar su calendario de almuerzos. ¡Probablemente Paul! Típico de él. Jessie sabía que Yom Kipur era una fiesta judía muy solemne. No recordaba qué era, pero era muy solemne. *No* puedes escribir *¡súper-fiesta!* luego de Yom Kipur.

—Jessie, ¿estás lista? —preguntó la Sra. Treski mientras entraba en la cocina.

—Sip —dijo Jessie. Levantó su mochila, que pesaba casi tanto como ella, y se la puso sobre los hombros. Tuvo que inclinar la cintura un poco hacia adelante para evitar caer hacia atrás.

—Mami, no hace falta que sigas llevándome a la escuela. Estoy en cuarto grado, ¿sabes?

—Lo sé —dijo la Sra. Treski, mientras miraba hacia las escaleras del garaje en busca de sus zapatos—. Pero aún tienes solo ocho años.

—¡Cumpliré nueve el mes que viene!

La Sra. Treski la miró.

—¿Es tan importante?

—¿No puedo ir con Megan?

—¿Megan no llega siempre tarde?

—Pero yo siempre llego temprano, así que compensaremos.

—Puede ser mañana, pero hoy caminemos juntas. ¿De acuerdo?

—De acuerdo —dijo Jessie, a quien en realidad le gustaba caminar hasta la escuela con su madre, pero se preguntaba si los otros niños pensaban que ella era una chica aún más rara por eso—. Pero es la última vez.

Les tomó menos de diez minutos llegar a la escuela. Darlene, la guardia del cruce escolar, levantó sus manos enguantadas para detener el tránsito y les dijo:

—Bien. Ya pueden cruzar.

Jessie se volvió hacia su madre.

—Mami. Puedo continuar el resto del camino sola.

—Bueno —dijo la Sra. Treski, con un pie en el borde de la acera y un pie en la calle—. Está bien. Te veré a la salida de clase. Te esperaré aquí.

Retrocedió al cordón, y Jessie sabía que la miraría hasta que llegara al patio. *No me daré vuelta para saludar*, se dijo. *Los chicos de cuarto no hacen eso.* Evan se lo había explicado.

Jessie caminó hacia el patio buscando a Megan. Como a los niños no les permitían entrar a la escuela antes de que sonara la campana, se reunían fuera de la escuela. Se colgaban de los pasamanos, se deslizaban en el tobogán, conversaban en grupos u organizaban juegos cortos de fútbol o de básquetbol, si tenían la suerte de tener una maestra que les permitiera jugar con una pelota de la clase antes de entrar. Jessie recorrió el patio con la mirada. Megan no estaba. Probablemente llegaría tarde.

Jessie enganchó los pulgares en las correas de su mochila. Ya se había dado cuenta de que la mayoría de las chicas de cuarto grado no usaban mochila. Llevaban sus libros, carpetas, botellas de agua y almuerzos en morrales informales. Jessie pensaba que esos bolsos eran una tontería. La forma en que se golpeaban contra las rodillas y se hundían en el hombro. Las mochilas eran más prácticas.

Caminó hacia el patio donde Evan y un grupo de chicos estaban jugando HORSE. Algunos de los chicos eran de quinto grado y eran altos, pero Jessie no se sorprendió al descubrir que Evan iba ganando. Era bueno en básquetbol. El mejor de toda la clase, según Jessie. Quizás incluso el mejor de toda la escuela. Se sentó en la línea de banda para mirar.

—Bien, lanzaré un *fadeaway* —dijo Evan, nombrando su tiro para que el siguiente niño tuviera que copiarlo—. Un pie sobre la rajadura corta para empezar.

Botó la pelota un par de veces, y Jessie miró junto

con los demás niños para ver si podía hacer el tiro. Cuando por fin saltó, lanzando la pelota mientras caía hacia atrás, la pelota surcó el aire e hizo un tiro con gran arco perfecto, justo a través de la canasta.

—¡Ufff! —dijo Ryan, quien tenía que copiar el tiro. Botó la pelota un par de veces y dobló las rodillas, pero justo entonces sonó la campana. Era hora de formar fila.

—¡Ja! —dijo Ryan mientras arrojaba la pelota bien alto.

—Tienes mucha suerte —dijo Evan, mientras atrapaba la pelota en el aire y la ponía en el cajón de leche donde se guardaba el resto del equipo de patio del 4-O.

A Jessie le gustaban los amigos de Evan, y, por lo general, eran bastante buenos con ella, así que los siguió para ponerse en fila. Sabía que no debía formarse justo detrás de Evan. No estaba muy feliz de tener a su hermanita en la misma clase este año. La Sra. Treski había aconsejado a Jessie: *Dale espacio a Evan,* y era lo que estaba haciendo.

Jessie miró por todo el patio para ver si Megan

había aparecido, pero a quien vio fue a Scott Spencer saltando del carro de su padre. *¡Genial!*, farfulló Jessie. Para Jessie, Scott Spencer era un farsante y un fraude. Siempre estaba haciendo algo que no debía hacer a espaldas de la maestra y nunca lo pillaban. Como la vez que cortó los narcisos que estaban creciendo en la clase de arte. O como cuando borró estrellas del pizarrón para que su grupo de trabajo ganara el Premio por Equipo de la semana.

Cuando Scott llegó a la fila, se metió justo delante de Jessie y tocó a Ryan en el hombro.

—Hola —dijo.

—Hola —dijo Ryan, dándose vuelta y haciendo un movimiento con la cabeza.

—Perdona —dijo Jessie tocando a Scott en el brazo—. La fila termina ahí atrás. —Señaló con el pulgar hacia atrás.

—¿Y qué? —dijo Scott.

—No puedes colarte así.

—¿A quién le importa? Solo estamos entrando a la escuela.

—Es una fila —dijo Jessie—. La regla es que debes ir al final de la fila.

—¿A quién le importa lo que dices? —dijo Scott, encogiendo los hombros y dándole la espalda. La fila estaba comenzando a avanzar. Scott tocó a algunos otros niños en el brazo y los saludó. Algunos le respondieron, pero Jessie observó que Evan mantenía la vista al frente.

—Llegué tardísimo, ¿no? —dijo Scott a Ryan. Sonreía de oreja a oreja—. No podía dejar de jugar con mi nuevo Xbox 20/20.

—¿Tienes un 20/20? —preguntó Ryan.

Paul se dio vuelta.

—¿Quién? ¿Quién tiene uno?

—Él dice que tiene uno —dijo Ryan señalando a Scott.

—No puede ser —dijo Paul—. Ni siquiera ha salido a la venta.

—Bueno, no se puede conseguir en una tienda —dijo Scott—. Pero mi mamá conoce gente en Japón.

Jessie miró a Evan, que estaba en el frente de

la fila. Se daba cuenta de que no había escuchado lo que Scott había dicho, pero más y más chicos se dieron vuelta para escuchar sobre el 20/20. Era la última consola, con gafas envolventes y guantes sensibles al movimiento. La fila delante de Jessie comenzó a amontonarse.

Cuando Jessie llegó a la puerta del aula, la Sra. Overton estaba parada allí diciendo buenos días a cada alumno a medida que la fila ingresaba.

—Sra. Overton, Scott Spencer se coló en la fila. —Jessie no era una soplona, pero Scott debía aprender un par de cosas sobre las reglas.

La Sra. Overton puso una mano sobre el hombro de Jessie.

—Bueno, Jessie. Voy a controlar mañana para que no vuelva a ocurrir, por ahora, dejémoslo así.

¡Perfecto!, pensó Jessie mientras caminaba hacia su lugar y bajaba la silla. *Scott Spencer se sale con la suya nuevamente.*

Luego de poner su silla en el piso, salió al pasillo para colgar la mochila en su armario. Arrancó la esquina de una página de su Cuaderno de Escritura y escribió rápidamente una nota. Luego, al pasar por el asiento de Evan cuando iba hacia el suyo, deslizó la nota en su mano. No lo vio abrirla y leerla, pero ya sentada en su propio asiento, se dio cuenta de que la había leído. Evan estaba mirando a Scott Spencer, y casi se podía ver que sus ojos lanzaban rayos.

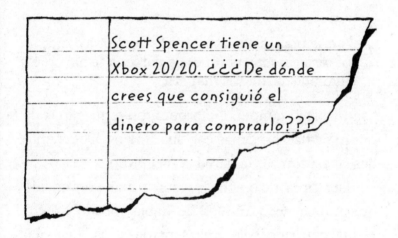

Scott Spencer tiene un Xbox 20/20. ¿¿¿De dónde crees que consiguió el dinero para comprarlo???

Capítulo 2
venganza

venganza, s. El acto de causar dolor o daño a otra persona porque esa persona te ha dañado de alguna manera.

Evan estrujó la nota. De pronto, no tenía ganas de reír ni de hacer bromas con sus amigos. De repente, deseaba atravesar la pared con el puño.

Esta es la razón: Evan estaba más convencido que nunca de que Scott le había robado dinero. Había ocurrido solo una semana atrás. Justo en medio de la ola de calor. Justo en medio de la guerra de la limonada con Jessie. Todos habían ido a casa de Jack. Todos los chicos —Paul y Ryan y Kevin y Malik y Scott— estaban jugando básquetbol en la piscina. Evan tenía $208 en el bolsillo de sus pantalones cortos. *¡Doscientos ocho dólares!* Era más dinero del que había visto en toda su vida. Había dejado sus pantalones cortos doblados sobre la cama en el cuarto de Jack mientras todos iban a nadar. Pero luego Scott salió de la piscina para ir al baño, y un minuto después, salió corriendo de la casa, diciendo que debía ir a su casa de inmediato. Y cuando Evan regresó a la casa para vestirse, el dinero había desaparecido.

Evan nunca se había sentido peor en toda su vida.

Hace muchos, muchos años, casi un millón de años, Scott y Evan habían sido amigos. O algo así. Evan iba con frecuencia a la casa de Scott, y cada tanto, Scott jugaba en la casa de Evan, aunque Scott decía que su casa era mejor porque había más cosas para hacer. Una vez, Evan incluso se había quedado a dormir en la casa de playa de Scott en el Cabo. Los Spencer tenían mucho dinero porque la mamá de Scott era abogada en una de las principales firmas de abogados del centro de la ciudad, y su papá dirigía una empresa de consultoría financiera desde su casa.

Pero, desde entonces, las cosas se habían enfriado. Muchísimo. La verdad es que Scott era un chico bastante latoso. El modo en que presumía, el modo en que hacía trampa cuando jugaban, incluso en jueguitos estúpidos como ¡Pesca! u Operando. ¿A quién le importaba ganar un juego como ¡Pesca!? Y el modo en que guardaba las cosas bajo llave, ¡como los bocadillos en su casa! Guardaba Yodels y Ring Dings bajo llave en un archivo metálico en el sótano. Si Evan lo pensaba bien, debía admitir que, en realidad, no lo soportaba. Y ahora tenía una razón para odiarlo.

—La tarea de la mañana, Evan —dijo la Sra. Overton dando unos golpecitos sobre la hoja que estaba en su escritorio cuando pasó a su lado. Evan se volvió hacia su escritorio y miró el problema de matemáticas del Doble Diario que tenía frente a él. Todos los otros chicos de la clase estaban trabajando en el mismo problema, y Evan se daba cuenta de que algunos ya habían terminado. Normalmente esto lo hubiera preocupado, pero esta mañana ni siquiera podía concentrarse lo suficiente en el problema como para quitarse el sentimiento de ¡ay, no! que tenía adentro.

Me compraría un Xbox. El nuevo. Eso es lo que Scott había dicho la semana pasada, justo antes de que desapareciera el dinero de los pantalones cortos de Evan. Estaban tratando de calcular cuánto dinero ganarían con un puesto de limonada y qué comprarían si se hacían ricos. Repentinamente ricos.

Y ahora él tenía un Xbox. Scott Spencer tenía un 20/20, y Evan estaba seguro de que lo había comprado con el dinero que había robado del bolsillo de Evan. Evan tenía ganas de levantar la cabeza y aullar de rabia.

Sh- sh- sh- sh- sh- sh- sh. Un sonido como el de una serpiente cascabel lista para atacar se deslizó por toda la clase. Evan levantó la vista. La Sra. Overton estaba sacudiendo el gran *shekere* africano que usaba para que todos prestaran atención. Las cuentas alrededor de la calabaza ahuecada producían un sonido susurrante, como el de un sonajero.

—Bien, Recolectores de Tareas —dijo la Sra.

Overton—, por favor, recojan los Dobles Diarios y pónganlos sobre mi escritorio.

Cada semana, a los alumnos de 4-O se les asignaba un trabajo. Algunos de los trabajos eran serios, como Recolector de Tareas, Encargado del Equipo y Supervisor de Asistencia, y algunos tenían nombres tontos, como Asistente de Vestuario del Pollo (la persona que elegía el traje del pollo de goma que estaba sentado en el escritorio de la Sra. Overton) y Creador de Caras Ridículas (la persona que hacía la cara que todos los chicos de 4-O tenían que copiar cada viernes al final del día).

—Todos los demás vengan a la alfombra para la Reunión de la Mañana.

Evan volvió a mirar el problema de matemáticas sin resolver que tenía adelante. Lo único que había escrito en la página era su nombre. Entregó la hoja a Sarah Monroe, luego caminó hasta la alfombra del rincón y se dejó caer al piso, sentado con la espalda contra el librero.

—Evan, siéntate bien, por favor —dijo la Sra.

Overton, sonriéndole—. No quiero encorvados en el círculo.

Evan cruzó las piernas y se sentó correctamente.

Primero, iban en círculo, y cada uno tenía que saludar a la persona de la derecha y a la persona de la izquierda, pero de una manera diferente. Cuando fue su turno, Evan dijo *"konichiwa"* a Adam, que estaba sentado a su lado. A Evan le gustaba decir esa palabra japonesa. Sentía como si estuviera jugando con una pelota dentro de la boca. Jessie usó lenguaje de señas para saludar a Megan. Scott Spencer saludó a Ryan con un *¿Qué onda?* e hizo reír a toda la clase. A todos menos a Evan.

Luego la Sra. Overton pasó a una página nueva del Tablón de la Mañana. Un ganso salvaje había aterrizado en el patio el día anterior a la mañana, y ese era el tema para conversar. La Sra. Overton quería saber qué sabían los chicos sobre los gansos en particular y sobre las aves migratorias en general. Por turno, cada uno escribió un dato en el atril. Evan escribió: *algunas aves vuelan durante días.* Iba a agregar *cuando migran*, pero estaba seguro de que tendría problemas al escribir la palabra *migrar* por lo que omitió esa parte.

Cuando terminaron de hablar sobre gansos y migración, la Sra. Overton tapó los Marcadores Mágicos y dijo:

—¿Alguien desea compartir algo con la clase antes de volver a los asientos? —Casi la mitad de los niños levantaron la mano, pero ninguna mano fue tan rápida como la de Scott Spencer.

—¿Scott? —dijo la Sra. Overton. Evan se desplomó sobre el librero. No quería escuchar lo que Scott quería compartir con la clase.

—Tengo un Xbox 20/20 —dijo Scott, mirando a los demás chicos.

De inmediato, la clase estalló. Los veintisiete alumnos de cuarto comenzaron a hablar a la vez. La Sra. Overton tuvo que sacudir su *shekere* durante casi diez segundos para lograr que los chicos hicieran silencio.

—¡Santo pollo de goma! —dijo la Sra. Overton. Los chicos de 4-O se rieron—. Veo que están todos interesados en el nuevo juego de Scott. Hagamos tres preguntas a Scott sobre su juego y luego continuemos con la siguiente persona.

La Sra. Overton llamó a Alyssa en primer lugar.

—¿Qué tiene de genial un 20/20? —preguntó.

—¿Es una broma? —dijo Paul—. Te pones las gafas y la tele se vuelve totalmente 3D.

—Paul, recuerda levantar la mano si deseas hablar —dijo la Sra. Overton. Scott asintió con la cabeza.

—Sí, es como si estuvieras realmente *en* la jungla —dijo Scott—. O en una persecución de carros. O adonde te lleve el juego. Y los controles son los guantes que tienes puestos. Según el modo en que mueves los dedos, así.

Scott extendió las manos y mostró cómo las movía de diferente manera para que ocurrieran las cosas en el juego. Ryan sacudió la cabeza como si no pudiera creerlo.

La Sra. Overton miró todas las manos que seguían levantadas.

—¿Segunda pregunta? ¿Jack?

—¿Qué juegos tienes? —preguntó Jack. Todos los chicos e incluso algunas chicas se habían dado vuelta y todo el círculo miraba a Scott.

—Por ahora, tengo Defenders, Road Rage y Crisis. Y luego tengo muchos que son japoneses, pero no tengo idea de qué son.

La clase comenzó a susurrar y a hablar de nuevo hasta que la Sra. Overton pidió la última pregunta antes de continuar.

—¿Jessie?

Evan se acomodó pensando qué preguntaría su hermanita. Los primeros días de clase, Jessie apenas había dicho palabra alguna. Ahora toda la clase se dio vuelta para escuchar lo que iba a decir.

—¿Cuánto costó? —preguntó Jessie.

Evan sonrió. Jessie preguntaba lo que todos querían saber, pero no se animaban a preguntar.

—Jessie, la pregunta no es apropiada —dijo la Sra. Overton.

Jessie arrugó la frente.

—¿Por qué no?

—No hablamos sobre dinero en la clase —dijo la Sra. Overton.

—Lo hacemos en matemáticas —dijo Jessie—. Todo el tiempo.

—Es diferente —dijo la Sra. Overton—. Quiero decir que no nos preguntamos unos a otros cuánto cuestan las cosas. No es de buena educación. Bien, avancemos. Evan, ¿deseas compartir algo con la clase?

Evan había levantado la mano, y ahora la dejaba caer.

—Ya que no contó la pregunta de Jessie, ¿puedo hacer la tercera pregunta?

La Sra. Overton se detuvo un minuto. Evan se dio cuenta de que la maestra quería pasar a otro tema, pero también quería cumplir con las reglas de la Reunión de la Mañana.

—De acuerdo —dijo ella—. Me parece justo.

Evan se dio vuelta hacia Scott y lo miró directamente a los ojos. Volvía a tener el mismo sentimiento, el mismo que tuvo cuando leyó la nota de Jessie. Era como una aplanadora gigante. Evan casi nunca sentía enojo o celos, pero ahora quería cruzar la sala y sacudir a Scott para que hablara.

—¿Quién lo compró? —preguntó—. ¿Tú o tus padres?

Scott levantó la barbilla, como hacía cuando desafiaba a Evan en la cancha de básquetbol.

—Yo lo compré. Con mi propio dinero.

La clase estalló otra vez, y la Sra. Overton no usó el *shekere*. Tan solo levantó las manos y dijo: "¡4-O!" Cuando bajaron la voz, dijo:

—Scott, qué bueno que hayas ahorrado dinero para algo que querías comprar. Ahora continuemos.

Pero Evan no podía continuar. No podía escuchar a Salley contar a la clase sobre el viaje que había hecho a la casa de sus abuelos. Ni siquiera a Paul hablar sobre el nido de serpientes que había encontrado en su patio. No podía escuchar nada ni ver nada. El sentimiento lo cubría, lo atravesaba y estaba dentro de él. Esas ganas de sacudir a Scott. Ahora sabía qué era lo que quería.

Evan quería venganza.

Capítulo 3
testigo presencial

testigo presencial, s. La persona que realmente ve ocurrir algo y por lo tanto puede relatar el evento.

Jessie se paró en la puerta, con un pie dentro del aula y un pie fuera, en el patio. Todos los demás chicos habían salido corriendo. Excepto Evan y Megan. Se habían quedado para terminar sus Dobles Diarios.

Jessie no quería salir si Megan y Evan no salían. Todavía no conocía a la mayoría de los de cuarto, no lo suficiente para saber quién era amable y quién no, y ella sabía que probablemente diría algo incorrecto a la persona incorrecta. Y se reirían. O serían crueles. O le dirigirían una de esas miradas, esas miradas que ella nunca entendía, y luego le darían la espalda.

Quizás Jessie podía quedarse en clase y leer el libro de Lectura Independiente en lugar de salir. Valía la pena preguntar.

Volvió a su asiento y sacó *Príncipe y mendigo*. Era un libro que le había regalado su abuelita. Dos veces, en realidad. Primero, abuelita lo envió a comienzos del verano con una nota que decía: *Jessie, me encantaba este libro cuando tenía tu edad*. Luego, un mes más tarde, envió otra copia del mismo libro con una nota: *Este libro me hizo pensar en ti, Jessie. ¡Espero que lo disfrutes!*

Jessie se había reído y había dicho:

—¡Espero que se olvide y me mande dos veces dinero por mi cumpleaños! —Pero la Sra. Treski no rio. Frunció el ceño, sacudió la cabeza y fue al teléfono para llamar a su madre, solo para ver cómo estaba.

—¿Sra. Overton? —dijo Jessie. Evan había ido al baño, y Megan estaba en el pasillo buscando agua, por lo que el salón estaba vacío. Solo estaban Jessie y la maestra.

—¿Sí, Jessie? —La Sra. Overton levantó la vista del escritorio, donde estaba leyendo lo que los alumnos habían escrito en sus Cuadernos de Escritura esa mañana. Jessie había escrito sobre los fuegos artificiales que ella, Evan y su mamá habían observado desde su casa el Día del Trabajo. Había usado muchas palabras largas, como *caleidoscopio* y *panorama,* y verbos enérgicos, como *explotó* y *caer en cascada.* Para ella, su texto era bastante bueno.

Jessie escuchó a Evan y a Megan riendo en el pasillo. Eso la detuvo, la manera en que estaban riendo juntos. No quería que ellos la vieran adentro con la maestra durante el recreo. Estaba bastante segura de lo que diría Evan: "Los de cuarto grado no hacen eso". Entonces balbuceó: "Eh, nada", y llevó el libro de vuelta a su asiento.

—Deberías salir, tesoro —dijo la Sra. Overton—. No te querrás perder el recreo de la mañana. ¿Cierto?

—Claro —dijo Jessie en voz muy baja. Fue rápidamente hacia la puerta trasera, la que se abría hacia el patio. Cuando se dio vuelta para cerrar la puerta, vio a Evan y a Megan entrando al aula desde el pasillo. Parecían bastante felices, considerando que se estaban perdiendo el recreo y que tenían que hacer la tarea de matemáticas.

Afuera, varias niñas estaban sentadas en la mesa de picnic, doblando flores de origami. Algunos niños de cuarto estaban columpiándose y deslizándose en la Máquina Verde. Unos ocho o nueve niños estaban jugando *kickball*. Todos los amigos de Evan —Paul y Ryan y Adam y Jack— estaban jugando básquetbol, junto con Scott Spencer. ¿A dónde debía ir Jessie? Se preguntó si los chicos todavía estaban hablando sobre el 20/20 y se dirigió a la canasta de básquetbol. Se sentó en el césped y fingió concentrarse en su libro, pero en realidad estaba escuchando la conversación de los chicos. Jessie escuchó que Paul preguntaba a Scott:

—¿Cómo ahorraste tanto? —No estaban jugando ningún juego, sino lanzando tiros libres desde la línea.

—De varias formas —dijo Scott. Paul le hizo un pase de pique a Scott y este hizo el tiro. Y falló. Eso alegró a Jessie.

—¿Por ejemplo? —preguntó Adam.

—Hice muchas tareas en toda la casa.

—No hay manera de ahorrar tanto dinero haciendo tareas —dijo Adam.

—Sí, lo hice —dijo Scott. Tomó la pelota y la hizo driblar en el lugar. Ryan levantó las manos —era su turno para tirar— pero Scott no se iba a rendir.

—¿Qué estás diciendo?

—Estoy diciendo lo que dije —dijo Adam—. *No hay manera* de que hayas ahorrado esa cantidad de dinero solo con tareas.

Lo que él está diciendo, pensó Jessie, *es que tú le robaste a Evan todo el dinero de nuestra limonada, y ¡todos lo saben!* Si al menos alguien lo hubiera visto tomarlo. ¡Si al menos hubiera un testigo presencial, como en las series de detectives en la tele! Así, Scott no se habría salvado del castigo.

Una sombra cruzó la página de su libro. Jessie

levantó la vista; ahí estaba David Kirkorian parado a su lado.

Jessie todavía no sabía mucho sobre los alumnos de cuarto, pero David Kirkorian era famoso en toda la escuela. Todos decían que tenía todo tipo de colecciones raras en su casa. Tenía una jarra con huesos de duraznos en su cómoda, y agregaba uno nuevo cada vez que comía un durazno. Tenía una caja llena de cordones de todos los zapatos que había usado en la vida. Incluso tenía un sobre marrón grande lleno de trozos de sus propias uñas del pie. Al menos, eso era lo que todos decían, si bien Jessie estaba segura de que nadie había visto realmente el sobre.

—Está prohibido leer afuera durante el recreo —dijo David.

—Nunca escuché esa regla —dijo Jessie.

—Que no conozcas una regla no significa que no sea una regla. —David comenzó a jugar con una de sus uñas, y Jessie se preguntó si también las coleccionaba.

—Es la regla más tonta que jamás he escuchado.

—No, no lo es —dijo David—. Te podrían atropellar si estás sentada acá. Ni siquiera estás prestando atención. Te podría golpear una pelota en la cabeza. Podrías *morir*.

Él comenzó a caminar hacia la maestra de turno. Jessie sintió que su cara enrojecía. ¿Qué le iba a decir David a la maestra de turno?

Jessie se paró y fue corriendo hacia la escuela. Diría que le dolía el estómago. Iría a la enfermería. La Sra. Graham siempre te dejaba recostar unos minutos antes de enviarte nuevamente a clase. Era un buen lugar para descansar y estar tranquila. Un buen lugar para pensar. Y Jessie tenía muchas cosas en las que pensar. No solo en reglas y recreos. Sino en que era injusto que Scott siempre escapara de los castigos y en qué podía hacer ella para cambiar eso.

—Coleccionista de uñas de pie —murmuró Jessie mientras entraba rápidamente.

Capítulo 4
RUMORES

rumores, s. Palabras de otra persona citadas cuando la persona no está presente para decir si las palabras son verdaderas; habladurías. Las habladurías no están permitidas como prueba en un tribunal.

—¿Entiendes? —preguntó Megan, recostándose en su silla—. Son iguales. ¿Ves?

El problema de matemáticas era sobre simetría. Había cinco formas diferentes dibujadas en la página, y, en cada caso, Evan debía resolver si la forma era simétrica o no. Si lo era, tenía que dibujar la línea de simetría. Megan ya había hecho la primera para mostrarle cómo hacerlo.

Pero a Evan le estaba costando pensar en la simetría sentado al lado de Megan Moriarty.

—Esa es fácil —dijo Evan, tratando de parecer astuto—. Todos saben que los corazones son simétricos.

—No todos los corazones —dijo Megan—. Mira este.

—Bueno, ese es raro —dijo Evan.

Las siguientes tres formas no eran muy difíciles, Evan pudo dibujar la línea de simetría para cada una.

Pero la última lo tenía confundido, y Megan finalmente tuvo que darle la solución: la forma no era para nada simétrica.

—Parece que sí —dijo Megan—, pero no, no importa dónde dibujes la línea. Jessie me lo mostró. Ella es una genia de las matemáticas, ¿verdad?

Evan no dijo nada. Tener una hermana lo suficientemente inteligente como para saltarse un grado completo era como si tu mejor amigo fuera una estrella del básquetbol. Por comparación, te hacía lucir mal.

—Ey, ¿Evan? —dijo Megan, bajando la voz e inclinándose para acercarse más. Ambos levantaron la vista hacia la Sra. Overton, que estaba hablando por el teléfono de la clase. Evan podía oler el champú de coco en el cabello de Megan. Le recordó el helado de Big Dipper—. ¿Cómo crees *tú* que Scott Spencer consiguió el dinero para el 20/20?

El sentimiento agradable y etéreo de Evan desapareció.

—¿Scott Spencer? ¡Bah! —dijo Evan.

—Sé a qué te refieres —dijo Megan, recostándose en la silla y jugando con su cabello—. Siempre es muy amable cuando la maestra está cerca, pero luego es malo en los pasillos.

—Sí, así es Scott —murmuró Evan.

—¿Sabes? —dijo Megan, inclinándose nuevamente—. Scott una vez me dijo que su madre gana diez dólares por *minuto*. ¿No es increíble?

Evan pensó en la casa de los Spencer y en las vacaciones que se tomaban cada año —esquiando y en el Caribe, e incluso en Europa— y no lo dudó ni un segundo.

—Seguro —dijo—. Deberías ver dónde vive.

—Escuché que tiene una nueva tele que es tan grande como la pizarra. —Megan señaló la pizarra grande que estaba en el frente de la clase.

—Probablemente —dijo Evan—. Nadie diría que un chico así puede robar.

Los ojos de Megan se abrieron mucho.

—¿Realmente roba? Alyssa me dijo que sí. Dijo que él tomó su pulsera de dijes de su armario y luego fingió que la había encontrado en el patio. Solo para impresionarla. Pero no sé si es verdad.

Evan se moría por contarle que Scott le había robado $208 a él, pero no podía.

—Le robó dinero del almuerzo a Ryan una vez. Y robó una barra de chocolate de Price Chopper. Roba muchas cosas.

Megan lo miró atentamente.

—¿Lo viste tomar el dinero o la barra de chocolate? —preguntó.

Evan sacudió la cabeza.

—No, pero Ryan dijo…

—Es solo un rumor, entonces —dijo Megan—. No puedes creer todo lo que escuchas. Eso es lo que mis padres siempre dicen.

—Si lo conocieras como yo, también pensarías que es cierto.

—Quizás —dijo Megan—. Pero no presto atención a los rumores. ¡Las personas probablemente dicen cosas sobre mí que no son ciertas! ¡Y sobre ti, también!

Evan se preguntó si sería cierto. ¿Qué diría la gente sobre él? ¿Hablaban sus amigos de él a sus espaldas? No le gustaba pensarlo.

Pero lo que Megan dijo lo dejó pensando en el dinero desaparecido. Evan en realidad nunca había visto a Scott tomar el dinero, pero él había dicho a todos —a Paul y Ryan y Adam y Jack— que Scott lo había tomado. Y todos le habían creído a él, porque… bueno, porque ¡era cierto! Evan estaba seguro.

—No conoces a Scott —dijo Evan, sacudiendo su cabeza otra vez. Pero podía escuchar la voz de su madre: *Los rumores son como las palomas. Vuelan por todos lados y causan problemas en todos los lugares a los que van.*

Capítulo 5
Acusado

acusado, s. Persona a quien se culpa por un delito o a quien se juzga por un delito.

Jessie y Megan caminaban hacia la escuela. Era tarde. Jessie había llamado a Megan a las 7:00 esa mañana, y nuevamente a las 7:30 y luego a las 7:55 y a las 8:10, pero a pesar de eso, Megan había salido tarde de su casa. ("Me atrasé porque no dejabas de llamarme", gruñó mientras salía por la puerta). *Diez minutos tarde.* Así que ahora iban un poco corriendo, un poco caminando, tratando de llegar a la escuela antes de que sonara la campana.

Normalmente, a Jessie no le hubiera importando perder el tiempo en el patio antes de clase, pero hoy tenía cosas que hacer. En el patio. Antes de la escuela. Sin adultos alrededor.

—Vamos, vamos —le decía a Megan. Las piernas de Megan eran más largas que las de Jessie, pero Megan era lenta porque su morral le iba golpeando las rodillas.

—¿Por qué tenemos que llegar tan temprano? —preguntó Megan. Iba dando zancadas, unos diez pies delante de Jessie.

—Lo sabrás cuando lleguemos. Sigue corriendo, sigue corriendo.

—Apúrense, chicas —dijo Darlene cuando llegaron al cruce peatonal—. Escuché la primera campana.

Jessie y Megan cruzaron rápidamente la calle. No estaba permitido correr.

—¡Oh, no! —dijo Jessie cuando doblaron la esquina y vieron el patio—. Ya se están formando. *¡Vamos!*

Cuando Jessie y Megan llegaron al patio, todo cuarto grado ya estaba formado, esperando la señal para ingresar a la escuela. Las chicas deberían haber ido al final de la fila, pero Jessie fue directamente al medio, donde Scott Spencer estaba tratando de quitarle la gorra de béisbol a Paul. Evan estaba parado más lejos, botando la pelota de básquetbol de la clase. Esta semana era el Encargado del Equipo, es decir que era responsable de todas las cosas del patio: pelotas, sogas, Frisbees.

—¡Ey! —dijo Scott al ver a Jessie—. ¡El final de la fila está *allá* atrás!

—¿Y? —dijo Jessie, mientras hurgaba en su mochila.

—Nada de colarse —dijo Scott—. ¿No es esa la *regla?*

Hasta Jessie se daba cuenta de que se estaba burlando de ella.

—No me estoy colando —dijo Jessie, sacando una hoja de papel de su mochila y sosteniéndola frente a sí—. Te estoy entregando una orden de detención.

Algunos de los chicos ubicados adelante de

Scott se dieron vuelta, y algunas de las chicas del final de la fila se movieron para poder ver también.

—¿Estás qué? —preguntó Scott.

—Ten —dijo Jessie, y ubicó el pedazo de papel más cerca de él. Scott se acercó y lo tomó como para romperlo en pedazos.

—¡Listo! —gritó Jessie—. Lo tocaste. Quiere decir que has sido notificado. Ahora debes presentarte ante el tribunal.

Jessie estaba bastante segura de que sabía lo que estaba haciendo. Había estado leyendo un folleto llamado "Juicio por jurado: El sistema legal estadounidense en pocas palabras". Era uno de los folletos del servicio público que su mamá escribía como parte de su trabajo como consultora de relaciones públicas.

Inmediatamente, Scott arrojó el papel al suelo como si quemara.

—¡No puedes hacer eso!

—Oh, claro que puedo —dijo Jessie—. Si lo tocas,

eso quiere decir que has sido notificado. No puedes librarte ahora.

—¿Librarme de qué? ¿De qué hablas? —Para entonces, toda la fila se había dado vuelta para observar. Evan había dejado de driblar la pelota, pero no se movió de la fila.

Jessie recogió la orden de detención del piso y la leyó en voz alta. La había escrito con la pluma de caligrafía que su abuela le había regalado para su último cumpleaños.

ORDEN DE DETENCIÓN PARA SCOTT SPENCER

Scott Spencer, por la presente, se lo acusa del delito de robar $208 del bolsillo de los pantalones cortos de Evan Treski el 5 de septiembre de este año.

El viernes debe comparecer ante el tribunal para presentar su defensa. Allí, un Jurado de Pares decidirá si es culpable o no. Si se lo declara culpable

Hasta ahí había llegado cuando Scott interrumpió.

—Esto es una broma —dijo cruzando los brazos y riendo—. ¿Es una broma, verdad?

Jessie sacudió la cabeza. Ninguno de los alumnos de cuarto hablaba. Todos estaban mirando a Jessie y a Scott. Ella continuó leyendo:

—Si se lo declara culpable...

—¿Estás diciendo —dijo Scott, achicando los ojos y con el ceño fruncido—, que yo robé dinero?

Jessie inspiró profundamente. Sabía que era grave acusar a alguien de esa manera.

—Sí. Eso digo —dijo. Se escucharon rumores entre los alumnos de cuarto grado.

—¿Y *tú*? —preguntó Scott volviéndose hacia Evan y dando unos pasos hacia adelante. Se acercó para tocar a Evan en el pecho, pero Evan apartó su mano de un manotazo antes de que pudiera tocarlo—. ¿*Tú* estás diciendo que yo robé tu dinero?

Jessie miró a Evan. Él dribló la pelota dos veces y luego la sostuvo en la mano, mirándola. De repente, Jessie comprendió que debía haber hablado con

Evan antes de hacer esto. Él había sido la víctima del delito. Él era el que tendría que seguir jugando en el recreo todos los días con Scott. Él era el que debería declarar en un tribunal en su contra.

Pero ya era muy tarde. Todos estaban mirándolos. Todos esperaban para ver qué ocurría luego.

Evan dribló la pelota nuevamente. Uno, dos, tres. Jessie sabía qué estaba pensando Evan. Evan pensaba con todo el cuerpo, no solo con el cerebro.

—Sí. Estoy diciendo eso —dijo en voz baja—. Digo que tú me robaste dinero.

La fila de los alumnos de cuarto se había doblado y formaba una C grande y desaliñada, y ambas puntas observaban lo que ocurría en el medio.

Ahora que Evan había acusado a Scott de robo, la fila comenzó a desarmarse a medida que los chicos se acercaban para escuchar lo que Scott diría luego. Pero fue Jessie quien habló primero.

—Si se lo declara culpable, su castigo será entregar su nuevo Xbox 20/20 a Evan Treski.

—¡De ninguna manera! —dijo Scott, pero apenas

se lo podía escuchar debido al ruido que estaban haciendo los alumnos de cuarto grado. Cada uno tenía su opinión sobre la justicia del castigo.

—Ey —dijo Ryan—. ¿Qué pasa si se lo declara inocente?

Jessie sacudió la cabeza.

—Eso no va a ocurrir.

—¡Sí va a ocurrir, tonta! —dijo Scott—. Y cuando ocurra, esto es lo que va a pasar. Los dos —señaló a Jessie y a Evan— van a pararse en la Reunión de la Mañana y dirán a todos, incluso a la Sra. Overton, que dijeron mentiras sobre mí y que no tomé nada de nadie. Y luego me van a pedir disculpas. Frente a *todos*.

—¡4-O! —La Sra. Overton estaba parada en la entrada, con una mirada de consternación—. ¿Qué clase de fila es esta?

Los chicos fueron rápidamente a sus lugares, y los que estaban adelante comenzaron a avanzar hacia el aula. Pero Evan, Jessie y Scott seguían mirándose unos a otros.

—¿Trato hecho? —preguntó Scott.

—Trato hecho —dijo Evan, le dio la espalda y entró al aula.

—Además, lo voy a poner por escrito —dijo Jessie. Agitó la orden de detención frente a Scott. Luego recogió su mochila y fue rápidamente al fondo de la fila, sonriendo.

Pronto se haría justicia.

ACUERDO DE RESARCIMIENTO POSTERIOR AL JUICIO DE SCOTT SPENCER

Si un tribunal determina que Scott Spencer es CULPABLE del delito de robar $208 del bolsillo de los pantalones cortos de Evan Treski el 5 de septiembre de este año, él le entregará su Xbox 20/20 a Evan Treski para siempre.

Si un tribunal determina que Scott Spencer es INOCENTE de robar $208 del bolsillo de los pantalones cortos de Evan Treski el 5 de septiembre de este año, Evan y Jessie Treski se pararán en la Reunión de la Mañana del lunes por la mañana y dirán a toda la clase que Scott Spencer no robó $208 del bolsillo de los pantalones cortos de Evan Treski el 5 de septiembre de este año, y se disculparán ante él por decir mentiras.

Evan Treski

Jessie Treski

Scott Spencer

imparcial

imparcial, adj. Que trata a todos por igual, sin tomar partido en una discusión; equitativo y justo.

En el recreo, Jessie no perdió tiempo. Evan la observó mientras sacaba las tarjetas, una por una, de un sobre grande. Todos los de cuarto se amontonaron a su alrededor.

—Tú eres el DEMANDANTE —le dijo a Evan, y le entregó una tarjeta verde en la que se leía DEMANDANTE—. Quiere decir que tú eres la víctima del delito.

Evan estudió la tarjeta, luego la metió en su bolsillo trasero. Un tribunal de niños le parecía una idea loca. Una idea loca de Jessie. Pero estaba acostumbrado, y gracias a esta podría tener un Xbox 20/20, y qué decir de la satisfacción de demostrar la culpa de Scott frente a todos. Por eso, estaba dispuesto a hacer el intento.

—Yo soy la abogada de Evan —dijo Jessie, y se asignó una tarjeta morada que decía ABOGADA DEL DEMANDANTE.

Luego se dirigió a Scott.

—Eres el demandado, es decir, el que está siendo juzgado.

Le dio una tarjeta amarilla que decía DEMANDADO.

Luego comenzó a entregar cinco tarjetas anaranjadas.

—¡Eh! —gritó Scott—. ¿Yo no tengo abogado?

—¡Espera! Tendrás uno en un minuto —dijo Jessie de manera cortante. Continuó repartiendo tarjetas.

—Quiero a Ryan —dijo Scott.

—Lo lamento —dijo Ryan, levantando una tarjeta anaranjada—. Soy testigo.

—Entonces quiero a Paul.

—Es testigo, también —dijo Jessie, dándole a Paul la última tarjeta anaranjada—. Todos los que estuvieron en la casa de Jack el día del delito son testigos.

—Bueno, pero ¿quién va a ser *mi* abogado? —preguntó Scott, arrugando su tarjeta de DEMANDADO.

Jessie ignoró la pregunta. Levantó una tarjeta morada.

—Megan, tú estás en el jurado —dijo. El corazón de Evan dio un brinco. Había un voto con el que podía contar.

—¿Cuándo es el juicio? —dijo Megan.

—Después de clase —dijo Jessie—. El viernes.

Megan sacudió la cabeza.

—Creo que nos vamos este fin de semana.

—¡No puedes perderte el juicio! —dijo Jessie.

Evan quería gritar lo mismo, pero mantuvo la boca cerrada.

—Hablaré con mi mamá —dijo Megan—. Quizás podamos salir más tarde. Pero sería mejor que le dieras esta tarjeta a otra persona.

Le devolvió la tarjeta morada a Jessie.

—Bueno, está bien —dijo Jessie, desilusionada—. Toma una de estas.

Le entregó a Megan una tarjeta blanca que decía PÚBLICO.

A Jessie solo le llevó otro minuto entregar las doce tarjetas del JURADO y el resto de las tarjetas del PÚBLICO. Todos los miembros del público eran niñas porque todos los testigos eran niños, y el jurado, como Jessie explicó a todos, tenía que ser cincuenta y cincuenta.

Evan miró a su alrededor. Era raro, la forma en que todos los chicos aceptaban la idea de Jessie. ¿No sabían que todo era falso? ¿Y cómo sabía Jessie todos estos temas legales? ¿Cómo hacía para saber siempre cosas que él no sabía?

Jessie reunió a las seis chicas que tenían las tarjetas blancas de público. Luego se volvió hacia Scott.

—Puedes elegir a cualquiera del público para que sea tu abogada. Técnicamente, ni siquiera necesitamos un público. No se ofen-

dan —dijo Jessie, volviéndose hacia las chicas.

—No quiero una chica como abogada —dijo
Scott.

—Haz lo que quieras —dijo Jessie, encogiéndose
de hombros—. Pero no vuelvas y te quejes de que
no se te ofreció asesoramiento legal.

—¡Chicas! —dijo Scott—. ¡Qué ofrecimiento!
Seré mi propio abogado. Me defenderé a mí
mismo.

Se volvió hacia Jessie.

—¡Y además te venceré! —dijo.

Típico de Scott, pensó Evan. Siempre pensando
que es el mejor. El chico que tiene las mejores cosas.
El que tiene las mejores vacaciones. El que tiene
todo.

—Bien —dijo Jessie—. Defiéndete solo. —Había
una sola tarjeta más en el sobre. Evan observó
mientras ella la sacaba lentamente. La tarjeta era
roja. Tenía una sola palabra.

Jessie miró a su alrededor como si estuviera
tomando una decisión muy importante, pero Evan

sabía que ella ya había decidido quién recibiría la tarjeta roja. Jessie nunca dejaba nada para último minuto.

—El juez va a ser... David Kirkorian.

Hubo un silencio sepulcral. Paul gritó:

—¿Es una broma?

—¡Él no puede ser juez! —dijo Ryan—. ¡Colecciona huesos humanos!

—¡No es verdad! —dijo David quien enrojeció, pero avanzó hacia Jessie y tomó la tarjeta de su mano.

Luego todos comenzaron a hablar al mismo tiempo. David, mientras tanto, sostenía la tarjeta roja y gritaba:

—¡Ja, ja! ¡Soy el juez! ¡Soy el juez! —Hicieron tanto ruido que la maestra de turno fue a ver qué estaba ocurriendo con la clase 4-O. Eso hizo callar a todos. Nadie quería que la maestra de turno participara. Una de las reglas tácitas del patio era *Nunca digas a la maestra de turno qué es lo que está pasando realmente*.

—¿Por qué él? —preguntó Paul cuando se fue la maestra de turno.

—Porque es el único en toda la clase que es *imparcial* —dijo Jessie—. No es amigo de Evan ni de Scott. Será justo. No tendrá favoritos. Y eso es lo más importante de un juez. Un juez debe tratar a todos de la misma manera.

David levantó la tarjeta roja con una mano y apoyó la otra sobre su corazón.

—Juro solemnemente que seré un juez justo —dijo.

—Bien —dijo Jessie.

Pero Evan no lo podía creer. ¿Quién iba a escuchar a un chico como David Kirkorian?

Para Evan, desde ese momento, el día fue cuesta abajo. Toda la tarde trabajaron en cosas que Evan odiaba: ejercicios de matemáticas, reglas de ortografía y el taller de escritores. Luego la Sra. Overton descubrió que faltaba una de las cuerdas de saltar del cajón de leche de 4-O, y ese era un error de Evan porque él era el Encargado del Equipo.

Pero lo que realmente arruinó el día, lo que hizo que un día horrible se convirtiera en uno de los peores diez días de su vida, ocurrió luego de la escuela.

Evan se estaba ajustando el casco de la bicicleta cuando Adam se acercó al rack y sacó su bicicleta.

—¿Quieres venir? —preguntó Evan.

—No puedo —dijo Adam—. Prometí a mi mamá que la ayudaría a preparar la casa para Yom Kipur.

—¿Es hoy? —preguntó Evan, ajustando la hebilla bajo la barbilla.

—Comienza el viernes por la noche, pero mi mamá quiere que limpie mi cuarto hoy y que haga otras cosas también.

Evan sabía que Yom Kipur es una fiesta en la que los adultos no comen durante todo el día. Se supone que los ayuda a pensar en sus pecados, pero Evan no podía comprenderlo. Cuando tenía hambre, no podía pensar en nada excepto en qué comería luego.

—¿Quieres venir a la fiesta del fin del ayuno? —preguntó Adam. Los Goldberg organizaban siempre una gran comida al atardecer una vez terminado el ayuno festivo.

—Claro —dijo Evan. Había estado en muchas cenas los viernes en la casa de Adam y en la de Paul. Le gustaban los candelabros e incluso las oraciones que no entendía, pero principalmente la comida: pan Jalá, pollo asado y pastel de compota de manzanas.

—¿Vas a estar todo el día entero sin comer este año? —preguntó Evan. El año anterior, Adam había presumido que haría ayuno el año siguiente para Yom Kipur.

Adam se encogió de hombros.

—Quizás lo intente—. Luego miró su bicicleta e hizo rebotar la rueda delantera un par de veces sobre el asfalto.

—Mira. Eh... Hay algo que quería decirte. ¿Recuerdas que el verano pasado Paul y Kevin y yo te abandonamos en el bosque?

—Sí —dijo Evan, preguntándose por qué Adam hablaba sobre algo que había ocurrido hacía meses. Evan se había enojado mucho entonces, pero ya había pasado.

—Bueno, lo lamento mucho. Y espero que me

perdones. —Evan parecía confundido. Adam se encogió de hombros.

—Amigo. Es Yom Kipur. El Día del Perdón. Debes salir y pedir a la gente que perdone tus pecados.

Evan se rio.

—¡Eres un tonto! —Empujó a Adam. Adam sonrió, simuló que iba a tirar un puñetazo, luego montó en su bici y se fue.

Evan estaba a punto de montar en su bici cuando vio a Ryan y a Paul caminando juntos hacia la acera. Atravesó el patio y cruzó frente a ellos antes de que llegaran a la verja. Antes de que Evan pudiera decir algo, Paul le puso el brazo alrededor y casi lo hace caer de la bici.

—Eh, Evan, realmente te debo una. Gracias por echarte la culpa cuando Charlie se soltó de la correa.

—Sí, bueno. No fue nada —dijo Evan, encogiéndose de hombros. Evan y Paul hacían eso todo el tiempo: intercambiaban culpas para no tener problemas con sus propios padres. Los padres siempre eran más benévolos con los otros niños que con los propios.

—¿Quieren venir? —preguntó Evan a Paul y Ryan, balanceándose en su bici sin pedalear.

Paul movió la cabeza.

—No, vamos a casa de Scott.

Evan se paró bruscamente y los miró a ambos.

—Dijo que podíamos probar el 20/20 —dijo Ryan—. Dice que es genial. Deberías venir también.

Evan sintió que le habían dado un golpe bajo.

—¡De ninguna manera! —gritó. Miró a Paul y a Ryan con una expresión que decía *¡Traidores!*, pero ninguno de ellos dijo nada. Finalmente, Evan dijo en voz baja:

—No puedo creer que vayan a su casa.

Paul se encogió de hombros.

—A nosotros no nos hizo nada.

—¡Qué buenos amigos! —dijo Evan.

—Vamos, Evan —dijo Paul—. Ni siquiera sabes con seguridad si él tomó el dinero...

—¡Sí, lo sé! —dijo Evan.

—Deberías venir —dijo Ryan—. Todos van luego de la escuela.

En la mente de Evan apareció la imagen de todo

cuarto grado marchando a la casa de Scott. Todos sus amigos. ¿Y él, dónde estaría? Estaría en su casa, con su hermanita.

—¿Quiénes? —preguntó—. Todos, ¿quiénes?

—Todos los chicos —dijo Paul—. Yo y Ryan y Jack y Kevin. Todos los chicos.

—Adam no —dijo Evan, pensando para sí que al menos tenía un amigo que era fiel.

—Bueno, tiene que ayudar a su madre con algunas cosas —dijo Ryan—, pero vendrá luego. Como en una hora.

Evan sacudió la cabeza sin poder creerlo. Su mejor amigo. Lo apuñalaba por la espalda. Jaló del manillar para alejarse de Paul y Ryan y se fue sin decir ni una palabra más.

Capítulo 7
Debida diligencia

debida diligencia, s. Dedicar tiempo y esforzarse para hacer un trabajo razonablemente bien, el opuesto de la negligencia.

—¿Podemos hacer una pausa ahora? —preguntó Megan, sentándose sobre las rodillas. Tenía el marcador azul en la mano como si fuera una vela encendida. Sus dedos estaban cubiertos de tinta de todos los colores y tenía un lápiz en la base de su cola de caballo.

Jessie estaba acostada boca abajo con toda su caja de lápices de colores esparcida frente a ella. ¡Imposible hacer una pausa ahora! El juicio era mañana. Todavía quedaba mucho por hacer.

Ya había hablado con los cinco testigos que darían testimonio —Paul, Ryan, Kevin, Malik y Jack— para determinar qué era exactamente lo que recordaban del día del delito cuando estaban en la casa de Jack. Había escrito tarjetas para David Kirkorian que le indicaban exactamente qué debía decir durante el juicio.

CUANDO COMIENZA EL JUICIO:

Golpeas con tu mazo y dices:

"¡Todos de pie! Comienza la sesión.

Preside el Juez David P. Kirkorian".

SI HABLA ALGUIEN QUE NO DEBE
HABLAR:

Dices: "¡Orden en la sala! ¡Orden

en la sala! Si no se queda callado,

lo declararé en desacato!".

CUANDO TOMAS JURAMENTO A LOS TESTIGOS:

Dices: "¿Jura decir la verdad,

toda la verdad y nada más que

la verdad?".

Jessie estaba terminando de pintar el mapa que mostraba dónde se pararía o se sentaría cada persona durante el juicio. ¡Y todavía tenía que escribir su alegato final!

Jessie sentía —por primera vez en la vida— que estaba a punto de hacer un examen y que no había estudiado lo suficiente.

—Trabajemos un poco más —dijo—. ¿Estás terminando con las credenciales?

Megan mostró a Jessie las doce credenciales del jurado,

las cinco credenciales de los testigos,

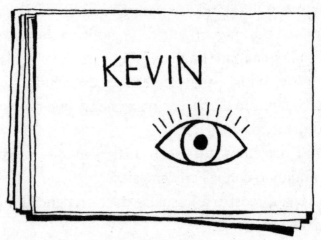

y la credencial del juez.

—Están bien —dijo Jessie—. Ahora solo tienes que hacer las del público.

Megan protestó:

—Por eso Evan te dice Jessie la Obsesiva.

Jessie odiaba ese apodo. ¡Odiaba todos los apodos! ¿Por qué Evan le había contado eso a Megan?

—No soy obsesiva. Soy responsable. Se llama *debida* —pensó un minuto, pero no podía recordar el nombre— "algo". Buscó entre los papeles que estaban esparcidos por el suelo y encontró "Juicio por jurado", el folleto que su madre había escrito. Comenzó a buscar entre las hojas.

—¡Hemos estado trabajando durante horas! —se lamentó Megan—. Quiero salir.

—¡Debida diligencia! —dijo Jessie—. Así se llama. Hacer el trabajo para que luego nadie pueda culparte ni decir que no has trabajado lo suficiente.

—Bueno, ¡la debida diligencia es ABURRIDA! —dijo Megan. Tomó la regla que Jessie había estado usando para dibujar líneas en el mapa y comenzó a balancearla verticalmente en la palma de la mano. Lo hacía bastante bien. Jessie quedó impresionada.

De repente, Megan preguntó:

—¿Piensas que realmente puedes probar que Scott robó el dinero de Evan?

Por un instante, Jessie sintió que se le cerraba la garganta.

Esa era la pregunta que más temía. Esa era la pregunta que había estado dando vueltas en su cabeza anoche, en la cama, mientras trataba de dormir.

—No lo sé. Más vale que sea capaz de hacerlo. —Jessie se imaginó parada frente a toda la clase disculpándose ante Scott. Le dieron ganas de vomitar.

Megan bajó la regla y se dejó caer al piso, y abrió los brazos y piernas como una estrella de mar. Levantó el mapa que Jessie había dibujado y que mostraba donde estarían todos en la sala del tribunal.

La sala del tribunal no era en verdad una "sala". Era la parte del patio de la escuela que tenía césped, la parte que estaba más alejada del edificio y de la zona del patio, y estaba cubierta por la sombra de

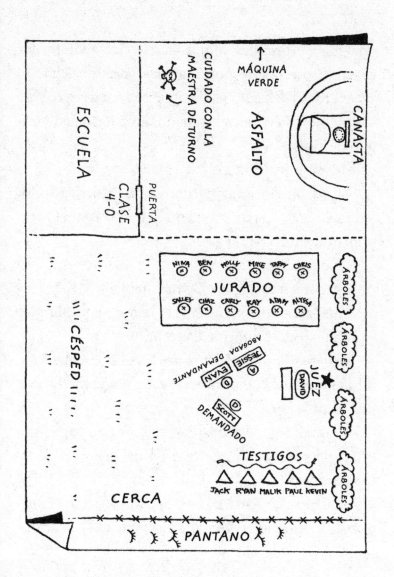

una fila de grandes olmos. Jessie había dibujado exactamente dónde pondrían las cajas de leche y las cuerdas y las pelotas y dónde se sentarían todos. Los nombres de todos estaban marcados con algún tipo de símbolo.

Megan miró el mapa.

—Casi puedo imaginarme cómo ocurrirá todo —dijo—. Solo hay un problema. Movió el papel para un lado y luego para el otro.

—No es simétrico. ¿Ves?

Jessie miró el mapa. ¿De qué hablaba Megan?

—Se supone que debería estar equilibrado, ¿verdad? Todo uniforme. Pero mira.

Megan se quitó el lápiz de la cola de caballo y dibujó una línea de puntos delgada por el medio del dibujo de Jessie.

—Scott no tiene abogado —dijo—. Las partes no están parejas por lo que esto no es, digamos, *justo*. No para Scott.

—Bueno, es su culpa —dijo Jessie. Había trabajado mucho en el mapa para que lo criticaran.

—Pero —dijo Megan—. ¿No dice la ley que todos

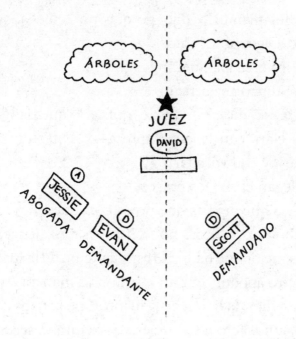

deben tener un abogado si son arrestados? Incluso si eres pobre y nadie te quiere. Incluso si todos creen que eres culpable. Debes tener un abogado. Así lo hacen siempre en la tele.

Jessie se encogió de hombros.

—Quiere defenderse solo. En un tribunal, está permitido hacerlo.

Megan sacudió la cabeza.

—Solamente lo dijo porque no tenía a quién elegir. Digo, ni un chico.

Miró el mapa nuevamente.

—No parece correcto.

—¿Qué dices? —Jessie quisiera que la gente fuera clara con lo que expresa—. ¿Estás diciendo que estoy equivocada?

Megan cruzó los brazos.

—Lo que digo es que no es *justo* que Evan tenga un abogado y Scott no. Y tú lo sabes, Jessie. Lo sabes mejor que nadie. Eres... la Reina de la Justicia.

¡Otro apodo! ¿Era un insulto? La manera en que Megan dijo "la Reina de la Justicia" no sonaba como un insulto. Pero Jessie no estaba segura. A veces, las personas dicen algo de una manera, pero quieren decir exactamente lo opuesto. Se llamaba *sarcasmo*, y Jessie siempre se lo perdía, como una pelota lanzada con mucha velocidad que la dejara bateando al aire.

Afuera, Jessie podía escuchar el rebote constante de una pelota de básquetbol en la entrada del garaje. Evan. Lanzando a la canasta. ¿Sabía cuánto estaba trabajando ella... por *él*?

Luego cesó el rebote, y escuchó que un carro entraba en el garaje. Megan también lo escuchó.

—Es mi mamá —dijo—. Debo irme.

Megan tenía cita con el dentista a las cuatro.

Por primera vez, Jessie estaba feliz de que Megan se fuera.

Capítulo 8
Defensa

defensa, s. Argumento presentado en un
tribunal para probar la inocencia de la
persona acusada; (en deportes) el acto de
proteger el propio arco contra el equipo
opuesto.

No hacía tanto calor como para sudar, pero Evan
estaba sudando. A los costados de la cara le caían
dos anchos ríos, y cada vez que giraba sentía que las
gotas salían volando desde las puntas de su cabello.

Iba a meter este tiro aunque se muriera en el
intento.

Había estado trabajando toda la tarde en el tiro.
En realidad, lo había estado practicando todo el mes.
Era un tiro en suspensión desde la parte superior de
la llave. Unos buenos quince pies desde el cesto, y

estaba lanzando con la mano izquierda. Eso era lo que los grandes podían hacer, lanzar con su mano débil y, a pesar de eso, encestar. El papá de Evan solía decirle: "Trabaja desde tu lado débil y nadie podrá defenderse de ti".

Evan se puso de espaldas al cesto y clavó los pies en las líneas pintadas de la entrada del garaje. Dribló la pelota una vez, dos veces, tres veces, luego, como un cohete que sale de la plataforma de despegue, saltó al aire y giró con todo el cuerpo. Incluso mientras el cuerpo estaba cayendo al suelo pudo lanzar el tiro, alejándose del cesto mientras la pelota volaba hacia el mástil y…

falló.

A veces, lo lograba; a veces, no. Acertaba aproximadamente uno de cada diez tiros. Evan quería que fuera al revés: *fallar* uno de cada diez intentos. Era un tiro magistral. Si tuviera ese tipo de tiros en su bolsillo, podría vencer a cualquiera en la cancha.

Dribló la pelota una vez, dos veces, tres veces…

—Hola, Evan.

Evan se enderezó y miró hacia la calle. Megan venía en bici hacia él.

Venía frenando, y saltó de la bici, que luego llevó del manillar. Evan se sacudió para quitarse el sudor de los ojos. Luego agachó la cabeza y se secó la cara en la manga de su camiseta. A las chicas no les gusta el sudor.

—Pensé que tenías cita con el dentista —dijo mientras ella entraba la bicicleta.

—Fue rápido. Solo un chequeo —dijo—. ¿Jessie todavía está? —Megan señaló con la cabeza en dirección a la casa.

—Sí. Todavía se está preparando para El Gran Día. —Evan temía el juicio. Todos los de cuarto grado estarían ahí, mañana, en el patio luego de la clase. ¿Y si Jessie no podía probar que Scott Spencer era culpable? Ella no era una abogada de verdad. ¿Podía Evan contar realmente con sus amigos? Aparentemente, Paul y Ryan habían ido todos los días a casa de Scott luego de la escuela. Quizás cuando llegara el juicio, todos los chicos estarían del lado de Scott. Evan se imaginó parado delante de toda la clase y disculpándose ante Scott. Dribló la pelota, como si pudiera sacarse la idea de su cabeza.

—Guau —dijo Megan—. Ella se pone un tanto...

—Obsesiva —dijo Evan. Nuevamente pensó en lo que *él* había estado haciendo toda la tarde. ¿Cuántas veces había practicado ese tiro? ¿Cien veces? ¿Doscientas? Y pensaba continuar hasta que fuera demasiado oscuro como para ver el cesto. Quizás fuera algo de familia.

Como si le estuviera leyendo el pensamiento, Megan preguntó:

—¿Estuviste acá afuera todo el tiempo?

—Estoy practicando un tiro. ¿Quieres ver?

Megan se encogió de hombros y sonrió, y Evan decidió que eso significaba sí. Preparó los pies y comenzó el ritmo de su dribleo. *Por favor, que entre, por favor que entre, por favor que entre,* se decía mientras botaba la pelota sobre el asfalto.

Pero no lo hizo. Cayó *con estruendo* del tablero y rebotó hacia la calle. Evan tuvo que correr velozmente para evitar que rodara hacia la calle.

—Estuvo cerca —dijo Megan—. Realmente eres muy bueno.

Evan sacudió la cabeza mientras botaba la pelota nuevamente al centro de la pintura.

—Cerca no cuenta en el básquetbol. Encestas o no.

—Bueno, fue mejor de lo que yo podría haber hecho —dijo ella—. Y soy la mejor tiradora de mi equipo.

Evan alzó las cejas.

—¿Juegas básquetbol?

—Y fútbol —dijo ella—. Pero soy mejor en básquetbol.

—¿En serio? ¿Puedes hacer una canasta de tres puntos?

Megan se rio.

—A veces.

—Entonces, veamos —dijo Evan. Le tiró la pelota y ella dribló por la entrada de automóviles para que sus pies estuvieran apenas fuera de la línea de tres puntos.

Evan observó cómo Megan tomaba la pelota, observó el modo en que su cola de caballo se movía para adelante y para atrás, y sus pulseras danzaban para arriba y para abajo en el brazo.

—Bien, aquí va —dijo ella—. Pero no te hagas ilusiones.

Levantó la pelota sobre su cabeza, y la envió cruzando el aire como sale el agua de la manguera del jardín. Aterrizó justo en el cesto.

—¡Increíble! —dijo Evan. Tomó la pelota que rebotaba e hizo un tiro fácil.

—¿Quieres hacer unos tiros? Podríamos jugar HORSE. O un uno contra uno, si...

Evan pensó en defenderse contra una chica y el estómago se le retorció. ¿Cómo te defiendes de una persona sin tocarla en ningún momento?

—No puedo —dijo Megan, mirando hacia la calle—. Voy a la casa de alguien.

—¿De quién? —preguntó Evan, botando la pelota entre sus piernas. Era un tirador bastante bueno, pero era un excelente base. Cuando jugara con los profesionales, probablemente sería un base. Sí, no reciben toda la gloria, pero los base mandan en la cancha.

Megan señaló con la mano hacia la calle, pero no dijo ningún nombre mientras se colocaba el casco de bici. Evan dejó de driblar.

—¿La casa de quién?

Megan pateó el pedal de su bici para que girara hacia atrás, y los frenos hicieron un chirrido como insectos en una noche de verano.

—A la casa de Scott. Dijo que podía probar su 20/20.

Un codazo en medio del rostro. Así se sintieron sus palabras. Evan apretó la pelota entre sus manos.

—¿Ahora es tu mejor amigo?

Megan lo miró.

—No es necesario ser mejores amigos para ir a la casa de alguien.

—Sí, bueno, realmente parece que de repente todos son amigos de Scott. —Parecía como si el 20/20 fuera la única cosa de la que todos hablaban. Scott era siempre el centro de atención. Y ahora...

Ahora Megan también iba. Evan alzó la pelota y la lanzó con fuerza contra la puerta del garaje. La golpeó con un ruido estrepitoso y de enfado. Tiró la pelota nuevamente.

—Lo único que les importa a todos ustedes es el estúpido 20/20. —De repente, Evan se dio cuenta de que Scott no necesitaba un abogado. Ya tenía la mejor defensa de la ciudad: el 20/20. Nadie diría que Scott era culpable si eso significaba perderse la oportunidad de jugar con el mejor juego de todos los tiempos.

—Oh, vamos —dijo Megan—. Apuesto a que mueres de ganas de probarlo también.

Evan no respondió. Simplemente continuó golpeando la pelota contra la puerta del garaje.

Megan se fue en su bici y dijo:

—Te veo en la escuela.

Cuando estaba en el medio de la calle, Evan le gritó:

—¡Te veo en el *tribunal*!

Capítulo 9
Auténtico

auténtico, adj. Del latín, significa "buena fe", genuino, "cosa real".

Jessie estaba colgada de la Máquina Verde, con las rodillas enganchadas en el pasamanos. Decidió que este sería el mejor viernes de su vida. Luego de la escuela, todos se juntarían en el patio para el juicio, incluso Megan, que había convencido a su madre de salir más tarde de viaje. La Sra. Overton les había dado permiso para usar el equipo del patio después de la clase. Jessie tenía su mapa. Tenía sus tarjetas. Había practicado su alegato final al menos veinte veces. Incluso Evan la había escuchado practicar y le había dado algunos buenos consejos sobre cómo mejorar el discurso. *Hoy será un gran día*, pensó.

En ese momento, Scott Spencer se aproximó y clavó su cara justo al lado de la suya.

—Mi *mamá* será mi abogada —dijo.

—¿Qué? —dijo Jessie. Se sujetó de la barra y se deslizó hacia el piso. Todos sabían que la mamá de Scott era una exitosa abogada que trabajaba en el centro. Jessie había escuchado un millón de veces lo hermosa que era su oficina. Scott decía que podías ver toda la ciudad desde su ventana. A veces, su nombre aparecía en el periódico.

—Así es. Mi mamá. Va a barrer contigo. ¡Te va a enterrar viva!

Jessie miró a Scott de reojo.

—¿Se toma un día de licencia en el trabajo?

—No —dijo Scott, mirando a Jessie con desdén—. Pero dijo que saldría temprano. Le dije que era importante, y ella dijo que aquí estaría.

—Bueno... ella... no puede —dijo Jessie, tartamudeando—. Es solo para chicos. No se permite la participación de adultos.

—¿Estás diciendo que no puedo tener una abogada?

—No dije eso —dijo Jessie. Pero estaba atrapada y lo sabía. Todos tienen derecho a un asesor legal. Estaba en la página dos de "Juicio por jurado". Lo decía la ley.

—Bien —dijo, apretando los labios—. Pero más vale que no llegue tarde.

Jessie recordó esas palabras esa tarde mientras corría de acá para allá en el patio, poniendo todo para armar la sala del tribunal para que el juicio comenzara a tiempo.

Por suerte, la Sra. Overton les había permitido usar el equipo del patio sin hacer ninguna pregunta. Había dejado en claro que era responsabilidad de Evan poner todo en su lugar cuando terminaran de jugar. Si bien era viernes por la tarde y ya la escuela había terminado, técnicamente Evan todavía era el Encargado del Equipo hasta el lunes por la mañana.

Para las tres menos cuarto, Jessie había llevado todo el equipo afuera y había instalado el cajón de leche bajo los olmos, apoyado sobre uno de los extremos para que pareciera un estrado. Sobre el cajón, colocó la pila de tarjetas que indicaban a David Kirkorian qué debía decir *exactamente*, luego llamó a David. Él tenía un mazo de madera en una mano y una bolsa de papel marrón en la otra.

—Mira lo que me prestó mi padre —dijo David, moviendo el mazo—. Era un mazo de broma, y dijo que podíamos usarlo.

—¿Qué hay ahí? —preguntó Jessie señalando la bolsa.

David tomó la bolsa y sacó una tela negra enrollada. La deslizó sobre su cabeza. La tela cayó hasta sus pies.

—Es la toga de graduación de mi hermano —dijo—. Sé que parece grande, pero espera.

Se paró detrás del estrado para que el cajón de leche tapara la tela sobrante que arrastraba en el piso. Jessie tuvo que admitirlo: lo hacía verse como un juez de verdad. Y cuando sacudió el mazo sobre el bloque de madera que había traído, Jessie sintió que podría contar con que David Kirkorian haría bien su parte.

Frente al cajón de leche, Jessie colocó dos pelotas de básquetbol, una para que se sentara Evan y otra para Scott. La "silla" de Jessie era la pelota de jugar al quemado, y la puso al lado de la de Evan. ¿Debía poner la otra pelota del quemado para que se sentara la madre de Scott? No podía imaginar una adulta sentada en una pelota como lo hacen los niños por lo que dejó la segunda pelota del quemado en el cajón. Para un lado, estiró las cuerdas de saltar para formar un cuadrado en el césped donde se sentaría el jurado, y del otro lado puso una vieja soga que marcaba el lugar en que se pararían los testigos mientras esperaban para dar su testimonio. Había solamente seis personas en el público, por lo que Jessie se imaginó que se sentarían detrás de los tres Frisbees que había colocado con mucho cuidado sobre el césped.

—¡Se ve genial! —dijo Megan, acercándose a Jessie. Jessie miró alrededor. Por primera vez, podía ver realmente la sala del tribunal. No era solamente una imagen en su cabeza. No era solamente un mapa dibujado sobre un pedazo de papel. Era un tribunal auténtico. Verdadero.

Asintió, y una mariposa le hizo cosquillas en el estómago.

—Por ahora, todo bien.

Capítulo 10
Juicio por jurado

juicio por jurado, s. Un proceso legal en el cual la culpabilidad o la inocencia de una persona acusada de un delito es decidida por un grupo de sus pares, y no por un juez o un panel de jueces.

Evan miró alrededor y sintió como si hubiera caído en un universo paralelo.

En primer lugar, estaba sentado sobre una pelota de básquetbol, y eso era extraño.

En segundo lugar, su hermana estaba allí, actuando como si fuera la líder del mundo libre. En casa, Jessie a veces era algo mandona, pero en la escuela Evan estaba acostumbrado a verla a un costado. Al margen de lo que estuviera ocurriendo en el patio. Comiendo en silencio en la mesa de la cafetería. Sentada con las manos sobre las piernas en las asambleas escolares.

De repente, era la líder. Era raro.

Evan miró a los doce niños sentados en el banco del jurado y también le resultó extraño. Si los miraba uno por uno, solo veía las caras de chicos a los que conocía de toda la vida. Nada nuevo. Sin embargo, cuando los veía en conjunto, sentados en el cuadrado que Jessie había hecho con cuerdas de saltar, se veían distintos. Hasta Adam, su mejor amigo, era casi un desconocido. Ellos eran los miembros del jurado, podrían darle un nuevo Xbox 20/20 o hacer que tuviera que disculparse en clase frente a todos. De pronto, no se parecían a los niños que conocía de toda la vida. Se habían convertido en algo mucho más importante.

Los ojos de Evan fueron de una punta a otra de la sala del tribunal: desde los testigos detrás de la línea de la cuerda, hasta el público que esperaba pacientemente el comienzo del juicio, y David Kirkorian de pie en su estrado hecho con un cajón de leche.

Y eso era lo más extraño de todo. Cada uno de los niños de cuarto grado se había presentado luego de la escuela y llevaba una credencial con su nombre (bueno, Malik se había colocado la credencial en el trasero, pero estaba de pie en el banco de los testigos, listo para atestiguar). Todos estaban esperando que Jessie dijera qué debían hacer. Era como si de pronto hubiera un conjunto de reglas completamente nuevas en la escuela, y todos, *absolutamente todos*, hubieran aceptado seguirlas.

Scott Spencer estaba sentado sobre su pelota de básquetbol. Tenía las rodillas bien separadas y tamborileaba sobre la pelota. *Tun tun tun paf, tun tun tun paf, tun tun tun paf.* Tenía esa mirada. Esa mirada de Scott Spencer. La mirada que parecía decir: "Todo está bien, no hay problema, tengo el control".

Eso era lo que pasaba con Scott Spencer. De alguna manera, de alguna forma, siempre lograba dar vuelta las cosas para sacar ventaja. Evan recordó la vez que en primer grado estaban en el cuarto de juegos de Scott. La mamá de Scott estaba en el trabajo. Su papá trabajaba en casa, igual que la mamá de Evan, pero su oficina estaba en el otro extremo de la casa y era a prueba de ruidos. Evan recordó que solían jugar a ver quién hacía suficiente ruido como para que el Sr. Spencer saliera de su oficina. Casi era necesario poner una bomba para que saliera.

Ese día jugaban a los palitos chinos por monedas, apostaban un centavo por cada juego. Al principio, ganaba Scott. Evan había perdido unos siete centavos. Pero entonces Evan comenzó a alcanzarlo y luego lo superó, y Scott le debía once centavos, lo que parecía un montón de dinero en ese momento.

—Ey, vamos por un bocadillo —dijo Scott, y hubieran podido ir ellos mismos a buscar algo a la cocina, pero Scott fue a la oficina de su papá y le pidió que les llevara algo al cuarto de juegos. Por supuesto, cuando el papá de Scott vio que estaban apostando dinero, puso fin al juego y pidió a Evan que devolviera todo lo que había ganado.

—En esta casa está prohibido apostar —dijo. Pero Evan pensó: *Perder, eso es lo que no está permitido.*

Evan miró a Scott. Evan no era un niño

pendenciero. Solo había participado en dos peleas a puñetazos en toda su vida, y una de ellas había sido con Adam, su mejor amigo. Las dos peleas habían sido rápidas y explosivas, y luego habían terminado. Sin rencores. Disculpas y más disculpas. Todos estuvieron de acuerdo en no pelear más.

¿Por qué no podía ser así con Scott? ¿Qué tenía Scott que le hacía hervir la sangre a Evan, que llevó una cosa a la otra para que pasaran de una pelea por desaparición de dinero a un juicio con jurado? Evan abrió la boca para decirle algo a Scott...

En ese momento exacto, David K. levantó el mazo, lo golpeó contra el bloque de madera y leyó la primera tarjeta:

—¡Todos de pie! El tribunal entra en sesión. Preside el juez David P. Kirkorian.

Capítulo 11
perjurio

perjurio, s. Decir una mentira de manera intencional en un juicio luego de haber jurado decir la verdad y nada más que la verdad.

—¿Puede pasar al frente la abogada de la fiscalía? —dijo el juez Kirkorian. Todavía no había llegado la abogada de la defensa, la madre de Scott, pero no podían seguir esperando. Casi la mitad del jurado tenía que volver a su casa antes de las cuatro.

Jessie se puso de pie y se dirigió al tribunal. Habló con voz firme:

—Damas y caballeros del jurado, como primer testigo, llamo a Jack Bagdasarian.

Jack caminó hasta el estrado, y David le indicó que pusiera la mano derecha sobre el corazón y que sostuviera en alto la mano izquierda.

—¿Jura decir la verdad, toda la verdad y nada más que la verdad? —preguntó David.

—Lo juro —dijo Jack, de pie, firme como un soldado.

—Prosiga —dijo David, volviéndose hacia Jessie.

Jessie caminó hasta Jack.

—Sr. Bagdasarian —dijo—. ¿Dónde se encontraba usted el domingo, cinco de septiembre?

—¿Qué quieres decir? —preguntó Jack—. ¿Es ese el día en que Scott robó el dinero?

—¡Ey! ¡Yo no robé el dinero! —gritó Scott.

—¡Eso dices tú! —gritó Malik, y todos comenzaron a gritar.

—Ponga orden en la sala —chilló Jessie a David que estaba de pie, mirando la escena como si fuera una película en televisión.

David buscó entre sus tarjetas hasta que encontró la indicada. Entonces golpeó con el mazo sobre el bloque de madera.

—¡Orden en la sala! ¡Orden en la sala! Si no se callan, los voy a declarar en —miró su tarjeta más de cerca— ¡desacato!

David sacudió la tarjeta y agregó:

—Esto significa que serán enviados a casa. Y cuando vuelvan a la escuela el lunes, no les diremos qué ocurrió.

Entonces, todos se callaron.

Jessie se volvió a dirigir al testigo.

—El cinco de septiembre fue el día en el que todos fueron a su casa a nadar —dijo ella—. ¿Puede contarle al tribunal qué recuerda de ese día?

Entonces, Jack contó la historia: habían jugado al básquetbol en el patio, Evan y Jack, Paul y Ryan, y Kevin y Malik, pero hacía mucho calor, así que decidieron nadar en la casa de Jack. Entonces, Jack entró a preguntarle a su mamá si podían y cuando volvió al patio, Scott también estaba allí, y fueron todos a la casa de Jack.

—¿Y luego qué sucedió? —preguntó Jessie, caminando de atrás hacia delante frente al estrado. Tenía un lápiz y llevaba el Cuaderno de Escritura plegado debajo del brazo. La hacía sentirse más profesional.

—Jugamos al básquetbol en la piscina —dijo

Jack—. Tengo una canasta flotante, así que tonteamos y esas cosas.

—¿Evan nadó con su propio traje de baño o le pidió uno prestado a usted? —preguntó Jessie.

—Creo que me pidió uno —dijo Jack—. Sí, estoy seguro. Y también Scott.

—Entonces, Evan y Scott se pusieron trajes de baño prestados en su casa. ¿Correcto?

—Sip —dijo Jack, asintiendo con la cabeza.

—¿Y dónde dejaron la ropa cuando se fueron a nadar? —preguntó Jessie, señalando con el dedo a Jack para que el jurado supiera que estaban llegando a la parte crucial.

—En mi habitación, creo. Allí es donde todos dejan sus zapatos y calcetines y las cosas en casa, porque si dejan algo en el piso de abajo, el perro lo agarra.

—Entonces, aclaremos este punto —dijo Jessie, parada directamente frente a Jack—. Los pantalones cortos de Evan, y lo que fuera que tuviera en los bolsillos, estaban en su habitación. Y los pantalones cortos de Scott, y lo que fuera que tuviera en los bolsillos, también estaban en su habitación, ¿Correcto?

—Sí. Ya lo dije.

Jessie se volvió hacia el jurado.

—Solo quiero asegurarme de que todos conozcan ese hecho. Los pantalones cortos de Evan y los de Scott estaban en la misma habitación.

Le dio la espalda a Jack.

—Una pregunta más para usted, Sr. Bagdasarian. ¿Alguien salió de la piscina y entró a la casa?

—Claro —dijo Jack, riéndose—. Bueno, habíamos tomado como diez galones de limonada y habíamos comido sandía. No se puede retener *eso* para siempre.

La sala estalló en una carcajada, pero David golpeó con el mazo con tanta fuerza que todos se callaron de inmediato. Nadie quería ser enviado a casa antes de que hubiera un veredicto.

—¿Entró *Scott* a la casa? —preguntó Jessie.

—Sip —dijo Jack.

—¿Entró *solo*?

—Sí.

—¿Y durante cuánto tiempo estuvo solo en la casa?

—No lo sé —dijo Jack, encogiéndose de hombros.

—¿El suficiente como para que subiera las escaleras y robara un sobre lleno de dinero de los pantalones cortos de Evan? —preguntó Jessie.

—Sin duda —dijo Jack—. Estuvo allí un buen rato. Y sé que entró a mi cuarto porque se había cambiado de ropa.

—¿Cambiado? —preguntó Jessie—. ¿Por qué hizo eso?

—Dijo que tenía que irse de inmediato.

—¿Pero dijo por qué?

—No. Solo dijo que tenía que irse.

—¿Se fue de la casa con apuro?

—Tendrías que haberlo visto. Salió corriendo. Creo que ni siquiera tenía las dos zapatillas puestas cuando se fue.

—Imagino que no revisó sus bolsillos antes de que saliera, ¿verdad?

—Eh, no —dijo Jack.

—Qué lástima —murmuró Evan. Jessie miró a su hermano. No parecía contento.

—Eso es todo —dijo Jessie.

—El testigo puede retirarse —dijo David con su voz seria de juez, y como Jack no se movía, agregó:

—Puede retirarse.

—¿Retirarme? —preguntó Jack, mirando el piso.

—Puede volver a la zona de testigos —dijo David, y miró a Jack de una manera que le hizo a Jack cerrar la boca y obedecer.

Jessie llamó a los testigos uno por uno, y cada uno de los chicos dijo lo mismo: Scott había entrado a la casa para usar el baño, había salido poco después ya cambiado y luego se había ido rápido. Escuchar la historia cinco veces hacía que pareciera una verdad absoluta. Jessie estaba contenta. Tanto que decidió llamar a Evan a declarar. No tenía preguntas pensadas para él, pero no importaba. Todos querían a Evan, y Jessie sabía que era una buena estrategia poner a un testigo querido a declarar.

Sin embargo, cuando ella dijo, "Como siguiente testigo, llamo a Evan Treski a declarar", Evan la miró furioso. Caminó hasta el estrado del juez como si estuviera yendo a la horca. Cuando se volvió hacia el tribunal, sus pulgares le colgaban de los bolsillos, y tenía los hombros encorvados hacia delante. *¿Cuál era el problema?*, pensó Jessie. *¡Iban a ganar!*

—Sr. Treski —comenzó Jessie—. ¿Podría, por favor, decirle al tribunal dónde se encontraba la tarde del cinco de septiembre?

—¡Eso ya lo sabemos! —gritó Taffy Morgan, que estaba sentada en la segunda fila del banco del jurado.

—¡Pregúntale *otra cosa*!

—¡Sí! —gritó Tessa James desde el público.

—Pregúntale de dónde sacó todo ese dinero. Eso quisiera yo saber.

Ben Lesser gritó lo mismo:

—¡Pregúntale eso!

Y Nina Lee se hizo eco:

—¡Sí, pregúntale eso!

Lentamente, Jessie sintió que el calor le subía al rostro. Eso era lo *último* que quería preguntarle a

Evan mientras estuviera en el banquillo. Si el jurado descubría que Evan le había robado el dinero a ella, sería el fin. Algunos de los chicos del banco del jurado comenzaron a gritar:

—¡Pregúntale!, ¡pregúntale!

—¡Orden en la sala! —gritó David.

Cuando todos se quedaron callados, le dijo a Jessie: —Es una buena pregunta. ¿Por qué no le pregunta eso?

—Él es *mi* testigo —dijo Jessie—, y soy yo quien hace las preguntas.

Jessie conocía las reglas: ella era la abogada, y nadie podía obligarla a hacer preguntas a su testigo que ella no quisiera hacer.

—Preguntaré lo que quiera y no quiero preguntarle eso.

—¿Qué pasa? —dijo Scott—. ¿Tienes algo que ocultar?

—Déjala en paz —dijo Evan.

—Sí, déjenme en paz —dijo Jessie, pasando la mirada de David a Scott a Evan.

—Bien —dijo Scott, cruzando los brazos con sorna—. No le preguntes. Le pediré a mi mamá que le pregunte de dónde sacó el dinero.

—Tu mamá ni siquiera está aquí —dijo Jessie con rabia—. Y estoy segura de que no va a aparecer, tampoco.

Scott se puso de pie de un salto, parecía estar a punto de darle un puñetazo a Jessie.

—Va a venir. Está demorada, eso es todo. Porque es una abogada *de verdad*, con un trabajo *de verdad*. ¡No como tú! ¡Farsante!

—Orden en la sala o los voy a echar a ambos —gritó David.

Se paró frente al estrado y sacudió el mazo sobre su cabeza como si fuera a golpear a alguien con él. Luego se volvió hacia Jessie y dijo:

—Podrías preguntarle eso a Evan, Jessie. Va a terminar contestándolo de todas maneras.

Y Jessie supo que tenía razón.

Había metido la pata. Pensar que se sentía tan bien... Tan confiada. Tan segura de sí misma.

—Sr. Treski —dijo—, ¿de dónde sacó usted el dinero, los doscientos ocho dólares que tenía en el bolsillo ese día?

Perfectamente se habría podido oír la caída de un alfiler, aunque un alfiler no hubiera hecho ruido debido al césped. Pero la sala estaba en *silencio*. Hasta los pájaros parecían haberse callado, como esperando la respuesta.

Evan murmuró algo, y Jessie tuvo que pedirle que repitiera lo que había dicho.

—Lo saqué de tu caja —dijo Evan, mirándola como si quisiera aplastarla como a un insecto.

Nadie dijo ni una palabra. Todos miraron a Evan, y Evan miró a Jessie.

—¿Lo *robaste*? —preguntó Paul, abriendo los ojos con asombro.

—Ey, nunca nos contaste *esa* parte de la historia —dijo Adam, sacudiendo la cabeza.

—Guau. ¿Le robaste dinero a tu hermanita? —dijo Scott, sonriendo por primera vez en toda la tarde—. Eso es muy *bajo*.

Jessie agachó la mirada. Sabía que Evan la estaba mirando de una manera que parecía decir *"ojalá no hubieras nacido".*

—¿Perdón? —dijo una voz desde el público. Jessie se dio vuelta. Era Megan, y estaba levantando la mano como en clase.

—El juez le da la palabra a Megan Moriarty —dijo David.

—El juez no puede darle la palabra a una persona del público —dijo Jessie—. El público no tiene permiso para intervenir en un juicio. Está mal.

—Bueno —dijo David—. Yo soy el juez, yo decido. ¡Megan!

—¿Ese era mi dinero también? —preguntó Megan. Miró fijamente a Evan—. ¿Era mía la mitad de esos doscientos ocho dólares del puesto de limonada?

Jessie abrió la boca, pero no emitió sonido alguno. Evan dejó caer la cabeza sobre las manos.

En el juicio estaban apareciendo temas que Jessie jamás había pensado que fueran a aparecer. Como el hecho de que Evan había robado el dinero a Jessie antes de que Scott lo robara a Evan. O el hecho de que la mitad del dinero que él había perdido era de Megan. Pero que Evan planeaba devolver el dinero a Jessie un día después y que ella lo había perdonado por haber tomado el dinero, que Jessie y Evan habían trabajado duro para ganar el dinero de Megan para que *nunca supiera* que lo había perdido, nada de esto parecía importar demasiado. A la vista de todos, Evan era un ladrón. Un mentiroso ladrón.

De pronto, las palabras comenzaron a subir a los labios de Jessie.

—Él no lo robó —dijo ella—. *Yo* le dije que tomara el dinero. Se lo di para que lo cuidara. Él *no* lo robó.

Jessie se volvió hacia Megan.

—Es mi culpa que tu dinero haya sido robado.

Evan la miró. Megan la miró. Scott la miró. Toda la sala del tribunal se volvió hacia Jessie. Y lo único que Jessie podía pensar era que acababa de mentir en juicio. Y todos lo sabían.

Capítulo 12
sexta enmienda

Sexta Enmienda, s. Parte de la Constitución de los Estados Unidos que explica los derechos de toda persona acusada de un delito y llevada a juicio, incluso el derecho a contar con un abogado.

Jessie susurró:

—La fiscalía ha finalizado con las pruebas, —y ella y Evan volvieron a sus asientos. Evan no despegó la vista del suelo. No podía mirar a Jessie. Si lo hacía, sabía que su ira iba a desencadenarse sobre ella como lava de una grieta en la tierra. Había sido humillado frente a todo cuarto grado. Y aunque sabía que Jessie no lo había hecho a propósito, *todo era culpa de ella*. Si no lo hubiera llamado como testigo. Si no hubiera puesto a David como juez. Si no le hubiera dado a Scott Spencer esa tonta orden de detención, en primer lugar, nada de esto habría ocurrido.

David golpeó con el mazo tres veces.

—¿Puede pasar al frente la abogada de la defensa?

Evan vio a Scott girar la cabeza y mirar hacia el estacionamiento.

—Tenemos que esperar unos minutos más —dijo Scott, como si nada—. Todavía no ha llegado mi mamá.

—Si ella no viene... —dijo Paul—, ¿Scott pierde?

David buscó entre sus tarjetas.

—¿Jessie? ¿Scott pierde si su mamá no viene?

—¡Aquí llegó! —gritó Scott, saltando de su pelota—. ¡Les dije! ¡Les dije!

Se volvió hacia Jessie.

—Ahora van a ver a una *verdadera* abogada. Te hará quedar como una tonta.

Scott salió corriendo hacia el estacionamiento, donde una camioneta realizaba una maniobra.

Evan vio a Scott correr hasta el carro e inclinarse sobre la ventanilla abierta, hablándole a su mamá.

Scott se dio vuelta y señaló a los niños, sentados en la sala del tribunal. Evan apenas podía ver a la Sra. Spencer, las manos al volante, el motor del carro todavía encendido. Entonces, Scott se apartó del carro, y este se alejó.

Scott volvió y se sentó sobre su pelota. Se encogió de hombros. Evan notó que le pasaba algo.

—No puede quedarse —dijo Scott—. Tiene una reunión importante. Cosas de verdad, no cosas de niños.

Se encogió de hombros nuevamente y miró de frente a David, evitando la mirada de todos.

—¿Entonces? —dijo David—. ¿Qué hacemos ahora? —Todo el tribunal se volvió hacia Jessie que había estado callada desde que se sentó.

Evan miró a Jessie. Ella no sonreía, lo que lo sorprendió. Después de todo, esto significaba que habían ganado, ¿verdad? Al menos así es en el básquetbol. Si el otro equipo no aparece o no tiene suficientes jugadores, abandonan el juego, y eso significa que tu equipo gana automáticamente. En general, Evan odiaba los juegos ganados por abandono, incluso si le tocaba a él. Prefería jugar y perder, antes que ganar por abandono. Sin embargo, esta vez, Evan aceptaría la victoria de cualquier manera. La imagen que lo había estado persiguiendo por días, él en la Reunión de la Mañana disculpándose ante Scott, comenzó a desaparecer, y una nueva imagen ocupó su lugar. Evan con su nuevo Xbox 20/20 jugando con todos sus amigos en *su* casa.

Jessie dijo:

—David, tú dices: "¿Puede pasar al frente el abogado de la defensa"? Y Scott dirá... bueno, lo que quiera decir en su defensa, y después deberá decir: "La defensa ha finalizado con la presentación de pruebas", y eso es todo.

—Y después, el veredicto —dijo Salley Knight, desde el jurado—. Entonces, votamos y damos el veredicto.

—Correcto —dijo Jessie, con aire sombrío.

¿Cuál era su problema?, se preguntaba Evan. Era seguro que ganarían si Scott no tenía un abogado que lo defendiera.

—Ejem. —David se aclaró la voz.

—¿Puede pasar al frente el abogado de la defensa?

Todos volvieron la mirada hacia Scott, pero una voz desde el fondo de la sala rompió el silencio.

—Esa soy yo. —Megan se puso de pie desde el público y caminó hasta el frente de la sala.

¿Cómo?

Al principio, Evan pensó que había escuchado mal.

¿Megan Moriarty acababa de decir que iba a defender a Scott Spencer?

—No puedes hacer eso —dijo Evan, saltando desde su asiento—. Estás… estás… Quería gritar: *¡Se supone que estás de mi lado, no del suyo!,* pero no podía hacerlo. No frente a todo cuarto grado.

—¡Ey! —gritó David, golpeando su mazo una vez—. Orden en la sala. Demandante, siéntese. Si sigue causando disturbios, lo mandaré echar de la sala.

—Sí, claro. Como si pudieras —dijo Evan, pero se sentó sobre su pelota.

—Jessie —dijo David sosteniendo el reloj—. Son

las tres y media. Tengo que irme en diez minutos. ¿Esto está permitido?

Jessie asintió con la cabeza.

—Sí. Es... justo.

Evan no podía creerlo. ¿Estaba ocurriendo de verdad? ¿La chica de la que estaba *enamorado* estaba a punto de destruir su única oportunidad de vengarse de su mayor enemigo?

Megan se volvió hacia Scott.

—¿Sigues sin querer que una niña te defienda?

Scott volvió a encogerse de hombros.

—Eres lo único que tengo. Supongo que está bien.

—Bueno —dijo Megan—. No llevará mucho. ¿Puedo llamar a mi primer testigo?

David asintió, y Megan pasó al frente de la sala del tribunal.

Capítulo 13
Prueba
circunstancial

prueba circunstancial, s. Prueba indirecta
que *indica* la culpabilidad de una persona.
Por ejemplo, si un sospechoso es visto esca-
pando de la escena del delito, el jurado
podría asumir que es culpable del delito,
aunque nadie lo hubiera visto cometerlo.

Megan comenzó con Jack. Le hizo tres preguntas
sencillas y le dijo que contestara con una sola
palabra: *sí* o *no*.

—Jack, ¿viste alguna vez el dinero en el bolsillo
de Evan?

—No.

—¿Viste a Scott Spencer tomar algo del bolsillo de Evan?

—No.

—Desde ese día, ¿has visto a Scott Spencer llevar doscientos ocho dólares?

—No.

Entonces, uno por uno, fue llamando a Kevin, a Malik, a Ryan y a Paul al banquillo de testigos y les hizo las mismas tres preguntas. Todos respondieron lo mismo: *no*.

Jessie se sentía miserable escuchándolos, pero estaba impactada. En menos de cinco minutos, Megan había desarmado todo su argumento contra Scott Spencer. La verdad era que nadie había *visto* nada ese día en la piscina. Eran todas suposiciones sobre lo que había pasado con el dinero de Evan.

Mientras Megan interrogaba a los testigos, Jessie estaba preocupada de que Megan llamara a Evan para interrogarlo. Sabía que Evan habría preferido arrancarse los pelos, uno por uno, y no volver al banquillo de testigos. Pero Megan llamó a otro testigo, uno que ni siquiera Jessie había imaginado.

—Mi último testigo —dijo Megan al jurado— es Scott Spencer.

Scott Spencer estaba encorvado hacia adelante, sentado sobre la pelota, los codos sobre las rodillas, la mirada fija en el suelo. Entonces se irguió y acomodó los hombros. Parecía tan sorprendido como todos los demás de ser llamado ante el tribunal.

—No quiero —dijo. Miró de manera provocadora a Megan y luego a David, como si fuera a desafiar a ambos a una pelea.

David le apuntó con el mazo.

—Bueno, tiene que hacerlo. Debe hacer lo que su abogada indica.

Jessie estaba bastante segura de que eso no era verdad. Creía recordar una regla que decía que no es necesario declarar en tu contra en un tribunal, pero no estaba segura, así que no dijo nada.

Scott se puso de pie y pateó la pelota con el talón, de modo que esta rodó unos pies al fondo del tribunal. Caminó hasta el estrado y puso la mano derecha sobre su corazón y alzó la izquierda.

—¿Jura decir la verdad, toda la verdad y nada más que la verdad? —preguntó el juez.

—Sí —dijo Scott, pero de manera lenta y en voz baja, como si le estuvieran arrancando las palabras de la boca con una cuerda.

—Solo tengo una pregunta —dijo Megan—, y es sencilla. —Puso las manos en sus caderas y lo miró de frente.

—¿De verdad pagó usted el Xbox 20/20 con su propio dinero?

—¿Qué? —dijo Scott, como si no pudiera creer lo que acababa de oír. Se volvió hacia David K.—. No voy a contestar eso. No tengo por qué contestar esa pregunta.

—Sí, tiene que hacerlo —dijo David—. O lo declararé en desacato.

Golpeó el mazo con firmeza una vez para que Scott supiera que hablaba en serio.

Jessie miró a Scott y supo exactamente cómo se sentía. *Todos* lo miraban.

—Bueno, yo…

Nadie hacía un solo ruido. Hasta las ramas de los olmos dejaron de moverse, y el gentil sonido de las hojas se fue apagando hasta el silencio.

—Recuerda —dijo Megan con calma—. Estás bajo juramento.

Scott puso una expresión amarga.

—*No*. No lo hice. ¿Estás feliz?

Sonrió a Megan con sorna.

—Mis padres me lo compraron.

Todos comenzaron a gritar.

—¡Lo sabía! ¡Lo sabía! —dijo Adam.

David tuvo que golpear con el mazo unas diez veces para que el 4-O se callara.

—El testigo puede retirarse. Alegatos finales. La fiscalía primero. ¡Apúrense!

Jessie se puso de pie. Este se suponía que iba a ser su gran momento.

—Escribí un alegato final realmente excelente —dijo, tomando unas tarjetas de su bolsillo trasero—, pero creo que no tendremos tiempo. Así que solo diré lo siguiente.

Caminó hasta el banco del jurado. Doce pares de ojos la miraban. A algunos del jurado los conocía, como a Adam y a Salley, pero a la mayoría apenas los había visto alguna vez. Ahora todos la miraban. Todo el banco del jurado esperaba oír lo que ella tenía para decir.

—Damas y caballeros del jurado —comenzó—. Los hechos son los hechos. El dinero estaba en los pantalones cortos de Evan, doblado cuidadosamente en la habitación de Jack. Scott fue a la habitación de Jack, y luego entró corriendo a la casa como un bandido. Cuando Evan se dirigió al piso de arriba, su pantalón estaba desdoblado y el dinero no estaba. No hace falta ser un genio para resolver este caso. En definitiva, todo se reduce a quién dice la verdad. Entonces, piensen hace cuánto conocen a Evan Treski y hace cuánto conocen a Scott Spencer, y pregúntense: ¿a quién creen *ustedes*?

Jessie volvió a guardar las tarjetas en el bolsillo trasero de su pantalón. Ni siquiera había tenido oportunidad de usarlas. Pensar que le había llevado tanto tiempo escribir un alegato final tan fantástico.

Este juicio no se parecía en nada a lo que ella había pensado.

—Bueno, hecho —dijo David—. Ahora, los alegatos finales de la defensa. *Rápido,* Megan.

Megan se puso de pie y caminó hasta el jurado.

—Esta es la situación —dijo ella—. No se puede condenar a Scott porque no hay ninguna prueba. Solo estamos imaginando lo que sucedió. No lo sabemos con certeza porque nadie *vio* nada, y el dinero nunca apareció, así que... no sabemos. Y supongo que nunca sabremos qué ocurrió realmente esa tarde.

Megan miró a David.

—Eso es todo —dijo ella.

—¡Listo! —gritó David, golpeando con su mazo otra vez.

—Jurado, tome su decisión.

—¡Llegó mi mamá! —dijo Salley Knight, al ver un carro en el estacionamiento.

—También la mía —dijo Carly Brownell.

—¡Jurado! ¡Reúnase! —gritó Adam.

Los doce miembros del jurado formaron un

círculo estrecho, juntando las cabezas, de espaldas a la sala.

Jessie se puso de pie, luego se sentó, luego se volvió a poner de pie. Tenía esa sensación peligrosamente efervescente que a veces sentía en el estómago. Comenzó a pensar: si tuviera que vomitar, ¿dónde sería el mejor lugar para hacerlo? ¿Detrás del estrado? ¿Cerca de los árboles? ¿Podría llegar a tiempo al baño? Deseaba hablar con Evan, pero con solo mirarlo una vez entendió que era mejor mantenerse alejada. Él tenía la mandíbula tan apretada que parecía querer morder su propia boca.

—¡Listo! —gritó Adam, aplaudiendo con fuerza. Los miembros del jurado se separaron, y Jessie vio a Adam hacer un garabato rápidamente sobre un pedacito de papel que luego le dio a David.

—Todos de pie para escuchar el veredicto del jurado —dijo David.

Todos se pusieron de pie.

Jessie sentía un nudo en la garganta. Intentó tragar, pero era como si los músculos de su cuello estuvieran paralizados. Una imagen cruzó su mente:

ella de pie frente a toda la clase disculpándose ante Scott Spencer.

—Viene mi mamá —dijo Carly, señalando el estacionamiento.

Jessie se volvió y vio a una mujer alta con gafas de sol y una gorra de béisbol que se dirigía a ellos.

—¡Apúrense! —dijo Adam.

—Bueno —dijo David, subiendo la voz hasta gritar.

—Se supone que tengo que decir un montón de cosas oficiales, pero simplemente voy a leer el veredicto en voz alta. El veredicto es: ¡inocente!

—¡Sí! —gritó Scott Spencer, saltando en el aire y golpeando dos veces los puños sobre su cabeza—. ¡Gané! ¡No veo la hora de que sea lunes por la mañana.

Pero nadie más se movió. Y nadie más dijo ni una palabra.

Algo había salido terriblemente mal en el patio. A la sombra de los olmos, lejos de la mirada regañona de maestros de turno y padres, los niños de 4-O habían creado su propio tribunal y habían seguido todas las reglas, pero por algún motivo habían llegado a la respuesta incorrecta. Jessie lo sentía, y lo mismo les ocurría a los demás. Jessie estaba segura.

—¿Hemos terminado? —preguntó David, con el mazo en alto—. ¿Jessie?

Jessie asintió.

—Se levanta la sesión —dijo David, y golpeó con el mazo una vez sobre el bloque de madera, justo cuando la mamá de Carly Brownell se paraba al lado de su hija.

—¿A qué están jugando, chicos? —preguntó.

—A nada —dijo Carly.

Ella agarró su mochila y se dirigió al estacionamiento con su madre. David guardó la toga y el mazo en su bolsa de papel marrón y se dirigió a la acera. Casi la mitad de los otros niños lo siguieron, pero el resto de los niños de cuarto grado se quedaron en donde estaban.

De pronto, una voz cortó el silencio.

—¡Esto *no* ha terminado!

Evan estaba parado con la pelota de básquetbol entre las manos.

—¡Tú y yo! —dijo, empujando a Scott Spencer en el pecho con tanta fuerza que Scott retrocedió un paso—. A la cancha. A la cancha de básquetbol.

Capítulo 14
Palabras amenazantes

palabras amenazantes, s. Palabras que son tan venenosas y llenas de malicia que hacen que la otra persona reaccione físicamente. Las palabras amenazantes no están protegidas en el marco de la libertad de expression de la Primera Enmienda.

—Acepto el desafío —dijo Scott.

Nadie se molestó en recoger nada del equipo. Las cuerdas de saltar, los Frisbees, el cajón de leche, las pelotas extra quedaron en el mismo lugar en el que estaban. Todos los chicos de 4-O que no habían ido a sus casas se pusieron en línea a cada lado de la cancha de básquetbol.

Evan dribló la pelota, intentando lograr esa soltura que lo ayudaba a jugar mejor.

—Vamos a jugar siete a uno. Sin más. El rey de la cancha. Y tienes que ir detrás de la rajadura grande para despejar.

Evan señaló la gran rajadura en el patio a veinte pies de la cancha. Esa era la línea que siempre usaban para despejar la pelota en partidos de media cancha.

—¿Quién es el árbitro? —preguntó Scott.

—No hay árbitro, ni faltas —dijo Evan—. Solo jugamos. Si la pelota atraviesa la canasta, es un punto. Si no, ve a casa y llórale a tu madre. ¿Está bien?

Evan practicaba su dribleo cruzado mientras hablaba. Empezaba a entrar en ritmo. Miró a Scott de pie en lo alto de la zona de tiro libre. Allí estaba, la mirada en la cara de Scott que parecía decir: *¿Para qué molestarse? Siempre gano.* Más que ninguna otra cosa, Evan quería borrar esa mirada de la cara de Scott Spencer de una vez por todas.

—Bueno, está bien —dijo Scott—. Pero, ¿quién va primero?

—Tú —dijo Evan, y le hizo un pase al pecho tan rápido que Scott no tuvo siquiera tiempo de levantar los brazos. La pelota le golpeó en el pecho y cayó a sus pies.

Evan oyó reír a algunos niños y se dio cuenta de que Megan tenía los brazos cruzados y el ceño fruncido.

—¡Buen comienzo! —gritó Paul desde los laterales, mientras Scott tomaba la pelota y despejaba detrás de la línea.

—Muy bien, Treski —dijo Scott—. Muy bien.

Evan corrió a la línea de despeje y se agachó, listo para defender.

Scott dribló la pelota, esperando detrás de la línea. Entonces fingió ir hacia la izquierda y fue hacia la derecha, y dejó a Evan detrás.

Scott era rápido, pero Evan era más rápido. Llegó por detrás, y justo cuando Scott lanzaba la pelota, Evan la alcanzó en el aire, con tanta fuerza que la estrelló contra el suelo. En el movimiento, sus manos golpearon la cara de Scott. Scott se desplomó sobre el piso. Sin defensa, Evan hizo un tiro sencillo y anotó su primer punto.

—¡No puedes hacer eso! —dijo Scott—. ¡*Cometiste una falta*! —Se sentó en el patio, con las piernas extendidas. Parecía que nunca iba a ponerse de pie.

Evan rebotó y dribló hacia la línea de despeje. Puso una mano en la oreja y simuló concentrarse.

—¿Escuchas algún silbato, Scott? Supongo que no, porque no lo hay. *Madura de una vez*.

Scott se puso de pie de un salto, y Ryan gritó:

—¡Farsante!

—Uno a cero —gritó Adam—. La pelota es de Evan.

Evan no se molestó en esquivar. Simplemente chocó a Scott de frente y lo llevó a la zona del asfalto antes de cargar la pelota para hacer una bandeja sencilla.

—Oh, vamos —gritó Ryan.

Megan sacudió la cabeza.

—¿Para qué llamarlo básquetbol si vas a jugar así?

Evan observó a Scott que comenzaba a levantarse lentamente. Pero ya había despejado la pelota en la línea y apuntaba al cesto antes de que Scott se pusiera de pie. Hizo otra bandeja sencilla, bella como un ave.

—Tres a cero —gritó Adam.

—Scott —dijo Ryan—. Vamos, pon un poco de garra.

Esta vez, cuando Evan comenzó su movimiento hacia el cesto, Scott arremetió contra la pelota. La arrancó de las manos de Evan, pero la pelota salió botando.

—Fuera —gritó Adam—. La pelota es de Evan.

Entonces, Evan la tomó otra vez, y esta vez fingió ir a izquierda, a derecha, a izquierda, y Scott estaba inclinado en el sentido equivocado cuando Evan finalmente hizo su movimiento.

—Es básquetbol, Scott. No el congelado —gritó Kevin.

Evan lentamente dribló la pelota hacia atrás. Scott lo miró desde la línea con el ceño fruncido y las manos en las caderas.

—Todo esto no cuenta —dijo Scott—. Es juego sucio. Es basura. Nada de esto cuenta.

—¿Por qué no? —dijo Evan, driblando continuamente—. Estabas de acuerdo. Sin faltas. Tú lo dijiste, ¿cierto?

Dio un paso adelante de la línea de despeje, todavía driblando la pelota lentamente frente a sí. Entonces Evan extendió las manos, la pelota rebotando entre ambos, sin defensa.

—Vamos, ¡tómala!

Cuando Scott se movió, intentando tomar la pelota en el aire, Evan estaba listo. Más rápido que un águila tirándose a pique, atrapó la pelota otra vez, dio un giro alrededor de Scott y se dirigió al cesto. Saltó lo más alto que pudo, y apenas pudo colocar la pelota con ambas manos a través de la canasta.

—¡Humillado! —gritó Paul, haciendo un baile al costado.

—Esto es desagradable —dijo Megan—. Me voy a casa. Tomó su morral y lo colgó sobre el hombro.

—Jessie, ¿vienes?

—No —dijo Jessie en voz baja. Estaba sentada en el césped, las rodillas apoyadas contra el pecho—. Me quedo.

Megan asintió y caminó hacia el estacionamiento. Evan la vio alejarse, pero se dijo a sí mismo, *¿a quién le importa?*

—Cuatro a cero —dijo Adam—. Ey, Evan. Ya termina, ¿está bien? Tengo que ir a casa.

Evan pasó rápidamente el puntaje a seis a cero, con un tiro con salto desde media cancha y un flotante justo frente al cesto.

Todos los niños al costado gritaban *¡invicto, invicto!,* y Evan driblaba la pelota al ritmo de sus cantos. Miró a Scott. Scott respiraba con dificultad, parecía querer vomitar. Le sangraban las rodillas y un hombro. *Tiene razón*, pensó Evan. *Esto no es básquetbol. Esto es venganzapelota.*

—¿Quieres la pelota? —preguntó Evan—. Toma. Aquí está.

Dejó la pelota rodar desde la punta de sus dedos de manera que dribló hasta Scott.

—No digas que no tuve piedad —dijo Evan mientras Scott tomaba la pelota y cambiaban lugares y Evan pasó a la defensa—. Vamos, retrocederé. Te daré todo el espacio del mundo. Ni así puedes hacer un punto en mi contra.

Scott dribló la pelota lentamente, y Evan se dio cuenta de que estaba intentando pensar una estrategia. No había manera de que pudiera pasar a Evan, por el peso de Evan y porque no había forma de que pudiera ganarle en velocidad, porque Evan era más rápido. La única manera en la que Scott Spencer podía lograr el punto era engañándolo. Eso era lo único que tenía Scott, pensó Evan. Eso era lo único que siempre había tenido Scott.

Scott comenzó a driblar lentamente hacia el cesto. Evan se puso en posición, bloqueando la línea, pero dándole bastante espacio a Scott. Mantuvo la mirada fija en la de Scott.

De pronto, Scott se quedó con la boca abierta. Dejó de driblar la pelota y gritó:

—Oh, Dios mío. Jessie, ¿estás bien?

Evan se dio vuelta. ¿Dónde estaba? ¿Estaba en la Máquina Verde? ¿Se había caído? Qué torpe era. Apenas podía pasar por una habitación sin tropezarse.

Evan vio a Jessie sentada al costado, sentada como siempre, con el mentón apoyado en sus rodillas dobladas, mirando el juego atentamente, cuando se dio cuenta. Pero entonces, Scott ya lo había pasado y se dirigía hacia el aro. Evan llegó casi a tiempo para bloquear el tiro, pero casi no cuenta. El tiro de Scott fue apurado y débil. Dio vueltas alrededor de la canasta y la atravesó.

—No puedo creer que hayas caído en esa trampa, amigo —gritó Kevin.

—El truco más viejo de la historia —dijo Paul, sacudiendo la cabeza.

—Seis a uno —gritó Adam—. La pelota es de Scott.

Scott tomó la pelota y se encogió de hombros mientras pasaba por detrás de Evan driblando.

—El rey de la cancha, ¿no?

Evan nunca se había sentido así en toda su vida. Ni siquiera cuando se rompió la pierna. Ni siquiera cuando su padre se había ido. Ni siquiera cuando Jessie puso insectos en su limonada. Esto era peor. Esto era más fuerte. Esto era todo para él.

Entonces, cuando Scott se dirigió a la canasta, Evan llegó hasta él con ambas manos hacia arriba, y debe haber sido la mirada en su rostro que hizo que Scott se congelara y detuviera el paso. Fue todo lo que hizo falta. Evan despejó la pelota y se dirigió a la parte delantera de la cancha.

Podía haber llegado a la canasta driblando y hacer el tiro, y allí habría terminado todo. El juego habría terminado. Y él habría ganado.

Pero no.

Él quería que Scott pagara. Quería asegurarse de que cuando contaran la historia durante días, semanas, años de cómo Scott Spencer había sido *aplastado* en la cancha de básquetbol, hablaran sobre el tiro final que hizo Evan Treski.

Entonces, dirigiéndose hacia la parte superior de la cancha, se plantó sobre sus pies para hacer el hermoso giro con salto que había practicado durante meses. Se quedó allí, driblando la pelota, prácticamente gritando a Scott, Sí, *ven a buscarme*. Y cuando Scott lo hizo, Evan se dio vuelta y tiró un codazo que alcanzó a Scott en el costado de la cara.

Scott salió volando y aterrizó de espaldas. Sus manos se rasparon contra el piso. Evan ni siquiera miró para ver si Scott estaba bien. Dribló una, dos, tres veces, y saltó en el aire, giró el cuerpo y tiró la pelota al aire. Todos miraron mientras surcaba el aire y atravesaba la canasta.

Solo red.

La pelota cayó en el asfalto y rebotó.

Nadie hizo ni un solo movimiento. Nadie dijo ni una sola palabra. Scott seguía sentado en el suelo, la sangre de sus manos era de un rojo brillante. Evan estaba de pie, las manos a los costados. Sentía como si hubiera peleado a los puñetazos.

Scott se puso de pie lentamente, tomó la pelota y la pateó con toda su fuerza para que volara por encima de la cerca y desapareciera en el pantano. Entonces, corrió.

Capítulo 15
BaIanza

balanza, s. Un dispositivo utilizado para pesar que tiene una barra que se sostiene de manera horizontal de la que cuelgan dos platillos. En estatuas y pinturas, a la figura de la Justicia a menudo se la representa sosteniendo una balanza.

—Abuelita, ¿podemos hablar un minuto? —Jessie puso una almohada súper blanda detrás de su cabeza y acomodó el teléfono en su oreja.

—Claro, pequeña Jessie. ¿Qué ocurre? —La abuela de Jessie vivía a unas horas de distancia, por lo que Jessie la llamaba muy a menudo por teléfono.

—Todo esto es horrible —dijo Jessie, tomando de la esquina de su cuarto un pedazo de papel que se despegaba de la pared.

Le contó a su abuela sobre el juicio del día anterior, el juego de básquetbol y cómo Scott había pateado la pelota al pantano. Le contó cómo Evan había tenido que buscar la pelota durante media hora hasta que finalmente la encontró, y cómo les había dicho a todos sus amigos que se fueran a casa, que él la encontraría, que simplemente *se fueran a casa*. Y así lo habían hecho. Y cómo Evan y Jessie se habían quedado buscando la pelota y que Evan no había hablado durante todo ese tiempo.

—Y ahora ni siquiera *come*, no hace nada —dijo Jessie—. ¿Sabías que es Yom Kipur?

—Yom Kipur... ¿Es esa fecha en la que los niños se ponen ropas especiales? —preguntó la abuela de Jessie.

—No, eso es Purim—. La abuelita siempre mezclaba las cosas, cosas que sonaban parecidas, pero eran diferentes. La última vez que habían hablado por teléfono, hablaba con Jessie sobre los árboles secuoyas en California, pero no dejaba de usar la palabra *secuestro* en su lugar.

—Yom Kipur es el día en que los judíos piden perdón y no comen.

—¿Ahora Evan es judío? —preguntó la abuela.

—No, pero no quiere comer. Dice que no tiene hambre —dijo Jessie.

—A veces me pasa eso —dijo la abuela—. Prácticamente me olvido de comer.

—Pero Evan *siempre* tiene hambre —dijo Jessie—. Mamá dice que es un barril sin fondo.

—Comerá cuando tenga ganas —dijo la abuela—. Déjalo.

Jessie odiaba cuando la abuela decía eso. Siempre estaba diciéndole a Jessie *que se tranquilizara* y *que fuera el árbol*. La abuela era una fanática del yoga. ¿Cómo podía alguien ser un árbol?

—Pero... quiero hacer algo para ayudar —dijo Jessie.

—¿Por qué no preparas unas galletas? —dijo la abuela—. Eso lo hará comer. ¿Cierto?

—No lo creo —dijo Jessie—. No esta vez.

Esto era más que un tema de galletas. ¿Cómo

podía explicarle a su abuela la gravedad de la situación?

Jessie había creído en el juicio. Ella pensaba que el juicio iba a revelar la verdad y que la verdad traería justicia.

En cambio, en lugar de verdad, en el juicio hubo mentiras, incluso suyas. En vez de justicia, había un delito sin castigo. Y ahora ella y Evan iban a tener que ponerse frente a todo el cuarto grado y decir que se habían equivocado, incluso a pesar de que Jessie sabía que eso no era verdad.

—Abuelita, es muy injusto —dijo Jessie—. Yo sé que Scott Spencer tomó el dinero. Sé que está mintiendo. Y ahora siento como si hubiera hecho todo este trabajo solo para que él parezca inocente.

—Hay cosas que están fuera de tu control, Jessie —dijo su abuela—. Tienes que aprender a aceptar eso. No puedes manejarlo todo.

Ojalá pudiera, pensó Jessie. El mundo sería un lugar mejor si ella estuviera a cargo. Pero entonces… ella pensó en aquello terrible que había hecho.

—Abuelita —soltó abruptamente—. Mentí en el juicio.

Le contó lo que había pasado. Su abuela escuchó toda la historia sin interrumpir.

—Mentir está mal —dijo la abuela—, pero al menos lo hiciste desde un buen lugar en tu corazón. No debes sentirte avergonzada por querer a tu hermano.

—Igual me siento muy mal —dijo Jessie.

—Eso es bueno —dijo la abuela—. Me preocuparía si no te sintieras mal por haber mentido. *Sí tienes* control sobre eso. Nadie puede obligarte a mentir. Entonces, siéntete mal y siempre recuerda lo que aprendiste y avanza para ser una mejor persona. Pero no seas tan dura contigo misma, Jessie. Solo tienes siete años.

—¡Abuelita! ¡Tengo ocho años! —dijo Jessie. ¿Cómo podía su abuela olvidar cuántos años tenía?

—¿En serio? —dijo la abuela—. ¿Estás segura?

—Tengo ocho años hace casi un año. Mi cumpleaños es el mes próximo.

—Bueno —dijo la abuela—, tengo un libro que quiero mandarte, y será el regalo perfecto.

—Abuelita —dijo Jessie, con un tono de advertencia—. No me enviarás *Príncipe y mendigo* otra vez, ¿verdad?

—No, cerebrito. Recuerdo que te envié ese libro dos veces. Nunca me lo perdonarás, ¿verdad?

—¿Por qué te olvidas de las cosas? —preguntó Jessie—. Antes no lo hacías.

—Ah, pequeña Jessie, estoy envejeciendo. —Su abuela se rio despacio, y Jessie se aferró al teléfono—. Y eso es algo que ninguna de las dos puede controlar. Lamentablemente.

Jessie oyó el timbre que sonaba abajo. Sabía que su madre no lo escucharía porque estaba en la oficina del ático y estaba segura de que Evan no iba a contestar, incluso si lo oía.

—Tengo que irme, Abuelita —dijo Jessie—. Hay alguien en la puerta.

—Bueno, tesoro. Sé el árbol. ¡Y prepara galletas! Te quiero.

Jessie corrió escaleras abajo y abrió la puerta del frente. Era Megan.

—Hola —dijo Megan.

Jessie levantó la mano en un saludo breve, pero no invitó a Megan a entrar.

—Pensé que estarías enojada conmigo —dijo Megan.

—Un poco —dijo Jessie. Hubo un breve silencio.

—¿Por qué lo hiciste? —Jessie no había querido creer que estaba enojada con su mejor amiga, pero ahora todas las preguntas que había intentado ignorar desde el juicio inundaron su cabeza. *¿Por qué arruinaste todo mi trabajo? ¿Por qué dejaste que Scott se saliera con la suya? ¿Por qué me traicionaste a mí y a Evan?*

—Lo siento, Jessie —dijo Megan—. No quería que te enojaras y no quería arruinar tu juicio, pero sucede que no era tu juicio. Era de todos.

Megan la miró a los ojos.

—Hiciste algo increíble, Jessie. Nos diste un juicio de verdad. No algo falso, con disfraces, de mentira. Uno de verdad. Pero en un juicio de verdad, todos tienen derecho a un abogado. Entonces, alguien tenía que defender a Scott. De otra manera, el juicio habría sido una gran farsa.

Jessie no dijo nada, pero entendía perfectamente lo que Megan le estaba diciendo. En el fondo, lo había sabido todo el tiempo.

—Quería ganar —dijo finalmente, sintiendo una y otra vez el dolor de haber perdido—. Pero tienes razón. Hiciste lo correcto.

Las dos se quedaron allí, mirándose los pies. ¿Por qué era tan difícil hablar sobre los sentimientos?

—Ya no estoy enojada contigo —dijo Jessie, sabiendo que era casi cierto y que para el día siguiente sería totalmente cierto.

Megan sonrió.

—Nos vemos el lunes, Jess.

Se fue saltando los escalones del frente.

—Ey, Megan —dijo Jessie—. ¿Crees que Scott tomó el dinero?

—Sí, lo creo —dijo Megan. Se encogió de hombros, con una mirada que parecía decir *así es la vida*.

Jessie vio a su amiga caminar por la acera. Era un magnífico fin del verano y un día casi otoñal. Los árboles se mecían con la brisa. El cielo tenía el color de las flores de los acianos. Era agradable sentir el sol sobre la piel.

Jessie corrió escaleras arriba hasta su cuarto y encontró el libro de yoga que su abuela le había dado la Navidad anterior. Fue a la página 48 y miró la imagen.

Ser el árbol, se dijo Jessie. Lentamente, tomó su pie izquierdo y lo apoyó sobre la rodilla derecha, encontrando y manteniendo el equilibrio durante todo un mágico instante.

Capítulo 16
ResarcimienTo

resarcimiento, s. Compensación legal (de dinero u otros activos valiosos) como reparación por una pérdida, daño o perjuicio de cualquier tipo.

Jamás en la vida Evan había pasado tanto tiempo sin comer. Y lo más extraño de todo era que ya ni siquiera tenía hambre. En algún momento alrededor de las dos de la tarde del sábado, su hambre había desaparecido. Como se apaga una luz. Se sentía vacío y ligero y con la cabeza un poco confundida. Pero no tenía hambre.

Ni siquiera lo había planificado. El día anterior, había llegado a su casa y había cenado, como siempre. Y luego se puso el sol y pensó en Adam y Paul, y se preguntó si ellos habían comenzado a ayunar y si lo harían hasta la noche siguiente. Y entonces quiso saber si él podía hacerlo. Pasar veinticuatro horas sin comer. Solo quería ver cómo se sentía y si tenía la fuerza para hacerlo.

Y eso le hizo pensar en el Día del Perdón. Cuanto menos comía, más pensaba, hasta que estuvo allí, sentado en su rama del Árbol para Trepar, bien arriba con las hojas susurrándole y los pájaros cayendo en picada sobre su último bocadillo del día y las sombras de la tarde comenzando a estirarse por el campo.

Empezó a reflexionar sobre sus pecados. Y era difícil pensar en eso. ¿Había pecado realmente? No lo sabía. Pero había algo que sí sabía. En ese preciso instante, se sentía triste. Y Evan sabía que cuando se sentía muy mal, eso solía significar que había hecho algo que lamentaba. Evan se arrepentía de todo el juego de básquetbol. Deseaba no haber jugado así. Deseaba que Megan no lo hubiera visto jugar de esa manera. Ni Jessie. Ni nadie. Deseaba no haber sido tan patán. El juego volvía una y otra vez a su mente, cada tiro perfecto en su cabeza, y lo hacía sentirse muy mal. Nunca iba a saber lo que había pasado con el dinero desaparecido, pero destruir a Scott en la cancha de básquetbol no cambiaba nada.

Evan bajó del árbol y entró a la casa. Jessie estaba en la cocina con un bol y unos ingredientes dispersos sobre el mostrador: harina, azúcar, mantequilla y huevos.

—¿Qué estás preparando? —preguntó al entrar.

—Lo que más te gusta. Galletas con chips de chocolate.

—Gracias —dijo Evan, tomando su gorra de béisbol del vestidor de la entrada y caminando hacia la puerta.

—¿A dónde vas? —preguntó Jessie.

—A la casa de Scott.

—¡No! —dijo Jessie—. No lo hagas.

—No te preocupes. Dile a mamá a dónde voy, ¿está bien?

Jessie lo siguió hasta la puerta.

—Y no te comas todas las galletas antes de que vuelva —gritó por encima del hombro.

En verdad no tenía un plan. En el fondo de su

mente, imaginaba un apretón de manos y algo como un "lo siento" en algún momento futuro. Más allá de eso, no sabía qué ocurriría.

La casa de Scott estaba cerca de la casa de Evan como para ir en bicicleta, pero su vecindad parecía otro mundo. Allí las casas eran enormes y tenían elegantes arbustos plantados en pequeños grupos, estacionamientos de dos carros y un césped que parecía cortado con navaja. Mientras Evan iba por el camino de ladrillo hasta la puerta del frente, notó que los dos arces grandes del jardín comenzaban a cambiar de color. Dejarían caer un montón de hojas el próximo mes, pero Evan sabía que Scott nunca rastrillaba porque su familia tenía un servicio que se ocupaba del jardín.

Cuando se abrió la puerta del frente, Evan no se sorprendió al ver a Scott parado allí. Evan casi no recordaba haber visto a los padres de Scott abrir la puerta.

Se veía mejor que el día anterior, eso era seguro. Limpio, sin sangre, con jeans que le cubrían hasta las rodillas. Pero la mirada en su rostro era la misma, una mirada de odio. Odio puro hacia Evan.

—Hola —dijo Evan.

—¿Qué pasa? —dijo Scott—. ¿Qué quieres?

Evan no había practicado qué iba a decir, y ahora que estaba frente al enojado rostro de Scott, era difícil pensar algo en el momento. Se quedó allí un minuto, con la mente en blanco. ¿Para qué *había* ido?

Y entonces dijo lo único que se le ocurrió:

—Quería ver tu nuevo 20/20.

Eso cambió todo. El entrecejo fruncido de Scott se aflojó y soltó los brazos. Esperó solo un segundo antes de decir "está bien". Entonces dio un paso atrás para dejar pasar a Evan. Así había sido siempre desde que eran pequeños: a Scott Spencer le gustaba alardear con sus juguetes nuevos.

Evan siguió a Scott por las escaleras hasta el sótano, que era una mezcla entre un salón de juegos y un salón familiar. Se parecía bastante a cómo lo recordaba Evan: dos sillones, el escritorio de la computadora, el gabinete de archivo con bocadillos guardados bajo llave, cajas de juguetes y de construcción, equipos deportivos, la silla mecedora que colgaba del techo, un teclado electrónico y una cinta caminadora. Lo que llamó su atención, sin embargo, fue la nueva tele. Era enorme, la pantalla plana más grande que Evan había visto en toda su vida.

—¡Guau! —dijo Evan.

Scott sonrió.

—Sí, mi papá la compró hace unas semanas. Es genial, ¿no?

Evan observó la caja blanca brillante conectada a la tele.

—¿Ese es el 20/20? —preguntó—. Guau, es tan pequeño.

—Sí, pero mira lo que puede hacer.

Scott le dio dos guantes gruesos que parecían guantes de hockey, pero blancos, y un par de pesadas gafas oscuras que se ajustaban alrededor de la cabeza. Evan se quitó la gorra de béisbol y se puso los guantes y las gafas, entonces Scott apretó un botón de la caja. Lo siguiente que supo Evan fue que estaba manejando un carro en una pista de carrera y otros carros lo pasaban a unas 120 millas por hora.

—¡Guau! —gritó Evan.

—¡Dobla a la derecha! ¡Con los guantes! Imagina que estás al mando de un volante y dobla a la derecha —gritó Scott.

Evan había evitado chocar por poco contra una barrera de paja que protegía las curvas de la pista. Rápidamente tomó un volante imaginario y volvió a la pista.

—Aprieta la mano derecha para ir más rápido y la mano izquierda para desacelerar —dijo Scott, subiendo el volumen para que el rugido de los automóviles llenara los oídos de Evan. Evan casi podía oler los gases de escape.

Durante los siguientes cinco minutos, Evan disfrutó el paseo de su vida. Nunca había jugado con una consola tan divertida. Ahora entendía por qué Scott no paraba de hablar de ella.

—Scott. ¡Scott! —gritó una voz desde atrás.

Evan se volvió y se quitó rápidamente las gafas. El Sr. Spencer estaba de pie en lo alto de las escaleras. Scott dio un salto para bajar el volumen de la televisión.

—Te estoy llamando desde hace cinco minutos. ¿Podrías bajar eso? ¿Tienes idea de lo fuerte que está?

—Lo siento, Papá —dijo Scott—. Estábamos jugando a *Road Rage.*

—Bueno, vas a arruinar las bocinas de la tele, y *serás tú* quien me compre una nueva. Y no te creas que te lo dejaré pasar. No gasté cinco mil dólares en una televisión nueva para que la destruyas con tus videojuegos. Es un equipo caro, y tienes que aprender a tratarlo con respeto. Ahora, baja el volumen. Estoy intentando trabajar.

—Sí, señor —dijo Scott.

El Sr. Spencer se dio vuelta y desapareció en lo alto de las escaleras. Scott tomó una pelota de béisbol y comenzó a tirarla y atraparla una y otra vez con la mano. Evan no sabía qué hacer. Dejó los guantes y las gafas en el suelo. Los carros todavía pasaban a gran velocidad en la televisión; sin sonido, parecían algo tonto y falso.

—Tu papá trabaja mucho, ¿verdad? —dijo Evan.

—Hasta los sábados —dijo Scott, lanzando la pelota.

—Mi mamá trabaja mucho, también —dijo Evan, pero pensó *al menos ella no nos grita por hacer ruido*.

—Sí, como sea —dijo Scott—. ¿Quieres jugar a *Crisis*? Es genial.

Y tras eso, lanzó la pelota de béisbol al rincón de la habitación. Pero lo hizo con demasiada fuerza y apuntó mal. Muy mal. La pelota dio una vuelta y golpeó el borde de la pantalla del televisor. Hubo un estallido fuerte, y la tele se apagó.

Los dos niños se quedaron helados. Evan no podía emitir sonido alguno. Sentía como si tuviera un calcetín atorado en la garganta. Había una rajadura de un pie en la pantalla del televisor y un puñado de rajaduras que parecían una telaraña. La casa estaba en total silencio, excepto por los pasos del Sr. Spencer que bajaba corriendo las escaleras. Y ahí estaba, de pie junto a la puerta, observando el televisor.

—¿Lo hiciste a propósito? —le gritó a Scott.

—¡No! —dijo Scott—. Yo no...

—Porque vas a pagar el precio. Cada centavo. Tu mesada, el dinero de tu cumpleaños, olvida los regalos de Navidad de este año. ¿Lo entiendes? Al Sr. Spencer se le marcaba una vena en la frente, como en una película de extraterrestres. Cada palabra que decía que comenzaba con *p* (*porque, pagar, precio*) salpicaba hilos de saliva blanca.

Evan pensó que iba a explotar o algo así.

—Papá, yo no...

—El televisor es nuevo. *Nue-vo*, ¿me escuchas?

Evan dio un medio paso hacia Scott.

—Lo sentimos. No quisimos hacerlo. Fue un accidente.

El Sr. Spencer vio a Evan por primera vez desde que bajó las escaleras. Era como si hubiera olvidado que había alguien más en la habitación. Lentamente, inspiró y exhaló. Sus dientes crujieron, tenía la mandíbula rígida como una pared de piedra.

—¿*Tú* arrojaste la pelota?

—No, pero estábamos, bueno, jugábamos, y la pelota... golpeó la tele por error. No lo hicimos a propósito—. Evan estaba asustado, pero no podía evitar pensar que el Sr. Spencer era un patán. Claro, su mamá se enojaba (miles de veces) y a veces gritaba, pero no cuando era un accidente de verdad.

—Lo sentimos, Papá —dijo Scott en voz baja.

—Bueno, eso no arregla el televisor, ¿no es así? —dijo el Sr. Spencer. Sin decir otra palabra, se fue.

La habitación quedó en silencio.

—Bien —dijo Evan, solo para llenar el incómodo silencio.

Scott miraba hacia el suelo.

—Sí —dijo. Parecía como si acabara de morir su perro.

Evan tomó su gorra de béisbol y la ajustó a su cabeza, colocada hacia atrás.

—Bueno, fue divertido —dijo simplemente, pero

Scott no sonrió ni quitó la vista del suelo. Evan lo entendía. Era horrible cuando tu padre te gritaba así frente a otro niño. Te hacía sentir como si toda tu familia fuera lo peor. Seguramente Scott deseaba que él se fuera.

—Bueno, mejor me voy a casa.

—Bueno —dijo Scott—. Y gracias. Sabes. Por intervenir.

—Nada que agradecer.

—Mi papá ama esa tele. Digo, en serio. Así que gracias.

—Para eso están los amigos —dijo Evan, girando para salir.

Eso lo tomó por sorpresa. No había querido decir *eso*. Era un poco difícil pensar en Scott como un amigo después de todo lo que había ocurrido. Sin embargo, ¿qué eran? Él y Scott. No eran amigos. Pero no eran enemigos. Algo intermedio. Algo que no tenía nombre ni reglas.

Evan se rascó la parte trasera del cuello.

—Ah, y, lo siento —dijo—. Lamento lo del juego

de básquetbol de ayer y el juicio y todo eso. Mira, tú dices que no tomaste el dinero, y eso significa que no tomaste el dinero. Y lamento haber hecho tanto lío y haber sido tan patán.

Scott asintió una vez con la cabeza.

—Sí, bueno, olvida lo de la Reunión de la Mañana. Tú y Jessie disculpándose. Simplemente lo dejaremos atrás.

Está bien. Evan se sentía mejor. Se sentía mejor de lo que se había sentido durante toda la semana. Era como si hubiera llevado una mochila llena de piedras durante días y días, pero ahora estaba tan liviano que casi podía volar. Y guau, tenía un *hambre*. Podía sentir el llamado de las galletas con chips de chocolate desde el otro lado de la calle.

Scott todavía parecía triste. Evan dijo simplemente "Nos vemos", y se volvió para salir.

Estaba en lo alto de las escaleras cuando Scott lo llamó:

—Espera. —Evan se dio vuelta y vio a Scott poner la mano en su bolsillo y sacar una llave, abrió entonces el gabinete del rincón. Evan esperaba que fuera a ofrecerle un Yodel para el camino. Un Yodel sería muy bueno en ese momento.

Pero no era un Yodel lo que Scott sacó del gabinete. Era un sobre que Evan reconoció de inmediato.

Era el sobre de Jessie. El sobre que tenía $208 adentro.

Scott se lo dio.

—Siento haber robado tu dinero.

Evan tomó el sobre gordo. Había olvidado lo ancho que era un fajo de $208. Tanto trabajo. Tanto sacrificio. Preparar la limonada y llevarla por todo el pueblo bajo el caluroso sol del verano. Y luego tener que decirle a Jessie que había perdido el dinero. Eso había sido lo peor.

—Imagino que estás bastante enojado, ¿no? —dijo Scott.

Evan se sorprendió al escucharse diciendo "no". Y se sorprendió porque sabía que lo decía en serio. Quizás había sido ese horrible juicio o el sucio juego de básquetbol o el hecho de que no había comido nada durante casi veinticuatro horas. Por lo que fuera, Evan se sentía vacío. No había nada de enojo dentro suyo.

—¿Por qué lo tomaste? —preguntó, mirando el dinero.

Scott se encogió de hombros.

—No lo sé. Porque tú lo tenías, supongo.

—Ah —dijo Evan. Eso no tenía sentido para él. No es que Scott necesitara el dinero. Después de todo, sus padres le compraban todo lo que quería: el nuevo iPod, los mejores patines de hockey, la tele más grande. No tenía ningún sentido para Evan.

Pero algunas cosas no tienen sentido.

—Tengo que irme —dijo Evan, metiendo el sobre en la parte delantera de sus pantalones. El sol estaba bajo en el cielo, y su madre no le permitía andar en bicicleta cuando oscurecía. Pronto, iría a la casa de Adam para la gran cena del fin del Día del Perdón.

—Nos vemos —le dijo a Scott.

—Sí, adiós—. Se separaron en el jardín, luego Evan montó su bicicleta.

—¡Ey! —gritó Evan mientras pedaleaba por la

calle—. La próxima vez que la pelota pase por sobre la cerca, tiene *tu* nombre. Me debes una.

Evan no se quedó para escuchar la respuesta de Scott. La pelota volvería a caer en el pantano, la próxima vez que estuvieran jugando en la cancha de básquetbol.

PACTO SOLEMNE DE SILENCIO

Este contrato es <u>legal</u> y <u>obligatorio</u> para todas las partes que firman más abajo.

Quienes firman abajo juran solemnemente no revelar jamás a los miembros de la clase del 4-O, ni a ningún adulto que pudiera hacer preguntas, lo que ocurrió realmente con los doscientos ocho dólares que desaparecieron de los pantalones cortos de Evan Treski el 5 de septiembre.

Este asunto se considera cerrado, ahora y para siempre, y los detalles quedan cerrados para siempre

Evan Treski

Jessie Treski

Scott Spencer

EL BANDIDO DE LA CAMPANA

Jacqueline Davies

Serie La Guerra de la Limonada: tercer libro

En el tercer libro de la serie de *La guerra de la limonada*, los hermanos Evan y Jessie deben resolver el misterio de un preciado tesoro familiar que desaparece, mientras asimilan el preocupante comportamiento de su amada abuela.

Sigue leyendo un capítulo de muestra de
El bandido de la campana
de Jacqueline Davies
hmhco.com

HOUGHTON MIFFLIN HARCOURT

Capítulo 1
Atrapada en el asiento trasero

—¿Cuánto falta? —preguntó Jessie desde el asiento trasero mientras golpeaba el vidrio de la ventanilla tres veces. Jessie siempre golpeaba la ventanilla tres veces cuando pasaban por debajo de un puente.

—Una hora más —dijo la Sra. Treski. Miró el reloj del panel—. Como mínimo.

Ya habían viajado tres horas, subían cada vez más y más alto en las montañas, y Jessie se daba cuenta de que estaba poniéndose de mal humor. En este viaje a la casa de la abuela todo era distinto.

Primero, Evan estaba sentado en el asiento delantero. Jessie sabía que estaba escuchando su iPod. Desde atrás, podía ver su cabeza sacudiéndose ligeramente al ritmo de la música, mientras miraba por la ventanilla.

A Evan nunca le habían permitido sentarse adelante. Pero esta vez, cuando lo pidió (por vez número diez mil), la Sra. Treski lo miró de manera reflexiva durante un buen rato y dijo "sí". Tenía diez años y era alto para su edad, por lo que la Sra. Treski pensó que ya tenía edad suficiente para ir adelante.

Jessie tenía nueve y estaba atrapada en el asiento trasero.

—¡Ey! —dijo Jessie, intentando que Evan se volteara y le prestara atención. Pero no lo hizo. No podía escucharla. Era como si ni siquiera estuviera en el carro.

Jessie miró el campo a través de la ventanilla mientras lo cruzaban. Normalmente, le encantaba ese viaje. Le gustaba contar objetos en el camino: vacas, halcones, Mini Coopers, placas de carros de otros estados. Llevaba una cuenta en su cuaderno, y al final del viaje, sumaba el total para ver quién había ganado. Casi siempre ganaban las vacas.

También registraba el avance buscando puntos de referencia importantes en el camino, como el edificio del control de pestes que tenía una cucaracha de fibra de vidrio de cuarenta pies en el techo, o el tótem de dos pisos tallado en madera que en verdad era una torre telefónica, o la marquesina de una cafetería que tenía una gran tetera de donde salía vapor de verdad.

LO QUE VEO	LUGARES ESPECIALES
VACAS ЦНТ ЦНТ lll	☑ CUCARACHA
HALCONES ll	☑ TÓTEM
CABALLOS llll	☑ TETERA
OVEJAS ЦНТ ll	☐ MARIQUITAS
CABRAS l	
MINI COOPERS ЦТ l	

PLACAS DE CARROS AL OESTE DEL MISISIPI

   ✳ Nebraska l
   ✳ Kansas l
   ✳ Idaho ‼
   ✳ Missouri l

Antes, Evan también buscaba estos puntos de referencia, y la carrera era por ver quién los encontraba primero. Sin embargo, este año, no parecía importarle. Incluso cuando apareció el tanque gigante de almacenamiento de agua pintado como una mariquita, y Jessie se lo señaló, él simplemente se encogió de hombros, como si no le importara. No jugaba, y de pronto el viaje se hacía largo.

Pasaron debajo de otro puente, y Jessie golpeó tres veces la ventanilla.

—¿Por qué la abuelita prendió fuego a la casa? —preguntó.

La mirada de la Sra. Treski pasó de la ruta al espejo retrovisor, y se detuvo en el reflejo de Jessie un instante antes de volver al camino.

—No lo hizo a propósito. Fue un accidente.

—Lo sé —dijo Jessie—. Pero... ¿por qué pasó *esta vez?*

La Sra. Treski inclinó la cabeza hacia un lado.

—Son accidentes. A veces no hay razones. Dejó

algo en el horno, y se prendió fuego. Le puede pasar a cualquiera.

Pero nunca le había pasado antes a su abuela. Jessie pensó en todas las veces en las que Abuelita le había preparado fideos y chocolate caliente o calentado una sopa. Ni una sola vez había prendido fuego la casa.

Por el incendio iban a la casa de la abuela dos días *después* de la Navidad, en vez de ir el día *anterior*, como siempre. Y era por el incendio que no sabían con certeza si se quedarían en la casa de la abuelita para la víspera de Año Nuevo como lo hacían siempre. Esa era la gran diferencia este año.

Desde que Jessie tenía memoria, la víspera de Año Nuevo se quedaban en la casa de la abuela, había una larga y lenta escalada hasta lo alto del monte Lovell, donde los árboles se separaban y el cielo se abría y estaba la vieja campana de hierro con su pesada viga transversal de madera.

Justo antes de la medianoche se reunían, caminaban por los bosques cubiertos de nieve, con vecinos y amigos, familiares y a veces incluso desconocidos que venían de todas partes de la colina para cantar las viejas canciones y hablar sobre el año que se iba.

Entonces, justo antes de la medianoche, el más pequeño del grupo y el más viejo pasaban al frente y ambos tomaban la soga que colgaba del badajo de la oscura y pesada campana, y en el momento preciso, la hacían sonar en Año Nuevo, fuerte y alegremente y durante todo el tiempo que desearan.

Jessie recordaba el año en que *ella* había sido la más pequeña y la sensación que tuvo cuando la Sra. Lewis, que tenía ochenta y cuatro años ese año, cerró sus manos suaves y delicadas como un papel sobre las suyas. Habían sacudido la soga hacia atrás y adelante, una y otra vez, hasta que el sonido de la campana llenó el valle cubierto de nieve y los ecos de cada repiqueteo rebotaron desde el monte Black Bear y regresaron hasta ellos, como el viejo perro fiel que siempre vuelve a casa.

Pero este año, todo era al revés. Quizás ni siquiera pasarían la víspera de Año Nuevo en la casa de la abuela. Todo dependía, dijo la Sra. Treski. ¿De qué? Se preguntaba Jessie. Golpeó dos veces su rodilla derecha. ¿No pasar la víspera de Año Nuevo en la casa de Abuelita? ¿Quién haría sonar la campana?

Jessie sacudió las piernas hacia arriba y hacia abajo. Sentía un cosquilleo en el pie izquierdo porque lo había dejado doblado debajo suyo durante media hora.

—¿Cuánto falta para la tienda Crossroads? —preguntó.

—Oh, Jessie... —dijo su madre, mirando nuevamente por el espejo retrovisor—. ¿Necesitas que nos detengamos?

—¿Qué quieres decir? —preguntó Jessie. No era que lo *necesitara*, aunque ahora que lo pensaba, ir al baño parecía una buena idea.

—Siempre nos detenemos en la tienda Crossroads —dijo ella, con un dejo de queja en la voz.

—Es solo que pensé que esta vez iríamos directamente —dijo la Sra. Treski—. Vamos bien de tiempo, y ya sabes cómo es el clima en las montañas. Nunca se sabe qué puede pasar.

—¡Mamáaa! —dijo Jessie. Todo era raro este viaje—. Evan, tú quieres que paremos en Crossroads, ¿no?

Evan seguía mirando por la ventanilla, asintiendo con la cabeza al ritmo de la música de su iPod.

—¡Evan! —Jessie no había querido golpearlo tan fuerte en el hombro.

—¡Basta! —dijo él, volviéndose hacia ella.

—Te estoy haciendo una pregunta —gritó ella. Evan se quitó uno de sus auriculares y lo dejó colgando sobre la oreja como un gusano muerto en un gancho.

—¿Quieres parar en Crossroads? —Jessie no podía evitar pensar que la pregunta sonaba tonta. Por supuesto que quería.

Pero Evan simplemente se encogió de hombros y volvió a ponerse el auricular en su oído.

—Me da igual.

Jessie se arrojó sobre el asiento y cruzó las manos sobre el pecho.

—Cálmate, Jessie —dijo la Sra. Treski—. Nos detendremos. Puedo aprovechar para estirar las piernas. Pero no podemos quedarnos mucho tiempo. No quiero llegar a la casa de Abuelita cuando haya oscurecido.

La tienda Crossroads era un desvío de diez minutos de la ruta principal. Estaba en el cruce de dos caminos tan insignificantes que la Sra. Treski lo llamaba el cruce entre Ningún Lado y Olvido. Pero la tienda en sí era hermosa. Era una mezcla entre una estación de gasolina, una tienda gourmet, una panadería, una tienda de regalos, una librería, una tienda de caza y pesca, una tienda de ropa y una oficina postal. Vendían kayaks, rifles, animales embalsamados, cuchillos de caza, tarjetas de saludos, paraguas, libros de humor, lombrices, golosinas y calendarios decorativos para la pared. Jessie podía pasearse por la tienda durante horas deseando tener el dinero para comprar todo.

Pero solo tenía cinco dólares en el bolsillo. Era todo el dinero que se había permitido llevar de viaje. En su caja fuerte en casa tenía casi treinta dólares. La mayor parte de ese dinero lo había ganado durante la guerra de la limonada, o al menos lo que quedaba luego de que hiciera un aporte de $104 a la Liga de Rescate de Animales ("No hace falta que des tanto como yo", había dicho Megan, pero Jessie había insistido. "Dije que lo iba a hacer y lo voy a hacer", dijo, a pesar de que casi la mataba entregar todo ese dinero, ¡y a animales!).

Pero no importaba que la tienda Crossroads fuera muy atractiva para ella (¡un cascanueces ardilla! ¡bigotes falsos!), Jessie no iba a gastar treinta dólares. Le gustaba tener dinero ahorrado. Por si acaso.

Luego de ir al baño, caminó hasta donde estaba Evan, a mitad de camino entre los productos gourmet y la panadería. Él miraba bolsas de regalos, todas hechas con moños de florituras.

—¡Mira! —dijo él, sosteniendo una bolsa. La etiqueta de la bolsa decía "Caca de Alce".

—¿Quieres? —preguntó, sacudiendo la bolsa frente a su cara.

—¡Qué asco! —dijo Jessie. Pero le encantaba.

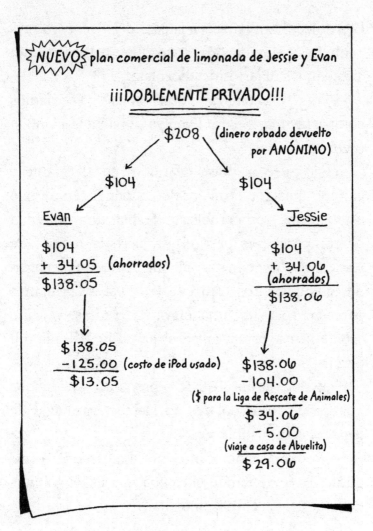

Los dulces eran iguales a la caca del alce, pero más pequeños. Más de cerca, vio que en verdad eran arándanos cubiertos de chocolate.

—¿Vas a comprar una bolsa? Podríamos compartir una. —Pero Evan ya se había ido y no la escuchaba.

Jessie puso la bolsa de nuevo en el estante y caminó hasta el rincón de la tienda en donde estaban los rompecabezas. Había una variedad de rompecabezas para elegir, pero la mirada de Jessie fue directamente al que tenía una imagen de gomitas. Los dulces de colores brillantes parecían rocas de una playa de piedras, y Jessie sabía que ese rompecabezas sería difícil. Tenía mil piezas.

—Jessie, ¿estás lista? —preguntó su madre, guardando unos dólares en la billetera, luego de pagar el combustible.

—¿Podemos comprar este? ¿Por favor? —preguntó Jessie, tomando el rompecabezas de gomitas del estante—. ¿Para la abuelita?

Jessie y la abuela siempre armaban rompecabezas

en las visitas familiares, y Jessie a menudo llevaba un rompecabezas nuevo para armar. Pero nunca habían hecho un rompecabezas de mil piezas.

La mamá de Jessie se detuvo; el dinero todavía sobresalía de su billetera. Jessie sabía que su mamá era cuidadosa con el dinero, y se esforzaba por no pedirle nada que no necesitara.

—Tengo cinco dólares —dijo Jessie—. Podría aportarlos.

La Sra. Treski tomó el rompecabezas y dijo:

—Es una buena idea, Jess. Tú y la abuela pueden hacerlo cuando ella vuelva a casa del hospital.

Jessie sonrió, contenta de poder llevar el rompecabezas sin tener que gastar su propio dinero, y se volvió hacia el exhibidor giratorio de tarjetas postales que estaba junto a los rompecabezas. Había ocho columnas de tarjetas, y a Jessie le gustaba hacer rechinar el estante cuando lo giraba lentamente. Comenzó desde arriba y bajó hasta la primera columna, y volvió a subir hasta lo más alto de la siguiente columna. No quería perderse ni una sola postal.

—Jess, ¿podemos irnos? —preguntó su madre, mirando a través de los distintos compartimentos de su billetera, como si el dinero pudiera aparecer mágicamente si miraba lo suficiente.

—No, estoy mirando las postales.

—Seguro tienes todas las postales de ese exhibidor.

—A veces tienen una nueva —dijo Jessie.

—Cinco minutos, ¿está bien? Quiero que en cinco minutos estemos saliendo del estacionamiento. —La Sra. Treski caminó hasta el rincón de la caja para pagar el rompecabezas.

¿Por qué estaba tan impaciente su mamá? A ella le encantaba parar en Crossroads, pero esta vez solo decía que había que llegar a tiempo y retomar el camino. Bueno, Jessie no se iba a apurar. Terminó de ver la segunda columna de postales y comenzó con la tercera.

—¿Has estado alguna vez allí?

Jessie miró hacia arriba. Un anciano con barba descuidada entornaba los ojos a través de sus lentes viendo la postal del Estadio Olímpico del Lago Placid. Jessie notó que tenía los lentes rotos.

—El estadio en donde se realizaron las Olimpíadas. ¿Has ido alguna vez?

Jessie sacudió la cabeza.

—No.

El hombre tocó la tarjeta.

—Yo estuve allí en 1980 *y* en 1932. Sí. Vi a Sonja Henie ganar la medalla de oro de patinaje artístico. ¿Puedes creerlo?

Sacudió la cabeza hacia arriba y hacia abajo como si así pudiera hacer que Jessie lo hiciera también.

Jessie vio de cerca al hombre que estaba a su lado. Él comenzó a rascarse la cara como si tuviera una reacción alérgica.

—¿Estuvo en las Olimpíadas? —preguntó ella.

—¡No! —dijo el hombre—. Pero tuve sueños.

Sacudía la cabeza más vigorosamente ahora, asintiendo y rascándose, y sus ojos estaban fijos en el otro extremo de la tienda.

—Ey, Jess, vamos —dijo Evan, tomándola de un hombro y alejándola hacia la puerta.

—¡No terminé! —dijo ella. Pero Evan no la soltó hasta que no salieron. Cuando Jessie miró atrás por la ventanilla, vio al hombre todavía rascándose el rostro y hablando, a pesar de que no había nadie cerca.

—Ese tipo estaba loco —dijo Evan, simplemente.

—¿Cómo lo sabes? —preguntó Jessie, mirando a su hermano mayor.

Evan se encogió de hombros y se volvió a poner los auriculares.

—Se nota.

Pero Jessie no se había dado cuenta. No se le había ocurrido que hubiera nada raro en el anciano. ¿Por qué se volvían así las personas mayores? ¿Algo se rompe en sus cabezas, como un cordón del calzado que a veces se suelta después de haber estado atado mucho tiempo? Y... ¿cómo lo sabía Evan?

Apenas volvieron a la carretera, comenzó a nevar. Al principio los copos de nieve eran grandes y húmedos, se pegaban un instante al parabrisas como polillas blancas gigantes antes de disolverse en gotas del tamaño de una moneda de 25 centavos. Luego la nieve se volvió más constante y fuerte, y el suelo a cada lado de la carretera se tornó blanco y sin forma. Era de noche cuando llegaron al final del largo y serpenteante camino de entrada a la casa de la abuela y pudieron ver por primera vez la casa.

—Oh, Dios mío —dijo la Sra. Treski mientras apagaba el motor y las luces.